Alex George live
historic Mediter
draws his inspira f
London graduate now fully devoted to his writing. You can learn more about the world of Thalagia and the Heartstone Talisman series by visiting www.alexgeorgebooks.com.

UNDER THE DRAGON'S CLAW

HEARTSTONE TALISMAN
BOOK ONE

Alex George

α

Alphapex

This novel is entirely a work of fiction.
The names, characters and incidents portrayed in it are the work of the author's imagination. Any resemblance to actual persons, living or dead, events or localities is entirely coincidental.

alphapex

An Imprint of Alphapex Publishing
2 Langdon Court, City Road,
Islington, London EC1V 1LH

www.alexgeorgebooks.com

Published by Alphapex Publishing 2008
1st

A CIP catalogue record for this book is available from the British Library

ISBN-13 978 0 9558777 0 4

Printed and bound in Great Britain by
CPI Cox & Wyman, Reading, RG1 8EX

Acknowledgements

To Theo for his adroitness, Nem for his wit and steadfastness, Serilia for her tenacity and to Nestor for being the rock on which they are all anchored.

To my children George and Stavriana for their pleasant distractions and unconditional love.

To my wife for her patience.

To the Master of the Web, Arch Mage of computing, Gus.

To Stuart and Eliana for their support.

And to my readers for sharing this world of Thalagia with me.

Alex George
June 2007

To the bravest woman I know,
Maria Nicolette

Contents

LAKE CHAD
CRYSTAL ISLE
URID OCEA
GULF OF DUNS
Borget
KEL
GULF
CRATER OF ILLIATH
EMERALD FOREST
SILVER LAKE
SILVER
MESAL
MARASSIA
Aldorn
Ameron
Ramila
Balsovia
Sandora
TWINS
VALDORIC SEA
NERUS OCEAN
GIANTS FIORD
KERTA
CYRUS
Nubis
SNAKE EYES
FALSE SISTERS

URID OCEAN
LAKE
CRYSTAL ISLE
GULF OF
GULF OF KOLGA
LAKE OMIRA
PLAINS OF ARDUR
Gate
Caymden
Mingory
COZANDIR SEA
Hold
Algashar
Aldorn
Baltovia
Amaron
ORIC SEA
KERTA
CYRUS

♦ CHAPTER 1 ♦

Strangers

Theo moved over to the mantelpiece placing his favourite bow and quiver at its usual place–*there*–in the snug corner formed by the projecting fireplace and the adjoining wall closest to his armchair where he could reach out for it with ease. All the while he stared accusingly at the stranger who had entered their lives uninvited. It was because of *him* that Theo had lost his chance at claiming the best prize the Triad Woods had to offer: the buck had been the only one to sense the presence of the strangers.

Theo stared from one to the other. Their appearance in the woods in the dawn light had been grey, shapeless and threatening. The fire from the hearth provided the male with some colour, playing games of light and shadow on his angular face. The female still managed to remain in the least lit corner of the room furthest away from the rest of the group and closest to the door. Dark eyes blinked at the flickering tongues of flame whilst jet-black hair hung loosely about her face smothering her features. She gave the impression of a wild animal ready to bolt at the slightest provocation.

Theo looked across the room at his boyhood friend. They locked eyes. Nemarchus, or Nem as he was known to his friends, was still a bit jittery from their experience in the woods. He nervously fingered the dagger hanging from his belt whilst listening with the rest of them to what the male stranger had to say.

"I still can't believe how easily our ranks have been infiltrated," the stranger named Archon was saying. "For their agents to have managed to track me down–even here–to this remote part of the island...that shows they are growing bolder, Elron." Archon threw a sinister look at Theo's father.

Elron looked over at his wife Russilda and smiled encouragingly. He was trying to divert her thoughts from the gloomy image the mage was painting. Elron weighed heavily on his walking stick as he shuffled over to his father's armchair. He laid a comforting hand on Nestor's bony shoulder. Theo's grandfather reached up and patted his son's proffered hand squeezing it tightly.

"We will survive this and any other threats," Elron said turning to the mage with conviction. The smile was still fixed on his face although, even by the dim light of the hearth, Theo could see some of the sparkle abandoning his eyes. Every word the mage uttered was like a hammer's blow on the protective shell Elron had built around his family.

Theo tried to recall everything the mage had said. Archon was Arch Mage of Aldorn, the capital city of the four kingdoms of Seldavia. He had been recalled from his position by the king's side and sent on a mission by the Coucil of Light. Archon was cryptic about his mission. Instead he chose to elaborate on events transpiring in the four kingdoms.

Theo absorbed everything Archon was saying with interest as the mage filled the gaps in his knowledge of the world. The conversation moved on to matters about the Church of Athud, the largest ecumenical body encompassing Leonium, Seldavia and Renderon. The Ecumenical Patriarch was old and ailing and had for the past few years reduced his public appearances substantially. Evidently he had withdrawn from the governing of the church to a large extent and was confined to his quarters by an illness that kept him bedridden. The rest of the spiritual leaders were vying for position to fill the gap, forming alliances that were most likely to improve their influence, simultaneously emptying the church's coffers to supply their individual campaigns.

Archon moved on to the business of the Council of Light, which was experiencing similar problems, since the High Sorcerer who led the council was fast approaching retirement with various candidates presenting themselves to take his place. Elron scoffed at the goings-on of the council.

"Your views on the Council of Light are well known, Elron," Archon was saying. Theo's mother had explained to him in the past that the Council of Light was a body ruled by the "gifted", as those who could wield magic were otherwise known. This body of sorcerers and sorceresses was established to monitor Thalagia, the name given to the known and mapped world, to address any problems that could not be solved by conventional means. It was widely rumoured that this group produced the problems so they could manipulate events and exercise control over the rest of humanity. Theo did not know what to believe. He had gifted people in his family and as a rule they never misused their talent to cause hurt or disrupt the lives of others. However his father vehemently supported the rumours about the council and did not fear to express his view.

Theo took the opportunity to scrutinise Archon's appearance. The mage wore his hair in the fashion of the earls at court, with the top half in a knot and the rest left to spill over his shoulders. He kept his beard neatly trimmed above his bare neckline revealed by the open collar of his linen shirt. His sleeves, rolled up so as not to encumber him, revealed strong arms, a fighter's arms. Wisps of grey intermingled with his blond hair, placing him in his mid-forties. He had the appearance of a mountain eagle with a beak of a nose crested by twin peaks of heavy blond eyebrows above intelligent stone grey eyes. His gaze panned across the room soaking in his surroundings like a sponge, cataloguing information that might prove useful at a later stage. Theo could almost sense the mage's mind ticking, planning behind his piercing, calculating gaze. His woollen grey trousers were well worn by his travels and his traditional brown leather riding boots, that had been dust-coated, were now polished and shiny.

"And not without reason!" Elron answered the mage heatedly, snapping Theo's attention back to the conversation. "*You* were not left unaffected by the machinations of the Council–and I got this!" Elron exclaimed, pointing to the patch covering his left empty eye socket and the side of his face that had been badly burnt in the past. Vivid memories of that fateful day lit up in his mind's eye and for a moment his eyes glazed over as he stood there, unmoving.

"Elron, that's unfair," Russilda spoke in a hushed voice, a pained look crossing her face as she gazed worriedly at Nestor. The old man was looking off with a mournful, dejected expression. "You promised not to bring this up in front of the children," she accused. "I'm only thankful that Serilia is away with your aunt, Emeralda."

"They are children no longer, Russilda. Theo is twenty-two and Serilia is just two years younger. It's about time they learnt the truth." Elron focused his one-eyed gaze on his son. Theo had asked in the past how his father had received his scarred face and limp but the answers, when given, had been vague and evasive. His father blamed the council for his afflictions. His mother refused to expand on the matter, saying simply that Elron would explain when the time was right.

"If it wasn't for the rest of us in the council, Elron, none of you would be alive," Archon argued.

"I take care of myself and my own!" Elron smacked his palm on the table, meeting Archon's gaze. His scarred face was red, more noticeably now than ever before. Elron, who at the cottage was easy-going and always ready with a smile, was self-conscious in public because of his affliction and did not often venture out, sending his father or the boys to the fishing town when they needed supplies. In summer even at home he would always wear long pants to cover his scars and he never took off his shirt, no matter how soaked it got from his sweat whilst he toiled.

Archon stood up to his full height, half a head taller than Theo's father. "Not all in the council are perfect, I grant you that Elron, but you can't blame the works of the Dark on my colleagues and myself who risk our lives daily in waging our battle against them. *We* keep the rest of you out of harm's way. We've had infiltrators before but we've always managed to wheedle them out, or force them to flee."

"That's what we thought twenty one years ago, when I almost got burnt to a crisp. I still have the limp, as you must have noticed, and this patch itches like crazy." He wasn't about to let Archon off that easily. Years of bitterness were coming to the fore and he had found a recipient to vent it on.

"I lost loved ones too that year, Elron," Archon raged. "Do you think I can forget? Do you think I haven't blamed myself and the rest of them a hundred–no, a thousand–times for not realizing sooner what our enemies were up to that day... for the death of my parents? But I've come to realize that we, the gifted, are only human as well ... and mortal. I've come to learn it the hard way." Russilda took Archon's hand reassuringly and turned a reproachful look on her husband.

Theo felt uncomfortable at having so much revealed about Archon's innermost private life, a man he had only just met. He looked around uneasily, waiting for a reason to present itself for him to leave the sitting area. But the two men had their attention trained on one another and were oblivious to their surroundings as they peeled away painful memories of the past.

"A lot has changed in the world since you were last in it," Archon continued.

"What's that supposed to mean?"

"Admit it. We've kept you concealed here at the cottage in safety. I only pray it remains that way," he added in a lowered voice.

"Archon is right, Elron." Nestor, who had been silent all this time turned to look at his son with tears brimming in his eyes.

Both men halted, looking at him as if they had just noticed he was there. They lowered their eyes ashamedly and backed away from each other taking their seats once more.

"You know as well as I that I am an authority on pain, so what I have to say I say with conviction. I am through blaming others for the acts of Evil! Evil exists and so does Good to combat Evil. We are given a choice which side we intend to fight for. I choose to fight alongside anyone who supports our cause. A mortal Council of Light which makes mistakes is better than no council at all. I'm sorry son, but this is the truth of the matter."

Elron limped over to his father and reached out to cradle the old man's head in his embrace. "I'm the one who should apologize, father, for bringing up painful memories. I remember only too well how you suffered... how we all suffered from mother's untimely death at the hands of our enemies ... which is yet another reason why I think of all that has happened and feel despair." Russilda moved up closer and hugged them both from behind. Elron opened his arms to include her in his embrace.

Archon cleared his throat. "Well I suppose we'd best get some sleep," he said, turning to his companion. "Roxette?" The nymph, who had remained unobtrusive throughout the conversation, stood up and looked towards Russilda.

"I'll show you to your rooms and get you pillows and blankets for your beds," Russilda offered.

Archon and the nymph were given separate rooms, even though out in the plains they had had to sleep close to one another for added safety. He was thankful for the chance to sleep in a real bed. He had been out in the open for several weeks now. Russilda had given him a bar of soap and a towel which he soon put to good use, grabbing the opportunity to bathe in a tub filled with hot water. The cottage hadn't changed all that much in twenty odd years since he had left them all in the care of old Nestor. Now, *there* was a tough nut to crack! There was more to that old man than first met the eye. If Theo turned out to be half as tough as the old man, then Archon would be well pleased ... as would the council. The boy possessed the gift. Archon was able to ascertain this twice back in the woods when he had probed the boy's mind. However Russilda had not managed to awaken his talent. Maybe a man's touch was needed. He would get down to it soon. Time was precious and he didn't have much of it. Elron could be a problem though... As for Russilda, she had been in league with the council from the start.

Archon woke instantly to the insistent knocking on his door. He flung himself out of bed and tore on his trousers before opening the door.

Roxette was standing at the doorway fully dressed and ready for action, bristling like a stuffed porcupine with *two* swords strapped behind her back and with twin daggers hanging from her leather belt. Archon imagined that beneath her black leather tunic and matching riding pants she was hiding more surprises. She arched an eyebrow upon seeing Archon's semi-naked body.

"Don't you ever sleep?" he grumbled, stretching out his limbs. Looking outside his window he could see the sky faintly illuminated by the twin moons and the starlight–it was the middle of the night!

"We Mountain nymphs do not need a lot of sleep," she answered informatively.

"So you have told me many times before. What is it?" he asked on a more serious note, reading uneasiness in the nymph's brown eyes.

"We've had visitors. I found footprints all around the cottage with some leading to the stables. I believe they were made by Pithiks."

"Pithiks!" Archon exclaimed grabbing at his shirt. "Damn! Are the horses ok?"

"The horses are fine though both hounds have had their throats slit. Archon, we need to hurry before they bring their masters."

"You're right," he said, his face creased with concern. Pithiks were half human, half beast and were well known in the eastern kingdoms of Renderon as vicious beings that fought ferociously and hated man with a vengeance. They walked on two legs but when they ran they loped on all fours, covering great distances with their powerful bounds. Their chests were wide like a bear's and their bodies were covered with long grey-brown hairs. Almost always they travelled in the company of Dark nymphs who used them to track down their quarry. The mage and his nymph companion had known they were being followed from the moment they had reached Cyrus's shores.

"We don't want to endanger the cottage any more than we already have. Let's just take the boy and be on our way." Then he added, as an after-thought, "Go break your fast. I'll be out in a minute. Oh, and leave those blades behind. We don't want to upset Russilda more than is necessary." Roxette nodded grudgingly, turning to go. He grabbed her by the arm. "I thought we had lost them... when we entered the forest, I mean," he said, studying her intently.

"They must have picked up our scent when we left its confines. They were probably combing its outskirts for hours before they came upon our trail."

Archon nodded, letting her go.

Down at the breakfast table Nestor had a lantern lit and was chewing on some bread and fruit. The old man tilted his silver head in greeting to Archon as he entered. "Bright and early," he said, without much cheer in his voice.

Archon looked around the kitchen noticing that the cloak stand held one, not two, grey cloaks. "Where's Roxette?"

"She said she was going to the stables to get the horses ready."

"You know?" Archon asked simply.

"I saw the footprints," Nestor nodded. He had encountered pithiks in the past when he had been journeying close to the border of Renderon with Kalkador and recalled it was not an experience he relished. "I've taken care of the dogs. No need to mention them to the boy, though," he said, his blue eyes looking intently at the mage.

Archon acquiesced and took a moment to study the old man. He hadn't changed much in twenty-one years. He still left to spill over his shoulders the same long hair that Archon remembered had been blond shot through with grey, whereas now the old man's head looked like it was surrounded by a silver halo. His blue veins showed beneath the outstretched skin of his hands like streams crossing a pale yellowy terrain. They were firm hands, however, like the rest of him and there were no tell-tale signs of weakness, as was the fate of most men his age. His face and skin were taut canvass, weather-hardened by years spent out at sea. Staring into his blue eyes one was drawn into them, like a vessel to a whirlpool. There was no hump to his back but instead he carried himself with a proud bearing and his limbs, though slim, were devoid of fat, being sinewy, like well-tended rope used to tack the sails of a ship. He bent over his breakfast chewing slowly, staring at Archon like a hawk that recognizes its own kind and is therefore more wary of what its next move might be. There was no fooling this one! That's one thing Archon remembered acutely about Nestor of the Alunda Sea race.

"So what's your plan, now that you've brought them down on us?" Nestor asked, his knobbed fingers closing firmly around his coffee cup.

Archon paused at the accusation before answering truthfully. "We do what we came here for and be on our way. They'll follow us and leave the cottage alone."

"You hope," the old man added.

Just then Russilda walked into the kitchen carrying a candelabrum and wearing her green gown from before. It matched her emerald-green eyes and did little to conceal her ample bosom and lithe waist that was accentuated by the velvet belt she wore.

Doesn't anybody get a good night's sleep around here? Archon thought but said instead, "You're breathtaking." He beamed a smile at her appreciatively. He remembered the way she had been as a young girl. The passing years had added to her beauty. Her features were more mature, fuller, *more womanly,* he mused. She reminded him a lot of her mother, Serilia.

She pursed her lips. "Well I'm not dressed for the day yet, and my head feels like a sack of sand from too little sleep, and I probably look the way I feel, but thanks for the compliment." She answered modestly but smiled back nonetheless.

"Elron is lucky to have you."

"And I to have him." Russilda stared at his grey eyes searchingly before asking, "What about you then? Is there anybody special in your life?"

"Ha!' Archon exclaimed dismissively. "In my line of work there can be none." He had long decided that doing the Council's bidding and keeping up a relationship were two things that did not blend together, like oil and water.

"What about Roxette?" she asked, now the nymph was nowhere in sight.

"No," Archon answered firmly. "She is my guide and protector."

"How did you meet?" Russilda poured him milk and coffee and laid a platter of bread and jam nearby, along with some fruit and a slice of salted meat.

"Aren't we the nosy one this morning?" Archon retorted, biting into his bread hungrily and gulping down the milk and coffee. He was famished from the evening's events.

"Still a few hours yet till morning," Russilda said pointedly, laying the candelabrum on the kitchen bench to add its light to the lantern on the table. "Well?" she pressed insistently.

"Women!" Archon flung his arms up in mock exasperation. "In your minds, a man is not allowed to remain solitary as soon as he is of what you like to call, marrying age," he teased. Russilda grinned back but waited for an answer. He went on, "I met her at the Apalachus River, west of Ramila."

"Apalachus River!" Nestor exclaimed. "What was a Mountain nymph doing near Alcavia? They're mortal enemies with the Dragon's Foot Mountains."

Roxette overheard as she entered and stood at the doorway. The kitchen lantern cast its light on her oval face, highlighting her sharp nose and reflecting in her dark cat-like eyes. Russilda studied her intently. She reminded her of the large black panthers one could find in the jungles of the Hadir. She moved with the same feline grace, her ebony leather tunic and pants tightly worn accentuating her firm, fine-tuned physique but at the same time giving her a freedom of movement Russilda could only envy. She kept her jet-black hair well groomed and, as was the custom among the nymph hill tribes, dyed the tips with bands of red beside her temple emphasizing her exotic look. Russilda looked down at her own brown hair and decided it was drab and needed a change. She looked back at the nymph's eyes: fearless and scrutinizing. *What secrets hide behind those eyes?* Russilda thought. *What are you holding back?* Then realizing she was staring and remembering the context of her conversation with Archon she blushed guiltily and looked away.

"The horses are fed and ready to be saddled," Roxette said to her travel companion. Russilda looked sharply at Archon at the mention of them leaving. The nymph ignored her and turned to Nestor, saying in a calm controlled voice, "As for your question, I was leading a group of nymphs from the mountains on an assassination attempt on one of the Alcavian lords who was rumoured to be travelling in those parts at the time." Nestor stared at her coldly.

Roxette carried on unperturbed, "I was instead waylaid by the same nymphs at the command of their leader who felt threatened by my rising station in the assassins' ranks. All the exercise had been a sham to lure me into their trap. I never saw it coming. Such is the way of the Dark," she added in explanation. "I was left for dead until Archon came upon me and took pity on me. I was given treatment at the hands of the healing Sisters of Athud who at first did not want to admit me but Archon's sister, Lucinda, a member of their order, convinced them to allow me in."

"Fortunate for you," Nestor commented dryly, looking at her with steely blue eyes.

"To conclude, Roxette has been with me for the past four years and has saved my neck on several occasions," Archon added, looking meaningfully at both Nestor and Russilda.

They remained silent until Elron limped into the room leaning heavily on his walking staff. Archon stared at his limp quietly but said not a word. The late evening's conversation was still a freshly opened wound.

"You're all up and about unusually early," Elron said, stating the obvious. He sensed the mood in the room and looked from one to the other, then fixed his gaze on Russilda, who was drinking her coffee silently.

"Roxette and I are leaving," Archon replied, looking up at him.

"Archon, you don't need to leave so soon." Elron placed a hand on the mage's shoulder.

"I'm afraid we do." Archon got up from the table and moved around to stand beside Roxette.

"We had more visitors during the night," Nestor explained.

"Visitors?" Russilda and Elron spoke simultaneously, looking at the old man worriedly.

"Yes, and not the kind we would want at the cottage either."

"Father, stop beating about the bush and tell me what's going on."

"Me and the Mountain nymph,"–he chose not to use her name but stressed her origins–"found tracks all around the cottage. Full posses of what we believe are Pithiks were nosing around the grounds close to the stables."

"Pithiks! Here in Cyrus?" Elron asked incredulously. "What are Pithiks doing so far south? They seldom leave Kalkador and when they do it's to harass Renderon's border then make a quick retreat."

"Are the boys alright?" Russilda asked in alarm, grabbing the candelabrum and getting ready to rush to the rooms.

"Hold, Russilda. I checked up on them right after I saw the tracks. The boys are both fast asleep and undisturbed and will remain so for several more hours, if I know anything about young boys, which I do." Russilda looked at her father-in-law uncertainly but sat back down again.

"What about the horses and the rest of the animals?" Elron asked, looking accusingly at Archon, whom he was obviously blaming for this.

"The stables are unharmed but we're missing a few lambs and maybe some chickens," Nestor said. In a lower voice he added, "The hounds are both dead and buried."

Elron stared at him, the dismay openly showing on his face. He had raised those hounds from pups. They had become members of the family. He had glimpses of them when they were little, falling over one another in their attempt to suckle at the bottle of milk he and Theodor had used to feed them, yapping and wagging their little tails with delight as some of the milk trickled down their soft furry chins. He combed a hand through his long blond hair, his angry wound showing red beneath his eye patch. He added as an afterthought, "What are we going to tell Theo?" Russilda stared at him, silently sharing his feelings of despair.

"Nothing." This from Archon. "He won't have time to notice the dogs missing." Taking a deep breath he came to stand opposite Russilda, who had joined Elron hugging his waist. They both looked questioningly at him. "Elron, I'm here to take Theo away with me."

That stunned them both.

"Not on your life!" Elron answered vehemently, tensing his muscles. Russilda covered her mouth to hide her dismay. Nestor stood up slowly, only now realizing the purpose of Archon's visit.

"It's no longer up to you, Elron," the mage ploughed on, not giving them a chance to recover. "Theo will need to decide for himself. He is a man now and needs to go out into the world and shape his future."

"He was shaping his future just fine here at the cottage," Elron said, hardening his stance. *So that's what has brought you to the cottage,'* he thought angrily. *'Twenty-one years and not a word from you and those blasted 'gifted' of yours. Now this!* He wasn't about to let his son get involved with them. As he had pointed out to Russilda in the past, it was not wise to meddle with the affairs of the Council of Light. To do so was to invite trouble to your doorstep.

"How long do you think he will remain here?" Archon asked, taking them all in with his look, studying as was his nature the expressions on their faces, picking up the tell-tale signs that would aid him in his task of winning them over to his point of view.

"Elron, you left the cottage when you were barely eighteen years old to join the military–and you were alone, whereas Theodor will have both me and Roxette by his side."

Tears were forming in Russilda's eyes and Archon felt sure she had realized the time had come for the boy to discover his hidden talent. She was won over already. Nestor was studying him with clear blue eyes probably thinking back on the time Elron had wanted to leave the cottage. Would he deny his grandson that which he had not denied his son? Archon realized he needed to play on this point more convincingly.

"The boy needs to learn as much as he can about the pitfalls that may be set before him. He can't do that tucked away at the cottage. How long will you be around to shield him from outside threats, at the same time keeping him cut off from life's experiences? Do you have a right to quash his inquisitive young spirit?" Elron probably used the same arguments back then to disarm the old man's resolve. Nestor was already turning away, deep in thought. Elron, however...

"Bravo," Elron said, clapping his hands. "A fine performance but you didn't fool me one bit." His face was beetroot red and his voice quivered with the rage that was boiling up inside. "I decide for Theo and I say, NO!"

Archon turned to Russilda for support. "Deep down inside you know I am right. You can't keep it bottled up inside him." He was making reference to Theo's gift which all wizards inevitably came to use to some extent, depending on their strength. It was a flood that no dam could contain, not even Elron. Russilda knew that if a male wizard did not help the boy come to terms with the gift, he would walk through life maimed or as though his other half, his gifted half, was faulty. Russilda herself could not imagine life without her gift. It made her feel whole. She had been lucky in that her mentor had taught her patiently and completely how to wield every aspect of her unnatural power and Russilda could well appreciate the consequences had her mentor not been there for her.

"Roxette will see to the boy's weapons training and I'll deal with the rest." Archon said, lighting his own lantern and leaving the kitchen to make his way to the stables. The nymph followed closely at his heels.

"What did he mean by the rest?" Elron said, turning accusingly to his wife. "And what was all that about you knowing he is right?" His blue eyes searched hers beseechingly, trying to find some comfort in them ... anything to set him at ease. Instead Russilda, unable to withhold her tears, turned her back on him and walked out into the morning darkness sobbing uncontrollably. He exchanged a look of guilt with his father. "I'll go after her and calm her down," he offered in compensation, taking a cloak from the stand.

"Yes. You do that, son," Nestor replied. He continued drinking his coffee, deep in thought.

Outside the morning air was chill. Elron came beside her slowly and placed the cloak over her shoulders, taking her slender hand in his. "Let's leave the boy to decide," he said, staring up at the twin moons. The grey one was in its final stage in the waning cycle whereas the smaller blue moon was full and matched the couple's mood.

Elron stared off to his left at the envelope of light that was being cast at the open stable door by the mage's lantern. "Archon is right about Theo being old enough to decide," he offered grudgingly, "but I still don't trust his methods, and the way he manipulates people."

Elron thought back to when he and Archon were younger. Perhaps he was being unfair. But the mage was talking about taking his boy away from him. Even if he meant well; Elron knew Archon would do everything in his power to look after the boy and to teach him properly about the goings-on of the world, but he still remembered clearly the dangers he and Russilda had faced daily before seeking sanctuary at the cottage. And now, not even the cottage was safe.

Theo walked into the kitchen wearing a thick cotton robe and his woolly socks. He stretched his limbs like a hound that's been disturbed from its nap and managed to greet his grandfather between jaw-breaking yawns.

"What's all the commotion about?" he asked, rubbing at his half-open eyes and blinking at the lantern light before sitting himself down at the table. He was about to ask what was for breakfast when he caught the look on his grandfather's face.

The old man looked at him sullenly. Instead of answering him he finished his coffee and left his breakfast mostly untouched.

The cottage rocked violently like a ship in a rough stormy sea, the kitchen cutlery rattling to the *Boom! Boom!* noises coming from outside. A couple of pots and pans perched on the bench fell to the ground as the resounding noises continued to shake the premises. Flashes of blue and white light pierced the kitchen windows illuminating the walls like fireworks.

Elron stormed into the kitchen, his crippled form silhouetted against the ephemeral lights from outside.

Nestor stood up clutching at the table not knowing when to expect the next tremor. "What in Nerus's name is going on?" he bawled at his son.

"Father, go with Theodor to the rooms and get him and Nemarch packed." Nestor stared at his son unblinking. "Hurry man!" Elron exclaimed. "Archon and Russilda are out there with the nymph holding them at bay." Then he shoved the old man and the boy towards the rooms, almost knocking Nem over, who was racing in the opposite direction in his nightclothes, wild-eyed with hair dishevelled.

"What's happening?" Nem asked as they were being led hurriedly back to the bedrooms.

"Father, I'm going out there to help!" Elron shouted from the living room where he had gone to retrieve his sword. "Pack only the essentials and take the boys to the stables. I'll have horses saddled and waiting for you."

Theodor had no time to answer his friend's question but the sounds of fighting outside were all the explanation Nem needed. In no time at all they had managed to put on their woodsman clothes, fling cloaks over their shoulders and rush to the kitchen carrying their bows and short swords; they had been using the very same since boyhood in their military training with Elron. Theodor was trembling uncontrollably and looked towards his friend who looked no better off.

Nestor was packing salted meat and other such food and drink to last them for a short trip. Every now and then he peered out the door to take stock of the situation outside. He motioned the boys to remain low and clear of the windows and door–not that they needed much encouragement.

There was a cacophony of sounds coming from outside: beastlike voices howling with bloodlust and barking commands in a foreign, guttural speech intermingled with yelps and inhuman shrieks as the voices were abruptly cut off; and crackling noises, like the breaking of a thousand twigs, accompanied by bolts of light. Theo thought he could make out his father's voice calling urgently over the noise. His heart leaped in his throat as he envisaged horrific scenarios in his mind.

But nothing could have prepared them for what they witnessed as the three of them flung themselves out of the kitchen door; Archon and his mother were standing midway between the cottage and the stables bracing themselves, as if against a storm, arms flung out. From their hands beams of continuous blinding light were flowing in all directions like a giant web. All around the cottage, dark shapes milled around, snarling and biting, like predators waiting for their chosen bull to tire before going for its jugular. The grounds were already littered with the bodies of the creatures that had ventured too close to the sorcerers' web of fire. Theo almost retched, overcome by the stench of burnt flesh. There were so many of them. Everywhere he looked, a sea of teeth and furry limbs was racing towards them.

His grandfather fired arrows incessantly at the beasts that were getting too close. At some point he shouted something at the boys but they stood frozen, like newborn lambs staring at predators closing in for the kill. One of the grey furred pithiks reared up tall in front of Theo wielding a wicked-looking blade in its right hand. The beast was easily two heads taller than Theo, its chest massive like a wine barrel and its hands and feet, though manlike, covered in brownish grey fur. It smelled foul and that together with Theo's crippling fear brought back the feelings of nausea he had felt earlier. It lifted its saw-edged weapon readying for the strike. Theo looked into its dark eyes and fell back in surprise and confusion. He recognized in them a man's intelligent look, albeit a look of utter hatred.

"Die human," it barked in its guttural tongue with a voice like rocks being ground together. All the time it grinned, huge incisors jutting out of its mouth, twisting it even further out of shape.

Theo crouched low and shut his eyes, trembling and waiting for his life to be snuffed out. He opened them when he felt his shoulder being shaken none too gently.

"Boy, what's the matter with you?" Nestor was screaming at him. "Get yourself together and use that thing you're carrying before you get us all killed!" He pointed at Theo's short sword.

Nestor retrieved his own sword from the back of the pithik that a moment before had held Theo's life by a thread. Nem's face was drenched of colour. Saliva was dribbling from the side of his trembling mouth. He looked up at Theo, eyes wide and disbelieving at having witnessed a life being taken for the first time. That seemed to break the spell and they rushed behind Nestor who was nearing the stables.

Nestor let loose another arrow, catching a pithik in the chest before it had a chance to strike at them. Elron stepped out of the darkness finishing the beast off from behind with a quick slice across its throat from his dagger. This time

Theo did throw up. He looked up in time to see Nem emptying his stomach.

"What took you so long?" Elron complained to his dad.

"The boys had a run-in with some Pithiks," Nestor sneered as he followed his son into the stables.

The horses were whinnying and rearing with fright as the company of four approached them. Elron went into the stalls picking out horses and calming them with a soothing word and a comforting stroke to the neck and hindquarters. But every time the booming noises were heard the horses would start up again.

"Nestor, you take the gelding. Theo will take the roan mare and Nem the brown one."

"What about you and Russilda? Not to mention Archon? Where's the Nymph?" Nestor added as an afterthought.

"Roxette is quietly disposing of some of them, striking at them from behind whilst they have their attention trained on Archon and Russilda. She's very thorough," he said, not hiding his admiration for her. "As for me and the mages, we will remain a while longer to keep them busy while you make your escape. Now hurry! We're running out of time and I want you gone before sunrise." He saddled the horses aided by Nestor and the boys. Then he turned to his father and clasped his arm before pulling him into a hug. "Don't worry about us, father. I'll take care of things."

Nestor managed a brave face, even though he knew the situation outside was bordering on the impossible. "I know you will. You always do."

Elron limped over to the boys. He hugged Nem offering him consoling words. Then he turned his gaze on Theo. Father and son looked at one another, emotions welling up inside, now the time had come to part.

"Oh, Theo, how quickly you have grown, son. I haven't told you this as often as I should but I'm proud of the man you've become...and I love you."

Elron took his boy in his firm embrace and hugged him lovingly.

Theo returned the hug. "I love you too, father," he croaked, letting tears wash over him in a flood. That seemed to relieve some of the tension. He felt readier to face the dangers outside. Another boom resounded shaking the stable like an axe blow on a tree. "Mother!" Theo exclaimed. "I have to say goodbye to her."

"I can't let you do that," Elron said firmly. "In the predicament she is in, you would only distract her from her task –and that could be fatal. Just remember she is fighting to buy you some precious time. Now mount up and leave. And don't look back." He helped the boys with their steeds and pulled Nestor close. "Ride to port Paliphea and seek out my brother. Tell him to get you off the island. We'll hold them for as long as we can and try to join you when it's safe to do so."

Nestor nodded solemnly. He heeled his chestnut gelding and they sprang out of the stable closely followed by the two mares and a fourth pack horse. They veered sharply to the right, away from the fighting and noise, and plummeted down the hill at break-neck speed. Theo glanced back to see his father taking on two pithiks that had approached the stables. Further behind he could make out the two mages, who at this distance looked like matchstick men, maintaining their web of death with all around them crouching figures forming an undulating line just as the sun was creeping over the horizon.

The horses leaped over the cottage fencing and continued down the road without slacking their speed. Soon what had been Theo's home vanished behind the hill.

The solitary figure clad in black sat atop his steed in silence casting his gaze over the tumult that had erupted at his command around the little cottage that was so near to the woods.

"Archon." He said the name aloud chuckling. *The young fool thought he had lost us when he boarded the ship at Hendon's port,* he mused. *Granted it was tough to work around the pithiks' fear of the sea, but what beast can deny its master's will?* Those that did were killed gruesomely on the spot, as a warning to the rest. *And then, when he had entered the forest with that traitorous bitch! How naïve of him to believe we would not instantly pick up his trail once he left the forest's confines. But he is full of surprises. Who is this new friend he has found at the cottage? Her use of the gift is notable, however on the larger scale of things she is a fly on an elephant's hide, but still, annoying. What's this?* The dark rider rose in his stirrups to take a closer look. Three figures on horseback were being outlined by the first rays of the rising sun which cast their shadows in elongated lines before them as they rode down the hill from the direction of the cottage. *A diversion then! But why would Archon place himself in so much danger for these three?* This would need looking into.

♦ CHAPTER 2 ♦

Escape

Archon cast his gaze around the carnage surrounding him and Russilda. With the coming dawn the number of dead was suddenly illuminated, like gazing upon the inside of a freshly opened tomb. The web had done its destructive work but he could make out many more beasts massing around at the periphery of his vision–they kept coming!

Elron had been backed to the stable doors, fighting desperately to keep the pithiks away from the horses. Several times during the night they had almost succeeded in setting the stables alight but were thwarted in their efforts by the man's powerful sword strokes: it was as if some invisible hand had set up a large scale and was adding the bodies of the beasts on one end of the scales to counter Elron's skill and will to stand firm on the other. The pile of dead outside the stable doors proved they were close to tipping the balance in their favour. Elron looked exhausted, his clothes ripped and tattered. Archon could see a blotch of blood blooming like a red rose on Elron's shirt just beneath his useless left arm. He would not last another determined attack.

Roxette was nowhere to be seen but Archon wasn't worrying about her. Many times during the night he had seen her skilfully dispatch several pithiks from behind, then disappear into the dark before they could organize themselves into a counter attack; hit and run tactics were her specialty.

He looked at Russilda who stood in her green gown, arms flung out fighting for her life. The beads of sweat that had formed on her creased brow were now trickling down her neck and cleavage and her breathing was grating. Their bolts of blue and white flame were disintegrating, like the strands of a spider's web in a storm. The pithiks sensed their weakening and were getting bolder.

"Russilda, we can't keep this up much longer," Archon called out.

"What do you suggest?" she asked, taking in big gulps of air.

"We'll need to split up and run whilst we still have the chance."

Archon heard Roxette's scream from behind, close to where Elron had been. He turned in time to see Elron down on the ground and Roxette kneeling beside him. He and Russilda broke off their defence and ran towards the stables.

Elron heaved himself up just as they reached him. The blood from his side wound had stained his entire left leg. The wound was gaping open every time he moved.

"I'll be alright," he said weakly to the nymph as his wife ran to his side, tearing off a piece of her gown to wrap around the wound.

"Roxette, go get our horses. It's time to get out of here." Archon ordered. "Russilda, you and Elron will have to make your way to the forest with Roxette. I'll hold them off for a while longer to give you a chance to escape."

"But, Archon," Russilda started to object. "You're almost spent, yourself. We must all leave together. And my son has gone south, not north to the woods."

"Russilda, we can't have them going in the direction of the boy. We must lure them away, in the opposite direction. And as for us leaving together, we can't all make a break for it at the same time, or we risk being run down before reaching the safety of the woods. Let's just keep to the plan."

"I'm not leaving my cottage to these beasts," Elron growled.

"Forget the cottage, man! Save your lives. That's all that matters now. Roxette, where are those blasted horses?"

"I'm almost finished getting them saddled," the nymph called from inside the stable. "Russilda, I'll need your help."

She looked at her husband but he motioned her away with his good hand–his sword hand. "Go," he wheezed, "help the nymph saddle up our horses. Archon is right...and let the rest of the horses run free as well."

They exited the stable simultaneously: Archon was in the lead astride his tall grey stallion. He headed, like an arrow shot from a bow, into the body of the beasts that fanned out like a net thrown to catch and bring them down. Roxette followed on her shabby mare but veered off sharply to the left followed by Elron and Russilda. The sorceress took up a defensive position at the back, hurling balls of flame at any beast that dared to follow in their wake as they sped towards the forest.

Archon raised his head to gaze at the solitary figure that stood crow-like at the top of the hill on the far side of the cottage opposite the direction Roxette had taken. Whoever he was he stood there, a general overseeing a successful campaign. Archon cast a mind search at the figure. He recoiled instantly with disgust upon sensing the evil intent oozing from the being like puss from an infected wound; it had intentionally allowed him a glimpse of its thoughts to impress upon him all the vile things it had in store for him and how indifferent it was to his performance. The deflective spell it had set up with astonishing ease to counter Archon's mind search had shaken the mage; he hadn't felt this way since he had been a young sorcerer's apprentice learning his first steps in the use of the gift, greatly humbled before the vast knowledge and prowess of his experienced teachers. He looked in the direction of his companions, realising they had managed to make a clean break. The stable horses had largely managed to scatter into the fields: the enemy wasn't interested in horseflesh at this point. Those few pithiks that had hobbled behind the three riders heading for the woods gave up on them and were returning to him like shavings to a magnet.

Archon made a final desperate attempt to disrupt his foe's advance and gain a few precious moments to make good his escape. The pithiks closest to him fell back clutching at their burning faces, howling with dismay as a shockwave of fire, its epicentre at Archon's outstretched hands, hit them head-on bowling them over like boulders toppling in an earthquake. Grabbing the reins he heeled Mist away from the black rider on the hill and fled in the direction of his friends. Behind him he could hear his name being called out from the hilltop followed by a cackling laugh that chilled him to the bone.

He turned in time to see the cottage and stables going up in flames like twin bonfires.

***

They arrived at port Paliphea shortly after they had fled the cottage; it was only about fifteen miles. The port was bathed in an orange yellow colour under the early morning sun, making its buildings look like amber coals burning in an oven. They entered the northern gate at a walk to rest the horses which were letting off steam from their earlier exertion. They had galloped for most of the way and sheens of sweat had formed on the horses' glistening flanks.

Theo patted his soft roan mare on the neck to express his thanks. She was a good-tempered beast that gave all her effort and did not encumber him with vicious bites or a jolty ride. Nestor's tall chestnut gelding with a white band on his nose and white fetlocks was a favourite at the cottage for his sleek, war-horse looks and swiftness. But even Brigadier was breathing hard with tendrils of vapour trailing from his nostrils.

Theo looked inquisitively around the port that was already bustling with people in the streets; the fishermen were early risers so the shop owners opened their stores early to sell their morning produce to them. They passed a bakery that was exuding tantalizing smells, making the boys' stomachs rumble. They had not had the time or the appetite to eat any of the food that Nestor had so hastily packed. They had only drunk from the water skin to quench their thirst. But now they realized just how famished they were from the morning's ordeal.

Paliphea, like most trading ports, was scarce on living space so the wooden residences were aligned side by side, sharing their boundary walls with a few breaks here and there for the little side roads that criss-crossed the main cobble-stoned road. The buildings stood in line like soldiers, each painted in its own bright colour, giving the overall impression of a poppy field bursting with flowers. It was no wonder that so many oil painters had ventured to the port over the years to capture the chromatic scene on canvas.

"I wonder what my mom and dad are up to," Nem was saying, now they were approaching the side street that led to his home. His parents lived on the outskirts of town in a tall three-storey house. Nem's dad was usually away on his trading business which involved shipping goods via Cyrus to and from other cities, mostly to be found close to the Meldenyan Sea.

"Nem, there's no reason for you to stay with us and endanger yourself. Go to your parents' home and lay low for a while until this all blows over," Nestor urged.

Nem stared back at him for a while clearing the thoughts in his mind, then brightened as he made his final decision. "I'll go say my farewells and join you later at Tiber's place," he said firmly.

"Are you sure?" Nestor asked, his blue eyes intense.

Nem, unable to speak through the lump in his throat, simply nodded.

"Alright then. That settles it. Make sure you're with us in a couple of hours at most. We can't afford to hang around. Those pithiks could be coming at us any moment now. They are not known to enter towns for they hate but also fear humans. However, their masters may come concealed so the locals won't pay any heed. We want to avoid a confrontation." With that said, the group split up.

Theo stared around at the townsfolk who were beginning to fill the streets, running about searching for their morning bread, milk, and other such produce they needed to start their day. *The Blue Mermaid*, as the sign swinging outside the tavern door read, was filling with fishermen taking their morning coffee or other more potent beverages prior to setting out on their daily routine. Some were carrying creels whistling a merry tune whilst heading for the docks wearing bright-coloured kerchiefs or flat sailors' caps with a jolly expression on their sun-kissed faces as they bounded along to their fishing boats. A couple of them offered their greetings on seeing the riders.

Paliphea was a booming merchant town but at such early hours it converted to a fishing town; the merchants began their day a lot later and carried on their trading well into the night. The locals were a close-knit society. They were good-natured and friendly to strangers, who mostly visited for trading purposes, leaving behind plenty of their much appreciated coin as they haggled with the many owners who lined the roads with their stalls and shops.

They halted before a tall, yellow, well-tended house off the main cobbled road and tied up their horses outside. Nestor rapped on the front entrance door waiting patiently. It was not long before they heard the noise of the owner's footsteps approaching from the other side. The door swung open to reveal a blond, slightly chubby, middle-aged woman who was beaming a pleasantly surprised smile at them.

"Nestor! Theo! How nice to see you again," she said, hugging them fondly. "What brings you so early? Have you come for Serilia and Emeralda?" then before they could answer, "Come on in. I've just prepared breakfast."

She helped them remove their cloaks and stopped at the stairs to call out loudly, "Boys, come on down. Breakfast is ready and your grandpa and cousin Theo are here." She turned to Theo and his grandfather and added, "We'll let Serilia and aunt Emeralda sleep a while longer. They're not used to our early mornings. Theo you're looking taller and more handsome by the day."

"Thanks aunt Fiona." Theo blushed slightly.

"Nestor you've lost weight." She looked disapprovingly at the old man. "No matter, we'll soon fix that. How long are you staying for?"

Nestor was about to answer when Theo's uncle Tiber came rushing into the corridor.

"Father, Theo, welcome," he said hugging them both. There was only one word to describe uncle Tiber: Big. He had a broad back and a barrel chest like a wrestler, his arms were as huge as a blacksmith's and he was tall; his head almost reached the ceiling. His rich plentiful head of hair and fierce beard were ginger, unlike Theo's father who had blond hair. However, in his blue eyes and facial expressions one could see the resemblance to his brother, Elron.

Tiber put a large arm on each of his guests' shoulders and led them to the kitchen. Before Nestor had a chance to sit down, two young girls with long blond hair rushed into the room crashing into him, hugging him fiercely.

"Grandfather!" they both cried with glee. He patted and stroked their golden heads, bending to give each one an affectionate kiss on the cheek.

"My sweets," he murmured, his face beaming with happiness.

"Girls, let your grandfather relax after his journey," Fiona urged, bringing food and hot drink to the table.

"Oh, they're no bother, Fiona," Nestor answered as he sat down placing the girls on his knees. "So, what have my two little darlings been up to then? Tell me all about it."

That was all the encouragement the girls needed. They burst, like water released from a fountain, into a long account of their latest adventures, the one eagerly intercepting the other in their willingness to be heard, especially Jenny who was the youngest.

Theo looked up from his breakfast just as the twins entered the kitchen. They grinned at him through freckled faces covered over with long curly ginger hair.

"Cousin!" they both exclaimed gleefully.

"Hello, Neil, Keel," he replied nodding at each one in turn. Nina left her grandfather's side and came over to give Theo a hug, closely followed by Jenny who kept chattering, like a squirrel talking about its acorns, all the way. She did not settle for only a hug but climbed onto Theo's knee.

"Boys, I want you to take the horses over to Robin's stable and tell her to care for them whilst your grandpa and Theo break their fast." Fiona wiped her hands on her apron.

They both rushed away to get their chore done as soon as possible so they could return to their cousin.

"We won't be staying very long, Fiona." Nestor helped himself to some toast and cheese and a hot mug of coffee.

"What's the rush?" Tiber looked from his father to his nephew. "Serilia and aunt Emeralda are still sleeping anyway."

"We've had an incident at the cottage," Nestor explained, his face darkening.

"What kind of incident? Are Elron and Russilda ok?"

"We don't know. We left them with Archon and a Mountain nymph he had brought along as a companion back at the cottage. We were raided by Pithiks last night. When we were making our escape things were looking pretty fired up."

"What are Pithiks doing out of Kalkador?" Tiber's beard seemed to bristle. "No need to ask why they were after Archon; he is always on some errand for the Council that gets him in trouble with some very dodgy characters."

Fiona and her daughters were listening attentively, the shock visible on the youngsters' faces. Even little Jenny had stopped her chattering, sensing the mood rather than understanding the conversation.

"They followed him from Hendon's shores," Nestor answered.

"Pithiks, boarding a boat? How absurd!"

"Well, would you like to go back to the cottage to see the bodies for yourself?"

"No father. I don't think you would make a joke about something this serious, but what's your plan? Are we going to call for aid and go back for my brother and Russilda?"

"No,' Nestor replied firmly. "We were told to get off the island as soon as possible and that they would meet up with us later. We don't have much time. We'll eat quickly and leave. We don't want to endanger you and your family. Serilia and Emeralda can stay here."

"I'll come with you and we'll set sail on the *Sea Breeze.* Fiona can stay here to take care of things for a while."

Nestor nodded in agreement.

"We're coming too," the twins shouted as they entered the kitchen.

"Mom, we want to go as well,' the girls pleaded.

"Where's everyone going?" Serilia asked as she entered rubbing at her eyes and stretching. "Hello Theo, grandpa." She was dressed in her night gown and slippers and was still looking sleepy. She was a tall girl with a body shaping to maturity. Her blue eyes twinkled with intelligence and her easy smile gave a clue as to her generally cheerful disposition. She had the same brown hair as her brother though it was thicker and longer: it now spilt loosely over her shoulders down to her back.

Nestor returned Serilia's smile though its warmth was absent from his eyes. "Theo and I are leaving the island. Your uncle is going to take us with his fishing boat."

"Why are you leaving?"

Fiona came over and laid her arms gently around Serilia's shoulders. "Come and sit down dear and have something to eat whilst your grandpa explains." All eyes turned on Serilia as Nestor retold the events of the previous night. Her face changed from an astonished and worried expression to one of grim determination.

"Father will take care of these raiders, I have no doubt," she said putting on a brave face. "Grandpa is right though, we need to get going as soon as possible."

"We?" Theo asked. "Serilia you're not coming. It's too dangerous."

"If you're going then so am I,' she answered with finality.

"Serilia, your brother is right. You'll be safer here until your parents come and take you away with them. Theo and I will lead our pursuers away from all of you."

"Grandfather, I'm going and that's the end of it."

They ate the rest of their breakfast in a rush. Serilia went upstairs to get changed and pack for the journey. Aunt

Emeralda was going with them as well. Nestor tried to convince her otherwise but he was having no luck with the women this morning. Soon they had said their goodbyes to a tearful Fiona and were off to the stables.

Stable Master Robin kept her stalls neat and tidy and well supplied. The horses were chewing contentedly at their fodder when the group arrived. They had been rubbed down and Robin, who was also a blacksmith, had shoed Brigadier's left hoof.

Theo had met Robin before. She never ceased to amaze him with her benign manner that defied her tough physique. She took Tiber's hand firmly in her own and shook it with vigour like two comrades meeting on equal grounds. She was of average height with shoulder length hair tied back in a ponytail, revealing a pleasant, pretty face.

"Everything ready?" Tiber smiled at her, knowing the answer to his question already.

"Do you have any doubt?" She asked back playfully.

"It's such a pleasure to see a master at work getting the job done right."

"Watch you don't bump your head on my rafter. Your father must have had something put in your food when you were growing up for you to get so tall and clumsy." She winked at Nestor who returned her smile.

Theo couldn't help grinning at them exchanging remarks. For as long as he could remember Tiber and Robin had been close friends. Tiber admired Robin's zest for her work, something he could identify with, since he too was fond of his fishing career.

"Robin I'll need Serilia's and aunt Emeralda's horses as well."

"Going somewhere?"

"We're going for a boat trip. Keep it to yourself though. We're expecting some bad company."

"Say no more."

They left the stables with their mounts and headed hastily for the dockyard. There they found the women waiting for them with the twins. Theo cast his gaze around taking in all the sights. There were several fishing boats of varying sizes moored to the dock, bobbing and swaying to the sea currents. The Meldenyian Sea was abundant with sea life and fishing was a main source of food for the surrounding islands and lands bordering its shores. Theo's eye was drawn to the larger trading vessels and the awe-inspiring battleships that were set apart and dwarfed the fishermen's boats like full grown whales next to a young calf. The merchantmen were wide and sat low in the water. Their varying designs and shapes depended on their origins and at the top of their masts they displayed their homeland's flags proudly.

Paliphea's main harbour, used for unloading the merchantmen, was overlooked by Fort Parthos which was essentially a sheer twelve-foot-high stone wall running along the length of the coast bordering the dockyard and bristling with catapults and giant stone-throwing trebuchets. It made for a formidable defence that together with the staggered wall summit could provide cover and firing positions for numerous archers should the need arise; indeed Fort Parthos had successfully rebuffed, in the past, naval forces intent on invading Cyrus Island's southern shores.

As the group progressed along the foot of the fort wall, they approached what could only be described as a small ship rather than a boat. Tiber's fishing 'boat', the *Sea Breeze,* was a seventy-foot cutter with a well-oiled dark wooden hull and a tall single mast that supported a swivelling triangular main sail and small square top sail both of which were now reefed by the rigging to their yards. Two lateens, one flying the boom and the other behind and above the foredeck, provided additional sailing power to propel the ship forward at high speeds. It had a wide beam and sat in the water with plenty of freeboard signifying its ability to store large quantities of cargo. Unlike the rest of the fishing boats that had smaller hulls and rude sails, the *Sea Breeze* was built for the open seas and could be used as a cruiser. The ship was a huissier, meaning that its stern, facing the docks, had a specially contrived keel piece above the rudder which pivoted on hinges and lowered to form a wide boarding platform for horses–and passengers. The boarding door now rested on the docks, shifting ever so slightly with the boat's leisurely movements.

Tiber let the women and children board the ship first then helped Nestor and Theo coax the horses into stepping on deck. The bulwarks were almost a man's height adding to the ship's depth and its passengers' feeling of safety. The chestnut gelding whinnied but was soon settled down with comforting strokes to its dark temple and neck and soothing words in its ear from Nestor.

"Grandfather, what about Nem?" Theo asked anxiously.

"There's no time to wait for him, Theo. Besides, he might have had a change of heart and decided to stay with his parents."

Just as they were untying the ropes that held the boat fast to the docks and were preparing to lift the platform, they heard someone shouting. They looked up at a young, curly-haired man sprinting down the docks, working his way through a crowd of sailors, all the time shouting at the group on the boat and waving his arms about. It was Nem, urgently leading his brown mare behind him, a bundle of supplies hanging from his saddle.

Theo smiled in relief as his friend was aided by Tiber to board the boat.

"So eager to be off on adventures without me?" Nem managed between gulps of air.

"I wouldn't dream of it." Theo patted his back.

"Well if it isn't the Foresight boy," Serilia teased, beaming an affectionate smile at the new addition to the group.

"What's she doing here?" Nem asked Theo with false annoyance. Serilia thumped him on the arm playfully. "Ouch! That hurts."

"It's supposed to. Now mind your manners on this trip, Foresight."

"The name is Nem. Where are we off to, Theo?"

"Grandfather hasn't told us yet," Theo answered, looking at an albatross dipping into the sea to retrieve a fish successfully from the waters.

Tiber was at the helm manoeuvring the ship out of the shallow dock waters, avoiding collisions with the smaller fishing boats on either side. The twins responded to his unspoken demands, lowering the lateen sail allowing it to catch the aft wind that drove the ship forward as the sail strained against its tack.

Emeralda was standing by Nestor speaking in a low voice, her hand resting on the keel. She was suitably attired for a sea voyage, wearing a white cotton shirt opened at the collar and tight brown trousers revealing her slim curves. These were tucked into her heeled leather boots. She was tall and had the same proud bearing as her half-brother. Her long green cloak was flapping in the wind and loose strands of her red hair–the rest were tied in a bun revealing her pointy nymph ears–were blowing in her face. She brushed them aside as the three youngsters approached.

"That colour suits you," she said, looking approvingly at Serilia's blue velvet tunic and pants. "It matches your eyes and accentuates them, dear." She nodded a greeting at Nem and took Serilia's arm, walking away with her and speaking in hushed conspiratorial tones. Every so often they would turn to look at the boys and Serilia would laugh, probably at some clever remark from Emeralda at the boys' expense.

"Women," Nem scoffed, his ears reddening.

"Grandfather, where are we headed?" Theo asked.

"I've decided we'll make our way due south westerly to the island of Alunda. We can remain there until your parents arrive. I informed Fiona of my decision so she could point them in the right direction. We should be safe with the Sea nymphs until your parents catch up with us. Our pursuers will not be able to follow us there. Alunda is a safe haven against Darklings."

"I've heard the Sea nymphs are a remote people who don't suffer strangers to their shores," Nem said with caution.

"Dolphins!" Neil was shouting from the mast head, pointing to starboard. He had used the ship's shroud as a ladder to climb to the top of the mast.

The crew made their way to the right flank of the ship. Theo peered over the keel in the direction Neil was pointing. The ship was making good progress with the prevailing wind pushing it steadily forward causing waves to be formed in its wake. Swimming side by side with the ship was a school of dolphins clearing the water with huge leaps, re-entering only to repeat the leaps a moment later. They kept pace easily, blowing spray through their blow-holes making clicking noises and splashing water playfully at their audience.

"They're beautiful," Emeralda called out. She waved at the dolphins and spoke in nymphish to them which they seemed to understand for they answered her with clicks and responded to her praise with eager bounds.

Theo could tell his aunt was in her element. He too was enjoying the fresh sea air and the salty taste on his lips from the spray. The morning sun lit up their faces as they stared at the dolphins in their play.

It was close to midday when they approached the shores of Alunda. Its beaches stretched out before them: golden white sand washed over by clear blue waters, coconut and palm trees spreading into the inland green, soft rolling hills covered in luscious green vegetation at the island centre. It seemed deserted with no signs of human habitation, giving it an eerie, mysterious feel.

The twins reefed the sails as Tiber gently led the *Sea Breeze* into a shallow bay. It was a tricky feat getting the vessel turned about and in a position to unload the horses while at the same time ensuring the boat did not run aground, but one which Tiber carried out with mastery at the helm that was hard to match. Soon the ship was anchored and tied down safely with pegs driven deep into sturdy ground on shore. The twins lowered the platform so the crew could jump off. The women took off their shoes and plunged knee deep into the waters followed by the men who led the horses, which stepped gingerly off the boat and sloshed behind.

A fire was soon lit and everyone was drying their wet clothes. Emeralda sent the twins to the boat to retrieve the cooking pots and busied herself stirring a broth she had made containing hake that Keel had caught on his line during the sea trip and a variety of herbs and vegetables she had packed from Fiona's house. They all sat around the fire getting warm and waited eagerly for the meal.

Theo sat to one side with his sister. An exotic bird balancing at the edge of a tree limb was calling out to its mate, ruffling its multicoloured feathers and peering at him with one eye as it held its head askance.

"Theo," Serilia said, turning towards him. She straightened her blue velvet tunic and was fussing with her sleeve. She wiped a tear from her cheek and an involuntary sob escaped her throat.

"What's the matter, Serilia?" Theo gently cradled her in his arms. She buried her face in his embrace, sighing, then turned her head away and began to remove stray threads from Theo's cotton shirt absent-mindedly. Theo passed a consoling hand through her hair thinking of how much he treasured her. It was only the two of them now. He felt he had a responsibility to protect her, even though Serilia was a tough girl with a sharp mind and mature manner that made him feel childlike and feeble in return. She had grown from a young playful girl with skirts and ponytails into a calm and collected woman aware of her developing maturity and budding beauty.

"Do you think our parents will be alright?" she murmured softly, her face close to his so her eyes, like deep pools of water, completely filled his vision.

"Of course they will be alright," Theo cooed, holding her tightly. *Father is a worldly man with many talents,* he thought. His military training had toughened him like rough hide and their mother had proven more resilient than Theo could ever have imagined. "Weren't you the one that said our dad could take care of things?" he asked, willing it to be so. He had to think positive and give strength to his sister, just like his father gave *them* strength. Elron had never used his affliction as an excuse to live life lackadaisically, but instead he had kept up his work at the cottage in earnest, tending his flock of sheep and raising herds of horses, pastimes he enjoyed from his days as a youth when he had been in the service of the royal stables. He had managed to move up from stable boy and squire, to full knighthood and then on to become a commander of a cavalry regiment in the Hendon army. *Of course the cottage is probably destroyed by now, but we are alive and that's what counts.* Theo kissed his sister on the head. *Buildings can be erected again whereas people cannot be mended when broken.*

"I suppose you're right," Serilia conceded, putting on a brave face and resuming her normal collected self which exuded confidence and gave courage to those near her. "I shouldn't worry," she said firmly, patting Theo's hand in thanks. "Was it terrible?" she added in a more controlled inquisitor's voice.

"What? The raid you mean?"

She nodded. "Yes. Did you get a good look at them before you escaped?"

"Unfortunately, yes," he said, shivering involuntarily as the previous night's images flashed before him.

"Were mom and dad ok? I mean...were they alright when you left them?"

"Dad was fine and mom was doing well with the Mage Archon."

"A real sorcerer!" Serilia exclaimed with wonder. "Mom often told us stories about the Council and the Sorcerers but I never thought we would meet one."

"Well mom's a sorceress."

"Yes but that's different. I mean she's our mother so we don't think of her that way."

Theo wished he could go back to feeling that way about his mother too, but he knew better now. He said as much, sadly.

"What's changed?" Serilia looked at him with a spark of interest in her eye.

"If you were there last night you would have understood what I mean," Theo said, his face lighting up. Even though he would have preferred to have remained blissfully ignorant of his mother's sinister, more mysterious side, he could not help recalling how he had stood dumbfounded and awestruck as she artfully carried out her arcane battle on their attackers. "I saw a completely different side of her, one she has been downplaying for a long while."

"Mom doesn't believe in using the gift without just cause," Serilia explained, then asked eagerly. "Was she good? I mean was she any different from the sorcerer at using the gift?"

"Serilia," Theo looked at her intently, "she was magnificent. You would have been proud." Killing was wrong but defending one's family from an oppressor was a sacred duty and one that his mother had carried out without regard for her own safety.

"I hope she managed to kill the whole lot of them," Serilia said with fervour, surprising Theo with her bitterness. His sister had mettle. He felt sorry for anyone who might cross her.

Theo was silent for a while as his mind wondered. He thought involuntarily of how he had been sick from the smell of death at the cottage and his face lost some of its colour. Serilia sensing his unease changed the subject.

"Shall we go for a walk whilst the food gets ready?" she offered, getting up and straightening her velvet trousers.

"Yes. Why not?"

Theo joined her followed by Nem and the twins who had been pretending not to hear their private conversation.

"Children, don't stray too far because dinner will be ready soon," Emeralda called from the campfire where she was bent over her pot stirring the brew.

"We'll always be children to her," Theo said, grinning.

"She loves us dearly as we do her," Serilia agreed.

They approached the horses, which had been let loose to nibble at fresh shoots sprouting from the ground. Theo stroked Brigadier's neck fondly, admiring his muscled, sleek form. Aunt Emeralda's and Serilia's ponies were off to one side nibbling contentedly at some roots they had uncovered, whilst the mares stood huddled close to the gelding feeling safety in numbers. The chestnut nudged at Theo's shoulder with his white-banded nose seeking attention. Theo obliged, scratching him tenderly behind the ears.

"So what do you make of this island?" Nem asked, looking about with interest. Theo looked at the green surrounding them. Alunda was alive with the sounds of birds chirping contently. Further into the woods he could hear the calls of small mammals: squirrels, chipmunks or even small monkeys; once or twice he spotted the little creatures staring at them with their pink faces and bands of blue around the eyes, giving them the appearance of robbers wearing scarves to hide their identity; their silver heads of hair stood on end round their faces, like lion's manes. When startled they raised their long silver tails revealing pink rear ends as they flew through the trees, calling out with loud yelps and leaving the disturbed tree branches swinging to and fro in their wake.

"Aunt Emeralda is from this island, you know," Serilia said.

"Yes. She's a Sea nymph isn't she?" Nem asked with interest, stroking his chin thoughtfully.

"Yes, though she came to live with grandpa when grandmother Rubin died."

"So you never met your grandmother, then," he said carefully, not wanting to stir up bad memories or to cause offence.

"No. Dad and Uncle Tiber were teenagers when she died."

"And Emeralda stayed with you all this time?" It was more a statement than a question. "Didn't she miss her home?"

"We became her family and home, though every couple of years or so she would venture to this island to visit her relatives."

"She has family here? I mean does she have more brothers and sisters living on the island?"

"She has one more brother named Rufous and a sister named Dextra, whom she seldom mentions in front of our grandpa."

"Your grandfather is related to them also?"

"Yes, they share the same father, but grandpa's mother—our great grandmother Maritha—was human."

"That explains why Nestor and Emeralda look alike, except for the ears. Has your grandfather ever returned to Alunda?"

"Not from what I know. He left when he was in his late teens and never returned. Aunt Emeralda says there's bad blood between grandpa Nestor and his half-brother King Rufous and half-sister Dextra."

"A king no less!" Nem raised his eyebrows.

"Yes, Prium, their father, was king of the Sea nymphs before he retired."

"How do you know all this?" Theo was amazed by what he had just heard and the extent of his sister's knowledge of their grandfather's and aunt's family.

"We women learn from a young age to communicate, unlike you men who keep things bottled up inside," Serilia rebuked Theo, as if by doing so she was reprimanding all men. She looked pointedly at Nem, who blushed and averted his eyes.

"We're royalty." The twins lifted their chins up and strutted about with their thumbs tucked below their tunics like roosters.

"Oh stop that," Serilia and Theo spoke up together.

"Alright. Don't get your feathers ruffled. It's not everyday one learns one is blue-blooded," Neil explained. "Yeah, that's right," Keel added.

"Come. Let's get back. I'm starving." Nem lifted his nose, smelling the aroma drifting over to them from Emeralda's cooking pot.

"That hole in your stomach will never mend," Theo chided teasingly.

They ate their meal in silence enjoying its rich, savoury taste. When they had finished, they napped under the trees till afternoon wore off into evening.

♦ CHAPTER 3 ♦

Alunda Sea nymphs

Theo was awakened by a sense of being watched. He sat up straight and peered into the forest. Rubbing the sleep from his eyes he stared more keenly at the undergrowth beneath the palm trees and was startled by what he saw. He stood up the same time Nem did. The rest of the group was looking intently in the direction of the trees.

"No need to be afraid," Emeralda reassured them.

Theo thought he was looking at fish with legs –at least that was what the strangers appeared to be. They wore scaled swimsuits that covered their entire body, apart from their hands, feet and faces. The suits extended over their heads and shark teeth lined the perimeter of the hole left for the face. In their left hands they held flippers and in their right pointed spears like javelins for skewering fish.

Emeralda greeted the strangers in the traditional manner used by the nymphs that involved touching one's temple and heart to signify good intentions. The sea nymphs greeted her in kind, moving closer. There were nine of them.

The lead nymph, a tall slender man with fine features and blue eyes like Emeralda's, pulled back his hood revealing copper hair that tumbled over his shoulders. He held a triad in his right hand to mark him as leader.

"Your Highness, welcome back to your homeland. I am named Alorn and am at your service for however long you may require me," he said, bowing low formally. He was speaking Galipan, the tongue most commonly used by Cyrus and the surrounding lands though as he spoke the ear was deceived into thinking he was singing the words. Aunt Emeralda was the only member in Theo's family who spoke with such a singing lilt to her voice–it was a characteristic trait of nymphkind; even Roxette had spoken with the same mannerism, though her accent was harsher–rougher–somehow.

The rest of Alorn's companions followed suit in bowing respectfully to Emeralda. "Our welcome extends to your guests as well," he added straightening up.

"You are most kind, Alorn. I recognize you from my previous visits to Alunda and am glad once more to be under your care. Now, please be a dear and escort us to the hidden kingdom and to my brother the king. We need his aid and require his counsel on a grave matter that has caused us some measure of grief."

"May our gracious king shed some light on your problem and dispel your grief."

"I thank you, Alorn. Please lead the way."

The sea nymphs escorted them around the bay away from the ship's berth to a rocky point where in the past lava had caused the igneous rock to form in sharp, jutting edges. In the centre of the rock there was an opening roughly fifteen yards in diameter that led into a cave. The small red pebbles lining its entrance seemed to extend all the way into its darker depths.

The group stepped tentatively past the jutting rocks. Inside, the cave was surprisingly well lit by numerous lanterns. Hanging on the walls were additional shark swimsuits which Alorn handed out to the visitors.

"Put these on," he instructed. "They will prevent hypothermia in the deep where the water is cold."

"We're just going to strip right here... in the middle of the cave... with you watching?" Serilia asked incredulously.

Alorn grinned at her, his eyes sparkling with amusement.

"These humans are a bashful lot," he said, turning to one of his comrades who was also grinning.

"I don't understand," a young she-nymph said, approaching Serilia. "You have a nice figure. Why are you ashamed to show it?"

Serilia blushed profusely and turned in exasperation to her aunt.

"The Sea nymphs have different ideals and perspectives on what is ethical or not, dear" her aunt explained. "Don't let it upset you. Just take off your clothes and I'll make sure *all* the men," and she looked pointedly at Alorn and his companions and then at the boys, "turn around and remain so until you wear your suit."

"The young lady's wish is our command," Alorn said mischievously motioning to his men to turn around.

It was not long before everyone was wearing their suits—even the twins had found ones their size.

"Now listen carefully, everyone," Alorn called out beckoning for the visitors to huddle closer. "This," he said, picking up a round shell the size of a fist, "is a breathing clam. You wear it like this so it covers your nose and mouth. As soon as you're submerged it will filter air through so you can breathe."

"There's no way I'm putting that thing on my face," Serilia said, pinching her mouth with disgust.

"Don't be so squeamish," said the she-nymph that had spoken to her before, as she placed the clam to her mouth. She dipped her head under the water releasing air bubbles as she breathed. She came up again and removed the clam. "See. It's easy."

"What's your name?" Serilia asked, feeling she could trust the nymph.

"My name is Yiora."

"Pleased to meet you, Yiora. I am Serilia."

"Likewise." They shook hands.

"Uncle Tiber, what about the horses?" Theo remembered abruptly.

"They'll be fine, Theo. There's plenty of grazing foliage and, from what I know, there are no large predators on the island that can harm them," he said, turning to Alorn who nodded in agreement.

They immersed themselves in a world unlike any they could have imagined. The breathing clams were very effective. Theo at first did not appreciate the mucus feel of the clam's fleshy body on his nose and mouth; his initial feelings were of revulsion but once he began to breathe fresh air below the water surface he forgot all about the clam and concentrated on all the wonders that surrounded him. To his surprise the swimsuit kept him warm and made him feel protected from anything sharp that might scratch his naked skin.

They worked their way in and out of a series of tunnels and caves that interconnected forming a complex maze. It was as if a crazed artist had burst on the scene with his brush and palette, splashing the multitude of plant and animal life forms with all the shades of the spectrum. Small fish darted in and out of the anemones looking inquisitively at the divers whilst blowing bubbles contentedly from their mouths. The rocks were covered over with coral and long-leafed vegetation that moved about leisurely to the sea currents in wave-like motions. As the sea nymphs passed by with their harpoon-shaped spears, the fish scattered away like flocks of birds taking to the air after being startled by a predator.

At one point a small shark was burrowing in the rocks searching for crabs. It looked at the divers and thrashed its powerful tail, propelling itself away. A couple of dolphins also approached and allowed Theo and Nem to move beside them. They clicked with contentment as the boys scratched at their noses and stroked their heads. The dolphins, at a command from Alorn, swam behind him placing their noses to his feet and pushed him forward at great speed.

Yiora motioned for the group to follow. They were moving into openings ever increasing in size and Theo felt they were beginning to climb; the direction of the air bubbles as they rose indicated up from down. The tunnels were surprisingly well lit by the sun's rays which trickled their way through openings in the tunnel roofs. Then at one particular tunnel the group halted.

The dolphins returned with Alorn and four more nymphs carrying what looked like underwater lanterns; they were in fact glass containers which at close inspection were filled with little plankton-like life forms that gave off a phosphorescent white light. Alorn pointed at the 'lanterns', then at the group of divers, and then at the dark tunnel opening. The group nodded in understanding, flipping their feet to propel themselves into the tunnel.

The walls were wide apart so two divers could comfortably swim side by side. They reflected the phosphorescent light from the plankton in shades of green, blue, red, then back to green again. Theo realized in amazement that this lining of the walls was made of precious stones, quite possibly emeralds, rubies and sapphires. He looked at Nem and could see the astonished expression on his friend's face revealed by the uncanny plankton light. Nem grabbed at a green stone that was jutting out but couldn't dislodge it. Instead he cut his finger on the razor sharp surface. Yiora waved a scolding finger in his face motioning for him to keep moving. A sea serpent darting in and out of its lair frightened the wits out of Serilia but she soon recovered and flipped her feet.

After what seemed like ages they emerged out the other side to a brightly lit chamber with a dark green marble basin floor and reddish, intermingled with black, flecked marble steps that climbed upwards. It took a while for them to adjust to the natural light that was far brighter than the plankton light had been. They blinked and swam close to the edge of the first steps where they were motioned to remove their flippers. They did so, holding them in their hands and climbing cautiously, like a toddler taking its first tentative steps; their legs needed a moment to recollect how walking was done, since they had been pushing with the flippers for so long.

Theo emerged from the water almost losing consciousness. He was trying to suck in breath but the clam blocked his airways. Alorn, seeing his distress, ripped the clam away from his face. He gulped in the precious air, filling his lungs.

"You're supposed to take the clam off when emerging from the water," Alorn pointed out dryly.

"Thanks for the warning," Theo answered accusingly between breaths. He didn't dwell on the subject however, but gazed around open-mouthed at the spectacle before him. He was in the largest cave dwelling he had ever seen. The roof of the cave was sloping away many feet above them and was dome-shaped with its apex open to allow an inward flood of light that illuminated the entire city that lay richly sprawled before them. A gathering of tall trees bathed in the sun's pool of light and were dressed in their spring shoots of green leaves, decorated further with splashes of the red and blue plumage of exotic birds which filled the cave with their symphony of shrill, chirping sounds. Amongst the trees stood, interspersed, a variety of white marble stone buildings, with their sloping gable roofs supported by great round columns. The triangular roof pediments and the column metopes were ornately decorated in gold, silver and all manner of precious stones so a feeling of shameless opulence exuded from the city.

Theo had never seen such splendour. Bountiful supplies of diamonds, rubies, emeralds, black and white pearls and many, many more decorative stones were used to make mosaic patterns on the walls and floors depicting various sea creatures such as: sea horses, dolphins, large octopi and many others. Sea nymphs were also depicted in their every day life undertaking various activities: playing musical instruments, laughing, feasting and, to Theo's astonishment, coupling.

The stairs they had climbed continued on for about another ten steps. They ended at a grand courtyard lined with neatly kept hedges and here and there benches occupied by young nymphs embracing or chatting to one another. Children were running on the lawn, their merry voices filling the courtyard with their playful shouting and laughing. In its centre, beige stones were neatly placed to form a pathway that was lined on either side with flowers. The path was easily over thirty feet wide and led to a grand palace that stood taller than the rest of the buildings.

The group moved on in silence, taking in all the sights and exchanging glances with the young nymphs who were occupying the gardens. The nymphs looked at the visitors with interest and were friendly in their demeanour, sensing by the expression of the escort that all was well. Some of the younger nymph maidens greeted Alorn fondly and quite a few of them cast eager, inviting looks at Theo and Nem, who blushed profusely. The children halted from their play and stood in line to gaze nosily at the group. Two of them broke away from the line and ran towards Emeralda, falling into her embrace.

"Aunt Emeralda," they cried out gleefully. "We missed you."

"I missed you dearly as well, my sweets," she answered, giving each one a peck on the cheek. Then turning to the others she said fondly, "This red-haired young man is Timothy, and this little bundle of joy is Pearl."

They greeted one another and Theo was informed by his aunt that he was related to the children from his grandfather's side. They walked along the path accompanied by the children who chattered incessantly with Emeralda, filling her in on the goings-on of the royal family whilst she had been away. Soon they arrived at a group of columns that did not support a structure but stood like worshippers in the centre of the path surrounding a dais. Sitting on the dais was a larger than life statue three storeys high made from the finest white marble depicting a nymph deity who wore a golden crown on his head with three spokes on the front. In his right hand he held a large bronze trident and in his left he carried the reigns to his sea chariot which was made of gold and was being drawn by six dolphins so one could almost imagine the sea spray forming from their thrashing tail fins. His upper torso was bare revealing large shoulders, a broad chest and muscular arms and from the waist down he was covered in scales; instead of legs he had a long fish-like tail. For eyes he had sapphires and his eyebrows were heavy and arched on either side of his nose below which he had a long beard forked into three points with each tied by a golden clip.

"Impressive, isn't he?" Emeralda whispered, not wanting to intrude on the silence that had befallen the group.

"Very," Theo said with awe.

"It's a statue of the sea god, Nerus, crafted by one of our most skilled sculptors who, alas, is long dead but thankfully has left many examples of his fine works of art behind."

Nem blew out a whistle of amazement whilst Alorn escorted them to the palace entrance that was beyond the dais. The stone path gave way to a white marble floor with grey striations and intermittently dispersed in the marble were mosaic decorations depicting nymphs bordered in gold.

They entered through an open iron gate that was painted in black with golden leaf shapes of dolphins and other sea creatures attached to the gate bars. To either side of the gate stood large, square pillars for gate posts and atop the pillars rested bronze braziers filled with burning coals letting off a steady undulating flame.

They were led through the gates and through an external corridor lined on either side by guards who saluted as Alorn passed with his group. The guards were dressed in their customary grey uniforms covered over by blue cloaks and in their hands they held spears or tridents. Strapped to their free arm they carried square iron shields large enough to protect their chests. Each shield was slightly concave with projecting ridges forming an "X" that joined the corners of the shield. In its centre there was a semi-spherical projection designed to deflect strikes from a sword or axe blow.

"Here we are then," Alorn said, as they approached the palace doors that were surprisingly made of simple wood but also ornately decorated with gold patterns. Emeralda spoke softly in Alorn's ear. He nodded, and in turn spoke discreetly to the door guards. They swung open the heavy doors.

"His Royal Highness Prince Nestor of Alunda and Her Royal Highness Princess Emeralda of Alunda," the guard on the right called out loudly so his voice carried well into the throne room.

The courtroom was filled with people dressed in simple but colourful robes so most of the men's upper torsos were naked apart from a toga thrown over one shoulder and the women's silk dresses were thin with low bosom lines. Most of the women wore their hair up so as to show their swanlike necks, that together with their wrists were dripping with jewellery. The courtiers were moving around gracefully, like dancers at a ball, talking amongst themselves and listening to the sweet voices of a young male and female nymph pair who were singing in harmony with a musician playing the harp. All fell silent as the royal visitors were announced and all eyes turned to look at the group as it was led forward by Alorn. The group stopped before the throne of Rufous, King of Alunda, Lord of the Sea nymphs. Alorn genuflected, everyone following suit.

"My King," the tall red-haired warrior called out in a strong voice that carried to all corners of the throne room. "I present to you your sister Emeralda, your brother Nestor and their entourage, who seek asylum and your majesty's counsel."

Theo looked closely at Rufous and was surprised to find that he resembled his grandfather; his blue eyes had the same hawk-like gaze and he sat straight and proud. Unlike Nestor he looked just over fifty and his hair, like his name implied, retained its red colour with only some wisps of grey. He too was attired like his courtiers with a simple white toga thrown over his left shoulder. It was clasped at the waist by a broad belt studded with jewels with the rest of the robe left to spill over his legs to his ankles. In his right hand he held a triad similar to the one Theo had seen the statue of Nerus holding.

"Alorn. You should know better than to announce our half brother Nestor as a prince of Alunda." All turned to the tall figure that stood to the right of the king. She bore a resemblance to the king but appeared slightly younger.

"It was I who bade Alorn introduce our brother," the word *brother* was stressed, "with his correct title, Dextra," Emeralda said, rising to her full height as she stood squarely facing her sister.

"Always the one to stir trouble in the family, Emeralda," said Dextra, who was dressed in deep blue velvet garments. Her intense violet eyes were hate-filled and she made no attempt to hide her disdain for Emeralda and Nestor.

"This was a mistake," Nestor said submissively turning around as if to leave.

"Will you not grant me a chance to express my feelings on the matter, brother?" the king asked, his eyes sullen with sadness.

Nestor turned slowly to face his brother the king. "You made your feelings on the matter quite clear, brother," he said firmly, "when we last parted all those years ago."

"Times change, brother," the king insisted. "A man should be allowed to mend his errors. I sent for you shortly after my wife Kaprine died, but you wouldn't come."

"There's no need for you to explain yourself to him, brother," Dextra said vehemently, her face scarlet.

"It's time to put the past behind us, Dextra," the king insisted sorrowfully. "We aren't getting any younger and in the end family is all that remains." Young Pearl and Timothy, sensing their father's anguish, ran to him. The king took them in his arms placing one on either knee. "As I was saying, family is what we cherish most."

"I will not stand around listening to any more of this," Dextra said, turning about so she was facing Theo and his companions. She had short cropped red hair combed forward so it ended in tips around her pinched mouth and sharp cheekbones. Theo stood transfixed by her gaze, like a sparrow before a venomous snake. His hackles rose as he sensed that familiar feeling of someone searching the borders of his mind. The woman lifted a lip to sneer at him. "I wouldn't want to be the cause of ruining this joyous reunion," she added sarcastically, before walking away. She was followed by those courtiers faithful to her as she left the hall by a side door.

"What a creepy woman," Serilia whispered slowly.

"You felt it too?" Theo asked astonished.

"Why brother! You have begun to awaken the gift in you. I'm impressed," she said mockingly.

Theo felt like an idiot. His sister was far more advanced than he was at using the gift and had displayed her talents several times in the past when she was receiving instruction by their mother. He was taken out of his musing by the king's grim voice.

"You must forgive our sister, Nestor," the king was saying. "She will come around eventually. Now please, make yourselves at home in the palace and after you've been shown to your rooms and had a chance to refresh yourselves, join me in the dining hall where we can sit and discuss what ails you."

He clapped his hands and two young maiden nymphs approached signalling for the group to follow them. Tiber and the twins walked behind Nestor and Emeralda. Theo followed with his sister and Nem.

"I thought they'd never get the talking over with so we could get down to the serious stuff," Nem complained.

"Which is?" Theo asked.

"Why, dinner of course."

"Foresight, you're impossible." Serilia scolded.

"Nem, remember? Just plain old Nem."

Serilia raised her chin, ignoring him.

The rooms they were shown to were large and well-lit with candelabrums and torches hanging from the walls. The windows looked out into the woods which were silent, now nightfall had fallen. They bathed with the hot water the nymph maidens supplied for them and changed into evening wear in preparation for dinner.

"Serilia, Emeralda, you look stunning," Tiber was saying, as the two women made their way down the corridor to where the others were awaiting them. Emeralda wore a dark blue velvet gown that complemented her eyes and hugged her form whilst Serilia wore a green frock with a low hem line that formed a "V" at her bosom line, revealing parts of her womanliness. Nem blushed furiously but did not avert his eyes.

"You are planning on going in that?" Theo asked in an admonishing big brother tone.

"I wouldn't have worn it otherwise, would I silly?" Serilia tsussed, grinning impishly.

At the table, they sat with the king and several of the higher ranking nobility. On the other side of the table, and as far away from Nestor as possible, sat Dextra dressed in a black dress looking intently at Theo, a haughty smirk on her face.

Seeing Theo returning Dextra's look, Emeralda leaned over to caution him. "I'd stay away from her if I were you. She is known to dabble in witchcraft and most folk give her a wide berth."

"So I was right about her being a sorceress."

"Not a sorceress boy–witch. There's a difference."

They turned to listen more attentively to the conversation between the king and their uncle Tiber.

"Do you own any ships on this island, King Rufous?"

"We have no need of ships, nephew. All our trading is done directly at our shores. We provide precious stones from our underwater tunnels and the traders, once they unload their goods, cast away. We do not allow more than one ship at a time to berth at our shores–for safety reasons."

"How do you enforce your rules?"

"We are not without our own vessels. We have sea chariots scouring the seas keeping them safe from intruders."

"Oh? I have not seen any vessels on my way here."

"You weren't paying attention. Ours are submersibles so they cannot be seen from above unless they are very close or driven to the surface."

"How do you propel such craft?" Tiber asked with growing interest.

"We use the dolphins. We keep a lot here under our care from young porpoises and train them to fulfil a variety of tasks. If you like, Alorn can show you around later so you can visit our submersibles and study the dolphins at work," the king said, turning to his warrior who nodded.

Theo turned to where Timothy was chatting excitedly with the twins about the joys of spear fishing. Neil and Keel sat chewing at their meal listening closely to Timothy relating how on one of his fishing trips he had caught a giant skate. They told him in turn about the hake Keel had caught earlier during the day. Theo could see a strong resemblance between the twins and their newly discovered cousins. They had the same curly red hair and blue eyes and seemed to share the same interests.

"I've taken a look at your fishing ship, Tiber," Alorn was saying, "and I must admit it's amongst the best I've seen. It is an all-rounder, capable of both short fishing trips at sea but also built for long ocean voyages."

"Yes, the *Sea Breeze* is our family's most prized possession," Tiber said with pride. "And one never knows when one might need to make a long trip."

They were halfway through the meal when an elderly, bent over couple walked into the dining hall. The woman was dressed in thick black silks and approached Emeralda giving her a peck on the cheek. "Nice to see you again, daughter," she said, then looked at Nestor for a long while, as if recollecting something in her past. Finally, recognizing him, she stepped away. 'You!" she exclaimed with distaste then turned away to walk over and join Dextra on the other side of the table. The old man hobbled over slowly, clutching his walking stick with a trembling hand bent over like a beggar. His long grey hair was dishevelled and he wore a simple grey woollen toga. He approached wearily and stood studying the people around the table who had fallen silent at his entry.

"Father, come sit by us," King Rufous said.

Nestor rose slowly as the old man squinted up at him, unable to straighten his back. Nestor's eyes brimmed over with tears and a gasp escaped the old man.

"Praise Nerus!" The old man exclaimed. "Is it you, my son? My quiet, young Nestor?"

"It's me father," Nestor managed through a lump in his throat. He worked his way around the table and took his father into a loving embrace.

"My boy," the old man sobbed. "It's been so long. I've missed you so much, Nestor my child. Why did you not come sooner?"

"I couldn't father. I...I needed time to come to terms with myself. When Rubin died...I lost the will to live. But Emeralda and the boys helped me overcome my grief. Come over and meet my son, Tiber."

Nestor introduced his father, Prium, to his son and then to Theo, Serilia and the rest of the family and friends. To his family he said, "The lady over there is my father's first wife, Ziana," his voice neutral so as not to offend, as he pointed to the old woman who had gone to sit beside her youngest daughter Dextra.

"My heart is brimming over with happiness," old Prium said, wiping away at his moist cheeks. "Oh, how I miss my Maritha," he added, looking at Nestor.

"I miss mother too." Nestor lowered his eyes sadly.

"Emeralda told me you had another son, one that looks like my Maritha. Where is young Elron?"

There was a hushed silence whilst the companions stared at one another.

"That's the main reason for our visit," Nestor said after a long pause, turning to include the king in the conversation. "My cottage at Cyrus was attacked by Darklings and for all I know is destroyed. My son and daughter-in-law, I pray, have managed to make good their escape. We will remain here for a few days, provided you will have us, in the hope that they got away and will manage to come after us. Archon, the Wizard from Aldorn is with them, so I feel more assured they will make it."

Dextra, from across the table made a "hah" sound to give her opinion about Archon's ability to shape the outcome of events.

"I know of this Archon you speak of," said the king, placing a hand thoughtfully below his chin. "He has visited us at times, searching through our libraries for various bits of information about the goings-on around our island. We keep catalogued the events taking place in the Meldenyan waters, such as pirate raids from Ishbad or Neba and many other happenings that are worth writing down. Our history books are quite extensive. He was quite close to my daughter Nethida, before she was lost at sea on one of her expeditions." He looked away with a pained look on his face.

"When was that?" Nestor faintly remembered Emeralda mentioning the incident.

"It has gone on to fourteen years now," the king muttered, looking morosely at his younger children who hugged him lovingly. "From what I recall, you did not see eye to eye with the wizard, Dextra." He turned to his sister who scoffed, giving him a flat look.

The rest of the evening was spent with Nestor reciting the events of the previous night.

♦ CHAPTER 4 ♦

Lords of the sky

Theo was tossing and turning in bed. He had drawn his curtains and had extinguished his candelabrum so he could be lulled into sleep, but to no avail. So much had occurred the previous evening when they had been in the Triad Woods. In just one day he had been separated from his parents and gotten whisked away to a remote island with inhabitants and an underwater kingdom that fables were made from. He was still very much on edge. Where were Archon and his parents? Would he see them again any time soon? Why did Nestor's step-mother hate him so much–well actually that was the only question he could hazard a guess at answering: it was plain to see that Theo's grandfather was a constant reminder to Ziana of Prium's infidelity when he was younger. Was that why Dextra shared that hatred–because she felt defensive of her mother's honour? But that was a long time ago, and King Rufous did not feel that way any more, so why should she? He bolted upright, startled by a knock at his door. The knocking continued until he opened up wearing only his night clothes and woolly socks.

It was Nem, dressed shabbily with half his shirt left hanging outside his trousers. His hair was in a mess and one trouserleg was tucked into his boots whilst the other was left hanging out, as if he had put them on in irritation.

"I can't sleep," he said simply, entering the room and lighting Theo's candelabrum with his own fat candle.

"Me neither." Theo sat on his bed looking at his friend. He rubbed at his sides with his hands to warm himself against the draft.

Nem stared back at him. "Well?"

"Well what?"

"You're going to sit there all night? Get dressed. We're going exploring."

"Nem, I don't want to get into any trouble," Theo said disapprovingly, but started to pull on his trousers and changed into his shirt.

"Trouble?" Nem grinned impishly. "I don't intentionally go about looking for it."

"Yes. It kind of has a way of finding you on its own," Theo replied dryly.

Nem shrugged his shoulders as they stepped into the corridor. Serilia's door creaked open.

"What are you two up to?" She looked suspicious.

"Nothing," the boys answered innocently. "We just thought we'd go for a short walk, that's all."

"I see," she answered, as if she understood exactly what they meant by "nothing". "I'm going with you. Stay here while I put something on," she ordered, as she went back into her room leaving the door slightly ajar.

Theo groaned.

Very soon Serilia tip-toed out of the room she was sharing with her aunt Emeralda. She wore a long coat thrown over her nightgown, tied at the waist.

"Come on," she said, taking charge as she led the way down the corridor.

"Where are we going?" Theo asked, as they passed by their friends' rooms. Loud snoring was coming from their uncle Tiber's room and Theo found himself wondering if the twins were going to be able to get any sleep.

They left the corridor and stepped into the throne room which was faintly lit by a few torches. Theo stood staring at the paintings and the richly embroidered carpets on the walls depicting fighting scenes out at sea. Red-haired, fair-skinned sea nymphs were struggling against foes who were bronze skinned in contrast, with dark hair and curved moustaches. They wore coned hats on their heads with cloths wrapped around the base and were brandishing broad sabres in one hand to strike at the sea nymphs whilst in the other they held ropes by which they swung from their ships. The sea nymphs in turn were defending themselves with triads and spears from their sea chariots drawn by dolphins.

"These must be the pirates King Rufous mentioned at dinner," Theo whispered in awe.

"The ones from Ishbad and Neba, you mean?" Nem asked.

"Yes, do you know these people?"

"You forget that my father is a ship trader, Theo. The Ishbadese and Nebese are well known for their spice products and their fine silks and gold deposits. The Harim Mountains are a rich supplier of the priceless metal and they uncover rubies and other jewels from their mountains that the lords and ladies of the Midlands admire and desire. It pays to be on good terms with them and for the time being they are not all that hostile, apart from the occasional raid, so trading relations are quite good."

Theo stared at his friend in astonishment and looked on him in a new light. Nem was a lot more knowledgeable of the neighbouring lands than Theo had originally given him credit for.

"Let's get going," Serilia pressed on impatiently. "We'll go that way." She pointed off to an archway that led out of the throne room. "I saw the royal family leaving from there earlier on."

"Let's not startle any of the guards on the way," Theo cautioned.

They entered another hall less broad with a lower ceiling that had both of its walls covered with paintings. To the sides of the hall and lining it to form a corridor a variety of statues of sea nymphs stood on the marbled floor in different poses. Tall windows in the left wall had their curtains drawn so the twinkling from the precious stones lining the insides of the cave reflected the moonlight coming in from the cave opening on top.

They slid behind one of the curtains as they heard footsteps coming towards them. Theo held his breath. The footsteps halted in the hall a few feet away from where the three of them were hiding.

"Have you fed them?" asked a deep voice that sounded like Alorn's.

"Yes, sir," answered a second.

"Everything's well?" Alorn prodded.

"Well...I'm not sure, Commander. The male seemed a bit on edge tonight."

"Really? I'll go check up on him."

Theo and his companions waited till the footsteps faded away in opposite directions.

"Hurry," Serilia hissed, moving swiftly in the direction Alorn had taken.

The boys had no time to object but followed after her. They kept to the shadows whenever they could and tried not to lose sight of Alorn but at the same time not to get too close, to avoid discovery. He led them through several more halls and then out from the side of the palace and into the gardens. They ducked through the trees and rushed to catch up with Alorn who was opening the distance between them. Alorn climbed the steps to a building standing off to one side. It was supported by taller columns than the rest of the buildings. The entrance step treads were deep, as if made for a giant's feet and the youths had to leap ahead to climb them.

They entered. Braziers filled with burning coals provided sparse light. The floor was made of plain unadorned stone which surprised Theo who had grown accustomed to seeing marble floors, and the walls were bare. A soft rumbling sound was coming from the depths of the building and smoke tendrils filled the chamber making it warm and stuffy.

Serilia moved forward cautiously on the tips of her toes. Theo and Nem looked about warily as they followed. Alorn had gone ahead into the source of the smoke vanishing from sight. They came to a flight of broad steps that led downwards into a darkened passageway. They took the steps one at a time till they were submerged in the murky, smoke-filled atmosphere that was moist like a steaming hot spring. Their clothes were dampened, clinging to their skin, their breathing becoming laboured–they tried not to cough and alert anyone of their trespassing. Theo could not distinguish shapes from within the murky depths. The rumbling noise was louder now, underlain by a thumping sound like the beating of a large drum.

Suddenly the smoke cleared–Alorn stood before them, his blue eyes hard and accusing. Behind him rose a giant blue head with twin slits from which stared yellow reptilian eyes. Theo stood petrified. He opened his mouth to warn the sea nymph but his throat was constricted–no sound came from it. The head was followed by a scaled body that hovered above the nymph, spreading its wings wide so that they completely enveloped the steam-filled room. From its nostrils trailed smoke and from its sealed lips protruded long sharp teeth.

"Alorn look out!" Serilia squealed, almost falling over as she tripped on one of the numerous bones littering the floor. She stepped back jerkily, whilst keeping her eyes trained on the reptilian being.

Alorn turned to look behind him and extended a hand to stroke the beast's beaked nose. He seemed perfectly at ease. The blue creature lowered its head, acknowledging his attentions with contentment; rumbling noises of pleasure escaped its throat as Alorn continued to scratch it on the nose and behind the ears. Theo realized the thumping sounds he had heard were the giant creature's heart beating.

"Step closer," Alorn beckoned to the youths. "Don't be afraid."

Theo looked at Nem, who looked equally uneasy, and then at Serilia, who had regained her composure and was fidgeting with the hem of her cloak. Serilia was the first to move. Alorn took her hand and placed it on the beast's nose.

"It's warm." Serilia said surprisingly. "With all those scales I expected it to be cooler, like a fish."

"I am no fish, young maiden." The creature rumbled, like a dozen blow horns all calling at once. Serilia, startled, stepped back hastily.

Alorn laughed. "No, Vracho. You certainly are not, my friend," he said, stroking the dragon's snout fondly.

"A dragon!" Nem was breathless. "My father described them to me once. He had seen a red one during his travels to Hieradon."

"The reds are our enemy," rumbled the blue dragon with contempt, spewing forth jets of flame and smoke from his gaping maw.

"I'm sorry if I offended you," Nem put in quickly, shrinking back with unease.

"No need to be so uptight, Nem," Alorn said, soothingly. "Vracho is simply expressing his view. He will not harm you. Theo, step closer. You may as well make the most of it, since you have decided not to sleep tonight."

Theo joined Serilia in stroking the dragon's ears and nose. He peered closely at the dragon's defenses. Scales were neatly arranged forming a continuous defensive barrier, like a mail shirt, even covering the dragon's feet that ended in sharp dagger-like claws. Its long tail extended well beyond its hind legs, curling back past its underbelly and reaching back up to its forepaws where it forked into a three-pointed tip.

"Vracho, Shanus said you were feeling a bit nervous today." Alorn looked into the dragon's unblinking golden eyes that had black slits for pupils, like a snake's.

"I sense an intruder to my domain, young Alorn," the dragon said, menacingly.

"An intruder? You mean another male dragon?" Alorn asked disbelievingly.

"Yes."

"But how is that possible? There is a moratorium banning dragons from flying skies that are not in their flight domain. No dragon, except during a war, has been known to break this law, and we are not at war."

"I know my senses judge true, Dragonstrider," growled the dragon with slight irritation.

"I didn't mean to question your word, my friend. It's just that this type of thing has never happened before....not since the last Great War.... over one thousand years ago."

Theo did not expect to see the nymph warrior so troubled. It heightened his feelings of unease.

"Well, it looks like we'll be taking a short ride," Alorn said in a resigned voice. He had come to his decision.

"Ride?" Nem asked apprehensively.

"Yes," Alorn was brooking no objections. "You and Theo will ride on Celeste. Serilia and I will ride on Vracho."

"Who's Celeste?" Theo asked only to be startled by a nudge from behind. He turned around in time to come face to face with a second dragon, its snout inches away from his face. Overcoming his initial shock he studied Celeste intently. She looked much like Vracho, only she had a more slender snout and she was not as large and as thick-limbed as the male dragon. "Pleased to meet you, ma'am." Theo was unsure as to the correct way to address a female dragon.

"The boy has good manners," Celeste observed looking at Alorn. "I will allow him to straddle my back."

"Well. Enjoy your ride," said Nem as he turned to leave.

"Nemarchus! I thought I had made myself perfectly clear." Alorn halted the curly haired youth in his tracks. "I said *everyone* will be taking a ride."

When they had climbed upon their respective dragons, Alorn nudged Vracho with his feet. Theo noticed for the first time that the living chamber of the dragons was open at the top to the star-filled sky. With a few powerful beats of their massive webbed wings the dragons rose into the air in unison, clumsily at first like large, sluggish birds, then more swiftly. They approached the gaping hole of the cave apex and flew through it into the cool night.

Theo's eyes were running from the biting cold of the wind blowing in his face. He felt a oneness with Celeste he could only relate to the feeling he had when riding his horse, only he felt a deeper connection with the dragon, as though they shared the same mind; also the thrill of flying was like nothing he had ever experienced before. He turned around to find Nem shivering and cowering over the dragon's back with his eyes tightly shut.

Theo looked down to find they were circling above Alunda Island. Gentle waves were splashing on its shores reflecting the blue light from the smaller moon. The silver moon had not yet come out of its waning cycle and was a thin sliver in the sky. Theo recognized the bay where they had docked the *Sea Breeze*. To his surprise he saw a second smaller boat docked next to it. His heart fluttered with excitement. He dared not raise his hopes too high. He looked over at Vracho who was flapping his gigantic wings riddled with nerve endings; they kept his great body airborne with mighty strokes. He was like a creature from a distant past, belonging to an era when lizards and their kind dominated the earth.

Theo shivered in spite of himself at the archaic visions that the image in his mind's eye had evoked. He recovered and called out so he could be heard above the whistling wind. "Alorn, I need to take a closer look at the boat docked by my uncle's ship," he said, pointing down at the bay.

Serilia cupped a hand to Alorn's ear and said something to him. He nodded and the dragons began their descent.

"Not again," Nem moaned from behind Theo, as his face visibly paled.

"Hang on, Nem," Theo urged, as they plummeted from the sky. They were approaching the boats quickly. From small specks on the sea they were speedily blowing up in size. When they were right on top of the boats the dragons veered sharply upwards beating their powerful wings to gain height once more. Theo looked behind him to see the ships tossing wildly from the turbulence the dragons had left in their wake. The little craft beside uncle Tiber's ship was a small fishing boat with a single triangular sail.

"Theo I can't take any more of this," Nem was saying between clenched teeth.

"Nem, open your eyes. It will help to settle your stomach."

His friend did as he was told and remained silent, not giving any indication whether opening his eyes had aided him in any way. As they were gaining height, Theo saw a red flash from the corner of his eye.

"There!" Alorn shouted, pointing due west to the other side of the island.

Theo could just make out a red form that was fleeing from the island as if it had a full score of pursuing dragons on its tail.

"Vracho, you were right." The dragon let out a derisive snort. "But he's too far away for us to catch him up," Alorn pointed out. "And we will run the risk, if we set out to follow him, of entering foreign flying grounds."

"We'll stay on his tail a while longer to make sure he leaves our area," Vracho commanded. After a few leagues, and when it was plain to see that the red dragon had no intention of remaining in Vracho's domain, the pair of blue dragons banked away to the left and made their way back to the island.

Soon the dragons were back through the cave opening. They alighted with surprising gentleness unto their sleeping chamber stone floor. Alorn let the siblings stroke and pat the dragons before leading them away. Nem couldn't wait to distance himself from the dragons and with each stride they took, the colour returned to his cheeks.

They were about to exit the grounds and enter the palace when they came across Dextra wearing a tight fitting black tunic, black pants and tall, black leather boots with high heels. She had blood on her fingers and held a small mutilated animal in her right hand.

At first she was startled, like a child that's been caught doing something mischievous but soon recovered. Her initial surprise changed to irritation. "Well if it isn't the bustard's grandchildren," she snarled, looking malevolently at Theo and his sister.

"You have no right to speak of grandfather in that way," Serilia answered sternly, her face turning red with annoyance.

"Silence girl!" Dextra snapped. "Learn to know your place. You are on my turf now."

"Princess Dextra, this is not necessary, I was just..." Alorn's voice was cut off like a thread snipped by scissors. His face went blue and he was gasping for breath. Serilia took him in her arms and turned to Dextra. "Please release him. We're sorry for any wrong we may have done. Alorn was just escorting us back to our rooms," she pleaded.

Dextra complied, smiling spitefully–viper-like.

Alorn coughed and spluttered as he tried to regain his breath.

"You should learn, Alorn," Dextra bent close to him, threateningly, "to speak to royalty, only when you are given permission. Now take these dreadful children out of my sight, and teach them to remain in their rooms after dark."

Serilia and Theo tucked themselves underneath Alorn's arms and helped carry him as they walked away grimly without uttering another word.

"That was a cheerful end to our evening," Nem said scornfully, when they had progressed far enough to be sure Dextra was far out of hearing range.

"I'm alright now," Alorn said, removing his arms from the two youngsters' shoulders.

"Are you sure?" Serilia asked, concerned.

Alorn nodded.

"Alorn, why does she hate grandfather so much?" Serilia looked into his blue eyes searchingly.

"Her heart has been poisoned by her blind hatred for all who are not nymph kind."

"But that's absurd. How can one hate someone else for what nature has preordained them to be?"

"It's irrational, I know, and most of us don't share this point of view."

"Well, as long as it's not widely held–this xenophobia–I suppose we ought to be thankful."

"It's not only a question of hostility or blind fear towards humans, though, that drives even nymphs with moderate views on the matter to avoid contact with your kind."

"Oh?"

"Well," Alorn fidgeted and cast uneasy glances at Serilia. "Has not your grandfather told you?"

"Told us what?"

"Well...I mean, about what happens when humans and nymphs interbreed," he added, waiting for her response.

"I don't quite follow." Serilia and Theo were waiting for Alorn to come clean with his explanation.

Alorn stopped and stared at them both for a while trying to find the right words. "The offspring resulting from the union of a nymph and human lives *your* lifespan."

Theo and Serilia exchanged puzzled looks. "And ...?" Serilia said, showing she was missing the point. So what if the child of a human and nymph lived a normal lifespan? Then she had a thought, *how long was considered a normal life span for nymphs?* Come to think of it, *how old was aunt Emeralda?* Serilia had never thought to ask her. She had heard stories about nymphs–that they aged slowly. Aunt Emeralda had always looked the same for as long as she could remember–around her early sixties–though she dressed provocatively and had the energy of a woman at least twenty years younger.

"Serilia, you may not have been told, but on average we nymphs live at least ten of your lifetimes."

Serilia looked at him in stunned silence. *Ten lifetimes*! That would explain matters. No parent wanted to outlive their children or to outlive their spouses for that matter. The situation became crystal clear to her now. But was that enough for one to feel hatred? Could a human not experience love and the pleasures of companionship in their short, in comparison, lifespan? Nestor was proof of that... or he was a reminder of all that was opposite to the nymphs.

They approached the corridor leading to their rooms. Alorn bade them a good night.

♦ CHAPTER 5 ♦

Princely gifts

Theo woke in a haze to find Serilia pulling open his curtains fully dressed in the blue velvet tunic and pants she had worn on the trip to Alunda. He squinted at the sunlight flooding into the room and stretched his arms out, yawning. By the intensity of the light he estimated it was late in the morning.

"You've been sleeping for hours," Serilia said curtly. She moved beside his bed and stood there staring at him.

"Yeah. Last night's little excursion took its toll," Theo offered in explanation.

"Theo," Serilia said seriously, drawing his gaze. "Archon has arrived."

"Archon!" Theo sat up in bed. "So you've met him?" He was hesitant, sensing from Serilia's tone of voice that something was wrong.

She nodded.

"What is it?"

"He's alone."

Theo's face paled. "What about mom and dad?" he asked, fearing the worst.

"They're alright," Serilia assured him quickly, "but they did not come with him."

"Why not?"

"He wouldn't say. He was breaking his fast when I found him talking in hushed tones with King Rufous. He promised to explain later. Grandfather and aunt Emeralda are with him, and uncle Tiber. The twins and Nem are asleep."

Theo's door opened and Nem walked in as if answering to the mention of his name. He was dressed in a white shirt and plain pants. His curly hair was tied back in his customary ponytail style. "Have you heard?" he asked the siblings.

"I thought you were asleep, Foresight," Serilia snickered ignoring his agitated look, adding a mocking smile for good measure.

Nem blew an irritated breath out of his nose and approached his friend. "Well?"

"What is it, again?"

"Get dressed," Nem and Serilia both said at once.

"Alright, keep your shirts on. I need a moment to wash and I'll be out in a minute."

Soon they were making their way down the corridor and passed the halls they had ventured into the previous night until they arrived at the dining hall. King Rufous was sitting at the head of the table with Nestor and Tiber. To his right sat Archon. They were all in deep conversation with grave expressions on their faces. Emeralda was sitting a little way off staring out of the window at the sun's rays.

Archon looked up as they entered, halting his speech.

"You're all here. Good. Come sit with us. We have a lot to discuss and prepare for. Time, as always, is not on our side."

Quick and straight to the point, Theo observed. Well that was just as well. He didn't want any beating around the bush. He looked closely at the wizard who looked none the worse for wear after the raid on the cottage, except for some soot marks on his white shirt and the drawn look to his eyes: they had a haunted look as if he hadn't gotten a decent night's rest since the cottage incident.

They ate the bountiful meal the royal cooks prepared then sat drinking morning tea whilst Archon related past events. Theo's parents had remained with Archon and the Mountain nymph in the Triad Forest for most of that fateful day hiding away from their pursuers. At nightfall his parents had fled the forest for Nusia where they stopped for supplies prior to setting out for Seldavia's shores. From there they would make their way to the capital city of Aldorn way up north. Archon and Roxette caused a diversion drawing the pithiks' attention away from Theo's parents fleeing south, in the opposite direction, retracing Nestor's steps back to the trading port, Paliphea. They made a quick stop at Fiona's for supplies before buying a small fishing boat and setting off for Alunda with the darklings still searching for them.

"Will Fiona be in any danger?" Tiber asked concerned.

"We were not followed into the fishing village," Archon assured him. "Pithiks tend to stay away from human habitats. However they've already shown they can be persuaded to enter ships and give chase. I didn't see any boats following us on the way here but they may still catch up with us. That's why we have to hurry."

"When are we going after mother and father?" Serilia asked. Unlike her brother, she had been away from home a week before the raid on the cottage and was anxious to see for herself that her parents were alright. Archon's word–the word of a man whom until today she had not met–was somehow not enough to allay her fears. She fidgeted with the sleeve of her blue tunic and returned Archon's scrutinizing look.

"We will meet up with them eventually but for the time being I must stick to my original plan. Your brother was the only one who I figured on taking with me but I now see that I got more than I bargained for."

"Sorry to have burdened you with our presence." Nestor cocked a bushy eyebrow at him.

"I didn't mean to put it so bluntly, and you did help with getting the boy away to safety but we're on a dangerous mission. I don't want to involve anyone else."

"Archon, you already have. Elron was right, though I would not admit it in front of him. Needless to say the cottage is lost and I've become a refugee overnight. Now whether you like it or not we're involved, so make the best of the situation never forgetting your promise to take care of the youngsters. I for one can take care of myself as can Emeralda. In any case my sister is going to remain here when we leave."

"Thanks for asking me, brother," Emeralda answered sourly, puffing herself up like a guinea fowl readying for a fight.

"Emeralda there's no need for you to get involved in any of this. I will take care of the boys. You and Serilia can meet up with us at Aldorn when we're done and things have settled down."

"I'm going wherever my brother's going," Serilia snapped. She eyed her grandfather and pushed up her sleeves so he now had two women glaring at him.

"We're both going along until I say any different," Emeralda said, with cool determination.

Nestor averted his eyes, turning to Archon for support. "Say something."

Archon looked at both Serilia and Emeralda, contemplating. "Serilia will not be separated from her brother or you, Nestor. You're her last link to her family. And Roxette and I will not have any time to spare for a young woman who ought to be somewhere else getting on with whatever young women do at this age," he said, staring pointedly at Serilia who snuffed her nose at him, "so Emeralda's help will be necessary as well on this trip."

"What do you intend to do now?" Theo asked, attempting to stay on the subject that interested him the most. He felt he was being forced into teaming up with the mage rather than being allowed to make his own decisions. Archon kept mentioning him in his plans without revealing his true intentions. Theo felt as though he were caught up in events larger than him, like a young blind pup wandering aimlessly led on only by its sense of smell.

"For now I intend to use the time allotted to me to complete some unfinished business with the king," the mage said evasively. He turned to the Sea nymph king. "We'll need one of your chambers where we can talk in private. We've confidential matters to discuss," he said, in hushed tones so Theo could barely hear.

"We'll go to my study. We won't be disturbed there or be overheard," the king answered, in the same low tone.

Theo had a thought. "Where's Roxette?" he asked, looking around.

"If you mean the Mountain nymph, we left her at the bay," Alorn answered, entering the dining hall, his cloak fanning out behind him as he strode forward. He was attired in the officers' garb worn by the Alunda Military Guard: a light grey tunic held at the waist by a black leather belt fastened by a gold clip, darker grey trousers tucked into black leather boots, polished so they gleamed; thrown over it all a deep blue cloak held around the neck by a golden brooch. His hair was kept from his face by a hair lock.

"My Lord." He bowed formally to his king. "I have sent sentries out with sea chariots. Nobody will be able to come within twelve nautical miles of the island without us being alerted. The Mountain nymph," he said sternly, turning to Theo, "is under guard and will remain so for the duration of her stay. Human visitors are one thing, her *kind* quite another."

Theo recalled that the Mountain nymphs were not friendly with their sea cousins so it didn't surprise him that Alorn was being cautious. Alorn was probably wary of the

Mountain nymph discovering the cave entrance to the sea kingdom. It was his duty to protect Alunda from any possible threat.

"You've done well, Alorn," the king responded thoughtfully, his mind occupied on other matters. *I wonder what they were talking about before we entered,* thought Theo. Alorn thumped his fist on his chest in salute and turned on his heel to leave.

"A moment, Alorn, if you can spare it," Tiber recalled the young officer.

"Yes Tiber? How may I be of service?" The tall nymph waited patiently for the bearded man to make his request. Tiber was slightly shorter than the nymph but apart from his human ears he looked astonishingly similar to Alorn. In fact he resembled all the sea nymphs with his ginger hair and blue eyes; it was not surprising if one considered that Prium was Tiber's grandfather. In Theo's father, Elron, the nymph blood ran thinner, since his hair was brown like his human mother.

"Last night you never got the chance to show me those submersible chariots you mentioned. If the offer still stands I would very much like to see them up close. The sea is my life, apart from my family, and all aquatic craft hold a special interest for me, seeing as I've been a sailor all my life."

Alorn grinned broadly at the opportunity presented to him to share his interests with a man of his own heart. "My dear friend Tiber, I would be more than happy to show you our submersibles. If my king has no objection?" King Rufous gave his consent with a wave of his hand.

Just then Neil and Keel ran into the room closely followed by King Rufous's son and daughter. They were red and hot from their exertions and breathing hard. Tiber laid a hand on each of the twins' heads, roughing up their ginger hair fondly, whilst Timothy ran to give his father a quick hug before returning to the twins' side, eager for whatever they would think of doing next. Pearl ran to her father who took her up in his arms and placed her on his knee.

"Boys, we were getting ready to visit the king's sea chariots with Alorn. Do you want to come along?" Tiber asked the twins. The boys shouted with glee and waited anxiously for him to set off. Pearl remained behind and was handed over to her nanny's arms whilst King Rufous and Archon made their way to the king's study. Archon beckoned for Nestor to join them as they left the hall. Serilia and Emeralda were led by Yiola to a room in the palace where nymph women were accustomed to taking their tea. Theo stood staring at Nem.

"Are you coming?" Alorn called from the exit to the dining hall.

"Wait up," the youths replied as they followed.

"How long have you and Alorn been together?" Serilia was asking Yiora. She studied her host over the brim of her cup taking a few sips of the scented tea. It was very tasty and hot, just the way she liked it. Yiora was wearing a long brown dress laced around the neckline and sleeves and embroidered with flower patterns all down the front.

"Did I mention us being together?" Yiora sounded shocked, caught off guard by the direct question. She picked at a loose thread that was not there, averting her eyes and blushing ever so slightly. It made Serilia smile inwardly. *That will teach you to embarrass me,* she thought remembering the previous evening when she had stripped in front of all the Sea nymph divers to put on her swim suit.

"It shows in the vexed way you look at other women who dare to flutter their eyelids at Alorn," Serilia continued, giggling shamelessly. Emeralda too was smiling over her tea cup.

"It's that obvious," Yiora sighed with mock disappointment, then laughed. "But he *is* handsome is he not? And gifted, if you know what I mean."

Serilia's cheeks were crimson. *Yes I do know what you mean,* she thought but kept it to herself.

"If you're referring to the tightness of his buttocks and his long, leisurely stride, not to mention his gorgeous long hair and those eyes of his," Emeralda was saying, her eyes sparkling with delight, "then yes, I must agree."

"Aunt Emeralda, that's quite enough!" Serilia gasped in shock. Who would have thought aunt Emeralda harboured such thoughts, *at her age*!

"I'm sorry, dearest. It's my nymphish blood you know. I'll try to be good, I promise," she said teasingly.

Tiber, the twins and Timothy made their way back to the palace from their trip with the sea chariots whilst Alorn escorted Theo and Nem to another building that was surrounded by a courtyard filled with white sand. Young nymph warriors were standing in the sand, their chests bare wearing loose trousers reaching up to their ankles. They were exchanging blows as they weaved in and out with tridents and nets like combatants in a ring. Some of them fought using spears and the square shields of the house guard with their characteristic veined corners and projecting centres. All were breathing heavily, red-faced from their exertions during the morning's training. They saluted fleetingly as Alorn passed them by then resumed their sparring without further pause. Theo was reminded, with a pang of nostalgia, of his weapons practices with Nem under the scrutinizing supervision of his father back at the cottage.

They left the courtyard and entered a building with a long hall whose walls were lined with racks supporting an assortment of spears, tridents, swords and other such paraphernalia.

"Where are you taking us?" Theo asked, coming up close to the tall nymph so he would not have to shout.

"I have been instructed to take you to the armoury," Alorn said, continuing with his easy long strides. "There is someone waiting for you there," he added mysteriously, his face an unrevealing mask.

Theo looked at Nem who just shrugged as they followed after the sea nymph. They reached the end of the hall and walked down a flight of stairs into a basement lit by torches hanging from the walls. The floor was simple stone, the walls bare apart from spears crossing diagonally with the square Alunda shields set at their centres. Alorn approached a door made of plain wood knocking twice before opening it. They walked into another well-lit room.

"Wait here," Alorn commanded, getting ready to leave. "And please feel free to look around," he added, before closing the door behind him.

Theo and Nem took Alorn's advice and searched the room with great interest. There were countless racks filled with all types of weapons: from daggers, to spears, to mean looking maces, to double-edged axes with sharpened blades and well-oiled handles. There was also a collection of swords of varying lengths and shapes: some were curved, others were straight, whilst still others were man-high and heavy looking. These last were probably similar to those used by armoured knights fighting horseback where a heavy sword with a long blade was required to reach one's foe and dent or penetrate their armour. All the weapons were well tended, revealing the Sea nymph's readiness to defend themselves.

Theo picked up a sword with a blade that was just over arm's length. He hefted it in both hands to test its weight and slashed at the air to accustom his arms to balancing it in his grip. The sword was light enough to wield swiftly but heavy enough to cause damage. Its double-edged blade was sharp and free of chinks or dents. This characterized it as a sword of superior quality. Running almost the entire length of the blade starting from the cross guard was a fuller with markings etched on the surface. The hilt of the sword was fashioned to be held single-handedly; it was of shiny metal with the grip wound around tightly with fine silver wire. The pommel was also of silver ending in an inverted cone with the point of the cone facing inwards towards the hilt. The cross guard was built up from a solid écusson with straight, slender, hexagonal arms tapering inwards.

Nem was comparing a sabre he had found with the dagger at his belt. The sabre's single-edged blade was two feet long and slightly curved. Its hilt was of ivory and adorned with silver gilt inlaid by a variety of jewels, mostly rubies and emeralds; some form of text was inscribed on the blade, the writing of which was exotic looking. Its scabbard was made of dark teak wood overlaid with pierced gold which was also studded with rubies and emeralds. The sword Theo held had a simple leather scabbard that was meagre in comparison, but practical. Theo liked practical things. Nem preferred his prized possessions to reflect his appreciation for the finer things in life.

"Ah, I see you have already chosen your weapons," a voice said from behind.

Theo and Nem turned abruptly. When they saw who it was, they reclined their heads respectfully and made to place the weapons back where they had found them.

"No, please," Prium pleaded, approaching them. "It was my intention to bring you here for just this purpose. I wish for you to have the weapons of your choice. They will aid you in the difficult tasks you have lying before you as you set off on your adventures–for life is just that, you know, one large adventure. I see, young Nemarchus, that the Nebese scimitar has attracted your attention."

"Yes, my lord," Nem answered, looking at the scimitar appreciatively.

"It belonged to a young Nebese prince, you know?" The old man came up close to inspect the weapon. "He was one of many sons of the Neban king who had ventured foolhardily in our waters seeking glory and to plunder our island. Not one of his crew, including the prince, lived to return to Neba. We, however, were left with a ship full of booty."

Nem returned the old man's grin. All was permissible in the name of self-defence.

"Keep it." Prium motioned to Nem.

"My lord...I couldn't accept such a fine gift. It belongs to your people who have rightly earned it."

"The sword is ours to give. And in any case, you, I am sure, will put it to good use. Now take it, please."

Nem bowed deeply. "I thank you for your most gracious gift, my lord."

Then Prium turned to study Theo. A smile crossed his face and his eyes clouded over with emotion. This tall young man reminded him of the days when he too was of that age and full of vigour. The youth's features were more like his great grandmother's: green eyes and wavy brown hair. Prium felt a wave of longing as he recalled his feelings for Maritha. The young man had the same proud bearing and intriguing persona, the same ability to captivate the eye; some day he would evolve into an imposing figure with men waiting on his every command. His father Elron could marshal such faithful followers around him–so Prium had heard from his daughter Emeralda. Such was the destiny of the Alunda royal line–to be leaders amongst men.

But leadership meant responsibility and Theo was young and scarcely prepared for what was in store. Prium was no stranger to the challenges facing Theo's generation. With each passing century he had lived, the last was the most troubled. He did not need the young mage, Archon, to tell him that Thalagia was facing a storm that would be difficult to ride. But the free kingdoms had been through turbulent times before and had come through in the end. For many, freedom and the right to live one's own life with dignity required the ultimate sacrifice.

"Theo. Have you chosen something for yourself, my son?"

Theo lifted the sword for the nymph lord to see. "If I am to choose a weapon, then it must be this sword, my lord. It fits my hand well and has a balance and poise that feels just right."

"A sword worthy of a prince, young Theo." Prium looked approvingly at the weapon Theo held. "It was fashioned by nymphs, forged patiently with devotion using *lithureal* which in nymphish means 'silver metal'. It is the toughest ore in all of Thalagia and priceless because of its rarity. Look closer and tell me what you see."

Theo gave the weapon a scrutinizing look. Markings he had not noticed before were etched on its face–close to the guard above the hilt. "I see some lettering I do not understand, my lord," he said, examining the writing more carefully. It was in a fluid hand composed of seven words.

"It's written in the tongue of the Ancients," Prium explained. "It says, '*A spark of light in the dark*'. May it protect you in the years ahead and may its blade find its way to your foe's lifeblood." It was the address used between fighting men. Theo had often heard his father using it when describing how men in battle exchanged words of encouragement before preparing to meet their enemy on the field.

"I thank you, my lord," Theo said, touching the blade to his forehead in the customary salute.

"Your father has taught you well." The elderly man gave his great grandson a contemplative look. He dipped a bony hand into his robe and fished out an amulet hanging from a silver chain. "This is for you," he said, handing the amulet to

Theo. "When you cast it into the sea it will invoke Nerus's protection should you ever encounter trouble out at sea. Use it wisely." Theo looked closely at the amulet which depicted a small dolphin with tiny sapphires for eyes. "The chain and amulet are both made of white gold."

"White gold!" Nem whistled. "That's extremely precious and can only be found at the mouth of the Silver River." Theo looked at his friend admiring him once more for his erudition.

"That's right, young Nemarchus. We trade from time to time our precious gems in exchange for the gold. Now, knowing the appetites of young men your age, I will return to my quarters and allow Alorn to escort you to the dining hall where the noon meal has been prepared." And with that said, the old nymph turned about and walked out of the room supported by his staff.

Alorn was waiting for them in the corridor and led them swiftly to the dining hall. There they met up with the rest of their companions. The table was laden, as on the previous evening, with an assortment of crustacean and shell fish delicacies, as well as refreshing white wine, not to mention a plenitude of fruits, yoghurt and honey. After they had eaten to their heart's content, the mage rose from the table.

"My king," Archon said. "I wish to thank you for your hospitality but must inform you that we will need to take your leave for reasons I have already mentioned. I believe it's best that by nightfall we are on our way. It will be much easier for us to slip away from our pursuers concealed by night."

"About time too," Theo heard Dextra murmuring, so that *he* at least had heard. She got up and left the dining hall in a hurry.

At a sign from Archon the rest of the group made their way to their rooms where they started to pack their belongings. Nestor took care of the supplies he was given by the head cook. Soon they were being led by Alorn to the marble basin where they had first entered the under-sea kingdom of Alunda. They said their farewells to the king and to Prium who had come out of his quarters to see off his son.

The sun was low in the sky by the time they located the animals and were safely boarded on the *Sea Breeze*. Roxette, glad to be off the island, was introduced to the rest of the group by the mage. She was wearing her customary black leather covered by her grey cloak that hid away her many blades.

"She's a dodgy-looking one," Emeralda said to her brother, not hiding her inbred distaste for the Mountain nymphs.

It was going to be a long trip.

They withdrew the anchor and unfastened the sails which caught the evening breeze, gently pushing the ship out of the bay. The small boat Archon had purchased at Port Lund was tied to the ship's stern and tugged along behind. Tiber gave his orders to the twins from up close so his voice would not carry over in the approaching twilight. Stealth was required for their get-away. Theo noticed a half dozen sea chariots escorting them. One of the charioteers waved. It was Alorn. They waved back and set course towards the setting sun.

That night on the ship Theo's sleep was troubled.

He was on a mountain, overlooking its sheer sides dropping away into cloudy mist. Theo held his newly acquired nymph sword aloft and pointed it southwards. Suddenly he was transported above a dense forest that judging by the size and bent shape of the trees was ancient. His gaze fell on a small winding line of silver, like a ribbon lying on a velvety green cloth, separating the forest in two halves; nearing it, he could discern it was a river. Downstream, midway through the forest, he could now see a large lake that mirrored the blue sky and clouds above. To the east of the lake stood a wooden structure built into the trees so it looked like a natural extension of the forest, fusing with it to make an enclave. Theo ghosted through the wooden walls of the fort like an ethereal spirit and was assailed by a splashing of colour and gracefully designed structures made from carved wood intermingled with silver décor.

He glided into a large hall and approached the end where stood a tall throne made of wood studded with emeralds and ornately decorated in silver and gold.

Sitting regally on the throne was a woman as tall as the throne with long flowing brown hair dressed in a simple thin pale dress. The dress was embroidered with silver silk strands and revealed her voluptuous body. In front of the forest queen stood three retainers: a broad-shouldered warrior dressed in military garb covered with heavy chain mail, a tall sinewy man who also wore military garb but of light leather, and a third man with silver hair dressed in a colourful velvet tunic and pants and holding a harp. All three were looking adoringly at their queen who raised her emerald eyes to gaze intently at Theo. He felt naked under the scrutiny of those eyes, as if they could see to the very depths of his soul.

"You have strength in you, Islander," she said. "But strength and courage alone will not avail you in your struggle against the Dark One."

Suddenly he was wrenched away from the great hall and hurtled eastwards faster than any beast could fly. He continued his mad flight over a range of grey mountains and crossed a round sea like a colossal plate and began to descend on a smaller sea connected to the larger one at its north eastern tip. This sea was dark and devoid of light.

He passed into a dimly lit chamber.

There was a faint humming sound. Before him he could see what seemed to be two boxes the length of a man's coffin pulsing with red light. As he approached he saw several black robed figures kneeling before the coffins. The humming sound was in fact their incoherent monotone chanting. He looked at the coffins and found to his surprise that they were not that at all but altars upon which rested two figures, one clad in black robes trimmed in red lace and the other fully dressed in black armour of a peculiar design. The armour clung to the figure's body and was segmented following his muscular form with bulging chest plates, upon which were stamped twin red dragons, and a central stomach plate that was curved into a six pack. The armour on his legs and arms was similarly shaped.

Upon closer inspection Theo realized what he had thought was a red glow surrounding the altars was a glass-like ruby red screen. He looked at the robed figure. He was a pale man with long silver hair and beard and a calm noble looking face with a sharp nose and prominent cheekbones. Theo placed him in his mid-seventies. His gaze was drawn back to the armoured warrior lord. He could not see his face that was covered by a black visor and a helmet crested by long red hairs like a horse's tail. The helmet creaked as the concealed face turned to look at him.

"You will bow down to *me*, Athuddir!" Theo clasped his head tightly with the palms of his hands doubling over in pain at the booming sound of the voice.

"All will bow down to the might of Ushud."

♦ CHAPTER 6 ♦

Message in the stars

Morning dawned grey and oppressive. The sun was obscured by a mist that had descended upon them during the night. It added to Theo's sultry mood. He looked around into the gloomy fog; he could only see about three paces away. The group was moving on deck slowly, speaking intermittently in hushed tones.

"How far are we from Jade Island?" Theo moved beside his uncle who was peering out at the dense fog steering the ship whilst listening intently for any sign of waves breaking on protruding rocks.

"Oh we still have a long trip ahead of us, nephew. By my estimate we aren't too far from Galipa's eastern shores," he answered, stroking his ginger beard. "We're sailing the Pardenian Sea and are at least a good two days voyage from Jade Island."

Just then Nem stepped on deck. "Perfect morning," he said mordantly, gazing around resentfully. He had donned a white linen shirt tucked roughly into his pants. His curly hair was loose so it fanned about his head. Coming up to Theo he combed it back with his hand, tying it into a ponytail. "You look like you've been thrown out of bed and dragged backwards by your boots for a mile," he said, turning to Theo.

Theo cocked an eyebrow at him. "You look like a fresh bouquet of roses yourself."

"What's for breakfast? I'm starving." He looked in the direction of Nestor who had packed their supplies.

"Dried meat and bread," Nestor answered curtly, "and Emeralda's warmed some milk for you teething youngsters," he added, grinning.

"Milk is good. The dried meat is your idea of cooking I suppose?"

"You've eaten Alunda out of her supplies for a year," Nestor replied. "Some frugality will do you good. By the way, you two are cooking lunch. I've taken my turn."

Nem muttered under his breath. Nestor simply ignored him, but the grin remained. The youngsters made their way towards Emeralda and Serilia who were back in travelling pants and tunics. They were leaning on the ship's starboard gunwale speaking in hushed tones. They greeted the men briefly then resumed their conversation.

"Emeralda and I were saying that we don't know much more about our mission than when we started," Serilia commented dryly.

"That Archon is a secretive one. Always has been," Emeralda said, looking to port where the mage and his Mountain nymph companion were standing alone in silence.

"Aunt Emeralda, how long have you known the wizard?" Theo asked.

"Archon and I go way back. I first met him when he was a young man in his mid-twenties. I remember that, even at that age, it had struck me how enigmatic he was about his business. Archon has always been on one or other mission for the Council of Light and is known in many lands where his duties have taken him. In Alunda, he would spend weeks buried in our archives searching for Nerus knows what. He was close to my niece, Nethida...that was before she died at sea. They were of the same age, though if Nethida was alive today she would look in her early thirties.

"You've been told about Dextra's feelings towards the mage by King Rufous. Dextra's hatred for mankind does not end where sorcerers are concerned, and being a witch there is an inherent enmity between them."

"Oh? How's that?" Serilia asked. "Being from similar schools...I mean they both use the gift. I would have thought they would share a level of respect for one another...even feel they had something in common."

"They respect each other alright, but it's a respect between opposing factions, like mountain cats and wolves. I've already explained that sorcerers do not believe in using dead things to achieve their aims. Whereas witches delight in it."

"But that's still a very thin line to draw."

"From the little I understand about it, that's all that separates magic. You know very well from your mother's instructions that all sorcerers can tap into the Dark and Light source of the gift. It's what they do with the sources...the final outcome that separates friend from foe." Emeralda turned to Theo. "Tell me what *her* story is," she said, nodding in the Mountain nymph's direction with her chin.

"There's not very much to tell," he replied. "Archon never said anything about her, so we assumed she's a friend."

"I'll ask Nestor. Maybe he knows something we don't," said Emeralda, walking towards the old man who was standing next to his son at the helm.

Roxette was staring at the three youngsters and beckoned to them. They approached silently trying to read the expression on her face but found it as devoid of emotion as Archon's.

"Theodor and Nemarchus," said the nymph, rolling up her tunic sleeves. "I'd like to have a word with you. Let's go to the fore of the ship."

"Serilia, a moment please," Archon said, as she prepared to leave.

The young men followed behind the nymph as she passed by the horses tethered to the port side. She inspected the horses' limbs and hooves and patted them on their flanks reassuringly. The steeds continued munching their fodder contentedly, Nestor's gelding nudging Theo with its nose. He rubbed it beneath the chin. Nem kept his distance, looking with distaste at the animals. One of the ponies tried to nuzzle his shoulder but he backed away shoeing it with one hand.

"Awful stinky brutes," he said, holding his nose in disgust.

"Don't say that," Theo reprimanded him. "You'll hurt their feelings."

"Don't be ridiculous, Theo. Horses don't understand Seldavish."

"Maybe so, but they can sense your mood and feelings towards them. They are very sensitive in that respect."

"Come along," Roxette beckoned, moving forward.

She stood looking at them critically, like a seamstress measuring with a once-over look prior to setting down to the serious bits. She rubbed her oval chin thoughtfully as she looked at the boys' arms and chests.

"There's a lot of room for improvement," she said. "Elron has done a good job with you both but you still need to put a few pounds around the shoulders and arms. I'll take care of that soon enough. Now, let me have a look at those weapons you picked up in Alunda."

They handed them over grudgingly to their new teacher. She tested their weight and balance in her hands, cutting through the air in circular motions. "That's a mean-looking sabre you have there, Nemarchus." She looked along the sword's curved blade with one eye closed. She moved with feline grace as she turned on her heel and made several slicing and jabbing thrusts in the air, her muscles rippling beneath her dark leather. "This weapon was invented as an in-between of the cavalry sword and the traditional short bladed dagger," she instructed. "It can be very effective when you are up close and can also be used at arm's length to deflect and parry with an opponent holding a sword."

After a few more jabs and twirls she handed the blade back to its owner. She turned her attention to Theo's sword. "A *spark of light in the dark.*" She read aloud the inscription on the fuller. She hefted the sword with one hand, falling into a series of dance-like motions with bent knees and elbows as she sparred with an invisible foe. She ended by saluting with the blade held before her forehead, her head slightly inclined. "A fine nymph blade crafted by master swordsmiths using *lithureal*–'silver metal'. Take good care of it. It will save your life someday," she said, handing the sword back to Theo. "As of today, you will begin your training with me on the correct stance to take when fighting with a blade and how to end a confrontation in the most simple and effective way. Quick, graceful, and precise motions that deliver the correct pressure are the keys to success when facing an enemy. One often has to face more than one foe so you must learn to dispatch your enemy swiftly and efficiently so that you will have time to move on to the next before they can organize their counter attack."

They spent the rest of the morning sparring, at times with Roxette and at others pairing with each other. She corrected their stance, teaching them new moves. It seemed the nymph was as skilled as Elron...maybe more so where close combat was concerned. Unlike Elron's teachings that were concentrated on keeping the enemy at bay with sword or mace strokes designed to decapitate or sever an opponent's limbs, Roxette's style was centred on making use of the hands, fists and feet to get up close with kicks, punches, chops and tripping techniques, so as to bring the opponent into a position of feebleness where one could deliver an easy blow to the vital organs, finishing him off without the excessive, energy-wasting movements employed by knights in battlefield warfare. It was very much an assassin's method of fighting.

After a couple of hours both men had taken off their shirts and were sweating profusely. Their breath was steamy as they gulped in air. The mist had lifted. Theo cast his gaze forward and could discern the Galipan coastline not too far off. Sparkling drops of sea spray reflected the sun's light as the waves crashed ashore.

"Land ahoy," Neil shouted, pointing in the direction of the coast.

"Aye," Tiber acknowledged. "We'll be steering well away from the Kylada Hills and those rocks, son."

It was the third day when they tentatively approached Jade Island's western shore. Tiber was weary of running into one of the smaller shipping boats that were scattered around a mile or so from the shore. The island fishermen paid them little heed as they busily cast their nets.

Jade Island was substantially larger than Alunda but smaller than Cyrus. The island was made up of sheer cliffs on all sides. White buildings huddled closely together at its only bay which was overlooked by a large fortress hanging from the cliffs like a giant raptor clinging to its perch. A soft breeze was blowing from astern pushing the *Sea Breeze* towards the bay at a leisurely pace. They entered the port and cast anchor beside a trading vessel that was near twice the length of the *Sea Breeze* and with a deeper draft.

Tiber reversed the ship so the horses could be led ashore. They disembarked aided by the twins and made their way away from the wharf towards the white painted buildings lining the docks. Archon led Nestor and Tiber with the twins whilst Roxette was followed by Theo, Nem, Emeralda and Serilia.

"I need to go up into the fortress to visit some friends of mine," Archon said, turning to his companions. "Roxette, you can stay with the group. Theo, you may accompany me. We have some things to discuss on the way."

"Good," Tiber said. "I'll remain close to shore so I can keep an eye on our ship with the twins. Dad, shall we make our way to a nearby tavern?"

"Sounds good to me," the old man grinned.

"Hey, what about us?" Emeralda placed her fists on her slim waist giving her brother a withering look. Serilia tapped her toe reproachfully, folding her arms beneath her bosom.

"Young Nem is the lady's man. What do you need us old prunes for?" Nestor said.

"Yes. You're right about that," Emeralda agreed. "Come young Nemarchus, lead the way to the nearest inn. There's a good lad."

Nem groaned, giving his friend a scorching look. Theo shrugged, smiling back apologetically.

"Some people have all the luck," Nem grumbled in a low voice.

"What was that?" Emeralda asked curtly.

"Nothing."

"I thought so. Now move it, Foresight! We're tired and in need of a hot bath."

"Yes ma'am. As your royalty commands." Serilia landed a punch on his arm.

"Ouch, that hurt you ninny!"

"It was supposed to."

"Good, that settles it then," Archon said. "Roxette you can take care of the rest of the horses. I'll ride the grey and Theo can take his roan mare."

They made their way through the cobbled streets of the fishing town that was much like Paliphea but with buildings all painted in white. Theo realized he had never ventured so far from home and felt a pang of nostalgia for the quiet cottage, not for the first time since beginning his journey. As a boy he had always dreamed of setting out for different places, like his grandfather Nestor, but now he was away he missed the seclusion of his home.

They began their ascent up the cliffside road that was barely wide enough to fit two wagons side by side. To Theo's surprise many people were braving the sheer climb, moving on foot or riding astride their steeds. There were even a few supply wagons heading up the gravel path.

"What's up there?" Theo asked the mage, pointing at the complex on the cliff. It was built overhanging with sheer walls reaching down and around the rocky face for support, like an eagle's claws around a branch. The entire structure was made up of levels, each having its own precipice walls behind which hid the main structures, punctured here and there by slender windows affording slots for archers.

"This is the residence of the Astrologer's and Astronomer's Guilds," the mage answered, gazing up the cliff with his piercing grey eyes. "The building was first erected in 850 AA to house all the scholars interested in the study of the cosmos and has stood against attacks from Hieradon, Neba and Ishbadese invaders from time to time, which explains the slotted windows one can discern on the faces of the defensive walls. Entrance is gained via a large platform that is hoisted using ropes and pulleys hanging from the brink of the walls."

"Why would someone wish to invade a group of scholars?" Theo asked perplexed.

"Theo, you must stop being so insular and start thinking more broadly, in terms of politics, as to what is profitable and of importance to the kingdoms that are in constant conflict trying to gain advantage over one another. Why do you suppose anyone would want to annex any island in the middle of the Valdoric Sea?"

"Trade I suppose. The islands offer an in-between stop for trade."

"There you have it. The islands also control their surrounding seas so they can impose taxes or other measures on the traders. They can be used as a first defensive post in times of war; think of them as a base from which one can launch an attack by air or by sea."

They rode in silence looking down at the port that lay sprawled before them like a miniature toy model. Theo could just discern the *Sea Breeze* in the harbour next to the larger trading vessel. He craned his neck upwards to gaze with awe at the overhanging structure that seemed to float above them as it cantilevered from the cliff's edge supported by giant wooden beams from below embedded into the rock face.

"Good morning, sirs," said a chubby short fellow with a bald head as the two travellers approached the boarding platform.

"A good morning to you too." Archon looked down at the fellow who was riding a bay pony that had a build like its master with short legs forced to move twice as fast as Archon's grey gelding.

"My name is Griffin. I am a trader from Ameron returning from my journeys to Hieradon," the man wheezed mopping his brow with a handkerchief.

"From Hieradon, really?" Archon cocked an eyebrow at him. "So how go things at the Desert Empire these days?"

"Business is booming as usual but the raids from the blasted pirates are more frequent. I've filed a complaint with the authorities at Lisandria but I doubt they'll be able to do anything about it. All they are interested in is imposing taxes on the working class who are trying to run an honest business," he added, wiping sweat from his upper lip with fingers laden with rings set with precious gems of all shades and colours.

"Indeed master Griffin," Archon sighed in feigned agreement. "So what brings a gentleman like you to the Astrologers' Guild?"

"Oh, I'm not here to have my fortunes read." Griffin waggled a fat finger supporting a ruby ring. "Jade Island is known for its excellent clocks and looking glasses you know?"

"Aah. Business then."

"Yes master...?"

"Longman and this young man is my apprentice, Flin. We are pilgrims searching for life's deeper meaning."

"Really? Well have you discovered anything yet?"

"Not much, master Griffin. Man is such a strange being with so many hidden attributes and contradictory emotions. We will need to work a while longer at untangling that puzzle, but in the meantime we are enjoying meeting up with new people."

"Well you don't seem to have done too badly for yourselves." The merchant looked at them appraisingly.

"How so, master Griffin?"

"Well, that stallion you are riding is a fine beast. Sandorish I would say or maybe even from Balsovia's royal stock. And the mare the young man is riding is not bad either, though it is not of any known stock–still it is a fine enough beast."

"You know your horseflesh, master Griffin. You're right about the stallion. It was a gift from a Balsovian noblewoman whom I had the good fortune of becoming acquainted with."

"Oh?" Griffin looked astonished.

"No, nothing like that master Griffin. She and her husband were struggling to have a child and asked for my aid."

"So what happened?"

"I brewed a potion for the young lady and, a month after she'd drunk it, she fell pregnant."

"You could make a fortune with that potion. What was in it, if I may ask?"

"Tea."

"Tea? You're not serious!"

"Oh, I am absolutely serious my friend. You see in her case the problem was purely psychological."

"Why, master Longman, you are more devious than you look."

"Well, everyone gained from the whole affair, did they not?"

"Indeed," the fat man laughed heartily, slapping his thigh with a meaty hand.

They reached the platform and dismounted. Stable hands waited to take their horses. The visitors were ushered to the platform by two clean-shaven young men with close-cropped hair. They allowed a score of people to enter the platform before closing its iron gate. Yanking on a rope they signalled to those above that all were aboard and ready.

"Hold tight," Archon warned, stepping close to Theo. "I hope you're not afraid of heights–but what am I saying? I forget that you're secretly a dragonstrider."

Theo looked at him astounded, turning crimson at having his little adventure of four nights ago revealed. He recovered, biting his lower lip.

Archon was wrong. Riding on a dragon was one thing. Hanging from a man-made contraption that lurched upwards and swung with the slightest breeze was quite another. He looked at Griffin who was sweating profusely from his previous effort at dismounting his pony and noticed that his face was pale. Archon stood perfectly still, statue-like and impassive. After a while Theo paid more attention to his surroundings and forgot his fear to some small degree. He noticed a small shape flying through the air above them with a wing span larger than any sparrow or dove. As the bird soared closer Theo could discern its reddish brown top plumage. When it tilted its outspread wings to bank away from them, calling out in a shrill voice that echoed from the rocks, he could see its light yellow under-plumage and rufous coloured tail.

"It's striking," he whispered to the mage, who nodded his agreement.

"It is a red-tailed Valdoric sea hawk," Archon informed him.

Soon another larger hawk joined the first one and they circled around each other calling out to one another.

"It has found a mate." Archon sounded pleased. "You know the females are larger than the males, though like most birds the males are more beautiful, to attract the females."

Theo gathered the mage was fond of the birds and had to admit that he too was enthralled. He closed his eyes daydreaming he was soaring with the birds.

"Theo, stop that!" Archon's voice sounded harsh even though he had whispered.

"I'm sorry," Theo opened his eyes perplexed. "What did I do wrong?"

"I'll explain later." Archon looked around carefully. "Just don't do it again–at least not in public."

They reached the top of the cliff after what seemed like ages but was in fact only a few minutes. The platform came to a grinding halt. The two operators pulled a lever acting as a break and opened the gate to let a very relieved group of passengers get off. Theo discovered the mechanism employed to raise the platform: a large room next to the dock held twin ropes as thick as a man's legs wound around a hefty wooden ratchet wheel that was being turned by four large draft-horses with hairy fetlocks and coarse long-haired coats.

"This way please," a young woman with flaxen hair beckoned to the visitors. She led the way through a corridor enclosed by stone walls that were recessed at intermittent intervals so a variety of mantlepiece clocks, pocket watches and an assortment of looking lenses were on display behind closed panes of glass. Theo's attention was riveted to a grandfather clock standing at the end of the corridor like a solemn officer guarding the exit. Its face was golden surmounted by three black hands. Its wooden encasing was ruddy brown rosewood exquisitely carved with vertical rod-like pieces standing in the front on either side of the clock with alternately bulging and thinning stems. Just beneath the circular clock face were two tiny doors above which were engraved in gold writing the words, "*Time can be a friendly companion in the present. Use him wisely to build a brighter future, or suffer him in reminiscence as your most bitter enemy.*" The clock struck twelve and the twin doors opened allowing two finely crafted figurines to exit. It was a young man and woman who met halfway and exchanged kisses in time with the clock chimes.

"How delightful." Theo turned to the mage who was smiling in agreement.

"Yes lad, and the message on the clock should be heeded. Now come along Theo, we're falling behind."

They were led into a courtyard filled with people from various parts of Thalagia. There were blond-haired Renderons and blue-eyed northlanders, and there were olive-skinned Galipans and dark folk with brown or black hair from the Hieradon Empire. And there were, of course, Leonese and Seldavians with fairer skins with a range of hair colours dyed–or not–depending on the fashion trends of each kingdom.

"This is where I'll take my leave of you, my friends." The merchant placed a fat purse in the palm of one hand.

"May the business guru shine upon you, master Griffin," Archon said.

"Longman, my most gracious fellow, we will discuss the matter of your grey stallion when we are finished, yes?" The merchant beamed his most precious smile.

"I wouldn't get your hopes up," the mage said. "That animal has sentimental value."

"Everything has its price my friend...but perhaps you might prove refreshingly different."

And with that they made their way past the trading stalls that–apart from the clocks–were filled with all other manner of trade: there were wines, spices, fine silks and much more. Archon seemed to know his way about. He led them towards an archway that provided entrance to the higher apartments.

"Did you mean what you said to the merchant, about the stallion being a gift from a lady in Balsovia?" Theo asked, his curiosity getting the better of him.

"Every word was true, but I never explained that the lady in question is none other than Princess Matrice of Balsovia. She is one of two daughters of King Sebastione Deleviere of Balsovia. Maybe our travels will take us there some day and you will get to meet her."

"Did she have her baby in the end?"

"Yes, she gave birth to a baby girl and five years later to another one. They are the same age roughly as Tiber's girls. Ah, here we are," said the mage, reaching an opening that led to a spiral staircase. They climbed the winding steps lit by sunlight streaming through the slotted windows. By the time they reached the tower top they were panting for breath. "This is the highest point in the entire complex and houses the sky lenses."

"Sky lenses?" Theo asked, intrigued.

"Yes. They are giant contraptions used to stare up at the heavens. You'll see soon enough," Archon said, leading the way through an open walkway. Theo preferred to stay away from the parapet wall on the left due to the dizzying height to the bottom of the cliff. They arrived at two large doors tall enough to fit an ogre. Archon knocked twice. Someone from inside worked on the locks and one of the doors creaked slowly open, its weight pivoting on bulky iron hinges.

"And you are?" asked a bald man with a head like an inverted pot. The door was opened a bare crack as he stood barring their entrance.

"Tell old Achalcanoras that Archon requests a viewing," the mage said, looking directly at the man.

"Wait here." The bald fellow left them standing near the doorway. He returned soon after. "Come with me. Our Principal will see you at his stargazer."

They made their way through a large hall filled with a variety of instruments used for gazing up at the sky. Behind these sat scholarly men jotting notes and sketches down on drawing paper using pencils, compasses and scaled metal rulers. Finally they arrived at the largest stargazer, standing supreme in the centre of the hall surrounded by all the rest of the smaller looking glasses like a spider surrounded by her hatchlings. It was three storeys high resting on twin steel columns and a circular base toothed like the inner wheel workings of a clock and was kept well greased so it could be revolved into any position. The stargazer was entirely made up of a black metal tubular casing except for the brass eyepiece and the huge ten-foot objective lens that poked like a rude finger at the night sky. It was lacquered with care so its shaft shone like polished ebony.

"Archon, my young friend, I knew you would come," said an elderly man with a long silver beard that reached down to his knees and a silver crown of hair around his bald head. He was dressed in a plain grey moth-ridden woollen cloak. The bags beneath his eyes bore witness to his insomnia.

"Master Achalcanoras," Archon said reverently, bowing low to the old man. Theo followed suit, sensing the need to show respect.

"Who is this delightful young man with you, Sir Archon?" the aged astrologer asked.

"A pupil of mine I picked up during my travels," the mage answered obscurely.

"Ever the secretive one, aren't you my dear Wizard? But such is your profession and like astrology it has its own rules and regulations," said the old man, stroking his long beard thoughtfully whilst keeping his grey eyes trained on Archon and Theo.

"Do you have a name lad or should I just call you the sorcerer's apprentice?"

Theo was taken aback by the question; it was somehow shocking to be described in that way. Up until now he had not given it much thought.

"My name is Theo, sir," he answered, meeting the astrologer's gaze.

"Do you have any interest in the constellations, boy?"

"I have an interest in learning many things, sir, as is natural for someone my age," Theo answered carefully, trying to unravel where this conversation was leading.

"We might be able to steal you away from the Council of Light yet," Achalcanoras answered, rubbing his palms together and looking triumphantly at Archon.

"Still on the look-out for scholars to join your guild, master Achalcanoras?" Archon asked, hiding a smile.

"I thought for a while that we had made *you* one of us, but at the last you slipped away."

"Yes, I remember my days at the end of a lens when my curiosity got the better of me, but sitting at a stargazer for most of my life does not suit my style of living."

"Well I suppose you are not here on a social call then?" The astrologer sat on a worn chair at the base of his looking lens and peered at the mage in anticipation. The chair seemed to suit him, moulded over years of use to his form, like an old snail's shell.

"I was hoping you might be able to shed some light on what the near future has in stall for us," Archon said, taking one of two seats proffered by the bald scholar who had led them to the viewing hall. Theo sat on the other. "Perhaps your stargazer can give us a clue to the problems plaguing our world and early warning on forthcoming events so we can best prepare ourselves; I realize though from my previous experiences at studying the constellations that such hope is slim."

"Archon, to be fair, the study of the stars does not provide clear answers to direct questions," Achalcanoras agreed, "however their messages are always truthful, albeit general and vague in their nature, and may have different meanings for different people." The aged astrologer went back to gazing intently through his eye piece. "Aah, here we are then, have a look," he said, placing a frail hand on Archon's shoulder drawing him close so he could gaze through the lens. "Tell me what you see."

"Hmm, I've never seen such a constellation before, master Achalcanoras. It looks like a hole in the sky apart from those stars on the left that are almost in a straight line –and those top three that are slightly askew. And the other five form an arch from the tip like a scythe."

"I see you have not lost your touch, my mage friend." The Astrologer beamed with pleasure at the might-have-been student of the Guild. "Do you see anything else close to this constellation?"

Archon worked a wheel at the side of the astrologer's chair and the giant stargazer began to turn on its well-greased base. "Seven stars forming three peaks, like a crown and below smaller stars shrouded in star dust forming a man-like shape. Here, Theo, take a look."

Theo leaned closer and gazed through the lens. The far-off stars suddenly filled his vision, causing him to gasp in surprise and wonder. He had looked through Tiber's lens in the past, that his uncle used to steer his ship but the stargazer zoomed the stars so much closer and made them appear clearer and more impressive. "I see it," he said excitedly, as he was able to distinguish the regal form with the three pointed crown atop its head. "What does it mean?" he asked, handing the lens back to its owner.

The ancient astrologer peered through his lens muttering. "Yes, very disturbing indeed." Archon and Theo remained sitting at their seats whilst the astrologer was immersed in thought, oblivious to his surroundings and the two that sat next to him.

"Master Achalcanoras," the mage called out gently. No answer was forthcoming. "Master Achalcanoras," he repeated, louder.

The astrologer gave a start. "Hmm? Oh I apologize. I sometimes get completely absorbed in my work. You know I can sit for hours looking at my stars. They hold a special fascination for me. Every time I gaze through the stargazer I see something new."

Archon waited patiently for him to finish. When the astrologer remained silent, he offered, "What is it you see that's so disturbing?"

"Hmm?" the astrologer repeated with a blank expression. "Disturbing? Oh, yes, quite unusual. It's not often we see the Grim Reaper hanging with his scythe above Regal. We are going to witness the death of a royal figure this year, I fear," he stated informatively in a matter-of-fact tone.

Archon pricked his ears, all his attention suddenly focusing on the old astrologer. "Are you sure?" he asked, his eyes hard as stones.

"The stars never lie, my young friend. I'm quite positive."

"Who will die, how, and when?" the mage pressed. The death of a monarch always upset the balance in the kingdoms and led to a period of uncertainty until another took the throne. Most of the time, this change was brought about with squabbles between the varying factions trying to gain favour with the new monarch. It was the business of the Council of Light to keep watch over the free lands in such cases and ensure the transitions were made swiftly and with as little disruption as possible. And of course the extent of the disruptions was directly related to the events surrounding the monarch's death.

"Archon, you have been an observer of the stars long enough to know that I cannot answer those questions for you," Achalcanoras said grimly. "The only certainty is that before this year is out, the monarch will die."

They left the astrologer's hall shortly after. On their way out Achalcanoras informed them the good news was that the harvests this year would be bountiful once more. Archon did not respond. He was troubled and chose to move silently through the corridors of the guild.

It was late afternoon before the mage and Theo joined their companions at the inn where Emeralda and Serilia had rented rooms.

"You're late," Nestor said, as Archon came to sit at the common room table.

"We got caught up with some business I had with the Guild."

"Never mind." Nestor waved a hand at him indifferently. "Here lass," he called to a serving maid. She smiled at him as she approached, dimples showing on her cheeks. "Be a good girl and bring these two some of that stew your kitchen prepared for us earlier."

Theo ate his stew ravenously, dipping in it great chunks of bread spread with butter. His ride through the hills had worked up his appetite. The innkeeper kept his establishment clean and running efficiently. He had arranged entertainment for the evening. A flute player accompanied by a young lady with a sweet voice added cheer to the dining room patrons.

Nobody paid attention to the door of the inn opening or to the slim hooded figure entering–nobody, that is, apart from the mage and Roxette who were always on their guard. The figure was shrouded in a dark brown cloak with the hood turning here and there as it scanned the room. Finally the figure found who it sought and made its way towards Archon's table. Roxette went for her sword but Archon stayed her, placing his hand firmly on her sword arm. The figure bowed at the mage before removing her hood.

"You are Lord Archon?"

"I am," answered the mage, looking intently at the young girl who stood before him with curly brown hair. Theo felt a tingling sensation and knew Archon was searching the girl's mind.

"My lord, the Council requests you pass by Jandaea Island and pick up a woman named Zoi. She has asked to be escorted to Ghiadon."

Archon paled visibly. "Who sent you?" the mage asked directly.

"Our master from Ramila, First Sorcerer Sharman."

"How is Sharman these days?"

"He is well, my lord, though King Ionid of Ramila keeps him away from his work with one or other musical or theatrical event."

"Yes, that sounds like Ionid. He is very much a patron of the arts. Will you have a drink with us?"

"No, my lord. I must be back in Ramila by tomorrow to resume my training at my master's side. I got the first ship over as soon as we received the Council's message by pigeon."

"How did you know where to find me?"

"We were told you had a mission in Cyrus and that you were forced to flee westward, so we posted our people at the triplet isles to alert us to your arrival. Your reputation precedes you so you were easy to spot."

Roxette looked darkly at her companion, shaking her head.

"So we might get to see you again at Ramilla, young...?"

"My name is Jameira, my lord."

"Just call me Archon."

"Yes–Archon," she said the name stiffly, not used to speaking on an equal basis with a sorcerer of Archon's stature.

Jameira left soon after. The night wore on and they remained to enjoy the singer's music. She kept throwing Theo inviting looks but his attention was trained on the mage who, ever since receiving the council's request for a detour, was whispering in Roxette's ear, his mood foul. When it was well past midnight they all made their way to their beds except for Nestor and Tiber who remained behind to smoke their pipes one last time.

Theo fell asleep almost as soon as his head rested on his pillow. He dreamt he was soaring on the wings of a hawk above the triplet islands. The hawk banked sharply towards the island furthest to the south. As it soared it could make out a man nest hanging from a cliff face. The hawk had the urge to take a closer look and descended till it was in line with it. It cast its gaze at the man nest that was rising slowly from the ground, bearing with it the two-legged man things. There was one in particular that caught the hawk's attention. It was a tall man thing with broad shoulders and brown wavy "plumage" on its head. It was staring at the hawk as it flew. The hawk gave out a cry and banked away from the man made contraption. Then it felt as if it was not alone but was sharing its flight experience with the man thing in the man nest. Then, just as suddenly, the link was broken. The hawk circled around looking at the female that had joined it in its flight. She was a good-looking specimen fit for mating but the hawk was more interested in exploring, for the moment.

It banked away from the cliff and headed out to sea leaving the female behind. As it approached the sea front, it could see several man trees with their white sails sitting on the water next to more man nests onshore. Man things were disembarking from the man trees and going towards their nests, some riding the four legs. The hawk looked up and was attracted by a man tree that was far away on the horizon in the direction of where the sun rose. The hawk flapped its wings vigorously to gain speed and height. Soon it was above the man tree with the black sails that helped it move forward in the water. The commotion on the man tree drew the hawk's attention and it started its descent.

Before it had lost too much height the hawk felt a sense of danger and beat its wings to gain height again. From the man tree he discerned man things with long grey plumage that covered their bodies. These man things were unlike any the hawk had ever seen before. One of them at the command of a man thing dressed in black threw a death stick at the hawk and forced it to turn somersaults to avoid being torn by the death stick. The hawk cried out its hatred for the grey haired man things and their black clad leader as it fled back to the safety of the islands.

♦ CHAPTER 7 ♦

Incident at Jandaea

Theo woke with a start, feeling uneasy. He got out of bed, washed his face, put on his clothes and made his way quickly to the inn common room. Archon was in a corner speaking in hushed tones with Nestor, Tiber and Roxette. Nem and the rest of the group were still sleeping.

"Morning," Theo said, sitting by his companions. They greeted him in turn and Nestor ordered some breakfast for him.

"We'll need to leave very soon," the mage was saying to Tiber. "Did you have any problems last night with the ship?"

"No, I checked up on it several times. Were you expecting any?"

"I'm not sure. I've been feeling unsettled ever since that girl recognized us the previous night. She was right, we're easy to spot and those Darklings might be close by. The fog that descended whilst we left Alunda might have thrown them off for a while but I'm sure they've picked up our trail."

"Do you think they will dock at the port?"

"No, I don't imagine they would brave such a thing. They like to come up on their quarry from behind in the open waters."

"Well, we'll need to be extra careful as we make our way out of the harbour," Tiber said in conclusion.

"Yes. Theo be a good lad and go wake the rest. We need to get going."

Theo found his companions preparing for breakfast. They ate their meal quickly, sensing the mage's irritation. Before long they had retrieved their horses from the inn owner's stable and were leading them towards the wharf. Merchantmen were trading early with the shop keepers as the group made their way to their ship.

"Ahoy there, master Longman! I see you've picked up some fellow travellers. Are they pilgrims as well?"

"Why, master Griffin! How has your business venture faired?" Archon replied, as the jolly plump man approached the group. "No, these are not pilgrims but fellow travellers on this captain's ship," he said, pointing at Tiber. "He's been kind enough to offer us passage aboard his vessel."

"Longman?" Nem whispered in Theo's ear.

"I'll tell you about it later."

"Business in Jade Island, as always, has proved a profitable affair, my young friend," the merchant was saying. "So have you had a change of heart concerning the dappled grey?"

"I'm afraid not, master Griffin. I have grown somewhat attached to the beast," Archon replied, stroking his steed's nose gently.

"Oh well, maybe the next time we meet up you may feel differently," the chubby man said hopefully, wiping at his sweaty brow. "I'm heading for Ramila. Perhaps our paths will cross."

"Perhaps."

Master Griffin boarded the large plush trading vessel that was anchored next to the *Sea Breeze*. His man servants unloaded the merchant's acquisitions on the ship whilst he gave orders in a shrill, wheezing voice for them to handle the items with care. Nem looked on with great interest at the items Griffin had purchased and paid particular attention to the ship's dark lines and build. The letters on the side of the ship read the *Flying Duchess*, an appropriate name signifying the ship's ability to move at great speed, judging from the many sails that hung from her yards.

"That's a fine ship," he said, placing a hand below his chin. "My father trades with wealthy merchants but Master Griffin seems particularly affluent. And his taste is impeccable, judging by his wares. Every item will fetch a good price at the right places."

Tiber barked his orders to Neel and Keil who responded even before the words left his mouth. In no time at all they were manoeuvring out of the harbour. The *Flying Duchess* was still being loaded as they began to put some distance between them. Tiber turned his wheel setting a course due north along Jade Island's coastline.

Archon peered up at the sky, spotting high up above the solitary form of a red-tailed sea hawk. Theo was unsure of how he knew but he sensed it was the same hawk they had met near the Astrologer's complex. The bird soared high above them giving out a shrill cry in greeting as it followed in their wake. Theo squinted up at the morning sun that was shining brightly then at a few wisps of white cloud in the clear blue sky. It was going to be a fine day after all.

Theo and Nem spent the morning training under Roxette's instruction, working out the stiffness that had developed in their limbs and shoulders from their previous day's session. Serilia and Emeralda decided to join them and were looking appreciatively at the young men's upper torsos. Nem was grinning foolishly, blushing both self-consciously and from his efforts. Theo landed him some choice blows sending him reeling across the deck floor by a throwing manoeuvre. Nem recovered and got to his feet slowly, rubbing at his head. Serilia burst out laughing and Emeralda concealed her grin behind her hand, murmuring something in Serilia's ear that made her laugh even louder.

"Pay attention, Nemarchus!" Roxette snapped, rapping him on the head with her knuckles. She was wearing her black leather tunic and tight-fitting trousers and her black hair was brushed back and gleaming, the red tips shining as they caught the morning sun's rays. Theo decided she was definitely not a bad-looking woman, especially in those high heels that added to her femininity; he rubbed at his bruises, reminded of the wicked blows she could deliver during hand-to-hand combat. She pointed a scolding finger at Nem. "Always keep your mind focused when you are fighting, even during sparring practice. In a real life encounter there will be a lot of distractions, so you must learn to keep your senses trained on your opponent at all times."

After their two-hour bout the young men retired to the stern where they sat down to gain their breath and to towel dry their sweaty bodies. Archon stood in his clean shirt and grey travel trousers looking off to the east, his brow knitted and his chin set as he concentrated on something on the horizon that to Theo was invisible. As he turned his face away he glimpsed Theo looking in his direction.

"We didn't get the chance to speak yesterday," he said to the young man, looking agitated with himself. "There just never seems to be enough of the day to go around, does there?"

"We spoke at length with the astrologer and about the guild and other things," Theo offered in recompense.

"I know, but that's not what I meant, Theo. I wanted to speak to you about your gift."

"Er, you will excuse me." Nem looked at the mage and his friend with trepidation. "I just remembered I have to go ask Emeralda if she needs me for anything: to shine her boots, peel potatoes, fetch her comb–anything!" He made his way swiftly to the aft section of the ship, as far as possible from Theo and the mage.

"You don't realize it-" the mage started to say, not paying the departed youth any attention, then corrected himself, "–well how could you? You've been thrown into all this from one day to the next. However, time is running out, Theo," he finished, with rising urgency in his voice. "I feel as if we've wasted these past few days without you making any progress. It's hardly your fault but your enemy doesn't care if you weren't given the chance to prepare yourself. They're out there, Theo. I can sense them. And they are bent on their task and will stop at nothing to achieve it. You still haven't seen the worst of it. Back there at the cottage: that was nothing."

Theo stared at him with rising unease. His feelings of fear gave way to anger–anger at being forced out of his home–anger at being separated from his loved ones–anger at the mage for not solving the problem there and then. *He* was the one who had brought it down on them after all. *What does he want from me?* Theo thought, preparing to answer the mage with a few choice words.

"Theo, I am not trying to frighten you needlessly, or to blame you for anything," Archon explained, placing his hands on either side of the young man's shoulders. "It's just that you have so much to learn in so little time. Please believe me when I say I am on your side. I have taken a vow to do everything in my power to protect you and I will do just that, no matter how hard I have to drive you lad, and no matter how much you will feel at times that I am being pushy and unfair. I'd much rather you felt that way about me than allow harm to befall you because I was too lackadaisical with your training–you're too important for that." The mage stood a long time staring at him with his stone grey eyes, contemplating. "Your training with Roxette is going well but you need to start learning how to use your gift."

"So I've been told before." Theo blurted the words out before he could check himself. He wasn't ready to reveal to anyone the messages in the dreams that had been haunting him for the past few days. Not even to the mage.

"Oh?" Archon asked with interest, sensing that Theo was concealing something.

Theo thought quickly and answered, "Yes, mother has been telling me that of late."

It seemed to satisfy the mage, his expression softening. "You miss her don't you?"

"Yes,' Theo admitted. "Serilia is having a harder time with it than I, though."

"She's a tough girl. I wouldn't worry about her. I agree with your mother, though, about you learning to use your gift. Tell me Theo," he said, moving closer. "What have you been taught so far by your mother?"

"Not much, I'm afraid. Serilia has proven to be the talented one in the family and is more adept at using the gift than I. She can produce balls of flame and lift objects from the ground and propel them to wherever she chooses."

"The first you mentioned is the elementary step in learning to use the fire agent of the gift. The principle behind producing the flame however is what's important. It requires that you, as apprentice, learn to focus your life force so you can unlock the gift within you. Once that is achieved, your talent and henceforth your strength in the gift depends entirely on how often you use it, how eager you are to learn, and, something that nobody can control, your inborn ability. Practice makes you stronger but to become adept at using the gift requires patience and hard work. You *do* have talent in the gift." When Theo did not respond, he added, "I sensed it when we first met in the Triad Forest and again yesterday on the platform at the guild complex."

"I never realized what I was doing when we were on the platform."

"You shouldn't need to. The gift and its use should come to you like second nature...like breathing. You don't consciously do it; it just comes to you when you need it."

"Have you been a sorcerer long?" Theo asked, clutching his legs and resting his chin on his knees. He stared up at the mage.

Archon's gaze took on a far-off look as he recalled his past. His usually composed face changed countenance several times, surprising Theo, as it displayed conflicting emotions of sadness and joy. "I have been a sorcerer since birth, as a fish is born to water. My whole life from infancy was spent in the presence of Wizards and Sorceresses as an integral part of their work, often coaxed to use my gift in their presence. Whilst other youngsters were out playing games in the fields, I was with my parents learning the deepest mysteries of being a sorcerer. When I reached adulthood I joined the Wizard's Keep as a trainee sorcerer but was already way ahead of the rest of my class. I became a full member by the age of twenty-two–your age–and left the keep soon after to begin my term in the service of the Council of Light. I have been one of their High Sorcerers and most prized possessions ever since." Archon spat the words *"most prized possessions"*.

Theo did not expect this level of bitterness to be expressed by the mage, especially in his presence; after all, this was the Archon who had supported his creed so strongly before at the cottage and had probably been called upon to defend their name in other circumstances as well. It made Theo feel uncomfortable and obligated to divulge to the mage at least one of his own secrets in turn. "Well, I can't light a single spark, unless striking a match counts for anything," he said, in an attempt to bring Archon out of his reminiscences.

The mage let out a long breath recovering his composure. He stared at Theo for a while before speaking. "Tell me everything you know about the gift," he urged softly.

Theo scratched his head in thought and answered, "It has nine agents." He proceeded to name them. "That's all I know."

Archon stared then pointed at a small dot in the sky, off the stern side. "You see that hawk soaring above us?" he asked. Theo nodded. "Yesterday you used the Fauna and Spirit agents to fuse your mind with it. Had I left you alone you would have seen everything the hawk saw and felt everything it felt. Your senses for that fleeting moment would have become as one. You know more than you realize, Theo."

"But how did I do it?" Theo looked surprised, but thinking back on the event and his dreams the previous night, it began to make sense to him.

Archon sat opposite folding his legs and placing his hands on his knees like a Nebese meditator. He motioned for Theo to do the same. "I'll show you. Shut your eyes and clear your mind of all thoughts," he ordered. Theo did as ordered, shutting his eyes, but his thoughts remained on his parents and on the events of the past week. "Just let yourself go, Theo," the mage said, in a soft hypnotizing voice. "Listen to the sounds of the sea and the creaking of the ship. Don't generate thought but let your senses respond without restraint to their surroundings. Smell the freshness of the air as the gentle sea breeze carries over the faint scent of island blossoms. Taste the salt on your lips from the sea spray. Feel the air as it tingles the fine hairs on your arms. Immerse yourself in a warm world devoid of turmoil concentrating on the murky brown canvass of your mind's eye. You see, hear, smell, feel, and taste exactly what I tell you to. You *are* calm and at peace."

"I am calm and at peace," Theo murmured, responding to the mage's ever so delicate prompting.

"Your eyes see nothing but darkness." Theo was completely relaxed and sat for a long while absorbing the stimulating effects on his senses from the surrounding sea, listening to the soft tones of the mage's voice instructing him on how to let down his barriers. He found himself floating in a world of blue, rocking as one with the gentle motion of the ship as the waves buffeted its hull.

"Stay focused on emptying your mind of all thought," the mage continued and repeated, "you see nothing but darkness."

Theo's mind let go of the floating blue and dissolved into darkness devoid of thought and impulse, a darkness just as it had been before the beginning of time, before the Creator had given birth to all life and light.

"That's it," the mage murmured. "Keep concentrating. There is nothing but the darkness. Feel its warm embrace, let yourself go completely... nothing but darkness... warmth... darkness... warm... dark... warm... dark."

Theo was dimly aware of his surroundings. He could only respond to the mage's voice that kept murmuring, guiding him along. Time passed but had lost all meaning. After what seemed like fleeting moments to Theo but was in fact a long time, the mage spoke. "In the centre of the darkness you can now see a small spark of light. Do you see it?"

The darkness of Theo's mind continued... then after a while he could indeed see a spark of blinding white light. "I see it," he answered excitedly.

"Good. The spark of light now grows into a walnut sized ball of flame." Theo did not respond. "Nurture the spark," the mage continued in his soft commanding voice, "feed it with your gift, give it life, *make* it grow."

"I see the ball of flame," Theo said, a tremor entering his voice.

"Good. Now stretch out your hand towards me Theo but keep your eyes closed and focused on the small ball of flame." Theo did as he was told, responding mechanically. "Do you still see the ball of flame?"

"Yes."

"Now visualize the small ball of flame resting in the palm of your hand. Do you still see the ball of flame?"

"Yes."

"Open your eyes, my apprentice."

Theo opened his eyes and for a moment blinked at the sun's light trying to get accustomed to it after having kept his eyes closed for so long. Then as they adjusted to the daylight he looked at his hand. A small white sphere was hovering above his palm emitting a light so strong that it hurt his eyes. Theo screamed in utter terror flinging himself backwards and bumping against the gunwales of the ship. He shook his hand vigorously and did not stop screaming until he realized the ball of flame had been extinguished.

Serilia was the first of the crew to reach them. "What's going on?" she asked, looking fretful.

"Nothing anyone needs to worry about," Archon consoled her with a waving gesture.

More of their companions came to the stern. Archon asked them all to give him and Theo a moment alone. He explained that they had some sorcerer business to take care of. That was enough to convince everyone but Serilia to leave hastily.

"Theo, what happened?" Serilia asked, placing a comforting arm around her brother's shoulders.

"Your brother has just successfully taken his first step at becoming a sorcerer," Archon replied in Theo's stead.

Serilia rubbed her brother's trembling arms. "Oh that," she said, understanding dawning on her. "It's always frightening at first. But you need to keep at it till you get used to it," she said encouragingly to her brother.

"I'm never doing that again!" Theo said vehemently. It had been like taking a first plunge in icy cold water or like a baby must feel when it's born and forced to use its lungs for the first time. Theo had unlocked a part of himself he had never thought existed; a part he now wished he could ignore. He was terrified.

"Here," Serilia said, releasing his shoulders and leaving a space between them. She extended her hand turning her palm upwards. A ball of blue flame the size of an apple appeared in her right palm. She extended her left hand and the ball bounced from one hand to the other. "See, there's nothing to it."

Theo stared at the blue ball bouncing from hand to hand and at his sister then back again. "Why is yours blue?" he asked, his mind reaching for the question as a means of overcoming his initial shock.

"Each sorcerer is naturally inclined towards one or other agent of the gift," Archon explained. "Your sister is probably strongest in the use of the Water agent though her blue is much darker than any I've seen before. Serilia it's almost purple in colour. Do you have any idea why?"

"Well mother couldn't explain it. I'm not sure if I'm any stronger in the use of water than any other agent. It's too early to tell."

"Yes," Archon mused, stroking his neatly trimmed blond beard. "With time we may be able to explain it. Your light is easy to explain though, Theo. You're a natural at wielding the Light agent."

"You use white flame as well," Theo said, recalling the incident at the cottage, "and mother uses blue."

"Your mother is a sorceress skilled at using Water. My light however has a different explanation." Theo and Serilia were waiting for more but Archon remained silent and mystical.

Nem came up to the three of them and stopped before the mage, fidgeting uncomfortably with his shirt sleeve. "I don't mean to intrude in whatever it is you are doing," he said, waving his fingers about like a conjurer and rolling his eyes mockingly.

"What do you want, Foresight?" Serilia asked short-temperedly, flicking a lock of her hair over her shoulder with one hand.

"Tiber wants you at the cockpit," he said to the mage.

"We're done here," the mage said, gathering his grey cloak about him. "Theo." He turned to the young man. "You've made a fundamental first step today in the right direction. Keep it up and don't give in to fear." He left a lot unsaid and made his way to the ship's captain. Theo and his friends followed shortly after.

"Tiber, what is it?" Archon asked, nearing him.

Tiber stroked his beard and ran a hand through hair. He pointed to the fore of the ship at a small body of green jutting out of the sea's surface. "That's Jandaea Island," he said. "We should be there within the hour."

"Good, and not a moment to spare. I want to retrieve our new member as soon as possible and be off straight away for Sulicia Island," the mage answered.

"You know we're being followed, don't you?" Tiber asked abruptly.

Archon did not seem surprised or at least he wasn't showing it. "They've been on our tail for the past hour or so, but have tried to keep out of sight."

"I wouldn't have known had Keel not spotted them from the mast head. He's a sharp eyed-one, my Keel," Tiber said with pride.

"I had some help myself," the mage admitted, looking up at the red-tailed sea hawk.

They left the rest of the group on the ship and made their way swiftly through the dense undergrowth of the island. Jandaea was very much like the Sea nymphs' island of Alunda, with similar exotic plant and animal life...and just as devoid of human presence. As soon as Theo set his foot on the island he had the unsettling feeling he was entering a numinous setting that existed simultaneously apart from and together with the rest of the world. The island wildlife seemed to respond to the three companions' alien, invasive presence and sent shrill warning calls further inland as the group waded through the bushes. They were being led by the Mountain nymph clearing the way for the mage who looked about searchingly, followed a few paces behind by Theo.

"Archon, who is this Zoi person we're here to pick up?" Theo whispered, disinclined to let his voice be heard more than was necessary in this eerie place.

"She is an old acquaintance of mine," Archon said evasively. "The Council owes her a favour or two which is why we are here, to repay the debt to some small extent."

They were getting deeper into the island green that was gradually changing to a forest with high trees that a moment ago had been full of birdsong; the birds had taken flight in large flocks at the group's approach. The woods were now silent as they walked below them. They searched around but saw no one.

"This is getting us nowhere," Roxette said, looking about frustrated. She was wearing her grey cloak over her leather and had opted for some stout climbing boots rather than her high-heeled ones. She stared at Theo with dark brown eyes and, reading his feelings of disquiet, looked back at the mage accusingly.

"Sash," Archon said, raising a finger. "Do you not hear it?" Theo cocked an ear but could not hear anything. However Roxette nodded.

"It's very faint but sounds like a woman's voice," she said shortly. She drew her hood low over her face and placed a hand in her robe fingering her sword hilt as she prepared to move forward.

"We'll let her come to us." Archon placed a restraining hand on the nymph. They waited until even Theo could make out the singing voice. As it grew louder Theo realized it sang in an old dialect that, although he could not understand, had a profound soothing effect on him. He stared ahead in the direction of the voice in anticipation, picturing it in his mind belonging to a fair lady.

Roxette however was deeply distressed by the words expressed by the singing voice, which she understood as it sang in an ancient form of nymphish.

"The nymph from the mountain reborn to the plane,
but tell me young she-nymph are you aware of the pain,
that follow the betrayer of blood and kinship,
and brand one as traitor and slayer of friendship,
to whom will your loyalties lie when you're forced,
from family and forebear to be divorced,
will you again your new comrades beguile,
deceive, and cheat by nature so vile,
as a nymph of the Dragon's Foot Mountains to live,
a daughter redeemed to the darkness to give,
her heart, her soul, to be forfeited,
her spirit eternally abdicated?"

"Young Archon, shall we be off then?" They all swung about, caught unawares by the stranger. Theo found he was staring at the most gnarled old woman he had ever seen in his entire life. She croaked a laugh, a sound like grating wood on sand, at the look of astonishment on their faces. Roxette went for her sword but Archon snatched her by the wrist. "This is Zoi," he explained. "You won't need that."

Theo realized the singing had stopped. He looked more closely at the old woman who stood hunched over in her black cloak that covered her entirely. She had a face like an old water skin and two small hazel eyes that peered out at him beneath droopy eyebrows that sagged like the rest of her in folds.

"That was a neat trick, Zoi, but we're in kind of a hurry," Archon chided.

"The great Archon is irate that an old woman has managed to sneak up on him," said Zoi, cackling with delight. "Now who might your companions be, wizardling, or have your manners forsaken you since last we met?"

Archon bowed his head in a sign of respect, his companions following suit as they were introduced in turn. "This is my guide and companion, Roxette," he said, "and this is my apprentice, Theodor, from Cyrus Island."

"I am aware of your most recent Mountain nymph acquisition," the old woman said provocatively, peering at Roxette with a beady eye whilst crouching low, hag-like, in her dark garments. Theo could sense there would be no love lost between these two. Then she turned her gaze askance staring at him and grinned, toothless but for a few blackened front incisors still stubbornly holding on.

"So this young shoot is Theodor," she said, looking at him appraisingly, like a horse master does when purchasing a new steed. Theo almost expected her to prod him in the ribs with her walking staff to test his reflexes and to ask him to open his mouth so she could see the state of his teeth to decide if he was a healthy enough specimen. Instead she smiled roguishly then turning to the mage she locked her arm inside Theo's and said, "Come along then, young

Archon. Time's wasting. Instruct your Mountain nymph guide to get a move on instead of standing around like a pretty, gazing about vacantly."

Roxette threw her an icy look that could have frozen over the hot desert sands of Hieradon but bit down hard on her lower lip in an effort to control her chagrin. Instead she turned about wordlessly and led the way, her hands balled into fists as she walked with stiff shoulders.

I wonder who that sweet voice belonged to, Theo mused. He was about to ask the old woman if she was alone on the island but thought better of it, not wanting to pry. They made better time going back to the beach as it was all downhill. The old woman with her hunched back and thin skeletal limbs, though frail-looking, moved with an energy that defied her years.

Archon's premonition had proven correct: they cleared the edge of the bushes in time to witness a scene they had been dreading for most of the day. The *Sea Breeze* was bobbing in the water with her sails reefed like a goose caught napping. Behind her, and looming at easily double the size, was a ship dressed in black sails stretched out to capture the prevailing wind. It was a battle cruiser, fully rigged with two widespread triangular lateen sails affixed to long crossbars extending aft well above the masts to which they were mounted and angling forward low, near the deck with their free corners secured to the stern. It looked like a crouching bird of prey with a dark, sleek hull banded by a thin white line bordering the top edge of the gunwales accentuating its streamlined looks and signifying its speed and agility. It made the *Sea Breeze* look like a toy ship in comparison. Its approach was fast closing the distance between them in huge forward bounds, like a vulture closing in on carrion.

"Hurry!" Archon yelled, throwing himself forward, his cloak flapping behind him. He paired with the nymph as they raced towards the ship closely followed by Theo and Zoi who had abandoned the use of her staff and was sprinting ahead like a young girl.

They hit the water's edge and plunged into the sea swimming hard, urged on by the flailing arms and screams of their companions who were waiting for them anxiously aboard the *Sea Breeze*. They reached the hull on the port side and were lifted bodily over the ship's edge by the aid of Tiber's strong arms.

"What's kept you?" Tiber reproached the mage, whilst barking orders to the twins who had already unfastened the sails and were drawing in the anchor. The *Sea Breeze* lurched forward into life as it caught a strong wind blowing off the island.

Archon quickly introduced the new passenger to the rest of the crew.

"Where to, Archon?" Tiber asked, taking the wheel of the ship.

"We'll head west for Sulicia Island," the mage answered, casting his gaze nervously behind at their pursuers.

"That's not where I want to be taken," Zoi exclaimed, frantically. "My understanding was that you were to lead me to Ghiadon, so I assumed that we would strike out for Ramila, not go heading west for an island-hopping cruise."

"That's where the dragon we've been following is going and that's where we'll go as well. I'm not about to lose him now that we're so close," the mage insisted.

So that's what he's been after, Theo thought, exchanging glances with his sister and Nem who nodded back at him.

"Dragon? What dragon?" Emeralda asked. Nestor approached and explained in her ear what the mage had discussed with King Rufous in his study two days before. Tiber remained silent. He had enough on his hands navigating the ship with a Battle Cruiser breathing down his neck. He let others worry about the mage's business.

"Marvellous, that's just great!" Zoi flung her thin arms up into the air in exasperation. "We're being dogged by a ship full of Darklings and all our brilliant Wizard is interested in doing is going after some lizard. Don't they teach you anything about setting your priorities straight at that council of yours? I'll have to have a long word with the prefect of your order. Meldwin must have gone soft on you."

"Zoi, with all due respect, I will not be bullied on this trip into doing what you or anyone else here believes I should do. I have my orders and will stick to them." When it was plain that Zoi had accepted who was in charge, the mage turned to Tiber. "Can you outrun that cruiser?" he asked, pointing aft where the black ship was gaining on them.

"I doubt it," Tiber answered truthfully.

"Zoi, I need your help." The mage turned to the old woman beseechingly. She nodded grudgingly as they moved to the stern. "Theo, Serilia come with me! You may be needed."

Theo gazed with mixed feelings of awe and terror at the approaching Battle Cruiser. It was so close now he could discern figures moving around on deck shouting in their guttural speech as they manipulated the running rigging to make the most of the wind flying their sails. Standing at the keel of the ship near the bow were four black-cloaked figures shrouded by hoods. Theo heard the lead figure laughing, a scornful, intimidating laugh that set him on edge and his skin crawling. Written in black writing on the white band crowning the gunwales were the words, "*Unrelenting Condor*", a fitting name it seemed for a ship that had stood steadfast and resolute in its hunt for the mage and his friends.

"Serilia and Theo, I want you to link with me," Archon instructed, taking them by the hand. "We are going to form what's called a Sorcerers' Circle," he explained. "Now empty your minds, like you did this morning Theo."

"Archon, this could be dangerous for them," Zoi cautioned. "They're too new at this and you might injure them irrevocably."

Archon shook his head. "I won't let harm come to them, Zoi. I'll break the link if things get out of hand."

"But severing of the link entails its own dangers and you'll be left more vulnerable and weakened after you break the bond."

"Zoi, I have no choice. There's four of them and only two of us. I need you to concentrate on providing a supporting wind to push us forward whilst I divert their attention on me. It's our only hope."

Zoi nodded reluctantly.

"Alright," Archon said, turning his attention to the siblings. "Just relax and follow my instructions and everything will go smoothly. Don't worry," he added, beaming a confident smile of encouragement at them. "You both have more strength than you realise, so there's no need to fear. Now, shut your eyes and clear your minds of all thought."

Theo followed his mentor's instructions trying to push away his dread but even with eyes closed he could still see the four dark figures in his mind's eye standing there, like grim reapers, feeding off his fear and feelings of inadequacy.

"Don't let them intimidate you," Archon murmured softly, sensing their waning resolve. "Their greatest weapon is your fear which makes them larger than they are. Just keep focused on your task at hand. Good," he said, as he sensed their apprehensions dwindling, being replaced by a more self-assured calm.

"Now envisage the gift within you as being enclosed in a box. You are the box. The gift wants to get out but you are keeping it in." Theo felt a sense of tingling running through his entire body, as if he was straining against a force that wanted to overwhelm him. "Open the box and release your gift. Do it now!" Archon commanded his voice like a slap in the face.

Theo let go of his gift and felt it race through him like a flood bursting through an overflowing dam. His arms ached as energy in its purest form pulsed through them and entered the mage like multiple springs of gushing water entering a raging river torrent. His eyelids snapped open and he saw a luminous blinding white light surrounding him like a cocoon. He looked at his sister and found that she too was enclosed but in a deep blue essence. Her eyes were ablaze like twin sapphires.

Archon felt strength coursing through his veins unlike anything he had ever felt before. He almost lost the link when the siblings laid so much energy at his disposal. He felt for that moment like a god. The four dark beings before him could not possibly match this much power. He extended his arms flinging a white scolding beam of continuous light at the taunting pursuers. They erected a red ethereal shield instantaneously to deflect the beam of light. As it hit them, the white beam shattered their ruby shield hurling them to the back of their ship. Zoi meanwhile had begun an incantation that raised a body of wind from the sea filling their ship's sail causing it to surge ahead like a racing yacht.

Back on the deck of the *Unrelenting Condor* there was a lot of distressed shouting and waving of angry fists as its crew went to the aft section of the ship to check on their fallen masters. Neil and Keel were whooping in delight sticking their rude tongues out at the opposite crew. Soon the distance between the *Sea Breeze* and the pursuing ship got larger as they sped away till eventually it was nothing but a dot on the horizon.

The dark sorcerer rose from the deck floor pushing away with disgust the surrounding pithiks that had milled around him like lap dogs round their master, whimpering and sneezing as they worried over his still form. He located the cloaks of his three dark disciples, still steaming from having been burnt to ash along with their owners. He shook his head scolding himself for having underestimated his opponent. Had his disciples not channelled all their energy to him in time, he might also have suffered their fate.

That boy and the girl that looked so much like him–she must be his sibling–had surprised him with the amount of energy they stored, though he realised in the short conflict that they were simply being used by the mage as conveying vessels to enhance his attack.

A reward will be given for handing over those two to the Dark Lord. Perhaps they could even be turned to the Dark in time, under the proper encouragement. The sorcerer laughed out loud causing the pithiks nearest him to crouch back in confusion and nervousness. He laughed all the more. *Yes, I will not make the same mistake twice with Archon,* he thought, moving through the mob of pithiks that cleared a path for him quickly. But first he would need to turn north to Ramila and pick up a few more gifted disciples. The previous ones, evidently, were all burnt out.

It was nightfall by the time the *Sea Breeze* entered the north harbour of Sulicia to dock. The lights from the lanterns of the cobbled stone streets reflected on the sea surface like fire flies in the night, illuminating the port and beckoning to approaching ships with their welcoming glow. Archon's group disembarked making their way to an inn close to the docks.

The innkeeper was a lady in her mid-forties who ran her establishment with military-like efficiency. Her serving girls wore skirts with clean white linen aprons and hair tied back in ponytails. They stood alert, waiting to carry out her commands at a moment's notice. Emeralda looked around pleased with the tidy inn tablecloths.

"Be a good girl and bring me some warm tea, dear," Zoi said to the serving girl nearest to her, as she sat at one of the neat round tables. "Would you like one as well, my darlings?" she asked Emeralda and Serilia, who both nodded. "You and I will get along just fine," she said, smiling at them appreciatively. "Emeralda, I'd be obliged if you could accompany me tomorrow in buying a few new frocks. Nothing as beautiful as the one you're wearing, of course, which by the way matches the blue of your eyes perfectly. At my age women tend to prefer darker garments, though I'm afraid I left my change of clothing behind at Jandaea Island in all the rush."

"Sounds like Archon, to sweep a lady away on one of his errands without a moment's thought as to her more delicate needs," Emeralda said in a reprimanding tone, casting an accusatory glance at the mage. "Of course I will go with you, my dear, and if you wish I can lend you a night gown for tonight. I have a light green one that will fit you nicely since we seem to be the same size."

"Apart from my hump, yes?" Zoi smiled her near toothless grin.

The men ordered beer. Neil and Keel ordered ginger ale whilst they waited for the inn keeper to prepare their rooms. Dinner was served as steaming platters were brought before them filled with roast lamb chops, boiled vegetables, and mashed potatoes topped with savoury garnish accompanied by a loaf of bread thickly spread with butter. They ate ravenously till they were gorged, after which they sat contentedly with the rest of the inn's guests listening to a musician playing his flute whilst another sang softly a melancholy tune: it was about the journey of a young man who ventured across the seas searching for the woman he had fallen in love with after setting eyes on her for the first time; he had not had the nerve to approach and tell her how he felt. He finds his beloved at last only to discover that she has wed another and departs broken hearted for his home land. He gets lost in a storm never to be heard of again. The song went on to tell how on a windy day out at sea, if one listened closely, one could hear the young man calling out the name of the woman who had stolen his heart–Violanda.

Neil and Keel were the first to seek the comfort of their beds, worn out by the sea chase. They bid everyone a meek goodnight making their way to the room they would be sharing with Tiber.

A couple of hours after the twins had gone to sleep, Archon rose. "Get some rest tonight," he instructed Theo and Serilia. "Tomorrow we rise early to visit the Sisters of Athud."

Roxette sat alone to one side drinking her beer quietly, her look blank and wandering. Nem thought to make some light conversation with her but she kept answering him in monosyllables. In the end he gave up and returned to Theo's side.

"What's the matter with *her*?" he asked his tall friend.

"She's just had a rough day, Nem. I'd let her be for tonight. Maybe tomorrow she'll be in a brighter mood."

Nem grunted his agreement.

"So what happened back there with you two?" he asked, looking at the siblings. "I mean, what was that on the ship? This hanging around with mages has turned you both weird."

"What did you expect us to do Foresight, sit around and wait for those Darklings to finish us off?" Serilia answered, vexed.

"Of course not, it's just that..." he began to answer ruefully.

"It's just what?" Serilia interrupted.

"Well I'm not used to you two behaving this way, well not Theo in any case, and you always used to do ...your stuff somewhere in private so we seldom noticed."

"You *did* notice, Foresight, but you just *chose* to ignore it." Serilia flicked a strand of her hair irritably above her shoulder. "We are who we are and you'll have to find a way to accept it."

"This young Nemarchus has a talent at getting under one's skin," Zoi said sternly, turning to Emeralda.

"Yes, he can be quite obnoxious at times," Emeralda agreed.

Nem found himself being stared at by four scolding pairs of female eyes. *How do I manage to get myself into such predicaments?* he chided himself, getting up and excusing himself with a quick exit for his bedroom.

"I believe Nem has a point, to some extent," Theo ventured.

"Don't you start now!" Emeralda warned.

"Theo, come and sit by us," Nestor said, from the table he was sharing with Tiber close to the fireplace. They were both smoking their pipes, listening to the voice of the young singer. "You boys should learn when to avoid the womenfolk," the old man said, bending over to Theo's ear as he sat down so they would not be overheard. He was wearing a white shirt he had opened almost to his stomach revealing the curly hairs of his chest. He smiled appreciatively at one of the serving girls who smiled back whilst looking worriedly at the inn keeper who for the time being was busy pouring drinks from the bar.

"So what's this story about us going on a wild goose chase after a dragon, then?" Tiber asked, turning his attention back to his father and nephew. He waited, blue eyes trained on Theo, the young man returning his gaze.

"I'm not too sure but we spotted a red dragon when we were flying with Alorn above Alunda," Theo answered shortly.

"Yes, King Rufous told us about your gallivanting across the skies of Alunda when we were locked up in his study with the mage," Nestor said curtly. Theo blushed slightly and made to explain, but was waved to silence, the old man's face softening. "I too would have done the same at your age and in fact when I was living at the island I would often visit Vracho, although I don't suppose he would remember; it was so long ago. Then again..." he mused, clutching his pipe stem with one hand, "...dragons, they say, have long memories. Did you know they live to be over a thousand?"

"I thought they lived forever," Tiber answered, scraping shards from his pipe into the fireplace. His cheeks were red from sitting close to the fire and from the tankards of ale he had consumed. The chair beneath him creaked as he moved his ample body. One of the serving girls, appreciating his large chest and rough sailor look was throwing him inviting looks but he ignored her, unlike his father who was grinning shamelessly.

Theo got up, feeling that he might be in the way. It was well past his bed-time, bearing in mind the early start Archon had in store for them on the morrow. Serilia caught his gesture nodding her acquiescence as they bade their companions a good night.

Theo felt the beast beating its veined wings, stretching them out extensively as it laboured to pull its winding body higher into the night sky. The creature looked up at the twin moons, the light of the smaller moon turning its scaled body a shimmering blue. It laughed at the irony of it all, its body trembling to the rumbling sounds emitted by its throat. *What I would give to be this colour by day*, it thought, finding it amusing that so much importance was given by its kin to such a trivial feature. Was not one's beliefs and the values held in one's heart more significant than something so...of-the-flesh?

He snorted blowing jets of flame into the night air. His senses warned him that he was approaching another's territory. He would have to be more careful this time. He had been lucky before with the blue, island pair: by the time they had gained their altitude he had been well away and beyond their reach. He banked sharply towards the right following the shoreline. The wind was blowing north easterly, so if he kept his present course his silver cousins would hopefully not sense his intrusion. They were a mean lot these silver ones but then again his own kindred did not show any mercy either when they encountered any of them.

The red and the silver had always been mortal enemies since the dawning of time when their kind first took to the air leaving their heavier lizard relatives to dominate the earth whilst they became lords of the skies. And then when the meteor had struck forming the Ring Mountains at Kalkador all the great lizards had been exterminated by the falling temperatures and absence of light created by the dense mass of material the meteor boulder had thrown into the air. Only the fire breathing sky lizards had been able to survive the sudden depletion of vegetation in the midland areas by flying to the poles where they preyed on herbivorous mammals that lived in abundance there.

However the rest of the land lizards could not reach the poles, as the lands of Thalagia had long since become separated from them by earthquakes and the gradual shifting of the tectonic plates of the earth, leaving oceans behind that could not be traversed. The land lizards were amongst those creatures that had chosen all those millions of years ago to migrate to the warmer equatorial regions, thus sealing their fate.

And that's how we came to dominate the earth, Dragonstrider. Theo heard the dragon talking directly to him and was sufficiently startled for the mind link to break. He continued to soar bodiless. Casting his gaze below at the long thin strip of land, he recognized it as Sulicia Island. He hurtled forward, westwards, to a kingdom that lay at the foot of a series of mountains. He looked down upon the sheer fortified walls of the kingdom and could see in the blue moonlight the night guards standing with their pikes erect gazing attentively at the mountains that loomed threateningly before them.

Theo shivered as he felt the cold wind blowing off from the snow-capped peaks–*how is it possible to feel the cold in one's dreams?* he wondered, perplexed. He was losing altitude quickly and braced himself for the impact with the fortress walls. He shut his eyes in anticipation of the collision. Nothing happened. He opened them to find he was in a dimly lit room built from grey stone like the rest of the fortress. On its walls hung two solitary torches giving off their light as they splattered in the wind blowing in from the open window.

He looked around at the room furniture that was sparse and functional. There was a crude dressing table that was nothing more than a flat surface with four simple legs for supports upon which was placed within easy reach a comb, a brush, and a single box. The box was open and resting within it was a single swan brooch made of white gold. Next to the brooch was a ring fashioned from the same metal with an emerald stone set upon it.

His attention was diverted to a large body-height mirror next to the dressing table. He stared into the mirror and was surprised by what he saw. His hair was getting long, down to his shoulders so he would soon be able to hang it in a ponytail and his eyes were wilder and more care-ridden than he remembered before. He turned about to the bed that sat against the opposite wall, with posts extending above forming a canopy over which spilled a fine lacy fabric; it completely enclosed the bed mattress that was plush and made to provide warmth against the chilly mountain temperatures.

A noise, as of the beating of giant wings, drew his attention to the open window where the curtains fanned out from the on-blowing wind. Shadows were cast into the room in relief against the moonlight and his interest was piqued by the solitary figure that stood at the balcony. He could see a slim body silhouetted against the blue light. His pulse raced as he realized his intrusion into the woman's private quarters might be discovered.

"We will continue our rounds early tomorrow morning, Assima," the figure said, in a feminine voice that intrigued Theo with the air of command but at the same time gentleness in it. Theo found that he could understand the words she spoke, though they were like an ancient form of Galipan.

"That red dragon we saw tonight was alone and, by the way it was flying, had no intention of entering your domain," the figure said. "However, to be on the safe side we will fly over the same spot in the morning to make sure he has gone."

"You should have let me take a dive for him," growled a voice that thundered and rocked the room furniture but which Theo recognized strangely as belonging to a female.

"We could not have been certain of the outcome, my zealous friend, and in any case he posed no significant threat where he was."

"I could have taken him, even one as large as he; we had the element of surprise on our side."

"Maybe next time. Now go seek your lair. I am tired and in need of my rest." And with that dismissal she whirled around entering the room, the torch light illuminating her face. Behind her the beating of wings dwindled away into the darkness as the female dragon sped away.

The young woman standing before Theo had a body and face every sculptor would dream of capturing in white marble: fairy-like pastel skin, a dancer's poise and balance, and a perfectly proportioned nymph oval face. Above full, kissable lips her eyes were a shade of pale blue which alternated to light green, like cyan gemstones, depending on how light and shadow played on her face. Her dark hair reached down low to the hollow of her back and was tied back behind her surprisingly human rather than nymph ears. Her clothing was both decorative but at the same time military style in its efficiency: she wore a crimson blouse that left her shoulders and neckline bare; criss-crossing over it were several black leather belts fastening scabbards to her back from which protruded the hilts of two swords. The blouse was tied by a wide leather belt sporting a collection of daggers round her lithe waist. She wore plain black trousers that were tucked into soldiers' boots; they were tied up with laces and small buckles up to her knees with slim pin-like throwing knives protruding from the top. She wore matching leather gloves to protect her hands and arms up to her elbows, cut to reveal the fingers so they could be more dexterous in the handling of weapons.

As she approached her bed she removed from her slender neck a silver necklace upon which hung a sapphire pendant the size of a walnut. She fingered it softly, laying it tenderly on a small velvet pillow next to her bedside. Theo was surprised to feel pangs of jealousy he had never felt before. The woman was perhaps Serilia's age. She stepped over to her mirror taking a look at her reflection. Theo approached from behind drawn to her by an invisible force he could not deny. She sensed his presence and swung about.

"How did you get into my room, boy?" she asked, drawing her twin swords without a moment's hesitation.

The image of the room became blurred as Theo was enveloped in a world of darkness. *Boy?* he thought in disappointment, as he sped away from the fortress.

The young girl approached the balcony and shut her windows to the cold night air, drawing the curtains. She inspected her bedroom door and found it securely locked. The boy–well he was a young man actually, she admitted grudgingly–must have gotten in by the window. *Don't be absurd!* she corrected herself. Spirits don't have body mass so they're not bound by the laws that govern solid matter. Brave of the boy to attempt such a feat. Her mother had often told her that wizards were wary of travelling out of their body because it left them unprotected and vulnerable to attack from another possessing the gift. Maybe the boy wizard had an accomplice guarding him whilst he spirit-travelled.

Who is he? Well, whoever he was he had no right sneaking into other people's rooms. *He's not my type either.* She found herself considering. His hair was a lighter brown than she liked and his eyes were green–not brown which was her preference. His face was handsome enough, albeit too young looking, but she confessed his shoulders and arms were solid enough though there was room for further improvement. *What am I thinking?* She chided herself. If she ever caught him she'd give him a piece of her mind, *and maybe something more*, she reflected passing her finger gingerly along the edge of her sword blade.

♦ CHAPTER 8 ♦

Sisters of Athud

Archon, true to his word, woke Theo and his sister early the next morning. Before the sun was above the horizon, they had finished their breakfast and were drinking morning coffee whilst the inn keeper busily cleared their table of empty dishes. Roxette had changed into another of her leather suits. *I wonder if she ever wears anything else*, Serilia thought, fidgeting with her cream coloured cow hide riding tunic and pants.

"That was a hearty breakfast ma'am," Archon said with approval. "Dinner last night was fabulous as well. You run a very neat establishment."

"Why, thank you sir," the inn keeper smiled contentedly. "I try to keep my girls on their toes. They're good hearted lasses but like all young people they require a firm guiding hand. It's for their own welfare in the end because a happy customer is one that returns again. Talking of returning, I've seen you here before, sir," she said.

"Yes, I've dealings with the good sisters here. I travel a lot in my line of work so I often need the services of a healer to tend a bruised limb or a cut leg."

"It's a dangerous business travelling abroad," the inn keeper nodded in agreement. "The name is Vicky," she said, extending her hand.

"I'm Longman and these are my companions, Flin, Jodie, and Linda." Archon took her hand and shook it.

She was tall with broad shoulders for a woman and had a firm handshake. Her dress code was frugal: plain brown tunic with matching pants, and calf-high low-heeled boots. Her white cotton apron covered it all and her hair was tied back in a bun revealing a face that was stern but with tell-tale smile lines at the corners of the mouth and eyes. She was not beautiful but neither was she unpleasant to look at. "And the rest of your companions?" she asked, more in the way of conversation than from any special interest.

Archon decided to reveal some of the truth. "Family and friends who have decided to accompany us on this trip."

"Well enjoy your stay," Vicky said, nodding as she walked to the kitchen with the dishes.

"Jodie?" Serilia asked in a low voice. Archon simply shrugged.

"You prefer Linda?" Roxette offered, giving one of her rare smiles.

"You should do that more often," Serilia answered.

"What?"

"Smile. It suits you." Roxette blushed ever so slightly.

"Leave your weapons behind on today's trip," Archon instructed. Roxette exchanged glances with him but nodded in the end.

Just as the sun was lifting over the horizon, bathing the port with its amber light, the companions set off on horseback following the cobbled road that passed by shops and more inns before turning inland towards the low hills of Sulicia. They left the cobbled road entering a track covered with crushed stones laid in a neat thick layer above the dirt sub-surface. This ensured that the road would remain free of mud and be traversable in rainy weather. To either side of the road were positioned, neatly and equally spaced, small rocks painted white that led all the way up to the highest peak upon which was built a long sprawling complex covering most of the hill's crest. Archon explained that the rocks were painted thus in an inspired endeavour to aid travellers so they could find their way in the night by the reflection of the moon or starlight on the rocks. The sign read "*Abbey Road*" and pointed south in the direction of the cliff top.

They arrived at the abbey after being halted twice by the church paramilitary guards wearing the distinctive regalia of the Templar Order: white surcoats marked above the right breast with Athud's yellow flame, laid over chain mail and black trousers.

"You may leave your steeds with me," said a young novice dressed in white, as they entered the outer courtyard. They dismounted, handing her the reins. She promptly led the horses away to the stables whilst a second novice approached.

"We're here to see the Mother Superior," Archon explained.

"Please follow me," she said politely, as they proceeded to the first stone alleyway on the left hand side of the courtyard. They passed the novitiate where they could hear the loud clear voices of the nuns carrying over from the open windows instructing several of the neophytes listening attentively on the virtues of self-abasement and humility. Further on at the infirmary there were nuns hunched over examining the progress of a few of their patients. They reached the end of the corridor, coming to a halt before a gatehouse where a nun was waiting for them.

"Sister, Prissila," said the novice, curtsying and reclining her head reverently, "these travellers have come to see the Mother Superior."

The austere sister's gaze remained fixed for a moment on the mage and his nymph companion before recognition dawned on her. Clapping her hands together in delight, she stepped towards the nymph and placed her arm about her shoulders. "How have you been, my dear?" she asked familiarly. "Have your wounds completely healed?"

"Yes thank you, sister Prissila," Roxette said, smiling. "I will be eternally in your debt."

"May the Creator protect you child and guide you to safer paths in the future. When they brought you to us, I personally doubted there was anything we could have done. You were fortunate that his sister," she said, nodding in Archon's direction, "proved such an adept healer, even though we do not usually condone the use of the dark arts at our convent."

"The gift may be used by the forces of both the Dark and the Light, sister," Archon said defensively. "When one has the gift it is sinful not to use it when the need arises."

"Well, that has been a matter of much debate among the laity and one that we will not solve here," the sister answered resolutely, as she opened the door to the Mother Superior's office. "Please take a seat whilst I send for the abbess."

They entered the room and sat on crude chairs opposite an unadorned desk with a pile of papers resting on one end and an ink bottle with a feathered pen on the other. Theo looked around at the stark white walls where portraits of previous abbesses with stern faces hung, dressed in their black garments concealing all but their faces, their hands folded neatly in their laps. On the third finger of their left hands were the prominent rings that signified their consummation to a life of devotion to the Creator. The only decorative piece visible that could be identified as belonging to the abbess was a small silver statue of a mountain eagle resting on the dark polished surface of the office table.

Two large windows at opposite ends of the room, the one facing towards the outer courtyard and the other inwards to the abbey proper, let in the sun's rays causing the minute dust particles hanging in the air to be illuminated.

The door swung open and a woman in her mid-fifties walked in. She beamed a smile at the mage and his nymph companion, then scrutinised Theo and Serilia with interest.

"Mother Superior," Archon said, getting up from his chair and reclining his head respectfully. His companions did likewise.

"Archon, let's dispense with the formalities," the abbess said, returning the mage's greeting. "Please take your seats," she said, motioning with one hand as she moved around her desk to sit on her high-backed chair.

"So what brings you to the convent, Archon? It's been a while since you last came, with Roxette cradled in your arms in dire need of our healing skills."

"Close to four years if memory serves me correctly," said the mage, straightening in his chair.

"So how have you been, my dear?" The abbess asked, turning her attention to the nymph.

"None the worse for wear, thanks to you and the sisters, Mother Superior."

"Emilia, please," the abbess insisted, studying her carefully, like a healer her patient. "Your wounds seem to have sealed on the surface without scarring, but it's the damage to your inner organs which had us worried. Lucinda did a fine job healing you in the end, though she was unable to stand for a week after her exertions. Is it always so taxing...using *it*, I mean?" she asked, turning to the mage again.

"It can be very strenuous when so much of the energy from the gift is expended," Archon explained, "and in the case of healing, one needs to use the five agents of Fire, Water, Spirit, Fauna and Light simultaneously in a complex weave to help reconstruct the damaged tissues of the body. Only the most knowledgeable amongst us in human anatomy and the arcane skills of healing would dare to attempt such a feat, which is why I came to you for aid and more specifically to Lucinda."

"The end result justifies the means, I suppose," the abbess said resignedly, placing a hand under her chin. "So, are you here on a social call, to see your sister?"

"That and to visit your archives," Archon nodded.

"Ever the searching mage bent over his volumes trying to unravel whatever mysteries lie hidden in the chronicles." She smiled at him briefly before her eyes wandered over to Theo and his sister. Theo sat gazing at her calm face that was slightly wrinkled around the corners of the eyes and mouth. It was a face exuding confidence and authority though as she fingered the little statue on her table Theo could also sense a gentler, sadder side to her nature.

"So who are your young companions?" she asked.

"This here is Theo and this is Serilia, Elron's and Russilda's son and daughter," Archon replied, introducing the siblings.

The Mother Superior's eyes widened. She looked disbelievingly at the pair, as if at an apparition. "Why, I thought their parents were dead," she said, her voice trembling slightly.

"Well, I must confess I am largely responsible for spreading that false rumour. As you might remember at the time, there was a conspiracy to wipe out the *Sorcerers* of Aldorn," the mage stressed the word "sorcerers". Theo imagined he caught a look passing between him and the abbess. "My first priority was to save Russilda at all costs." He halted, a pained look crossing his face. "I just wish I had been in time to save *them* as well," he finished softly, as if speaking to himself.

"You knew our parents?" Theo ventured to ask the abbess, eager to find out whatever he could about their shrouded past.

"I am from Hendon, which is where your mother Russilda received her apprenticeship as a sorceress of the Council of Light," the abbess answered carefully, giving Archon another of those looks. "I met your mother at the king's court when she was accompanying a group of her colleagues acting as representatives of the Wizard's Keep. I remember she made an impression on the courtiers, being the daughter of the sorceress Serilia. Your grandmother was an impressive, intelligent woman, Theodor. I remember I was very little when I met her but she left a lasting impression on me. I am truly sorry you did not have the opportunity to meet her."

"There's no need to apologize," Theo answered, clearing the lump in his throat. "We never got to meet my mother's parents. They both died before we were born." Theo thought he saw something pass in the mother superior's eyes, as if she wanted to tell him something. But when she remained silent he realized she must have wanted to offer words of support, so he added quickly, "Mother has told us all about them so we feel as if we knew them. That will have to be enough, I suppose." He looked at his sister who nodded.

"I was named after grandmother in memory of her," Serilia said, smiling in an attempt to lift the mood.

"My dear children," the mother superior said, getting up and coming round to give each of them a hug and a peck on the temple. "The Creator has truly blessed your parents with two children they can be proud of. For every life he takes he gives a new one in return." Then she turned to the nymph and said, "Roxette, please be a dear and call Sister Prissila to my office. She should be in the almonry, stock-taking–you remember where that is, don't you child?" The nymph nodded as she got up and left the room.

Then turning back to the siblings she said, "Sister Prissila will take you around for a tour of the convent whilst Archon and I catch up on some business that you most probably would find mundane. Now, whilst we wait for the sister, tell me what I can order for you to drink. Tea or some juice perhaps? We have wine as well that we produce here and which they tell me is very good."

Roxette returned shortly, she and the mage remaining with the mother superior whilst Sister Prissila escorted the siblings out of the room. Once the sister had closed the door behind her and the sound of their footsteps had receded the abbess leaned closer to the mage. "Do you realize the implications of what you have done?" she asked, giving him a searching look.

"What would you have had me do, Emilia?" the mage answered softly, pinning her with his stone grey eyes. "At the time, we could not recognize friend from foe. I still often wonder if we managed to get all of them or if there are some lurking behind masks waiting to strike at the opportune moment. Even after so many years I fear for Elron's and Russilda's safety–and for their children."

"But they have you to protect them," Emilia answered, looking out her window at the inner court where she could see Sister Prissila taking the siblings to the east wing so they could pass in front of the church on their way to the kitchens located at the south end of the convent. *Good-looking lad that Theo–his sister too, just like their grandmother Serilia, though the girl's eyes are the same colour as her grandfather from the other side of the family. What was his name again?* she mused, turning the ring on her finger. *Nestor, that's it!* she remembered.

"Will you tell them?" she asked, turning to the mage.

"They've been through a lot, Emilia. In time, all will be revealed to them. For the time being though it's best they remain blissfully ignorant."

"Your ways and ours don't differ all that much, in the end." She laughed ironically. "We carry out our work the way we do, all in the name of duty, and hope that people will understand it was for their own good." She stroked her statue of the eagle and sighed.

A knock at the door interrupted them. "Come," said the abbess, as a white-dressed novice entered carrying three goblets and a wine pitcher on a tray that she placed on a small table in front of the mother superior's desk before curtsying and leaving the room.

"Do you wish you had chosen another path to follow?" the mage asked gently.

"No, I do not regret my choice," she answered, taking a deep breath and reclining in her high-backed chair. "It's just that the burden of responsibility lies heavily on my shoulders. It's no easy task running the abbey, making sure the novices and sisters are kept well supplied. The toughest matter to deal with though is not their material needs, for the life of a nun is one of frugality, but tending to their spiritual needs. I try to augment their teaching by not using too much chastisement in my classes, which I have found cripples the spirit, but through appealing to the girls' natural desire to open their young minds and hearts to learning. The girls, when allowed to choose on their own rather than being bullied into it, are drawn to a life in the service of our Creator, to the virtues of a life free of gluttonous excesses and destructive external influences that confuse the mind and imprison the soul to a life of sin and darkness.

"I don't mean to rumble on, Archon, but the point I am driving at is that for the past few years less girls have been arriving at our gates to espouse our ways and live a life close to the Light. Our sisters report that our people are becoming used to a life of excess where there can never be enough of anything. There is a large influx of gold and diamonds entering the midland kingdoms from the slave mines of the Hieradon Empire and from the dark dungeons of the Warlock of the Dragon's Foot Mountains, not to mention precious stones from the Ice Queen of Galandir–and

Kalkador has been exporting gold for centuries. Our aristocracies grow ever greedier on the luxuries the Darklings provide, plotting one against the other in a desperate attempt to rise in station. We have had reports of women being used by the dark forces to seduce men into committing acts of atrocity that do not fall short of even murder."

"These matters you mention have always been occurring, Emilia. For example the aristocracy has always been vying for position and for the favour of the royal families ruling their lands. It is not uncommon for them to scheme and conspire; in fact it has come to be expected."

"Yes, Archon, but they grow bolder in their methods and are losing all sense of what is permissible in their pursuit of personal profit to the detriment and attrition of their homelands, which is what the Dark desires. Unless something is done, and done soon, we will begin to lose control of the situation entirely and we'll become susceptible to our enemies. Surely in your travels you have seen this for yourself?"

"I'm afraid, to some extent, that you are right, Mother," the mage admitted sternly at last, a resigned sigh escaping him just before he placed his wine glass to his lips. He took a few long gulps, finishing it off before proffering it to the abbess for a refill. She obliged him. "I have witnessed the events your sisters have reported, first hand. I was simply harbouring the lame hope that we are not too far gone down our self-destructive road—too much past redemption."

"*You* never used to be such a cynic." The abbess smiled ironically, bringing the conversation round full circle, realizing her message had gotten across but much preferring that the sorcerer would have had something to say to allay her fears or counter her reports. Still, she was not one to be disillusioned and preferred to dwell in the real world, however much it might hurt. "Have you been to Hendon recently?" she asked, suddenly changing subject, her eyes taking on the look of longing they showed every time she fingered the statue on her desk.

Archon nodded in response.

"Tell me, how is he?" she asked simply.

"The boy or his father?" he returned her look, his face expressionless. Roxette also did not show any emotion.

They're a matched pair, the abbess mused. "I want to know about them both but start with the boy."

"Lepidar is well, Mother. He has been well cared for by the royal household, his uncle treating him as a son, making available to him all the opportunities and resources his kingdom has to offer, the same as he does for his own son, Prince Achelor, who has grown up to be very fond of his cousin and has set him up as his role model."

"That pleases me–that he has grown up so well. Tell me, how is his career in the military progressing?"

"It's going very well, actually. He is a man with ambitions and aspires to rise to the very top."

"Like his father," the abbess interrupted, smiling fondly.

"Yes...like his father," the mage repeated gently. "Lepidar has recently become a colonel and now leads his own battalion. He is one of Hendon's finest and has proven his strategic skills time and again on sea expeditions against the pirate forces of Ishbad and Neba."

"He has served our kingdom as a sailor as well?" the abbess asked, surprised.

"Why yes. Hendon is fortunate, as is the rest of Seldavia, in that we are flanked on three sides by lands that are friendly towards us. Our only weaknesses are our seas that are troubled, like the rest of our allies' shores, by the marauding pirates of the Anvil kingdoms. The military have thus often been called upon to support the navy, though in your son's case he has served in reconnaissance missions and in supportive roles with the land forces of Renderon as well. In fact it was for bravery shown well above what's considered the norm, in skirmishes with Kalkador's forces on the eastern borders of Renderon and at Darion's Hold, that Lepidar gained recognition as a fighting man. He spent five years in Renderon assigned to the defending army there, prior to returning two years ago to his post in the Hendon army. He was made a colonel this year in light of his achievements whilst serving in Renderon and before that as a naval lieutenant fighting alongside Hendon's sailors in the Valdoric Sea."

"And his father? How go things for Primate Alistrat of Hendon? Last I heard, he was stipulating that he might announce his candidacy for Patriarch of Seldavia, seeing as the position will soon be vacated by the current Patriarch of Hendon, who it is rumoured will support Alistrat."

"Your reports are very accurate once more, Mother. The old Patriarch Ischillus has long been hinting that he is approaching his retirement and that he wishes to lead a quieter life at his lodge back in his home city of Aldorn. He has often said in jest that sixty years is enough for any man to offer for the needs of others and that he now wishes to enjoy the few years left to him in the tranquillity of his residence, tending his vineyards. I believe that, by this summer, Alistrat will have begun his campaign in the kingdoms of Seldavia to rally support for his candidacy."

"Does he have time for his son?" the abbess asked, with intense interest. She straightened her shawl and sat up straighter in her chair.

"Alistrat and Lepidar seldom meet, Emilia. The secret has been well kept to protect the primate's position but as a consequence father and son have grown apart. By the time Lepidar discovered his true father's identity, he no longer cared. Alistrat has tried to reconcile his relationship with his son but I think without much success. Lepidar feels bitter about not having had his real father close by when he was younger. Even though the king was gentle and affectionate with him as a boy, the love of a father cannot be replaced. He feels betrayed. Alistrat has always been kept away, filling his varying posts all across Seldavia as he worked his way up through the clergy hierarchy, so he was seldom in Hendon and etiquette prevented him from approaching the boy when he was. I don't know though...maybe with time."

"Thank you for being blunt and truthful with me Archon," the abbess said, deeply moved. She fought back tears and cleared her throat. "Just look at me rambling on and on. You have been here for an hour and still haven't had the chance to meet with your sister," she said, getting up from her chair. "Please follow me to the central courtyard. We'll sit by the fountain and I'll send a novice to notify your sister that you have come to call on her. She'll be pleased to see you. You too, Roxette."

Roxette bowed her head in acknowledgement as the three of them filed out of the office.

Theo and Serilia were shown around the convent to the brewery where the nuns produced their wines and to the church that fascinated them with its high arched ceiling and tall lancet windows infilled with colourful glass depicting various scenes from Creation. They finished up at the central courtyard adorned with a fountain surrounded by a rectangular, well-kept lawn bordered by stone paving. Sitting at a wooden bench by the fountain, they found their other two companions chatting with the abbess.

"Ah, there you are my dears," she said, beckoning to them. "Come and sit by us whilst Sister Prissila summons Lucinda."

Archon looked up towards the sky gazing intently northwards. Theo followed his gaze and caught sight of a small object like a dark dot in the distance fast growing larger. Archon produced a leather glove from his cloak and wore it on his left hand. He whistled and the object in the sky plummeted towards them. Theo could now discern from its yellow under-plumage and rufous tail that it was the Valdoric sea hawk. The bird flapped its wings at the last to break its speed and alighted with a flutter of feathers on the mage's gloved hand.

"This is a friend of mine, a fellow traveller whom I have named Farwing," the mage said fondly, stroking the hawk's throat feathers beneath its hooked beak. He motioned to Theo and Serlia and they took turns stroking the majestic bird.

"You are full of surprises, Archon." The abbess giggled with delight like a schoolgirl as she tenderly reached out a hand to stroke the hawk's back. Farwing peered at them with one golden eye cocking its head from side to side as it gazed at its surroundings with keen interest.

Just then the hawk noticed one of the nuns approaching and gave out a welcoming cry. It flapped its wings a couple of times and shook its head before settling down once again on the mage's hand.

"Farwing, you show off. Where have you and my restless brother been?" the nun asked, grinning broadly as she approached. She bowed her head low to the abbess. "Mother Superior," she greeted her and was greeted back with a nod and a smile. "Dearest brother, welcome back." She hugged her brother lovingly, giving him a peck on each cheek. "Roxette, how have you been?" she asked, turning to the nymph and standing back to look at her appraisingly. "You look well."

"Thanks to you Lucinda," Roxette answered, surprising the siblings by taking the nun in a warm embrace.

"Has this old fox been giving you much trouble?" Lucinda smiled playfully at her brother as she put an arm around his waist. The sea hawk fluttered its wings once more and peered at her with interest.

Archon placed his free arm around his sister's shoulders whilst balancing the bird with the other. "Old?" He feigned hurt feelings whilst concealing a grin.

"Nothing I couldn't handle," Roxette answered meaningfully. "I'm used to walking with foxes and wolves and have learned their habits well."

Lucinda laughed wholeheartedly and seeming to notice the siblings turned towards them. "Hello there. Brother, won't you introduce me to your friends?"

Archon looked at the siblings, considering, then introduced them. "Lucinda of Sulicia Abbey, meet Theo and Serilia of Cyrus Island."

Lucinda seemed to be taken aback at the mention of their names and her eyes widened. "Elron's and Russilda's boy and girl," she exhaled, looking at the siblings more closely. "Yes, now you mention it, I see the resemblance." The mage and the abbess exchanged a look.

"Well I'll leave you to get acquainted," the abbess offered. "Lucinda can show you around the rest of the convent and may take *you*, Archon, to the library as well."

"Thank you Mother," Archon replied. "We'll speak later on."

"Yes, we'll do so," she said, turning away.

They were left on their own with the mage's sister who was still staring at the siblings, who likewise were returning the stare with interest at this woman who, with her blue eyes and fair complexion, looked so much like her brother. "I'm very pleased to finally meet you." She extended her hand to shake Theo's and Serilia's firmly in return and gave each a hug.

Strangely, Theo could sense he was in the presence of a gifted one by the faint tingling sensation on his skin. It was the same he had felt, since the age of sixteen, every time he was approached by either his mother or sister. Lucinda too seemed to sense something, for he could see it in her body stance and the look of recognition in her eyes.

"Shall we make our way to the library?" she asked.

They spent the better part of the day being shown around the convent.

Archon meanwhile chose to remain immersed in his archives searching for who-knew-what in the ancient, brown, weathered tomes. He spent most of the day there, skipping lunch, whilst the siblings, Roxette and Lucinda ate at the refectory in the company of the nuns. Finishing their meal the siblings were escorted to the lawn where they sat down to enjoy the measured pace and tranquillity of their surroundings.

"Have you found it safe living here, amongst the nuns?" Serilia asked, turning to Lucinda. "Have you been able to get away from the stigma that follows the gifted wherever they might go?" Theo wondered if any place in the world was safe from attack by their enemy. Being on the run, he decided, was not a life worth living.

"I have lived a relatively sheltered life and the church's militia keeps a watchful eye on the comings and goings of our various visitors, though, even here, I have not been entirely without mishap."

"Indeed you haven't," Archon interrupted, overhearing as he approached them from the direction of the library.

"My brother feels a slight bitterness at losing an ally to the convent, but I can still be of much use when needed." Lucinda turned to her brother, offering her hand for him to aid her in getting up. "What happened before had nothing to do with the sisters."

"Yes, but it just goes to show that you can never be safe, no matter where you go." Archon kept his eyes on her and they exchanged a brief look before Lucinda turned away silently.

Lucinda stood staring at the dormitory alleyway and lifted her finger to point at a stone column that was charred black. "It still bears your mark."

Archon stared at the column for a long while, reminiscing on how he had just been on time to save his sister from a sorceress of the Dark who had dressed as a nun to get close to Lucinda and dispose of her. That time, Archon had been the swifter, and the darkling was left as a charred pile of ashes next to the column that still bore testament to the event. The sisters had never managed to remove the soot marks, no matter how much they scrubbed at them.

"Have you found what you were looking for in the archives?" Lucinda brought the mage out of his musing.

"What? Oh, not quite...but I learned a few other things of interest." Then turning to the siblings and the nymph, he said, "We're leaving."

"Why don't you stay for the night?" Lucinda offered. "We have guest rooms and you can make a fresh start in the morning."

Archon shook his head. "No, our companions are waiting at the port. It's better we return and see that everything is alright. They too will be worried about us."

Lucinda shrugged. "As you wish. Will I see you again any time soon?"

"Perhaps, I cannot tell at present where my journeys will take me." Lucinda placed an arm around his neck and gave him a peck on the cheek then led them to the Mother Superior's office to say their farewells.

They were out of the convent gate by dusk, just as the sun was beginning to lower over the hills. They started their easy descent passing by the Templar guards before continuing on their way. By the time they reached the inn nightfall had overtaken them.

♦ CHAPTER 9 ♦

Mountain nymph's bane

He awoke with a groan, his head feeling as though it was stuffed with sand, his entire body aching as if he had been battered by a thousand unseen fists. He dragged his feet as he approached to stare at his reflection in the mirror. His eyes were red and puffed up, his face a sickly yellow. He stuck out his tongue to find it was swollen and covered by a whitish mucous film. *It's all worth it in the end,* he thought, splashing water on his face from a bowl resting by the basin below his mirror. He turned his naked arm staring at the needle marks spread there. He would have to find a new vein today. The one he had been using was turning blue and was bruised from extensive use.

Will she come to the training grounds today? he mused, kneeling at his bedside to pull out the small unadorned tin box. He opened it and brought out the needle and his dose. *"The finest the market can provide,"* his rat-faced friend had assured him. *"Only the best for my prince."* Armend had begun to use the stuff when he was still in his late teens. It was well named: "lifeweed". He remembered how, when he had taken his first injection, he had felt like he could achieve anything. Taking his dose, he could go on for hours without tiring but the mornings after were always the worst. Still, being the best, performing in combat like no other could, made it all worth while.

Armend was born the son of a king, and not just any king, but Philander himself, Lord of Ameron and High King of Leonium. Philander had taught his son from a young age to strive to reach the top, to distinguish himself.

"You will be the next High King of Leonium so you must act like one. There is no room for failure where you are concerned. Pay attention to your tutors and make me proud, boy." King Philander did not often get a chance to speak with his son because the ruling of the kingdom and the lands of Leonium took up most of his time. But when, on those rare occasions, he did pay attention to him, he would push him to his limits, always asking for more and Armend would respond with all his heart.

After all, was he not his father's favourite? Armend felt sorry for his only other sibling, his elder sister Diomeda. *"She's too much like your mother,"* his father would often comment frigidly, most of the time showing no qualms in mentioning it to her directly. Diomeda was a bland overly tall girl, very ordinary to look at and timid in her ways. First child of the king from an arranged marriage with the Princess Paula of Ramila, Diomeda had never been shown affection by her father who likewise had never shown any love for her mother either. When Armend was born, the king was pleased he had acquired a son and heir, even one born to him by his wife Paula. When he did have time to express affection, which was nowhere near often enough, he would give it sparingly to his son with none left for his daughter.

And so Armend took every opportunity given to him to remain in his father's good graces, working hard to be just what his father willed him to be: a thoroughbred. At the age of twenty he moved to the Military School in Alcavia, the best of its kind that Leonium had to offer and there became fast friends with Prince Leon of Alcavia. Leon was everything Armend aspired to be. He was bright, good looking, tall with a muscular build and he was an expert fighter. Their tutor had teamed them up together from the start but under normal circumstances Armend with his average height and build was no match for Prince Leon–which is where the life weed came into play. "*You have a speed and energy reserve that astounds me,*" their tutor would say to Armend, when the young men sparred together. But even with the drug, Armend was only just about able to keep up with Leon.

He bit the inside of his cheek as he injected the dirty green liquid into his system. It affected him almost instantly as it entered his blood stream. He began to shake violently but waited, knowing that the trembling would soon subside. When the initial shock to his system had lessened he got up smiling to himself. *Maybe today will be the day that I throw Leon flat on his back...and hopefully Leon's sister will be there to witness the whole thing.* "My dear, sweet Adelayne," he said out loud, as he dressed in his pants and a tunic bearing the insignia of the Royal House of Ameron: a gold lion set against a brown background.

The princess was in a sour mood this morning. She had woken from a nightmare again. She still remembered the details–how could she forget? It was the same dream recurring every night she laid herself to rest. Actually it was not a dream at all but the events of that fateful day. *Will I never be able to forget? Will the pain never lessen?* She nodded to the guards who snapped to attention as she passed them by in the corridor on her way to the lower levels of the fortress.

Adelayne had always thought of her uncle as invincible. He had developed into a killing machine so proficient that he came to be known in Alcavia as "*the Mountain nymphs' bane*". Only brother to the king, Eschalion had left his homeland when he was eighteen and travelled east to Kamtai Island to learn, under the strict instructions of the masters there, the art of self defence and more importantly how to be efficient at dispatching an opponent. He returned ten years later, from the Shion Temple, no longer the young boy he had been but a fully skilled Grand Master in the use of weapons. He pledged his sword to his brother the king to protect Alcavia from the marauding Mountain nymphs. His opposition to the foe became legendary and all Alcavia had proclaimed him a hero.

Eschalion took it upon himself to teach everything he knew to his niece. Under Shion Temple law he was permitted to take only one student and, since his male nephew was already receiving instruction by his tutors at the military school, the next obvious choice was Adelayne, whom Eschalion cherished, so it suited him fine. He was a firm believer that women should learn equally as men do to defend themselves. He set out to make Adelayne as skilled in using the hidden arts as he himself was.

Eschalion would always say when Adelayne began to feel overconfident, "*No matter how good you become, there will always be someone out there who is better than you, so always be on your guard and when you train do so in earnest to reduce the chances of coming across your better.*"

How prophetic those words had proven.

It was a grey, dreary day when they set out for the hills south of the Ankadar River. Adelayne had a premonition that day. It was drizzling and the moisture was seeping through their cloaks into their garments, soaking them to the bone. She remembered how she trembled like a new born babe as she rode on the back of her silver dragon paired up with her uncle and peering through the dense fog, trying to distinguish the terrain below. They were combing the hills, as they often did, looking for possible intruders. Eschalion was not going to let a simple thing like the weather get between him and his duty.

They came at them from above–four of them. Before Adelayne had a chance to respond the red dragons tore into their flanks, almost knocking her dragon out of the sky. The riders astride the red beasts recognized her uncle and ignored the princess, concentrating on *"the Mountain nymphs' bane"*. Adelayne turned her dragon in an attempt to aid her uncle but one of the reds kept her at bay whilst the other three descended on her uncle's lone dragon. The odds were mounted against him and in no time at all Eschalion and his silver male were in trouble.

"Run Adelayne! Save yourself to avenge me another day." Eschalion had shouted at her, as he tried desperately to fend off his attackers...but he knew his time had come.

She had turned around and raced for the safety of her fortress. Looking back she had seen the four red dragons tearing the silver male apart like wolves a stag. The shame and guilt of having left her uncle to his fate would haunt her for the rest of her days.

She reached the lower levels in time to see her brother and Prince Armend sparring under the close scrutiny of their tutor. They were both sweating from their efforts their tunics soaked. Armend, noticing her, beamed a smile. She didn't feel in good cheer but made an effort not to seem rude and smiled back briefly. Armend attacked with renewed vigour but her brother skilfully deflected his blows. She couldn't help but admire Armend's courage, however. He just kept at it, never surrendering.

Their tutor had taught them well, Adelayne thought, as she followed their movements. Her training with her uncle had made her a prudent judge of other men's fighting techniques; had she been granted another four years with him she would have earned her title as Grand Master. Perhaps some day she would find a way to learn the rest of the secret moves...then she could hunt down and destroy her uncle's murderers.

"There's only one person who could beat me in a fight one on one," her brother Prince Leon was saying, as he and his friend took a breather from their efforts. "And she's standing there looking at us. Just look at that body, look at her stance, the way her eyes don't miss a single move."

"Oh brother, you are such a tease." Adelayne waved a hand for him to stop. "Your fighting skills are not as legendary as you think, so my matching them is no great feat. You've grown too tall, too quickly, and you move around like a clumsy oaf." She stuck her tongue out rudely at him, forgetting her dreary mood as she ran laughing in a mock attempt to get away from her brother who caught her up, lifting her bodily into the air.

He turned her around giving her a hug and a moist peck on the cheek.

"Phew, you stink," she said, waving a hand before her nose.

Armend came from behind, grinning foolishly like her brother. "Adelayne," he breathed, bending low formally.

"Hello, Armend." She glanced at him. She was wearing a dark tunic and pants and was fully armed with an assortment of blades, their handles jutting out from different places.

"Where are you off to?" Armend rubbed the sweat from his eyes and stared at her, waiting for her reply. His gaze caressed the lines of her form appreciatively.

Adelayne did not respond to his look. She was not interested in men for the time being. "I'm off to the stables to saddle my horse. By day I prefer to go out hunting on horseback. I leave flying for the night."

"Can I come?"

Armend sounded so eager she did not want to disappoint him. "I suppose it wouldn't hurt to have an extra helping hand come along. But don't expect me to lag behind for you."

"No, ma'am." Armend grabbed his cloak and followed after her.

♦ CHAPTER 10 ♦

Sworn enemies

The *Sea Breeze* had left Sulicia's shores in the morning and was sailing westwards led on by Farwing who soared above them, his pale under-plumage contrasting with his rusty red tail. Zoi was wearing her new frock, black as she had said it would be, and was moving about on deck accompanied by Emeralda and Serilia. They approached the keel on the starboard side and stared out at the Leonese coastline which the ship was hugging as it moved along aided by the prevailing wind.

"Serilia, how long has it been since you last practiced using your gift?" Zoi moved up close to her younger companion who was wearing cowhide traveller's clothes.

Serilia looked at the old woman's wrinkly face and her hazel eyes that sparkled with intelligence. *They say the eyes are the mirror to a person's soul,* Serilia mused. It was definitely the case with Zoi but mixed with the clever mind there were also secrets. *Who is this woman who lives alone on a remote island in the middle of the Valdoric Sea, a woman to whom the Council owes service and one whom, it is obvious, gifted people like Archon revere?* She brought herself out of her musing. "I used to practice all the time with my mother."

"Hmm." Zoi placed a gnarled hand on her chin. "There's something about your gift which baffles me. There's nothing wrong with it, mind," she added, noticing Serilia tensing. "In fact on the contrary you have a natural knack at drawing all of it at once, unlike many apprentices who need to keep at it and struggle in order to reach your stage. It is strong in you. I sensed it when you and your brother bonded with Archon to aid him in throwing off our pursuers. It is rare indeed to find such strength in ones so young. But that is not what puzzles me. Firstly your gift's colouring is unlike any I have ever seen: it's a much darker shade of blue, almost purple I would say, than the Water agent which is a purer blue."

"So you think there's something wrong with me, then?" Serilia looked at the old woman in earnest. Her mother too had commented when she had produced her first ball of flame. But she hadn't dwelled on it and so they had forgotten all about it. Archon was the next to bring it up...and now Zoi.

"Somewhere in my subconscious I know I have encountered this before, so don't worry dear. I am simply making my observations. In any case, who is to say that the gift manifests itself in the nine forms only? Magic is as diverse as nature itself and much that has been forgotten over the years resurfaces later on."

"Emeralda dear, I just need Serilia for a moment." Emeralda nodded in understanding as Zoi motioned for Serilia to follow her leaving their companion behind to stare out at the sea. They made their way to the stern of the ship where Zoi indicated for Serilia to take a sitting position on the ship's deck. They sat in the way Serilia had been taught by her mother when meditating: legs crossed, back straight and palms on the knees.

"Will you exchange flames with me, dear?" Zoi asked, her grey hair lifting in the sea breeze, fanning out around her slender neck.

"Yes Mother." The words just came out. She felt right saying them. Perhaps Serilia saw Zoi as a mother to all, because of her age which commanded that level of respect...*or is it something deeper I feel?*

Zoi smiled appreciatively, cupping Serilia's chin in her hand. "You are a treasure. Your intuitive senses are sharper than is usual for an apprentice. Archon is fortunate to have such...companions."

Serilia caught the hesitation, however slight it had been. She didn't understand for the moment what had brought it on, so she filed it away in her memory. Serilia felt a tingling on her skin and realized Zoi was embracing her gift. Twin spheres of emerald fire appeared above each of her outstretched palms. Somehow Serilia had known she would be a Flora gifted. She produced her own purply blue balls of flame and they began their exchange, letting them float across the air.

Serilia felt completely at ease; this act of exchanging fire spheres with another gifted always preceded any other exercises that followed. Its main use was to make the apprentice familiar with the feel of their own gift but at the same time be able to work together with a colleague. The effort of two sorcerers united was far stronger than acting individually.

They spent the rest of the morning expanding on Serilia's new found knowledge of the gift. Theodor joined them with Archon, after he had spent a couple of hours' weapons training with Roxette, and the four of them shared in the learning experience. Theodor had gradually overcome his initial fear of using his gift and produced his own spheres of magical white flame.

By late afternoon the *Sea Breeze* had reached Alcavia's shores and they called in to port alongside the other merchant and fishing boats. They disembarked and made their way to the nearest inn whilst the twins were charged with the responsibility of guiding the horses to the port stable master.

After they had their lunch at the inn, they retrieved their horses from the stables and prepared to follow the route west to the furthest kingdom of the Thalagian Alliance. Alcavia loomed large and imposing ahead of them. It was a fortress surrounded by mountains forming a crescent beneath their much taller cousins: those of the Dragon's Foot which were the highest peaks in all of Thalagia, taller even than the Brakkand's Throne Mountains to the north east.

"What a dark and dreary place." Tiber looked to the black fortress that could be seen from the port where they stood. "Father," he said, turning to the old man. "This is where the boys and I will have to leave you. Fiona is waiting for us back home and it looks like you'll be travelling by land from now on."

It hit Theo like a shockwave. His uncle Tiber was right. After travelling for more than a week by sea sailing from island to island he realized he would, for the first time in many years, be roaming on land that was not part of an island. In fact he had lived secluded on Cyrus for most of his life but all that was changing; he was seeing the world. He remembered all the stories his grandfather had told him about his adventures, *and now I will get to see these lands for myself*, he thought with mixed emotions. With Archon leading the way, any destination was possible and Theo was none the wiser now on where they were going and why than he had been when they started. He wasn't that gullible to believe their sole purpose was to locate a fugitive dragon. *Why does he need to be so secretive?*

Theo was going to miss his uncle Tiber, and the twins too–wit and all. He gave the large man a warm farewell hug and made a manly hand shake with the twins. They were growing by the day it seemed. "You look out for your old man." He rubbed them ever so lightly on the chin, playfully, with his fists.

They grinned back at him. "The old boy couldn't last a minute without us on deck. The ship needs our gentle touch to get going. All he does is stand at the cockpit playing captain." They winked at him and ducked to miss being cuffed by their father who reached out with a large arm, his face feigning a reproving look.

When the companions had all said their farewells to the captain and crew of the *Sea Breeze* they mounted their horses and made their way slowly out of the port. Roxette led the way on her shaggy mare accompanied by Theo on his roan whilst Archon and Nestor followed from a good distance behind, the mage on his grey dappled stallion and the old man on his chestnut gelding. Aunt Emeralda, Serilia, and Zoi were close behind on their mares; Zoi's mare had been purchased by Archon from the port. Nem brought up the rear pulling behind him the pack horse that was bulging with the ladies' clothing.

"Uncle Tiber was right about the fortress." Theo pointed at the structure ahead. Even at this distance he could tell the walls were many feet high.

"It was built to keep at bay a formidable foe." Roxette's eyes took on a far-off look as she stared beyond the fortress to the mountains behind. *Was that a feeling of nostalgia that crossed her face?* Theo wondered. She turned to peer, fixing him with her alien gaze. Theo remembered their first meeting and shuddered.

"We Mountain nymphs are vast in numbers and fearless in battle," Roxette said with unveiled pride, "unlike many of our Darkling allies. Leonium erected the fort of Alcavia at the end of the Dark Age to keep our people at bay and the designers of the fort and their stone masons built the walls tall and thick so they could not be breached. The outer wall was built shortly after the Great War, taller and wider than the other two and about a third of a league away from the middle wall. Now two leagues across, this has enlarged the living capacity of the city with the workmen and their families occupying the outer and middle rings, whilst the nobility have taken up residence behind the third and final wall that also encloses the royal palace citadel with its gardens.

"For almost three millennia the fortress has withstood our best efforts, though recently our master has grown bolder and watches the lands of Leonium from his mountain perch with a greedy eye. The Witch Lord has managed to unite our feuding tribes, a feat no other leader has accomplished, so now our enemies tremble at the might of the Dragon's Foot Mountain nymphs."

She caught the look in his eye. "Would you have preferred if I had lied to you manling, telling you that you and your kind are safe from the nymph hordes?" she asked, and when he didn't answer she scoffed at him. "I didn't think so." Then, in answer to Theo's uneasy look, her countenance became gentler and she spoke with conviction, "I made my decision, Theo, four years ago when I was rejected by my kind, to leave the service of the Dark. There is no going back for me now. I couldn't do that to Archon; he has given too much to me." She said it as though she were trying to convince herself.

They rode on in silence, the nymph deep in thought and Theo mulling over everything she had told him. *It must be difficult*, he mused, *to turn away from family and friends, to join up with a people who have been sworn enemies of your kin for so long.* He could understand she was bitter with the nymphs responsible for her ambush and near death but was that enough to turn her against her own kind? *Why has Archon taken the risk of having her by his side?* He felt wretched, and regretted his thoughts almost as soon as he formed them. Roxette was a solitary person who did not open up to people and was hard to approach. But during the trip she had shown nothing but respect for Theo and his companions, even though some of them had not bothered to hide their disdain towards her. They had categorized her without due consideration as just another despised Mountain nymph.

But Roxette had put her life in danger for Theo and his family back at the cottage and she was making the effort to teach him all she knew about combat. Even though his training had started but one week ago he was learning fighting techniques he knew he could not have gleaned from any other tutor. His family, at least, owed a debt of gratitude to the nymph who had sacrificed so much.

From a distance, a pair of riders was fast closing the distance between the nymph and her companion. Roxette's sharp eyesight saw them first when they were but a dot on the horizon. She loosened her swords in their scabbards, Theo responding likewise.

"Leave the talking to me," she said, eyeing the approaching riders with her predatory gaze. Her shaggy mare sensed her mistress's mood and pranced on the spot, her skin quivering with anticipation. "Easy." The nymph spoke softly in the mare's ear and stroked her neck.

Theo turned to look at the approaching riders. Their faces could be distinguished now. It was a man and a woman with the woman in the lead astride a tall white steed that had a large war horse chest and hooves that beat the ground so Theo could feel the reverberations from where he sat on his mare. The woman's face, upon seeing Roxette, changed from an expression of curiosity to one of pure hatred. She dug her heels into her stallion's flanks causing the big animal to career forward in large leaps leaving behind her astonished companion.

It all happened so fast. One minute Theo was trying to keep his roan calm, the next Roxette had drawn her swords and heeled her mare forward to meet the stranger's unprovoked attack. Roxette gave out a shrill "la, la, la," war cry increasing in pitch as she closed with her opponent. The two women exchanged sword blows in mid-stride, Roxette just managing to turn her mare at the last moment in order to save herself and her steed from being knocked over by the large stallion. The attacking woman fought with the frenzy of a crazed animal, striking out so fast Theo was amazed Roxette's reflexes were swift enough to deflect the blows.

Theo had no chance to move in closer. The rider accompanying the mad woman on the white horse remained in his saddle, an expression of shock on his face. Theo could hear the rest of his companions shouting from behind.

Then Roxette leaped from her mare bearing down on her opponent, knocking her off her steed. They tumbled in the dirt, like a pair of wild cats, bristling with drawn weapons. They got up quickly, swords flashing in the air lighting sparks as they struck. Roxette bent low, coming up with a kick to her opponent's stomach that sent her sprawling. In an instant the Mountain nymph was above her opponent who had lost one of her swords and was in a tricky predicament with her other sword arm pinned down beneath the nymph's heeled boot.

"Noooo!" Theo shouted, just as Roxette raised her sword in a backhand action, about to deliver her killing blow. She snapped her head around to look at him for a fraction of a moment, her face distorted by her blood lust. That moment was enough for her opponent to throw her off her feet.

The attacker got up retrieving her second sword and made ready to strike once more. She was the woman in Theo's dreams, the one he had seen the night before, the one that had caused feelings to surface in him he did not realise he possessed. He looked anxiously at the pair and made his decision.

He placed himself in the middle of the two combatants and turned to look at the young woman who had attacked them without hesitation. “We are not your enemy.” He spread his arms out in a gesture of goodwill.

“You!” Her eyes grew larger as recognition dawned on her. “You’re that intruder from last night. I’ve been saving this for you,” she sneered, licking her finger and passing it along her sword tip. “I’ll dispatch two Darklings before the day is out.”

“Theo, get out of the way!” Roxette hissed, as she crouched down low like a jungle cat ready to pounce. “I’ll deal with you and your interruptions later,” she promised, throwing him an ominous look.

“No, this is ending here and now.” Theo stood resolute.

“What is the meaning of this?” Archon dismounted his grey and approached the three of them. The rest of the companions had arrived and were forming a ring around the combatants. “Young lady, put down your swords. We are not here to quarrel with you.”

“I am not leaving till I finish my work.” The young woman had her eyes trained on Roxette, completely ignoring the rest of them, as if their numbers did not matter to her. “I have sworn to kill every Mountain nymph that crosses my path.”

“Well, that may be so but you’ve found one Mountain nymph you’ll not be dispatching,” Roxette sneered. “You’ve been weighed and measured and found lacking the required skill.” Roxette had a haughty expression as a malevolent grin crossed her face.

“Boy, take your friend’s advice and get out of the way or I’ll finish you off first, even if you’re too much of a coward to draw your weapon in your defence.” Theo could see in the young woman’s eyes that she meant what she said but he stood his ground.

“Adelayne, let’s reconsider.” The woman’s companion spoke up, eyeing Theo’s group uneasily as they prepared to intervene. Nem had drawn his golden scimitar and even aunt Emeralda had fished out a small blade from beneath her cloak. "These people have done nothing to provoke us."

"Armend, I did not let you ride with me so you could tell me what to do. Now stay silent! There's more to this than you know. Why would they keep company with a Mountain nymph if they were not paying homage to the Dark."

"Young lady, if you are Adelayne, daughter of King Dreyfus and Queen Crystal of Ghiadon, then you have a lot to learn from your parents about treating visitors and friends to your lands with the proper respect." Archon's stone grey eyes were hard like blades of steel as he took his place next to Theo. He motioned for Roxette to step down. A frustrated look crossed her face as conflicting emotions took hold of her: to obey her lord or to submit to her killing lust. She fought down her anger and stepped back in a pose of semi-readiness.

"Who do *you* presume to be, mentioning my parents' names as if that alone will shield you?" Adelayne recovered from her crouching position and stood erect to her full height. The wind coming down from the mountains was blowing through her dark hair fanning it around her shoulders as she stood defiant, swords drawn–a warrior princess in all her splendour.

"I am Archon, friend to King Dreyfus of Alcavia, and High Sorcerer of Aldorn, and I will endure no more of this behaviour." The mage turned about leaving Adelayne to stare at his back. He ordered his companions to mount up, including Roxette. "Prince Armend of Ameron," he bawled at the young man. "Will you, at least, be gracious enough to lead us on to Alcavia? We have pressing business with the king and I don't have time for idle chatter, or to teach young whelps how to conduct themselves properly." He turned a stony gaze at the young warrior woman who looked a bit flustered, especially since the mage seemed to know not only her family but Armend's family as well.

They all mounted their steeds. The young warrior woman passed by the nymph on her way to retrieve her white stallion. "This doesn't change anything," she said menacingly.

"I'll be happy to oblige any time you're ready." Roxette's voice dripped venom.

They rode in silence, this time Archon taking the lead in front with Prince Armend. Roxette rode with the rest of the group and Princess Adelayne rode off alone to one side keeping her distance from them. Theo urged his roan mare forward, coming up beside the white stallion. Adelayne made to ignore him not acknowledging his presence.

He cleared his throat. "I want to apologize if I offended you...I don't mean about the incident back there," he nodded behind, "I mean for having intruded into your room last night. I don't know how it happened, honestly. I was dreaming that I was soaring on the wings of a dragon, then the next moment I was in your bedroom." He imagined how strange he must sound and kicked himself mentally. *What a dolt I am*, he thought. *A great first impression I must be making.*

Adelayne however, did not seem to respond but just kept riding in silence. Theo rubbed his palms on his pants. They were sweaty. His soft roan was trembling beneath him at being so close to a strange stallion and her ears were flat on her head. Theo bent down and rubbed her on the side of her neck to put her at ease. She flicked her ears at him and seemed to settle down a bit. The stallion, like its mistress, ignored the mare beside him.

"That's a fine animal you have there," Theo ventured again to break the uncomfortable silence, looking appreciatively at the princess's steed that stood two hands taller than his mare.

The princess looked at him, her eyes altering from green to blue depending on how the light played on them. He was drawn like a firefly to a candle. Then she turned her gaze ahead to the mage leaving Theo breathless and feeling like a child that has been shown a sweet then cheated from having it. "Is he really the Sorcerer Archon or was that just another Darkling lie?" But before Theo had the chance to answer, she added, "What am I asking you for? It's not as if a peepster like you would tell the truth, now is it?" She sneered at him.

"When you do that," Theo hardened his look, "you ruin your pretty features." She arched an eyebrow at him with some measure of surprise. He built up his courage; what he had to say he would say and damn the consequences. "Look, I already explained that what I did last night was an accident. I am from a family that respects other people and their privacy. I don't know how it happened and I wish I could remedy the situation; then again, if I hadn't met you last night you probably would be lying dead right now. Roxette got the better of you back there."

Adelayne shot him a look of chagrin, the blood rising to her temple. Then she seemed to compose herself, releasing the tension from her shoulders. She laughed, surprising him. "Theo, was it?" She looked down at him from her larger steed. "You have a strange way of making friends–showing them their weaknesses, I mean."

"I aim to please princess, and yes, I am Theodor Marentherin of Cyrus Island," he answered, bowing in a mock sign of deference. Let her chew on that for a while. He felt slightly out of breath and sat on his horse uncomfortably. Had he been too offensive just now? *I wonder what she would make of my woodsman's clothes,* he thought, looking down at his dingy garments. They were tough and well worn, just the kind for a long travel but not like Prince Armend's fine tunic and pants that were the norm among the more genteel men. *Who am I fooling?* Princess Adelayne probably had a score of men lined up waiting for her at the royal palace. Maybe she was even more than friends with this Prince Armend from Ameron.

"Theodor Maren 'therin." It had a good ring to it the way she said it; the sarcasm had gone out of her voice and was replaced by curiosity. She had spoken his family name breaking it into two words. "It means 'Far Strider' in the old tongue," she mused. "You have Nymphish blood; there's more to you than first meets the eye." Her gaze was not unpleasant any more. "I will give you the benefit of the doubt, though a scholar of the hidden arts should be more careful when spirit travelling and ignorance is no excuse for bad manners."

Theo looked at her perplexed. *"Hidden arts? Spirit travelling?"* He was unsure of what she meant and it showed on his face. Then it dawned on him: by hidden arts she probably meant the use of the gift. But what was this spirit travelling she had mentioned?

Seeming to read his thoughts, she explained, "When a sorcerer's apprentice leaves his body behind to travel abroad we call it spirit travelling. It is an old form of magic that not all apprentices and indeed not many sorcerers practice unless they are so inclined. Tutors of the arcane arts choose not to teach it because it has inherent dangers. Most sorcerers who attempt such a feat retain a link with their body in order not to leave it vulnerable to an invading spirit. I sincerely hope your mage friend was by your side and protecting you when you were off soaring like a bird."

Theo opened his mouth to say something but didn't know how to reply.

Adelayne stared down at him in shock disbelief and shook her head admonishingly. "Really, Theodor, if you're going to dip your finger in the honey pot, at least learn about the dangers beforehand."

"You're gifted as well?" For her to have been speaking about magic with so much familiarity meant she should be, though the tingling sensation that usually accompanied him when he was close to a gifted was not there to prove the fact.

Adelayne considered his question before answering. "I am what you might call an 'inactive' gifted. We are commonly known in some wizard circles as 'dormants'." When Theo did not show any signs of understanding she continued. "Dormants are able to experience the effects of the gift with all their senses but are unable to use the gift. I was able to see your spirit travelling the other night but could not respond to it in the way another sorcerer might."

"So the gift is dead in you?" Theo asked, thinking on whether he would have preferred the gift to have been dead in him as well. It seemed to complicate his life so.

"No, it's not exactly dead to us or we wouldn't be able to sense it being used. It is more correct to say that it exists in us but is asleep, so we may not touch it. I feel its presence like a second awareness but I have grown accustomed to not being able to use it."

"Do you feel incomplete, somehow?"

Adelayne stared at him as she thought it over. "No, I wouldn't say I feel that way. You cannot feel you miss something you never had in the first place. It's like asking someone who has never been in the water whether they miss swimming."

"Do you wish you could have been able to use it?" Theo insisted. In effect he had asked himself the same questions, which was why he was so interested in Adelayne's response.

"I do not dwell on what might have been Theodor Marentherin but on what I can achieve. I need only these to get by in life," she said, pointing to the twin blades behind her back.

They approached the towering walls of thc city in silence. The dirt road, which was fifteen yards wide, led in a straight line from the port to the city gate and was being traversed by many a wagon on its left shoulder bearing supplies and goods to trade with the city dwellers. The middle lanes were left for men on horseback whilst people on foot walked on the extreme left trying to avoid being run down by the passing wagons and looking enviously at the riders and wagon handlers. In the opposite direction the same order was repeated for folk leaving the city to go to port.

The sun shone brightly. On either side of the road workers wearing straw hats were bent over with baskets cradled in their arms sowing the spring grain into the rich soil of the plains whilst they sang a merry tune to aid them in their chores. Other parts of the plain had been ploughed and tilled but left unsown. Land for growing grain was plentiful in these parts so the farmers could afford to let a portion of the land lie fallow so it could absorb lost nutrients and moisture to be used for the next year's crop.

Soon they were passing through the main gate. Theo stared around with awe at the city sprawled before him. It was much larger than Nusia, the capital city of Cyrus, and rows of houses stood on either side of the road which was now cobbled causing the horses' hooves to make clopping sounds as they struck the stones. Merchant stalls filled the main road and there was a cacophony of sound as shopkeepers and traders tried to sell their wares.

"They seem oblivious to the proximity of the Dragon's Foot Mountains." Theo turned to Adelayne riding by his side. Several people turned to look at them but none seemed to recognize their princess as she was not wearing the royal household distinctive regalia.

"People have very short memories and tend to ignore that which can unsettle them. Our patrols keep the Mountain nymph raids far from the city so the inhabitants don't pay much attention to them. Life goes on, Theodor."

They moved carefully through the throng of people who were crossing the road whenever there was a break in the wagons. The road seemed to rise gradually, seeing as Alcavia was built on a gently sloping hill with the central ring occupying the crest. They approached the middle wall, more ancient than the outer one had been with chips missing from its stones where time had eroded some of it away. It was still formidable-looking, standing thirty feet high and several yards thick. They passed through its portcullis to more houses and more stalls; Alcavia seemed to go on for ever.

Within this second wall a church stood not far from the main road with its central dome and two bell towers on either side. Templar soldiers in white surcoats and bearing the flame of Athud on their right breasts were massed around the church yard keeping watch whilst worshippers passed in and out of the arched entrance.

"Adelayne, I've been meaning to ask you," Theo said, prodding his mare in the ribs to bring her beside the princess's white stallion.

"Yes, Theodor?"

"How is it you speak Galipan? I mean, how is it your common tongue is so akin to ours?"

"You're a bit rusty on history, Theodor," Adelayne observed without scorn. "We Alcavians and you Cyriots have common ancestors," she said. "In the ninth century before the Great War, the Galipans began to settle on Leonese soil. In 446 BA, the Galipans built Alcavia as a defence post against the Mountain nymph raiders. We and the inhabitants of Ramila and Ameron to the north are the direct descendants of those Galipans."

"That explains a great many things," Theo said.

At last the group reached the final gate to the third wall which was as tall as the middle wall but had been restored to its former glory with its stone work gleaming in the afternoon sunlight. At the gate stood sentries dressed in the livery of the Alcavian guards: red surcoats with a silver dragon crouching on their chest laid above chain mail. They snapped to attention as Prince Armend passed them by with his entourage, and nodded to their princess in welcome.

They made their way straight for the palace grounds and passed by large houses that sat on either side of the road like ladies at court dressing in their finest garments to impress. Each house was splendidly and lavishly adorned with spiralling steps and fancy columns, chandeliers hanging behind large curtained windows. There was no doubt that they were in the more affluent part of the city.

The fortress loomed dark and imposing before them as they neared. Theo could just about make out its cone-shaped spire with its tall mast from which was flapping a large red banner with a silver dragon sprawled across it. "No wonder it can be seen from the port," Theo thought out loud.

"Yes," Adelayne agreed. "You can see the entire kingdom from the top windows of the tower. There are four towers on each corner of the fortress which occupies thirteen acres with the centre of the rectangle left open forming the king's private grounds."

Theo and his companions passed into the long shadow cast by the tower blotting out the sun. Tall elm trees on either side of the road led them to the fortress main gate which the guards opened for them recognizing their princess. A tall man was waiting at the gate beaming a smile at Prince Armend and Adelayne and looking with intrigue at the group accompanying them. His look darkened as his eyes fell upon Roxette.

"What is the meaning of this, Adelayne?" He had a muscular build and his shirt buttons were opened to reveal his large hairy chest. He had long wavy hair that fell behind his back like the mane of a horse and his brown eyes gazed searchingly at the princess. "It's not like you to leave a

Mountain nymph alive. Have you grown slack in your duties?"

"Brother, I bring Archon the Mage who is calling upon our father to discuss matters of grave importance–so he claims. The nymph is under his protection." Roxette scoffed at that comment. "I will leave it up to the king to decide what is to be her fate. If his decision is that she should seize to breathe I will be more than happy to oblige." Adelayne threw an icy look at the nymph who in response seemed to bristle, cat-like.

"Prince Leon, you have grown since last I laid eyes on you at the summit meeting of the free lands of Thalagia. That was five years ago at Ameron," said the mage, from atop his tall steed as he led his companions through the citadel gate. Then he shouted behind him as he moved forward, "From what I recall you were better mannered then."

They passed through the entrance vault with arched walls running on either side for forty yards, the sounds of their horses' hooves ricocheted against the masonry walls before they emerged into sunlight on the other side. The sweet perfume of roses assailed them. Spread before them was a neatly cropped lawn bordered by stone paving that led all the way round and separated the lawn from the steps that led further down to the east quarter. Adelayne explained to Theo that the eastern grounds were used for putting horses through their paces and also as a training area for men employing a variety of weapons: the sword, pike, axe or longbow. The royal stables were to the left of the citadel. At a sign from Archon the companions dismounted, handing the reins of their horses to the stable boys.

Soon Prince Leon was leading them through the corridors of the palace straight to the throne room with the mage keeping pace by his side matching him stride for stride. They passed several of the royal household staff on the way that curtsied politely or bowed their heads depending on their gender. The palace guards snapped to attention as they were approached by their prince until he made a sign for them to take the at ease position.

Prince Leon swung open the large doors at the entrance to the throne room. The grim-faced guards standing on either side held their pikes erect with their eyes trained forward. The grand hall was largely empty apart from a few courtiers and city officials who were massed around the throne. As they approached, Theo saw sitting on the great throne, raised a few steps higher than the rest of the hall, a man with similar features to Prince Leon. He had the same broad shoulders and long brown hair, only his face was more careworn, his eyes revealing the soul of a man accustomed to pain. The body was that of a fighting man, the eyes proud but with a hint of restraint, the kind one recognises in someone who has lost a loved one.

"Your Majesty," Leon genuflected, the group of companions responding likewise. "I bring before thee the Mage Archon of Aldorn who has come seeking an audience with my king."

As the companions rose, Theo turned his gaze to a second throne paired up with the king's upon which sat a woman with long hair twined with stalks bearing flowers. She stared at each of the companions with eyes like pools of deep blue water with a hint of violet. Theo's heart skipped a beat as he realized where Adelayne got her good looks from. But this woman did not look much older than her daughter! Upon closer scrutiny he could discern pointed ears protruding slightly from the queen's straight brown hair which gleamed as if it had just been combed. Her faintly coloured dress made from an almost diaphanous fabric bejewelled with small sapphires matching her eyes hugged her body closely revealing a form that brought a blush to Theo's cheeks and a quickening of his pulse.

She turned her eyes upon him just as he blushed. He felt like a court fool, like the cottage boy he was, but she smiled pleasantly at him then her gaze shifted, lingering for a while on Roxette before it finally fell on Zoi, remaining there for a substantial amount of time. A look crossed between the two, the queen nodding so indistinctly that one had to be paying attention to have noticed. *So they are acquainted but why all this prudence?* Once more Theo felt a sense of unease about the new addition to their group. Did all people using the gift veil themselves in so much mystery?

"We are glad to have Archon Thendelin, First Wizard of King Daron of Aldorn, calling upon us gracing our humble court with his presence." The royal couple got up simultaneously from their thrones, the king holding his hand aloft so his queen could place her slender hand above his as they made their way towards their guests.

The courtiers and city officials bowed, opening up to allow the royal couple space, encompassing the guests in a ring as they fell back to staring with interest at the new arrivals, particularly the mage. They observed his long golden, intermingled with silver, hair that surrounded him like a lion's mane tied back in a gentleman's top knot. He was a well dressed man with a neatly trimmed beard and a clean white tunic opened at the top for comfort. Soft pants made for journeying were tucked into boots worn by men accustomed to riding.

His companions were an odd bunch. There was an elderly lady dressed in a black dress that covered her all the way to her ankles who was bent over and wrinkled, though her eyes twinkled with an energy seldom encountered in one her age.

The other three women were younger: the older of the three had hair the colour of a burning flame with blond and ginger streaks intermingled with grey in her tightly wound bun atop her head. She was attired in a white shirt opened at the neckline, and wore tight trousers that hugged her form and were tucked into tall heeled boots. Her pointy ears identified her as nymph kind.

The other nymph woman was the most striking of the lot. Most noticeably, she was a Mountain nymph, causing many a sharp comment amongst the courtiers to be murmured behind a covering hand in an attempt to conceal the speaker. She was like a wild thing, untamed and running loose amongst them; like a cat amongst closed pigeons in a pen, bristling with weaponry and ready to pounce, her jet-black hair tinged with red adding to her mystique and her menacing countenance.

The younger woman, who bared a resemblance to the tall youth with the sword strapped to his hip, was a pretty thing with long flowing brown hair and blue eyes like their princess, only they were a deeper shade of blue and she wore a fetching velvet suit which matched her eyes. Next to her stood a handsome youth with dark curly hair tied in a ponytail. He was dressed in plain woodsman's clothing so austere that it made the golden-hilted scimitar hanging from his belt all the more conspicuous.

The other youth, the one who had accompanied Princess Adelayne into the great hall and looked like the young maiden with the velvet suit, was as tall as Prince Leon and almost as broad in the shoulders with wavy hair. If he let it grow a bit more he would be able to tie it back in the fashion of the lords at court. He stood with a proud bearing that one identified in men of noble birth and, though he wore the same dreary clothing as his companion, had something very compelling, very unique about him: that quality, that look in his eye that held one captivated. Not much could escape those probing eyes the colour of an evergreen forest in late spring.

Finally to complete the group was an elderly man with silver hair tumbling down his shoulders to his back.

Surprisingly, he bore a resemblance with the nymph lady with the ginger hair: the same sharp nose and intelligent look in the eyes. Though his tough skin revealed he was a travel-worn man he stood firm and straight as a plank exhibiting a strength in his movements that younger men might well envy.

"I am glad to be here amongst friends once more after having travelled so great a distance." It was the mage, addressing the king who took him in a warm embrace.

The mage turned to his companions introducing them one by one to the royal couple. They were greeted in turn and were offered refreshments and some fruit by the serving maids whilst the royal chamberlain was requested to oversee the readying of hot baths and rooms for the palace guests. It was not long before the companions were shown to their rooms where they could wash and change into their evening wear for the royal banquet that was to be held in their honour.

♦ CHAPTER 11 ♦

A banquet amongst friends

Theo and Nem were the first to emerge dressed in their finest clothes which they had brought with them from Cyrus. Nestor was next to appear chewing an unlit pipe in his mouth and wearing a golden tunic and pants fit for a king. Zoi had changed into another of her ankle-length black frocks whilst Emeralda exited her room wearing an embroidered dress dripping with small precious stones.

"Aunt Emeralda, you look stunning." Theo smiled, adding to the happiness that was evident on her face.

She placed a hand gently in a show of coyness on the silver pendant around her throat and continued to stare at him returning his smile. "Why thank you, dear. It's just a little something I picked up whilst Zoi and I went shopping at Sulicia Island. It was a bit on the expensive side but I think it was well worth it in the end."

"Yes, my sweet, it's very becoming on you," Zoi agreed in a motherly fashion.

Just then Serilia emerged with her hair tied up wearing a gown that was low cut and sleeveless revealing her pale shoulders and slender neck adorned with white pearls.

"Shall we be off then?" she asked, lifting her skirts so she could walk more easily in her high-heeled boots. She had a twinkle in her eye as she looked with satisfaction at Nem's wide grin. She waited till he offered her his arm then took the lead as they made their way to the dining hall followed by the rest of the group.

There, they were greeted by Archon who had donned a full length tunic with a high collar that rose at the back, covering the nape of his neck, giving him the appearance of a priest dressed in ceremonious clothing. The king stood by his side along with some other men of import. One of them, a tall man in his mid-forties, was obviously a cleric, judging from his dress.

The group gasped catching sight of Roxette who was dressed in a blood red gown that hugged her feline form provocatively. She was being approached by many a courtier who wished to learn more about this mysterious nymph who had been accepted as a friend and guest of the royal couple.

Zoi made her way towards the queen who stood a little further off on her own and was wearing a dress which left very little to the imagination. All eyes were trained on the queen as she moved amongst her guests, the long split along the front of her dress revealing her shapely legs. Theo couldn't help but stare and she caught him at it once more. She smiled cheekily at him causing him to blush like a young pimply boy. He turned around only to come face to face with Prince Leon, attired in a red tunic with a silver dragon on the left breast over black trousers with a stripe running up the sides–the Alcavian Royal House garb. Prince Armend was also by his side but attired in the Ameron garb: brown tunic with a gold lion covering the front and green pants.

"My sister tells me you're an apprentice of the Hidden Arts." The prince looked at him with interest. They stood at eye level measuring each other's strength subconsciously; the prince was the same age as Theo though he was more muscular and his chest was surely broader. It seemed as though he must spend a lot of his time exercising.

But was there an intelligent mind behind the robust body? "Yes, Your Highness. It's true that I am a practicing sorcerer." There. He had said it. He may as well come to terms with it sooner rather than later. Back on the *Sea Breeze*, when he and Archon were training together with Zoi and Serilia, he had managed to produce the white balls of flame again and this time he did not panic and extinguish them but held them in his palms feeling the gift flowing through his limbs, making him feel elated and more whole than he had ever felt before.

"None of that Your Highness business around me, if you please. It makes me feel like a pompous ass. Just Leon will do nicely. Your mage tutor is notorious in all of Thalagia for his skill at wielding the gift. I myself have not a spark of it. My sister has the gift, I am told, though she is unable to use it. She explained to me once about it being asleep but I don't pretend to understand much about magic. Our mother, however, is a third degree sorceress; I believe that's what they call those who manage to reach the first level."

"She knows how to use the gift well enough to get by." Adelayne approached from behind. Theo's breath caught as he stared at the dazzling creature that stood filling his vision. Adelayne had opted for a dress that hang from the shoulders revealing her slender but muscled arms and which was open round the neck forming a low "V" reaching to just below her belly button that was pierced with a tiny diamond stud. Theo noticed she wore the swan brooch he had seen last night lying on her dressing table. She also wore the large sapphire pendant that had caused such feelings of jealousy to stir in his heart. She reached round to grab a wine glass and bared her tantalizing back–all of it–down to just above her buttocks. Theo and Prince Armend couldn't help but stare in appreciation.

Then she turned and rested her gaze on Theo. He suddenly felt very weak in the knees flushing with hot and cold spells. Adelayne seemed to notice his rosy cheeks. She smiled faintly. Prince Armend noticed their brief exchange and pinned Theo with a sinister stare. Theo, sensing the prince's eyes boring into his scalp, tried to avert his eyes from Princess Adelayne though he glimpsed her bosom that was showing slightly from the sides of her dress. A *fine pickle this is*, he thought, feeling awkward.

"Our parents have suggested that Adelayne visit the Wizard's Keep to see if they can help awaken her gift," Leon continued, smiling at his sister.

"Have they been able to do that before?" Theo asked with renewed interest.

"No. Never," Adelayne answered in her brother's stead. "Father is simply hoping that he can lure me away from my duties that bind me to the war front of Alcavia, for we are at war with the Dragon's Foot Mountains, even if most people here seem to have forgotten it." Adelayne took a sip from her wine glass and stared around at the courtiers moving amongst the guests exchanging idle chatter. "I must pay my dues here before I can move on," she added, a pained look crossing her face.

"What happened to our uncle was no fault of yours, Adelayne," Prince Leon said, placing an arm gently around his sister's waist.

She slid her slender arm around his. "I still feel responsible, though. How could I not? I was there when it happened and I fled like a coward when things got complicated–just when he needed me most, Leon." Her eyes glazed over, her lips trembling slightly.

Theo envied her brother who comforted her by pressing her close to him and kissing her on her long soft hair. "You had no choice but to do as our uncle Eschalion had commanded you. If you had not obeyed him we would have been recovering two bodies from the foot of the mountains. It's a senseless way to go, sister. Better to live to fight another day." Prince Leon's eyes burnt like hot coals and Theo felt glad he was not on the receiving end of that look.

"Tell me, Islander,' he said, turning his gaze back to Theo. "Are your people a fierce warrior race, like us Alcavians? We pride ourselves in being the best fighting men in all Leonium." He turned meaningfully to Prince Armend who stared back at him, tight lipped, obviously unwilling to dispute the fact in favour of Ameron.

"We are not by nature a warring race, Your–Prince Leon," Theo corrected, at the last. "Our people are more of a trading folk or fishermen. You see, our position in the centre of the Meldenyan and Valdoric Seas makes us a favourite entrepôt. There have been wars in our land in more ancient times but always we have relied on the Seldavian Kingdoms to come to our aid."

"You'll be surprised what a humble fisherman or trader can do when his back is put against a wall, my friend. You look like a fighting man," Prince Leon said, placing a hand to his chin contemplatively. "Your muscle tone is not poor by any standard and you are well shaped for wielding that sword you had strapped by your hip earlier. A fine weapon too, by the looks of it. Your friend's scimitar was quite impressive as well. I'll wager any amount that he acquired it from a Nebese or Ishbadese merchant."

"Actually both weapons were given to us by my great grandfather, Prium, father to King Rufous of the Alunda Sea nymphs. The scimitar belonged to a Nebese prince and my sword was forged by nymph blacksmiths using lithureal metal."

"Lithureal metal!" Prince Leon exclaimed with interest. "We have learnt about the nymphs' use of this metal at the academy. Perhaps later on you might let me take a closer look at your sword."

"I'd be glad to if you could show me and Nem around the academy."

"Done." They shook hands on it.

"So you and your sister are of a royal bloodline?" the prince murmured, a pleased grin lighting his features as he stared with interest at Serilia's low cut dress.

"I wouldn't go as far as that, Leon."

"You still haven't told us how you and your friend acquired your build. Surely not by carrying out farming chores?" Prince Armend butted in, grabbing the opportunity to let out a scornful laugh.

Theo ignored the Ameron prince and turned his gaze to Prince Leon. "My father, Elron, served in the Hendonian army before he retired to Cyrus and his father's cottage. He taught Nem and I how to handle various weapons in a fight. I suppose after a while it begins to show."

"Indeed I am sure of it," Leon confirmed. "So, have you been given the chance to use your training?" Seeing that Theo did not understand he continued. "I mean to say have you drawn first blood? Have you ever *killed* someone?"

Theo paled visibly. Images flashed before his eyes on how close he himself had come in the past few days to being killed. He remembered the incident with the *Unrelenting Condor*. No, that didn't count, since he was simply being used as an energy vessel to be laid at Archon's disposal. Any killing that may have been done was strictly the mage's work.

"Leon, that's enough about killing for the night." Adelayne caught Theo's sickly look and ventured to change the subject. "Let us mingle with the rest of our guests. Theodor will you be gracious enough to escort me? I am certain my brother does not wish to be burdened with me at a time like this with so many young girls around." She winked naughtily at her brother who returned a toothy grin.

"Yes, Yo–princess," Theo blurted. He remained standing stock still, so Adelayne lifted one of his arms and placed her own in his. Theo realized he was behaving like a ninny and coughed nervously whilst trying without much success to recover his posture; Adelayne's perfume assailed his nostrils and his eyes wandered to the fine hairs on the nape of her neck and to her soft ear lobes; what he would give to be able to nuzzle them. *Stop that!* he chided himself mentally. *She's a princess and you're a cottage oaf without a title to your name.* He had to save himself from needless pain and embarrassment. To pursue the princess was folly. *But how nice it would be to exchange a tender kiss with those luscious full lips.*

Adelayne stared at Theo with interest as he escorted her around the room. *He's not bad, really,* she thought, looking at his long brown hair and those–oh so–beautiful green eyes. *Yes, he's not bad looking at all, actually.* What was she thinking? Had she forgotten so quickly her obligation to her uncle–her duty to her country? This Theodor was a nice enough lad but he also would have to wait like the rest of them till she was finished with what she had to do. *Still, no reason why I shouldn't at least enjoy this night of pleasure,* she concluded, smiling inwardly.

"Tell me, Sir Wizard, how go things for the church at your neighbouring city of Hendon? My last visit there two years ago, and the reports I have been sent, seem to hint that Patriarch Iscillus will not remain at his post for the remainder of the year." The man standing in priestly robes beside Archon was tall and slim with a long face and a dark beard reaching his chest. He was dark haired with dark penetrating eyes behind which was concealed a clever and observant mind, from what the mage had been able to ascertain on his previous visits and had reconfirmed now during their short conversation.

"Your Eminence, indeed the patriarch is worn out by old age and seeks retirement and a less demanding lifestyle. He has served Seldavia well and is mentioned by the laity there with high praise and honour, but fifteen years is not a negligible time to hold the highest post Seldavia has to offer to a clergyman." Archon took a sip from his wine glass and peered carefully at the primate of Alcavia trying to establish his feelings on the matter.

"I hear that my colleague, Primate Alistrat, may announce his candidacy for Patriarch of Seldavia. Being of royal blood and with the support of his brother, King Apandor of Hendon, his chances of taking up the post are strong."

"I can personally vouch for Primate Alistrat. I met him a while back, when I was on official Templar business to Hendon, and spoke with the man at length." The rough voice belonged to a man dressed in the livery of the Templar Knights, the flame of Athud pressed on his chest. "I recall from our conversation that he was an erudite man with strong views and beliefs but that he was also willing to observe the ideologies and pay heed to the suggestions of worldly figures; he would listen attentively to the opinions of the ruling nobility and heads of institutions, for example the learned professors at universities and even your own leaders of the Council of Light, Sir Archon. One recognizes that he incorporates those views he feels do not come into conflict with church doctrine but at the same time offers a more diversifying and less harsh set of ideals for the religious community to follow.

"I believe, Primate Zerum, that Primate Alistrat is a good choice and will offer valuable service to the Church of Athud in Seldavia, like his predecessor Patriarch Ischillus before him, however Alistrat is a more flexible man and I am of the opinion that the church needs such men who bear in mind the changes that are being wrought in our time."

"I couldn't agree more, Templar Commander Baxter," Primate Zerum said, stroking his long beard, "for I too have met my colleague when the church hierarchy assembled in Ameron to be addressed by the Ecumenical Patriarch there. We share many views with the primate, but tell me, Sir

Archon," he turned his dark-eyed gaze on the mage. "What are the feelings of the other seven kingdoms in Seldavia concerning Alistrat's candidacy?"

"Your Eminence, Lithudon and Aldorn, and–of course–his home city of Hendon firmly support him. Sandora and Balsovia have not offered their own candidate but neither have they expressed their preference so the primate will need to campaign there. Nusia has offered a candidate but he is not well known amongst the Seldavians. Lisandria's candidate is a strong opponent. He served for a while in Sandora and Balsovia before being sent to Lisandria to become primate there and it is told that he has the backing of the Hieradon empress who is said to hold him in high esteem."

"Pah," Primate Zerum waved a hand in disgust. "What business do heathens have with the Creator's church. All know that the empress follows the pagan teachings of the followers of Ssul in Zaldessa. However, not even she knows the extent of her wealth, so if she is offering Primate Castiogne financial aid for his campaign then it's anybody's guess who will prevail in the end, and the fact that he served in Sandora and Balsovia will play an important role in the elections.

"Tell me, what does your Council of Light make of all this? Do they have a preference?"

Archon contemplated, carefully weighing the answer he would give. These were matters needing delicate handling; no doubt Primate Zerum was testing his skills at the dirty game of politics. "The Council of Light looks on with great interest at the elections as we cannot do otherwise for we have always supported the church and the critical role she plays in our society in shaping our future. We believe all the candidates have something to offer and are gladdened that our sister church has such capable people manning its ranks.

"But we do not believe in interfering with the Church's business and respect her right to handle her own affairs and wish her well in her endeavours. Naturally, depending on a sorcerer's background and the ideals he has formed in his journey through life our members do have their own views but they do not express our council's as a whole."

Primate Zerum smiled, almost slyly. "So what is your own personal opinion on the matter then, Mage Archon?"

"I believe it is well known that I am born of Aldorn and have spent most of my years growing up in Hendon, so my preferences, however biased they may seem, can be guessed at your Eminence."

"Indeed," Primate Zerum answered cunningly. He had caught himself a wizard, hook, line and sinker.

"And your opinion on the matter, your Eminence?" Archon offered in return.

"I also do not claim to represent all of Leonium, by no means, but as primate of Alcavia and friend to Hendon I believe my preferences can also be guessed at," he answered, looking around to make sure only the three of them had heard.

Archon lifted his wine glass. "Touché," he saluted the clergyman and his protector knight.

They ate from the buffet and drank various spirits till the early morning hours, enjoying the music of the orchestra. There was an opportunity to dance. Nem took Serilia in his arms then moved on to Emeralda, then he even danced with Roxette who had been the one to ask him if he would oblige her, to which he had assented pleasantly surprised.

Theo too had danced for a while with Adelayne before Prince Armend cut in. But no sooner had he released Adelayne's hand when Queen Crystal appeared before him. They danced for a long while, Theo clutching her by her naked waist feeling that at any moment he might step on her dress's lacy tail. He managed the dance well enough and was actually beginning to enjoy it before the king cleared his throat and stepped in to take the queen from him smiling with amusement. Serilia was there to fill the void and brother and sister shared a tender moment before retiring to the sidelines to take a breather.

Theo exited the hall and made his way to the parapet walls forming the citadel's rectangular enclosure. He stared up at the night sky where both moons were in their mid cycle forming twin half spheres in the sky, the one silver and looming, the other dark blue and dwindling. He cast his gaze westward, to the dark spot in the sky were all the stars were blotted out as if by a giant curtain. It was the huge bulk of the Dragon's Foot Mountains, the tallest peaks in all Thalagia. He shivered involuntarily as the cold wind blew from the icy caps, passing over his thin cotton shirt chilling him to his bones.

"They never melt, you know." He swung about coming face to face with Adelayne. She looked at the mountain peaks, her eyes an indistinguishable dark shade apart from the twinkle in them as they reflected the starlight. "Even in the heart of summer they are forever shrouded in cloud. The few that have endeavoured to climb them and have not perished have brought back tales of blizzards that can wrench a man from his perch and of a vast whiteness that goes on endlessly. Not even we dragonstriders dare to venture close to those peaks but rather choose to fly around them. The Mountain nymphs themselves do not surface there but remain hidden in their tunnels where they live huddled in close knit communities for safety and warmth."

"How often are you harassed by their raids?" Theo asked, accepting the cloak she had brought for him from the hall.

"They are incessant. At times it is only a few groups scattered here and there seeking to steal a farmer's livestock.

At other times their efforts are more organized and they use specially trained assassins, like your friend back there," she said, motioning with her chin towards the hall where Roxette was with the rest of the companions. "Those are the raids that cause us the most damage."

"Have you long been actively involved in the defence of the city?" Theo tried to ignore her comment about Roxette.

"From the age of sixteen when I drew first blood. Alcavian warriors learn from a young age to wield their weapons and we are brought into service almost as soon as we have mastered the use of one or other weapon. We are outnumbered by our enemy so no soldier can be spared, no matter how young they might be."

"It's a tough life," Theo noted, "having to keep vigil at all times and deflect an enemy bent on killing you. I admire your resilience and your ability to shed your fears. I'm not sure I could keep that up for long." Here he was only a week without the protection of the cottage and his parents, and he already felt overwhelmed.

"We don't have much choice in the matter, Theodor. And like my brother explained, when given no other choice people adapt to their circumstances...or they die. We are not the dying breed."

"No, I wouldn't have said you were."

They stood in silence for a long while. Theo felt more at ease with Adelayne now. Having shared an evening with her, he was beginning to get over his initial coyness. It was not as if he was not used to the company of girls. Back at Paliphea Port he had met plenty of them. One year, when he was but twelve years old, he had shared holding hands and a light peck on the cheek with a fisherman's daughter. Well, actually she was two years older than him, and she was the one who had kissed him. He had his first affair with a shop keeper's daughter when he was sixteen and that lasted all summer.

Then later when he had reached adulthood he had thought he'd met the woman he was going to marry. She had come over to the port for the summer, from Nusia, to make an oil painting of the houses and shops. Their relationship went on for a year before she decided she wanted to migrate to Ramila to join the School of Arts there. Theo had opted to remain at the cottage which was probably a sign that she was not the one for him. They still exchanged letters, though it had been six months since her last.

However, Adelayne made him feel different. He felt like a boy of twelve again. She woke feelings in him he knew he had not felt for any woman before. Now he had found her, he did not want to lose sight of her. But what would he do when Archon inevitably decided to move on? Every day they delayed was another the crew of the *Unrelenting Condor* had to recover and lick their wounds before regrouping to strike.

"Come, it is late and I have an early day tomorrow," Adelayne said, turning to leave.

"Adelayne." She halted and turned about. She stared at him, the moonlight falling on her face as she waited for him to speak. "I want to thank you and...and your family for having us. I had a good time tonight. I hope we'll get another chance soon to enjoy each other's company." He breathed a sigh of relief inwardly. *That went better than I thought it would.*

Adelayne stared at him for a long while as if fighting with her inner feelings. Finally she answered. "You're welcome, Theodor. I too have had more fun than I can recall having for any length of time. We'll see each other again tomorrow. I'm sure my brother and Prince Armend will be eager to put you through your paces," she promised him.

◆ CHAPTER 12 ◆

A lesson well learnt

He was standing on the parapet once more, gazing eastwards this time to a small star twinkling in the night sky just above a winding river that emptied into an isolated bay. Within the bay were concealed ten sleek battleships with sails reefed, however their red flags bearing the dragon banner were flapping in the wind. The small star was moving! Oblivious for his own safety he leaped off the parapet. The ground below rushed towards him and he braced expecting to smack into it. Instead he flew in the direction of the silver star.

As he approached, he realized it was not a star at all. He looked upon the reflection of the starlight on the scales of the large beast. It was beating its bat-like wings and twisting its long winding body to soar in the frosty night air like a snake moving on water. Its rider looked petite in comparison and was searching the terrain below, longbow held in one hand and a quiver full of feathered arrows in the other. Her hair was streaked behind her revealing her beautiful features; her lips were moist and drained of colour from the cold and her skin was pale reflecting the moonlight.

At a mental sign from her, which was barely discernible, the beast banked its bulky form towards the meandering river. They descended upon their prey before it had a chance to respond and the woman released a series of arrows rapidly following one other, all hitting their mark. A dozen bodies lay sprawled on the ground twitching, the shafts of the feathered arrows protruding from their point of impact. She turned a satisfied smile towards him then her face darkened.

"I thought I told you it is dangerous to do that unsupervised."

He had no time to respond however and in the dreamy state he was in he did not fully comprehend what she was telling him.

He soared once more, only this time he felt he was suspended from feathered wings. He stared at his bronze coloured plumage and looked beneath his wings to the peninsula below. Off to the south his sharp eyes could distinguish the Triplet Islands which he had passed on his journey westwards. He searched carefully down at the hills that bordered the sea looking for any signs of his quarry—well it was not his quarry exactly—it couldn't be—not a beast of that size. But he had been monitoring its progress for the past week and was sure it had doubled back.

There! Behind that pile of rocks. The red tail was unmistakable. The man thing with the blond "plumage" on his head would be pleased with him. He circled once above the fire breathing lizard then fled towards the man dwelling on the hill due west. He would have to report to his man thing companion that he had rediscovered their prey.

He broke contact with the hawk and sped over tall peaks veiled in a thick blanket of snow and continued his mad flight until the mountains gave way to hills and the hills gave way to a plain that led to another range of mountains. He had traversed these parts before; he knew where he was heading but could not halt or control his flight.

Inevitably he found himself standing in the dark chamber lit by a few torches hanging from the cold, bleak walls. The monotone chanting continued as before and the dark robed figures knelt before their lords' altars that were enclosed by the protective ruby glass screens. He looked upon the black armoured figure with the twin red dragons imprinted on his bulging chest plates and shivered involuntarily remembering their last encounter.

A pair of the kneeling robed figures stood and climbed the steps to approach the altars. They were hooded so he could not see their faces. They seemed to be in a trance for they walked stiffly. They reached out with their hands towards the red screens, their fingers getting closer. The chanting increased in pitch and urgency. Then their hands pressed against the screens.

He felt a shockwave and saw the torches on the walls spluttering as a gust of wind that seemed to originate from nowhere blew through the dark chamber. The hoods of the two robed figures were thrown back to reveal their faces frozen in a silent scream, the terror locked in their eyes. They began to shake violently but could not dislodge their hands from the screens.

Then the skin of their faces undulated and blisters began to form in their eyes, cheeks, and mouths. The blisters turned from red to a sickly yellow then burst open, spewing forth puss intermingled with blood. They were being devoured alive by an unseen malicious force that fed off their living body tissue. They began to dissolve like flesh dipped in acid. With a "poof" their heads and bodies collapsed leaving behind hunks of skin that hung from the glass screens. Then they too slid to the floor.

Another of the robed figures stepped forward coolly removing from the floor the rags of skin that moments before had been his brethren. He resumed his place on the bottom of the steps kneeling and chanting in synch with the rest.

The armoured warrior lord turned his helmet towards the intruder. The black visor lifted and abnormally large pupils set in blood red eyes without irises stared at Theo.

"Your time will come soon, Athuddir. I hunger for you. Bow down to me. Bow down to the Dark Lord and you will be spared."

Theo couldn't breathe. He felt like his throat was being constricted by an unseen hand. He was suffocating. He opened his mouth but no air would enter his lungs. It was as if his windpipe had ceased to exist, like a fish trying to breathe out of water. He was losing his senses. Darkness enveloped him.

He felt himself being shaken violently. A voice was calling to him in earnest bringing him back from the brink. From the oppressive darkness that weighed heavily upon him like a blanket of death he could see a spot of burning white flame. The flame grew larger till it gradually caused the darkness to recede.

"Theodor! Theodor it's me. It's Archon. Theodor can you hear me, boy?" He opened his eyes and stared at the mage's stone grey eyes for a good long while before he understood where he was. Archon was searching his face with the worry plain to be seen in his eyes.

"Archon, is he alright?" It was the princess, fully dressed in the warrior pants and tunic he had seen her wearing when he had first laid eyes on her. She entered the room out of breath.

"I'm not sure." Archon placed a hand on Theo's temple. "He's not cold any more and some of the vibrancy is returning to his cheeks. Theo can you speak lad. Tell us if you are well."

"I...I'm alright, I think," he managed to croak. "What happened?" He stared at the mage then at Adelayne's disturbed eyes. She was holding a candelabrum above his bed and the torches in his room were lit.

Achon cleared his throat. "You don't remember?"

The look of those eyes would remain seared into his memory for as long as he lived. He shivered and Archon, taking it to mean that he was cold, pulled his blankets around him.

"Adelayne," the mage turned to look at the princess who stood casting anxious glances at Theo. "Please be a dear and fetch a cup of hot tea from the kitchen. It should help calm his nerves and warm his limbs. He seems to be in a state of shock."

Adelayne nodded and left the room carrying her candelabrum to light her way.

Archon turned back to the young man lying on the bed. *Who would have thought he had learned to spirit travel on his own?* he mused, chastising himself for not being more alert and aware of what his charge was up to. Archon made his decision instantly. The group was going to remain in Alcavia till summer, until he had the chance to progress the boy's training to a level where he would feel confident the boy could at least keep himself out of harm's way. Magic was a dangerous thing, even when used by a skilled wielder, so in the hands of a novice was deadly.

"Adelayne located me in the gardens whilst I was taking a stroll and warned me that you were spirit travelling in your sleep. Theodor, how long have you been doing this?" There was a sound of urgency in his voice.

Adelayne walked into the room carrying a tray with three cups of the hot fuming brew. "Here, drink this herbal tea." She placed a cup gently into Theo's hand and offered the other to the mage.

"Theo, I need to know." The mage was insistent. He was still wearing his ceremonial cream gown with the silver embroidery. As he sat there on the bed, he reminded Theo of a priest listening to a confession.

"It happened shortly after we began our travels. I don't know how. Sometimes when I sleep I feel as if I am dreaming but I see things that are taking place in real life. I know this to be true for I saw Adelayne a day before we met her on the port road to Alcavia."

The mage idly stroked his short cropped beard with one hand whilst staring at Theo, his face devoid of emotion, quite calm now, like a researcher studying a laboratory rat. "Spirit travelling may take two forms," he began instructively. "One method is to retain a link with one's body and to send the spirit soaring either on its own or on the wings of a beast. Indeed one can bond momentarily with any creature of the land, sea or air. But there is a fine line between spirit travelling and bonding. That entails its own dangers but we will not dwell on the subject of animal bonding now.

"Spirit travelling without retaining a link with your body is the second and most dangerous of the two forms of outer body travel. In this case you leave your body open to attack from another gifted or from any of the numerous evil spirits that are known to plague the world. Many a sorcerer who has ventured to travel without retaining the link has returned to their body only to find that they've been sealed from it. It is not an experience that you would relish. I have had to exorcise bodies that have been possessed by demons and return them to their original owners. However, an after-effect remains forever; the body's owner never feels the same again; many in fact are driven to suicide by their nightmares.

"Theo I don't want you spirit travelling until you have learnt to retain a strong link with your body."

Theo had a horrifying image forming in his mind at the words Archon had just uttered. He shuddered at the thought of demons occupying his body with his spirit left to wander aimlessly as a ghost. "How do I stop it?" he asked. "It happens spontaneously."

"That may be so, only because you are strong in the Spirit agent of the gift, something I did not realize before. But you can stop it the moment it begins. When you feel that you are about to spirit travel you must concentrate on your present surroundings and picture them in your mind. That will keep your spirit anchored down and will cause the spell to cease." Archon stood and prepared to leave.

"Theo, I intend over the next few weeks to increase our training sessions. We must learn what other aspects of the gift you are strong at and where your weaknesses lie, to teach you to be able to control your gift." He bade Theo a good and trouble-free night then left them alone.

Adelayne sat at his bed and took his hand in hers. "When you were away on your spirit travelling you kept shouting *'Sed Muthin'*. Who is *'Sed Muthin'*, Theodor?"

"I don't know. I honestly don't know Adelayne." He shook his head in dismay. He did not feel like talking about it. He felt a bit agitated but at the same time was glad for Adelayne's company.

"Theodor, it means in the ancient tongue, 'Blood Eyes'."

He froze. The trembling returned to his limbs. Adelayne saw the sudden change and took him in her arms, cradling his head against her shoulder. "Hush. I will not trouble you any longer. Please forgive me." Then she let go of him and regained her composure, feeling a bit awkward at her show of tenderness.

She got up and prepared to extinguish the torches to Theo's room before leaving.

"No. Leave the torches." Theo was ashamed of himself almost as soon as he spoke, but he did not take a word back.

Adelayne nodded, approaching the door.

"Adelayne?"

"Hmm?" She murmured turning to him.

"Did you really kill all those nymphs tonight?"

She looked at him with cold pale eyes, green like an ice glacier dipped in murky waters. She left without answering.

♦ CHAPTER 13 ♦

Forging a tool

As the weeks passed by, Theo and Nem were drilled hard by the two princes who kept their vow, sparring with them every evening in the king's training grounds. It soon became evident that Leon was the strongest in the group after delivering Theo a few choice blows. But to Prince Armend's despair Theo had bested him on several occasions and on others had come very close, despite the shorter lad's most ardent attempts. With Prince Leon it was a case of pride and being the best, whereas it went much deeper than that with Armend. He had a grudge with the tall youth that had entered their lives so suddenly and who seemed to be getting along so well with Princess Adelayne.

Back at the citadel, King Dreyfus had recognized Nem's interest in trade and provided him with his personal Minister of Commerce as a tutor. The minister was a short bald man named Slade, responsible for informing the king, among other matters, on issues concerning the yearly yield of the wheat fields as well as the returns from the livestock.

Nem learnt much under the guidance of Slade who was more than willing to divulge his knowledge to a young and eager mind. They spent much time together visiting the port merchants and the aristocratic sector within the third inner ring of the city where the owners of the major city businesses and largest plots of land could be located.

Theo arrived on the grounds where he had earlier spent the day sparring with Prince Armend who, as always, had fought with all the energy he could muster a sneer permanently etched on his face throughout the two hour ordeal. Theo flexed his muscles looking at his arms and biceps: they were getting firmer. Today he had come close to outdoing Prince Leon –almost.

He smelled her lavender perfume before he heard her. She was light footed, toying with him by trying to sneak up on him unawares; he always turned around just before she reached him, like now.

"How do you manage to do that?" she asked. Adelayne stood before him dressed in tight pants and a long sleeved tunic. She had both her swords strapped on and her dagger hilts protruded from various parts of her body.

He grinned absorbed by her eyes which were now a light shade of blue, like the afternoon sky. "A man is permitted to keep a few secrets from a beautiful woman."

She returned a timid smile then, drawing her swords, swirled around abruptly just as Roxette approached. The nymph was dressed in her customary black leather outfit and high-heeled boots. The tension between the two was a taught string ready to break even though they had been training together for the past four weeks. Roxette had conceded to Adelayne's meek request to continue her training in the secret fighting arts of the Eastern Temples which her uncle had left incomplete on his untimely death.

The significance of Roxette's compromise was not lost on Adelayne, recognizing it as the nymph's method of paying her dues for the damage her people were inflicting on Alcavia. In return Adelayne was more relenting in her views of the nymph, accepting her now without comment though her weariness of her still remained.

When Theo and Adelayne had finished their training with Roxette, the nymph excused herself, leaving the two alone.

"Theo, walk with me to the gardens, will you?" Adelayne retrieved her swords and a selection of daggers which she managed to conceal in various parts of her clothing in locations Theo would never have dreamed of.

"I'll be glad to, Adelayne." He offered his arm and they exited the training grounds. The king's gardens were truly a magnificent sight with neat pathways covered by a layer of fine aggregate that crunched beneath their boots. On either side the roses formed a hedge with breaks providing entry to the lawns that were square or rectangular in plan with a variety of trees growing neatly in the centre of each lawn: there were oak and weeping willows, chestnut and cherry trees with their rosy blossoms, and other varieties Theo was less familiar with.

It was a peaceful place away from the world's cares where one could relax and take a much needed breather. Theo and Adelayne visited the gardens often, on occasion meeting up there with the king and queen who were pleasant to Theo, talking idly with him without prying or pressing for information about him and his companions. Every time Queen Crystal gazed at Theo, he would recall the banquet and blush to which the queen responded with a satisfied smile. She knew she was beautiful but appreciated being reminded of it by one so young.

She looks so much like the lady of the forest, Theo mused, thinking back on the queen. *She has the same long wavy brown hair and they are both nymph kind, but Queen Crystal's eyes are like the deep blue waters of the Urid Ocean;* this ocean, bordering the frosty northern lands, they said, was so deep and violet blue that songs were written about it and the creatures that were fabled to inhabit its depths. *Whereas the lady of the forest has light green eyes, a bit like Adelayne's.*

Theo had a thought. He turned his gaze on Adelayne who was leading him through a break in the rose hedge towards a bench underneath a tree with white blossoms. "Your mother is a Forest nymph, is she not?"

Adelayne sat down on the bench and patted the empty space beside her. As Theo took his seat she looked at him closely. "I don't believe I've ever told you about that, but yes she is one of two daughters of the late Queen of the Ghiadon Forest. My aunt, Queen Viola, being the elder sister inherited the crown. We used to visit her and the forest kingdom more often when I was younger. It's a good two weeks' ride from here if one presses matters. But with the increasing raids by the Mountain nymphs we do not venture north any more."

They talked about their families at length.

Theo stared at his hands which he clenched tightly between his knees. "I don't know all that much about my mother's family apart from that her mother died giving birth to her and that her father died from grief soon after." An uncomfortable silence followed.

Adelayne reached out and hugged him close. She kissed him lightly on the top of his head. He raised his head and their eyes met. Adelayne hesitated for just a moment before pressing her lips against his, opening them up to probe his warm mouth. They exchanged a long lingering kiss. Theo could feel her heart beating faster as she pressed her bosom against his chest that was heaving in response. He placed an arm about her waist and hugged her back fiercely.

They broke off with her nestling her head in his embrace.

"My sweet, precious Adelayne," he whispered. "How my heart has yearned for this moment but common sense got the better of me every time."

She looked up inquiringly at him. "How so?" she asked, perplexed.

"Adelayne let's face it: you are a princess and I am a...a cottage nobody from an island miles away with no titles to my name and no means to sustain myself."

"You think titles mean anything to me, Theodor? If they did I would have succumbed to Armend's advances ages ago." Adelayne seemed downstricken, her pale skin turning red with anger. She shook her head throwing him a frosty look with eyes like blue daggers. He recoiled from that look. "Theodor Marentherin, if you feel you're too high and mighty for me or that I do not please you in some way then be a man and say so, but don't sit there finding excuses only little boys use: A *'cottage nobody'*, *'no titles to your name'* and that last one, *'no means to sustain yourself'*. What a snivelling boy you are. I have misjudged you." She pushed him away and stood up to leave.

"Adelayne, wait!" Theo shouted as she fled from him. He made to run after her but found his path blocked by Prince Armend who had appeared in the hedge opening.

"Here, what have you done to the princess, farm boy?" The prince was red in the face and the dark rings around his blood-shot eyes were more prominent than ever. He stormed towards Theo who responded by raising his chin defiantly, bracing for a fight.

"I'm in no mood right now, Armend. Don't push me!"

"You village oafs are all the same," Armend retorted, fervently. "And it's *Prince* Armend to you, commoner. Give a man more credit than his birth permits and he'll soon prance around acting high and mighty. Don't think I haven't seen the way you drool over the princess. What could you possibly hope to achieve with her? Are you lustful for her family's dowry, for her titles, her lands? Do you think *we* of royal blood mix with *your* kind?"

"I do not seek the things that obviously seem to matter to you, Armend. I care for her for who she is, not for her station!" Theo replied hotly. He balled his hands into fists but tried to keep his temper under control. His vision was becoming blurry with the white hot anger that was welling up inside.

Armend sneered at him. "Don't think I've been idle, farm boy," he said in a cool, icy voice. "I know about your bustard grandfather, and my friends tell me your mother is of an obscure background. You're a nobody, of poor stock and unworthy of the princess. Why do you torment her so without reason? If you truly cared for her, as you claim, you would save her from unnecessary pain and humiliation. Are you selfish as well as blind?" The prince smiled a sly triumphant smile at the changing look on Theo's face.

Theo's anger was beginning to dissipate. After all, was Armend telling him anything he did not already know? The prince was right. He had no claim on the princess. Better to save her and himself from a lot of embarrassment. Better to stick to what he was good at doing, following behind the tail skirts of a mage who dealt with him condescendingly, not considering him worthy enough to entrust him with the truth of their mission. His grandfather had fed him false hope. They *were* better than him and his lot after all.

"I'll see you at training practice tomorrow, Islander. Make sure you are prepared. I will not deal with you mercifully for taking advantage of our princess." Prince Armend whirled his cloak around him as he left Theo alone with his thoughts.

The rest of the week passed with Theo being soundly thrashed during the morning training sessions by both princes. Prince Armend was in the best mood he had ever been since the arrival of the strangers. By day he would soundly beat the "farm boy" at sword practice and his evenings were free for him to seek out the company of Princess Adelayne who seemed to have turned frosty towards Theo.

"Theo, you are not concentrating the way you should be," Roxette scolded. Adelayne had just left after throwing him several times on the ground and delivering a couple of sound kicks to his head and stomach. "You were awful during your bout with the princes. Whatever's the matter with you?"

"Leave it alone, Roxette. I'm in no mood. You wouldn't understand in any case. What does a Mountain nymph assassin know about matters of the heart? Just forget it." He started to walk away but Roxette grabbed him by the arm, whirling him about.

"I understand more than you think, Theodor. You forget that I was betrayed by the one I loved. Now stop being such an ass and tell me what's wrong. I thought things were going well for you and Adelayne–well at least they were till a week ago."

"Is everyone missing the point here, except me?" Theo asked lifting his arms in exasperation then letting them flop to his sides again.

"Which is?"

"Adelayne is royalty, and I...I am a nobody."

Roxette looked at him with dark eyes, like a cat which doesn't know whether to cuff a cub or offer it support. "Is that what Adelayne told you?"

"Well, not exactly," Theo admitted softly, kicking at a protruding stone. His eyes were downcast as he placed his hands in his pockets looking fed-up and confused.

"Come, walk beside me and we can talk it over." Roxette placed her arm in his and led him towards the gardens. They walked side by side along the garden path till they found a bench to sit down on. "Tell me what happened. I have found in my experience that it helps to talk."

Theo looked at the nymph dubiously. Could there possibly be a more sensitive side to Roxette's tough exterior? She was the last person he was expecting to be discussing this with. Usually his aunt Emeralda would serve that role, replacing his own mother whom he had not approached for advice on similar issues since he had turned sixteen. Somehow he did not feel comfortable discussing his private life with his parents whereas he considered aunt Emeralda to be an impartial friend who knew how to be discreet.

He caught the nymph's expectant glance and blew out his pent up breath. "Adelayne and I had a quarrel a week ago. I told her we couldn't be together because we were from different backgrounds. She called me a coward and said I was looking for excuses to avoid her," he said, then added with frustration, "Roxette, I don't know what to do or how to behave. I'm trying to do what's right by all of you but end up doing exactly the opposite."

Roxette's face was pinched in concentration. She cleared her throat. "It seems to me, Theodor, that you are complicating matters more than is necessary. Adelayne likes you. That much is obvious. Why not let her decide if your backgrounds are an obstacle to you becoming friends. In any case it's not as if anyone is forcing you into anything. My advice is to let your friendship continue and take it from there. The least that can happen is that you become steadfast friends. Is that such a bad thing?"

Theo considered her words. She was right. Nobody was forcing him and Adelayne into doing anything they did not want to. Maybe he was placing too much of a burden on himself. Armend was partly to blame. Theo decided he would not play the prince's game any more. Roxette was right. He and the princess could be friends. "Thanks Roxette. I believe I've cleared a few things in my mind."

She nodded her agreement gifting him with one of her rare smiles.

♦ CHAPTER 14 ♦

Dancing maiden

Adelayne changed into something more comfortable and made her way to the palace sitting area next to the throne room. She entered finding who she was searching for. The two women nodded at her and she returned their greeting in kind.

"Come sit by us, Adelayne." Emeralda was drinking her tea with Serilia who was sprawled on a comfortable couch. Emeralda offered the princess some of the tea which she graciously accepted. She inquired as to the whereabouts of her mother and was informed that she had last been seen in the company of Zoi.

"They seem to be spending a lot of time together," Adelayne remarked, sipping her tea and staring out the window towards the central courtyard.

"Yes, they're like old acquaintances, wouldn't you say?" Emeralda agreed.

"Well, I never laid eyes on her before you arrived," Adelayne informed them. "Perhaps they met somewhere when I was away on an errand. My time is spent mostly away from the palace. I seldom have any time to be idle."

"Yes, I've noticed that about you, Adelayne. Do your parents agree with you placing yourself in so much danger on a daily basis?"

"It's not as if I give them much choice, Emeralda. Circumstances are such that my aid is necessary. Of course they argue that we have others to do the patrols but I cannot allow myself not to face the same dangers that my brother and our kinsmen are forced to. There can be no room for weakness in a land like ours." *And I have a score to settle.*

"It's a tough way to live. I suppose we should count ourselves lucky in Cyrus. At least we were till the attack on our cottage. Maybe there is no safe haven left anywhere," she mused sadly. "We lived well for the past twenty odd years. My brother's the one who has suffered the most from all this though, not to mention Theo and Serilia." She placed a hand lovingly beneath Serilia's chin. The young woman kissed her hand in return.

"At least you have each other." Adelayne was overcome with grief as memories of her uncle flooded her. She tried desperately to hold back the tears. It would do no good to cry in front of her guests. All her crying was done at night in her private chamber.

Emeralda sensing her mood tried to put on a cheerful face, changing the subject. "Tell me, Adelayne. What do you do for entertainment around here? I have not had a chance to visit your fine city and to see what your night life has to offer."

It worked, for Adelayne was shocked into a grin. She did not expect to hear such a request from one Emeralda's age. But then again Emeralda was no ordinary woman. She gazed at the Sea nymph and smiled, her eyes sparkling with interest. "Well, we'll just have to correct that, won't we?"

"I couldn't agree more, dear. What say you we meet again later on, say about an hour before midnight? I'll tell the boys to escort us, shall I?" Adelayne nodded her agreement as Emeralda finished off her tea.

That night Theo was feeling a bit jittery. He had so much explaining to do but was glad Adelayne had accepted Emeralda's proposal to go for a drink at a bar of her choosing. He shaved his week-old beard and dressed in his best clothing that he had purchased from the city stalls. He felt renewed as he stared at his bedroom mirror. The small dolphin amulet was hanging from his neck revealed by his open shirt. He rolled up his sleeves to free his arms. It was a pleasant spring evening.

He exited the room closing the door behind him and made his way to the sitting area where Adelayne had met with his sister and aunt earlier on. He found Nem and his grandfather there sitting on their armchairs chatting idly. They were both dressed in their finest and had an expectant glint in their eyes. They smiled at him as he entered and Nem poured him a drink as he took a seat beside them.

"Do you know who'll be coming tonight?" Nem asked. He had his curly black hair in a knot and wore a small earring in his left ear. From his waist hung the small dagger which he had been carrying that day in the Triad Woods. He had not put it on since he had been given the scimitar by Prium, but there was no need to carry the larger weapon in the city. They felt safe within the walls where the patrols kept the city under close surveillance. Still, Nem was not one to take chances so he at least carried the dagger.

"I know that Emeralda, Serilia and Adelayne will be coming, and the princess might invite her brother. Where's Archon?" Theo asked suddenly. He had not seen the mage since their lesson at midday.

"He's been in the company of the king and queen all day discussing matters of state and the affairs of neighbouring kingdoms," Nestor replied. "Since it didn't much involve me I left them to it hours ago. I doubt he'll be in any mood for entertainment tonight."

The ladies appeared soon after wearing their evening dresses covered over by light shawls. Surprisingly, Roxette joined the group dressed in a daring reddish-brown leather suit cut at the shoulders, hugging her slim form. She looked almost naked without her twin swords and her collection of daggers. Like Nem, she had opted to carry a small blade in her boot. The other three had chosen to wear evening dresses low-cut to reveal their shoulders and necks that were adorned with necklaces. They shared a single drink with the men to warm up for the night before setting off.

Adelayne led the group to a small bar on the posh side of the inner circle. The *Dancing Maiden* was in a side street off the main citadel road surrounded by trees and lit by several street lanterns. It was a cosy establishment with a fireplace and wooden benches and tables set around a dancing area that for the moment was empty as the guests were only now arriving. The group filed in handing their cloaks to the doorman who escorted them to their reserved table.

A couple of minstrels, a young man at the harp and a girl singer, kept the group entertained whilst they ordered their drinks. Soon the place began to fill and the guests joined the minstrel in song. She had a pleasant enough voice, managing to bring cheer to the customers with her witty performances on stage. Nestor clapped with glee and even winked at a passing maid who grinned back at him. To keep her brother out of trouble Emeralda asked him for a dance. Soon Serilia and Nem joined them leaving Theo alone with Roxette and Adelayne.

Theo felt a bit uncomfortable and kept looking in Adelayne's direction. She stared back waiting whilst taking a sip from her tankard of ale. When he looked at Roxette she motioned for him to leave saying she would be alright on her own. He offered Adelayne his hand and they proceeded to the dance floor. The minstrel with the harp was playing a lively tune so they danced with vigour exchanging partners every now and then, keeping in rhythm with the song. The bar was full almost to bursting point with a variety of folk whom Adelayne informed him were mostly employees at the citadel or young soldiers with their beloveds. She also explained it was not uncommon for young lords and ladies to seek this bar, which had become well known for its fair prices and ample entertainment.

"Did one such lord offer you this?" Theo asked, fingering the sapphire pendant around Adelayne's neck. He regretted uttering the words as soon as he saw the pained expression crossing Adelayne's face. "I'm sorry...I didn't mean to pry," he added softly.

She shook her head wiping at the corner of her eye. "You could not have known, Theo," she countered taking a deep breath and smiling bravely. "The wound is still fresh," she explained. "It was a gift from my uncle Eschalion."

You idiot, Theo chastised himself. "Adelayne, I...I don't know what to say–I'm sorry," he offered hastily.

Adelayne waved away his apology burying her head in his neck. Theo held her tightly in his arms moving gently with her on the dance floor. At some point the music became livelier and their mood was lifted as they left their troubled thoughts behind.

Theo locked arms with Adelayne and changed partner to come face to face with Roxette who had a tiny grin on her face that she was unable to conceal. They danced for a while till he handed her back to her partner. It was colonel Ajax who must have arrived whilst Theo was on the dance floor with Adelayne. He looked around and spotted Prince Leon butting in to relieve a disgruntled Nem from his partner. Serilia laughed at the look on Nem's face. Nem however did not have time to sulk for a young lady provocatively dressed and having eyes only for him fell into his arms, whirling him about as they danced together.

It was not long before Theo returned to the table huffing to regain his breath. Adelayne sat next to him enfolded in his arms, her perfume wakening his desire. She looked up into his eyes and they remained locked in each others' embrace, exchanging a private moment where words were unnecessary. Just then, Nem flopped beside them with his new-found companion bringing them out of their daze. "Theo, Adelayne, I'd like you to meet Lady Irene," he said, introducing his dame who appeared to be in her mid-thirties. They greeted each other with Irene asking Nem to drop the "lady" part.

When Irene was busy chatting with Adelayne, Theo grabbed his chance, moving closer to his friend. "So where did you meet up with this one, then?" he asked discreetly so he could not be overheard.

"You remember those ladies I told you about, the ones that Slade introduced me to when we were visiting the houses in the inner circle?" Nem was grinning shamelessly.

"Yes, I remember, the ones of high rank; you mentioned that Slade said it was good for a trader to mingle and make friends with those who had influence in the city."

"Precisely, my fine friend. Irene's father happens to be one of the wealthiest men in all of Alcavia, seeing as he owns large plots of wheat-filled land. Apparently last year's winter yield was particularly bountiful and the forecasts for this spring are encouraging as well." Nem had a smug look on his face.

"Yes, but what is a thirty-year-old woman doing with a man more than ten years younger?" Theo retorted.

Nem winced, placing a finger to his lips and looking cautiously at Irene to make sure she had not overheard. "Keep your voice down, Theo. Do you want to blow it all for me? Slade has told her that I am a merchant gentleman travelling abroad to make new contacts for my fledgling shipping business. I've told her that I am in my late twenties and that people in my family age slowly. She thought about it at first, but then she said that five or six years' difference in age did not matter to her."

Theo shook his head disapprovingly. "What if one of the girls accidentally reveals the truth? What then?"

"Theo, learn to live a little, take a risk or two. We won't be twenty again, you know. In any case, what is life without a bit of spice?" Nem clapped his friend on the shoulder, lifting his mug to the girls before draining it.

Theo stared at the dance floor. Roxette and the colonel seemed to be getting along well. At some point the two of them came and sat down at the table, Ajax ordering a round of drinks for all. Prince Leon and Serilia, followed by Nestor and Emeralda, joined the group and they spent the rest of the night chatting, singing and drinking. Theo could not remember the last time he had felt so good and care-free. He had mended his friendship with Adelayne and felt good about Roxette pairing up with Ajax. She deserved companionship.

"Leon, where is Armend tonight?" Adelayne asked at some point, and was told that the prince was not feeling well and had been looking a bit pale.

They left the *Dancing Maiden* in high spirits making their way back to the citadel. Nem opted to stay a while longer at the bar with Irene, as did Ajax and Roxette. Prince Leon offered to escort Emeralda and Serilia to their rooms whilst Nestor made for the sitting room to smoke his pipe and drink a nightcap. Theo was at last left alone with Adelayne. They chose to walk for a while in the king's gardens.

"Adelayne, I'm glad we are friends once more. The past week has been very trying for me. I realize that I haven't treated you properly. Your companionship means a lot to me and I want the time we spend together to be pleasant for both of us."

Adelayne took his hand gently in hers, staring into his green eyes. *How they remind me of father's*, she thought on impulse. She realized that Theo looked like a younger version of her father in many ways. They had the same facial features, the same proud bearing, and their mannerisms were similar. Her father in his youth had also travelled abroad searching for adventure. He had come across her mother on one of his trips to the Emerald Forest. Her parents had almost come to grips that day, she recalled. Her father had ventured into the forest searching for game and had almost killed one of her mother's favourite silver-maned bucks.

Their relationship, once Dreyfus had apologized, soon took a turn for the better. The young prince was smitten by the beauty of the Forest nymph princess. A couple of years later, Dreyfus married Crystal and they moved to Alcavia where they settled down to ruling the kingdom together.

"I too am glad that you have had a change of heart." Adelayne smiled up at Theo, deciding that her taste in men was shifting from darker-haired, dark brown eyed men to someone more closely resembling the young man that stood beside her. She had taken a vow to avenge her uncle's death and not to get involved with anyone until her task was completed. But with Theo she was finding it increasingly difficult. It was true that in the past week she had been harsh with him at training and had avoided speaking with him, but not because she had tired of him; on the contrary she was intrigued by his strange ways and the mystery that seemed to shroud him.

"Perhaps I have pressed you too hard before, Theodor. I will not bring you into a difficult situation again. At least not until you're ready."

"Adelayne, you haven't been pushy with me at all. I've been doing that to myself. That day in the gardens, after the training, when we kissed...I felt like I was never going to be as happy again in my life. I ruined everything with what I said after. I know now there's no rush. We can enjoy each other's company and decide later what we'll make of it."

Adelayne stopped abruptly. "Theodor, I too enjoyed what we shared."

Theo felt himself melt like ice on a hot blade as he stared deeply into her eyes like twin pools. He could lose himself in her gaze forever, shedding all awareness of his surroundings and immersing himself into her, filling his senses with her: her perfume, her soft embrace, the way her hair lifted lightly in the springtime breeze, the paleness of her slender neck contrasting with her dark hair which spilled down to the curve of her back. He blushed as he let his eyes wander over to her full bosom and her firm behind which was hugged by her tight dress.

He had an uncontrollable urge to kiss her. She sensed it. Parting her lips she brought her perfect oval face close to his so she filled his vision. They were merged as one as they embraced, their lips meeting, their hearts beating in unison as they shared their moment of closeness. Theo felt this was right, that he and Adelayne belonged together, that their backgrounds no longer mattered. Somehow he would find a way to make it work. He would make himself worthy of her love.

They stayed in each others' arms staring up at the starlight. It was a wondrous evening with not a cloud in the sky. The late spring scents from the garden flowers filled the night air which was fresh but not cold. They found a bench and sat down to enjoy each other's company for a while longer. Theo stroked Adelayne's hair gently as he contemplated what his next move might be.

"Assima will be worried that I did not go to her tonight," Adelayne murmured as Theo hugged her.

"Assima?" Theo responded, absent-minded.

"Yes, she's my silver dragon companion. We meet every night close to midnight and make our rounds before I retire to my room. I seldom ever miss a flight with her. It helps keep me sharp and it gives Assima the chance to spread her wings and do what she enjoys most–fly."

"How long have you been a Dragonstrider?" Theo asked, placing a gentle hand to her chin.

"For as long as I can remember. I was introduced to the dragons as a toddler and at twelve my father took me for my first flight."

"Your father rides a dragon as well?" He had never heard the king mention it and assumed the king's time was preoccupied with the ruling of the kingdom.

"All rulers of Alcavia have been Dragonstriders," Adelayne answered him, matter-of-factly. "My brother also has a dragon companion, though he doesn't fly with him as often as I do with Assima."

"How many dragons do you have in Alcavia?" Theo had felt awed to discover that the Sea Kingdom of Alunda had two dragons. Now Adelayne had already mentioned three.

"We had a full family of four–that is until the dominant male was killed...along with my uncle," Adelayne replied sadly, burying her face in Theo's shoulder as the painful memory of her uncle was stirred. She remembered being tougher than this but in Theo's company she felt she had nothing to hide...no need to suppress her distress. She wanted to let her emotions run free with Theo. She did not want to pretend to be more than she was with him. She felt comfortable leaning on him for support.

They stayed silent for a while listening to the sounds of the night. An owl hooted somewhere in the trees, not far off, and there was a rustling in the bushes as some small animal was scampering about. It was a very peaceful time in Theo's life. He wished it could always remain so. But he knew it would not go on for long. The mage had already hinted that they would have to be on their way soon, and then what would become of Adelayne? Theo felt a wrench in his heart as he realized that before he would be able to claim Adelayne he would need to complete whatever mission he had been thrown into with the mage.

"Theodor, that beautiful pendant hanging from your neck looks like it's made from white gold. Who gave it to you?"

Theo clutched at the small trinket, memories of the Sea Kingdom flooding back to him. "It was a gift from Prium, my great grandfather from my father's side. You're right about it being made from the Silver River metal."

Adelayne placed a finger on the dolphin and kissed him on the neck softly. He hugged her to him and they remained in each other's embrace.

Then they heard the sound of another couple laughing and sat up straighter. Peering at the lights flooding from the citadel windows, Theo was able to make out the familiar form of Roxette. She was in the arms of colonel Ajax.

"She's not the woman I at first thought she was," Adelayne admitted. "She is a good friend and ally to you all. The wizard was right in the end. You are fortunate indeed to be surrounded by such people, Theodor. Colonel Ajax is a good man also. He has been alone for quite some time now. I am happy they found each other." She drew Theo closer placing her slim hands on his collar and gave him another lingering kiss.

They remained there for the rest of the night. With the first rays of the morning they made their way each to their respective rooms. Theo, on a whim, cracked open Nem's door only to find that his friend's bed had not been slept in. *Well at least one of us has the nerve to carry it through,* he thought wryly. But then he didn't think Roxette would be sleeping in her bed tonight either.

He was pleased with his latest acquisitions. Whereas his previous three disciples had been blind followers without minds of their own and totally devoid of imagination, Ramila had proven to be a viper's pit filled with the Dark Lord's followers eager to prove their worth. The sorceress displayed a gratifying talent at using the gift and had a shrewd mind to go with it as a bonus. The cleric too in his sheep's clothing and affable appearance would prove a useful tool on missions where they would need to get close to the enemy. His Templar knight was a man to be reckoned with as well.

He was tired of leading these brainless animals he had been lumbered with. Pithiks were alright for an ambush where one required brute strength and overpowering numbers but otherwise they were a problem to feed and offered little else in terms of strategy. Whereas the Templar knight and the other three military trained Darklings would prove more resourceful and would allow him to concentrate on the task at hand. The other three were typical of the Gathzul, or "enslaved souls". Even the mindless Pithiks avoided going near the walking dead. Gathzuls were useful when one wanted to instil fear into the enemy. They could not be killed by any man-made blade except for those forged using *Lithureal* which was a rare silver metal to be found solely at the crater of Illiath.

Gathzuls could also be destroyed by one using the gift, if their opponent proved strong enough, for the Gathzul were themselves sorcerers that had sold their soul to the Dark One in exchange for power and eternal life. To defeat a Gathzul one had to overcome the fear they instilled–most could not.

Yes, I am well pleased with my new group of followers. Now I can finish what I started. Archon will either bow down to my lord or meet with the same fate as his parents. As for his two gifted pups, there is always room for new blood in the ranks of the Dark. And that old hag is not going to be a problem either. He would deal with her when the time was right–her and all of her kind. He laughed aloud as the *Unrelenting Condor* set course due south from Ramila's shores.

♦ CHAPTER 15 ♦

A short repose

It was a pleasant summer's evening. Theo turned at the soft knock on his bedroom door.

"Come," he called, pulling on his pants and a shirt.

Adelayne entered wearing pants that were cut off at the knees, which was the growing trend with the ladies, and a plain blouse on top. "Were you sleeping?"

"No. It's too early for sleep. Is everything alright?"

"Fine. I was going to go for a walk through the city. Want to come along? It's a lovely evening."

"I'd love to."

Theo turned to Adelayne breathing in deeply her lavender-scented perfume. They followed the street lamps lining the main road and headed steadily away from the palace grounds.

"Where are we going?" Theo asked.

"I wish to give thanks for the peace and happiness I have been granted these past few months with you," Adelayne answered, giving him a soft kiss on the lips.

They went round the city to its eastern side until they arrived at a small park near the outskirts of the second city wall.

"This is a small haven of green secluded from the rest of the city dwellings and protected by city law from being violated," Adelayne said, pointing to the park. "It is strictly prohibited for any citizen to cause damage to the trees here. It is a sacred place." She took Theo by the hand and led him through the park till they arrived before what looked like a stone dwelling. It was a rudimentary structure composed of stone walls and a large slab resting horizontally to form a roof. Numerous small slits in the walls formed windows that allowed air and light to enter the interior. They entered.

As they descended the few stone steps Theo could hear gentle singing voices. Reaching the bottom of the stairs they stood looking around the room at the small group of people gathered in prayer. The rock temple was surprisingly large inside, contrary to its deceptive outer appearance, and well-lit. Theo picked up the faint smell of incense and flowers. He looked towards the centre of the room and saw what looked like an altar upon which rested a fresh bouquet of flowers and a solitary fat candle. Theo's breath caught as he sighted *the woman* standing behind the altar. It was the tall lady in his dreams, the one with the hazel eyes and the olive wreath in her hair. She was singing in unison with the worshippers. Her eyes focused on Theo's.

"What is it, Theo?" Adelayne asked, sensing his unease.

"That woman...I've...seen her before."

"You mean the statue of Ellodiere?" Adelayne nodded towards the woman behind the altar.

"Statue?" Theo asked, recovering from his initial shock. *Statue...yes. It's only a statue.* He could see that now. Though it had looked so life-like before.

"Theo, do you want to leave?" Adelayne asked, concerned.

"No...It's quite alright. It's just that it was a bit unexpected, that's all. She looks so real."

Adelayne smiled at him. "It is said the sculptor who created her likeness was amongst the best of his time and that he was madly in love with the flora goddess. Sadly, another tale tells how the sculptor went mad with grief because he could not come to terms with his mortality and the fact that he would not be able to live by her side for ever. The gods can be cruel, I suppose."

"Had it been in the goddess's power she might have granted her lover immortality or given up her god-given gift of eternal life." They both whirled around at the sound of the unexpected voice. Theo went for his sword but remembered he had not worn it tonight. They relaxed upon recognizing the speaker.

It was Zoi.

"You gave us a fright!" Theo rubbed Adelayne's shoulders to reassure her.

"I'm sorry. I didn't mean to intrude. I hadn't expected to find anyone else at the goddess's altar. You see the old nymph gods are a dying breed. Not many remain now to remember their works and their contribution to the world. However it seems that the nymphs that accompanied Queen Crystal to Alcavia have kept their faith."

"There are close to a thousand nymphs living in Alcavia and they all worship the green goddess," Adelayne said, informatively. "You worship her as well?" Adelayne asked, grabbing at the chance to learn something more about the aged woman.

"Yes, I come from a family line that pays homage to the old gods," Zoi admitted. "May I enquire the same question of you, princess?"

"I worship Athud, like the rest of my people, but I still revere my mother's goddess. I am caught between two worlds, Zoi. My love for the one does not diminish my respect for the other."

Zoi stepped up to the princess and placed a gnarled hand beneath her chin. "My dear, sweet, precious child. Be certain that Ellodiere has heard your words uttered in her temple this day and will not forget them. The lady of the green protects those beloved to her."

Theo had a thought. "Zoi, what was that you said before about the goddess and her lover?"

Zoi turned to her young companion and smiled. "Why, it's quite simple really, Theodor. The gods are unable to grant immortality to man. Only the Creator can do that. As for the gods giving up their immortality, that is equally impossible for the same reasons."

Adelayne knelt by Ellodiere's altar together with Zoi and they joined in fleeting prayer. Then the two of them got up and ventured close to Theo. They locked arms with him, one on either side, and the three of them walked out of the goddess's temple nodding at the nymphs that stood hunched over in prayer.

"Tell me Zoi, how long have you been acquainted with my mother?" Adelayne enquired as they exited the park and headed for the inner wall.

"I have known Queen Crystal of the Ghiadon Forest nymphs since her birth, my child," Zoi answered, smiling gently at the princess.

"That would make you over two hundred years old!" The princess was aware of her mother's age and had come to terms with the fact that her father would age more swiftly than his queen.

"I am old, as you put it child and it shows as well, wouldn't you say?" Zoi laughed as she showed them her wrinkles and the floppy skin of her arms. Theo had the feeling she was making fun of them.

"I don't believe I have seen you at the palace before," Adelayne pressed on.

"My presence is always with your mother and her family, my child, though I may choose to be discreet about it."

Adelayne felt a sudden warming to the old woman and on impulse gave her a hug. She was like the grandmother she had never known. Adelayne's grandmother died, grief-stricken, shortly after her husband's murder.

"Zoi, has Archon told you when we will be moving on?" Theo asked concerned. He was in no hurry to leave the princess and the city behind.

"I believe we have 'till the start of autumn before our mage decides to make his move. You're being given the chance to rest, Theodor, so don't let it go to waste." Zoi bade them good night, leaving the two of them to exchange a few tender moments before returning to their quarters.

Nem lifted the crystal glass to his lips and sipped the cool wine, glancing with apprehension at the other end of the table where a man with thin white hair and a clean shaven chin, apart from his long white moustache, was staring at him. It wasn't the man's stare that annoyed him so. It was the glint in his eye and the grin on his face every time Irene bent to whisper in Nem's ear. He had seen that look before; it was a look fathers gave him when they had plans for him and their daughters.

Eular belonged to the Alcavian aristocracy and some said he owned as many fields as the royal household -an overstatement to be sure but there was no doubt of him being wealthy. One had only to look around the lord's house to confirm this was so. On the walls hung a variety of portraits in rich oil paints and long tapestries made from the finest Hieradon silks. The room they were dining in was one of many the duke used to entertain his guests. From the ceiling hung a tall chandelier dressed in priceless crystals, probably smuggled over from Galandir; Nem made a point of being knowledgeable on precious stones and their origins; his father had taught him from a young age all a merchant needed to know.

The arched walls that led to the adjoining rooms and to the veranda were decorated with gold filigrees shaped like vine leaves. Beside the balcony doors, tall velvet drapes trimmed in golden braids hung on either side drawn to reveal the lush gardens beyond. The floor was decorated in white marble with rose striations mostly concealed beneath thick carpets originating from the far eastern Kamtai or Jed Zul Islands. The furniture was all made of heavily crafted mahogany and cherry wood. Silverware, crystal bowls, glasses and jugs filled the room in a shameless display of affluence.

"Nem, what's the matter? You look pale."

Nem turned to look at his golden-haired companion. She stared back at him with large blue innocent eyes. She had styled her hair in locks for the evening, leaving it to hang loose to her shoulders that were left bare by her dress that barely covered her bosom line and back. "Nothing's the matter, my sweet," he said, bending over to give her a light peck on the cheek. "I was just thinking how fortunate I am to be here with you tonight."

Irene winked at him and beamed a smile as she lifted her wine glass to her lips to take a long swig. She turned to look at her father's guests, smiling and leaned in the other direction to exchange conversation with a brunette lady who had been looking at Nem hungrily all night as if he were a tart ready to be devoured. Nem tried as best he could to avoid the woman's sultry looks.

"Aah, welcome, Your Eminence." Duke Eular rose from his seat and saluted as the Alcavian primate made his entrance.

"I'm honoured to be here among you, Your Grace," Primate Zerum answered in kind, accepting a glass of wine being proffered on a silver tray by one of the serving maids.

When all the guests had taken their fill of the bountiful meal that followed, the duke rose once more and beckoned to his guests to make their way out of the dining hall and into the ballroom where he promised more refreshments and entertainment. A small band forming a string quartet was playing eloquently. Two young women were playing the violin accompanied by two youths on the viola and cello. It was not long before everyone was on the dance floor with their partners.

Nem stared down at his tight black pants that were knee-high and his white socks that covered his legs to his toes. He shook his head in disbelief. He had been dressed by Irene earlier on before the event. His white shirt was laced in frills down the front and sleeves and he wore a crimson tunic that added a bit of flair to his attire. All in all, he decided he looked quite the pompous ass.

"Nem, I'd like to introduce you to His Excellency of Ramila, Sir Cleon and his lady wife Alanda." The duke approached with the official couple whilst Nem's attention had been diverted by a young girl on the dance floor. Nem turned to greet them bowing to the Ambassador. Lady Alanda extended her hand for Nem to plaster a kiss on. As Nem rose from his crouching position the coquettish woman butted her eyelids at him and stared with large brown eyes. Nem's gaze however was not on her eyes but wandered to her dress which she must have taken hours to squeeze into. Her waist was held to bursting point, it seemed, for it was hardly wider than a slim tree branch and her bosom was threatening to explode from her dress that was adorned with white pearls forming flowery patterns along the front and back. Irene noticed the fleeting exchange and tore Nem away, taking him towards the other end of the ballroom. There they encountered Primate Zerum who was dressed in his customary black robes but with a golden hem reserved for official outings.

"Young Nemarchus," said the priest. "Duke Eular tells me that you are a trader's son and that your interests lie in that direction. I've had a word with the Minister of Commerce, Slade, on the matter and he confirms that you are an apt student."

"It's true, Your Eminence, that I wish to follow in my father's footsteps but rather than being a trader I prefer to own my own fleet of ships."

"I wish you the best of luck in your endeavours...oh, and please call me Zerum. Your Eminence tends to keep me at too much of a distance from my friends."

"In that case, Zerum, call me Nem. It's the name my friends use."

"Deal." They raised their glasses. "Nem, I'd like you to meet an old acquaintance of mine."

Nem turned round to come face to face with a chubby man overly dressed in silks with a round face smiling pleasantly beneath a sweaty brow. On all his obese fingers he wore rings of gold capped by a variety of precious stones.

"You are Longman's friend, are you not?" asked the chubby fellow.

It took Nem a while to realize whom the man meant by "Longman". "Oh, you must mean Archon the mage."

"Archon...the High Sorcerer of Aldorn?"

"None other. I must apologize on his behalf for his little lie but the mage is a secretive character and distrustful of people he meets for the first time. You are Master Griffin, are you not?"

"I am, and pleased to make the acquaintance of a fellow up-and-coming merchant."

Nem took the man's plump hand in a handshake. He decided he liked the pleasant fellow. "Is *the Flying Duchess* the pride of your fleet, Master Griffin?"

"She is the *only* ship in my fleet, my dear fellow, though in the past I used to own five trading vessels. Keeping an eye out on five ships and their captains proved a taxing experience, so I opted to sell them all and bought *the Flying Duchess* fresh out of the fabricating dockyards of Balsovia. She went on her first maiden voyage to Ameron one year ago and I've been travelling with her ever since."

"I had a hunch she was of Balsovian stock," Nem said. "Nobody in Thalagia makes finer and more beautiful ships–if one excludes the river cruisers of the Ghiadon Forest nymphs."

"It's true that no ship can compete in beauty with the nymphs' river vessels but you will agree that the clipper ships of the Midlands are a lot more practical for a voyage out at sea."

"Undoubtedly." Nem nodded emphatically. "The nymph river ships are made for manoeuvring in close quarters and require skilled operators at the rudder whereas the clipper ships rely heavily on the rigging crew and the steersman at the cockpit making them easier to commandeer at sea."

"Nem," the primate ventured to draw his attention. "I have spoken with Slade and the king. We all agree that you will need a helping hand to achieve your objectives. Since the church is always looking out for talented men like yourself I have a business proposition for you."

Nem's attention was riveted on the clergyman. "I'm listening."

"The church of Alcavia is willing to fund your training provided that you are willing to offer service to the church."

"I'm afraid I'm not very religious, Your–Zerum. In what way could the church possibly benefit from a man of my background and talents?"

"Why not leave that up to us to decide?"

"Ok, but it's your funeral–please forgive the pun."

"We have a deal then?"

"Only for as long as I am training, and not for more than, shall we say, a four-year traineeship?"

"Deal." They sealed it with a handshake. Nem looked over at Griffin who smiled in approval then back at the primate who had a wicked twinkle in his eye. Had he gotten more than he bargained for?

♦ CHAPTER 16 ♦

Disruption

Summer came and went far swifter than Theo could have imagined possible. He had grown stronger over the past six months under the careful training of both colonel Ajax and Roxette. He was feeling more vigorous than he had ever felt before and his ability at using the gift was improving also, albeit at a slower rate than his physical strength.

He waited for his friend and the princes to arrive for early morning practice. Colonel Ajax had informed them they would be using their swords today. They had fought using all types of weapons. Last week they had been training with axes and the week before with spears. Every week they tried something new until they completed the circle back to the sword.

Ajax approached, standing before Theo, measuring the young man with a gaze that left no weakness undetected. "I see you're packing your *Lithureal* blade. Good, you'll need it today."

Nem arrived with Prince Leon wearing his dragon shirt and long pants. The prince was looking more and more like his namesake with each passing day. His mane of hair combined with his pristine physique to give him the look of a young lion. He had no equal amongst the cadets at the Alcavian Military Academy.

At the academy, Leon was given the chance to increase his strength all the more. In Alcavia, Ajax had explained, there was no other way to lead. The king and his heirs had to be every bit as skilled in fighting as the best of their military men, and the ability to rule was judged by the ruler's ability at wielding his sword. King Dreyfus himself, in his youth, had been a skilled swordsman and still was, though he now relied more on cunning and experience gained on the field.

Armend arrived wearing a freshly pressed shirt with the lion emblem blazed across the front. In his right hand he carried a long sword which he must have spent the morning tending, for the blade gleamed in the sunlight. He threw Theo an ominous look placing himself squarely before him. "Time to find out what you're made of, farm boy." He spat the words in greeting, his upper lip curling above barred teeth like a jackal's, his eyes set deep beneath his brows with darkened circles as though he had not slept in weeks. His face was much paler than Theo ever remembered it to have been.

"Alright," Ajax cut in. "Theo, you team up with Armend, and Nem, you team up with Leon. I want a clean fight, try not to cut each other and halt as soon as you hear my call. Keep your nerve and your tempers under control and remember we are training for when it will be needed. We are not each other's enemy." Ajax's words seemed to fall on deaf ears where Armend was concerned. He sneered at Theo, swerving his sword dangerously.

Before Ajax had the chance to call out for them to commence, Armend pounced forward delivering blows at an impossible speed. Theo, caught off guard, was just about able to repel the onslaught. Armend pressed him without repose. He was like a demon possessed. Theo put all his skill, everything he had learned from his father Elron, and from Ajax and Roxette into deflecting the prince's blows. Inch by inch he was being forced to give ground. Armend laughed triumphantly at Theo's futility and carried on hammering him relentlessly.

After the first few moments Theo was sweating profusely his breathing coming in huge gulps. He knew that if he dropped his guard Armend would not hesitate to cut him. The confidence he had felt in the morning, before practice, was being shattered. *Where did Armend get such strength?* It was inhuman, the way he just kept coming. At some point, when Theo was beginning to see stars in his vision from his exertions, he thought he heard Ajax call out it was time for them to take a five-minute break.

"We don't need a break, do we farm boy?" Armend grunted coming in for a new blow to Theo's head. Theo just managed to deflect the blow before it would have decapitated him. He was too out of breath to answer. All his efforts were being expended fending off his attacker. He was near the end of his strength and was using up his reserves to keep on his feet.

Armend lunged at him from the side, changing tactics. Theo brought down his sword deflecting the full strength of the blow but his opponent's blade sliced his arm causing blood to gush out of the wound. Ajax called out again but was incoherent; Theo was too dazed from the sight of his own blood and from his fatigue to be able to hear clearly what Ajax was saying.

Armend kept coming. On and on he pressed causing Theo to fall back. Theo stumbled as he tried to distance himself from his attacker's blade. Then with a quick twist of his wrist Armend took another slice out of Theo's thigh. Theo shivered, realizing that Armend was out of control. He was in a killing frenzy and Ajax was unable to interfere for fear of making matters worse. He had no choice but to continue shouting at the prince in the hope that he would be able to draw his attention.

Theo saw from the corner of his eye that the other two had stopped their sparring. Nem was anxiously waiting for his chance to cut in and save his friend. But Theo and

Armend were firmly locked in combat. Anyone who interfered now would either have to kill or be killed. He panicked. He moved backwards faster in his attempt to flee from Armend's wrath. He tripped and fell. His sword was knocked away from him. He turned just as Armend placed both feet on either side of him. Armend's eyes were wide with blood lust as he placed both hands on the hilt of his sword readying to deliver the underhand death blow. Theo waited. It seemed an eternity passed. The blade began its descent. Theo knew it was all over.

Just as Theo braced himself for the blade to enter his chest, the sword flew from Armend's hand. The prince was thrown by an invisible force backwards several yards away. He fell hard and began to kick, convulsing and clutching at his throat. Foam began to dribble from his mouth, his eyes bulging as if they were going to pop out of his head. Theo was confused and his stomach was churning. *What happened?* By all accounts he should be dead.

Archon materialized out of nowhere. Roxette was by his side, a worried frown crossing her face as she knelt beside Theo, lifting his head and shoulders gently into her lap. She passed her fingers over Theo's torso and limbs searching for any wounds. She found the small gush on his arm and thigh.

"Is he alright?" Archon asked worriedly, his face dark with consternation.

"Nothing broken," Roxette answered firmly. "His cuts are not deep and will mend quickly. He will have nothing but bruises to show for it but if you hadn't intervened it would have ended badly. Armend was completely crazed! I have never seen such hatred expressed amongst allies."

Archon looked worriedly in the direction of the prince who had gone still and was breathing hoarsely with laboured breaths. He was still foaming at the mouth. Prince Leon bent over him cradling his friend's head in his arms.

"Theo, I'm sorry but I couldn't cut in." Nem approached and knelt down beside Theo taking his hand in his. The worry was plain to be seen on his face. "It happened so fast we had no time to react."

Theo got up slowly shaking off the trembling that overwhelmed him after his narrow escape with death. He looked at the prince sprawled on the ground. Archon approached the prince apprehensively and knelt down beside him.

Leon looked at him fiercely. "What have you done to him, wizard?"

"This is not my work," Archon replied, shaking his head whilst examining the fallen prince closely. He placed a hand above the prince's face and murmured a few words. Theo felt a tickling sensation as the gift was employed. He looked at Armend and noticed that whereas before his eyes had been staring vacantly, now they were shut. He was no longer foaming at the mouth. Leon wiped Armend's drool away with his shirt. However the prince's body was still convulsing.

Archon pulled Armend's sleeves up and turned the prince's wrists towards him. "Here is our culprit," he said, pointing at the needle marks on the prince's arms and looked directly at Ajax. "You never realized?"

Ajax looked incredulously at the prince's yellow punctured arms. He shook his head in disbelief and dismay. "He never took off his shirt or rolled up his sleeves in practice. I suppose I should have realized from his ailing condition and from the off days when he was as strong as an ox that something was wrong".

"Can you tell if he'll recover?" Leon asked, his anger replaced by worry.

"Bring him to his quarters and I'll have Zoi take a look at him. She is more familiar with poisons and their remedies. She might be able to do something for him with her herbs."

They led the prince to his room. As soon as Adelayne heard about the prince's condition she raced to his side taking his pale hands into hers. Armend was not responding to his surroundings but continued to tremble. His breathing was ragged. Zoi and Queen Crystal were in the room bent over Prince Armend's form examining his eyes, lips and arms. Zoi knelt beside Armend's bed and discovered, concealed beneath it, the tin box containing the drugs and needles.

"It's very difficult to recognize the symptoms of salith weed," Zoi replied to colonel Ajax's question on the contents of the tin box, thus granting him, in a way, absolution for his oversight with the prince. The colonel felt responsible for the prince's plight and was blaming himself for what had happened.

"Salith weed?" Leon asked, looking at the old woman with puzzlement.

"Yes. It's a rare herb cultivated in the Sul Mountains by the snake races. Salith means 'slow death' in Zaldese. It is highly addictive and, if taken over long periods of time, leads to the deterioration of the lungs and poisoning of the blood stream. It used to be administered in small doses to the Zaldese military in the past to give them increased vigour and to heighten their malice just before entering battle. It proved very effective but led to the snake peoples' death after a decade of using the weed, so its use was banned. In humans the poisonous weed acts more swiftly."

"Zoi, I'll see what I can do with the gift whilst you prepare a salve to extract the poison from his blood," Queen Crystal said, looking at the mage then at the old woman who nodded back at her. The queen placed both hands over the prince's body and moved them over his trembling form letting her fingers hover above him. Once again Theo felt that tingling sensation. "Archon, have you used the gift on him?" she asked, whilst continuing to move her hands above the youth. They all turned to look at the mage; Leon looked with some measure of suspicion. Adelayne simply looked anxious.

"Yes. I tried to set the flows of his positive life force straight. They were tangled around him like thread round a ball."

"I can discern your attempts to set the threads straight," Crystal said, bending over the prince with concentration. "However it's going to need a subtler hand and a lot more effort. I believe I know what is required to set his energy flows right, though I have become a bit rusty at using the gift. In any case, I'll give it my best."

"I'll keep watch over you and help in any way I can," Archon offered. Zoi looked up at them both and smiled encouragingly at the queen.

Crystal shut her eyes in concentration. Her hands emanated a soft amber glow as she began her healing weaves.

Serilia looked on with interest. "A sorceress of the Fauna agent," she whispered, looking at Crystal's orange light in surprise. She had never seen this side of the gift at work before. She was more familiar with the sorcerers using the blue light of Water, like her mother, or white of the Light agent, like her brother and Archon, though Archon's light was more silvery than white.

Theo was completely perplexed by Crystal's procedures. Archon had been right about healing being a form of magic which not all could comprehend. Theo was sufficiently advanced at using the gift now to be able to see the flows of Crystal's life force, like the threads of a spinster at her wheel. The problem for him was that the 'tapestry' Crystal was weaving was so complex and utilised so many different agents of the gift simultaneously that he could not follow the procedures. *Ah, there she is using the Water agent*, he affirmed, recognizing that part of the gift. *But where does Earth belong in all this?* he wondered, as Crystal called upon the agent. Zoi meanwhile was giving commands to colonel Ajax to keep him preoccupied and to make him feel he was contributing somehow.

"He has a fever and his heart is beating too fast," Zoi commented, placing the back of one gnarled hand to Armend's temple, that was wet with drops of perspiration, whilst with her other hand she held the prince's wrist and was measuring his pulse rate. "I will administer red leaf hemlock to reduce the fever and cripple jack ivy leaf to help calm his spasms."

Crystal threw a sceptical glance at the old woman. "Are you sure about those two? They're both very poisonous from the little I know about plants."

"Yeah, mother's right," Leon added, looking suspiciously at the old woman. "We use the sap from cripple jack ivy to taint our arrows with its poison. It leads to paralysis and death in our victims."

"Well then hurry up and get me some if you want to aid your friend," Zoi answered tartly. "If administered in minute doses it leads to a relaxation of the muscles which is what he needs right now."

Leon looked at his mother who nodded back at him then set off to find some of the leaf.

"Now where do I get red leaf hemlock from?" Zoi asked, looking at the queen.

"I think I have some stashed away somewhere in my room," Ajax answered. "I collected some when I was on my rounds. You never know when you might need it against your foe," he added to Crystal's questioning look. "We like to keep our Mountain nymph friends on their toes, no offence meant," he said, turning to Roxette.

"None taken," she answered from a corner of the room where she was standing looking at the healers at work. Ajax left in search of the remedy.

"What do you suggest we use to draw the poison out of his veins?" Crystal turned to the old woman, releasing her spell for a minute whilst she recovered her breath. She was breathing hard as if she had been labouring in the fields.

"Hmm. We could try to use a night lily leaf with a salve."

"I'll go and find the maidservants," Archon suggested. "There should be plenty of the leaf stashed away in the kitchens. No household is complete without it; after all it is used for the slightest cuts and abrasions."

Theo left the prince's room when he made certain the young man was not in any immediate danger. Zoi had explained to him that the salith weed was probably responsible for the prince's hostile attitude towards him but Theo was not convinced. He looked out of Armend's bedroom window only to discover that he was gazing upon the king's gardens and the bench where he and Adelayne had been meeting every night for the past few weeks.

Later during the day Queen Crystal and Zoi emerged from the prince's bedroom looking exhausted. Adelayne remained behind to keep Armend company, though the prince could not sense her presence and according to Zoi was in a deep slumber from which he was not going to wake up any time soon.

They met in the king's throne room and seated themselves. The serving maids moved amongst them, and sensing the dark mood, offered them refreshments in silence. The king sat on his throne listening to his wife who was relating the events that had led to the prince's current state. His face was grave at the news. He turned to his guests, his eyes coming to rest on colonel Ajax.

"My wife tells me that the prince will take a long while to recover. He may need till next spring before he is able to move around unaided and twice that long under close supervision to recover from his dependency on the drug. And there's no guarantee that he will overcome his addiction. You must take a team of men, colonel, and head for Ameron with the prince. It is only right that he spend this time with his family."

Archon got up from his chair and cleared his throat. "My lord, I beg to differ with this suggestion though at first glance it seems to have merit. You see, I believe the prince will not be able to make the long trip. It's a good ten days hard riding to get to Ameron and the prince should not be subjected to such a strenuous journey in his current condition."

"Then what is it you suggest, mage?"

"My king, the prince must be taken with all haste to the Sisters of Athud where I suggest he remains until he completely recovers from his illness and until the sisters are convinced that he has overcome his desire for the drug."

"I must agree with Sir Archon, my lord," Primate Zerum said. He had come to seek the king's aid on matters concerning the church. "The sisters are well known for their healing skills and for their patience and perseverance which are all qualities that will be required to achieve the task at hand. I will provide an escort of church soldiers to accompany the prince to his destination."

"That settles it then." The king stood up and cast his gaze around the throne room. "The prince leaves for Sulicia Island on the morrow and will be accompanied by the church paramilitary escort."

"My lord, I too will accompany the prince to the Sisters of Athud," said the mage, causing a murmur amongst his companions. "The Council of Light would not allow me to stand idly by in such a matter. I too feel an obligation towards the boy and his family."

"Then so be it." And with that the king left the throne room accompanied by his wife and some of his courtiers.

The group looked with astonishment at Archon. They had been expecting to leave in the other direction now that summer was over; Roxette stated as much.

"I'll be gone for a short period only," Archon answered. "If I'm not back in ten days then set off for Ghiadon without me. I'll catch up with you."

"But Archon, what are we to do in Ghiadon?" Nestor came to stand close to the mage peering at him with a hawk-like expression reading every hint of emotion that crossed the mage's face.

"I've been commanded to deliver Zoi safely to the Forest nymph's kingdom. You will have to finish the task in my stead if I am late in returning."

"Why all the haste?" Theo joined in the conversation. He wanted to delay leaving Alcavia as much as possible. He felt safe here, *and there is one more reason to stay*; his thoughts went to Adelayne.

"You forget our reason for coming to Alcavia, Theodor." The mage stared at him meaningfully. "Our red dragon will soon be on the move, and there is the other matter we discussed in private." He turned to the group and said decisively. "Should I not return in the time we agreed, then you will obey Zoi like you have done with me. Roxette will guide you safely to your destination. Theodor!" He turned to concentrate on his apprentice. "Seek the guidance of the Emerald Forest Queen. She is a corner stone to the Council of Light and will relay to you what is needed for us to achieve our goal. Do exactly as she instructs without questioning her decisions. She works for the benefit of all Thalagia and knows best how you can serve our people."

With that grim note they left the hall. Theo felt uncomfortable with what had been said. He was supposed to trust his future to a woman he had never met. But then again, he had only known Archon for a few months. Once again he felt the decisions governing his future were not his to make.

It had been four weeks since Archon had set off with the prince and the church soldiers to seek the aid of the Sisters of Athud. They had taken a battleship belonging to the Templar knights based at Jade Island. Theo and Nem had stood on the docks of Alcavia's port admiring the ship as it set sail eastbound, its white flag marked by the yellow flame of Athud flapping in the wind. They had remained there casting their gaze out at sea reflectively till the large ship dwindled to a small spot on the golden early morning horizon.

Now the time had come, Theo was loath to leave Alcavia and begin the journey east to Ghiadon and the Emerald Forest. He felt secure at the fortress even under the constant shadow of the Dragon's Foot Mountains. And he was tired of being on the run. He had found a refuge where he had a chance to rest and get stronger...and to indulge in pleasantries that had been denied him for a long while. His mind wandered as it often did to Adelayne. They had become very close. He couldn't help the feelings that welled up inside him every time he thought of her. Everything about her excited him: her brightness, her beauty, the gracefulness of her movements, her gentle manner which contrasted sharply with her sharp military appearance.

When she smiled at him her eyes would sparkle like gemstones and his pulse would race, the way it did the very first time he set eyes on her. His palms still sweated when she approached and his eyes focused on her lips of their own volition. He felt he could spend day and night with her and still not get his fill, like a man travelling through the desert who never seems to quench his thirst, no matter how much water he drinks.

He was going to meet with Adelayne again tonight. He walked over to the chest in his room and pulled out a small box, placing it carefully in his cloak. Then he approached the bedroom window and looked out to the gardens below that were bathed in starlight. There were also a few lantern posts kept with their fires burning throughout the night to light the pathways close to the citadel perimeter. Adelayne had requested they meet at the citadel entrance vault, close to midnight. She commented that she had been neglecting her care of Assima, her silver female dragon, and that she was going to go on her rounds tonight to give the dragon the chance to stretch her wings.

There was an unwritten but millennia old law that stated that no dragon was permitted to fly without the escort of its dragonstrider, which was why the red dragon that had fled the Witch Lord's realm was considered so dangerous. He was a free spirit running wild and contrary to the laws set down by man and beast, laws hidden in the dark passages of time when the great lizards had bowed to man's supremacy. The red was a renegade, like a wild stallion upsetting the balance amongst the tamed horses in a pen. He had to be cornered and made to submit or he would have to be destroyed.

Theo placed his sturdy woollen woodsman's cloak around his shoulders and prepared to leave his room. It was autumn time once more and the nights were getting colder. He had purchased a few new garments from the stalls around Alcavia and a suit from the port but had also kept his woodsman's clothes in a bundle in his room cupboard ready for when he would inevitably have to set out on his journey east. Zoi was the one who had caused the most commotion; she had wanted to leave as soon as the ten days since Archon's departure for Sulicia expired. However, Nestor and Emeralda had been a great help in convincing Zoi to wait a few more days. They both sensed the youngsters' reluctance to leave Alcavia so soon and Roxette wanted to give Archon more time before they were forced to set off without him.

Roxette had been on edge ever since she had been parted from Archon. She had wanted to accompany him to Sulicia Island but he had commanded her to stay with the group. As the days wore on and still bore no sign of Archon's return, Roxette grew all the more anxious. If it wasn't for Archon's direct orders to the contrary, Roxette would have found a ship weeks ago and set sail to find her mage lord. But as it was, the king sent a small party in the fourth week to find out what was keeping the mage and to bring news on the prince's progress. That was a couple of days ago. By all accounts they should be returning to Alcavia soon.

Theo mulled over these thoughts as he made his way to the citadel entrance. He gazed into the shadows and was startled as a figure separated from the sides of the wall and came towards him. It had been well concealed. He placed his hand to his sword beneath his cloak in readiness but released his grip on the hilt when his nostrils recognised the soft lavender scent assailing them.

Adelayne melted into his embrace, pressing her lips against his, her bosom flattened against his chest, her protruding dagger hilts poking his ribs; he hardly felt them. They remained locked together thus for what seemed like fleeting moments to Theo but in reality was much longer. He wanted to take her up to his room and forget all about the night prowl. She was all that was on his mind right now.

"Are you ready?" Adelayne inquired bringing him out of his stupor.

"What? Oh, yes, my mind was wandering." He reached into his coat pocket and pulled out the small box placing it gently in Adelayne's hand.

"What's this?" There was a tremor in her voice.

"Open it," he said evasively.

"Oh Theo..." She placed her hand over her mouth in astonished delight. "They're beautiful," she said, as she withdrew the earrings from their gift box to study them. They were fashioned in white gold and studded with tiny emeralds.

"They match the rest of your jewellery. Emeralda and Serilia helped me pick them out from Port Alcavia."

"They're lovely." Adelayne drew him towards her and planted a kiss on his lips. She placed the earrings gingerly back in their box and hid them in her cloak. "I have nothing to offer you in return," she said, dismayed.

Theo stole another lingering kiss. "That's all I require from you," he answered softly. The princess blushed happily.

Adelayne led him to the west wing of Alcavia's inner circle where the dragons occupied their lair. The king had chosen to place them close to the citadel so they would be within easy reach when their services were required. Alcavia's only defence against attack from the skies was its three remaining silver dragons. Their proximity to the fortress was far more important than the stretch of land they occupied in the wealthiest part of the city.

Soon they arrived at the dragons' lair. It was a natural outcrop formed by large granite rocks jutting out of the ground forming a pyramid with an opening to one side –the entrance to the lair. Vapour was rising from the pyramid entrance like the fumes from a hot spring. Adelayne approached with determination whereas Theo followed with apprehension. He had met, in the last year, several dragons – if one counted his trip with the blue dragons and his short encounters with the red, albeit in his dreams. But he still felt overly awed by their presence. His senses warned him that the beasts could extinguish his existence as easily as a Hadir alligator could squash a river rodent.

He believed deep down inside that he would never overcome the fear, intermingled with awe and excitement that overwhelmed him whenever he was close to the great lizards. To him they belonged to another era, when man was no more than an ape-form seeking the shelter of the mountain caves to avoid being devoured by the beasts that ruled the earth at a time when she was young and spewing forth poisonous fumes and red hot lava like a pregnant woman labouring to give birth. When the earth was going through her changes, millions of years before her crust cooled to form what was now Thalagia, the lizards had reigned supreme both on land and in the skies.

These descendants of the dragon race were living proof of those times. Somewhere in the distant past the land lizards had met with their extinction; their flying cousins had for reasons unknown chosen to relinquish their domination of the earth and had allowed mankind to gain a foothold. Dragons however were not to be taken lightly. They were highly intelligent beasts with a past shrouded in mystery and with senses highly tuned. They knew how to speak in several human tongues and were also fluent in the language of the Ancients. It was said that a dragon could not be lied to. They were masters at unveiling deception and were ruthless in their punishment of those who did not treat them with the respect they deserved.

They entered the dark lair and waited for their eyes to adjust to the pitch black interior. Theo could hear what sounded like the rumbling of mini earthquakes. The air was heavy with vapour, like a descending mist, causing Theo to cough and gulp more air into his lungs. As his eyes began to adjust he saw three pairs of yellow lights. One pair moved towards him and Adelayne. He clutched at her arm preparing to pull her back out of the lair.

"You come to me once more, mistress." The walls of the lair lit up in reddish light as the dragon's breath blew towards Theo and Adelayne. Then they were thrown back into darkness with the temporary sharp light imprinted on their vision.

"Yes, Assima, I come to ride the skies with you and I bring a friend. Will you accept Theodor Maren'therin on your back, my sister?" It was the customary way with which a dragonstrider addressed their dragon companion. The link between dragon and strider was age old. A dragon chose their strider and not the other way round. There was a special bond between them and a respect as of peers and equals.

The twin globes of yellow moved closer through the darkness of the lair. Theodor could feel the dragon's warm breath upon his face and trembled involuntarily at her proximity. The dragon sniffed at him like a hound. He felt his hair rise towards her snout as she drew in deep breaths that sounded like the north wind.

"He has your scent on him, this Far Strider of yours." *Was that the sound of jealousy in her voice?* Theodor stood staring into the dragon's eyes which filled his vision. He was mesmerized by them like a deer is paralyzed before a crouching panther.

"Don't look directly into her eyes," Adelayne whispered in his ear, bringing him out of his hypnosis.

"The boy may ride with us." The dragon decided at last. "Come let us take to the skies." The other two dragons came close to take in Theo's scent and to greet their princess.

Soon Assima and her pair of human riders were soaring above Alcavia with Theo sitting behind Adelayne holding her slim waist firmly. He felt the thrill of riding on a dragon's back once more and let the autumn wind blow through his hair and face. He clutched his woollen cloak closer about him, bending to the dragon's banking motions. They were following an easterly route across the Valdoric Sea, heading towards the peninsula that separated Alcavia from Ramila's shores. Before long they were above the small hills north of the Twin Isles. The silver dragon circled around the hills, the moonlight reflecting upon its scales that shimmered like drops of crystal, making the dragon seem like it was made of liquid mercury.

"Is he still at his cave?" Adelayne shouted above the noise of the wind so she could be heard. Theo wandered which "he" she meant before realization dawned upon him.

"The red is no longer in the hills, mistress. I do not sense his presence and his scent has grown weaker. He has been gone for a week by my estimate." Theo felt the rumbling between his legs as the dragon spoke in her deep booming voice.

The dragon beat its large canvas-like wings that appeared to be made of toughened hide. They gained the height they had lost whilst circling the hills and headed north westerly, following the line of the Apalachus River that was a dark mass in the night. Theo remembered the river from having seen it on the map in the king's study. He and the rest of the group had been shown the map by Colonel Ajax in preparation for their journey east. But to look upon Leonium from the wings of a dragon was to absorb in detail what no map could provide. Even in darkness he could distinguish from the starlight the varying contours of the winding rivers and gently rolling hills; Theo could smell in the air the scents of the coniferous trees in the mountains as opposed to that of the harvested grain fields below.

As they approached the foot of the Dragon's Foot Mountains, Theo sensed a change in the wind blowing from the north. It held the promise of a cold winter approaching. They were passing the Apalachus River when Adelayne gave a signal to her dragon to start her descent towards a small dark spot that appeared to be in the centre of a glade in the forest. As they lost altitude the spot grew in size, materialising into the shape of a horse and a man spread on the ground motionless. Assima approached with caution. Theo could sense Adelayne's trepidation by the set of her shoulders. The princess reached behind drawing both her swords from their scabbards. The blades sang as they were released from their sheaths, filling the night air with their ringing song.

"Be careful mistress, it may be a trap," the dragon cautioned, as it alighted on the ground and Adelayne prepared to jump from its back. Theo cast his gaze warily about the clearing but could see no danger hidden in the surrounding trees. He realized with trepidation that it was at just such a spot near the same river that his grandmother Rubin had been murdered. *Is that why I am tormented with this sense of foreboding?* Maybe it was the sight of the dead man and horse on the ground.

They approached the still forms slowly. Theo drew his *lithureal* blade. The man on the ground had several arrows protruding from his back and neck. The blood was dry on his body so he had probably lain there for several hours. His steed too had many arrow shafts protruding from its flanks, shoulders and belly. From the look of the steed and the clothing of the dead man he was someone of import.

"I know this man," Adelayne said, bending down to take a closer look at him. "This is lord Geramir. He was a friend of my father's and was from one of the oldest Alcavian families of the inner circle. But what would he be doing so far north of the trade road, and alone at the foot of the mountains?"

Adelayne had no sooner uttered her question before Theo was brought to his knees clutching his fists to his ears in an attempt to squeeze out the horrid screech that filled the air. He looked in the direction of the screeching sound and realized it was being emanated from Assima who was beating her torn left wing and crying out in pain. By the look of her wing bones that had pierced the skin, the damage to her wing was extensive. A red blur was whirling around the silver dragon and for a moment Theo thought it was the red dragon of his dreams. Then he realized that there were three of the beasts. These were older creatures.

Theo cast his gaze around as hunching shapes yielding an assortment of weapons materialised from the surrounding forest. Several held torches to light their way as they closed in on their prey. Adelayne had already crossed swords with three of their assailants. Theo was being approached by men intent on harming him from all directions. His previous sense of foreboding had turned into a red beacon of warning in his mind's eye. *Danger, danger*, it kept sending to him. He was conscious of the fact that he had discovered a new side to his gift, but the warning had come too late.

As they approached, he realised his attackers were all similarly attired in stout black clothing and boots. In their hands they held wicked-looking blades and daggers. A few held long-handled axes with jutting points like spear heads. Others held morningstars which they whirled in anticipation. All had evil grins on their faces their eyes slits as they concentrated on their prey. Theo held his blade before him in a futile attempt to ward off his attackers. From the corner of his eye he could see Adelayne had dispatched her three but more fell in to fill the void left by the fallen.

Theo's pulse raced and his limbs trembled. Assima was screeching like a mad creature to his right as the red dragons lunged and snapped at her. One of the dark figures flew at Theo with his sword. In a reflex action Theo met the onslaught and the two blades rang with the sound of metal on metal. Others advanced from the sides. Theo swung his sword in all directions. He knew he was doomed. He had never faced so many opponents before; during training it had always been one on one. He avoided a sword swipe that would have beheaded him and met an axe blow capable of severing a limb. He made to move backwards to avoid the onslaught but realized there was nowhere to go; there were four more behind. His opponents grinned triumphantly. They had realized in the first few moments that their quarry was no match for them and were toying with him.

Suddenly one with a morningstar loosed his weapon. It flew towards Theo hitting him squarely in the arm, just where it met the shoulder. Theo cried out with pain as the vile spikes punched his skin. He felt a jarring, as of bone being dislocated. His sword fell from his useless fingers. Tears welled up in his eyes and stars began to dance in his vision. He fainted.

When Theo came round he was being clutched painfully by the hair, his arms firmly held behind his back. The pain in his dislocated shoulder was horrendous causing him to feel nauseous. He almost lost his senses again. He looked towards Adelayne and was surprised to find she was still keeping her assailants at bay. Several bodies were littered around her and she was breathing hoarsely. Theo felt an overpowering shame at having succumbed so soon to his opponents without having taken even one life. Looking to the silver dragon he could see that the beast was in mortal danger. One of the red dragons had leaned its full weight on her broken wing whilst another pressed down on her tail to keep it from thrashing about with its deadly end spikes. The third dragon straddled her silver back and clutched her by the nape.

One of Theo's assailants held a sword to his neck and pressed it hard, causing a gash that sent blood trickling down Theo's throat.

"Princess Adelayne." The calm voice belonged to a tall man attired similarly to the rest of the attackers, though he had a more commanding presence. The light from the torches revealed his face and gold streaks that tipped his otherwise jet-black hair. Theo only just realized from their pointy ears that his assailants were nymph kind. "Princess, do not carry on so for you might hurt yourself, and our master would not be pleased."

Adelayne turned a hate-filled glare in the direction of the speaker. She drew her blade across the neck of another of her opponents, causing his blood to spurt out in front of her before she released him to fall lifeless at her feet.

The man with the gold-tipped hair sneered at her and pointed at Theo. "My princess, the choice is entirely your own. Would you have us kill your friend and your dragon?" As if to reinforce his words the nymphs holding Theo's arms pulled them back tighter, forcing him to cry out in pain. The nymph with the sword to his throat let the tip cut deeper. "Come now, be a good girl, surrender and we will spare their lives. We are not after this feeble boy or your dragon. The dragon will not be able to give chase with that broken wing of hers anyway so we'll spare her if you behave. Come, save your friends. Our master, Zarzbudin, is already preparing a warm reception for you in his mountain hall. Decide, quickly!" He motioned to his red dragons. They bit into Assima.

"Do not surrender on my account to these brigand dogs, mistress," the dragon hissed from between clenched teeth. Once again Theo felt a pang of guilt at the dragon's show of courage. He himself felt terrified at the prospect of dying.

The man motioned to the nymphs holding Theo. However hard he tried he could not help screaming with pain. Adelayne's eyes softened as she looked towards him and Assima with compassion. Theo could tell she was being torn between her desire to slay more of her enemy before being taken down, and her wish to save her friends.

"How do I know you will keep your word?" Adelayne asked. The nymphs surrounding her kept their eyes trained on her swords which were dripping with their fallen comrades' blood.

"I give you my word, as general in the ranks of the Dragon's Foot Mountain troops. In any case, we will need a courier to deliver our message to your father," he said, smiling triumphantly as he pulled out a small paper scroll from inside his dark tunic. "If you come with us we will relinquish our hold on your friends. I swear this as a nymph–and on my ancestors."

Theo realized that Adelayne did not have much of a choice. She was not going to be able to keep up her struggle for long, and the man's words had a ring of truth in them. It was plain that their intent was to abduct the princess and be off. If they had wanted to dispatch them all they could have done so, at least where he and the dragon were concerned.

Adelayne looked at Theo as something passed between them. It hurt Theo deep down inside turning his bowels to water. He felt utterly wretched as he clung to that look. "Tell my father, that whatever is in that letter, he is not to come after me. Tell him never to surrender even one square inch of Alcavia to the Witch Lord and his minions," she said, spitting at the nearest Mountain nymph. She stepped forward causing the nymphs around her to tense and bare their weapons. She reversed her grip on her swords and held them out to the nymphs directly before her. They tentatively reached out and snatched the blades from her grasp. Another two moved behind the princess gripping her by the arms firmly so she could not move.

"Careful with our prize," the gold-haired nymph commanded. "Our orders were to deliver the princess without a scratch and I intend to do just that." Then he turned his gaze to Adelayne's companions. Theo found himself staring into the eyes of a man who exuded confidence and pride. His muscled form and controlled movements gave witness to his training. He had an assassin's way of moving that reminded Theo of Roxette. His eyes were dark like the rest of the Mountain nymphs, below thin eyebrows crossing over a small hawk-like nose. As he approached, Theo expected him to give the order for the nymph with the blade tip at his throat to sink it in and end his puny life.

"Tell King Dreyfus that I, Barack, Commander of the Mountain Nymph forces, am the one responsible for his brother's death." Theo heard a commotion as Adelayne tried to wriggle out of her captors' grasp.

"You filthy swine! I should have killed you first, you son of a mountain whore!"

"There, there now princess. Calm down and put a hold on your acid tongue or I'll be forced to defy my orders and deliver you mute to our lord." Then turning to Theo he continued. "Tell Dreyfus that I await him if he's man enough to leave the safety of his citadel and venture forth to challenge me one on one." Then the Mountain nymph whirled around and approached the red dragon holding Assima by the nape of the neck. "We are done here, Voltan. Release her. Let it not be said that Barack cannot keep his word to a royal princess," he said, his voice thick with sarcasm.

The red dragon was noticeably larger than the other two. He released Assima's neck grudgingly, keeping just out of reach of her snapping jaws. "You ask too much of me strider. Her blood is sweet like her father's was before I took away his last breath."

Assima roared and heaved her body, managing to inch forward a couple of steps before being borne down by the weight of the other two. Voltan placed a clawed paw with contempt on Assima's head, pinning her to the ground like a handler a snake's head with his cloven stick.

"You *will* obey me, Voltan," Barack said with a menacingly low voice which brooked no disobedience. Voltan craned his neck and blew out a jet of flame that lit the night sky as he screamed with frustrated fury. He let go of Assima lowering his large frame so Barack could straddle his back.

Adelayne was tied hand and foot with rope and thrown unceremoniously across Voltan's back in front of Barack. She kicked and shouted choice curses at the Mountain nymphs who just laughed back at her. The way she was tied, she could do no more than squirm. The rest of the Mountain nymphs dissolved into the surrounding woods whilst the three red dragons with their masters took to the air. The last thing Theo remembered before blackness covered his vision was a thump followed by a blinding white light.

He woke with his head ringing and felt a small bump at the back of his head. He rolled on his back and opened his eyes to find himself staring into twin golden globes. He gave a start and rolled away. As he tried to get up, his head reeled forcing him to fall back again.

"Where did Adelayne discover you?" The sound of contempt was plain in the dragon's voice.

Theo allowed himself a few moments to focus and for his surroundings to stop swirling about. Finally he got up and began to search for his sword. *It has not proved of much use in my hands*, he thought bitterly, however he did not intend to leave it lying around; it was a gift he had no right to discard. He found it along with Adelayne's twin blades and a collection of her daggers. He almost threw up at the sight of the bodies littering the opening in the woods, testament to Adelayne's struggle before she submitted to her attackers to save his wretched life.

They made their way slowly away from the clearing towards the foot of the mountains. Assima was searching for a cave of some sort to shelter in. She was in no condition to fly and her thick blue blood was trickling over her left wing, tainting it as it spread. They found what they were looking for. Littered with the bones of large game, it had probably been occupied by a mountain bear. It would serve. Its lip was just high enough to admit entrance to the dragon that filled the interior with its long scaled frame. Theo sat in the centre of the cave at the dragon's feet staring out at the night sky.

"I'll stay with you the night, then tomorrow I will set off for Alcavia to fetch aid. That wing of yours will require the skills of a healer," he said, pointing at the useless wing.

"Do as you will," the dragon answered half-heartedly, sinking her long snout between her forepaws. She shut her eyes to the pain leaving Theo alone with his brooding thoughts.

He took off his cloak awkwardly with one hand. His dislocated shoulder was on fire and the pain almost brought him to his knees. Eventually he managed to curl up the blanket into a makeshift pillow for him to sleep on. The dragon's breath made the building of a fire unnecessary.

♦ CHAPTER 17 ♦

A king's ransom

Theo slept fitfully, awakened several times by the throbbing pain in his shoulder. Morning dawned dull and grey with a wind blowing off the mountains. He was cold and miserable and without food. He searched amongst the woods managing to forage some acorns and a few berries to eat but they only served to increase his hunger. Back in the cave, he placed his cloak over his back with his good hand and gathered his sword placing it in its sheath. He would leave Adelayne's weapons with the dragon. They would only encumber him on the trip he was about to undertake one-armed.

He set out just as the sun rose above the horizon making his way through the woods heading south in the general direction of Alcavia. Autumn leaves were beginning to litter the forest floor as he made his way through the trees dressed in their golden brown leaves. He tried pulling his cloak tighter about his neck to guard against the chill morning wind; his fingers came across something soft in his pocket. Pulling it out, he held it to the light. It was the scroll from the Witch Lord. Theo felt foul just at the thought of touching the same parchment the Witch Lord had been handling. He looked at the wax seal that held the scroll sealed and recognized the clawed paw of a dragon–the Witch Lord's mark.

As the day wore on into evening, he grew weary, his shoulder aching with every jarring step he took. He cleared the trees by midday and passed through the fields. Whereas in the spring tall stalks of grain had stood covering the rich Leonese plains, short stumps now protruded rudely from the earth like poking fingers. It wouldn't be long before the plough was brought to bear and preparations made for the winter seed-sowing.

He was encumbered in his walk through the fields by ridges the plough had formed in early spring. His stomach rumbled to remind him that he hadn't eaten since the night before. But worst of all was his thirst. He chided himself for the umpteenth time for setting out from Alcavia without a water skin.

Theo had been lucky enough to come across a farmer's cottage two days after Adelayne's kidnapping. The farmer lent him a fast horse and he covered the rest of the distance to Alcavia at thrice the rate he had been going before. By the fourth day he sighted the stark walls of Alcavia's outer ring. He murmured a prayer of thanks to whatever god might be listening as he approached the glum city walls.

The guards at the gates hardly noticed him among the throng of travellers entering the city. He made his way along the road he had traversed so often over the past seven months. He felt a loneliness such as he had not experienced since he parted from his parents. He wondered where Adelayne might be right now and in what dark and dreary dungeon she had been thrown into. He would not desert her even though he had acted cowardly thus far. When he approached the entrance vault to the citadel, the guards wearing the livery of Alcavia made to stop him until they realized who he was. Most of the palace guards knew him by now so he moved freely amongst them.

"A good evening to you, Master Theodor," one of the young guards greeted him as he passed by the gate.

He nodded his response not trusting his voice to answer. His mouth was parched dry and he did not feel like engaging anyone in idle chatter. In any case, what would the guard think of his failure to protect their princess? He had to find Emeralda or Nestor quickly. They would know how to approach the king about this.

"Theodor!" It was Leon who first greeted him. He had a worried look on his face as he approached Theo. "Where have you been? You've been gone for four days. Your companions have turned Alcavia inside out searching for you. Your aunt and grandfather are beside themselves and Roxette is ready to split at the seams. Have you seen my sister?"

Theo stared at the prince considering carefully what he was about to say. There was no easy way of putting it. "Leon I have had a trying day. Will you please take me to my grandfather?" Leon escorted him to the king's lounge where he found the rest of his companions sitting gloomily looking about with nervous expressions.

"Theo, you're back! Praise Athud!" Nem sprang to his feet and came to stand by his friend, clapping a hand to his shoulder. Theo winced with pain, crying out. Zoi immediately sprang into action asking Nem to step aside whilst she helped remove Theo's cloak. Emeralda gasped as she laid eyes on Theo's shoulder. The rest of the group approached huddling close to Theo with concern.

"Give us some breathing room please," Zoi requested, as she proceeded to remove Theo's shirt. Theo felt the shock of pain from the small movements his shoulder was being subjected to. The room whirled about him before he lost consciousness.

He awoke with Zoi and Emeralda crouched on top of him. His shoulder hurt but looking at it he realized it no longer looked out of place. A purple bruise the size of a melon had formed on the skin where it had been punctured by the Mountain nymph's spiked sphere.

"We set it straight whilst you were out cold," Zoi answered his questioning gaze.

"Theo what happened?" His sister kneeled beside his couch taking his hand into hers. He could feel his fingers again though with the returning feeling the pain from his shoulder redoubled.

Leon was staring at him worried as he stood to one side of the room, the light from the fireplace playing on his pale face. Nestor also waited quietly for Zoi to administer her healing salve. It had an awful stink and was a sickly brown colour.

"This will help the tissue surrounding the bone to heal," she said, as she applied more of the salve.

Moments later Roxette entered the room and rushed to Theo's side. She looked down at his wound but did not say a word. "Here are the bandages you requested," she said, handing over the cloth to the old woman.

"Help me with this," Zoi said to Emeralda, as she motioned for her to pull Theo forward whilst she tied them tightly around the wounded shoulder. Theo tried not to scream. He barely managed it though; he saw stars in his vision. When he was all bandaged up and drinking a bitter concoction that Zoi had brewed, his friends stood around waiting anxiously for him to tell his tale.

"Adelayne and I went flying with her silver dragon four nights ago," he began. As he recalled the events of that night, Leon's face became ashen. Nestor was shaking his head, clutching at his chin with one hand. The rest of the group remained silent, shocked at the news of the princess's abduction. "I promised Assima I would send her aid," Theo finished, looking at Zoi urgently.

"We cannot set out into the night," Zoi replied. "We may not be able to locate the cave you speak of and we cannot disregard the danger of another attack by the Mountain nymphs in the dark."

"Theo, where is this scroll you mentioned?" Leon, who had remained silent up until now spoke up. His stare was filled with dismay, his voice thick with emotion. Theo could only guess at what must be going on in his mind.

"There, in my coat pocket," Theo pointed with his good hand.

"Don't break the seal!" Roxette warned, as the prince laid his fingers on the parchment. "The Witch Lord may have placed a spell on the scroll to activate when the seal is breached."

"She's right," Zoi agreed. "Such a thing is possible with magic. Better you give it to me for safekeeping until we go to meet with the king."

The king called for Theo as soon as he heard of his return. He had been informed by his son of Adelayne's abduction and sat his throne with a weary heart now weighed down not only by the loss of his brother but also that of his daughter. Queen Crystal was sitting beside him sobbing uncontrollably with Zoi clutching her in her embrace caressing her hair like a mother her weeping child. Colonel Ajax stood on the other side of Zoi, close to his king, his top knot gleaming with the oils he had applied, his shaved head accentuating his warrior looks.

Theo's heart was wrenched by the sorry scene. He felt once more the pangs of guilt at having been spared...and at his failure.

"Where is the scroll, young Theodor?" the king asked in a low voice, gazing with an unfocused stare at the youth before him.

"I have it, my king," Zoi answered, from beside the queen's throne.

"Then step forward mistress and allow me to read what my foe has to say."

"I ask your forgiveness, my king, but I will open the scroll myself, for it has been sent by a wizard with a treacherous heart and may conceal a trap designed to harm you, my lord."

"Then pray, go on and open it. The sooner we know what's on our enemy's mind the sooner we can find a way to counter his plans."

Zoi walked away from the royal couple and stood alone in a corner of the hall far from the rest of them. She placed the parchment on the floor and backed away from it. Theo felt a slight tingling as Zoi produced a small thread of magic which tugged at the seal, melting it away to allow the scroll to roll open. After it was plain that it was not going to erupt or cause any other harm, she approached and lifted the parchment to study it more closely. She brought it to her nose and sniffed it. She did not detect any poison.

"It is safe to handle, my Lord,' she said, as she approached and laid the scroll in King Dreyfus's waiting hands.

The king read the message on the scroll once to himself then read it out loud.

> "My dear King Dreyfus,
>
> For you to be reading this means that my commander's trap has been sprung and your daughter is safely on her way to my tower. Too long has she been a thorn in our side separating our two kingdoms from coming together in friendship. You see my king I wish for us to live in peace and prosperity and for our two nations

to end this age-old useless feud which has no logical explanation or benefit for either of us.

I grieve with you, that your brother forced my hand and gave me no other choice but to remove him from our midst. I will endeavour in the time allotted to me to extract the poison which he has instilled in your daughter and to show her the error of her uncle's ways. I am confident that you too will acknowledge that I am not the one to blame for all this.

My terms are simple. I want free passage of my gold and gemstones from your port and a small part of your yearly produce of grain–say half of it–to be distributed to my forces as payment for the protection we will provide for your lands. You are also to allow my forces to move unhindered and to set up fortifications along the east bank of the Apalachus River.

In return I will order my troops to cease harassing your trade routes. If you agree to my terms, then deliver your message to me with one of your dragon striders. He will be allowed safe passage to and from my fortress.

Do not delay too long my king, for I cannot hold back my troops without some proof of your good will,

Zarzbudin."

"Outrageous!" Prince Leon shouted from across the hall. "Father, allow me to take a small party into the hills and locate this Witch Lord. I will return with his head as a trophy. How dare he lay his terms to us as if we had already succumbed to him?"

The king lifted his hand motioning his son to stay his temper. "Let us not make any hasty decisions. The Warlock has already managed to slay your uncle and one of our dragons through careful planning, and has left the other dragon incapacitated and holds your dear sister captive. This is proof that we can no longer act individually. We need a united front to tackle this threat. The time has come to call upon Ameron's aid."

"Ameron!" the prince shouted in disbelief. "What does Ameron care about our border dispute with the Dragon's Foot Mountains? Ameron has only a small stretch of land north of the Nesal River bordering with the mountains and does not even expend a small force to patrol that border but rather chooses to stay away from the conflict."

"Ameron is the chief city and ruler of Leonium. She has an obligation to answer our call for aid. The age-old agreements stand and cannot be denied. In any case, King Philander knows only too well that Alcavia's problem today, if not solved, will become his problem tomorrow. From the Warlock's letter it is plain to see that he has already turned his eye on the border with Ramila. Why else would he ask for free passage to set up fortifications along the Apalachus River? He intends to conquer all of the free lands of Leonium one by one.

"Ameron must be warned."

"What about Adelayne, my king? Will we do nothing?"

"My son, do you think I would leave your sister in the hands of this Witch Lord? We will send a party, as you have pointed out, to locate the princess and free her. But you may not lead it. I cannot afford to lose Alcavia's sole heir. The kingdom's needs must come before our own.

"And this party will not engage the Warlock for fear that it will fail and add to Adelayne's troubles. It must be a small force that can move unseen through the mountains and approach the Witch Lord in his dark fortress with stealth."

"This cannot be achieved by travelling above ground over the mountains," Roxette intervened. The king and prince turned towards her, waiting for her to go on. "This small party you speak of, King Dreyfus, must enter the Witch Lord's realm from below, through the network of tunnels beneath the Dragon's Foot Mountains."

The king stared at her, mulling over her words. "None of us know the entrance to these tunnels though we have oft tried to discover them but to no avail."

"That is because you did not know where to look," Roxette replied, a sly smile passing over her face. "All the entrances to the tunnels are on the other side of the Dragon's Foot Mountains, towards the Nerus Ocean."

"Hah, a great help that is to us," Prince Leon snorted derisively. "First you tell us we cannot travel above ground to the Witch Lord's lair undetected then you tell us we'll need to traverse the mountains to reach the other side. Or did you have in mind for us to go by ship through the Giants' Fiord into enemy territory?"

Roxette stared back at him, her dark eyes unperturbed by his scathing reply. "There is one more possibility you have not considered, my lord."

"Speak, my lady, for the hour grows late and I wish for us to reach a decision before the night is out," the king urged.

"The party must enter the tunnels from the Highlanders' realm. The Mountain nymphs and the Highland folk have shared borders for millennia. As each race has grown in strength and the other dwindled, the borders have shifted further east or west depending on who was the stronger. But the tunnels remain the same and are interlinked."

The king pondered Roxette's words. He passed a hand through his hair the streaks of white in it seeming more noticeable now. Finally he rested his hands on the carved arms of his throne and looked around at the companions in his hall before letting his eyes wander back to the nymph. "It is a long trip to the source of the Dolomidur River, and further on to the Brakkand's Throne Mountains. This party you speak of must set off at once with the dawning of the morrow. We cannot afford to wait any longer."

"It is not necessary to go the long way around, my king," Zoi said, from beside Queen Crystal. "We can enter the Dwarves' domain from the source of the Silver River."

"I agree." Roxette nodded. "That will place us closer to the border with the Dragon's Foot tunnels."

"That settles it then," the king said. "The party will set forth on the east road thus steering clear of the dangers present along the edge of the Dragon's Foot Mountains and will follow the road to Ramila then to Ameron before turning north for Ghiadon. A delegation will go with the group to rally the aid we need from our neighbouring allies for the impending war, for there is no doubt now that this Zarzbudin is preparing for war. All that remains now is to select who will form this party."

"My lord, we were on our way to Ghiadon and all that has kept us is Archon's disappearance," Zoi said. "We can form part of the envoy which will set out for the kingdoms east, though my journey must end at Ghiadon."

The king's face darkened as if he had remembered something which upset him. "That brings me to another disturbing piece of news. It seems that today is a black day in the history of our land. Fetch Primate Zerum," he shouted at the guards by the entrance doors to the hall.

The clergyman entered dressed in a simple black robe covering him from neck to toe. He looked about the great hall silently, his face bleak, his eyes saddened.

"Primate Zerum, will you please relate to our friends the grim news you brought to me earlier?"

The primate eyed the companions drawing their full attention. Theo felt his hackles rising. Something had gone horribly wrong. "My Lord, I am sorry to be the bearer of ill tidings. Our church's ship never made it back from her trip to Sulicia. Prince Armend was delivered safely to the capable hands of the Sisters of Athud but the ship met its unfortunate end on its return journey. Our scouts notified me as soon as they detected driftwood from the shipwreck littering the shoreline all the way to the mouth of the Ankadar River.

"I'm so sorry," he added shaking his head at the mage's companions. "We found no survivors."

The group stared in shocked silence at the patriarch. Theo knew his feelings of foreboding had come true. He felt at a loss wondering what was to become of him and his group of friends. The mage, though he had been secretive about their mission, had given them a direction, a purpose. It was Archon who had drawn him away from his previous quiet life at the cottage. The mage had turned the serenity of his world upside down and now he had forsaken him to their enemies just when his guidance and aid was needed most.

He looked at Roxette and his heart went out to her. Here he was thinking of his own problems and had selfishly not considered his friends. Roxette had turned away from her family and her nation to follow the new path upon which the mage had set her. Now she had lost the only lord she had known for the past four and a half years. "I should have gone with him," she said, bitterly.

"You would have been yet another body washed on the shore, my lady," the primate disagreed.

Colonel Ajax sensing Roxette's pain exchanged a look with the nymph as if to offer her support. She shook her head to signify that she wanted some time alone. Theo was torn between approaching her to comfort her and remaining where he was to allow her the solitude she desired. The look she gave the colonel convinced him to stay away. There might be a chance for him to speak with her later.

Nestor met Theo's eyes and Serilia's. The old man's first priority would be to lead the siblings to safety. He had been against Archon drawing the youths into his mission but had gone along to lend his support and to care for his grandchildren in the absence of their parents. Theo wondered what the old man would say when informed of his decision to go after Adelayne, no matter what the cost to his own life. Perhaps he could delay telling him for the time being. They would go to Ghiadon as was their original plan and he would take matters from there.

"Colonel Ajax, what is your opinion on all this? Who is to be part of the group that will rescue our princess from captivity?" the king asked his right hand man.

"I agree that Prince Leon should not be part of the rescue team, my king. It will be a mission fraught with danger and slim chances of success. The tunnels of the Mountain nymphs are well guarded and it will be very difficult to slip through them undetected, though I agree with Roxette that it is the best way to approach the Warlock's lair.

"I will head the mission, my lord, along with two of my best men. No more will be necessary. Zoi and her companions are welcome to come along with us up to Ghiadon, but from there we will go alone. A small group has a better chance to make it in and out of the Dragon's Foot Mountains."

"I too will go with Ajax on this mission," Roxette offered, startling her companions. "I'm best suited for the task since I know the tunnels better than anybody here," she explained.

The king nodded. "Primate Zerum, would you be willing to lead a delegation to Ameron to seek aid for our kingdom? I have not as yet informed you but we have been delivered an ultimatum by the Witch Lord Zarzbudin for my daughter's release. We must respond to this threat with all the might that Leonium can bring to bear."

The primate looked shocked. "My king is there no other way? There has not been an all-out war with the Mountain nymphs since the Great War."

"Your Eminence, I have not been given any other choice. The Witch Lord already considers us conquered and is turning his eye towards our neighbours." He handed the scroll to the clergyman who read it twice before handing it back to the king in disbelief.

"So we have come to it at last. The cauldron is about to boil over and woe unto those who will be alive to witness the events of this era." A chill settled on the hall.

The king was the first to speak. "I will convene with my counsellors to decide what measures we are to take over the coming period and who will be accompanying you on your trip, primate. You have not answered whether you are willing to be my envoy."

Primate Zerum nodded solemnly.

"My king, I have one more thing to add."

"Yes Colonel Ajax?"

"Roxette and I along with the rest of our group will set out early tomorrow morning at first light. We cannot afford to wait for the envoy. The delegation will have to follow after us. We will be travelling by land to more easily avoid being pursued by our enemy's spies."

"Agreed. Queen Crystal and I will head in the morning for the cave Theodor mentioned to administer the healing that Assima requires."

"My lord is that wise?"

"We will not be alone, colonel. My son will escort us with one of your most trusted knights. You may choose the man and let him know of his task before the night is out."

"Yes, my lord," the colonel saluted and turned on his heel to leave for the soldiers' barracks.

As the rest of the companions prepared to leave the throne room, Primate Zerum approached Nem pulling him off to one side.

"I have a request to make," the clergy man said, looking directly at the young man with his dark eyes.

"I'm listening, Zerum."

"I want you to leave with my group. I'll need your services on this task the king has charged me with."

Nem was distraught. What the primate was asking was for him to leave his friends to go on without him. Nem had never been separated from Theo before. Even after the cottage incident, he had abandoned family and friends to go off with Theo on his mission with the mage. The inevitable had come to pass. "I would be honoured to escort you and your delegation, Your Eminence." He could not let the primate down now that he was being given his first real chore.

"Good lad," the primate said, patting him on the shoulder approvingly.

♦ CHAPTER 18 ♦

On the move

It was a clear day, although a strong wind was blowing over Alcavia from the Dragons' Foot Mountains. The guards at the city gates clutched at their cloaks hiding their chins in their collars not giving much attention to the small group on horseback that was leaving the city just as the sun laboured to rise over the east. The tall outer walls were reflecting the amber morning light like giant mirrors contrasting with the bland brown colours of the surrounding fields that were barren at this time of year. As the riders began to distance themselves from the outer city gate another group of riders wearing dark cloaks with hoods drawn over their faces followed behind but kept at a distance.

By late evening a third group, led by soldiers wearing Templar white and the flame of Athud on their breasts, also headed in the direction of the previous two. A woman waited at the gate wrapped in a leather cloak with fox fur lining holding a kerchief to her nose. One of the riders broke away from the group of church knights drawing back the hood of his cloak to reveal his curly black hair tied back by a band. He kneeled down from his horse and held the sobbing woman in a lingering kiss. She reached up and hugged him fiercely. Then she whispered some words in his ear and stood back. The curly haired youth looked at her once more then heeled his mare to catch up with the group that had moved on.

Ajax's group travelled at a steady pace following the main trade road to Ramila. During the day they passed a few caravans daring enough to brave the road. Many of the caravans went under the escort of armed men. Their owners eyed the group with mistrust but Ajax's riders were not burdened by wagons so they soon outdistanced any convoys they met. Alcavia's soldiers were absent, kept in the city to guard her west flank and to patrol the road to the port. None could be spared for the routes east.

At night the group would make camp round the small fires they built under the cover of trees just off the road's right flank with the mountains looming opposite. Colonel Ajax and his men would take turns keeping night watch, their attention focused on the westerly wind and the bleak peaks beyond. Making good time, on the second day they arrived at the west bank of the Apalachus River. It was wide, fed by the melting ice caps from the heart of the Dragon's Foot Mountains. Theo admired its size. Its waters were a raging torrent hurrying to reach the sea though in their eagerness had eroded away the supporting valley so it meandered snake-like before spilling into the sea.

The trade road they descended was in utter disrepair, filled with potholes where the rain had torn away its lining. The group came across a series of deep excavations. They approached and stared in utter wonder at the ruins of the ancient city that lay sprawled and abandoned before them.

"What is this place, grandfather?" Theo whispered, not wanting to intrude on the silence that had befallen the group, gazing solemnly at the spectacle of this long extinct civilization.

"This is the ancient city of Phica, my son," Nestor said, laying his hand lovingly on a Phican column standing near the road side. It had centuries ago ceased to serve its purpose of supporting a building of high stature. Now it stood dejected–a soldier with no kingdom to belong to. Theo took a while to admire the column's capital which was composed of acanthus leaves crested by four slender volutes. "These ruins bear evidence to the most ancient city ever to have been built in Leonium by Galipan settlers back in 855 BA," Nestor added.

"You mean our ancestors arrived this far north?" Theo asked in wonder.

"Why of course, Theodor. At one time in Galipan history our nation had expanded its realm all across the southern coasts of Leonium and Seldavia."

"What your grandfather says is true," Ajax agreed. "We Leonese are descendants of the Galipans and the local tribes that farmed these lands at the time of the settlements. It was much later, after the Anvils conquered and annihilated the Galipan cities, that we emerged as a separate nation. Our first city of Ramila was built to bring together the nation of Leonium."

The group moved out of the ruins till they arrived at the river bank where they made camp for the night.

The next morning they paid a ferryman to take them to the other side and continued their journey. Towards midday Theo could smell the sea. As they approached the bay ahead, a small fishing port came into view a few leagues east of the Apalachus River mouth. It was the fort where Alcavia's navy resided. There were two battle cruisers anchored at the docks.

"The other two must be on their rounds," the colonel exclaimed, as they entered the port. "Keep together and hide your faces. I don't want to be recognized by any of the sailors. We cannot afford to waste any time and I don't want to spread the news of the princess's plight."

They found a bar and ordered their afternoon meal and drinks. It was a busy place with busty serving girls with a ready smile and flirty eyes. This probably accounted for the bar's popularity as well as its name: *The Willing Lass.*

They remained no more than a night at the port and with the crack of dawn were off again, which suited Theo fine; he was anxious to get to Ghiadon. His dreams were filled with thoughts of Adelayne. During the day he kept silent as he pondered what she might be going through. Roxette kept him busy in the mornings with an hour's training at the mystic fighting arts. She said the fact that they travelled all day until night time was no excuse for Theo to cease his training. Zoi also would occupy him before the midday meals, teaching him how to use different aspects of his gift and how to call upon it when needed, something he was unable to do just yet. Sure he could now form the fire balls with barely a thought but when he tried anything more intricate his concentration would waver and he would lose touch with the gift. It felt like groping in the dark to locate a match to light the way. He knew roughly where it was from having lighted it before but when extinguished he could not quite put his hands on it again.

"Colonel, do you intend to go north easterly on the Tuli Road instead of heading for Ramila via the ports of Ravensia and Acras?" Nestor was asking, as he heeled Brigadier to approach Ajax's sorrel stallion. The stallion reached out to nip at the chestnut's neck, so Nestor kept his distance.

"I want to avoid having to cross the Karpassa twice. And I want to avoid as many towns as possible."

They ate a hurried lunch of trout near the Karpassa River, just north of the town of Tuli, on the fifth day since setting out from Alcavia. Theo looked around at the autumn leaves carried by the wind. That wind brought with it a sense of foreboding; the kind he had felt when Archon left for Sulicia; the kind he felt the night he had ridden on Assima's back with Adelayne but was too preoccupied with the princess to heed.

They found who they were looking for. He was a weasel-faced man with dark beady eyes above a prominent nose. He took one look at them and their steeds and began to lick his lips.

"It's going to cost you, mister," he was saying to the colonel.

"My dear fellow, you propose to take us across with that sorry excuse of a raft and shamelessly claim it's going to cost us? What guarantee do I have that it will make it to the other side?" The colonel looked with contempt at the makeshift raft anchored to the river bank. It did not look large enough to carry the whole group over at once. Standing by the raft were two skinny fellows, haggard-looking with trousers torn at the knees. Their shoes appeared well-worn with the laces missing.

"Ain't another crossing for miles but you're welcome to try if you like." The weasel man smiled a near-toothless grin.

"Just pay him and be done," Zoi said to the colonel, staring back anxiously in the direction they had come. Theo's feelings of unease were heightened. He looked at his sister but she seemed unaware of any danger. The rest of the group was looking with foreboding at the raft. Roxette, however, seemed on edge and joined Zoi in staring behind.

"Well let's have it, how much will it cost us?"

"I think a silver shilling for each of your companions and twice that for every animal is more than fair," the fellow said, wringing his hands together with a glint in his eye.

"Why that's six gold crowns!" The colonel's face reddened.

"Not forgetting the shilling on top of that," the weasel man corrected him.

"Daylight robbery! I'll be sure to report to King Dreyfus the outrageous fees you people charge weary travellers when next I see him." The colonel shook his head reproachfully.

"King Dreyfus?" the weasel sneered. "Out here we don't know any King Dreyfus of Alcavia, or King Ionid of Ramila. None of their soldiers bother to come this far. We're left to fend for ourselves. Senator Dossa of Tuli doesn't venture out of town either, so pay up and stop your whining or be on your way."

"I'll pay you as soon as you get us over to the other side safely."

"Half now and half at the other side–or no deal."

"Two gold crowns now and three more when you get us to the other side," the colonel insisted, placing two of Alcavia's gold coins in the skinny man's hand. The weasely fellow bit the coin with his two remaining teeth then nodded grudgingly.

Nestor with Brigadier were the first to board the raft. It was only big enough to carry one horse and its rider at a time. The group watched as the raft owners pulled at their rope and pulley system to guide their craft slowly to the bank on the far side. The Karpassa was thankfully a lot narrower than the Apalachus had been but its waters were still rough. Theo heard Brigadier neigh as the raft rolled in the raging waters. After a while the raft returned.

"Serilia, you go next and then your brother, Theo," the colonel instructed.

Serilia made it safely across. Then it was Theo's turn. He boarded the raft with apprehension, stroking his strawberry roan to calm her down. He whispered in the mare's ear and rubbed her nose. The raft lurched forward and the horse bobbed its head in fright but did not move; instead it began to tremble all over. The far side of the east bank could not have been reached too soon. Theo was relieved when he finally stepped off to rejoin his grandfather and sister.

They turned to look at the raft that was going back for the rest of their companions. Then something completely unexpected happened. The ropes holding the raft sagged into the water and it began to float downstream with the current. The trio on the raft began to curse and shout at the group on the other side but their voices were soon lost as they got washed away. Nestor placed a hand to shield his eyes from the afternoon sun and peered intently across the water.

"There's something happening on the other side," he said with trepidation.

Theo looked on intently. His friends were forming a line along the river bank. Behind them he could see a milling of dark shapes. Then he saw arrows flying through the air at his friends and heard shrieks as two bodies hit the water's edge and were born downriver. His heart jumped to his throat as he wondered which of his friends had been hit by the arrows. Suddenly a blinding green light appeared. He heard screams coming from the attackers as they ran into the woods spreading flames from their bodies that had been lit up like live torches. It appeared to be Zoi's work. Soon the group opposite had split up and was moving away from the water's edge seeking shelter in the woods beyond.

Theo stared in stunned silence as his companions dissappeared. First Archon and now this. *Aunt Emeralda!* he thought suddenly, grief overcoming him. He turned to his grandfather and could see the same thoughts going through his mind. Serilia was sobbing uncontrollably as Theo placed his arm around her to comfort her.

"What do we do now?" Theo asked at a loss.

"First thing we do is get away from this river bank," Nestor replied, drawing himself forcefully out of his dark thoughts and occupying his mind with getting them all to safety. "Whoever those attackers were out there, they may find a way to cross further upstream, so let's get a move on.

The colonel bought us valuable time by cutting the rope supporting the raft. Let's not waste any of it."

They mounted their horses and rode hard for the rest of the day, heading easterly for Ramila till night cloaked them. When they were more or less sure they had put some distance between themselves and the crossing incident, they made camp. Nestor allowed them to make a small fire surrounded by rocks to shield its light as much as possible. They ate whatever they could find in their saddles. The pack horses had been left on the other side with their supplies. At least Nestor had thought to place some cheese and dry bread and meat in his saddle bag. They had mistress Freida to thank for that small comfort.

Nestor was staring at the fire, its flames lighting his face. Of a sudden he seemed much older and more wrinkled. His eyes reflected red from the flames as Theo sat down beside him. They were both quiet, absorbed in their thoughts. Serilia had been sobbing all day and only now had managed to fall asleep.

Finally Theo turned to his grandfather. "Do you think aunt Emeralda will be alright?"

Nestor looked at him with his piercing blue eyes and smiled encouragingly. "I'm sure of it. She's made from a tough breed, your aunt is. She has been through a lot, as have I, and survived. I wouldn't worry too much about her." But his eyes betrayed his inner feelings.

That night they curled up near the fire for its warmth but also because it made them feel safe the way it held back the encroaching darkness. Theo felt utterly wretched. He missed his parents terribly. And his thoughts never wondered away from Adelayne. Now he would add his aunt Emeralda to his list of missing friends. At least Nem was safe with the primate. What of Roxette? Had she met the same fate as her wizard master? Zoi might still be alive, since she had been able to offer resistance to their attackers. But was the colonel one of those unfortunate two who had been thrown into the river with an arrow in their backs? He dare not think his aunt might have been one of them.

He was experiencing a nightmare when he suddenly sprang up from his sleep, his eyes wide open. He looked around only to find that the fire was out. What had wakened him? He looked at the sleeping form of his sole companion. *ONE? Where is the other?* He was about to get up when he felt something sharp pressing on his throat.

"Make a move and I'll end your puny life right here," the voice hissed in his ear. His heart beat so fast he thought it would explode from his chest. He had been so startled by the voice that he had almost cut himself on the blade. The Mountain nymphs must have caught up with them during the night.

"Wake up the other and spread out to find the third," the voice whispered commandingly to three dark shapes huddled around Theo's remaining companion. He wanted to scream a warning but knew the owner of the voice would not hesitate to carry out the threat. Instead he got up slowly as the woman behind him pulled him by the arm.

"What about the girl? You said she was gifted?" asked one of the hunched figures as they approached.

"I'll take care of that as soon as you wake her."

"What's going on?" Serilia asked, coming awake. Theo felt a tingling sensation coming from his sister as she sensed the danger they were in but it was quenched by a force such as the slamming of a gate used to corner a young bull in its pen. Serilia gasped, her breathing coming in gulps from the strain.

"What are you doing to her?" Theo demanded and in reply felt a searing pain in his head that made him double over.

"Now that I have your full attention perhaps you can answer a few questions," the woman behind him said, releasing him. Theo realized she did not need to hold the blade to his throat to control him. She could inflict far more pain with whatever manner of witchery she was using. He reached out tentatively for his gift but felt instead like someone who had fallen into a well and was shut off from the rest of the world by thick walls. It was gone to him–truly gone. Even as a child he had always felt it lurking somewhere in the background, shadowing his every move. Now it was no longer there. Had the witch removed the gift from him altogether? He panicked.

"Stand still!" the woman commanded. Theo felt the pain in his head again. Serilia, who had meanwhile recovered, started choking again. "What happens to the one will happen to the other as well, so do as I say. Now tell me where your other companion is–the one that extinguished the fire–the old man?"

Theo could not distinguish her features in the dark but could see her form and the shape of her curly hair silhouetted against the moonlight. She smelled of jasmine. Theo smiled bitterly. *Funny how the mind works at times like these*, he thought ironically. "We don't know where he's gone. We went to sleep and hadn't noticed his absence till you woke us."

"Well, the Pithiks will take care of him–no doubt. Come, we have no time to lose in idle chatter. Keep up or I might decide you're not worth the effort."

Pithiks? Theo thought, a chill passing over him. That didn't sound right, unless pithiks were being employed by the Mountain nymphs as well.

The woman gave the command for the siblings' hands to be tied behind their backs before they were placed on their horses. They set off.

Theo noticed that Brigadier was missing. He felt relieved at the thought that a horse could outrun pithiks. At least his grandfather would be safe. He looked up at the night sky realizing from the constellations that they were still heading south towards Ramilla. Thankfully they were heading the right way. He wondered who this woman and her three companions might be and what they wanted from them. One thing was for sure, they weren't Mountain nymphs; if they took up company with pithiks they must be Darklings. Things seemed to get worse on this trip.

Sometime during the night they met up with more Darklings and a few posses of pithiks. The creatures stank. A few came to sniff at these new additions to their group lolling their tongues out like hounds. The horses would have bolted had they not been restrained by their captors; their steeds seemed to have grown immune to the foul beasts' smell.

"Grimshaw, keep them away from our captives," the woman shouted in an irritated voice. "In fact keep them away from me also and preferably downwind. Ugh, they're awful!"

"Do your own dirty work, Loxandra. I'm not your lap dog," answered one of the three figures that had been with the woman when they had captured Theo and his sister.

"If it wasn't for our master's protection, Grimshaw, I would teach you to be more civil around your betters." Grimshaw laughed back at her.

They rode all through the next day with hardly any stops. They ate cold meat and hardened brown bread and drank something mildly approaching warm coffee. At night their captors threw them unceremoniously on the ground beside a small campfire and untied their hands so they could eat the meagre meal provided.

Theo rubbed at his wrists and stared at his captors. Loxandra was a tall shapely woman who, under other circumstances, he would have found appealing. She wore a dark frock with a divided skirt for riding and leather boots laced up to the knees. Golden curls intermingled with copper streaks spilt down her back and surrounded her pretty face. *How misleading that face truly is,* Theo mused. He felt in his gut that she was a very dangerous woman. The tell-tale signs were all there: the way the rest of her companions avoided looking directly at her or speaking to her unless they had to.

Only Grimshaw was immune to her disconcerting gaze. Now *there* was an imposing figure! Easily as large as Theo's uncle Tiber, Grimshaw was undoubtedly a warrior: his huge biceps and the scars on his bearded face bore testament to his occupation. On his wrists he wore thick iron bands to guard them from being cut by a blade when in a skirmish. His nose looked as if it had been broken several times. The rest of the group were fighting men also but of smaller stature and obviously held Grimshaw in high esteem.

"Why are you so interested in me and my friends?" Theo ventured to ask the woman who was eyeing him thoughtfully. She held a leaf stalk in her mouth and was chewing at the tip. She stared at him considering whether she was in any mood to answer him. Finally she shrugged her shoulders.

"To be perfectly frank with you it's not I who am interested in you but my master, though I cannot see why. We've been keeping a watchful eye on you for the past three weeks. We would have moved sooner but you were too closely guarded in Alcavia, and my master wanted both you and your sister; you never seemed to be together at the right place and time–'til now."

"I don't understand," Theo said, looking baffled. "Why would anyone be interested in me and Serilia?" Then he had a thought. "Are you in league with the Witch Lord of the Dragon's Foot Mountains?"

Loxandra laughed. "Don't be absurd, boy. The reason we moved so fast since crossing the Apalachus River was to avoid any more confrontations with the Mountain nymphs.

We had to kill a few as we followed at your heels. But a twist of luck provided us the perfect opportunity at the next river crossing. We knew the nymphs would catch up with you there, for we saw them hunting you; so we moved ahead and crossed further upstream, doubling back before you reached your crossing. The rest you know already."

Theo waited for more. Loxandra just stared at him with an amused smile. She was toying with him, like a cat its prey when it has just finished gorging itself. Theo felt a tingling sensation and for a moment thought the gift had returned to him. Then he realized with disappointment that the feeling was his response to Loxandra's probing. He felt naked under her examination.

"Can't think why my master would take such an interest in you." Loxandra arched her brows as she finished her probing. "You're no more talented than any other young shoot your age and in fact you are trailing behind your sister in your ability to use the gift. You're not even worth gift draining." Theo didn't know what that meant but decided he did not like the sound of it. "But for the mage to take an interest in you means you must be worth something."

Theo sat up at the mention of the word "mage". A cold sweat washed over him at the possibilities that presented themselves. This Loxandra and her companions knew Archon, somehow. Had they simply asked around concerming the mage when they had seen him with Theo and his sister back at Alcavia? *Who is this master Loxandra keeps mentioning?*

Loxandra saw his face turn pale. Her smile crept back. "Yes, I know Archon the mage. He would come sometimes to visit Ramila; that is where I was stationed by the Council. I also met him when I was a scholar at the Wizard's Keep. He was quite talented. It's a shame really–that we had to kill him in the end."

Theo had no idea where he had mastered the courage to spring for Loxandra's throat. She saw him coming but made no move to avoid him. He was about to close his hands around her slim throat and squeeze that smirk off her beautiful face when he felt a jar, like being struck by a boulder. He fell back from her, five paces, as though he were a puppet pulled violently from behind by invisible strings. He groaned as he gathered enough strength to rise. His shoulder, which had been hurt at Adelayne's ambush, was aching terribly and his breathing was ragged. His attention was diverted to Serilia who was clutching at her head in agony.

"What happens to the one will happen to the other as well, Theodor Marentherin. Yes, I have learnt your name as well," she answered his questioning look. "I know most of what there is to know about you. My master explained how you and your sister aided Archon in killing three of his disciples." Theo felt a lurch in his stomach as realization dawned on him. "You will not find me so easy to deal with. Behave and I will not treat you harshly. Your only other option is for both of you to suffer." She pointed at Serilia who was still clutching at her ears as if to blot out a loud noise.

"Now we have the pleasantries over with, maybe we can get some sleep," Grimshaw growled, lying beside the campfire, his hand on his axe's hilt; it was never far from his grasp. The rest of the darkling soldiers spread around the campfire to sleep whilst a few remained awake to keep watch. The pithiks had gone off to hunt. They were nocturnal creatures by nature and only travelled by day when forced to.

Theo recovered from his battering and approached his sister timidly. "I'm sorry for all the pain she caused you." He gave her a kiss on the temple apologetically.

"Theo I'll be fine," she said, sounding a bit winded. The colour had drained from her cheeks. "But if you ever make her do that again I will personally kick you from here to Cyrus." She trembled in his grasp. "Theo it was awful. I've never experienced so much pain, and..." she looked into his eyes, tears staining her cheeks, standing out from the dirt surrounding the rest of her face. "Theo, I think I've lost my ability to feel the gift."

Theo cradled her head in his arms. "Hush little sister, don't worry. She has cut us off from it somehow. It will return, and when it does I swear..."

The next day they rode in silence keeping to Grimshaw's quick pace. He had awakened them before the sun crested the horizon. Theo felt his bones aching, especially around his shoulder. Zoi's medicinal care had mended the shoulder but not many days had passed since the damage had been inflicted. In the early mornings, when the surrounding air was chilly, it hurt him all the more. Now he sat stiffly in his saddle. He gazed at his sister yawning. Serilia looked drained, bent over morosely.

Loxandra was riding close atop a black stallion with a vicious bite. The strawberry roan steered well clear of the ill-tempered beast. Grimshaw was in the lead riding a tall charger with a buckskin coat and dark fetlocks. Behind followed three of his men who surrounded the two captives looking none too pleased at their proximity to the pithiks that were lumbering along on all fours beside them, their silvery brown coats trembling with the motion of their large limbs.

They followed the line of the Karpassa River riding on the dirt road that connected Tuli to Ramila. The weasely fellow with the raft had been right; Ramila's military had abandoned its patrolling of the surrounding lands. The countryside was very much the same as Alcavia's: rolling hills, rivers at frequent intervals, and acres of grassland and arable land suitable for growing grain. As they moved along they began to see a few farmsteads but steered well clear of them as they kept moving. On occasion, dogs picked up the scent of the pithiks and barked from afar till the group moved further on.

At times, Theo would see a hare or two crossing their path and in one instance, when they had surprised a young one, the pithiks sprang into action managing to chase it down. They fought amongst themselves as they tore the animal to pieces whilst it was still alive and kicking. When they had devoured the poor creature they caught up with the riders. Theo was sickened by the blood that was dripping from the pithiks' fangs as they grinned with pleasure.

"Fresh meat good," one of them said to him tauntingly, noticing his expression of revulsion.

A few of the pithiks had come too close for Loxandra's liking. She sent them off yelping after throwing a fire ball at their tails, causing them to bury their rear ends in the surrounding turf to extinguish the flames. They gave her a wide berth after that.

At midday they ate a quick lunch before launching themselves in the saddle once more; Theo was beginning to feel his bottom becoming moulded to the thing. He had a few sore points from the rubbing. Serilia gave him a salve that Zoi had prepared for her. It helped him somewhat but what he really needed was a short stop at an inn and some sleep in a real bed. He missed his accommodations in Alcavia. The royal family had been good to them. He felt he would remember their hospitality often on this trip. He wondered what would become of them when they finally met up with the Dark sorcerer. Loxandra was heading for the sea where the sorcerer's ship was doubtless waiting for them.

He tried once more to reach out to his gift. This time he did not push at the walls but rather probed them gently. It was of no use. He felt as though he were a small field mouse caught under a bucket that had been turned upside down on him. He could feel the rim all around but couldn't lift the weight to reach his gift. When he was straining till his veins stood out on his neck and he turned blue in the face, Loxandra turned to look at him shaking her head admonishingly. He stopped immediately, sensing her displeasure and not wanting her to take it out on his sister.

That night they camped near the river and Loxandra ordered Grimshaw's men to catch some fish. "They may as well make themselves useful instead of just riding pretty on their horses," Loxandra answered to Grimshaw's flat look.

Theo joined the three men and helped them catch some salmon and a few trout. They ate their best meal since they had been ambushed by Loxandra's lot. By the end of the meal Serilia was licking her fingers. Theo was glad he had been able to offer her this meagre comfort. Loxandra mocked him with her smile. Everything he did seemed to amuse her to no end. He promised himself he would find a way to wipe that smile off her face. As they prepared to go to sleep, Loxandra approached her pack horse. She drew out what looked like garments.

"Do you like it?" She held a dark purple dress before Serilia and her brother. "I purchased it at Alcavia. Cost me a fair sum as well."

Serilia at first was at a loss for words. Then she studied the dress more acutely appreciating its flowing lines and the quality of the fabric. "It's very pretty," she admitted grudgingly.

"Oh stop being such a grump," Loxandra scolded, placing the dress on her curvaceous form. Theo had to admit it suited her and her dark blue eyes. "Theo, come with me, please."

Serilia looked at her brother accusingly. He shrugged his shoulders. *What does she expect me to do? Wasn't she the one who had beseeched me to obey Loxandra's every command?* He followed Loxandra wearily as she led him away from the camp site towards the river bank. He found himself involuntarily gazing at Loxandra's rich curls glinting in the moonlight. He could not distinguish their reddish golden colour in the dark but he could see them tumbling over her shoulders to the curve of her bottom. Theo wondered at Loxandra's age and decided it was roughly the same as Roxette's–in her mid thirties. But whereas before he had found her beautiful, the thought of her having aided the Dark sorcerer in killing Archon made him hate her with an intensity that surprised him.

It would be so easy to place his hands around her neck right now; they were alone and far from the rest of her companions. But he knew he could not. He reached out and felt the walls to his gift as strong as ever. Loxandra turned around and stared up into his eyes. He was taller than her but not by much.

"Do you find me beautiful, Theodor?" He was shocked by her question. He recovered coughing in his hand. *What is she up to?* He had to be careful how he answered. He did not want to displease her and give her an excuse to hurt his sister. But at the same time he did not want to encourage her. She placed a hand to his collar and slid it inside his shirt, feeling his chest. Theo remained totally motionless, the same as he would have done if a poisonous spider was probing him with its hairy legs.

"You haven't answered my question, Islander." She undid two of his shirt buttons and passed a nailed finger across his chest down to his belly button.

"Yes." Theo let out his breath, swallowing hard.

Loxandra smiled but this time her smile was not mocking. She placed a finger to his mouth and pried his lips open before she turned around leaving him panting. He felt conflicting emotions. He wanted to choke her and at the same time run and, he admitted to himself, remain to see what else she would do.

"Undo my buttons," she commanded pulling her hair back from her neck as she remained standing before him by the river bank. The waters shimmered with the moonlight and somewhere he could hear an owl hoot. "Don't be afraid, boy, I will not bite you," she added, as he hesitated.

Theo obeyed placing his hands on the nape of her neck fumbling with her buttons in a vain attempt to undo them. He found his fingers were trembling and awkward but he calmed his racing pulse and managed to undo them one at a time. When he had finished Loxandra's pale neck was laid bare before him. She removed her sleeves with one slender hand and let the dark dress fall from her body. Theo swallowed. She was completely naked beneath. She turned around. He kept his eyes pinned to hers not daring to look down.

"Look at me!" she commanded. He hesitated, then let his gaze travel over her pale form that was lit by the moon. *She is magnificent!* he thought blushing, but instantly felt pangs of guilt remembering Adelayne. "This is what you can have, whenever you desire," she offered passionately. "All you have to do is stop your futile resistance to the Dark Lord. Theodor, there can be no victory against him. He is all powerful, all-consuming. Bow to him, only to him, and I will make you my disciple and teach you all I know. Your skill at using the gift is infantile but with me you will learn to unlock your talent and reach new heights. All you have to do is submit to our side. Better our ally than our enemy.

"Thalagia is at a crossroads Theo. The Dark Lord is preparing to strike and none will be able to stand before his might. Join us Theo. Join us and you may enjoy all the Dark Lord has to offer. Think on it well before you decide. My master will not again be so generous in his offer and neither will he be as patient. If you do not bow down to him he will destroy you. Don't throw your life away like this. You are young still and naïve. There is more to life than what you have been taught by your friends. The Dark Lord offers riches and power that men can only dream of. Do the smart thing. Join us and share in the spoils." Loxandra put on the dark purple dress, clutched the garments she had shed from the ground and led him back to the campsite.

Serilia was fuming when they returned. She threw Theo an icy look. The rest of the captors looked greedily at Loxandra's form but kept their distance. They were well aware of her ability to quash their life at a whim. Grimshaw sneered at her and carried on whittling away at a stick he had been working on.

"Well what do you think of it, Serilia?" Loxandra gave a whirl so the young girl could take a better look at it. She turned full circle and fixed Serilia with her gaze. The taunting smile had returned to her face.

"It's very becoming on you, Loxandra," Serilia answered at last, casting Theo a reproachful look. "What happened to your black riding dress?"

"Oh that droll thing? Theo helped me remove it. I will wear this to Ramila tomorrow. I am known there so it will not do for me to be seen in such drab clothing."

"Whatever. Now if you will excuse me I need to get some sleep. I suddenly feel very weary and the early morning ride will require me to be refreshed." Serilia stormed away with her back stiff. She lay by the fire and covered herself with her cloak, turning her back on her brother and the sorceress.

"Theo, will you assist me in putting back on the riding dress?" Loxandra laughed at the look on Theo's face.

Theo was left with his thoughts and the words she had spoken to him. Maybe she was right. Maybe it *was* futile to resist. Where had it gotten them? Archon was dead, the rest of his friends were missing, and Adelayne was being held by the Witch Lord as ransom.

When everyone was asleep, Loxandra went back to the river bank and changed back into her riding dress. Then she fished out the stone from her pocket. She let a trickle of energy flow into the stone and its milky surface began to clear. She held it at arms length and waited. The stone turned red then emitted the ethereal image of her master.

"Have you done as I commanded?" His face as usual was concealed by his hood so only his eagle-like nose protruded. In the background she could see the hull of the ship and the rigging.

"Yes master. I have given him a lot to think over, in my own unique way." However hard she tried to control it, her voice trembled slightly at the sight of her master—even if it was only a one-foot image of him.

The red image cackled with pleasure. "Yes, my pet. I'm sure you were very persuasive. Be careful with our prizes. We do not yet know their worth."

"The girl seems to be talented, master, but even her strength in the gift is nothing extraordinary."

"Do not underestimate your opponents, my dear. Just remember that with the aid of those two, Archon was able to overcome your master and three of my disciples."

"They were lucky, master."

"No, it was something more than luck. The siblings have great reserves of energy. If taught by the proper tutors they can become great. I believe this is what the mage saw in them...perhaps even more than that. Make haste and bring them to me. I will be waiting for you at the mouth of the Nesal River in three days. Don't be late. We have more tasks to accomplish after you finish delivering the siblings to me."

"Yes, master." The red image disappeared and the stone turned milky white once more. Loxandra was pleased with the outcome of recent events. All her dreams and aspirations were beginning to come to fruition. Her master had promised her much in the way of recompense for her services to the Dark Lord. The Dark Circle was beginning to sit up and take note of her.

She thought back on harder times when she had been growing up with her parents in Ameron. Her mother would often tell her she was from good stock and should make something of herself. She was the daughter of nobles; the combined wealth of her parents' lines was something to be reckoned with. She remembered with bitterness how her father's drinking problem had altered their lives. It was during this period that her father turned nasty and began to systematically batter his wife. Eventually one evening Loxandra's father did not return. He was found the following day in a ditch with his purse missing and a knife in his back.

Loxandra's mother took on a long line of lovers after that. They squandered Loxandra's heritage freely and by the time she was fifteen both her and her mother were thrown out of their residence by their financiers. At that age Loxandra did not know any craft, so she reverted to that most ancient of careers: she sold herself night after night to the highest bidder. She was very selective with whom she went. Her clientele included many men of high rank in the military, or merchant men with fat purses. On occasion she would be passed around from one lord to another. She was infamously known amongst the circle of the elite as "*the Duchess*". She had left her mother soon after her chosen line of work, feeling she had been betrayed by both parents. She never looked back again.

Finally when she turned eighteen, an opportunity presented itself to her to leave Ameron. Her competition had taken an unhealthy interest in her and was envious of her success. She feared for her life. It was not uncommon to find young women of her kind beaten senseless or worse still dead by a river bank, or lying in some alley with their throats cut. It went with the territory.

Her saviour came in the form of a young sorcerer who went by the name of Lethur. He had been visiting friends in Ameron. Lethur had recognized Loxandra's strength in the gift and came at an opportune moment in her life to offer her a way out. He had informed her that the Wizard's Keep was always looking out for new recruits and that in Hendon she would be well cared for and would rise to sorceress level if she worked hard and paid attention to her tutors.

And so, Loxandra set out for the Wizard's Keep where she began her training as a sorcerer's apprentice under the guidance of Lethur and the rest of her tutors. Lethur had asked from the onset to be her mentor and was granted permission. Seven years later, when Loxandra graduated as First degree sorceress, it was Lethur who had given her the first consignments. By the time she was thirty, Lethur had enlisted her into the secret society of the Dark Circle and managed to get her stationed in Ramila where she remained as a sorceress of the First rank.

During her time at Ramila, Loxandra had managed to seduce several men of high station. She married and then murdered with poison both her husbands but no evidence could be found to convict her. She retained their wealth and her high station in society. The only consequence of her actions was for the Council of Light to set up its own investigation. But Sharman, First sorcerer of Ramila, was unable to uncover a plot, so she was acquitted of any foul play. Sharman kept a close eye on her, and amongst the courtiers and nobility she had earned the name of "Black Widow", but other than that she carried on her tasks as before, only with greater care.

The orders always came from the most unlikely sources. At times the messages would be delivered by cutthroats and thieves, at other times they would come from people one would never suspect, such as healers, shop keepers and even lords and ladies of the court. The Dark Lord employed a range of people in his service. Every one of them had their own ambitions and aspirations. But nobody could have prepared Loxandra for the last bearer of her orders.

She remembered how she had felt the evil oozing from his presence before she had even approached the door. And then, when she had opened it, she knew he was the one everyone had spoken of. She felt like an infant beside him and remembered how she had cowered before him in obeisance. She still shivered when she thought of him. She hadn't dared to reach out with her gift and measure his strength; she didn't need to; it emanated from him, like dark clouds of smoke billowing from a burning bonfire. Just to be near him was like being close to an open furnace.

When her master had ordered her to follow him, she had done so willingly. She knew what he had in mind for her. He was searching for a new apprentice and was eager to divulge all the depth of his knowledge to her young mind, and she was prepared to soak it all up. When he had begun to show her what he already knew and took for granted, she was amazed at just how much her training at the Wizard's Keep had left out. There were huge gaps in her knowledge of the gift. He was like a supreme being amongst sorcerers, with no equal, much like a genius scientist who is born once in so many generations and drives his profession to new levels previously thought unattainable. It was small wonder that he was the High Sorcerer of the Dark Circle, leader of all the gifted serving the Dark.

Yes, she mused, *events have definitely taken a turn for the better.*

♦ CHAPTER 19 ♦

The twin thrones

It had taken them three days sailing with the *White Pilgrim*, closely followed by Master Griffin's *Flying Duchess*, to arrive at Ramila's port. They had made two stops on the way: one at Sulicia Island and the Sisters of Athud to inform them of the impending war and to ask them to evacuate the island. Templar Commander Baxter vowed to give aid to Alcavia when the time came and to escort the sisters to safety. The other visit had been to Jade Island but had proved frustrating. Even though the principal of the Astrologers' Guild, master Achalcanoras, had promised aid to Alcavia, he refused to evacuate the island with the rest of his colleagues stubbornly insisting that the mountain fortress was impregnable.

Nem had spent the past five days in Ramila under the supervision of Primate Zerum. Ramila was an ancient city that had been built by Ramile in 518 BA, before the Great War. At twice Alcavia's size, it was known as "the City of Light" in entertainment circles. The city was infamous for its many theatres and entertainment centres; it was an accepted fact that the best minstrels and actors graduated from Ramila's schools. In its large oblong circuses and its tall circular amphitheatres the best theatrical productions played daily.

"Ramila is renowned for its cultural history," Primate Zerum had informed the youth. "She is the mother of

Leonese civilization and rightfully holds the title of 'the Patron City of the Arts'."

Nem's father had told him that if ever he got to travel to Ramila he should visit the theatre at least once. *"It's an experience one never forgets,"* his father had said. Today they had been to the *Ramile Amphitheatre*, which was an open-air theatre with a maximum capacity of forty thousand spectators! There the repertoire had included a multitude of dancers, musicians and other such performers who set up a show to commemorate the founding of the city.

"Nem, would you mind if we made a stop at '*Dame Maldamona*'?" The primate straightened his dark robes and applied his heel, nudging his steed forward.

"I'd be glad to visit the church. My father told me she is the largest in all Ramila."

"She is the largest in the entire known world," the primate supplemented. "Construction of the cathedral began in AA 1445 during Philipus's reign and ended six decades later in AA 1505. You might recall from your history lessons, Nem, that this was well after the 'Golden Era', an epoch in Thalagia also known as 'The Years of Enlightenment'."

"Aah, here we are!" Nem and the primate were standing in the square directly in front of the basilica staring in mute awe and admiration at the various statues and fountains scattered in the square which was full of visitors from all parts of the world. One statue in particular caught Nem's attention. It was larger than the rest and instead of marble was sculpted in bronze.

"Ecumenical Patriarch Justice," the primate explained. "He was the first patriarch to order a call to arms, a Holy War, to cleanse the free cities from Anvil occupation." Next, Nem's gaze wandered over to the façade of "*Dame Maldamona*". The edifice was ornately decorated with marble columns supporting a continuous marble beam carved to depict various scenes of creation. In front of each column stood statues crafted by sculptors so talented they appeared life-like apart from their height which was twice that of an average man. Each statue held a small object in their outstretched hands which were cupped together. Nem approached one of the statues and saw it holding a dove. Another held a sword.

The primate followed Nem's gaze. "Each statue holds an object signifying the important aspects of our faith. The dove stands for peace, the sword for self-defence. That one over there with the measuring scales stands for justice and the lady with the rose stands for virtue. The other with the rolled parchment stands for knowledge and so on.

"Come, let us enter."

Nem followed by the primate's side, staring up at the tall columns which ended at the top in ornately crafted leaf patterns. They entered the nave of the church and stood to adjust to the change in light. The walls were punctured by large arched windows many of which were decorated in stained glass depicting Athud or Templar knights of ages past. Above, Nem stared with wonder at the dome which was masterfully painted and gave the feeling of staring up at the Creator and the inhabitants of his realm in the sky. There were various animals of creation as well as the more well-known heroes of Athudom.

"The cathedral was designed by Ugralgiros, chief architect of his time, and is shaped in plan like a sword with the dome positioned where the hilt joins the blade–so to speak–and the altar at the pommel. You will note that a thin line of bronze runs along the centre of the cathedral separating it into two identical halves." Nem stared at the marble floor and indeed there was a line of bronze roughly four inches thick running along the length of the cathedral. "That, my dear friend, is known as the Maldamona Timeline. You might recall from your studies of navigation that the Maldamona Timeline runs through Borgat in the north, Ramila in Leonium, Lithudon in Galipa and through the temple of Pahud near Hieradon in the south. It is the line from which we measure time across Thalagia."

"Yes," Nem agreed. "Every 15° on longitude east we lose an hour and in the opposite direction we gain one hour."

"Correct. Now Mersile, master sculptor and painter, is the designer of the interior paintings and of the statues outside which adorn the cathedral."

"It's magnificent." Nem felt fortunate to have been granted the opportunity during his lifetime to observe such marvels. He remembered how as a young boy he had listened in rapt attention whilst his father narrated tales of the places he had visited during his travels abroad. *I wish Theo could have seen this*, he thought, feeling a pang of longing as he remembered his friends.

"Nem, our visit to the basilica will serve a dual purpose. I believe it's this way." They exited the church from the west and headed for a long structure with arched isles in the front where clergymen and nuns were moving about in their dark robes.

"This way," the primate beckoned. They arrived before an office where two priests sat guard outside the official-looking entrance. The double doors were sealed and Nem recognized the three-star emblem of the church.

"Can we be of assistance?" one of the priests asked amiably, noticing the primate's garments.

Primate Zerum produced his official ring. "I am Primate Zerum of Alcavia and seek an audience with the Ecumenical Patriarch."

The priest at the patriarch's door bolted up, his eyes widening at the mention of "primate". Many officials sought an audience with the patriarch but it was not often that a primate visited; they tended to remain in their respective cities and to send clerics of lower ranks to do their errands.

"At once, Your Eminence." The priest disappeared behind the double doors. He returned shortly after, followed by a cleric wearing golden robes embroidered with priceless gems. On the front of his robe was imprinted the wolf of Ramila, the emblem of the city.

"Primate Zerum, how pleased we are to have you visiting us." The absence of warmth in the voice and eyes of the speaker was in sharp contrast to his words.

"Primate Orinor, I too am pleased to be here amongst you." The clerics exchanged kisses on both cheeks which was the formal method of greeting amongst priests.

"Come," Primate Orinor beckoned.

Nem entered the cool interior following on the primates' heels.

Looking around the corridor which led to the patriarch's office, Nem found a collection of portraits hanging on the walls. He guessed they belonged to previous patriarchs and indeed recognized the last as the portrait of Euphrand, the present Ecumenical Patriarch.

They entered a room at the end of the hall filled with dark wooden furniture lit by several arched windows. A large desk filled with official documents stood at the far end of the room with a luxurious dark brown leather armchair squatting behind the desk. The room smelled of wood and paper. Most of the granite floor was covered by a tapestry rich in earthy colours where red and amber featured prominently.

Primate Orinor removed his golden phelonion robe and placed it on a coat-stand next to the patriarch's desk. He took from the stand a black rhason robe and put it on, adjusting the collar before he turned to look at his colleague. "I have just completed the morning ceremony," he explained. The priests of the church of Athud wore their dark robes most of the time and only wore their ornate ceremonial ones when they were preaching at church or when they attended official events.

"Where is our ecumenical father?" Primate Zerum asked of his counterpart, looking a bit annoyed at being detained and in obvious disapproval of Primate Orinor's free use of the patriarch's office.

As if to stress how comfortable Orinor was with his surroundings, the flaxen-haired priest sat in the patriarch's armchair without flinching and beckoned to his guests to take a seat before him on the high-backed chairs that were placed in front of the patriarch's desk.

"I'm afraid, brother Zerum, that our father Euphrand has of late been feeling very poorly and has been kept secluded in his quarters where the medical staff are keeping constant vigil over him. We all pray he will recover soon, however it distresses me to inform you that the likelihood of that occuring is slim–short of a miracle." Ramila's primate smiled cordially at his colleague whilst he straightened his robes and shifted through the papers on what had now, it seemed, become his desk.

Primate Zerum coughed to clear his throat, recovering from his initial look of chagrin. He too was now showing his teeth pleasantly, concealing whatever thoughts were going on in his mind. "The church is most fortunate that a man bearing your acuteness and status was available and willing to fill the *temporary* void," Primate Zerum spoke sweetly, the smile never leaving his face as he stressed the word "temporary".

"Yes, yes, now to the point of your visit," Orinor said quickly, motioning with his right hand. It seemed he had other more pressing matters to take care of.

"We are on an official mission handed down to us by our king, Dreyfus of Alcavia. Our delegation has been sent with all due haste to warn our neighbours that the Warlock Zarzbudin is preparing to make his move and has already delivered into our hands an ultimatum." Zerum fished out of his pocket the parchment bearing the Witch Lord's seal and held it towards Orinor.

Orinor's eyes bulged till the whites of his eyes were showing and shrank from the parchment as if it was poisonous. "Has it been tested to make sure it's safe?"

"For me to be handing it to you, Your Emminence, you can be sure I have had it thoroughly examined," Zerum sneered, the contempt creeping back into his voice.

Orinor did not seem to be fully convinced but he stretched out a tentative hand and snatched the parchment shutting his eyes tightly for a long while, as if he expected to be burnt by it. When his worst fears did not materialize he opened his eyelids slowly and stared at the parchment. He caught the lofty look on Zerum's face and his blue eyes turned frosty in contrast to the red of his drawn cheeks which were bare of facial hair; Orinor was amongst an increasing group of priests that did not grow a beard.

He read the message on the scroll and handed it quite calmly back to his colleague. "Yes, it explains quite clearly here how your king's arrogance has delivered us to war's doorstep."

Zerum sprang to his feet almost knocking his chair over. "Explain yourself, Orinor!" Nem was surprised at the outrage imprinted on his companion's face. He had never seen the primate so vexed before.

"Why it's quite simple, brother. Zarzbudin explains in his letter that both the king's brother and his daughter were the cause of this impending war. Had Dreyfus been more prudent, and had he controlled his own family's hostile behaviour, none of this would have come to pass."

Nem could not believe what he was hearing.

"Only an infant would believe that the Warlock has not had his eye trained on Alcavia ever since he came into power," Zerum fumed. "Surely every king is entitled to defend his territory from attack? The king's brother, Eschalion, was murdered whilst defending our lands and the princess was abducted with no other purpose than to press our king into submission."

"That's not what it says in this scroll." Orinor held the parchment in plain view.

"You're missing the underlying message, Orinor. Even *you* will admit that the Warlock has not only eyes for Alcavia's lands. Your border with Alcavia at the Apalachus River is quite clearly mentioned in his list of demands," Zerum retorted pointedly.

"Yes. That part of the letter is most distressing." Orinor had not lost the frosty expression on his face. "So what do you require from the Patriarchy?"

"I would have thought *that* would be obvious, brother." Zerum's cool countenance had returned.

"Oh?" The corner of Orinor's mouth twitched. "Please enlighten me, brother."

"Alcavia's citizens who are followers of the one true faith deserve the church's protection just like every other of the Creator's flock. Our king asks of the Templars of the Ramilan Order to respond to the calling of their brothers at arms in the west. Furthermore I ask for the patriarchy's aid in approaching King Ionid to impress upon him the urgency of Alcavia's plight."

Orinor replied in a voice devoid of emotion. "Your first request I cannot answer as yet until the patriarchy has been given the chance to convene with the Ramilan clerical paramilitary. As for your second request I personally will see to it that before the day is out you will have been granted an audience with the king."

"I express Alcavia as a whole in thanking you in advance for your contribution to our holy cause." Zerum surprised Nem by reaching out to take Orinor's right hand, the one with the golden ring which all the clergy wore as a sign of their devotion to the Creator. Zerum placed his lips on the ring and kissed it then bowed his head to his colleague who reclined his head in turn ever so slightly, accepting this sign of deference with a self-satisfied smile.

Zerum rose and beckoned for Nem to do likewise. "I thank you, Your Eminence, for taking the time from your busy schedule to see us personally."

"A primate of our church deserves no less, brother." Orinor's sudden change in demeanour left Nem with a bitter taste in his mouth. He decided a thin almost non-existent line separated the clerical bureaucracy from other non-religious systems of government.

As they left the west wing of the church grounds, Zerum turned to murmur softly in Nem's ear. "I just remembered what I disliked about this Orinor. I doubt he will tire himself in persuading the Templars here to come to our aid."

"But he promised to arrange a meeting with King Ionid, though."

"Church etiquette does not give him much room to manoeuvre. It would have been considered a personal affront to Alcavia's sovereignty had he not offered this meagre assistance."

"He felt obliged to."

"Precisely, but come, my young companion. The day is yet young and I am not without friends in Ramila."

Meanwhile Orinor had summoned a close confidant to his office.

The priest standing before him had a well-kept dark beard and stared with fox-like brown eyes. A cunning mind was concealed behind the innocent look on father Xersil's face. Xersil had proven indispensable to the primate before and would prove so once again.

"I want you to follow the primate of Alcavia's every move and report to me."

Xersil kissed Orinor's hand, the one with the *ruby* ring, and left quietly. In private, all Darklings refrained from kissing the gold ring that signified loyalty to a Creator they did not pay homage to.

They ate a quick lunch at one of the king's many dining halls reserved for honoured guests. Nem looked around at the rest of their companions who formed Alcavia's delegation. Most important of all was the ambassador of Ramila, Sir Cleon and his lady wife Alanda. All the embassies in Alcavia had been instructed to evacuate their officials; the Ramilan ambassador had been gracious enough to lend his support to Alcavia's cause. Another prominent member in the group was Master Griffin who had offered to speak to his fellow merchant colleagues of Ramila and Ameron and to seek their assistance in rallying financial and military aid for Alcavia. The other four completed the delegation; they were the Alcavian Templar knights: Sir Duel, Sir Bold, Sir Evenar, and Dame Miranda.

"We are agreed then," Primate Zerum was saying, raising a crystal goblet filled with wine to his lips. He gulped down the wine whilst gazing at Griffin. "You and Ambassador Cleon with Lady Alanda will visit your merchant friends accompanied by Sir Bold and Sir Evenar. Nem and I will be accompanied by Sir Duel and Dame Miranda in our visit to the Ramilan Templar Order."

Nem sat with the rest of his companions and the primate in silence staring at the austere surroundings of the Templar Commander's office. Stone featured heavily in the construction of the walls and floor. Above, the roof was supported by wooden beams from which hung wooden candle holders in the shape of wagon wheels supporting eight fat candles that were lit, adding to the light coming through the tall windows positioned at opposite ends of the room.

The door opened and a large framed knight dressed in the white livery of the Templars entered. He bowed formally to the primate, kissing the proffered hand with the gold ring, as was the custom. He then extended a beefy hand to Nem and they exchanged a warm handshake before he moved on to grasp Sir Duel and Dame Miranda in a brotherly embrace.

"Primate Zerum, I am pleased to have you and your friends visit our humble establishment." The knight's voice was gruff and suited his tough outer appearance. He sent for refreshments, unlike primate Orinor who had been in a hurry to see them off.

"Have you been approached by Primate Orinor concerning our mission, Sir Dionar?" Zerum did not waste any time getting to the point. They had already been in Ramila for five days waiting to be admitted to the king's hall; Zerum was growing weary of the passing of time. Every moment the delegation wasted brought Alcavia closer to war unaided. They were Alcavia's only hope in rallying support.

"I am sorry to say that Orinor arrived shortly before you did." Sir Dionar did not look pleased at having been visited by his superior.

"You do not support our cause, sir knight?" Duel's look was downcast.

"You misunderstand me, brother knight," Dionar hastened to explain. "We of the Ramilan Order consider it our sacred duty and our honour to rally to your side in facing our joint enemy. However, my superior by church law is Primate Orinor. With the patriarch incapacitated I am given no other choice than to follow Orinor's command."

"And it is Orinor's command that you not aid us in our cause, Sir Knight?" Zerum asked, placing his glass of brandy on the office table.

"That Orinor is a crafty one, Your Eminence. I have been watching him for the past few years and his scheming to gain a position of power. What I now say remains between us," he said, casting a solemn gaze at his visitors.

"Go on, Sir Knight," Zerum prompted.

"I must have your oaths on this before I proceed, Your Eminence," the knight said resolutely.

They all swore to keep the Templar Commander's revelations a secret.

"I believe the primate may have something to do with our patriarch's ailing condition, though I have not been able to prove it."

"Poison, Sir Dionar?" Dame Miranda asked.

"Quite possibly, my lady."

"Can you arrange for us to visit the patriarch at his chambers, commander?" Miranda continued. "I am a resident of Sulicia Island and have served with the healing Sisters of Athud at the abbey. I have extensive knowledge in healing herbs as well as poisons and may be able to shed the light of truth on what you claim."

The large framed commander placed a beefy hand to his chin and thought well on what Dame Miranda was offering.

"Orinor will be furious," Dionar said drearily, just before a smile lit his face. "That alone should make it worthwhile. I'll see to it at once."

"Sir Dionar, you still haven't answered my question concerning Orinor's visit," Primate Zerum interceded.

The Templar commander stiffened. "I have been ordered not to voice my opinion on the matter of Alcavia's plight and not to offer any form of aid other than that which the Church of Ramila will order me to. I doubt the command to help will ever be given."

"Thank you for your candidness, Sir Dionar."

"I don't understand," Nem said. "Why is the primate so determined not to help us?"

"It's hard to explain, Nem," Zerum answered. "Perhaps the primate feels that Alcavia's plight might draw attention away from his campaign to become Ecumenical Patriarch."

"Athud forbid such a thing comes to pass!" Dionar interjected.

"Orinor is a strong candidate, commander," Zerum admitted ruefully. "However it is within my rights as Primate of Alcavia to ask for a postponement of the elections until the situation with the Witch Lord is resolved."

"Somehow I feel Primate Orinor will find a way to circumvent your objection, Primate Zerum, if you don't mind me saying so." Dionar shook his head in dismay. "I know him better than you do."

"We shall see," Zerum replied coolly.

Had it not been for Templar Commander Dionar, Primate Zerum would never have gained entrance to the Ecumenical Patriarch's room. The guards posted outside were given strict orders not to allow anybody–not even the king of Ramila–to enter without the previous consent of Primate Orinor. Primate Zerum had borne his ruby ring but to no avail. However, Templar Commander Dionar was not to be denied. When one of the guards made to halt his entry he drew his long sword and offered the guard two choices: to grant him entry or to offer his last prayers to whatever god he served.

"You may enter, my Lord, but please understand that we are under orders," the guard replied feebly.

"To Ushud with your orders!" Dionar swore, before flinging open the doors to the patriarch's room.

The group entered into darkness lit by a solitary candle resting on a side table beside a bed covered in heavy blankets. Nem felt intoxicated from the fumes that filled the room.

"What's the meaning of this!" screeched in a high nasal voice a pale thin man dressed in a white robe. He was bald apart from long wispy white hairs that clung stubbornly around his ears.

"I am Templar Commander Dionar and these are friends from Alcavia come to visit our father. The one over there with the ruby ring is Primate Zerum who has every right to be here. Now tell us who *you* are!"

The thin man shrank away from the burly knight clutching at his robes in fright. "I...I am the patriarch's personal physician," he stammered. "My...my name is Floose."

"Tell me, master Floose," Dame Miranda approached the gaunt man with a dangerous glint in her eye. "What exactly is it that ails our father?" She motioned to Duel to throw open the windows.

"Are you mad?" Floose raced to close the windows but was halted by the Templar commander who was blocking his way.

"I will report you to Primate Orinor for this outrage!"

"Do as you will," Dame Miranda answered, giving him a flat look. "Now answer my question."

At first it seemed as though Floose would not oblige but he cringed from Dionar's incensed look and decided it was not safe to ignore the lady knight's question. "Our father is an aged man who has been through many illnesses lately. His immune system is fatigued and unable to deal with even a common cold. He is currently suffering from a rare ailment I suspect may be the Harim virus." He grinned showing long thin teeth like a rodent's at Miranda's horrified look. Miranda went to the Ecumenical Patriarch's bed and removed the heavy blankets. Upon seeing the ill man she made the sign to ward off evil spirits. The cleric was suffering both from the baneful effects of the medicines administered to him by the physician and from the sinister disease that was ravaging his body.

"I see you are knowledgeable of the virus," Floose continued. "Good. Perhaps now you will let me continue with my therapy."

"I am aware of the virus you speak of. It originates from the Anvils and there is no known cure."

"That's correct."

"Tell me, physician Floose, how does administering forkleaf fumes aid in the father's recovery?"

"Oh, I am not harbouring any false hopes, my dear. We have already correctly established that our father is beyond redemption–if you will excuse the pun. And we also both know that forkleaf leads to a state of slumber and anaesthesia."

"In high doses it can also lead to death."

"That is correct but would you rather I left the father to suffer the symptoms of his disease?"

Miranda shook her head and turned her back on the physician. "He's right," she said, without turning to look at the physician. "But I suggest, Commander Dionar, that you remove this despicable man from the room and bring the patriarch's family to see him one last time. He does not have much longer to live."

"Is there any chance of the illness spreading, Dame Miranda?" Duel put voice to their concern.

"So long as contact with the patient's skin is avoided, the chances of the virus infecting someone this late in its cycle is rare. However, I suggest that visitors wear protective masks over their noses and gloves on their hands to be on the safe side."

"Come, my friends. Let us be away from this sorry place," Commander Dionar beckoned. "I will see to our father's further needs as Dame Miranda has advised. Floose, your services are no longer required!" The thin man opened his mouth to protest, but Dionar's expression and the set of his shoulders made the rat-faced man have a change of heart.

When the group was well away from the patriarch's quarters Primate Zerum bent close to Miranda. "Did you witness any signs of foul play?"

"Hard to tell, Your Eminence. Floose's diagnosis was flawless and the administering of forkleaf, though a drastic measure, under the circumstances can be justified. What puzzles me is how the virus managed to strike so far north and so much later than the last reported incident in Ishbad. I remember the outbreak of the plague occurring three years ago in the Anvil kingdoms. It was short-lived, however, and thankfully no symptoms of the virus were reported in the Midlands. I myself happened to come across the virus quite by chance when an Ishbadese merchant had asked for the sisters of Athud to nurse him until death overcame him. I remember we took all the prescribed measures to keep the merchant quarantined and to alleviate his pain."

"So what are you saying?"

"I am saying that I would have found it highly unlikely to come across the virus once more, and even more unlikely that it would choose to strike specifically the patriarch in a city full of people."

"You're suggesting they found a way to contaminate the father, somehow?"

"As I said before. Very hard to prove."

Primate Zerum nodded.

They arrived at the palace grounds and were admitted to one of the king's sitting chambers. There they found the rest of their party huddled together exchanging conversation whilst taking refreshments.

"Primate Zerum, you look like you've just visited a tomb," Master Griffin murmured, as soon as he caught sight of his friends.

"He has," Miranda spoke in the primate's stead.

"We've just come from the patriarch's sick bed," Duel explained to the puzzled look of the rest of their companions.

"That bad?" Sir Evenar asked, pushing back his blond hair.

Duel nodded in response. "Have you had any luck with the merchants here?"

"Master Griffin surprised us all with his powers of persuasion," Sir Bold entered the conversation, twirling his long moustache. "He is well known in the business circles here and has many influential friends. Griffin is a handy man to have around. He has managed to raise a fair sum in aid for Alcavia, to pay for food and arms and to finance his lobby for support amongst the ruling aristocracy here."

"At least our one group has proven successful," Primate Zerum stated in an atypical despondent manner.

"Primate, a word if I may?" Griffin bent his large frame to come closer to the cleric who was half his size.

"Yes Master Griffin?"

"My good father, would you consider it terribly rude of me if I left you and the rest of our companions in the delegation behind –now that I have completed our business here in Ramila? You see I have a shipment to pick up in Cyrus and some business to take care of. I will meet up with you in no more than a week's time in Ameron."

"My dear fellow, you have been more than helpful so far. Please feel free to conduct your business as you see fit. I'd be glad if you could meet up with us in Ameron though, as you say in a week's time. Sir Bold is absolutely correct in his assessment of your value to us."

The chubby merchant beamed a satisfied smile at the cleric then raised his large form slowly from the double couch he was occupying. "Whilst you're in Ameron, Your Eminence, seek out my cousin Solitair. He is a merchant like myself only much more established. Solitair will ensure you get an audience with King Philander as soon as possible and will help with the financial aid you will require from the lords of Ameron." He nodded to the primate and winked at Nem before excusing himself.

"Primate Zerum?" asked a palace guard.

"Yes?" The primate's face lit up expectantly.

"King Ionid will see you now, Your Eminence."

"At last!"

Just then Templar Commander Dionar walked into the room. "You have been summoned before the king," he said, gratified. "Good. I'll escort you myself if you will have me."

"Gladly commander." Primate Zerum clapped the burly knight on the shoulder in welcome.

The group was ushered to the throne room where the guards at the door announced them. "The Alcavian delegation led by Primate Zerum here to seek an audience with His Majesty King Ionid of Ramila."

The throne room they entered was like no other Nem had ever seen before. To approach the throne one had to traverse a hall long enough to hold a ball in. On either side of the hall, dark columns stood like sentinels made from the same ebony marble as the floor which was covered from the entrance doors up to the throne by a plush gold coloured carpet. The high vaulted ceiling was made of contrasting white marble and was carved in the shape of a variety of flower and leaf patterns. A collection of statues stood near each column reminding Nem of those outside cathedral Maldamona, only these were all of females dressed scantily in robes that revealed most of their curves.

The primate confirmed Nem's suspicions by murmuring in his ear. "The interior of the throne room was designed by Mersile, the same sculptor who designed the statues of Dame Maldamona."

Finally the delegation arrived before the king who was slouched on a lengthy couch. Off to one side, what could only be described as a mini orchestra was keeping the king and a party of his courtiers entertained. The king had his eyes shut and was humming in tune to the lead singer whilst a young maiden was busy feeding him grapes. A youth close to Nem's age was massaging his back. Behind the king stood neglected his throne and to the left of the king, where the queen should have sat, there was another throne of equal size and magnificence as the king's wherein sat none other than Primate Orinor. He had a smirk on his face as the delegation drew closer.

Templar Commander Dionar harrumphed to draw his lord's attention.

King Ionid lifted an eyelid, then as his eye focused on the delegation he sat up and opened both eyes.

"Welcome, friends from our sister city of Alcavia," the king said in a nasal voice that made the hairs rise at the back of Nem's neck.

The king was a tall, gaunt man with bland features. His face was elongated matching his long nose, making him look like one of the camel species of the Hadir Desert only his mouth, in contrast, was tiny. Nem was shocked to find upon closer inspection that the glistening effect on the king's face was due to the rouge on his pale cheeks and the lipstick on his lips. The king's dress was no less pampered: frills hung from his shirt sleeves and collar; his pants were short as were his pale tights which revealed his knobbly knees and slim calves.

Nem was absorbing the scene before him with such rapt attention that he almost forgot to genuflect before the king and the primate. Getting up from his bowing position he saw that Primate Zerum was unable to conceal the contemptuous look he was throwing his counterpart who in turn was sitting smugly and regally next to the king.

"My lord," Templar Commander Dionar called out in his bass-toned voice. "It is my honour to bring before you Primate Zerum of Alcavia who comes to us at a dark time in Leonium's history," he turned his gaze meaningfully towards Orinor whose face turned scarlet with rage, "and who seeks our aid in dealing with a common threat which has been a thorn in both our kingdoms' sides for too long."

"We'll let the king decide if the threat involves Ramila in any way," Orinor burst forth quickly.

The king looked from Orinor to Dionar, then to Zerum.

"Pray proceed, Your Eminence," the king requested in what would have been a genteel manner though the effect was ruined by his high-pitched child's voice.

Zerum coughed uncomfortably but soon regained his calm posture. "I thank you, Your Majesty. May I take this opportunity to express my feelings of gratitude to be here once more in your fine city of Ramila after such a long spell? They say a city's beauty and brightness of culture reflects upon its monarch. May Ramila never cease to shine for you, my king.

"Which brings me to the purpose of our delegation's visit to your fine city.

"I am sorry to be the bearer of ill tidings, my lord, but Leonium's recent years of relative peace have undoubtedly come to an end." Zerum handed the scroll to Dame Miranda who shifting forward with her head bowed down low in reverence placed it in the king's thin hand.

Zerum gave the king a chance to read the scroll. When he noticed the king's face was considerably paler than before he continued. "You will agree that from the contents of the Witch Lord's letter, my lord, Zarzbudin already considers Alcavia conquered and is making plans on Ramila. I am making reference to the part about him setting up fortifications along the west bank of the Apalachus River." This for Orinor's benefit who just scoffed at the comment.

"So our purpose here becomes quite clear. We, the delegation of Alcavia, request from what has been throughout the centuries our close neighbour and friend to dispatch a force forthwith to our city of Alcavia to aid us in meeting the rising threat from the west."

King Ionid stared dumbfounded at the primate standing before him. The mini orchestra, noticing the effect of the Warlock's letter on their king, had long since ceased to play. The king looked around the throne room at the horrified faces of his courtiers then turned and let his gaze linger on Orinor who sat in a cool manner like a boa constrictor who had just gorged itself on a meal.

"What are we to do, Orinor?" he asked, like a child turning to its father for guidance.

Orinor got up from his throne and walked towards the king. He spread out his hand and laid it on the king's locks. "Do not worry yourself on such insignificant matters, my son."

Primate Zerum spluttered out a cough in surprise; the rest of the courtiers gasped in astonishment.

Orinor let his frosty blue eyes roam the throne room and silence fell upon the hall as his gaze passed over the Ramilans one by one. Nem could sense the tension in the room but also the awe in which the Ramilans held their primate. Zerum must have only just realized the complete control Orinor exercised over the city officials; the look of exasperation he cast in Dionar's direction said it all. Nem had a bad feeling about the outcome of their visit to Ramila. Suddenly he wished they were well on their way to Ameron and leagues away from Orinor, who was proving a very powerful adversary.

"Why do you insist so with your misrepresentation of events, Zerum." He was not bothering to use the primate's title. "Do you feel our king has not enough to deal with here in Ramila and seek to lay your own troubles on our doorstep? Read the letter once more, my lord," he said, turning to the king. "Does not Zarzbudin extend a hand of friendship to King Dreyfus? But how does our proud neighbour respond? I'll tell you how: instead of learning a lesson from the needless death of his brother, and instead of mending his ways and sending out a peace party to seek the Dragon Lord's forgiveness for harassing *his* borders, our Dreyfus is blowing himself up like a rooster and is continuing his provocative behaviour."

"Outrageous!" and "Sacrilege!" were thrown at the primate by the visiting Alcavian knights.

"I must hasten to disagree with you, Your Eminence," Sir Cleon, the Ramilan ambassador hastened to add his own voice of protest but was torn away by his wife Alanda who whispered something in his ear and looked anxiously at Primate Orinor.

"Silence!" Primate Orinor's voice, unlike his king's, boomed with authority making the courtiers cringe with fear. "What would Ramila have done if Dreyfus had been harassing *our* borders? Would we not have been forced to send a similar letter to Dreyfus? When a child behaves insolently, is not a slap needed to reprimand it?"

"You seem to forget that it is the Warlock who has been harassing our people Orinor and not the other way around," Primate Zerum interrupted in a steady voice that gave his delegation more confidence. The fact that he was not using his colleague's titles was also not lost on the courtiers, and some of them–the boldest amongst them and those in opposition to the Ramilan primate–lifted a hand to cover their smirk. "How else do you explain Princess Adelayne's abduction and the constant reports of raids on our trade routes joining Alcavia and Ramila?"

"That too is explained in the letter, if you care to study it with an objective mind. Zarzbudin with the abduction of the princess is resorting to a final measure in the hope that he can sway Dreyfus from his wrongful ways. If his notions had been hostile he would have dispensed with the rebellious princess, whereas he clearly states that he will try his utmost to show the princess the error of her ways which stem from the upbringing her parents gave her. But Dreyfus is not solely to blame for the situation his kingdom now faces.

"No lady of the Alcavian or the Ramilan, or even Ameron's courts was suitable to serve as our King Dreyfus's wife–No! King Dreyfus, being the unruly-natured fellow that he is, arrogantly shunned his own people *and* religion and took to his royal bedchamber a heathen wife from Ghiadon."

Even the primate's closest allies remained open mouthed at the description the cleric had given to the Forest nymph queen.

Nem caught a dangerous undercurrent in Primate Orinor's words.

"Yes, friends of the Ramilan court. I ask you this: have you ever considered who is truly to blame for the ongoing feud between Leonium and our neighbours in the west? Who is responsible for bleeding our reserves and draining our cities' coffers dry for the sake of financing these futile wars? I'll tell you who: the heathens of the Emerald Forest with their accomplices in the Brakkand's Throne Mountains –that's who!

"Why should we follow in the heathens' wake? Why should we labour and offer our youths for the sake of the heathens' unexplainable animosity towards the Dragon's Foot Mountains? Well I say enough is enough. I say no to this delegation. I say no to Dreyfus who seeks to draw us into his personal conflict with Lord Zarzbudin."

"This is a disgraceful misrepresentation of how things stand in Leonium!" Zerum was barely keeping himself under control. His beard bristled as he vented his anger at the flaxen-haired primate who wore a calm expression and arched his brows scornfully at his counterpart. "You are a disgrace to your order and to the robes you wear. How our brethren of Ramila allowed you to rise to your station is beyond me."

"It is not Orinor who is a disgrace to our mother church but you and your meddling, Primate Zerum."

They all turned at once to observe to whom this new voice belonged that came at them from behind.

The speaker was a cleric with a neatly trimmed beard and a pointy chin and nose that together with the cunning twinkle in his eyes gave him a fox-like appearance. He walked aloof towards the twin thrones and reclined his head at the king then kissed the ground in front of Primate Orinor's throne before kissing the cleric's robe.

"Who is this worm of a man grovelling his way to the primate's throne?" Sir Bold asked of the Templar Commander, not concealing his contempt for the cleric.

"His name is Xersil; he is known as the primate's shadow; where Orinor goes Xersil is soon to follow."

"I see that church etiquette means very little to you and your kind, Orinor," Zerum stated, nodding at father Xersil. "You have not taught your clerics here the correct way to address a primate of the church. Stranger," he said, turning to the offensive cleric, "I did not get your name but would none the less ask you to explain yourself."

"Why it's quite simple, Your Eminence." Xersil's mouth twisted horribly as he scornfully uttered the primate's correct title. "Thanks to your meddling this afternoon with our Ecumenical Patriarch's health his situation has deteriorated drastically. By the way, Dionar," he sneered at the Templar Commander forgetting to use titles once more, "I have had physician Floose reinstated and have posted more guards faithful to our church of Ramila outside the patriarch's door with strict orders to execute any Templars who approach within a hundred paces." He smiled smugly when he saw the expression on the Templar Commander's face.

"I have heard of your unauthorized little trip to our father, Dionar," Primate Orinor added from his throne, "I will have your resignation letter before the end of the day on my desk."

Nem did not believe the large man's face could turn redder. The other four Templar knights seized the commander just as he jumped forward with arms extended ready to wring Primate Orinor's neck. Xersil hid behind the primate's throne upon seeing the commander's lunge; however Orinor stood up defiantly and met Dionar's bloodshot eyes with his own frosty gaze.

"Mount Sido's hot breath will freeze over before I lay my resignation at your feet, Orinor!" the burly knight bawled. "I know my rights, primate of Ramila, though you take me for a fool. Only the Ecumenical Patriarch or the Grand Master of our order may ask for my resignation. You are not the former yet and the latter will have my report on his desk in Ameron before the week is out. Then we'll see what Grand Master Samarass will have to say about your meddling with our ecumenical father's health and your scheming and plotting within the church of Ramila. I have been keeping a close eye on you and have catalogued a few choice pieces of information which will prove most useful in our master's hands."

Orinor, for the first time that day, looked flustered, his pale complexion turning several tones whiter. "My king," he said, turning to face King Ionid. "Order this man to be clamped in chains for high treason against the church. What he says is hearsay!"

King Ionid looked at his primate and then at his Templar Commander and shook his head. "I am afraid, Your Eminence, that the sovereign throne may not involve itself with matters of the church. I can no more order the Templar Commander to be clamped in chains than yourself."

Nem caught the faint smile crossing Primate Zerum's face. There was still hope perhaps for their expedition.

Then the king turned his long face to stare at Primate Zerum with droopy brown eyes. "Your Eminence, I am sorry to inform you that Ramila is in no situation to offer aid to our sister city of Alcavia. I have listened attentively to all that has been said today and feel that Ramila cannot afford to make more enemies. If it is King Dreyfus' wish to wage war with this Warlock then that is his choice. We on the other hand are a peaceful people who bare no ill feeling towards Alcavia or the Dragon's Foot Mountains and neither, may I hasten to add, to Ghiadon and the Forest nymphs. The views expressed by our primate are strictly his own."

Primate Zerum straightened wearing a calm exterior as he addressed the king. "Is that your final word, Your Majesty?"

"It is."

"Then we will not keep you much longer, my lord. We thank you for the opportunity you presented us to lay our plea before you."

The delegation bowed low to the king who responded with a nod. Then they made a quick exit followed by the excitable chatter amongst the courtiers. The king's mini orchestra resumed its playing.

♦ CHAPTER 20 ♦

A doll's house

Grimshaw set the same rapid pace. The river was beginning to get wider now and was moving more sluggishly, so Theo estimated they must be getting closer to the city. They were beginning to see cottages now, surrounded by large private fields that were fenced off to strangers by tall hedges and intermittent trees.

His mare snorted as she picked up the scent of the returning posse of pithiks. Grimshaw had sent them just before daybreak in the opposite direction to make sure they were not being followed. The large man approached one of the larger pithiks and for a while was listening to its harsh guttural tongue.

"Well, what did he tell you?" Loxandra approached her bearded companion. He looked at her sullenly and shook his head. "The old man is proving more resilient than we originally thought. You said the pithiks were sure to have caught him. It's been three days and still there is no sign of him. Do you think he may have gone ahead of us?"

"I doubt it," Grimshaw growled in answer. "We've been keeping a very quick pace so there's no way he is getting to the city before us."

"That may be so, Grimshaw, but when we reach the city it's going to take me a couple of days to finish off my work there and to make my preparations for the trip to the Nesal River. The old man might stir up trouble if he gets into the city. All he has to do is alert the guard and we'll have half of Ramila after us. I don't want to walk into a trap."

Theo felt a spark of hope at Loxandra's words. She was right. If his grandfather could get safely to the city and inform the authorities of their abduction, the least that would happen would be for an investigation to be made. That would cause Loxandra and her group some discomfort for sure, and her cover might be blown. However the spark of hope was quickly extinguished. "Don't worry about the old man. As soon as we reach the outskirts of the city walls I will remain behind with the pithiks to guard our trail. The old boy will not make it past me, or my name ain't Grimshaw!"

"Good, and look out for the rest of their friends," the sorceress said, pointing to Theo and his sister. "I believe it's too much to hope that they have all been captured by the Mountain nymphs. I don't believe in trusting to luck."

"This is all I believe in." Grimshaw pointed to his brain and to the edge of his axe blade. He gave Theo and Serilia a haughty grin. "The old man..." he began, and drew a line across his throat with his finger. He laughed as the blood drained from his captives' faces.

Theo no longer looked forward to approaching Ramila. It did not present any hope of escape for them but rather the possible death of his grandfather. *Well, we may as well get this over with,* he thought resignedly.

Grimshaw, true to his word, reined in, remaining just off the main road when they crested the hill and Ramila appeared. "Try not to dawdle too long with your boyfriends in Ramilla," he shouted after the sorceress who stiffened her back but did not grace him with an answer.

"Pig," she muttered so only Theo could hear. The pithiks dissolved into the woods where Theo was sure they would remain scouring the surrounding territory so not even a mouse would be able to squeeze through.

Theo could smell the sea once more as they approached Ramila. It was a huge sprawling city with most of it spilling outside its outer walls. It seemed as though over the years it had flourished and outgrown its boundaries. It was almost twice as large as Alcavia.

Theo looked with discomfort at Loxandra as she rode before them. She had changed into her purple dress and a lump caught in his throat as he remembered the events of the previous day. *Why is she being so pleasant with us today?* Perhaps she no longer felt they posed a threat. Or she was overly confident of her ability to handle any situation. He had to admit there was not much they could do. It was not as if they could approach any of the city dwellers and start yelling for help. Loxandra would cut them off with her gift straight away and the three soldiers that remained with them were more than able to handle any situation.

They passed into the city and moved towards the residences closest to the palace. The palace was separated from the rest of the city by tall iron fences and a gilded gate now closed to visitors. They turned into one of the side roads; it was more like the main road, seeing as it was the same width and just as well tended. They dismounted outside a large opulent house with lush gardens and entered through its main gate that was being well guarded.

"Welcome back mistress," one of the guards said, bowing formally to the sorceress. He was dressed in purple livery and on the front of his tunic was imprinted a small black spider. It seemed Loxandra had a sick sense of humour.

"It's good to be back, Fade," she answered the skinny fellow, as she led the rest of her companions through the entrance gates. "Tell me, is Rogue at the manor house?"

"No mistress. He went to purchase some supplies from the market place about an hour ago."

"As soon as he arrives, tell him to come see me. I'll need to have a chat with him and see how things have been going during my absence." When they reached the front courtyard to her manor, a young stable boy ran to them and took the reins of their horses. Loxandra motioned for Theo and his sister to follow. She ordered the three soldiers accompanying them to seek out the servants' quarters where they would be given something to eat from the kitchens.

The double doors to the manor house were painted white and were pierced by windows in their top half. Behind the windows hung small thin curtains, just like the ones hanging from the veranda doors which were also made from white frames. The slate roof and white wooden planks forming the walls to the structure made it look like a life sized doll's house.

"You seem to have done alright for yourself," Theo stated dryly, as they approached the entrance doors. They were opened from the inside before Loxandra reached them and a young maiden dressed in a black blouse and skirt covered by a clean white apron was standing at the door to welcome them inside.

"Yes, I believe I have. The house belonged to my second late husband." Loxandra's voice did not betray any irritation at Theo's tone or remorse at her husband's death.

"Your second husband?" Theo was a bit taken aback by the news that Loxandra had been married, and twice!

"Yes, I've been most unfortunate with my spouses. Both left me widowed. They died under the most mysterious of circumstances and I was left with the running of this," she said, spreading her arms around the manor. "Please make yourselves at home." She took their coats and offered them to a manservant. "Sophy, be a dear and fetch me two pairs of those bracelets."

Sophy, the girl that had shown them in, stood gawking at her mistress. She looked once at Theo and his sister and then turned quickly away, her eyes bulging in their sockets. "Yes ma'am, right away," she said, giving a small curtsy before she rushed to carry out her chore. *What odd behaviour*, Theo thought. His feeling of foreboding suddenly returned. He wondered why it chose this particular moment to warn him. He looked about the room and could not identify any threat, apart from the sorceress.

"Ah, there they are," Loxandra exclaimed, as Sophy arrived bearing two pairs of thin silver bracelets on a red velvet cushion. "Theo and Serilia, please extend your hands." Serilia looked at Theo questioningly. He shook his head at her. "Come now, don't ruin things. You've been behaving perfectly so far." Loxandra's voice sounded vexed. She was going to force them into doing this. Theo could find no way out of it, so he extended his arms. Better the sorceress try whatever she had in store for them on him first. Perhaps he would find a way to warn his sister if they were in imminent danger. Loxandra quickly placed two of the silver bracelets on his wrists and they snapped into position tightening their hold. He could not identify any seam or opening device on the bracelets. They were firmly attached to him now but at least he did not feel any pain. He nodded to Serilia and she followed suit. Soon Loxandra had clamped two silver bracelets on her as well.

"There, that wasn't so bad was it?" Loxandra beamed with pleasure.

Theo wondered if they had just made a serious mistake. His sixth sense was screaming, *danger!* at him. Well it was too late now. "What are these?" he asked holding his wrists up.

"These are called retainer bracelets. They're specifically designed for the gifted. The Council of Light has banned their use throughout the free lands on pain of death. However, one only needs to travel south to the Hieradon Desert Empire or east to Kalkador, or west to Dagorhind to purchase them. Even the Ice Queen, in Galandir, makes use of them. You see Theo, there is much more to the world than just the three midland kingdoms of Thalagia -four corners of the earth more, in fact."

"Why would the Council of Light ban the use of the bracelets?" Theo asked uneasily, his suspicions beginning to rise.

"Well you see the bracelets have been specifically designed to block the gifted from reaching out for their gift. To even think of touching your gift now would bring you so much pain that all I have done to you so far would seem like a blessing in comparison."

Theo's anger was boiling up inside him but he fought to keep it under control. The last time he had acted in haste it had caused his sister a lot of discomfort. He was not about to play Loxandra's sick game. "Alright. Now that you have taken care of our gift what's next?"

"Aah, I thought you would never ask. Sophy, please arrange for hot baths to be prepared for our guests. I am sure they would welcome the chance to freshen up. Also, go find the mistress of the kitchen and tell her to prepare us a generous meal."

Sophy curtsied once more and was off in a hurry. She had felt uneasy ever since she was ordered to bring the bracelets.

They were shown to separate rooms, the three soldiers posted outside their doors. Theo's room was much like the rest: it had an arched double window with thin lacy curtains that let in the afternoon sunlight and the walls were covered in flowered wallpaper. Arranged in tidy patterns hung small paintings of landscapes and animals such as horses and birds and there were even paintings depicting people in a garden or by the river having a picnic. The furniture was mostly white and definitely feminine.

Theo heard a gentle rapping on his door. He opened it tentatively. Loxandra's blue eyes met his own. "Your sister is in the guests' bathroom. That leaves you. I have a bath tub next to the master bedroom that you may use. Come now, don't be squeamish," she added, when Theo gave her a look of discomfort. "This way you will all finish at the same time and we can eat. Come on."

She took him by the hand and led him forcefully down the corridor. They arrived at a double door and Loxandra flung it open. They entered the room and on the double bed Theo could see lying on the duvet a clean shirt and trousers. The shirt was richly embroidered at the sleeves and the trousers were made of a velvety brown material.

"These should fit you nicely." Loxandra held the shirt and then the pants against Theo's frame. She was right. They were his size. "Their owner will not miss them," she assured him.

"They belonged to your husband," he croaked. His throat felt suddenly very dry.

Loxandra simply nodded, then she took him by the hand again and pushed him through to an adjacent room where a steaming bath was waiting for him. The sharp smell of jasmine assailed Theo's nostrils and he was reminded of Loxandra standing by his side. It was *her* smell. Loxandra led him to the mirror above her sink basin. He looked at his reflection and was surprised at the man that stared back at him. His face was the same as it had been at Alcavia, though it was covered in grime and the skin around his eyes was dark from lack of sleep. His hair too was greasy and tangled with a twig or two hanging from it.

He suddenly felt very unclean. Before he could react, Loxandra turned him around and started to remove his travel shirt which had become well soiled. Then, when he protested strongly, she turned around and waited whilst he removed his trousers and undergarments. He stepped gingerly into the bath and sunk thankfully into its warm waters. It felt good and he was sure it was going to work wonders for his aching bones. Loxandra took his clothing and left the bathroom. She returned soon after and grabbed a bar of soap and sponge and knelt beside Theo's bathtub.

"You have been wounded in the upper arm," she said, as she applied some soap to Theo's back. Theo nodded, not trusting his voice to answer. He was shaking like a leaf despite the warmth of the water. Loxandra continued to bathe him and to clean and then brush his hair. It had become long enough now to be tied in a knot.

"If you let me, I could take good care of you, Theo. All you need do is ask. You know, all of this could be yours someday too. *Our* side pays for services rendered handsomely."

"I could never live off someone else's riches," Theo answered, irritably. He could not hide the sound of contempt in his voice.

"Nobody is asking you to. I worked hard to get to where I am today, Theodor Marentherin. All this you see around you was paid for in kind. My husband died a very happy man."

"Well I have no intention of being your next victim." Theo knew he was treading on thin ice but he didn't care. Loxandra's advances were beginning to annoy him. His heart was given over to another woman. He would never dream of cheating on Adelayne and least of all with this Darkling. Loxandra however was not to be put off so easily. She removed her dress and stepped into the bathtub before he had a chance to react. She leaned over and grabbed his hair in her fingers pulling him towards her. Her nipples were hard against his chest as she parted his lips and delivered a long wet kiss. For a moment he felt lost in her grip, then built up the resolve to break away from her and wiped her kiss off his lips with the back of his hand.

"I told you I am not interested. I belong to someone else, don't you understand?"

Loxandra's face turned crimson and then pale as snow. "If you mean that vixen from Alcavia, I wouldn't harbour any false hopes of seeing her again. The Warlock of the Dragons' Foot Mountains is not known to be a merciful man. In your case I would take what's freely offered here and now, rather than live in a dream." Theo shook his head in reply. Loxandra got up slowly. The water formed rivulets down her naked breast line to her belly, womanhood and legs. She stepped out gracefully from the bathtub with her gazelle-like legs and threw a towel over her body. It did little to hide her alluring form.

After Theo finished his bath he stepped timidly into the room. Loxandra had left him alone. He searched for his own clothes but could not find them, so he was left with no option but to wear the clothes on the bed.

As he exited the room he found one of the soldiers waiting for him. They descended the steps, him in front and his guardian behind, and made their way to the dining hall where he found his sister wearing new garments also. They ate in silence and then were allowed to retire to the sitting area where Sophy had prepared them some hot tea. Theo looked outside the thin curtained windows to the garden beyond where he could see guards in Loxandra's household livery doing their rounds. At some point the sorceress got up and excused herself from their company.

"I have some business to take care of and will be back in the evening. You may remain here or visit the gardens outside but do not attempt to escape. I have posted guards everywhere with orders to kill you if need be. My foreman, Rogue, should be returning soon so just carry on behaving as you are now and everything will be alright for you. Before she turned to leave, Theo noticed she wore a small brooch of a spider on the hem of her purple dress. It was cast in black metal and the body and abdomen were adorned by two amethyst stones.

When Loxandra closed the door they were left on their own. Theo knew the three soldiers were not far -probably in an adjacent room. He looked about the sitting area but could not find anything that could be used as a weapon.

"That woman gives me the creeps." Serilia got up and paced around the room, casting her gaze outside the windows and listening at the door keyhole to see if she could hear anything. "I must say, Theo, your taste in women is quite astounding."

"I don't think I follow your meaning, Serilia. It's not as if I've been encouraging her. You saw how she has latched onto me like a leech. It's hardly my fault then, is it?" Theo's voice was agitated and he stared at his sister in challenge, daring her to go on.

"Don't give me any of that nonsense about you being all innocent in all this, Theodor." His sister chastised him. "You think I didn't notice the way you look at her every time she moves. A woman learns to sense these things. How could you do this to your friends? She's a Darkling for Athud's sake!"

"Serilia I am not responsible for the way she is behaving. She wants something from me. Her mind's made up, no matter what I say or do."

"Oh, she wants *something*, alright. That's what I am trying to tell you. I think you're enjoying all this." Serilia turned her back on him and stormed out of the room slamming the door behind her. Theo resorted to gazing through the sitting room windows. It was going to be a long and uncomfortable afternoon.

Loxandra had just finished reporting to her 'superior' in Ramila. Sharman, as always, had spent close to an hour interogating her with questions such as where she had been for the past six months, who she had been with and so on. It was a routine she was always subjected to whenever she arrived back in Ramila. Sharman was a thick skull, incapable of gleaning the information the Council of Light required. Loxandra had long since learnt how to deal with him.

She had one more stop to make before she returned to the manor house. She went east, towards the port, fast approaching the poorer sector known commonly as "Downside". It was a "viper's pit" where one could find all manner of people connected to the underground network. Here a different law ruled: the law of the toughest and meanest. She entered a pub with one door hanging lopsided. The sign above the entrance was sooty and almost illegible: *Nick's Slicer*.

She looked around fearlessly. She no longer had reason to feel threatened by these people. Most of them she knew already. A few had served in her employ as spies on her opponents or to murder those too stubborn to yield. They had proven very resourceful in the past and promised their new catch would be worth her while. She spotted the one she was looking for. He was holding a tankard in his left hand and with his right was fondling a wench sitting on his knee, her bosom ready to pop out of her low bust line.

Loxandra approached him, crossing the room to the bar where he sat. She looked down upon him as he kneeled forward to plaster a slobbery kiss on the wench's left breast. The wench laughed aloud and shoved his head away playfully. He grinned revealing a missing tooth, the rest blackened by ill-treatment. He nipped her ear then sat up sharply as he noticed the sorceress staring at him. The wench turned knitting her brows at the woman she thought was moving into her territory. The man shoved her off his knee and she flailed her arms to keep from falling as she lost her balance.

"Leave us," he said, turning to the wench with his one-eyed gaze. The other hollow socket was covered by a black patch. Whatever protests she had been preparing she swallowed at his look and made a hasty retreat, leaving the two of them alone.

Loxandra's attention was drawn to his ears protruding beneath the red kerchief covering his head; they were pierced in several places by half a dozen earrings. His skin was a dark brown–black almost–like the Makuri tribes of the Hadir Desert. Loxandra had discovered him about two years ago and found he was very thorough and professional at his work. "Well, will you take me to them?"

"Them?" he asked, a malevolent grin crossing his face.

"I was told three set out for Alcavia."

"Yes but only one survived the trip back to Ramila."

"Take me to him, now."

They left *Nick's Slicer* and made their way swiftly along the docks till they reached what looked like an abandoned shed. The dark man knocked twice at the door then scratched at it three times then knocked once more. They heard sounds of bolts being drawn and the large doors swung open. Another dark fellow was waiting inside, taller than the man with the red kerchief. This one had short curly black hair covering his head and bare chest. His top shirt had been left open down the front.

"What have you brought us, Maleb? She's a tasty looking morsel." The man took in Loxandra's lithe form revealed fully by her purple dress. He smiled in appreciation.

Loxandra smiled back: he was a dark and handsome man.

"She's not for your teeth, Hittat. This is the mistress I told you about: the one who pays our fees, so behave yourself!" He had given his friend fair warning. He had learnt in his dealings with the Black Widow that it was foolhardy to get too close to her.

Hittat continued to grin, ignoring his friend's warning. He motioned for them to enter before he closed and latched the door. He led them through the empty shed whose floor was littered with old smelly hay. Barely enough of the noon day sunlight streamed through gaps in the wooden walls for them to see. They arrived at a trap door in the centre of the room which Hittat lifted to reveal steps leading downwards.

"After you," Loxandra motioned. They descended carefully the narrow steps that seemed to have been carved out of the ground. When they arrived at the bottom, Hittat removed the torch from the wall and led them down the gently sloping tunnel. He informed Loxandra that this tunnel joined up with an interconnecting underground network beneath the city.

They soon arrived at an opening. Hittat entered the chamber and rested the torch on a bracket. Loxandra gazed around and was assailed by the smell of excrement, old and new blood and vomit. She stared at the far wall where a man hung limply from chains, dry blood crusting his head. He had cuts to his ribs and pelvis and on his wrists he wore thin silver bands with no sign of a seam. He was completely naked apart from his genital area that was covered by a dirty cloth. The man turned to look at her with his one eye that had not been closed by the bruising. The other bulged with an unhealthy purple colour.

"Loxandra is that you? Praise Athud!" he said, as his eyes adjusted to the torch light.

"My dearest Amus, what have they done to you?" Loxandra took out a handkerchief and wiped at his face. It was soon stained red and saturated with his blood. Amus was one of Sharman's most reliable third-rate sorcerers and had often been employed by his master on missions to the surrounding cities.

"How did you find me?" the man gasped. Blooded saliva was drooling from the corner of his misshapen mouth.

"They asked for a ransom to release you, Amus. They knew I was a colleague of yours and sent a message for me to meet them. They threatened to kill you if I did not respond. So here I am."

"Loxandra, they're using retainer bracelets on me. I can't light a spark without feeling as if my whole body is being set aflame. It's horrible."

"Hush now." Loxandra placed a hand gently on the side of his temple. He whimpered at her touch. "I'll get you out of here. Now tell me about your search. Did you find any signs of our friend? Was Archon's body amongst the wreckage?"

Amus nodded. "We found a man who fitted his description though all the bodies were bloated and barely recognizable. But I'm pretty sure it was him."

Loxandra smiled with elation. "Thank you Amus. You don't know how much pleasure you've given me."

Amus stared dumbly at her, not sure whether he had heard her correctly.

"Release him," she ordered. Hittat moved over to the man in the chains. He turned a key and the lock holding the chains to the wall opened. Amus crumbled to the floor in a heap like old rags. Loxandra bent close to him and sent a trickle of fire across his wrist bands. They sprang open.

"I can touch it once more," Amus whispered in wonder as he timidly reached for his gift.

"Yes, my dear." Loxandra placed a hand to his skull. A soft red light began to pulse beneath her fingers. It enveloped the man's head, his good eye goggling till it seemed it would pop out of its socket. He uttered an unearthly scream and arched his back. The vein at Loxandra's neck was throbbing as she fed off his life energy. His spinal cord snapped and he lay limp beneath her touch. Loxandra felt elated, like she had been taking a bath in waters filled with the primeval energies of life. She turned to Hittat with a coquettish smile. He smiled back eagerly.

"Maleb wait outside," she instructed.

Maleb nodded and went to stand a little further down from the torture room. There was nothing he could do now.

Loxandra undid her dress letting it fall next to Amus's corpse. She beckoned to Hittat. He came willingly to her open arms.

Maleb could hear the groans from the next room as the sorceress claimed her prize. He remained silent in the dark, as ordered.

As Hittat entered her, she envisaged it was Theodor. She responded with a passion to his touch that surprised him and heightened his desire for her. By the time they were finished they were both drenched in sweat.

Loxandra tried to push him away. "Get off me! Now!" she ordered, but he clutched her by the throat with one large hand that fitted easily around her slim neck.

"What is it, my sweet? You're finished with me already?"

"Get off me or I warn you I'll..."

"You'll what?"

No sooner had he spoken the words than he was propelled towards the ceiling as though an invisible hand had reached out and snatched him away. His skull hit the stone ceiling giving an audible crack. He fell on the floor beside Amus never to stir again.

Loxandra reached out calmly and put on her bloodied dress. Then she took the torch off its bracket and exited the dark room leaving the two bodies behind.

Maleb stared at her in the light of the torch. "It's not easy to come across men of Hittat's talent. He was one of the strongest men I have ever known and was useful for carrying out this line of work." His voice did not conceal his bitterness.

"You'll find another," Loxandra answered simply, as they made their way back to the stairs and to the trap door.

♦ CHAPTER 21 ♦

Puppeteer's strings

She had purchased the tickets from her usual source. The little man was a Darkling she could rely on to get her close to the lords and ladies. She would often use the theatre as an opportunity to make new contacts.

She entered the manor house from the servant's quarter so as not to be noticed and flung the dress in the bin pile just after she removed her spider brooch from the hem. She knew the blood would not wash away. Pity, it was a nice dress and had cost her a gold crown. She wrapped her nakedness in her cloak and passed through the kitchen to make her way upstairs to the bedrooms.

"I see you have gotten acquainted with Rogue," she announced a while later, as she entered to find the siblings and her foreman sitting at opposite ends of the sitting room. Loxandra looked down at her foreman whom she had employed shortly after the death of her first husband. He had arrived one day from Ameron on her husband's doorstep searching for work. Rogue had soon realized Loxandra was the one controlling the relationship with her husband and had aided her in poisoning him.

She had used him to get rid of the duke as well. Rogue kept his relationship with Loxandra on a strictly business level, which was probably why he lasted so long in her company. Before the end of his first year of service, and when he had realized how dark a heart beat in her bosom, he confided to his mistress the reason why he had left Ameron in a hurry.

He had not arrived that day at Loxandra's residence by chance. She had been recommended to him by his colleagues in Ramila. Since the death of her late husband, he had been running the manor house and Loxandra's affairs whilst she was away. The arrangement suited them both perfectly.

Theo's gaze followed the sorceress round the room as she poured four cups of tea from the pot Sophy had just brought in. She offered it to them before taking a seat beside Rogue. Theo sipped at his tea in silence. They had spent most of the afternoon in the garden searching for a means of escape. Loxandra had taken all the necessary precautions to ensure they remained trapped at the manor house. Then when they had retired to the sitting room they had found Rogue waiting for them. Theo looked at the triangular scar directly below Rogue's right eye. He also noticed the foreman walked with a slight limp.

He was almost relieved when the sorceress walked in. He did not feel comfortable being in the same room as this man with the dark eyes and thick head of hair that made him look like a wolverine ready to pounce.

Loxandra smiled brightly at her captives. "I have some pleasant news," she said, her eyes twinkling with pleasure. "I'll be taking you all to the theatre tonight. Herod Dromidus will be giving one of his rare performances."

Theo stared with disbelief at the sorceress. He turned to look at Serilia and realized she too was taken aback. Once more he felt as if the sorceress was overly confident of her control over their actions. Good, he would use the chance to draw some attention. Loxandra had surprisingly just made her first blunder.

"Is it wise to take these two with you?" Rogue asked. He shifted his broad shoulders with discomfort, his dark eyes gazing at the youths with contempt. "It will be difficult to keep an eye on them in the company of so many people and they're likely to call for aid at the first opportunity."

"I believe Theo and Serilia will be on their very best behaviour tonight," Loxandra replied with certainty. "You see I've placed a little something in their tea. Widow lace is a rare poison that, without the administering of the antidote every hour for at least the first seven hours, leads to death by constricting the wind pipe. If I so much as suspect that they are endangering me or are about to blow my cover I will leave them to perish."

Serilia's cup shattered as it hit the stone floor. She stared with horror and disgust at the sorceress. Theo's hand was trembling slightly and he placed the cup slowly on a side table. Rogue too stared at his cup and back at the sorceress but she shook her head to reassure him she had only placed it in the cups of the other two.

"Excellent. Now that we have taken care of matters let's all go upstairs and get dressed, shall we?" she said pleasantly.

The streets were filled with people. All were dressed in their finest as they made their way slowly towards the large circular building that stood just outside the city walls. It was crafted in the same old stone that adorned Ramila's more prestigious buildings. Outside the entrance, posters were plastered all over the ticket booth walls. The writing on the posters read, *"Herod Dromidus in: A Pauper's Tale"*. There were people from all levels of society flocking to see the theatrical production. Loxandra had led them to the aristocrats' entrance and held four golden coloured tickets in her hands.

They waited in the crowd patiently for the king and his royal entourage to arrive. The theatre commissionaires had placed movable bronze posts connected by a chain to keep the crowd back from the grand entrance and the walkway the nobles were to use. Theo felt a bit giddy from the ladies' perfumes. Loxandra had given them the first dose of antidote a few moments before they set out from the manor but he still felt the stomach upset brought on by the poison. He also felt drowsy, as did Serilia. All hopes of their escape had been quashed.

The honoured guests began to arrive one after the other, their shiny polished chariots stopping before the theatre entrance to release their exclusive passengers. The first group appeared to be lords and ladies wearing fanciful clothes with frilled sleeves for the gentlemen and long dress tails for the ladies who trod with high heels on the plush red carpet laid for their benefit. All wore hats with plumed décor and stepped forward with an erect elegant style like peacocks. Then followed a group dressed in black, like a flock of crows, with heavy pendants bearing Athud's flame hanging from their necks. They were clergymen from the Church of Athud and in their midst walked a clean-shaven man with flaxen hair who wore three pendants around his neck.

"That is the Primate of Ramila, Orinor, who could very well be the next Ecumenical Patriarch," Loxandra said to the two youths informatively. "The Ecumenical Patriarch is probably one of the most prominant and influential figures in all Thalagia."

"What do the pendants with the wolf and the one with that circular symbol imply?" Theodor asked, noticing the silver and gold pendants as the primate approached and passed them by. He knew what the flame pendant stood for. The crowd reclined their heads in unison as the fathers of the church led their leader inside the theatre.

"The wolf is Ramila's emblem, as you may have noticed from the flags flying at the mastheads of all the official buildings. The large Sovereign gold coin with the three stars signifies the dominion of the church, the three lands of Leonium, Seldavia and Renderon."

Next to alight from a black chariot carried forth by equally dark horses, was a solitary figure dressed in a plain grey cloak covering his stark brown tunic and pants. He had deep, inset brown eyes beneath heavy brows and a receding brow that went up to his bald crown, and around his head his dark hair with wisps of grey jutted out from the sides forming a ring around his baldness. He moved forward with a slight hunch and by his side stood a young slim girl with curly brown hair and a thin face. Theo's heart jumped to his throat as he recognized her. It was the girl that had visited Archon at the inn in Jade Island, the one that had delivered First Sorcerer Sharman's message that Archon was to make a detour to Jandaea Island to pick up Zoi.

Theo averted his eyes from sorcerer Sharman and his apprentice as they made their way forward. Loxandra had removed their retainer bracelets so, as the sorcerers passed by, he could sense a tingling, as when a cool breeze blows over the skin in the middle of a hot summer night. The tingling intermingled with his awareness of Serilia and Loxandra so he hoped the sorcerer would be confused by Loxandra's gift. The sorcerer moved closer when he spotted his colleague and nodded at her in greeting. Loxandra nodded back, forcing a lukewarm smile to form on her lips.

"Loxandra, I see you were able to make it. We'll chat once you come inside, then we can get better acquainted with your companions."

"Yes, Sharman," Loxandra spoke half-heartedly, casting a warning glance back at her charges. Serilia coughed beginning to feel the effects of the antidote wearing off. "We'll see what I can do to alleviate your cough once we are inside, dear," Loxandra said sweetly, but loud enough so Theo could hear. Sorcerer Sharman was unaware of the exchange and excused himself as he followed after the rest of the noble guests.

Then Theo heard the sound of a multitude of hooves as a large convoy of soldiers arrived on their freshly groomed steeds, dressed in shining armour glinting golden in the night, reflecting the light from the many torch lanterns lit around the theatre courtyard. Their shiny helmets were conical extending to the nape of their necks with openings in the front for the eyes and severe nose guards. Long flowing horse tails the colour of blood adorned their crest. They surely were the king's personal guard and on foot followed more soldiers dressed with Ramila's emblem of a crouching wolf imprinted in black on the front of their green tunics. They fanned out forming a line on either side from the courtyard to the theatre entrance. The knights alighted from their steeds whose steaming breaths formed tendrils from their flared nostrils.

Arriving at the rear of the column was a dark chariot with a lustrous finish. It was slightly curved in plan on both sides so it bulged like an oversized acorn and was set on springs mounted on wheels gilded with golden spirals, making a pleasant contrast with the dark chariot. The lackey swung down from his perch moving swiftly to open the door and to release the stair mechanism before genuflecting.

A figure richly adorned in frills wearing a golden coat and pants stepped gingerly down the chariot steps aided by one of his knights who had stepped forward to lend his arm to his liege. The king excused the knight when he reached the ground and in turn extended his hand to help his lady companion to alight from the chariot. She was dressed very plainly, in stark contrast to the king, in an austere dark green dress reaching up to her neckline, covering her arms and legs and reaching down to her calves. She wore black-heeled shoes with buckles similar to those of the king. Her only decoration was a thin silver-chained belt that held a pendant of an erect lion.

Theo was reminded quite suddenly of Prince Armend's emblem on his tunic and stared more intently at the woman who was half the age of the king. As the royal couple approached he realized they looked like brother and sister. *Odd*, he thought, *I feel like I have met her before*. He turned to his sister and saw the look of bewilderment on her face as well. "Who is she, and where is she from?" he asked the sorceress by his side.

"That's Princess Diomeda, daughter to King Philander of Ameron. She's our king's niece from her mother's side and spends most of her time in Ramila with her uncle." It all clicked into place for Theo. He found his heart raced faster as the princess approached. He almost expected her to look accusingly at him for what he had done to her brother. Then he remembered that he and his companions were meant to have broken the news to her family. He wondered where his friends might be now. Loxandra was taking risks delaying here at Ramila. If his companions had managed to get away from the Mountain nymphs they would come after him. Then he remembered with sinking heart Grimshaw and his posse of pithiks. He hoped his grandfather would have the sense to go back and team up with the group before coming for him.

"Come, they're letting us in." Loxandra ushered them before her and they joined the crowd moving in an orderly fashion; few people ventured to enter from the exclusive entrance so they soon passed the stewards and arrived at their booth. The theatre was a sealed arena with overhanging chandeliers supporting oil lamps providing light for the audience that was filing into it.

A steady murmuring noise filled the great hall with many voices chatting merrily as they were shown to their seats. Had Theo been alone, and his sister's life not in danger, he would have seriously considered jumping from the balcony. A few bruises and a cut or two would have been a small price to pay to escape from the sorceress's clutches.

"Ah Loxandra, there you are!" They turned around to find Sharman staring at them with his dark brown eyes. "I've asked the stewards to allow you to join us in our booth. It affords a better view of the stage and we have some brandy waiting."

Loxandra did not seem pleased but nodded, motioning to the youths to follow the sorcerer. He led them a few booths further on towards the front and pulled back the curtains. His young female companion smiled up at Theo and his sister, then nodded respectfully to Loxandra. Loxandra nodded ever so slightly in response. Theo sat quickly and tried not to look too directly at the slim girl. If she recognized him and said the wrong words, Loxandra might be backed into a corner with untold consequences.

"My name is Jameira." The young apprentice extended her hand in greeting. *Did she delay for a second more when she shook my hand?* But her eyes did not reveal she had recognized him. "Mistress Loxandra has told my master that you are from the Duchy of Varmondi," Jameira added, casually.

Loxandra threw Theo a fleeting hard look and quickly looked back at Jameira smiling without warmth. "Yes, that's correct," Theo said. "We live at a cottage there, my sister Lucy and I." He nodded at Serilia. "Mistress Loxandra was kind enough to offer us the opportunity to visit Ramila and stay at her residence. We are pleased to be afforded the chance to enjoy what our ruling city has to offer." He felt like a puppet with Loxandra pulling all the strings. He had told everything exactly the way she had made him recite before they arrived. She looked closely at him trying to decide whether he had given anything away then smiled with satisfaction. Theo felt the urge to slam his fist in her pretty face but restrained himself with great effort.

"You've never been to the city before, eh..."

"Tom," Theo added. "Yes we've been before to buy clothing and to visit the games but we've never been to the theatre before." It was the truth–the part about the theatre.

"Ah, you will enjoy it immensely. Herod Dromidus is famous for his performances." Jameira smiled sweetly at him. She was not an unpleasant girl though she was awfully thin and her cheeks were drawn. Her curly hair fell to her bony shoulders and around her bare neck she wore a small amulet. Theo was about to ask her where she was from but halted at the last. He did not want to jolt her memory of him.

Sharman stared at both him and his sister and placed a hairy hand to his large chin. Theo felt a tingling sensation as he sensed the sorcerer probing his mind. The sorcerer's eyes widened as realization dawned on him. "Loxandra are you aware that both Tom and Lucy are gifted?" He seemed well pleased with the results of his probe.

Loxandra kept her outer calm. "Why, of course I am, Sharman, which is one of the reasons why I have brought the two of them to visit Ramila. I was planning on bringing them over to our Chapter House over the coming days, to visit so we could show them around and perhaps convince them to give up farming and join our brotherhood in the service of the Council of Light."

"Why that's an excellent idea, Loxandra. Bring them to me tomorrow evening. No need to wait longer than that. It is highly unusual to find someone with so much of the gift waiting to be utilized, and here we have two candidates." Sharman's dark eyes were suddenly very bright. He gazed upon Theo and Serilia as if he were a treasure hunter who had just uncovered two precious stones.

A silence fell over the audience as the tall curtains to the stage were drawn back. Jameira offered them some brandy but Loxandra asked for a canter of water instead saying the two youths were suffering from a cold and she was administering medication to them. Serilia coughed unwittingly and Loxandra gave the two of them their next dose of the antidote. Neither Jameira nor Sharman recognized the drug in the dark.

A group of dancers began the show then a minstrel finished entertaining the crowd with several of his songs. When the audience's applause had died away, a tall slim man entered the stage. He had a black beard trimmed so it ran in a thin line along his jaw bone leaving his cheeks and throat clean-shaven and ending in a goatee at his mouth and chin. The crowd cheered and whistled at the site of the performer but he ignored them as he struck his pose. There would be time enough to acknowledge his fans at the end of the production. He lifted his right arm in the air and opened up his slender fingers pointing off to another female performer beside him.

The show had begun. "The Pauper's Tale", was a story about a young man who grew up in the poorer parts of the city. It went on to describe how he grew up from pauper to become a lord. He met the woman of his dreams but fate conspired against him and he lost his love to another man.

The crowd was riveted by Herod's performance and when the play ended they gave him a standing ovation. Serilia was shedding tears and even Jameira was feeling emotional. Loxandra smiled that ironic smile of hers. *She probably enjoyed the ending,* Theo thought acidly. Herod's performance had truly been magnificent. He felt a pang of longing for his princess and wondered, not for the first time, how she was coping with the Witch Lord. *No worse than we are with the Black Widow*, he thought miserably.

Loxandra gathered up her charges like a goose her chicks. They bade their farewells to Sharman and Jameira and made their way solemnly to the exit. Before leaving, Loxandra gave them the antidote once more just as they were beginning to feel their throats constricting.

"That went better than I thought," Loxandra said as they exited the theatre. They made their way back to her manor house in silence. The guard greeted them at the entrance and Rogue was waiting for them in the sitting room with the fireplace lit.

"How was it?" he asked, looking at the siblings meaningfully.

"The production was a howling success, and the rest of the evening was not too bad either. I was pleased with everyone's performances tonight." Loxandra had donned that sarcastic smile that so readily appeared on her lips. Theo and his sister asked to be excused but Loxandra had not finished with them yet.

"Do you have them?" she asked turning to her foreman. He produced the silver bracelets lying on the velvet cushion. "Here children, put these on, will you?" The sorceress held out the retaining bracelets. Serilia shook her head and Theo fixed Loxandra with a hate-filled gaze. "Come now we've been through this before. You still have one more dose of the antidote to take. You wouldn't want to ruin things now, would you?"

Theo felt those strings pulling at his hands, forcing him to place the bracelets around his wrists. His sister did likewise. Loxandra excused them at last and they went upstairs to their rooms feeling utterly wretched.

The poison had worn off during the night, leaving him with a sweat that had drenched his night garments. Now he stood on the front porch wearing the clothes the sorceress had provided for him. Loxandra had left early in the morning on one of her errands leaving the siblings alone with her foreman.

Theo looked at the guard at the entrance gate. There were others patrolling the grounds. He felt uneasy today for some reason. His senses warned him that something was amiss; he had learned to listen to his senses. The change in the wind promised foul weather was approaching. He wondered how Adelayne was faring up in the icy peaks of the Dragon's Foot Mountains. He rubbed at his arms as the cold air buffeted him. He was about to turn back inside when he heard the guard calling out to one of his colleagues. The other ran swiftly to the servants' quarters and returned soon after with foreman Rogue at his heels carrying a broadsword.

"What's going on?" Serilia was at Theo's side looking intently at the commotion at the gate.

"I don't know but get your coat, quickly!"

There was shouting and more of Loxandra's men with their purple livery were being summoned to the gate. Theo could distinguish the red tunics and green pants of the Ramilan city guard.

"Open up, in the name of the king!" one of the uniformed soldiers was commanding the foreman. "We have orders to search the premises."

"I will not allow a single man to enter without the permission of the mistress of the house," the foreman bawled in reply.

"Then fetch her as well. We have a warrant for her arrest," the same man answered. Theo could make out the insignia on the man's epaulet marking him as the officer of highest rank in the patrol.

"On what charge?" Rogue gave a wolverine growl, the muscles of his jaw line contracting as he clenched his teeth. Theo could see his knuckles go white on the hilt of his sword as he clutched it firmly in his hands.

"On the charge of kidnapping. Now do as the officer commands and open the gate!" Theo noticed from behind the patrol the bald head and out-flung hair of First Sorcerer Sharman. Theo also recognized the slim form of Jameira. *So she had recognized us after all!* Suddenly Theo felt elated at the possibility of them being freed from the sorceress's grasp.

"Don't let a single man inside or you'll suffer a fate worse than death at the hands of the master." Theo did not need to wonder at which "master" Rogue was referring to. He saw the rest of the purple liveried guards holding their weapons threateningly whilst Rogue placed a wooden bar across the gate to reinforce it from the inside.

"Battering ram!" The officer in the front growled.

"Get the pikes, and bring the archers to the front," Rogue commanded, falling back from the gate and clutching a shield that was provided for him by the stable hand. Soon Rogue's unit formed a few paces back from the gate, half of them equipped with pikes and the other half with bows and arrows. The half dozen men with the pikes held tall square shields and stood in the front to protect the equal number of archers. The three soldiers that had been in Grimshaw's company drew their swords and waited for Rogue's command, falling in line behind the foreman who seemed to know what he was doing.

"Fall back, NOW!" the officer called out urgently to his men, sensing the imminent danger. He had not counted on such an organized defence being mounted by the sorceress's house guard.

"Release!" Rogue gave the command in a calm voice and watched as the first group of soldiers of the city guard fell to the ground with arrow shafts protruding from their backs.

Theo's heart was racing with the events unfolding before him. Serilia bumped into him from behind as she ran out the front door. Theo's concentration was riveted on Rogue's every move, waiting for the chance to arrive for them to make their getaway. The foreman had his eyes trained on the city guard so he was not paying them any attention.

"Release!" Rogue shouted once more. The city guards had returned bearing shields with the wolf emblem of Ramila. Some of the arrows met their mark and the guards fell to the ground whilst the rest of the arrows pierced the remaining guards' shields and fixed into position with their shafts vibrating.

"Heave, hoooah!" the guards shouted in unison as they crashed into the gate with their battering ram.

Theo heard a whistling in the air then saw two of Rogue's archers falling to the ground struck by arrows. Somewhere he heard the "whoosh" of flaming arrows landing on the manor house roof and saw the stables catch fire. "The horses!" he shouted to his sister clutching her by the arm. "Come on, we need to get them out of there." They raced to the stables and were confronted by the stable boy who held a small dagger in his hand.

"Stay back," the stable boy snapped, holding the dagger threateningly before him.

"Let us help you," Theo pleaded. "Those animals will die unless we get them out of there."

"Nobody is going near the horses. Master's orders. Either Master Rogue comes for them or they remain there to burn." He was a young lad maybe just over sixteen years old but held the blade with a trained hand. The scars marking his face and the piece missing from his ear bore evidence that he had been forced to use the blade before.

"Don't be daft, man! What use will dead horses be to you or your master? This is senseless! Now stop being an ass and let us through." Theo made to move past the boy but had to spring back to avoid being cut by the young man's swiping action.

Theo made a sign to his sister, the way they did when she followed him and Nem on their hunting trips. Serilia nodded and circled around the boy from the right. The stable boy followed her every move and turned his body to face Serilia but at the same time was moving backwards to keep an eye on Theo who was approaching from his left.

This one is going to be tough, Theo thought. The stable boy was obviously accustomed to brawling. Loxandra had a skilled crew in her employ it seemed. He heard the horses' shrill neighing and began to feel jittery. They had to get around the boy somehow.

They backed him till they were almost by the stable door. At least they were getting closer. Theo panicked as he saw the flames licking the sides of the stable walls and the fire spreading from the roof. It wouldn't be long now before the whole thing was engulfed in flames. The seconds were ticking away. He could hear the horses smacking the sides of their stalls with their hooves. He coughed as the wind changed and the smoke from the fire blew in their direction.

The stable boy lifted one hand to cough and Theo decided to risk it. He moved in to attack knowing full well that he was at a disadvantage. He had to wrestle the dagger from the boy's grasp but at the same time avoid getting sliced by the sharp blade. The stable boy saw him coming and lunged at him. Theo employed the tactics of close-up combat Roxette had taught him and let the blade pass over his shoulder, too close to his neck for comfort. Then he grabbed his assailant's arm and delivered a downward chop with his hand on the boy's wrist. The boy gave out a yelping cry and dropped the blade. Theo kicked him on the side of the knee cap and heard a popping sound as the knee bone separated from the leg bones. The stable boy fell to the ground howling with pain.

Serilia was quick to snatch the dagger and the two of them rushed to enter the stables. Inside they came face to face with the full wrath of the blazing inferno. Flames were sprouting like hungry tongues from the wooden walls searching for fresh dry wood to engulf whilst from the base of the fire black poisonous fumes spewed forth as from the belly of a fire-breathing beast. Theo acted instinctively, going for the nearest stall and flung the doors wide open. His sister did the same on the opposite side and soon they were dodging the horses' hooves as the frightened animals raced for the stable exit. Thankfully they arrived at the last stalls and released those poor beasts as well.

They were about to leave when part of the roof subsided sending sparks flying everywhere. Theo was temporarily blinded. Above the sound of the falling timbers he thought he heard a shout. He rubbed at his eyes but the smoke would not allow them to clear. He was coughing continuously now and his every breath filled his lungs with more of the poisonous fumes. He was beginning to see stars in his vision as he fell to the ground spitting and coughing. He felt like he was swimming in dark waters and couldn't surface. For a moment he thought he was asleep and that he was reliving a nightmare.

Then he felt an arm reach out and pull him away from the worst of the smoke. The sinking feeling was beginning to recede and his vision was clearing. They burst out of the burning stables and into the daylight. He took huge gulps of air as his chest was racked by coughs. Then he looked up to see Serilia standing next to him, bent over and fighting for breath. Her face was black with soot and tears were streaming from her eyes. Theo saw the boy hobbling towards them with the three-pronged hay fork. He tried to force himself to rise but could not make his muscles respond. He was still suffering from the after-effects of the poisoned fumes. Serilia was still bent over, her hands to her bent knees, coughing. He opened his mouth to shout a warning but made a small croaking sound instead. The stable boy was hobbling closer in earnest and the prongs were suspended a few feet away from his sister's throat.

Theo saw a blur. *Am I losing my senses again?* He felt as if time had become suspended as he saw Serilia falling to the ground with the fork prong sticking out of her neck. Blood was splattered across her face. A sickening lurch assailed his guts. He had failed her miserably! No, something was not registering correctly in his brain. The prongs were by Serila's side and not near her throat. The blood spilt all over her face was not her own.

Beside her Theo could see the lifeless body of the stable boy. Serilia rose from behind the fallen boy and wiped the dagger blade on the dead boy's shirt. Her eyes were dilated and she jerked the blade over and over again across the boy's shirt well after the blood had been cleaned. Then she turned around and walked towards the well in the centre of the stable courtyard. She reached into the bucket next to the well and flung cold water over her head. She dropped the dagger and washed her hands in the bucket.

Theo pulled himself to his feet and stared in disbelief at the boy who lay on the cold stone floor. He was brought out of his stupor by the screaming and shouting coming from across the yard as the city patrol burst through the gate flinging it open as its chain and lock yielded.

Rogue's men were cut down to seven. Grimshaw's men were amongst the dead. Four of Rogue's men rushed forward scrambling over their fallen comrades and drove their pikes deep into the advancing soldiers' bellies. The other three remained behind with their foreman, clutching at their swords. Then mounted officers rushed into the grounds bearing lances and slammed into the pike men. Two of them were crushed beneath the horses' hooves whilst the other two were pinned to the riders' lances twitching in agony.

Theo approached Serilia and pulled her around to face him. He wiped the blood and soot away from her face with one sleeve. "Serilia, snap out of it. I need you to be strong now. We are still in danger." As if to reinforce his words, Sophy ran out of the manor house and flung herself at them screeching like a banshee, a sharp cooking knife held in her right hand. Theo reached out for the fork prong and slammed it into the young woman's chest. She stared at him in shocked surprise before she fell back and tumbled into the well.

Theo had reacted instinctively to protect his own. He could not believe he had taken a life, even if it belonged to a servant of the Dark. Now he knew exactly how Serilia felt. He realized he had crossed a line from whence there could be no return. He was brought out of his shock by a movement at the edge of his vision. He turned to see Rogue hacking away at the soldiers closest to him. Only he and one of his most hardened men were left. Theo recognized the second man as Fade, the guard they had first met upon coming to the manor house. The officers on horseback pressed their steeds forward. It was only a matter of time now before they would run down Rogue and his companion.

Then Theo met Jameira's eyes. The young girl apprentice ran towards them. "Let me help you out of those," she called as she approached. "My gift lies in the Earth agent," she explained as she placed a finger above Serilia's retaining bracelets. A soft brown glow emanated from Jameira's hands as she released her Earth weave. Serilia's bracelets sprang open. She threw them off as if they might reach out and bite her. She rubbed at her wrists and smiled at Theo encouragingly.

Jameira turned to Theo. He heard a loud cracking noise and felt a warmth on his face. Something was stuck in his hair and his right eye.

Why is there a hole in Jameira's chest? Theo's mind was working mechanically, disconnected from his emotions by the shock he had sustained. Jameira clutched at his shirt her eyes beginning to glaze over. She fell at his feet and lay lifeless.

Theo heard a howl of dismay from Sharman and noticed Loxandra standing at the gate her right hand pointing to where Jameira's chest had been. Sharman flung himself at her and they tumbled to the ground together, biting and snarling like curs. Sharman tore at the sorceress's dress with his large ape-like hands. He was enveloped in a brown glow that burned with the same intensity as Loxandra's red. The sorceress managed to get her knees between herself and the sorcerer and kicked at him furiously, sending him flying through the air.

She sprang to her feet and braced herself before sending twin bolts of red flame hurtling towards her opponent. Sharman flung up his shield but it disintegrated like glass struck by a rock. He was lifted into the air by the sorceress's red flame and flung away, like a monkey caught by a spear in the chest whilst springing in the air from one tree to the next. He fell to his side and remained motionless, smoke rising from his charred clothing. Loxandra stood to regain her breath, her dress torn on one side and her left breast hanging out with the marks of Sharman's nails red on her pale skin.

"Come on, are you waiting for her to take notice of you before making your getaway?" Theo threw an astonished gaze at the old man who held the reins to their horses.

"Grandfather, you're alive!" He embraced the old man in a warm hug and his sister joined them.

"Come we're still not free of her clutches," Nestor said, pointing in the direction of the sorceress.

Theo turned to look at Loxandra who had recovered and was throwing her bolts of red fire at the city patrol and the mounted officers. The horses screamed and some of them reared, throwing their riders off. The tables were being turned on the city guard once more.

Nestor led them from the side furthest away from the fighting. They pulled at their horses' reins as they led them along the manor house perimeter wall. The Black Widow was busy at her gruesome task and did not seem to notice them.

"Fall back!" one of the city officers was screaming. "We can't overpower her this way. Fall back and send forth the archers to finish her off." The remaining soldiers began to exit from the entrance and Nestor urged his companions to cross the yard and fall in with the retreating soldiers.

"Theodor, leaving so soon before the fun's over?" Theo felt like a noose was wrapped around his neck. He could see a thin red line fixed around his throat like a rope extending to Loxandra's hand. She yanked at the "rope" and he fell to his knees clutching at his neck. He could feel the flesh of his hands burning and the same sensation around his neck. Anger welled up inside him; anger that had been bottled up over the past five days of their captivity.

He reached out with all his strength to gather his gift, ignoring his sister's warning. Then it hit him–a pain like nothing he had ever felt before. It was like every fibre of his being, every nerve ending, however minute, had been scorched by a searing hot flame that burned him from within. Reaching for the gift was not supposed to feel this way–then he remembered: Jameira had been murdered before she could remove his retaining bracelets. So this was the pain Loxandra had promised them.

Nestor knelt beside him and was saying something incoherent to him; he could hear nothing other than a whistling sound in his ears. Loxandra approached from the other side of the courtyard, her sardonic smile fixed on her face.

Her hands extended before her as she prepared to deliver the killing blow.

Twin beacons of purply blue light flashed before his eyes. He saw, as if in a dream, the sorceress lifted into the air. Maybe he *was* dreaming. Loxandra had a look of disbelief in her eyes as she was flung away from them. She landed hard on her back, like a fat spider that had gotten its feet tangled up in its own web and fallen from its perch. Serilia stood with feet apart her arms stretched out in the direction of what had been their captor. She was breathing hard with the exertion of what she had just done. Theo felt himself thrown over his horse's back like a sack. As they rode out of the manor house he lifted his head and noticed from between the legs of his steed that the sorceress lay still. They passed what he mistook to be the charred remains of an animal. Then he saw the dark brown lifeless eyes staring back at him from behind the large snout and blackened lips. Ramila was going to need a new First Sorcerer.

♦ CHAPTER 22 ♦

The end of an era

He sat sprawled on his throne one foot left dangling over the arm of his chair. He looked with boredom at the large fellow who crouched before him informing him of his troubles. The obese man was attired in rich flowing garments and wore a king's fortune on his chubby fingers that were filled with rings surmounted by a variety of precious stones. He wiped at his bald forehead and spoke in a high-pitched nasal voice that cut off every time he drew a laboured breath.

"Master Solitair, I'm not exactly sure what it is you require of me," the king answered in a tired voice that showed plainly he would rather be dealing with other matters. "I already have ten of my warships patrolling Leonium's waters up to the northern shores of Galipa. Ramila has sent out another six aiding us in keeping the sea routes safe for you and the rest of our merchants."

"My king, forgive me if I carry on so, but even if we had twice that number they would still not be enough to keep the seas safe from the Anvil Kingdom pirates. What is required is for a delegation of high standing officials from both Leonium and Seldavia to make a voyage to Hieradon. They need to demand from the empress to honour the treaty she has signed for the safe passage of all ships, whether merchant or passenger."

"The empress will never admit to having any jurisdiction over the pirate ships, you know that well enough. She has oft claimed that the pirates act of their own volition and are a problem for her ships as well."

"Hah! Her ships are never harassed by the Ishbadese or Nebese. It is common knowledge that she receives a fat slice of the pirates' spoils. So far, my king, we were willing to put up with the raids because they were infrequent and our losses were down to an acceptable tenth of our produce. But lately for every four ships we send out one does not make it back safely. We will not be able to last under this strain and will have to increase our prices in the local markets to be able to compensate for our losses."

"That is unacceptable, master Solitair!" This time the king brought his leg down from the throne's arm and sat up with his attention riveted on the fat man. "Why do you not hire mercenaries to protect your wares?"

"We have tried that, my king, but mercenaries do not come cheap and when things turn nasty they prefer to lose their pay to save their necks."

"I will take your request to send a delegation seriously, master Solitair, but in the meantime I will not allow an increase in your prices on our markets. That will cause me problems I could well do without."

His mind wandered to the disturbing reports he was receiving from Alcavia and Ramila about increased raids from the Mountain nymphs of the west. The situation was so appalling that the caravan routes had almost been ground to a halt. Most of the produce waited at the docks for the first available ship to take them to their destination. There were just not enough ships to do the job. And the sea was no longer as safe as she had been in the past. He wondered how his son Armend was faring back at Alcavia's Military Academy. He had sent the youth there to learn how to wage war and to become stronger in body and spirit. That boy would become king of all Leonium one day.

"My king," the fat merchant said, in a voice like a squealing prairie dog. "I am afraid I will not be able to keep my prices at the same levels for more than two or three months at most. If the delegation delays or is not successful, then by spring my prices will have to go up and the rest of my colleagues will follow suit."

"Fine," the king answered, irritably. "Now leave me so I may ponder on your words." He knew the merchant was not to blame for his stance. It was no use being angry with the victim but rather he needed to face the problem and solve it. The door closed behind the fat merchant and King Philander of Ameron was left alone with his troubled thoughts.

He would need to send an urgent message to High King Daron of Aldorn. But would the aging king be able to respond? Daron was fast approaching retirement age and was rumoured amongst the nobles to have lost interest in politics ever since his daughter and son-in-law had been murdered twenty-odd years ago. Seldavia and her kings had other alternatives for their trading goods. They could send them north, through Aubenshorn Gate, or up in the Brakkand's Throne Mountains to the highlanders. They also traded with Renderon in the east. What need would the Seldavian Kingdoms have to come into direct conflict with the empress over the issue of the pirate raids when they had so many other options to choose from?

He thought about bringing his case forth to the Supreme Council of Thalagia that for the past three years had been residing in Hendon. By all rights the position of Supreme Chancellor usually went to either of three High Kings of Leonium, Seldavia or Renderon. But he had not expressed his desire to run for the post. Leonium was enough for him to handle and it seemed Renderon had proved more than enough for its late High King, who had this year met with his untimely death. That left Daron of

Aldorn, and he had been in no condition to take up the role of Supreme Chancellor. So he had left King Apandor of Hendon to fill the post.

Apandor was ill equipped to bring together the conflicting factions in Thalagia and to unite the races in a common cause against the enemy. The Wizards' Council of Light was doing everything in its power to keep the Dark's advance in check but they could not stem the Dark's tide. And the council was being weakened by infiltrators in its ranks. Stories of sorcerers previously thought of as allies turning to the other side were increasing.

The church also was not aiding the kingdoms as it had in the past. Too few of the church leaders truly cared about what was going on in the kingdoms of Thalagia. The clerics were more interested in gaining power. Of course there were still those amongst the laity who still cared. Such a one was Primate Karat, who now entered the High King's throne room, his dark garments flowing behind him as he advanced. He held a crosier in his right hand surmounted by the lion emblem which stood for the Leonese autocephalous seat of the church.

Karat nodded, one equal to another. The king acknowledged his presence with a nod of his own. The priest was a tall figure with a long beard Philander remembered had been filled with more black than grey hairs. He had aged considerably in the past eight years of his reign as primate of Ameron.

"My king, I have come to speak to you about a personal matter that will influence both of us, I believe." He fixed the king with a steady and sure gaze.

"Speak freely, father Karat, we are alone."

The cleric looked about uneasily and approached his king. "Even the walls have ears, my king," he said, bending closer to the king keeping his voice low so it did not carry. "I have come bearing sad tidings, my lord. Our Ecumenical

Patriarch's health has been reported to be deteriorating. He is not expected to make it through the week."

The king looked upon his cleric in astonishment. Everyone knew the old man was playing hide and seek with the reaper but the news of his impending death was shocking nonetheless.

"My king I will need for you to announce your support for my candidacy publicly as soon as the patriarch departs. I know this sounds cold-hearted, my lord, but you have known me for many years and have realized that I am a decent man."

"This is so, Primate Karat," King Philander answered genuinely. "Please feel free to express your thoughts."

"We will need to act fast to stay ahead of our opposition, Your Majesty. I will be in a better position to aid you if we are successful. Then you as High King and I as Ecumenical Patriarch can better rule Leonium side by side and solve the most prominent issues troubling our realm."

The king pondered on Karat's words. The church had often aided the monarchy in the past financially to squeeze through tough times. Perhaps he had found a way to gain some time for Leonium. If only the church could foot the bill for the merchants' losses for at least another year. Then by next year's elections for Supreme Chancellor, he could put down as a precondition for his giving his support that the chancellor send a delegation representing all of Thalagia to Hieradon. This united front of the three kingdoms could request that the empress fall in line with her signed agreements regarding safe passage to the Midlands' ships. "You have my full support Karat. In a week from now after we have buried our father, I will announce Ameron's full support to your candidacy for the ecumenical throne."

"I thank you, my king." The priest bowed low before exiting.

The king was about to leave when the door opened and a figure entered clad in a long dress covering her completely to her soft velvet slippers. She had her blond hair cut around her cheekbones accentuating her oval face that had once been very beautiful. Age had placed smile lines at the sides of her mouth and eyes, and her lips were puckered losing the fullness of their youth. She liked to dress stylishly which showed in the quality of the fabric of her red dress. Despite her age, which Philander placed at being somewhere around sixty, she retained a figure many younger women would have envied.

First Sorceress Narcissa was perhaps the most powerful figure in Ameron, after Philander and Primate Karat. She was born the daughter of a duke of Ameron and a sorceress from Ramila. Narcissa was rumoured to be even stronger in the gift than her mother and was widely respected; she was considered the most dominant figure amongst the gifted in Leonium.

"King Philander I have just received distressing news from our sister city in Alcavia. I've been informed that the body of Archon, First Wizard of Aldorn, has been found floating near the mouth of the Ankadar River. Apparently his ship was set upon by a Darkling battle cruiser that has been reported to be haunting our shores these past weeks.

As such we will be taking measures to ensure our enemies will not be able to repeat themselves here. I have asked my colleagues to be extra vigilant over the coming period and advise you to be careful in your movements around the palace and especially when you leave its protection to venture into the city. I ask your permission, my king, to post a guardian sorcerer by your side, at least for a couple of months–till we are certain that the threat has dissipated or the Darkling ship has been chased from our shores."

"Certainly not!" The king was in no mood to have a wizard of the council constantly shadowing his movements. "I will not be made a prisoner in my own palace."

"Philander stop behaving like an insolent boy." She was the only person the king allowed to speak to him this way. Narcissa was an old friend, and someone more than royalty; she was like a queen amongst her sisters and brothers in the Council of Light.

"I have nothing more to say on the matter, Narcissa. Now please leave me, I am feeling weary from my day's exertions."

Narcissa's hard blue eyes grew softer. "Would you like for me to arrange for some esselberry tea to be brought to you?"

"No Narcissa, my day's work is complete. I will be retiring to my quarters."

"Very well, my king, but please heed my words."

"I always do, Narcissa." The sorceress reclined her head and whirled around causing her dress to fan out as she left the hall.

At *last*, Philander thought to himself as the sorceress closed the door behind her. *At last I can have a moment for myself to visit my love.* He exited the throne room and made his way through the arcaded corridor to the east block. He stared down from the castle walls. He was many feet higher than the city that sprawled before him shining golden as it reflected the noonday sun. At six leagues across, it was easily the largest city in Leonium. Ameron had been built in 323 BA. It was the youngest city in Leonium and was a learning centre for merchants and men studying politics. Whereas Ramila was known for its affiliation with the arts, Ameron prided itself with producing leaders among men. The kings of Ameron had always ruled Leonium through the centuries and there was every indication that this was to continue.

He opened the door slowly and entered. It was not the bedchamber of his wife that he had come to visit, but that of his mistress. Whereas Paula was an overly tall woman clumsy as a stork and shapeless as a bark of wood, lady Evanthia had the proportions of a court dancer. Her long curly hair fanned about her pillow. She was wearing a skimpy gown so delicate he could see clearly her shapely form. He smiled at her belly which swelled slightly with the new life he had placed there. The baby was due in winter.

When the queen had closed the door behind her, Karat remained staring at the door. He had known, ever since Philander had been convinced to go through with his arranged marriage with Queen Paula of Ramila, that no good was to come of it. The king had begun to seek the attentions of other women from the third year of his marriage to Paula. He had treated the women as a pastime and an opportunity to stay away from the queen. This time, however, he threatened to sunder relations with Ramila just when Leonium required stability and unity most between the kingdoms.

There was a knock on his office door.

"Come," the primate called, half expecting the queen had returned to tell him something she had forgotten.

Instead, one of the fathers entered the office. He was a tall slim man, clean shaven.

"Ah, Father Prudent, I'm glad to see you're back from your travels. How go things in our sister city of Ramila?" Prudent had proven, over the years, to be a valuable asset to the primate. True to his name, he was a man who carried out his tasks with the care and finesse required.

"Your Eminence, as you are doubtless aware the Ecumenical Patriarch is gravely ill and is confined to his sickbed."

"Yes father, I have been informed of our spiritual father's ill health." The primate's gaze wandered from the portrait of the Ecumenical Patriarch to the calm impassive face of his charge.

Primate Karat cleared his throat, his stare hardening. "Father Prudent, I have a task for you that I believe fits you like a glove. I will expect you to be as discreet with this one as you have been with the others." The father's eyes lit up, the only indication he gave the primate that he was waiting for his master's orders. *Yes, he is the perfect man for the job.* "Father I want you to keep an eye out on the queen for me over the next week or so. Don't make it obvious but let me know straightaway if you notice anything odd in her behaviour."

"Yes, Your Eminence. Will that be all, father?"

That's what Primate Karat liked most about Father Prudent. He got on with his tasks without asking uncomfortable questions. "That will be all, father."

Father Prudent closed the door carefully behind him leaving Karat to ponder on the best way to approach his king. Queen Paula had been taken care of. Now it was the turn of the mistress. Gold coins would not be enough to convince this one to go away. Another, more subtle approach would be required.

♦ CHAPTER 23 ♦

Old acquaintances

They were moving on horseback through the ancient city of Ramila trying to remain concealed beneath their cloaks. Serilia felt dizzy and exhausted. Her mother had warned her about the after-effects of expending too much energy when applying the gift. She was thankful, however, that she had been able to call forth the aid of her gift just in time to save them from the Black Widow.

She was glad she had killed the Black Widow. That woman deserved to die. It was only fitting that she was dealt the same hand as she had her two colleagues. Serilia had shed tears for Jameira's sacrifice and that of her master. How many lives would be extinguished before the Dark's followers could be repelled? She recalled all those who had been dear to her. She knew for certain about Archon's death. She wondered if any survived from her aunt Emeralda's group. She worried over her parents as well; they had not had news of them for the past eight months.

She looked at her brother who was slumped in his saddle. He had been this way ever since he had tried to use the gift whilst wearing the retaining bracelets. He still wore them. Serilia moved her mare close to Theo's roan and wiped at his face with the seam of her dress. It was plastered with blood and bits of flesh from Jameira's exploded chest. *Odd how I no longer feel sickened by the sight of blood,* she thought, *and I'm beginning to get used to being around death.* She looked to the street to make sure nobody had seen the blood. Thankfully the Ramilans were too busy with their own chores to notice the strangers on horseback.

They chose to leave Ramila by the north exit. Her grandfather had retrieved Theo's blade from Grimshaw's pack horse by the side of the west road. Hopefully the warrior would not circle round and be waiting for them at the other exit.

Nestor clicked his tongue urging Brigadier to pick up his pace. They passed by circuses and art schools but did not delay and chose instead to admire them from their saddles. Nestor cast a worried glance at his grandson who was straddling his horse with eyes unfocused. His head swayed from side to side. They would have to make a stop soon to see if they could revive him.

They exited the gate, the guards ignoring them in the crowd, and urged their horses into a gallop. The sooner they got some distance between themselves and the city the better. Nestor knew the lay of the land well. He remembered it from his youth and his travels with his wife Rubin, and then when he had returned as a drunk, trying to drink himself to death; which was why he had been able to circle around and outwit Grimshaw to retrieve Theo's sword; he had no intention of leaving the fine weapon in the darkling's filthy hands.

Of course he had been forced to kill a pithik, strip and spread its blood all over his body to mask his own smell before he moved close to Grimshaw. He could still smell the stench of it on his skin even though he had bathed afterwards at the banks of the Karpassa.

It was well into the night when Nestor called a stop off the main road to Ameron. They hid themselves a little way into the bushes where they could be concealed by the branches of a weeping willow.

***

They had arrived close to five leagues from the west bank of the Silver River after only four days riding from Ramila. Theo, mercifully, had recovered.

That night, Theo was able to aid his grandfather in hunting small game to supplement their meal of cheese and hard bread. After they had eaten, Nestor smoked his pipe in silence, immersed in his brooding thoughts that went back to his half-sister Emeralda. Somehow he could not bring himself to believe that she may have been hurt in the ambush. He kept telling himself that Emeralda was smart enough to avoid any traps the Mountain nymphs may have set for her. Still, he had been there when those two bodies had hit the water floating down the Karpassa with arrow shafts sticking out their backs.

He shivered wrapping his cloak around him to keep the chill of the night out. His grandchildren were huddled round the fire and staring intently at the comforting flames. Nestor looked at them and sighed. From what he had seen back at the manor, they had both drawn first blood. He realized that with their first kill they had lost something precious in their lives forever–their innocence. But better they sacrifice that, than be felled by their enemy's blade.

Theo curled up in a ball close to the fire and remained awake thinking of the events that had transpired over the past few days. He rubbed at his wrists and fingered the bracelets once more. He could not find a seam and Serilia had not been successful in removing the bracelets with her gift. She was talented in the *other* agents, and could not perform the Earth weaves required. He could sense the gift, just out of reach, but dared not touch it. He appreciated fully now why the Council of Light had banned the use of these foul bracelets. The pain he had felt had run so deep he wondered whether he would ever be able to summon up the courage to draw on the gift again.

The next morning they made the short journey to the river bank where they descended the shallow valley leading to the mouth of the river accompanied by several more travellers who were making their way to the capital of Leonium. Theo was confronted by a majestic sight unlike anything he had ever experienced before as they approached the Silver River.

Ameron's Silver Bridge stood at the entrance to the city spanning at least sixty yards long, but that was not what inspired feelings of awe and stupefaction; it seemed to float above the water on wings like an elegant bird. The main structure above the river was held aloof, as if by some invisible, magical force, by delicate vertical strands of steel attached to cables as thick as a man's leg. These cables, under the weight of the vertical strands, formed a bow shape above the main span like an inverted arch. They were fashioned from steel so shiny that they seemed to be cast in silver; their reflection on the water surface made it shimmer as if it was being sprinkled by silver dust. The bridge on both sides of the river was flanked by tall towers built from the most resplendent granite stones of greyish, white colour in harmony with the rest of the suspended bridge. The cables passed through the towers at their summit and extended to the banks of the river where they were anchored in place by heavy stone foundations sunk deep into the ground.

"It was built by the Forest nymphs as a gift to the people of Ameron," Nestor informed them, clicking his tongue to urge Brigadier onwards. As the riders approached the twin towers on the west bank, Theo craned his neck to look up at the swan sculpture that adorned the face of the arch joining the towers. Below the swan was engraved the date "837 AA". They cleared the bridge and continued on the adjacent side. They congregated on the east bank waiting for traffic into the city to pass through the main gate. On either side and just outside the entrance lay, with their tails tucked around their hind quarters, two majestic bronze lions each as tall as a house.

"Come along, move on there." Theo was brought out of his trance by the gruff impatient voice of one of the gate guards. He almost fell back in shock when he laid eyes on the soldier; he was dressed in the Ameron livery of brown with a gold lion imprint. Theo was not prepared for it and had been startled as the image of Ameron's prince flashed before his mind's eye. Then realizing that he was drawing unwanted attention to himself he fell in beside his grandfather and sister.

They were *in* at last!

Ameron was a sprawling city packed with buildings that differed very little the one from the other so visitors arriving for the first time could easily lose themselves down the side streets that seemed to have no end. Nestor led them along the main road that rose steadily so at one point Theo could turn to cast his gaze around from his vantage point. He had a clear view, from the docks to the south that were inundated with ships, to the Silver Bridge shining in the west, to the king's palace that stood on a rock elevating the structure well above the rest of the city. Apart from the residents' homes that were all of similar size, Theo could distinguish the official buildings with ease; they were several floors taller than the rest of the residences and most were adorned with statues of marble and bronze and were supported by tall columns with ornate, flowery crowns.

"We'll make our way to the poorer, east side where I hope to locate a few friends of mine," Nestor murmured when he was up close to the siblings so nobody could overhear. He cast a weary gaze around the street but the rest of the folk around them were going on with their business keeping very much to themselves. Such was the nature of large cities.

"We'll need to lay low for a while in a quiet inn until I have had a chance to determine the situation in Ameron," Nestor continued. "I haven't been here for a while so I'll need some time to get reacquainted with events going on in the place. Ameron is a large city where it is easy for mishaps to occur –and to be forgotten. Be on your guard at all times and keep your possessions close by. We want to avoid becoming easy targets to the pickpockets that thrive in places like this one."

They headed down a road that was sloping gradually downwards so the smells of the city seemed to travel with them assailing their nostrils till they felt overwhelmed. Garbage heaps littered the sides of the street and swarms of flies were buzzing around getting in their clothing and hair. Curs were squabbling with cats for their share of the bits of rotting food intermingled with the rest of the garbage. People on foot were left with no other choice than to place their lives in jeopardy and move along the centre of the street where they had to shift in and out amongst the wagons and horses that sped past.

"Are you sure about this place?" Theo looked around with rising discomfort. He placed a hand protectively on the reins of Serilia's filly.

"We are safest here where our pursuers face the same dangers we do, only we have an edge," Nestor said, pointing at himself with his thumb.

"I hope your friends still remember you, grandfather," Serilia retorted dryly. She was hot and stuffy and in a foul mood; she desperately needed to soak in a hot bath and to get a good night's sleep in a real bed. All this travelling was wearing her nerves thin and to add to her problems Nestor was taking them further into what she considered to be perilous territory.

As if in answer to her concern, they rounded the street corner coming face to face with four characters with sly grins on their faces and eyes that darted about restlessly. The ruffians positioned their nags so they barred Brigadier's way. The gelding responded giving an irritated snort and stamped his front hooves on the cobbled road.

"'Ere. Look what the cat's dragged in," one of the shifty characters sneered. He had both front incisors missing. "Now there's a little pretty, wouldn't you say lads," he said, pointing at Serilia. "'Ere, you two! Yer not goin' to keep that morsel all for yerselves now is ya?"

Nestor reached over his saddle clasping Theo's arm firmly to stop him drawing his sword. He shook his head slowly at his grandson and turned to the character with the missing teeth. "I suppose you're friends of Kober Splitjaw?"

The louts stood back to examine Nestor more carefully. The fear was plainly inscribed on their faces.

"Whose askin'?" This time another of the four spoke. He was slightly taller than his companions and carried himself with an air of superiority. He wore a black band around his head to keep his long hair out of his eyes and in his right ear he wore a stud earring with a tiny diamond. A foot-long dagger hung in plain view from his belt.

"An old acquaintance," Nestor replied. "Is the street rat still king of the network?"

"That's dangerous talk, old timer." Hair Band took on a defensive posture and fingered his dagger hilt. "I suggest you identify yourself in the correct manner or be off with you!"

"The white swan swims above with no inkling of the black goose hiding below," Nestor voiced the words softly so he could not be overheard by anyone who might happen to pass by the same side street.

Hair Band cocked an amused eyebrow at Nestor. "I haven't heard that password in ages, old man. But I'm obliged by underground etiquette to admit you to my superiors who will soon wheedle out the truth about your identity. Follow me!"

Nestor and the siblings were surrounded by Hair Band's companions who placed their hands on Theo's and Serilia's reins. Hair Band took charge of Brigadier. Nestor nodded once more to Theo and his sister to allay their fears as they were led down the street at a brisk trot. One of the nags swished its tail and snapped at Theo's strawberry roan as they were led further along the east road.

Soon they arrived at a nondescript building with all its windows barred with wooden shutters. A lock and chain hung around the building's front gate and from the sorry state of the grounds that were weed-ridden the establishment looked to all casual observers to be abandoned. To Theo's surprise it was in front of this building that they halted. Hair Band fished out a bronze key from his pockets and placed it in the lock. It opened and they were ushered in.

"Come, old man. You and your companions climb down and follow me. Snitch here," he said, pointing to the ruffian with the missing teeth, "will make sure your animals are taken care of. If you are who you claim to be then they will be returned to you. I'll take these as well, if you please." He pointed at their weapons.

Having come all this way, it was futile to resist; Theo did not need his grandfather's coaching to do as he was told. It was too late for a change of heart now. They left the horses and their weapons with Snitch and followed behind Hair Band who led them to the front door of the derelict house. Theo noted with disapproval that the building was in desperate need of repairs and a fresh coat of paint. The door Hair Band knocked on was of solid enough wood but that too was weather beaten with large patches of green oil paint flaking away. Someone was working the locks from the inside and the door squeaked as it opened a hair's crack.

A fellow taller than Hair Band with a long nose and beady eyes like a rodent's peered from the slight gap of the doorway. "What is it again, Jewels? Your shift is not over for another couple of hours at least."

"I've brought visitors, Nose, to see the Fat Cat." Hair Band–or rather Jewels–side-stepped so Nose could get a good look at Nestor and the siblings.

Nose looked down scornfully at the three visitors and blew through his snout to show his annoyance. "You've asked for identification?" he enquired of Jewels.

"Er, in a way, yes." Jewels replied uncertainly.

"What's that supposed to mean?"

"Nose, just get on with it and let us in!" Jewels pushed the door open and motioned for the other three to follow him. "We'll leave the inquiries to the Hams."

They were passing through a narrow corridor which was dimly lit by Nose who held a lantern aloft as he led the way with Nestor behind and Jewels forming the rear. Theo felt claustrophobia from the tightness of the place and the low ceiling that was inches above Nose's wispy grey hair. It was with feelings of relief that they arrived at the end of the corridor. The way was barred by another wooden door, but this one was well-tended with its polished surface reflecting the feeble lantern light. A heavy lion knocker was positioned in the centre of the door at eye-level. Nose knocked twice, halted for three heartbeats then knocked a couple of times more.

Several locks were worked before the door swung open on heavy hinges.

As they were allowed entry, Theo peered behind and found that the inner face of the door was fortified with iron plating several inches thick and fixed to the door with large steel pins. Whatever this place was, it was well defended from an outside attack, however determined and well equipped the assailant might be.

He turned around to take in their new surroundings. They were in a square room five paces wide with a single door in the centre of each wall. The room served as a foyer and was lit from above by a bronze chandelier supporting half a dozen oil burners. The floor was of stone covered by a simple woollen rug and the walls were barren. A man wearing a blue shirt, left open at the front to his belly and with the sleeves rolled up to reveal his oversized biceps, was standing by a chair–the only furniture in the room. He held a bunch of keys in his hand and waited for Jewels to enter before he pushed the iron plated door shut then proceeded to lock it.

"What have we here, Jewels?" Biceps said, pointing with a fat thumb at the three outsiders.

"Visitors for Splitjaw. We're taking them to the Hams for questioning."

"Good luck to ya," Biceps snarled at Nestor. He then reached for his keys and opened the door to his right.

The door opened up to a short corridor that then led them down several flights of stairs. Theo felt even more hot and stuffy than when he had entered the first corridor. *What is it with these people and their narrow passageways?* He felt like a caged specimen that was being led by a mad scholar through a maze to see how he would react. When he felt as though he could go on no longer they descended the last flight of steps and he caught the scent of salt. This time they were pushed into what could only be described as a chamber–it was so large. They looked about with trepidation at the contraptions hanging from the walls. There were iron clamps, chains, saws, skewers and many other foul-looking instruments of torture. Theo realized that the smell of salt was from the dried up salt water that had been used with a mixture of ash to wash away the blood from past visitors to the dungeon.

"This is no way to treat friends of Kober." Nestor fixed Jewels with a cool blue-eyed stare. A vein was throbbing in his neck and his face was red with fury. Theo's hackles rose as he considered the precarious situation they had led themselves into. Perhaps his grandfather had been too sure of his old friendship with these thugs. His skin was tingling and he turned to Serilia, realizing that she had embraced her gift.

"You won't need to be doing that, my dear." They turned around sharply to confront the newcomer.

An old woman, as wrinkled as Zoi and dressed similarly in black, was pointing her walking stick at Jewels. "You're getting careless, Jewels. How could you bring a Spark in here without asking for a screen check?"

Jewels turned to look at Serilia in astonishment. "I never thought–"

"That's right!" The old woman cut him off, "You didn't think, and that can cost our community dearly. The boy is a Spark as well. You would have realized it instantly had you frisked him properly. He isn't wearing those bracelets as ornamental jewellery. Those are retainers used to curb the Sparks from using their talent."

"Er, excuse me for interrupting, my dear," Nestor ventured, "but–"

"I'll come to you shortly." Theo realized the old woman had a knack of not letting anyone finish their sentences. "But for now I must ask of your companion to release her hold on the source. It will do you no good down here, my dear. These dungeons are several yards below ground and you will never make it to the top unaided. I'm not the only Spark we have in our community," she warned.

Serilia looked to her grandfather who blew out the breath he was holding. He motioned for Serilia to comply with the old woman's wishes. Theo could sense from the absence of the tingling sensation on his skin that Serilia had relinquished her hold on the gift. No sooner had she done so than all three of them were elevated till they hovered several feet above the old woman and Jewels. Serilia gave out a cry but was unable to call her gift forth again. She had been cut off. Theo had a feeling of déjà vu. He was in the same appalling situation as he had been at the Black Widow's mansion where he had been unable to help his friends.

"Now, old man, I will hear what you have to say," the hag gave out a chuckle and folded her arms above her walking stick, kneeling on it for support whilst she peered with an amused toothless grin at her captives.

"We are not here to cause you any trouble," Nestor hastened to explain. "We have been on a gruelling journey from Ramila and I thought it prudent to seek out old acquaintances before I found a place for us to stay. You see we're being followed by a group of characters we prefer to avoid." He had decided to reveal some of the truth about their plight. "Since Kober and I departed on good terms over twenty years ago, I thought I should pay him a visit; he was leader of the network when I was last in–"

"Over twenty years ago?" The old woman placed a gnarled hand to her chin as she mulled over Nestor's words. "A lot can change in twenty-odd years. You took a chance coming to the east block of town bearing that in mind, especially since you say you are acquainted with the network and its erratic nature."

"We're desperately in need of help. We have nowhere else–"

"So say most sorry folk like yourselves who seek us out. But some are snitches. We don't take kindly to informers working for the authorities."

"My dear woman, I assure–"

"Yes, yes. I've heard it all before."

"Is everything under control here, Wecka?" Another character dressed in black leather with a sleeveless vest and arms covered in tattoos entered the dungeon walking over to the old woman. A black leather mask covered his scalp with holes for his eyes and ears and the mouthpiece cut away to reveal his heavy set chin.

"This here is Brass." Wecka introduced the dungeon master. "He's what we generally call a Ham because when he finishes with you that's what you'll look like. He'll be your entertainment for the duration of your stay if I'm not fully satisfied by your answers. Everything is dandy, Brass," she said, answering the torturer's question. "Our old friend here was about to give me his name and that of his companions." She waited expectantly.

"Nestor...my name is Nestor, but Kober's lot used to call me Bones."

"Bones..." Wecka looked thoughtful as she rubbed her hairy chin. "I don't seem to recall...wait a minute! Where are you from, did you say?"

"I didn't, but me and my grandchildren are from Cyrus. It's an island–"

"I know where Cyrus is, old man." Without warning she released them and they came crashing to the floor.

Nestor straightened his back slowly placing his hands on either side of it. "You could at least have–"

"Come closer. Let's have a look at you!" Wecka snapped. Nestor grudgingly shifted forward.

Wecka grabbed him by the chin turning his face hither and thither. "Yes, I remember you. You're a lot older now than you were back then but you still are a pretty one." She gave him a playful wink. Theo, surprised by the turn events were taking, almost broke into a grin at Nestor's tart expression. Wecka turned to look at Serilia, then at Theo. "She has your eyes but the boy looks nothing like you."

"They both took after their mother's side of the family," Nestor admitted. "That's no loss, of course, I'd much rather–"

"You talk too much," Wecka waved a hand in his face. "What are your names?"

Theo and Serilia introduced themselves.

"Come, we are done here." Wecka turned on her heel and left a very disappointed Brass looking at what had been his three potential victims.

They were led out of the dungeons from a side exit and took an easier, more spacious route back to the surface. Somehow they had bypassed the anteroom with the guard and had come up to the street facing the derelict building from the rear end. There behind the trees stood Snitch with their horses and weapons.

"We use the building to interrogate freshers like yourselves," Wecka answered the question that had been occupying their minds.

Theo had a thought. "Er, madame–"

"Plain old Wecka will do, young man."

"I was just wondering where the other two doors lead?"

"The other two...? What, you mean the ones at the anteroom...where you met the guard?"

"That's right."

"Are all the members of your family this curious?" Wecka cocked an eyebrow at Nestor.

"It's a family trait," Nestor nodded. "It's like a double-edged blade; on the one hand it has often aided us in getting out of difficult situations...on the other–"

"You wouldn't like to find out for yourself what's on the other side of those doors," Wecka hissed at Theo. "Few people ever come out of the central one, and none have survived who have gone through the left one." Then she turned to Nestor. "Our refuge is further away from here. You'll need to be blindfolded before Jewels takes you there – for you own safety, of course." In an unexpected change of behaviour, she pouted her lips and blew Nestor a kiss. This time both Theo and Serilia grinned broadly.

They were allowed to straddle their horses and then their blindfolds were put on. Wecka, Jewels and Snitch led them on. The rest of Jewel's group had disappeared. It was after several confusing turns that they finally came to a halt. They were guided off their saddles and shoved none too gently forward. Theo made to protest but was not given any notice.

As they moved forward, Theo felt a change in the surrounding air and realized they were indoors. They moved through a series of winding passages till they were brought to an abrupt standstill. Their blindfolds were removed and it took a while for Theo's eyes to adjust to the light. He looked around as did his companions and found they were in a large room with a high ceiling and tall windows with the drapes pulled shut. The room was well lit by several oil lamps perched on the walls and by an elaborately carved chandelier hanging in the centre of the room. *Nem would have appreciated this design*, Theo thought, gazing intently at the precious stones dripping from the brasswork of the candle holder. Ivory carvings rested on the mantelpiece of the marble fireplace that stood proudly in one corner dominating it completely. In another corner stood a life-size alabaster statue of a naked maiden taking a bath in running waters. In the centre was a richly embroidered carpet surrounded by comfortable looking armchairs.

"Sit," Wecka said simply. She was standing alone by the door and motioned towards the reclining chairs. "Kober will be here shortly." She proceeded to pour tea from a silver ewer shaped like a cockerel. She handed them each a cup of the steaming brew as they took their seats.

"Nice place you have here," Nestor said, looking around appreciatively. "All of these items look priceless."

"They are," Wecka replied. "Kober has an affinity for collectable items and has gathered a sizeable hoard over the years. That cup you're holding is twelfth century, made from the finest Kamtai porcelain; it used to belong to the Emperor of the East before they were reported stolen. It cost a fair sum to locate and smuggle them over to Leonium."

Just then the door opened. A large-framed man filled the doorway then entered looking with an intense gaze at his visitors. As he approached, Theo realized his left eye was fake so it remained stationary whilst his right roamed the room taking in his surroundings. A scar split his head literally in two, running down his forehead across his missing eye, passing through the middle of his upper lip causing a cleft and continuing down his lower lip and jaw. The hairs of his beard did not grow near the wide wound of his jaw so it looked like it was split in two. The man's gaze fell fleetingly upon Theo and his sister but came to rest on Nestor. He startled Theo giving out a loud sound, like the baying of a bear that rocked the room. Then Theo realized the sound was his laughter.

"Bones, you old jackal. It really is you!" he said, recovering from his mirth and clapping Nestor on his frail shoulders with a meaty paw.

"Easy there big fellow," Nestor winced, rubbing and rolling his shoulder to help alleviate the pain. "Of course it's me, Kober, you thug, though the way your toadies have been treating us, one would have thought we were on your hit list."

"Oh stop your whingeing, honeycakes." Wecka waved a hand dismissively.

"I see you've met my aunt." Kober took on a jolly expression.

"Yes, we've had the pleasure," Nestor replied tartly.

"Why did you keep this one hidden from me?" Wecka asked mockingly.

"If I'd have known he would take such a liking to you, aunt, I would have arranged a meeting much sooner. How long has it been, Bones?"

"A long time, my friend." Nestor's eyes misted over as the distant memories overwhelmed him.

Kober's face became very serious, his beard bristling around his chin. He had a knack, like his aunt, of shifting moods without warning. "Come, friends. I will order us something to eat and we'll catch up on lost times."

They remained in the sitting room whilst Wecka made lunch arrangements. Nestor related their story, starting from the attack on his cottage by darklings, to their flight across the Pardenian and Valdoric Seas with the *Unrelenting Condor* close on their heels.

"We've had an increase of activity from the agents of the Dark," Kober informed them. "Our folk out at sea have noticed this darkling ship you mention. So far it has not made an attack on any allied ships but has been kept at a distance."

Nestor went on to inform Kober of Adelayne's abduction and the delivering of the Witch Lord's ultimatum to Alcavia. He ended by revealing how their group was charged with the mission of retrieving the princess and how they had been waylaid at the Karpassa. He also mentioned the delegation that was sent after their group to rally support for Alcavia.

"We have heard of Princess Adelayne's abduction and of the precarious position Alcavia finds herself in. You say the delegation set off after you? They arrived in Ameron four days ago in a church missionary ship." At the mention of the delegation, Theo looked eagerly at the burly man. "They've been staying at the Templar Chapter House for the past two days enjoying the hospitality of Grand Master Samarass whilst awaiting an audience with King Philander who is currently out on his rounds with his admiral to determine the extent of the crisis with the Anvil corsairs. The king has his work cut out for him, I'll tell you that much for sure."

Theo felt elated by the fact that Nem was in the same city as they were. Finally they would get the chance to meet up with their friend after having been separated for two weeks, though it felt like months; so much had happened in such a short time. He looked over at Serilia who returned his smile. She had obviously been thinking the same thoughts.

"What do you believe King Philander's reaction will be to the delegation?" Nestor asked, as he helped himself to a slice of pig rump. Lunch was being served.

Kober swallowed and washed his food down with Ameron red. "Philander is one of the best rulers Ameron has ever had. He knows how to run a kingdom, even if he fails abysmally where the running of his family affairs is concerned. He will hasten to crush the nymphs before they have a chance to exit their mountain."

"What if Ramila and Ghiadon refuse to join forces with Ameron?"

"Ramila is under the firm control of Primate Orinor. However, King Ionid will not be able to deny a summons by Philander, and the church will be obliged to fall in line with its monarch's decision as a show of a united front. As for Ghiadon, the Forest nymphs are arch enemies with their mountain cousins. They will jump at the chance to deal the Dragon's Foot a decisive blow."

"Let's drink to Philander's health, then."

"To Philander and to our health–and to Ushud with Zarzbudin!" Kober bawled till the table cutlery shook.

When they had finished eating, Kober offered the siblings and their grandfather some tobacco. Theo and his sister reclined the offer courteously.

"Good for you," Kober murmured, though it sounded like a growl. "Nestor? From what I recall, you relish the leaf as much as I do."

"Indeed, your memory serves you well, old friend." Nestor accepted a healthy dose and fished out his pipe from his pockets. He tapped the pipe gently on the side of the coffee table then emptied its contents meticulously in an ashtray made of bronze depicting a head that reminded Nestor of the carvings the cannibals of Tegas made of their gods. He commented on the fact and was informed by Kober that the ashtray was indeed shaped in the likeness of the cannibal god, Tangatud, but was not bronze but solid gold from the mines of Tetinanka.

Nestor lit his pipe and puffed a few rings of smoke, savouring the sweet taste of the leaf. "It's excellent quality."

"Lisandrian. The best in the known world," Kober agreed.

When Wecka had returned with coffee and cakes, Nestor ventured to breach the subject for which they had ventured into the east block.

"Er, Kober. If I can have your attention for a moment on a matter that has been troubling us ever since we set out from Alcavia."

"Go on Bones. Spit it out," Kober rumbled like a volcano that was reminding nearby residents of its presence.

"You see, we seem to have drawn the attention of a group of darklings whilst on our way here to your city. In fact, Theo and Serilia had been taken from me for almost a week until, by a stroke of luck and determined effort, I managed to clutch them from the hands of our pursuers. When we destroyed the Black Widow we managed to escape but I fear that her colleagues are still alive and may be after us to wreak their revenge for the death of their mistress. In any case, our friends were separated from us as well, as I mentioned earlier, during the Mountain nymph ambush."

"Why do you beat around the bush so much, sweet cheeks?" Wecka intruded in their conversation, causing Nestor to gulp smoke the wrong way. He splattered and coughed with the old woman patting his back as if she was beating a dirty rug clean. Nestor waved her away impatiently, his blue eyes running from his exertions. "He wants you to set up spies to monitor the movements of new arrivals to the city," Wecka surmised, turning to her nephew who looked like a giant beside her. "If we match anybody with the description he will give us of his pursuers, then we are to dispatch them. As for his lost friends he would like us to inform him forthwith if we spot them. Oh, and lastly he would like to meet up with the delegation party to share his experiences with them and to offer what aid and words of caution he can before he sets off with his grandchildren and the rest of their group to save the princess."

Nestor remained with his mouth agape. Wecka extended a gnarled hand and lifted his chin till his teeth smacked shut. "There that wasn't so difficult, was it buttercup?" Nestor shook his head from side to side resignedly.

They spent the rest of the evening describing, first Loxandra's colleagues, and then the missing members of their group. When they were done, Kober rose from his couch and shook hands with each of them in turn before taking his leave.

"Now that your business with the Bear is finished," Wecka said, giving away Kober's nickname, "I'll see to your other needs. I suppose, young lady, that you'll be needing an inn with a hot bath to wash away the smell of horse on you?" Serilia expressed her emphatic agreement. "The old boy," she cast a mischievous look at Nestor, "would want it to be in a remote part of town where he can wander off on his skirt chasing undetected." Nestor grumbled that she was right about the first part but for the wrong reasons. Wecka simply grinned girlishly at him. "And you, young man." Theo was caught unawares, and found himself staring into her dark brown eyes till he was completely held by her gaze. "If I were several decades younger I would know how to treat your brown locks and those beautiful green eyes." She lifted her knobby hands placing them lightly on Theo's wrists. He felt a warm, tingling sensation course through his body and tried to tear his arms away from her vice-like grip but she was too strong for him. Then she pulled her hands away gently and the retaining bracelets on his wrists fell away.

"How did you do that?" he asked in shocked amazement. He lifted his wrists and stared at them disbelievingly.

"Old age has taught me a thing or two you young ones have yet to learn; some other time perhaps I will show you. Now please put your blindfolds back on." They did as they were instructed and Wecka led them out of Kober's hideout. They were guided to their saddles and helped to mount by Kober's people. Theo recognized one of the voices as belonging to Jewels. When they had been trotting along for some time, Wecka asked them to remove their blindfolds. They did so and blinked at the late afternoon light. The sky overhead was beginning to get clouded over.

"You remember the way to the blacksmiths' quarter?" Wecka asked Nestor.

"Yes. It's on the north west side of the city, close to the wall."

"That's correct. Go there and ask for the *Horse Shoe Inn*. It's owned by a discreet fellow who will not meddle in your affairs. His wife keeps a clean establishment and they charge a fair rate."

They said their farewells and Wecka faded ghostlike into one of the side streets. They were left alone with their thoughts as they guided Brigadier through the main streets of Ameron heading towards the setting sun. They arrived at the blacksmiths' quarter soon after their departure point with Kober's aunt. The first blacksmith they came upon gave them directions to the inn. Apparently it was favoured by decent folk. They reached the inn just before dusk and were warmly welcomed by the innkeeper who wore a clean white apron and took charge of their needs immediately.

Theo tossed and turned in his bed, his thoughts going from his aunt to his friend Nem who was so close and yet separated from them...and to his parents. Adelayne featured prominently in his dreams lately. She had been the centre of his attention for many months in Alcavia. He felt empty without her. She had said their coming together had given her a new purpose in life; he felt the same way. It ached deep down inside to think of what she must be going through shut away in the Warlock's dungeons.

There was one *more* reason why he did not want to sleep; the nightmares had returned with renewed fervour. They were like the hounds of the netherworld snapping and biting at his mind trying to drive him insane with fear. He had seen the lord with the red eyes over and over again ever since they had escaped from the Black Widow.

Eventually he did sleep.

He was in a large chamber with a ceiling carved out of rock. Torches hung from their perches on the walls, their flames illuminating the interior. A large hearth to one side provided scant protection from the fierce wind blowing in from a large opening looking out to tall ice-capped peaks. On a throne made from the same grey rock as the chamber sat a man with a long black beard and moustache. In his right hand he held a slim staff made from dark wood capped by a golden figurine of a dragon. The cloak that covered him completely to his neck with an upturned collar was a dark maroon embroidered with red dragons on both sides down the front.

He stared intently at the opening where snowflakes twirled like ice fairies making somersaults in the air. A few of the flakes fell on the stone floor melting from the heat of the hearth. The lord rose from his throne and walked towards the opening. He remained a few feet away from the edge that fell away to the chasm below. Theo heard a flapping of wings and identified four red shapes outlined against the white snow. They alighted on a peak, the chasm separating them from the lord. The beasts stared with yellow eyes at their master, like red parakeets perched on a tree limb.

"Report to me, my pets. What have you seen during your flight this day?" Theo felt odd that a mere man would treat the beasts with such familiarity and command in his voice. The slim figure stood with the wind buffeting his cloak. His beard streamed behind him along with his long black hair that reached down his back. In his right hand he held high the staff with the golden dragon that was glowing with a red light. The wizard was using the Fire agent to control the beasts on the rocks.

One of the dragons gave out a shrill cry that reverberated off the mountains, chilling Theo to his bones. It flapped large wings a couple of times before settling once more on its perch. "We have not encountered any of our enemy on the routes to the mountain, lord and master." Its voice was loud and grating. It was the largest of the four and, by the way the rest showed subservience towards it, was obviously the pack leader. "There will be no pursuit by the lowland dwellers."

"Keep searching the mountains," the cloaked figure ordered. "The king will not easily give up on his daughter. He will send out a rescue party, it is only a matter of time." He turned on his heel and returned to his throne. The red beasts took to the air and were soon lost to sight. The lord clapped his hands once. A door opened at the other end of the chamber and a figure dressed in black garments entered, bowing down low in reverence to the man on the throne. "Bring me our guest," the lord ordered.

The figure in black returned soon after. Theo's heart skipped a beat as he set eyes on the woman who walked into the chamber. She was scantily dressed in thin garments that did nothing to cover her naked breasts and hips. She walked proudly, barefoot, lifting her chin up defiantly to the lord on the throne. Around her neck was a hefty collar of iron with pointed studs in sharp contrast to the delicate pair of emerald earrings she wore. Hanging from the collar was a chain that trailed behind her and rattled on the stone floor every time she moved.

"Your family seem to have forgotten you already. I have received no answer to my letter. I believe they have decided you are not worth the effort." The lord blew at one of his long lacquered nails rubbing it against his cloak. He spread out the fingers of his hand like a hawk to study his nails.

"I told you there would be no response," the young woman stated in a neutral tone. "No one person in Alcavia is worth more than the safety of the kingdom. You will have no other choice but to kill me. I am worthless to you otherwise."

"Why are you so eager for your life to be expunged? We may find other uses for you yet. I will be bringing a friend of yours to stay with us soon, to keep you company."

"Bring whomever you wish! It makes no difference to me." Her eyes were a dark green, almost blue, as she threw a frosty glance at her arch enemy.

"Your resistance is admirable, my princess, but quite unnecessary and totally futile. Learn to admit when you have been defeated. Whether they send a rescue party or not, you will be in my service for the rest of your days; so make things easier for yourself and be more congenial in your manner. Defiance will only serve to enhance your discomfort." The warlock motioned to the nymph beside the young maiden and she was led out of the throne room, the chain rattling as she went.

♦ CHAPTER 24 ♦

Treachery

Father Prudent had been tailing the queen for four days. Her movements were fairly predictable. Each morning she would wake alone in her bedchamber–her king had abandoned her bedside long since. She would then make her way to the sitting area where she would spend much of her time with her ladies-in-waiting, knitting or reading poetry to pass the time. When she felt she could not stand being hemmed in by four walls any longer, she would go for long walks in the royal gardens to work off some of her tension. Lunch and dinner she would eat alone at the dining hall. Then she would almost welcome nightfall so she could rest her head on her pillow and drown her sorrows, weeping herself to sleep.

He approached her one day when she was walking in the rose gardens with one of her younger ladies-in-waiting. He bowed politely to the queen and bade her a good day. She smiled back at him but the warmth was lacking in her eyes. When she inquired as to his health he sighed morosely.

"My dear father, whatever is the matter? What ails your heart so, to bring such disillusionment to your countenance?" She looked genuinely worried, as did the delightful creature by her side.

Father Prudent, however, was not a man to admire what the opposite sex had to offer; not because he was bent on preserving his vows, but because he considered that it would complicate matters for him and interfere with his plots and ambitions.

"My queen, it is not a matter with which you should burden yourself."

"No, please tell me, I beseech you," the queen persisted. Her brown eyes were enlarged with worry like the eyes of a barn owl. The maiden also was looking intently at the cleric.

Father Prudent made a show of considering whether to reveal all to his queen, then his face took on the expression of one who is forced to succumb. "Only because you insist, Your Majesty. You see it's like this. I have a niece who is very ill and, being from a family with no means, we are unable to afford the treatment required to cure her ailment. I really do not feel comfortable telling you all this my queen. You do not need to be pestered with the problems of your servants."

"My dear Father Prudent, you have known me since I first arrived in Ramila and together with Primate Karat have always looked out for my welfare. In all this time have you found me to be heartless?"

"Quite on the contrary, my queen." The cleric lowered his head submissively.

"It is my royal duty and my wish to alleviate my friends' and my subjects' pain with whatever means I can. Tell me, how much will be needed to ensure your niece is healed and cared for till she is fully recovered?"

Father Prudent kept his head lowered and shook it from side to side. "I cannot, my queen. This is not right."

"Let *me* be the judge of that. Now tell me. I do not request father, but rather I command that you tell me the sum."

Father Prudent raised his head and stared deeply into her eyes. A pained look crossed his face and a blush formed at just the right instant. "No less than fifty gold sovereigns are required, my queen."

The lady in waiting flinched when she heard the amount, though the queen was barely flustered. "Father Prudent, you will come to my personal study just after lunch and I will give you the coins you need–no, no–I will hear no objections from you." Father Prudent fell to his knees and made to kiss his queen's feet. "Please father, do not make me feel ashamed for being in the privileged position to help. What I do for you and your family I do with all my heart. I would gladly give double the amount to learn that your niece is well again." She helped him to his feet and placed a consoling arm around his shoulders.

"My queen, I will be eternally in your debt but if I arrive at the healers with the sum, they are sure to report me to the city patrol for theft. Best we leave fate and our Lord to decide."

"Nonsense, my dear father. When you arrive at my study I will have a letter waiting for you with my seal explaining that I have given you the coin freely."

"My queen, may I trouble you a bit further and implore you to allow me to help you phrase the words correctly, so there can be no doubt of your consent."

"Of course, Father Prudent. I will meet you at my study at the designated time."

***

"Do you have it?" the large man asked. The wrist bands on his arms flashed in the torch light as he snatched the letter from the man with the triangular scar beneath his right eye. "Good. Don't tell the other two about the letter. We will decide later what to do with it."

"Who died and made you boss, Grimshaw?" asked the man with the limp, sourly. He had a couple of fresh scars now on his arms and legs but, other than his limp, did not seem to be permanently damaged.

"Nobody, Rogue, but seeing as you handled yourself so well back at the manor house our master has asked *me* to take care of this particular task." Grimshaw was at least a foot taller than Rogue and when he flexed his muscles dangerously the other man sneered at him but did not argue further. They made their way through the corridor that was lit by several torches hanging from the walls till they finally met up with the other two.

"Have you checked the premises to make sure there are no guards around?" asked Grimshaw.

"Yes, I have been through all the rooms. They're all empty except for this one," answered a man dressed with the Ameron royal guard livery.

"Very good, Fade. You'll remain out here to warn us if anybody comes along whilst these two and I get the job done. Let's see what you desert dogs are capable of," he added, looking disdainfully at the fourth man who wore a red scarf on his head and a patch across one missing eye. Fully a dozen earrings hung from both his ears and his skin was dark like the desert tribes south across the Meldenyan Sea.

"We are capable of much more than you fat, overfed white skins with your puffy flesh that bleeds like a bitch in heat in our sun," answered the dark man.

"I'm going to like working with this Maleb fellow," Grimshaw said, grinning at Rogue who was limping towards the door. Rogue placed his hand on the door knob and his other two companions drew their weapons. Fade was already holding a pike in his hands and stood guard a little further down the corridor where he was afforded an unobstructed view. Grimshaw held a short sword in his beefy hand as did Rogue, whereas Maleb held a small curved blade with a notched edge.

They entered softly, Grimshaw holding a lantern in his free hand, as they tiptoed towards the large bed that had twin mounds sleeping in it. Grimshaw left the lantern burning on a perch on the wall. Maleb went for the smaller mound whilst Rogue, closely followed by Grimshaw, advanced on the larger one.

Maleb was the first to act. A small whimpering sound was heard as he placed a black hand firmly over the mouth of the woman. Her gold curls were spread on her pillow and her pinky white skin seemed paler still against her assailant's darker form. Maleb grinned with relish as he dragged her out of the bed.

That was their first mistake.

The second sleeping form, sensing its companion's distress, awakened instantly and sprang out of the bed. He punched Rogue squarely in the face sending him crashing into the furniture that littered the room. Then, before Grimshaw could respond, he drew a sword from his garments that rested by the chair beside him and stood facing the tall warrior.

"Make a single sound and my man here will slit your young whore's throat from ear to ear," Grimshaw said, as his opponent prepared to scream for help.

"What is it you want?" the man asked, stalling for time and looking anxiously at his female companion. Maleb's dagger was held to her throat which was already bleeding weakly from a faint cut. With his other hand Maleb was holding her mouth sealed. Maleb, sensing how distraught the man was, licked the curly haired woman's neck and ears to further increase his victim's unease. "If its coin you want then I can provide it," the man urged. "Just don't hurt her, she's with child."

"It's not your coin we're after. Your wife has graciously provided for that. We want your kingly blood." Grimshaw crouched into a fighting position and held the short sword aloft. From the corner of his eye he could see Rogue righting himself and getting to his feet.

King Philander roared into action like a lion unleashed on a pack of wolves. He hammered at the warrior in front of him and at the same time fenced off the blows from the man behind him with the limp. He was trying to force Grimshaw back with every blow but he could not overcome the larger man and Rogue was like a thorn in his side.

The door flew open at some point and Fade walked in on the king being driven away from his mistress by the other two men.

"Guard! Save the woman!" the king shouted, mistaking Fade with his Ameron livery for one of his guards.

"Get this over with quickly," Fade said to his companions, ignoring the king's plea for help.

When the king realized that Fade was with his attackers he flung himself desperately for the door, managing to sink his sword into Fade's chest. Fade stared for a while with disbelief at the sword hilt that protruded from his chest. Then he collapsed on the floor. The king retrieved his sword and prepared to turn on Maleb but Grimshaw grabbed a hold of the scruff of his neck and hurled him across the room so he flew into Evanthia's dressing table.

The king rose slowly from the smashed furniture, still holding the double-handed sword in his grasp and advanced towards Rogue. They exchanged a few blows. The king moved in so he could come at Rogue from his weakened side, the side with the limp. He reversed his grip on the sword hilt and hammered the sword down into Rogue's damaged leg. Rogue howled with pain mixed with rage and fell to the floor clutching at his leg. The king left his sword in Rogue's leg and wrestled his opponent's sword from his hands. He advanced on the tall warrior who just grinned back at him.

The king fought with all the skill and strength he could muster. After it seemed as though they had been at it for hours, he fell back to catch his breath. He looked towards

Evanthia and was shocked to find that Maleb was fondling her breasts and her private parts. The rage awakening within him threatened to completely overwhelm him. His vision blurred so all he could see was Maleb and his groping hands. He screamed with loathing as he advanced towards the dark man. Maleb, seeing his approach, decided he had played enough with his victim and drew his blade across Evanthia's throat. Blood gushed from her jugular like water from a spring. Philander felt the warm flow of her life's blood splattering his face.

"Noooooo!" He raised his sword to strike at the dark man but, just then, his chest exploded from within. He felt a white hot pain in his spinal column and a trembling sensation overwhelmed his body as he twitched, supported by the blade that protruded from his chest. He felt the strength of the warrior that held the blade from behind.

Then he slid from the blade and fell to the floor. His blood intermingled with that of his mistress. He placed one hand on her golden curly hair that was mottled with dark red from the surrounding pool of blood.

"My darling Evanthia," he croaked with his dying breath, then, "my baby...my son Armend." His mind was becoming foggy. Was he forgetting anyone else precious to him? *No, there is no one else now but Armend. At least there is Armend.* "My poor Evanthia," he sighed once more as darkness enveloped him in its warm embrace.

"Quickly," Grimshaw hissed, as he retrieved his short sword from the dead king's back. "Rogue, come on man! Stop whimpering like a babe and get to your feet. Maleb help him. We need to get out of here. Quickly! He squealed like a wild boar whilst we butchered him. I'm sure half the palace must have heard. Come on!" He bent down to place a parchment in Fade's tunic and a few of the gold sovereigns in his pockets. Then he and Maleb moved Rogue between them supporting his arms over their shoulders as they made their way out of the room.

In the corridor they could already hear the noise of the approaching guards. They swung down the other end that led away from the palace and made their way swiftly down the steps. They reached the bottom and shuffled as fast as they could towards the grounds. There they found their horses waiting for them under the starlight. They hauled Rogue into his saddle then followed suit, heeling their horses so they were soon racing out of the gate the cleric had left open for them. As Father Prudent had promised, there was no one at the gate. Behind them they could hear the distressed calls of the palace guards who had located their king.

Grimshaw grinned as he kicked his buckskin charger viciously in the ribs. Their new master would be pleased with them. Their rewards would be great.

Nestor and his companions looked up from their evening meal as the young boy burst through the inn door. His eyes were wide with worry, his face ashen. He went straight for the bar and ordered a pint of ale. When he had drunk a few swigs he turned to the guests at the inn. "The king has been found murdered in his mistress's bedchamber," he proclaimed loudly. "The city patrol is searching the streets and the buildings closest to the palace for his murderers right this minute."

The guests at the inn gaped at the youth in disbelief. Theo gazed at Nestor who returned him the same troubled look. *Could this influence our mission in any way?* They would have to decide soon on their next course of action. Outside, Theo could hear people howling in the streets with dismay. He leaned over to his grandfather. "Maybe it's time we decided whether we ought to be on our way. I am anxious to leave this city, especially now it seems there will be trouble."

"I couldn't agree more, Theo, but we're too late." Nestor stared at him with cold blue eyes.

"What do you mean, we are too late?" Theo was beginning to feel nervous.

"In cases such as this, the remaining officials and ruling nobility seal the city and enforce a curfew until the matter is resolved. I have the uncomfortable feeling that we will be trapped in the city for a long spell."

The young lad stood at the entrance to the *Horse Shoe Inn* and waited patiently for the serving maid to return with the innkeeper. He was barefoot, wearing trousers he had outgrown at least a couple of years ago. He had a runny nose he wiped with his sleeve; his pullover was too large for him, hanging loosely from his arms so his hands were hidden. A smudge remained on his nose where his wiping action had removed the soot covering the rest of his face. He shivered like a fledgling bird as he stood in the open whilst the light drizzle soaked him thoroughly.

The door opened and a man with a round face and bulging belly peered down at him. "What can I do for you, young man?" he asked in a kindly tone.

"You have a man named Bon–I mean Nestor staying here?"

"Yes, that is correct," the innkeeper admitted grudgingly. The disclosing of even this meagre information went against his principles.

"I've been told to deliver this to him." The boy held out a letter which was sealed in a plain envelope with no inscriptions on it. The only identifying mark of the sender was the blue wax seal that bore an imprint of a bear.

The innkeeper's eyes widened in recognition and he stashed the letter promptly in his apron pocket. "I'll see he gets it as soon as he comes back from his excursions," he said sternly. Then seeming to note the boy's discomfort he added,

"Please wait here a moment." He soon returned with a hot pie that steamed in the cool morning air. "My wife baked these fresh at the crack of dawn. This one is for you."

The boy's face lit up with pleasure. He grabbed the pie and was soon lost to sight as he rushed off at a quick sprint.

Nestor returned from the Ameron court proceedings still numbed by the verdict against Queen Paula. He waited till both his grandchildren were seated at the library room before he proceeded to read the letter. He had requested of the innkeeper to keep the library off bounds for a while and was assured their privacy would be guaranteed for as long as they remained in the room. The innkeeper's wife had placed a tray filled with freshly baked cranberry pie on the table and a pot filled with tea. Nestor drunk deeply from his cup, appreciating the aromatic scent of the tea that the innkeeper had informed him was imported from Neba, a city infamous for producing the finest varieties.

"The letter is from Kober. It says,

> Nestor,
>
> I write this letter to set your mind at ease concerning the king's assassination and any thoughts you might have about our involvement in it. I can assure you it was an outside job. The queen is innocent. Our investigations so far lead us to believe that it was organized by persons familiar with the king's movements and who had planned it all very carefully over a long period of time.
>
> But this letter will serve another more urgent purpose. We have reason to believe that your pursuers were in the city at the time of the king's murder, but have not

been able to locate them. We believe they may have moved on and are hiding in the rural areas of Ameron, perhaps close by so they can keep an eye out on the traffic passing through the main routes east and north.

If you are going to be travelling in those directions be on your guard.

We have identified the Black Widow you mentioned as one Loxandra Lockhead of House Lockhead. Her father was a duke of Ameron. We were contracted out to arrange his murder when he was no longer able to pay his gambling debts. I'm afraid we inadvertently played a major role in moulding her future. She became a courtesan selling herself to the wealthy and earned the name Duchess. We were monitoring her movements closely for a while until one day she left, never to return. From what little we have been able to glean concerning her later dealings, the world is better off without her.

As for your man Grimshaw, he was a knight of the Ramilan Templar Order before managing to get thrown out for killing two of his comrades bare handed in a brawl. He was also charged on several accounts of rape but the authorities lost touch with him when he fled east to Ameron.

Your foreman fellow, the one named Rogue, had us puzzled for a while until we managed to uncover information concerning a man named Estephan that fits his description. About twelve years ago, Estephan fled his home city of Ameron but not before he had murdered the master of the house, whom he was serving as assistant foreman.

Nestor, I cannot caution you enough. Be wary of these characters. They are extremely dangerous men.

I'll be in touch when I have more news for you.

Kober, the Bear, Splitjaw.

P.S. Destroy this letter as soon as you finish reading it."

They remained in stunned silence for a while staring at the rivulets forming on the library windowpane. Nestor moved over and threw the letter in to the hearth watching it catch fire.

"Grandfather, we cannot delay any longer," Theo urged. "I suggest the three of us visit the Ameron Chapter House and find a way to gain entry. We must get in touch with the delegation and let them know that our mission has gone awry. If the colonel and the rest of our group don't arrive in Ameron soon, then the weight of saving the princess will fall upon our shoulders and the Templar knights from Alcavia."

Nestor passed a gnarled hand through his grey hair, his eyes falling upon a tiny figurine that rested on one of the library shelves. He stared into empty space deep in thought. Eventually he recovered from his pondering. "You're partly correct, Theo. When we set out from Cyrus, it was to get away from the Dark Sorcerer. Meanwhile Archon got us involved in his hunt to locate the red dragon, though we both know that that was not the main aim of his mission. What that mission might have been was lost with Archon when his body was found washed up on the Alcavian shore.

Only his superiors at the Council of Light in Hendon can shed light on the task assigned to Archon before his unfortunate demise. As for us, we then became involved in accompanying the group that was to set out on the rescue mission, but only as far as Ghiadon, I remind you. I therefore cannot and will not allow you to jeopardize your life or that of your sister on a mission fraught with danger and with little chances of success, Theodor," Nestor said candidly. "Your father placed your care in my hands and I will not disappoint him where your safety and well being are concerned."

Theo shook his head stubbornly. "Grandfather. You don't understand. You can't ask me to abandon Adelayne to the hands of the Witch Lord?"

"It's not our problem."

"But...I love her grandfather."

"Pah," Nestor motioned dismissively with a bony hand. "You are too young to know what true love is, Theodor. You have only known the princess for six months. You are infatuated with her. That is all. It will pass."

"I may be young, grandfather, but I'm old enough to decide which path I will follow. Archon helped me to understand that much."

"Archon was skilled in manipulating people, Theodor. A curse on the man–wherever in the Netherworld he may be–and for having shattered our peaceful existence. Your father Elron was right after all."

"Grandfather, you know that's not true!" Theo raised his voice as the anger and frustration he had felt at their inactivity surfaced.

"Not true, Theodor? Then, if I don't know what the truth is, please enlighten me. You've been away from Cyrus for less than a year and already you feel you know all there is to know about the world."

"Enough!" They turned a surprised look at Serilia who had been silent till now. She held her hands to her ears and was shaking uncontrollably. Theo reached out to her and cradled her in his arms.

"There, there," Nestor said, coming up beside his grandchildren and patting Serilia's hand reassuringly.

When Serilia's shaking had subsided she turned tearful eyes towards them. "I for one would like to believe that aunt Emeralda and our friends are still alive."

"Of course, my dear." Nestor placed a consoling arm around her shoulder.

"I say we take things one step at a time," Serilia added, straightening her hair with one hand. "We'll visit Nem at the Chapter House and decide our next course of action there."

"Agreed," Nestor murmured. Theo nodded averting his eyes.

***

Primate Karat held once more the letter of evidence Father Prudent had produced at court earlier on today that had lead to the queen's conviction for her husband's murder. It read,

> "I, Queen Paula of Ameron, do decree that these fifty gold sovereigns have been given by me to the bearer, and may be considered as payment in full for services rendered,
>
> Paula Avgerini."

Karat folded the letter and placed it back in his robes before turning his attention back to his colleague.

"You have arrived at a dark time in our city's history, Your Eminence." Karat drew together his bushy grey eyebrows, adding to his glum look. He had grown weary of carrying the weight of the faithful in Ameron. It was a large city with many demands, so large he had been forced to watch it become corrupted over the years. "It's unfortunate you arrived so late in our city. High King Philander was a great leader and would have rallied the support you need for the defence of your city," Karat stated with no hint of doubt.

"I couldn't agree with you more, Primate Karat." Zerum sat in his armchair staring out dismally from the paned Chapter House doors to the courtyard beyond. They were afforded an open view of the front portico. Between the columns one could see the grounds lined with gravel affording easy passage to wagons and riders on horseback. Forming the surround were low hedges kept neatly trimmed by the Templar page boys who also tended the numerous rose bushes that were in full blossom. Due to the rainfall, the gravel was looking slippery glistening like wet pebbles polished by the sea. The raindrops hanging from the leaves reflected the sun's rays like wood fairies dressed in frocks sprinkled with gemstones.

When Zerum had finished his musing, he turned his dark-eyed gaze back on the older primate. "We have been in Ameron for just over a week. Grand Master Samarass has been kind enough to extend his hospitality to us. During this time we have been kept confined to the Chapter House and strict orders given for us not to be allowed into the city without an escort.

"I understand this is for our own protection but in his zeal to keep us guarded, Samarass has inadvertently obstructed us from carrying out our role of rallying support for our cause. To our misfortune the king was unavailable when we arrived, since he was out at sea on a reconnaissance mission to ascertain the extent of the Anvil corsair threat. To our further dismay we were informed the morning after the king's arrival that he had been murdered by his wife, Queen Paula.

"And now we are forced to wait for the governing nobility to elect a new ruler, unless Prince Armend can be revived from his sickbed in Sulicia to assume the task of ruling the city. Only then will we be in a position to lay our claim before Ameron for military and financial aid. Meanwhile we lose precious time that could have been spent sending reinforcements to Alcavia."

"I share your grief on how events have unfolded, Primate Zerum. I see no other way to hasten matters."

Meanwhile the rest of the delegation knights and Nem were busy playing board games and lounging around the room looking very bored. During the day they practiced swordplay in the grounds with their colleagues from the Ameron Templar Order to keep themselves in fighting form, but in the evenings had very little to do.

A knock drew their eyes as the page boy entered.

"Visitors to see the primate of Alcavia," the young page announced, before genuflecting. He opened the door wider.

"Theo! Serilia!" Nem sprang to his feet and raced to greet his friends. Serilia fell into his arms and Theo patted him affectionately on the back. Nestor was with the siblings and gave Nem a quick hug before turning to greet Primate Zerum and the rest of the delegation who had swarmed around the trio. After they had exchanged words of greeting, Zerum was the first to enquire as to the absence of the rest of the group. They spent the rest of the evening together with Nestor relating the events from the moment they had left Alcavia to the ambush at the Karpassa River.

"Most unfortunate," Sir Duel voiced their concern. "However you are not to worry, my lady," he said turning to Serilia who was close to tears. "We will begin forthwith with a search of the city and the surrounding area up to the Silver River. We will not cease until they are found." The rest of the knights nodded and Sir Evenar from Jade Island and towering Brond exited the room to begin the search, whilst

Miranda took Serilia to one side to give her words of comfort, woman to woman.

Nestor carried on relating the story of what had transpired from the moment Loxandra had kidnapped his grandchildren, to their miraculous escape ending with their arrival in Ameron. He opted not to mention their trip to the east block. He threw Theo a meaningful look. He nodded faintly to show he understood. Nestor was uncertain, but felt as though Primate Zerum had caught the exchange, though the clergyman's calm demeanour had not altered in any way. They were offered refreshments in the form of tea and coffee supplemented with cookies. Nestor lit his pipe and shared smoke with Duel and Bold who both commented on the premium quality of his tobacco.

"It's a gift from a friend of mine," Nestor answered, smiling.

Zerum gave him a calculating look. *That man knows more than he reveals*, Nestor realized.

Another knock interrupted their gathering. This time, a tall slim priest entered, surprisingly with no beard. Nestor recognized him as the man in court two days ago, who had been called forth by the prosecuting officer as a witness against Queen Paula. He had disliked the man from the outset.

"Father Prudent. What an unexpected surprise!" Primate Karat beamed a smile at his subordinate who stood looking deceptively docile. "It's barely been two days since you left for Ramila."

"Your Eminence." The cleric's serene expression was replaced by a dejected one. "I'm afraid that no sooner had I set foot in Ramila when I was forced to leave prematurely. I got here as soon as I could to deliver personally to you the grim news."

"Pray go on, brother," Primate Karat urged, a grave expression on his face. Zerum also was completely focused on Father Prudent.

"The Ecumenical Patriarch was found dead in his sick bed yesterday morning." A stunned silence fell on the room.

"Athud rest his soul." Primate Karat made the sign of the flame as did Zerum. "He was a devout servant of our master and served our church altruistically. He will be sorely missed." There were nods of agreement from the knights in the room.

"He will be laid to rest a week after tomorrow," Prudent went on. "I set sail for Ameron immediately to deliver the news to you. I have come straight from the port where my ship docked just one hour ago."

"You have my appreciation, father, for not delaying," Karat expressed his gratitude. "Now please have a seat with us and I'll order some refreshments for you. You must be exhausted after your travels."

"Thank you, Your Eminence, but if I may have your permission, I would like to make my way to the church grounds to take a bath and change clothing."

"Yes, of course, father." The priest bowed formally to the primates and turned to leave.

"Father Prudent." Karat recalled his priest.

"Yes, Your Eminence?"

"I would appreciate it if you could accompany me and Primate Zerum tomorrow on our voyage to Ramila. We must set forth early if we are to have time to prepare for the funeral service."

"I live to serve, father." Prudent reclined his head before making his exit.

"I don't know what to say." Karat turned to look at his colleague. "I beg your forgiveness if I presumed too much when I included you in our voyage to Ramila, Your Eminence."

"On the contrary, Primate Karat. All who wish to express their respect to our Ecumenical Patriarch will be there. It will offer us the opportunity to meet with our brethren from far-off Renderon and neighbouring Seldavia. It has been a while since the heads of the church have congregated."

"Yes," Karat agreed. "It has been four years, in fact, since the Ecumenical Patriarch visited Ameron and made his address to the church fathers."

"Excuse me for interrupting, Your Eminence," Nestor said, coming closer to the primates. "I understand your need to be at the funeral procession, Primate Zerum, but we must also solve the issue of our rescue mission. You must agree with me that a decision should be taken soon."

"Yes, Nestor." Primate Zerum turned to look at the Alcavian knights. "Sir Duel, what is your opinion on the matter?"

Duel got up from his armchair and went to stand beside the porch doors. He stared out at the overcast sky. The steady drizzle had turned to a torrent. Fat drops of water were striking the porch door making '*tick, tick*' noises on the glass. "I suggest we begin our search efforts tomorrow. Let's just hope that this spell of foul weather will let up by the morrow. If we do not locate Ajax and his group by the end of two days from today, then it is my firm belief that the rescue attempt must be abandoned."

"What!" Theo yelled from across the room, raising eyebrows. His face turned red as soon as he realized everyone was staring at him. They were accustomed to him being a well-mannered youth. Theo coughed with discomfort but was determined to follow through with what he had to say. "Sir Duel, I must disagree strongly with you. We cannot abandon the princess to the Dragon Lord. Surely you must feel the same way?"

"I do, young Theodor." Duel's grim expression did not change. "But without Ajax and your Mountain nymph friend to guide us, what chances of success would such a rescue attempt have? Even with the colonel and the nymph, a positive conclusion to that endeavour was always a far-fetched affair. Ajax knew when he was assigned the mission that it was suicidal but chose to forfeit his life rather than face the humiliation of losing the princess. I am not as willing to jeopardize the lives of my men on such a futile effort."

Theo was about to protest but Zerum cut in. "Let's not hasten to come to a decision, my friends. Sir Duel, you are right to show caution. For the time being we will stick to your original plan of renewing our search for the colonel and his friends. If in two days they are not found then I will leave the final decision in your capable hands as to what should be our next course of action. For that purpose I will be taking with me only the Ramilan knights Dromid and Brand to their home city tomorrow. The rest of you are Alcavian knights and have till then to decide the fate of your princess's rescue mission."

Primate Karat excused himself and left to make his preparations for his voyage west. Nestor, Serilia and Theo declined Primate's Zerum's offer to remain at the Chapter House as guests.

"We have a busy day ahead of us," Nestor explained.

Nem approached the primate and stared down at the floor searching for the right words to say.

"Speak what's on your mind, Nem." The primate had gotten to know him over the time they had spent in each other's company.

"Your Eminence –Zerum," he added, as he caught the primate's look. "I was just thinking that, since you will be gone to Ramila for the funeral tomorrow, maybe I could..."

"Stay a while with your friends?" Zerum finished for him.

"Yes."

Zerum stood squarely facing the youth and placed his hands on his charge's shoulders. "Permission granted, my young friend. I hope I have not bored you with my affairs these past few days."

Nem shook his head vigorously. "No, no, please don't get the wrong idea..."

Zerum waved a hand at him to show he understood.

"I enjoyed our time together and have learnt a lot from you."

"As have I from you, Nem. For one so young in years you are a very talented and knowledgeable man. Now, go with your friends. They are waiting for you." He pointed at the door were the trio was standing looking at them.

Nem bowed before the primate and kissed the proffered hand with the gold ring. Then he turned on his heel and left with his friends.

***

He had gone to get supplies and entered a side road feeling a prickling sensation between his shoulder blades. He knew, from his travels before, what that meant. He moved faster and stepped into one of the less used alleys. It smelled of excrement and garbage to the extent that he gagged. He did not go far before he realized it was a dead end. He turned around and saw three hooded shapes approaching him purposefully. He drew his short sword balancing it in his hand. He would make them bleed before they took him down. His only thought was that he would not be there to guide his grandchildren out of the city.

Theo had that uneasy feeling again, the one he had learned not to ignore. He exited the inn leaving his sister alone and made his way in the direction of the palace. His grandfather had asked them to stay put until he returned for them. But Theo could not sit around and wait. His grandfather may have gotten into trouble. He had to help in any way he could. He had not gone far when his senses alerted him of impending danger.

The hand that was placed to his mouth was calloused, holding him firmly so he could not utter a single squeal. He tried to wriggle out of his opponent's grasp but it was too strong for him. He tried to kick with his legs but they had been locked by his attacker's knees. He could not break free. He panicked. He was contemplating using his gift but the memory of the pain he had experienced from the retaining bracelets came back to haunt him. He was trapped. The man pulled him into an alley bringing him before an old grey-haired man. The aged man looked up. "It's alright, Theo, you do not need to struggle." It was his grandfather.

The man holding him from behind let go of his mouth and pulled away. Theo turned around to come face to face with a tall figure with scars crossing his handsome face. The man smiled at him removing his hood. His head was shaved completely apart from his top knot.

"Colonel Ajax!" Theo exclaimed. "I am so relieved to see you!" He hugged the man causing him to fidget with uncomfortable shyness at the contact. "Where is the rest of our group?"

"I'm glad to see you also, Theo. Roxette and your aunt were here with Zoi before I left them."

"Aunt Emeralda is alive!" Theo exclaimed with uncontrolled joy.

"Easy lad," Ajax cautioned, looking apprehensively at the entrance to the side street to make sure they had not been overheard. Then he turned to Theo's grandfather. "Nestor, do you have any idea where they have gone?"

"They said they were going to fetch their horses so we could all go back to the inn. They should be here any moment now."

No sooner had Nestor spoken when the horses' hooves were heard on the cobbled stone road. Emeralda flew into Theo's arms. Roxette surprised him by giving him a fierce hug. Zoi lowered his head and planted a kiss on his brow then patted him fondly on the cheek. He was glad to discover that all his friends were in good health.

Back at the inn Serilia and Nem greeted their friends with the same enthusiasm as Theo. Overcome by her emotions Serilia could not hold back her tears of joy as she hugged her aunt. Nem grinned broadly.

"There, there, my sweet. You didn't honestly believe your aunt would let those Mountain nymphs harm her now, did you?" Emeralda cupped Serilia's chin in her hands.

They sat eating their evening meal together whilst Colonel Ajax related the events of the past two weeks of their separation. The colonel explained that his men had been the unfortunates shot with arrows that day, and that if it hadn't been for Zoi's magic they would all have perished. They had managed to throw off their pursuers by following the river bank south and had crossed the Karpassa following the main road. They had taken longer to get to Ramila but, once there, had spent the best part of four days searching for their friends.

Zoi had heard of First Sorcerer Sharman's and of Jameira's deaths. She had visited Loxandra's manor house finding nothing but piles of burned wood where the stables and house had stood. Of the sorceress's body there was no trace. A few believed that her Dark disciples had taken her remains away.

When it was apparent that Nestor and his group were no longer in Ramila they set off for Ameron. A little further out of Ramila's north gate they had come across a posse of pithiks that lay butchered on the plain. The vile beasts had been mauled by wolves to the extent that they were barely recognisable. Zoi had been able to revive for a few moments one of the beasts that still had its head attached to its shoulders but was missing its hindquarters. She managed to force it to confess that its posse had lost touch with Nestor's group and that they had been stationed near the gate exit to set an ambush for them should they come that way.

And so the colonel and his group had arrived outside the city gates, just after they had been shut to outsiders whilst the Ameron Committee searched for King Philander's murderers.

"A sorry state of affairs, this business with Philander's death," Zoi said, shaking her aged head morosely. "It could not have come at a worse time for Leonium."

"It's all happened just as the old astrologer at Jade Island foresaw," Theo murmured.

"What was that, dear?"

"Oh, nothing aunt Emeralda. I was just thinking out loud."

"Who would have believed that Queen Paula could be capable of committing such a crime?" Colonel Ajax expressed his disbelief.

"I don't believe anything they say about her," Zoi replied with conviction. "I met both the queen and her husband before on my journeys through Leonium. She was a plain, unobtrusive woman with not a bad bone in her body. I was there before she wed the king and bore witness to the ironic remarks expressed. It's true she was not an attractive woman, but what she lacked in beauty she made up for in kindness and character. Too bad that Philander was too preoccupied with appearances to notice her other attributes."

"I must admit, I too feel the queen has been at the receiving end of a plot against both her and her deceased husband." Nestor shook his head in sorrow. They spoke softly.

"Then we must do something to save the queen!" The colonel almost shouted. Nestor winced. Roxette threw Ajax a reproachful look before casting her gaze around. Thankfully the rest of the inn lodgers carried on with their meal and did not seem to have taken notice.

"I would willingly offer any help I can, but what can we eight do against the entire city patrol?" Nestor fixed the colonel with his unwavering stare.

"Nestor, I have read your heart. I do not believe you would sit idly by and allow an innocent life to be sacrificed leaving the way clear for others to seize the throne of Ameron." It was Zoi's turn to chastise Nestor.

He lifted his gaze from the colonel and rested it on Zoi, then he looked at Emeralda who was staring back at him as though she were measuring him to see if he was about to disappoint her. "Damn teeth of a Mountain Cave troll!" Nestor swore. He murmured a few more choice words and Zoi arched her brows at him grinning in amusement.

"Nestor! Not before the children." Emeralda scowled at him.

"Aunt Emeralda, you're beginning to sound just like mother," Theo complained and Serilia nodded her agreement.

They spent the rest of the night at the inn plotting how they would carry out what they had to do without stretching their necks out too dangerously. They kept going in circles till they decided there was no easy way out. If you wanted to retrieve a gold snippet from the hearth with no tongs, you just had to place your hands in the fire.

♦ CHAPTER 25 ♦

Ultimate sacrifice

They rode through the city gates under a heavy Ameron City Patrol escort. They were a hundred of Ramila's finest cavalry men and in their midst rode a tall woman with a determined expression on her face. They made their way swiftly through the main street leading to the palace on the hill that overlooked the city like an eagle nesting on its perch. When they had climbed the top they passed through the gates and the twin lion statues guarding the entrance. The cavalry men dismounted and remained by their horses, not allowing the stable boys to lead them away. They would remain where they were till their princess returned. Five of them were permitted to escort her inside the palace. The rest were surrounded by double their number of the Ameron Royal Guard.

The princess had not been in the palace since spring, when she had left to visit her uncle in Ramila. Ameron held no fond memories for her. Apart from her mother's love, there was nothing else for her here. She remembered with bitterness all the times she had argued with her father over trivial matters. He would find any excuse to belittle her and to make her look foolish in front of his courtiers and friends. When she had been younger, she would retire to her room and cry for hours till her mother would arrive to offer her a consoling hug and a kind word. But lately she had stood up to the man and had discovered that she was not as fearful of him as she had been as a young girl. Now, she had a rebellious streak and fed off the frustration and anger her father had planted deep in her heart.

It was not that she hadn't loved the man, but he had not been a proper father or husband to his wife. Diomeda had often advised her mother to divorce her father, but the queen would turn away and find excuses for Philander's behaviour, excuses such as that he was under a lot of strain and that he had not known love from his deceased father either. She justified his actions by laying the blame on herself and saying that she was not as understanding and caring with him as a wife should be. But Diomeda knew the king was a difficult man to live with and that he had no intention of saving his marriage. This recent affair with this Lady Evanthia had been the apex of the king's betrayal of his wife and children. And now he and his lover were both dead.

Diomeda wondered how Armend would cope with the death of their father. He and Philander had been close, though the king had often pushed the youth beyond his limits, which was another form of harassment and exercising of dominance over one's children. She wondered too if her mother had finally snapped at this last slap in the face by her husband, and if she could have brought herself to the point of arranging for the king and his lover to be murdered. Diomeda dismissed the thought from her mind almost as soon as it formed.

The guards standing on either side of the large doors leading to the throne room crossed their pikes barring her entrance.

"What is the meaning of this?" Diomeda's commanding voice was tinted with annoyance. She motioned for the five Ramilan soldiers to keep their swords sheathed. The ten Ameron guards escorting her placed their hands on their swords in anticipation.

"My princess, you may enter the hall freely," one of the Royal Guards explained, "but the Ramilan escort will not be allowed to enter." He was a tall officer with long curly hair tied back to reveal a bearded youthful face in its mid-thirties. He looked at Princess Diomeda respectfully but there was no hint of anything else in his eyes. Diomeda was used to the bland look men gave her. She had long since come to terms with the features she had inherited from her mother and was beyond the stage where she cared. She had resigned herself to the fact that she would not seek the admiration of men.

"Then lead the way officer. My escort will remain here with your men until my return." The lieutenant of the Ramilan cavalry nodded his acquiescence and stood at attention with his men a little further down the corridor so they were within earshot of the hall. The tall Ameron officer and his nine guards remained between the Ramilans and the throne room entrance.

"Her Royal Highness Princess Diomeda," one of the guards with the pikes announced, as he opened the large doors to admit the princess.

Diomeda entered the hall proud and erect. She kept her eyes trained on the man standing a little distance away from the throne. She purposefully ignored the sneering courtiers on either side of the hall. There were a few whispers of "the murderess's daughter" and "Paula's brat". Diomeda felt the tension in the room but was used to being the object of people's disdain. Her father had made sure of that. Even from his grave he still found a way to complicate their lives.

"Uncle Georgile, I demand to know by whose authority you passed judgment on your queen and with what evidence!" She would be direct. She knew it would not bring any results but she wanted to see for herself how deep the conspiracy ran and to bring out the culprits responsible for her mother's arranged conviction.

"You are in no position to demand anything, Diomeda." He was not even bothering to use her title.

"You forget who you are speaking down to, Georgile. My brother is the rightful heir to the throne and I represent his interests. You have an obligation to show me the respect I deserve. To act otherwise is to be treasonous." There were worried murmurs in the crowd at the mention of Prince Armend. It was true that he was by right the next in line for the throne. If Diomeda indeed spoke on his behalf, then to confront her was folly of the worst kind.

"Hah!" Georgile did not seem perturbed by the princess's words. "Have you not heard? Our prince has, over the past few weeks, been lying flat on his back in a sick bed in Sulicia, hidden away by the sisters there so we might not learn about the poisons he has been injecting in his veins. Who in their right mind would consider placing an addict on the throne?"

Diomeda's lower lip began to tremble. "You lie!" she replied vehemently. She could see by his look, however, that he did not. He would not dare to lie about something as serious as this. Poor Armend. How could he allow himself to end up so? What were they to do? She had sent a rider to Alcavia to summon her brother's help just before setting off in a hurry to halt the execution until her brother's arrival. A cold sweat washed over her as she realized that without her brother's aid there could be no saving their mother. Her world was collapsing around her. Her poor Armend, the only other member of her family she had truly loved, was lying all alone, sick and in pain without anybody to comfort him. And now her mother would be taken away from her also; she felt wretched. Georgile smiled triumphantly at the princess's obvious distress.

"I advise you to crawl back to your Ramilan hole, Diomeda, never to step foot in Ameron again. If you remain, then you will suffer your mother's fate as co-

conspirator for the murder of our king. Now leave us." The man was already behaving as if the throne was his! "We're done with you and your foreign influence. To think, that we had allowed your Ramilan bitch of a mother to have seduced our king into marrying her." There were murmured replies of agreement and most of the lords threw Diomeda venomous looks whilst their ladies raised their noses as if the sight of her offended their finer senses.

Diomeda was attentive enough to realize that it would only be a matter of time before Georgile would seize the throne for himself. She realized that, after her father's family, her uncle Georgile was the most powerful man in Ameron. The support he could rally from the ranks of the courtiers was overwhelming. Cousin to the king, his family was as ancient as Philander's so he was the next logical choice; the subjects of a kingdom needed to feel stability and that their rulers were in firm control. Georgile would be welcomed by the people by the time the nobles were finished spreading the word of the order he would bring to the kingdom.

"I'm not finished with you yet, Georgile!" She had one final slim chance to cause the courtiers to rethink their position. "If my mother is not given over to my custody, and given a fair trial by representatives of both the Ramilan and Ameron courts, then, by the authority invested in me by King Ionid of Ramila, I am forced to inform you that in four weeks from now Ramila will ride forth to lay siege to Ameron until you and your committee surrender yourselves to suffer the same fate as you propose for my mother."

There was a stunned silence in the hall. Ramila and Ameron had been the two strongest kingdoms in Leonium since before the Great War. Their relations had always been amiable. For matters to have reached such a point was beyond anyone's wildest fears. What Princess Diomeda threatened them with was a Leonese civil war with unknown consequences. For centuries the four kingdoms of Ameron, Ramila, Ghiadon and Alcavia had stood united against the threat from the west. Truly the brunt of the attacks from Leonium's arch enemies was borne by Alcavia, but all of Ameron's subjects were conscious of this threat and knew that a weakening of relations between the kingdoms of Leonium was just the opportunity the Mountain nymphs needed to assail them. Now the murmurs were filled with fear and many voices were suggesting a more prudent approach.

"Your ultimatum to us will not stay the hand of justice, Diomeda! We will not cower before the murderess's brother. Ramila has no say in Ameron's affairs and we do not recognize the authority of her representatives here. Tell your uncle to rethink what he is about to sacrifice over his traitorous sister. Our decision is final. Tomorrow at noon, Paula Avgerini will take her last treasonous breath. Guards! Please escort the princess out of the hall. My audience with her is over."

"You will pay for this sacrilege, Georgile!" Princess Diomeda screamed, as she was seized by the arms and led forcefully out of the hall. "Your lust for power will be the end of us all," she managed to shout before the doors to the throne room closed.

Outside, her escort was waiting anxiously for her. They had been able to hear her screaming and looked apprehensively at the Ameron Royal Guard standing by the entrance to the throne room. The princess snapped her arms away from the two guards that held her and straightened her clothes agitatedly. She nodded at her escort and they left followed close behind by the tall Ameron officer and his nine guards.

In the palace grounds, Princess Diomeda mounted her steed as her hundred followed suit. She was about to heel her mare forward when a bent-over cleric dressed in the traditional black of his occupation approached, calling out to her. "Princess Diomeda, wait!" He had run from the hall and was breathing heavily from his efforts. "Princess, I wish to express my condolences for your father's death and to clarify my feelings of sorrow for your mother's predicament."

He looked far more careworn than last the princess had set eyes on him. "You betrayed my mother's trust in you, Primate Karat. I will never forgive you the part you played in all this mess."

"Princess," he said softly, clutching at her cloak so she was forced to bend closer to him. One of her cavalry officers went for his sword but she shook her head at him. The primate stared at her with dark troubled eyes. "I have been left with no other choice. Your mother's actions cannot go unpunished. We all invested a lot of time, effort and love in your parents. In return we reaped sorrow from them both. My heart goes out to you and your grieving family, Princess Diomeda, but apart from being a cleric I am also an Amerian. I cannot betray my religion and my country to such a one as your mother who has betrayed us." His voice was choked with bitterness, barely audible as a whisper. Then he released her cloak and stepped back taking a deep breath. He fixed the princess with a hard stare she had never seen on his face before. "I'm sorry I had to go against you and your mother, princess," he said in a louder voice which carried across the grounds. "But I am bound by my oath to the church to speak the truth and to punish the guilty. Take Lord Georgile's advice and never return, and tell your uncle not to act foolishly, sacrificing Leonium for his sister. She has proven unworthy of us all." The primate had unequivocally chosen his side.

The princess turned her head away in disgust and slapped her mare's flanks. She rode at the fore with her cavalry unit. They soon exited the palace grounds and made their way to the buildings at the outskirts of the city. When they had exited the city gates and were well out of sight, Diomeda called for a halt. Her men dismounted and set up scouts to ensure they were no longer being followed by the city patrol.

"I am going back to the city," she informed her five commanding officers.

"My princess, that would be madness," the highest ranking officer said. "Georgile is sure to have given orders for you not to be admitted back into the city walls."

"I cannot allow them to murder my mother."

"Your Highness, what can you possibly hope to achieve against the entire City Guard? You did what you could back there. It would serve no purpose for you to offer your life to their headsman's axe as well."

"I do not intend to let either myself or my mother bow to the headsman's axe, lieutenant." She had made up her mind about this. She was going back for her mother.

***

The group made their way silently through the streets that led up to the palace grounds. The hooves of their horses as they were being led made clopping noises that carried through the night. They were dressed in heavy cloaks to keep out the late autumn chill. Winter was almost upon them and the icy air that blew from the Dragon's Foot Mountains stole away what little warmth their cloaks afforded them. The leader of the group was crouching low. Following him was a slight figure bent over like a hag. One of their number remained behind in the shadows with the horses. The rest approached the gate and were stopped by the guards.

"Halt, who goes there?" asked one of the guards, dressed with the brown tunic and the golden lion livery of Ameron. He held his pike threateningly at them whilst his companion held up his torch to take a closer look at the group outside the palace entrance.

"We are visitors to the palace and must be admitted in," Theo heard Zoi saying. He found himself thinking that it was not the cleverest of approaches. The rest of his companions seemed to share his view and stared at the old woman uncertainly. They were going to get themselves into trouble this way.

"Oh must you now," the guard jeered, fixing the old woman with a stare that expressed his disinclination. "Unless I see some identification and an official paper informing me that you have been summoned to the palace, then you can forget about passing, old woman."

Theo realized then that there was a faint humming noise in the background. He felt his senses being lulled and began to feel sleepy. Somewhere in the back of his mind an inner voice was shrieking at him that something was amiss.

"You must let us through," Zoi said again, this time with more conviction. Theo wondered how the guard could possibly deny her request.

"Yes, you're right," he heard the guard answering in a drowsy voice. "You must be allowed through." Somehow the guard's change of heart did not surprise Theo.

"You will not remember seeing us once we have passed," Zoi spoke softly but commandingly to the guard.

Theo felt like he was sleepwalking. He was dimly aware of his surroundings as they made their way to the palace grounds. All along their route he could hear the soft humming sound. He felt like a baby being lulled to sleep as he was enveloped in the humming's safe embrace. Somewhere along the way he realized they were descending steps. They entered a dark corridor lit by torches hanging from the walls. Zoi retrieved one of them with a bony hand and led her companions. They moved through the central corridor of the dungeon, the guards swinging open the intervening iron gates without paying them any attention. Nothing about their behaviour registered as odd to Theo's mind. Then they descended more steps till they were in the lowest levels of the prison. One of the guards informed Zoi in a monotone voice devoid of emotion that the queen was being held through the second door to the left. She commanded him to open the door and he did so without a moment's hesitation.

They entered the dark room to find a figure crouched in one corner with legs drawn close to its body and curled up into a ball. As they approached, Theo realized it was a woman. Her face was caked with mud formed from the dirt and tears that had dried on her cheeks. Her dress was blackened from the soot of the prison to the extent that its colour could not be recognised. In one corner of the room was a hole smelling of excrement. The woman blinked at the light of Zoi's torch. Theo realized the woman bore a strong resemblance to Princess Diomeda.

The humming had stopped and Theo was brought out of his hypnosis. He looked around the prison cell wondering how he had arrived there; he had no recollection of the events that had transpired. The last thing he remembered was the exchange with the guards at the palace entrance.

"Help her up, quickly!" Zoi ordered the colonel at her side, who stared around dazed like the rest of them.

Roxette aided the colonel in lifting the woman to her feet. She swayed in their grasp. Theo could see she was gaunt from her ill-treatment. Her lips were shrivelled and pale from dehydration. She was whimpering as the two at her side tried to lead her out of her cell. She planted her bony legs apart, pulling back with all the strength she could muster. Her body began to tremble and her whimpering turned into a wail.

"Shh, my queen," Zoi said, clamping the woman's mouth shut with one of her bony hands. "We are here to aid you," she whispered. To Roxette and Ajax she said, "Keep her silent or she'll get us all killed." She stroked the queen's dishevelled hair and spoke to her in a gentle voice till the queen's trembling subsided. This time they managed to persuade her to leave the cell where she had been kept locked up for the past week.

They made their way swiftly through the prison corridor. They kept walking, the guards closing the iron doors behind them, their eyes glazed over not registering their presence.

Then they heard the sound of a skirmish coming from outside the main gate leading to the underground prison. The guard closest to the gate seemed to snap out of his dazed condition and swung the door closed barring their exit.

"Sergeant I think I caught us some rats," he shouted to another guard who wore the insignia of his rank on his collar.

"Can you do whatever you did before with your humming?" the colonel asked, turning to the old woman and making weird motions with his hands.

"In the state of alert they are in now it wouldn't work." Zoi shook her head at him.

"Damn Ushud's teeth!" the colonel swore. "How do you propose to get us out of this then?"

From outside the prison they could see a group of men covered in dark cloaks swinging their swords at the palace guards. Their shadows danced around in the light of the torches hanging from the palace walls as the men moved around to avoid their opponents' blows. Their cloaks flapped open to reveal their undergarments. Theo realized from their red tunics and the black wolf imprinted on their uniform that they were Ramilan soldiers. *But what are they doing in Ameron?* No sooner had he formed the question in his mind when he spotted a woman he felt he recognized moving swiftly towards them. She was being closely followed by three of the Ramilan soldiers. It was Princess Diomeda!

The prison cell guard and his sergeant turned around to meet the new threat of the princess and her men. They managed to keep them at bay long enough for more of the guards to come to their aid.

"Zoi, we're running out of time!" Colonel Ajax yelled as the guards from within the prison awakened from their stupor. They were turning their keys in the locks to get at the group. Theo and his companions drew their weapons. Roxette placed Queen Paula gently in Emeralda's and Serilia's arms whilst she drew her weapons to aid the colonel.

Theo could see from the fighting outside that the princess was in trouble. They were hopelessly outnumbered and bodies with the Ramilan red were beginning to litter the grounds.

"Stand back!" Zoi yelled as she pulled her sleeves back from her arms.

Theo felt the tingling sensation as green light surrounded the old woman's gnarled hands that were outstretched towards the gate. Then he felt himself being sucked towards the sorceress like wind to the eye of a vortex. He braced himself to keep from being drawn in, then was flung backwards as Zoi reversed the flows of air. He heard a booming noise and the sound of metal scraping against rock.

He looked up to see the gate torn from its hinges and flying, together with some of the rubble from the blast, into the prison guards standing outside.

They wasted no time but sprang for the exit and came crashing into the Ameron guards who were massing all around them. Theo was in a daze as he cut and sliced with his sword. Before him he could see the soldiers giving way as he bore into them in a maddened frenzy. Then the guards regrouped to allow for the new group that had joined the fight. Somewhere at the edge of his vision, Theo saw red and blue lights streaking towards them and felt the hairs at the back of his neck rising. Ameron gifted had joined in the fight. Zoi flung up her green shield and was screaming for Theo and Serilia to give her aid.

"I cannot handle them alone! Theo, forget your toy sword and come over here," Zoi ordered. "Nestor, grab the queen's other arm so Serilia can help us."

"I'll help with the queen." Princess Diomeda was by her mother's side and placed her neck and shoulder below her mother's arm.

Theo's senses were on full alert. He found himself searching with his gift to locate his opponents. It came naturally to him, though he did not understand how, since he had never been taught to do so. There were five of them, up in the surrounding walls of the palace, crouching behind the defences weary of Zoi's retaliatory fire.

Theo still held his sword but the Ramilan soldiers and his companions were keeping the Ameron Guard away from him and the other two sorceresses. Serilia flung up a purply blue shield as one of the sorcerers on the wall threw a bolt of red fire at her. They hedged their way forward, towards the palace exit, like a crab moving sideways to avoid an opponent.

At the gate a dozen men with pikes were waiting for them. Theo looked around at his friends. Roxette, the colonel and his grandfather were fully engaged in combat. He counted ten of the princess's men still on their feet, all of them looking exhausted. He realized with a sinking heart that they would probably not be able to make it out of the palace grounds alive.

A blue bolt of flame exploded on a green shield a few feet away from him.

"Theo, concentrate on the task at hand or we're all doomed," he heard Zoi shouting at him. He looked up on the walls to see a young woman with a blue ball of light emerging from her hands. She was looking intently at his sister who was turned the other way defending herself against another of their attackers. If he didn't do something soon, Serilia would be in trouble.

He knew he had to call on his gift but the memory of the pain he had experienced when last he had done so was still burned in his mind.

The sorceress on the wall produced another ball of blue flame in her other hand. She pulled her arms back and was preparing to hurl her destructive force at Serilia. Theo stood transfixed by terror.

The sorceress looked up at him, their eyes meeting for the first time. She was maybe a few years older than him, her pretty features twisted by the bloodlust of combat. He could see in those eyes that she was ready to take Serilia's life. Then, instead of throwing the balls of flame at his sister she aimed them at him and let them loose. They grew larger in his vision as they approached till they were only a few feet away.

He brought up his arms expecting to feel the searing pain of his burning flesh being removed from his body. Instead he saw a blinding white light surround him. He looked up to find he was unscathed.

His gift had acted of its own volition in a desperate attempt at self-preservation and had made him inadvertently fling up a shield.

The woman standing on the wall was preparing to renew her attack.

He tried to summon the will from deep within him, ignoring his fear and the memory of the pain. This woman was going to kill him or his sister if he did not act to stop her.

He raised his arms. They were trained on the woman on the wall. She realized what he was about to do and formed a blue protective shell like a cocoon to completely surround her.

Twin bolts of light so intense they hurt his eyes arched towards the young sorceress on the wall; their colour was purply blue however; he realized the bolts of light had not originated from his hands.

The bolts impacted on the woman's shield and exploded causing a light far brighter than daylight.

Theo blinked as he was blinded momentarily. When he could see more clearly again, the woman on the wall had vanished. His senses could no longer detect her presence.

He turned and looked at his sister. Her eyes were burning with an inner icy flame, like sapphire stones emanating beacons of fluorescent light into the dark night. He shuddered realizing he would remember those eyes for the rest of his life.

"Quickly Theo." Roxette was beside him, pulling him by the arm. Somehow they had managed to break away from the main body of the palace guards. They exited the gate, treading over the bodies of the Ameron pike men who had fallen to their blades.

"We will remain behind and stall them." It was one of the Ramilan officers. Only five of their number remained and they were bleeding from multiple wounds.

"No, come with us and we'll all escape together," the princess called out.

"Princess, please go. We will buy you some time so you can get away. Please, don't argue."

"Come princess, he's right. We will never be able to get away otherwise." Colonel Ajax was at her side, his face streaming with blood from a cut across his forehead. A cut had grazed the tip of his nose and he was clutching at his side. Theo looked at his companions realizing they were all bleeding from their wounds.

"Come on," Roxette urged, as they made their way to their mounts. They found three Ramilan soldiers and Nem waiting for them.

They mounted their steeds flying into a neck-breaking canter as they sped through the empty streets of Ameron. Behind them they could hear the sound of pursuit. They were about a league away from the outer wall of the city when Theo heard Serilia screaming. The Ameron Guard had slain the remaining five Ramilan soldiers who had stayed behind; now they had closed the gap and were firing arrows at them. Theo heard his grandfather give a grunt of pain and saw an arrow protruding from his shoulder. Two of the three remaining Ramilan soldiers had fallen from their horses having been shot down by their pursuers. An arrow flew past Theo's head, inches away from his face. He bent lower in his saddle holding on with all the strength he could muster as his roan mare surged ahead. If she slipped now, at this speed, she would surely break her legs and he knew their pursuers would finish him off. The city outer gate was looming closer. He prayed fervently that the guards at the gate would be too slow to seal them. As they approached he felt a lurch. His mare fell from under him and he was sent tumbling to the ground. He flung out his arms and felt a searing pain as the jolt to his shoulder awakened the wound the Mountain nymphs had inflicted upon him the day they had kidnapped Adelayne.

He saw stars in his vision and could hear the sound of the pursuing horses' hooves getting closer. He stood up shakily on his feet but his vision would not clear.

Then he felt himself being yanked from behind.

The Ameron soldiers were upon him.

He was hurled up into the soldier's saddle and thrown across it like a sack of potatoes.

"Watch you don't hurt yourself with that sword." He looked up with relief to find Roxette's dark eyes staring back at him.

He righted himself on the saddle and looked down at Roxette's shaggy mare, her coat letting off steam into the chilly night air as she laboured to carry both of them on her back. "This is not good for your mare," he said, with concern.

"Would you rather I left you behind?" Roxette nodded behind her at the pursuing soldiers.

They flew past the gate and were heading across Ameron's bridge that shimmered ghostly silver in the moonlight.

Theo noticed a group of soldiers on horseback huddled close together with drawn weapons on the other side of the bridge waiting for them.

"It's all over," he whispered despairingly, as they approached their opponents. He was in no condition to put up a fight. He was going to surrender to them and let them do what they wished with him. His body ached with exhaustion.

Just as they were about to crash into them, the riders opened up to let them through. Then they closed ranks behind them and waited at the foot of the bridge.

Roxette and the rest of the group did not slacken pace but kept on going. Theo could hear shouting behind them and the sound of metal meeting metal. He realized the riders had been Ramilan. They would be offering their lives to ensure their princess and her mother managed to make good their escape.

He turned to look at the princess and saw tears glistening on her cheeks.

They had been riding for several hours guided by the moonlight. Behind them there was no sound of pursuit. As they approached some trees a good way back from the main road to Ramila, Roxette called for a halt and the group dismounted from their steeds. The horses stood trembling, their coats covered with a thick lather of sweat, their nostrils flaring with their heavy breathing. Theo rushed towards his grandfather and helped him before he fell to the ground. His shirt was heavily stained with blood on his shoulder and his face was deathly pale.

Aunt Emeralda had already pulled out her pots from the pack horse and Nem at her command had gone to fetch some wood to build a small fire. Roxette meanwhile was dabbing at the cut on the colonel's brow with a clean cloth.

"Zoi, can you do anything for him?" Serilia was by her grandfather's side and turned tearful, concerned eyes at his wound.

"Come bring him and lay him down here so I can take a closer look." Zoi pointed at a spot close to the fire. She opened Nestor's shirt and peered closely at the vicious puncture. She placed her hands gingerly on Nestor's shoulder moving his arm slightly whilst she studied the wound. The old man winced with pain but offered no more than a grunt in protest. "It's deep but his breathing is normal so I am certain the arrow has not punctured his lung, nor has it struck any other vital organs. Good, Emeralda I see you have the water boiling. Serilia, be a dear and fetch me my medicine bag from my saddle. It's hanging next to the water skin–oh, bring that as well."

"Theo, help me get this off him," she added, pulling at the torn shirt that was soaked with Nestor's blood. After they had removed the shirt she washed the wound and wrapped it loosely with a cloth she used as a temporary bandage. Then she threw a cloak over the old man to keep him warm. Nestor's lips were turning blue and he was shaking visibly. "Aah, thank you my sweet." Zoi retrieved her medicine bag from Serilia's hands and began to rummage inside. "We'll use this when we're done...or maybe this one," she was murmuring to herself as she searched her collection of herbs. "Here we are." She pulled out a flask and held it to the light. She poured some of the clear liquid into a tin cup she had borrowed from Emeralda and held it to Nestor's lips.

"What is it?" Serilia asked, whilst Nestor drank the liquid, coughing and wheezing at the same time.

"What–oh this? Just your everyday common spirit. It will help prepare him for what is to come." Zoi refilled the cup and placed it once more to Nestor's lips. A bit of colour was returning to his cheeks and his lips were no longer trembling.

"What are we going to do about the arrow?" Theo asked. He knew from having hunted before that once an arrow was lodged in it would not budge and could not be pulled out of the wound.

"We are going to force it out the other side."

Theo stared at the old woman in shock. "Is that the best you can come up with? Is there nothing else you can do for him?"

"Like what, Theodor? You want me to make it disappear? I cannot, so do you have another suggestion?" He did not, so Zoi went about her task of laying out strips of white cloth next to his grandfather. She placed some dried leaves in the water which Emeralda had brought to the boil. Theo smelled the vapours from the flavoured water and found they had a pleasant odour and revived him. Zoi placed the cloths in the water letting them soak. "Now, Nemarchus and Theodor, I will need for you to hold him by the shoulders. Mind you hold him fast. This is going to hurt him and he'll try to break your hold."

Nem and Theo sat next to the old man and held him by the shoulders firmly. Nestor was mumbling incoherently, having become intoxicated from the spirit Zoi had given him. He had finished half the bottle. "Here, Emeralda, put this in his mouth." Zoi gave Emeralda a thick stick to place between Nestor's teeth. Then she grabbed the shaft of the arrow and broke its tail end so only ten fingers width protruded from Nestor's back. She picked up a rounded rock about fist sized and looked at the youths. "Ready?" They nodded bleakly.

Nestor gave a bear-like growl as the rock struck the butt end of the shaft. He clenched his teeth on the piece of wood and pulled at his shoulders. Theo was surprised by the strength in his grandfather. It was all he could do to retain his grip on the old man's shoulder. Nem was not having a better time of it either. Zoi struck the arrow shaft once more and the tip broke through the skin on the other side. Then she got up and came around to the front. She placed a thin cord made from toughened rope around the tip so it closed around it like a noose. She looked at Theo and his friend and they nodded. Nestor was breathing hard and his brow was wet with sweat.

Zoi gave a tug on the cord as the arrow was wrenched out of Nestor's shoulder with blood gushing from the wound. "Let it flow for a while," Zoi urged Emeralda. "It will help to wash away the poison." When the blood no longer had traces of yellow, Zoi placed the heated cloths on the wound and began to soak up the blood. After she had washed it thoroughly she started to place a whitish paste on either end of the shoulder. Nestor meanwhile was breathing easier but had lost his senses and was lying in Theo's arms.

"Will he be alright?" Theo asked looking down at his grandfather with concern. Serilia was by his side sharing in his worry.

"The worst is over," Zoi answered. "Now, with this paste made from night lily, and the bandages we are going to place on him, the wound should be kept free of festering. We will need to change his bandages and apply the salve three times a day till the wound seals. After that there will only be a scar to remind him of the ordeal."

Zoi lost no time but moved on to her next patient. Roxette helped the colonel to lie on his back next to the fire. She then aided him in removing his shirt. A gaping wound was revealed in his side above the ribs.

"The cut is deep but it has not resulted in the breaking of any bones," Zoi said, looking at the worried nymph. She wiped away the blood with more of the cloths soaked in the incense water. Then, once she had washed the wound clean, she produced a thick needle from her sewing kit and began to tie the gaping skin together. When she was done, she placed some of the white paste she had prepared for Nestor on the colonel's side wound and moved on to the cut on his brow.

"That will not need any of your attention," the warrior dismissed the wound.

"Nonsense." Zoi shooed away his protesting hand and within a few moments had sewn his forehead back together and had applied some of the salve to his brow. The rest of the companions washed away their minor cuts with the remaining cloths and settled down to rest by the fire.

The queen and the princess stood off to one side looking dejected.

"So many lives lost and so many hurt, for what?" The queen looked at Theo's companions and turned an accusatory glance on her daughter.

"Mother, I don't understand. What did you expect me to do, leave you there to die?" Princess Diomeda looked pleadingly at her mother.

"The life of one is not worth more than the lives of many, daughter, even if I am a queen."

"My lady, I do not mean to intrude, but your daughter did the right thing." The colonel stood up and approached the two women.

The queen ignored him turning to her daughter instead. "How many Ramilans were with you, daughter? How many of our people gave their lives needlessly this day?"

Tears were streaming from the princess's cheeks as she fought to meet her mother's enraged gaze. "One hundred cavalry men," she answered stiffly.

"A hundred!" Queen Paula stared off into the distance in disbelief.

"And thirty more at the bridge," Diomeda snivelled.

The light from the fire did nothing to improve Queen Paula's darkened expression.

"My queen, if I may," the colonel tried to interject once more. "In Alcavia, my queen, our monarch is treasured above all. We rely on our king and queen to give us strength and the hope needed to face the troubles of our everyday lives. A blow struck against our monarchy is a blow struck against us personally. Those men back there gave their lives for their beliefs, my queen. By saving you from the unfair end the Amerians had in store for you, they did what they felt was their duty. Don't belittle what these men have offered because you are frustrated with your daughter. Those men were oath-bound to ensure your safety."

The queen stared at him for a while as if she was thinking over what he had said. Then she broke down and cried, her shoulders racked by her sobbing. Emeralda moved over to her offering words of comfort whilst Serilia brought some warmed water and a cloth to wipe clean the queen's face, which was still covered with the mud from the prison cell. Then Emeralda went to fetch one of her frocks from the pack horse. She returned with it and they went off aways so Queen Paula could change from her dirty torn dress to Emeralda's clean one. Water was supplied for her needs. She returned with the dress reaching to just below her knees whereas Theo had remembered that on Emeralda it had covered her to her ankles. Emeralda did not often wear this brown dress because she found it conservative but it seemed to match the queen's taste. She thanked Emeralda warmly for the gift.

As the first rays of sunlight began to rise on the horizon, the group huddled close to decide on their next move. The horses had been fed and were now rested, though there had been no water for them to quench their thirst. Theo had given them some apples to help them last till they could reach a spring. Nesal River was a day and a half away so the horses would have to be ridden with care.

"We are going to need to change direction and head for our original destination, north to Ghiadon," Zoi was saying to the group.

"My mother and I are not going to the Forest nymphs' kingdom," Princess Diomeda interjected. "I need to get mother to Ramila as soon as possible. Every moment we spend out in the open is an opportunity for our pursuers to catch up with us and reclaim the queen."

"Princess, I was not suggesting that you go with us. Before we had the fine notion of saving your mother's neck from the axe man's blade, we were on our way to the Emerald kingdom. You and your mother will continue on your journey west and my companions and I will make our way to our destination north."

"You will leave us alone to make the journey unaided!" The princess was incredulous.

"Why of course not, my dear. The fine colonel and Nestor will complete the task they began. They will be going with you."

Nestor and the colonel both muttered their complaint.

"I am not going to leave my grandchildren alone when they need me most," said the old man.

"And I will not forsake my mission at such a critical junction with time pressing on us," the colonel added.

“I’m afraid Zoi is right.” Roxette fixed Nestor and Ajax with her cat’s gaze. Her black leather shimmered in the morning light.

“Whatever do you mean, Roxette?” The colonel returned her gaze.

“You are both in a bad shape and will delay our journey. I feel that even the trip to Ramila will inflict more punishment on Nestor’s wound than he should allow in his present condition.”

“Yes, and what’s more, colonel, it would hardly be fitting for you to abandon the queen and the princess now, after you have gone through all this effort to save them.” Zoi placed a gnarled hand on the colonel’s shoulder.

He looked down at her in exasperation. A series of conflicting emotions could be seen on his face. He was torn on the one hand between his duty to his imprisoned princess and on the other felt the weight of his responsibility towards the Ramilan queen and princess. He sighed with resignation then turned back to Roxette. “I will deliver Queen Paula and the princess safely to Ramila, then I’ll meet you in Ghiadon.”

“I will not linger more than I have to in the Forest nymphs’ realm,” Roxette warned. “We’ll need to enter the mountains as soon as possible. We have already delayed more than we should have, and winter is almost upon us.”

“I do not expect you to delay on my account. If, when I arrive you are gone, then I will come after you and catch you up in the mountains.”

“What about you, Nestor?” Zoi asked.

Nestor looked first at the old woman, then at the Mountain nymph, then at his grandchildren, and finally to his sister.

“Nestor, maybe Roxette is right,” Emeralda said gently. “Maybe we should make it slowly to Ramila till you’ve had a chance to heal.”

Nestor considered her words and finally his shoulders drooped as he came to his decision. "Roxette is more right than she knows. I don't think I will be able to make it to Ramila either, Emeralda. Already I feel my shoulder going numb and my breathing is strained." He breathed in with difficulty a few times to regain his breath. "I will go back to Ameron and seek out accommodation at the inn we've been staying at for the past week, till the shoulder heals somewhat."

"Nestor is that wise?" Zoi asked concernedly. "You might be recognized by the guards."

Nestor shook his head. "I doubt the guards would have taken notice of one old man in all the confusion last night."

"Then I'm sure they would not have noticed one old woman either," Emeralda added. "I'm going to stay with you and make sure you get better."

Nestor smiled at her appreciatively. Emeralda had always been there to support him in the worst of times. Now was no exception. "What about you Serilia?" Nestor asked turning to his granddaughter. "Are you going to come along with us?"

Serilia looked troubled. She was being torn between following her grandfather and keeping close to her brother. Finally she seemed to make up her mind. "Aunt Emeralda I am sure will keep you safe, grandfather. My brother will need me by his side a while longer. In any case I have always wanted to meet the Forest nymphs and their queen."

"That may be so, Serilia, but once you are done visiting the Emerald kingdom, return to your aunt and I. We will be waiting for you here to take you east to your parents."

A look of longing crossed both Serilia's and Theo's face at the mention of their parents. They were only on the other side of the Hills of Halum. So near when one looked on the map but so far in reality. It was no easy feat travelling over the long road east to Seldavia's border. And once across the border it was still a long journey north to Aldorn.

"Will you also be coming with us once you've completed your journey to Ghiadon, Theodor?" The old man raised his eyes and searched his grandson's face, marking each line carefully in his memory. He already knew what the answer would be.

"No grandfather. I'm afraid I have an unfinished task to accomplish in the mountains with Roxette. Maybe when it's all over I will return to you in Aldorn and we can be united once more."

"My sweet boy." Nestor placed a hand with skin like taught canvas affectionately on his grandson's cheek. "How our lives changed that day you brought the mage to our cottage. But how were you to know what vicissitudes you would bring upon us."

Then his gaze became harder and his eyes took on that cool look of ice. "Be careful in the mountains, my son. There are all manner of creatures lurking in the shadows. Some are not known to mankind; many have never escaped into the light, which is just as well." Then he turned his frosty gaze on the Mountain nymph. "You have given us no reason to doubt you over the past few months. Your courage and commitment to your friends is clear. Do not forget where your loyalties lie when you take my flesh and blood with you into your homeland. I have lived a very long time and have grown tough and knowledgeable enough of this world to be able to track you down and kill you should you betray the trust I have placed in you."

Roxette bowed her head in respect to the old man, like a wild cat that realizes the damage a large bird of prey can inflict upon it. She recognized his ability to carry out his threat.

"Er, by the way," Nem butted in, drawing everyone's attention upon him. "Since nobody asked, I just thought I should mention that I too will be going to see the Forest nymphs."

"And your company will be most welcome," Theo said, placing his arm affectionately on his friend's shoulder.

After they had packed their belongings and saddled their horses, the group exchanged their goodbyes. Theo and Serilia hugged and kissed their aunt and grandfather. Even Zoi gave Nestor a peck on the cheek and Nestor ruffled Nem's hair. Roxette surprised them all by pulling colonel Ajax close and giving him a long lingering kiss.

Then they were off in their chosen directions.

♦ CHAPTER 26 ♦

Separate ways

Theo felt morose at the death of his strawberry roan. She had been a good, sturdy animal with a pleasant temperament. Riding on her back had been an effortless affair, unlike the black gelding he was now on. It had belonged to one of the Ramilan soldiers and was a nasty beast that pulled at the reins and trotted along awkwardly so he already felt saddle sore.

They kept along the west bank of the river opposite the direction of the lazy flow. The Silver River, which was the longest in Leonium, surged along like a serpent that had gorged itself and did not feel the need to change its sluggish pace. Along its length, the group had seen a few ships traversing the waters, long eloquent crafts shaped like giant swans. Zoi explained that the ships belonged to the Forest nymphs and were carrying their produce down to Ameron City where they would dock to unload. When Nem had suggested that they try to board one of the vessels going the other way, Zoi explained the obvious, that the deep hulled ships could not possibly approach the shore and that the proper docking area lay behind at the city. They had decided jointly that they would not risk going back to Ameron and that they would make the eight-day trip to Ghiadon on horseback.

There were smaller boats going up and down the river as well but they looked upon the group with distrust; it was not surprising, since they only carried passengers to and from the conventional boarding areas. Once or twice when Nem had hailed a boat, the owners had completely ignored him. So they carried on riding and Theo resigned himself to struggling with his dark gelding. He looked over enviously at Nem and Serilia, who were still riding upon the mares they had been given at the cottage back in Cyrus. Elron was a good judge of horses and would never have allowed an animal of inferior stock to reside at his farm. Theo felt a pang of remorse for the animals they had been forced to let loose when their stable had been set alight by the pithiks. He wondered if his father would have had the opportunity to round up the herd–*most probably not*. He hoped fervently that the animals had found a welcoming home somewhere at another farm; it was preferable to them being mauled by wild animals.

The weather was becoming decidedly colder with the promised kiss of winter upon the air's lips. Theo bent his head into the wind clutching his cloak tighter about him as they made their way forward. They had been travelling for three days on the plains–three days since they had split up with the rest of their companions. Zoi offered them encouragement informing them that by noon tomorrow they would reach the outskirts of the Emerald Forest. The trees should help break the wind and would offer them shelter from prying eyes as well. They were still not sure whether scouts had been sent out to try to locate them. Roxette had taken measures to conceal their tracks that first day when they split up, but an experienced tracker might still be able to figure out which way they had gone.

After a very tiring ride, they decided to call a halt. The sun was dipping over the Dragon's Foot Mountains and the night chill had arrived to envelope them in its cold embrace. Soon they had a small fire going. Theo sat on a log close to the fire to warm his hands. He placed both hands on his back and arched it to relieve some of the tension. He looked accusingly at the gelding. It snorted back at him, fixing him with a dark eye that seemed to glint with amusement.

When they had eaten from their supplies, they curled up around the fire and settled down to sleep. Roxette was going to take the first watch.

As soon as Theo rested his head on the ground he slept.

He was standing in the great hall, the thick limbs of the surrounding trees forming both the walls and the intervening columns upon which rested the torches that lit the hall. He noticed the floor was decorated with the rusty hues of autumn leaves resting on large carpets intricately woven with strange designs depicting otherworldly scenes: there were slender maidens with long brown hair fanning behind them in an echo of their thin gowns as they raced through the forest chased by young men with outstretched arms. A few of the young men had been successful and were in the arms of their lovers, merged together like doves.

The hall was empty, apart from the gilded throne which was decorated with precious metals contrasting with its dark wooden surface. Theo stared long and hard at the empty throne. Then he was startled as an ethereal shape materialized upon it. The shape solidified to become a woman of such beauty that it made his heart ache just to look at her. He was surprised that in his dream he could feel both his heart beating faster and his palms sweating. There was also a faint whiff in the air as of the scent of flowers. The forest queen fixed him with her eyes. Her lips parted slightly as her chest rose and fell with her breathing.

"Your arrival is imminent, young sorcerer's apprentice. You have been late in coming. Winter is almost upon you and I see in your heart that you are decided on the task you have set for yourself. You have yet to learn that the life of a servant of the Light is not his own."

Theo was about to protest but the lady raised her hand to silence him.

"We of the Council of Light have much need of the strength you and those of your kind can provide. Our enemies are battering at our defences mercilessly and seek to tear down the gates we have planted in their path to seal them from the Midlands and the free lands of Thalagia. It will not be long now before the Dark Champion will awaken from his slumber and will ride forth to reclaim that which was once his. But the thirst of the Dark Lord will not be quenched. His roving eye is already turned upon Leonium and he has set in motion the events that will lead to our downfall.

"Time is running out young apprentice. Your tasks lie elsewhere, yet without your mentor to guide you, one would expect that you would falter."

Again Theo sought to speak in defence of his decision but the queen leaned forward seeming to grow in his vision so she loomed before him like the trees that towered above.

"You are contemplating putting your life at great risk for a girl her own family has realized is beyond redemption. You venture forth with the blind overconfidence of youth. But *we* have lived in this world for too long and are aware of what awaits you in those tunnels. Many who have ventured into the Mountain nymphs' kingdom have never returned to tell the tale. And yet, even I, with my long years of servitude to the Light, cannot help wishing selfishly that you *do* make the wrong choice, and set out to rescue my niece."

His vision blurred and he felt the ground below him lurch as he was changing scenes once more. At first he thought he was back in the Forest hall but then he realized the tree walls were missing and so were the torches and the decorations on the walls and floor. He was deep in the Emerald Forest, or at least so he believed from the age of the trees. They were the same oak species of tall, thick limbed trees with large trunks that two men standing together could not encompass. He looked up but his vision was obscured by the canopy of the trees. He moved forward till he reached a small clearing in the trees so the silver and blue light from the twin moons was able to trickle through the forest, like cascading water falling through an opening in the rocks.

Something had drawn his attention to the clearing. He walked at the fringe of the trees and realized that a little further on they began to open up and become scattered. As he made his way towards the glade he realized the ground was no longer level but was rising upwards. Then he found himself standing at the edge of the woods staring up towards hills covered in green shrubs. From the arrangement of the stars, he realized he was looking eastwards. He remembered with fondness the lessons his uncle Tiber had given him on how to steer a ship by night using the key stars that had guided sailors over the millennia. There to the east, he could see the Hope Star, the brightest star in Thalagia's heavens. Now its bright light was almost entirely shrouded in cloud.

He turned as he caught the movement in the corner of his vision. There, it was! At the base of the hills, a shape darker than the surrounding rock was moving slowly forward. Its neck was arched like an elegant bird, or like that of the noble stallions of Balsovia, ending in a long snout. From its nostrils trailed its warm breath which solidified into mist in the chill night air. Its large wings were folded above its back, their tips reaching down to the ground covering its hindquarters from which extended a long tail ending in a three-tipped point. The beast arrived at the spot of its choice and bent its haunches to settle to the ground. It reminded Theo more of a mammal than a lizard, the way it lay there on the forest bed, its legs bent beneath its belly like a large cat with its long tail curled up to its tapering snout. Its scaled hide was resplendent in the moon and starlight, shimmering as if the beast was dressed in armour adorned with a multitude of sparkling gemstones.

It turned to look at him with yellow eyes like saucers reflecting the moonlight. In the centre of each eye were dark slits for pupils, like black seeds standing on their ends. He stood transfixed by the gaze; until you gazed in those eyes, you did not realize quite so acutely the origins of the beast. He managed to tear away his gaze from that of the dragon and looked to its horns instead that jutted from either side of its head like those of a bull, but were as large as an elephant's tusks. He still felt those eyes peering at him so he looked down at its feet instead. The feet were as large as a man and ended in five clawed toes, each claw the size of a dagger and kept just as sharp.

"You come to me in your shadow form once more, Dragonstrider. I seem unable to sever the link that binds us, though it is a mystery to me how it came to be. What manner of magic have you used to track me, boy?" A growl like the sound of a small avalanche escaped the dragon's throat. It had not stirred from its position but its gaze remained fixed on Theo.

Although he knew he was not standing bodily before the dragon, he still felt uneasy at his proximity. One bound would be enough to bring the beast on top of him. He thought about backing away but decided it would not do to act cowardly before it. He summoned up his courage and stood firm but with his eyes lowered to just below the reptilian gaze. His gifted senses warned him not to stare directly into those eyes.

He opened his mouth to speak but remembered that he could not, so he stood looking at the dragon without meeting its gaze.

The dragon let out a snort, blowing away the leaves closest to its snout. The lids of its eyes came closer together so it gazed distrustfully at him through narrowed slits. "I am not unfamiliar with your kind, wizardling. A far more powerful wizard than you has tried unsuccessfully to keep me servile to his whims, but I will not be enslaved by any man."

The dragon heaved its body from the ground with surprising ease, bringing its head inches before Theo's. It turned slightly askew so its one eye filled Theo's vision. The youth stood trembling before the beast. He found that even in his shadowy form he could still sense the stomach-wrenching effects of fear.

"Perhaps you are one of Zarzbudin's underlings sent to take me back?" Theo heard a rumbling noise and the dragon's body shook. He realized the beast was laughing at him. "Zarzbudin is desperate if he expects mere boys to carry out the task."

Theo shook his head emphatically to signify that he had nothing to do with the Witch King. Involuntarily he took a few steps back from the dragon. The beast stared at him for a long while then blew out a torrent of wind from its nostrils before deciding to return to its resting spot. "Perhaps when we next meet, you will be in the flesh and I will get the answers I want from you, wizardling." Then the dragon closed its eyes to sleep.

Theo's vision blurred once more and he felt his shoulder shaking. As he returned to his body he could hear a murmuring noise. The noise became clearer till he could hear his name being called over and over. Someone was trying to shake him awake. He opened his eyes to find Nem staring at him worriedly.

"Theo, you gave me a fright. I've been calling you for quite a spell. Your hands were so cold and your face pale. For a moment I thought something had happened to you."

Theo sat up and felt the blood return to his limbs and face. Nem was right. He did feel a bit numb. "I'm alright, Nem. I was just having a dream...that is all."

Nem's worry seemed to lessen and he nodded. "Alright, Theo. I suppose now that you are awake I have nothing to worry about. I am going to get some sleep. It's your turn to keep watch. Roxette said you are to awaken us with the first rays of daylight."

Theo nodded in return as he got up and placed his cloak about his shoulders. He went to check on the horses then settled down on a boulder that provided him with a good view of the camp site and the surrounding plains. The fire had burst back to life now Nem had placed more logs on it. Theo stared at the river that could just be seen from the camp spot. The starlight danced on its surface like fire flies and the sound of the rushing water filtered through to him from the surrounding bushes. Once or twice he could hear a small animal skitter along on small feet and then a squeaking sound followed by the hoot of an owl after a successful kill.

He was nodding off to sleep when he heard it. A howl pierced the night air causing the fine hairs of his back to stand on edge. A second and then a third howl followed the first. These were further away. He looked about anxiously till he fancied he saw a loping shape moving along the river bank. The horses began to snort and stamp their hooves nervously. He got up from his perch swiftly and moved to comfort the beasts. He passed a hand over their noses and whispered softly in their ears to calm them. But the loping shape at the edge of his vision was joined by two more. He wandered whether he should awaken his friends but decided to investigate first. He drew his nymph sword from its scabbard and stepped closer to his sleeping companions, at the same time peering out into the plains.

It approached him with no sign of fear. It stood perhaps fifteen feet away, its eyes reflecting the campfire light. As it caught his scent it folded back its lips to reveal sharp fangs. Its coat shone silver, bulging at the shoulders and around its neck to reveal the muscles there. It had long powerful limbs it used to carry it over great distances and a thick tail that now stood erect to signify its alertness. Theo replaced the sword slowly in its scabbard and stood perfectly still staring directly into the grey animal's eyes.

He was thrown into a world man had relinquished long ago when he had discovered fire and had chosen to leave the wild for the comfort of a shared dwelling with others of his kind. Visions of the wolf's hunting trips over the last few days flashed before his eyes. He saw the wolf pounce on hares and he was also witness to the pack hunting down and killing an old buck with long horns and a tough hide. The buck had fed the wolves well and had provided for the entire pack and the litter of young ones that waited back at the den. What he saw next caused him to draw in a sharp breath. The previous night the wolves had killed five ape-like creatures that loped along on all fours but that also reared on two legs and used mean-looking blades to cut and slice with. Two of the wolves had lost their lives in the skirmish but it had been worth it. They were age-old enemies with the furry two legs and were surprised to find them so far west. From tales passed down by their forebearers the wolves of the west knew that the furry two legs had been exterminated long ago and were forced to flee far to the east.

The wolf sensed Theo's loathing for the pithiks and the tension from its shoulders was released. It came a few paces closer till it was almost beside him. Theo stretched out his hand tentatively towards the wolf and waited. He was risking being bitten but he knew from having raised his hounds from pups that this was the only way to befriend their kind. The wolf brought its nose closer and sniffed at Theo's hand. Then it turned its gaze upon him and he saw in its eyes a vision of its fangs. The wolf was named Whitefang.

Whitefang turned its head to look behind and two more of its pack came closer to the camp to get acquainted with the human who seemed to be able to understand their way of communicating. The bitch with the dark coat stepped softly towards him. She smelled him once then bounded away to just beyond the light of the fire. A vision remained fixed in Theo's mind as he had briefly made eye contact with her. Softfoot was her name and she was the leader of the pack. The other wolf also came closer. Theo did not need the wolf vision to learn this one's name: Bigpaw.

Theo studied the three wolves for a while and marvelled at their smooth flowing motions. The other two had drawn back from him after they had introduced themselves and kept just far enough from the camp so only their eyes, reflecting the campfire light, could be seen. Whitefang engaged Theo's eyes once more and he saw visions of himself in those eyes striding ahead endlessly on a journey that took him to far away lands. Farstrider. Somehow he had conveyed to the wolf his name.

When the wolf had taken a few more sniffs at him and at the ground surrounding the camp site it turned at a silent signal from the lead bitch and they loped off together disappearing ghostlike into the night.

"How long have you been able to mind fuse with the beasts?" Theo jumped in surprise and turned to look at Zoi who was peering at him with her hazel eyes that missed nothing. Her absorbing gaze reminded him for a fleeting moment of the calculating looks Archon had sometimes given him, before he was killed.

"I've been aware of it for a few years now but I only found out what it was exactly when Archon explained it to me after our trip to Jade Island. I had mind fused there with a hawk for just an instant."

"You need to take care in your use of the gift, Theo. Mind fusing involves a releasing of your own senses and a becoming as one with the beast. If you are not careful you may lose yourself forever to it. Like all aspects of the gift this too needs careful handling. It is not something to indulge in freely. Many a wizard attuned to sharing his thoughts with an animal has reached beyond the point of no return only to spend the rest of their life loping along on all fours like an animal and having lost all links with humanity."

"How do I guard against it?" Theo sat beside the old woman and folded his knees so he could rest his arms upon them.

"If you pay attention to your warning senses you will know when you are reaching too far. The best way of course is to avoid the mind fusing as much as possible."

Theo nodded in understanding.

"And Theo," Zoi added.

"Yes."

"I suggest you refrain from spirit travelling as well." Theo's eyes widened as he looked at her in surprise. "Theo, don't act so shocked. You know I am gifted so you didn't honestly expect me not to notice, now did you?"

Theo looked down guiltily, then he turned his gaze back to the old woman. She studied him, her mouth a thin straight line, the wrinkles on her face becoming more prominent in the alternating light and shadow being cast by the campfire. "You're not the first to tell me to be careful of spirit travelling. Back in Alcavia, Archon had to use his gift to draw me back from the darkness. I have tried Zoi to refrain from it and for a long while now I have not spirit travelled. Archon said that when I feel it happening I must concentrate on where my body is at that particular moment so that I can keep myself...anchored down." Zoi nodded her agreement. "But I feel drawn to it like a fish to its breeding grounds, or a frog to a pool of water."

"You must fight it, Theo." Zoi looked at him in earnest. "Spirit travelling is a useful tool in the hands of a fully trained wizard but even then it is done in the company of another gifted. I suggest you refrain from it until you have been taught how to avoid the pitfalls."

Theo looked at her as if he had something more to say. Then he seemed to change his mind.

"Go on, Theo, tell me."

"Oh, I was just thinking."

"Yes?" She remained looking at him expectantly.

"Zoi I...I saw the queen of the Emerald Forest in my dreams." He decided to keep from her the encounter with the dragon. Somehow what had transpired between the dragon and himself was private, but he was curious to find out what Zoi would make of the queen of the Forest nymphs.

Zoi pulled her black cloak around her bony frame and placed her feet closer to the fire. She rubbed at her shoulders to warm them from the morning chill. It would be sunrise soon and this was the time of day when the surrounding air was at its coolest, and wettest. "What did you and the queen discuss?"

Theo returned the old woman's gaze. He had known Zoi for almost a year now and she was still an enigma to him. Who was Zoi? Where had she come from? Who were her family? He admitted he was glad of her company even though he still knew close to nothing about her. Apart from him and Serilia, she was the only other gifted in the group and she, at least, knew how to use her gift. "Queen Viola is not pleased with my decision to rescue the princess," Theo began. "She feels my efforts are better spent elsewhere."

"I understand that you are forced to respond to your heart's call," Zoi said. "That is often the way: our heart's desire gets in the way of prudence. But that is what makes us human." Zoi lifted her face just as the first rays of light begun to rise above the Silver River's banks making it shimmer like liquid gold. "Let's wake the others," she prompted. "We are still a two days' ride away from the edge of the forest."

♦ CHAPTER 27 ♦

Solidifying the bond

Nem craned his neck to gaze with awe at the ancient woods that surrounded them. He had never seen trees like these before. They stood to attention, tall giants, straight and erect, flaunting proudly their autumn coats that were adorned with amber and rust coloured leaves. Intermittently a solitary orange brown leaf would descend slowly from the tree tops, like a feather falling from a bird's nest, to settle on the ground. The noise of the horses' hooves was muffled completely by the fallen leaves, and only the sounds of the birds and small mammals, such as squirrels and chipmunks, could be heard.

Nem wondered how many ships could be built from such fine wood, or how many splendid pieces of furniture to adorn the lords' offices and lounges. But sensing Zoi's overwhelming love for these trees, he did not speak his mind. He looked at Zoi and marvelled at the look in her eye and the springiness of her step. Ever since they had stepped foot into the forest, Zoi appeared to be in her element. The first day, she had spent smiling with pleasure, cocking her head to one side, as if she could hear voices that the rest of them were unable to. She seemed perplexed that her companions could not sense the trees emitting their life energy. Nem had not wanted to admit it at the time, but since entering the ancient woods, he felt numbed, as if a buzzing noise was constantly ringing in his ears, though whenever he concentrated on the sound, he would hear absolutely nothing, apart from the noise of the small animals that lived in these woods.

That was another thing he found strange. They had been in the woods for two days now and he still had not seen any sign of the Forest nymphs that were meant to inhabit them. He found his mind wandering aplenty. With nothing but walking to occupy his time, he would wonder what Irene was doing. He felt a pang of regret, and not for the first time, at having been forced to leave Alcavia so soon. Life had been good with Irene. She knew they had no future together, so she was easy-going and gave of herself freely, and without the usual demands other women would have placed upon him. He remembered her fondly and the days they had spent together in the double bed of their favourite inn.

"What are you grinning about?" Serilia brought him out of his musing. She was walking beside him leading her mare next to his. He looked up at her and concealed the smile on his face.

"Oh, I was just thinking about how good life was for us before we left Alcavia." He decided it would not be a good idea to mention Irene in front of Serilia. She had not seemed to approve of their relationship. He had wondered in the past if anything might evolve between him and Serilia but realized soon enough that it was impossible. She was his best friend's sister and he had grown to look upon her as a close friend–nothing more complicated than that. True, Serilia would flirt with him or tease him at times, but it was just playful fun.

Serilia looked a bit thoughtful before she answered. "Yes, I must admit Alcavia was good for you both." She nodded towards Theo, who was walking side by side with Roxette in the lead. "And it gave me and aunt Emeralda a chance to rest. Zoi's aid in training me to use the gift during this time was useful. I learnt far more in these six months than I ever learnt with mother. Zoi says it's because I spent my younger years getting ready, and that now I am at the stage where I will begin to see the benefits of using the gift." She had gotten carried away with herself and one look at Nem's discomfort placed a check on what she had been saying. "But Alcavia has also placed new dilemmas and dangers in our path."

"Yes, that's true enough," Nem admitted. "There hasn't been a moment he hasn't been thinking about her." He looked at his friend who seemed oblivious to their conversation. They were speaking softly so it was doubtful he would overhear. "You know that at night he dreams about her?"

"He dreams about her ...or he sleep walks to her?" Nem gave her one of those looks, the one that said, *what are you talking about?* So she shrugged her shoulders instead. "I'll have to have a word with him later."

"Yes, I believe you should." Nem wiped at a stray strand of curly hair that had fallen in his eyes and clutched the golden scimitar tightly in his grasp. "These woods are beginning to give me the jitters." He looked around warily, as if he expected a wild animal to pounce upon him at any moment.

"I must admit I am getting a bit wary of walking, eating, sleeping and waking each day surrounded by these old trees." Serilia lifted her gaze to stare at the forest canopy. "Look how the light just manages to infiltrate through the leaves."

"Don't remind me. I already feel like a mouse stuck in an endless cornfield. By the way, have you not wondered at how we have been going on for two days without any sign of other inhabitants here?" He turned his brown eyes searchingly towards her blue.

"Yes, I have wondered, but when I asked Roxette she assured me that there are several Forest nymphs already trailing us."

"You're not serious!" Nem looked around uneasily. He tried to be discreet about it, but could not help gawking at the surrounding woods.

"It's no use, Nem. I've tried to detect their movements for most of our trip through the woods but have not been able to sight even one."

"How long have they been following us?"

"Roxette says they are not following us exactly but are ahead, beside and behind us."

"So we are trapped in their midst ...till they decide what they'll do with us," Nem muttered gruffly. He wasn't happy about this at all. He preferred to be able to see when an arrow might be making its way towards him. He felt an uneasy feeling between his shoulder blades but stiffened his resolve and kept moving, though more rigidly than before.

"Roxette says we are most definitely at a disadvantage, should the Forest nymphs decide to turn hostile."

"Great. Thanks for making me feel much better with your piece of enlightening news," he said ironically.

"Pleasure to be of service, Foresight." Serilia smiled at him impishly, dimples forming on her cheeks.

"Aren't you able to sense them with your ..." he waved his hands in the air to signify her gift.

"Of course I am silly. Why do you think I went to Roxette about it?"

"Oh," Nem answered resignedly. "And how is Roxette able to see them and we're not?"

Serilia stared at him as if he were daft. "She's *nymphish!*" She rolled her eyes to show what she thought of his ridiculous question.

"So I am the only one in the group that didn't know about them, then. I suppose even *he* could sense them?" He nodded in Theo's direction.

"Yes, even Theo could sense them, though it took him longer than the rest of us. Needless to say Zoi noticed them first with Roxette."

Much later in the day—at a spot where the trees seemed to clear somewhat—Roxette called a halt. A large beech tree was sprawled across the forest floor, which was the reason for the thinning of the trees. The age worn tree had occupied a sizable spot in the forest and so its downfall had provided a small glade in the continuous mass of woods. Nem and Theo set about clearing a space on the ground closest to the fallen tree. They would build a small fire for the night and had to make sure there were no leaves lying around in the vicinity of their campfire. They did not want to start a blaze.

"See if you can bring something back for us to eat," Zoi requested of the youths. Theo noticed all three women were staring at him. He realized that he and his friend were not wanted for a while. Then he saw Serilia bring out a bar of soap and Roxette searching for a change of clothing. He couldn't help blushing. He nodded and pulled Nem by the arm to bring him alongside him as they walked in the opposite direction to the river, which could be heard not so far away.

Nem smelled at his clothing and wrinkled his nose. "We're going to need a bath soon as well," he commented. "I don't know about you, but I smell like my horse, and these stains look like there going to need some scrubbing to get rid of."

"We'll try and wash up when we get back. Meanwhile let's concentrate on getting something to eat." Theo's belly grumbled in agreement. They were moving soft-footedly through the woods, searching for footprints of any small animal that might have crossed their way. Theo strained to hear any minute sound that might give away their prey. It reminded him of their hunting in the Triad Woods, only these trees were far older and more imposing in the way they towered above them, blotting out what little light there was. He found himself searching unintentionally with his gift the surrounding forest. He knew they were being watched. He sensed perhaps half a dozen forms, though he could not see them no matter how hard he peered into the woods. At first, when he had realized the group was being followed, he had felt a bit flustered, but as the days wore on and nothing happened he felt less wary.

Zoi had explained to him that as long as they did not make any threatening moves, the Forest nymphs would be content just to keep an eye on them. Later, when they would be closer to the nymph's dwelling in the forest, they would have to confront them and ask permission to be let through. So for now he concentrated on his hunting. He carried with him his favourite bow, which he had brought from the cottage, and which thankfully his grandfather had retrieved when they had been ambushed by Loxandra. He shivered at the memory of the sorceress. Nem shot him a quick glance to see if he was alright. He waved his friend onwards and cleared his mind of any thoughts of their experience back at Ramila. It was all over now, so there was no point dwelling on it.

What Theo saw next on the ground caused him much puzzlement. It looked to him as though in some areas the leaves of the forest had been punched into the ground, much like a runaway boulder would have done if it had rolled along the forest bed. He looked up to see the same perplexed look on Nem's face. "So, what do you make of this, then?" He placed his hand in the recess. It measured the length of a man lying down and had compressed the ground a good five inches.

"Theo, I can't say I've ever seen anything like this before, though my father told me stories of elephants that could leave tracks like this, but nowhere near this size, not to mention that the elephants I know are to be found in the Hadir Desert or to the far eastern isles of the Kalim Ocean."

"And this beast, whatever it is, has five claws on its feet." Theo motioned with a finger to the pointed recesses at the front edge of the paw prints.

They had no time to puzzle over it, however.

Somewhere up ahead of them they heard a resounding roar, like the voices of a score of lions sending out their call in unison. Theo felt the tremors of the earth, as whatever was out there pounded upon the ground. He and Nem crouched down lower instinctively, making themselves as small and as inconspicuous as possible. He heard the noises coming again, from not too far away, and the distinctive sound of trees being crashed into. He envisaged that this beast must be of gigantic proportions and, for a horrendous moment, wondered how he would respond if it came rushing towards them.

Surely all that racket can be heard from miles away? he thought, as he knocked an arrow. He shook his head in despair at what he had just done. No arrow was going to be enough to stop this beast. In his mind's eye he envisaged a towering giant coming towards them with large forearms and a club as large as a tree. *What if the giant troll, or whatever it is, bursts out of the trees and comes at us?* He did not have to strain his ears to hear the loud crushing noises again. They were close...real close.

His heart was beating faster and his lungs were filling with air rapidly as his breathing quickened. He rubbed his sweaty palms on his pants. It wouldn't do to have slippery hands if and when the beast came at them. If the arrow slipped whilst he tried to draw the bow, then he would not be given a second chance to re-knock it.

They waited anxiously behind the massive trunk of one of the trees. Nem had drawn his scimitar. It glistened golden as the feeble light infiltrated through the forest canopy leaves to fall upon it. Theo looked at his friend's pale face and wondered if his own was just as terrified–*probably more so.*

Then they saw it. A light, as of burning flame, was hurled into the dawn. It was so intense it reached them from between the tree trunks. Those trunks were all that stood between them and the beast now. Theo calculated that they were not more than a furlong away from it. So it was not a troll then; trolls did not breathe fire. Theo looked uneasily all around and crouched behind the tree trunk, clutching at its bark for comfort. He swallowed and tried to still his beating heart. His friend was right beside him with his back to the tree.

"Shall we make a run for it?" Nem asked, the trembling in his voice causing him to almost shout out loud.

"What if it sees us and comes after us?"

Nem considered for a moment, then turned to look at him with wide frightened eyes. "So, what do you suggest?"

Theo didn't know what to do. If they ran, the beast would spot them and come crashing after them. He already felt as though it was breathing down his neck. He placed a hand to his collar and pulled at his shirt to loosen it. He did not dare to look from the side of the tree trunk in the direction of the noises. *What if I step away from the trunk and come face to face with it? What if it throws its flaming breath on us and lights us up like dried bundles of hay?*

"Theo, we can't just stand here waiting for it to smell us out. We need to do something, and do it now."

Nem was right. Theo was about to tell him he was ready to sprint in the direction they had come, and hope the beast was too slow to react. But then his curiosity got the better of him. He felt he was about to make a big mistake, one he might not live to regret. "Go fetch Roxette and Zoi. I'm going to see what's happening."

"Are you crazy, Theo? Come on! Let's get out of here while we still have a chance." Nem stared at him incredulously, as if he had been hit on the head and was not thinking properly.

"Go on, I'll be fine. Honest! If he had been after us we wouldn't still be alive to escape."

Nem was torn between his loyalty to his friend and his need for self-preservation. The latter won him over. "Suit yourself, Theo, but this is madness." Theo nodded in reply but left his friend to go sprinting back into the woods till he was lost from sight. For an instant, he felt like he wanted to go sprinting after him but then he gathered up his resolve and peered past the tree trunk. There was no beast waiting behind the trunk, though he could hear its loud roar.

Theo was all alone.

He sent out a search with his gift and found that he had been abandoned by the nymphs that had been shadowing his movements. Perhaps they too had done the sensible thing and run away. As he inched his way slowly forward he heard more of the screaming noises, only now they seemed to be more laboured, as if the beast was trying to catch its breath. Maybe it was getting tired of knocking down trees.

This time, when he sent out a search weave with his gift, it came back at him with so much force he almost lost his footing. The beast filled his secondary vision, like a beacon of light that is shone suddenly on a dark canvass. The rest of the nymphs, the ones he had thought had run away, were smaller beacons scattered all around that of the beast, like ants around a grasshopper many times their size.

He burst through into the clearing and was completely caught unawares by what he saw.

There it was–the dragon in his dreams!

At first he thought it was about to stretch out its large red wings and launch itself into the air like a giant missile hurled by a catapult of war. But then the dragon fell back to the earth uttering its desolate cry. Its eyes were huge and bulging with thin red veins criss-crossing its irises as it cast its furious gaze at the Forest nymphs that stood all around it. The dragon opened its mouth to reveal jaws lined with teeth as large as daggers. It flicked out its snake-like tongue and hissed at the little men that moved all around it. Theo wondered why the dragon did not pounce on the Forest nymphs and crush them, or take flight to leave them behind.

Then he saw the thin silver strands that completely enveloped the dragon's body and wings. The ends of the strands, which made a net to ensnare the bellowing beast, were tied onto the surrounding trees so no matter how much the dragon pulled at the ropes, the trees, by their sheer numbers, held it down firmly. With each frustrated motion, Theo could see that it was tangling itself even further in the net. Soon it would not be able to lift even its huge head.

The nymphs seemed oblivious to the dragon's hissing and to its crazed movements. They made sure to keep away from its snout which was still spewing forth flame, and not to approach too near to its thrashing limbs. Gradually but decisively, the nymphs were tying more knots onto the dragon, like small baby spiders would have done with a moth, so the dragon eventually could not move its wings and tail at all. It was pinned down like a tent that is stretched out and held by its ropes firmly to the ground. The dragon opened its maw once more to cry out or to blow fire, but not a whiff of smoke escaped its throat. It had depleted its reserve of flame. Instead it made a sound like a deflating wine skin.

When the dragon was forced to its knees and its breathing was rasping, one of the nymphs stepped close to its head and held a spear a few feet away from its throat.

"Have you secured his head and his legs like I told you?" the nymph asked his companions. There were easily a score of them surrounding the dragon's large form.

"Yes, Commander Malgor," one of the nymphs closest to him answered.

"Then let's get this over with." The leading nymph with the spear in his hand lifted it and aimed at the soft spot on the dragon's throat.

"NO!"

Theo did not know what had made him call out. He just felt that he did not want harm to befall the dragon. Now the nymphs stood staring at him. A few of them moved closer to him and held spears aloft threateningly in their hands.

"What claim do you have over this dragon, manling?" The lead nymph asked, still holding his spear at the ready.

Theo looked around uneasily at the faces of the nymphs that aimed their spears at him. They had similar features to his aunt Emeralda, and to Roxette, though their hair was a lighter shade of brown than the Mountain nymph's and their eyes were the colour of emeralds. Their skin was fair like that of the Sea nymphs and they were just as tall, standing easily at Theo's height.

Theo stood wearily before the nymph commander. "My lord," he said loudly so he could be heard over the dragon's laboured breathing. "I do not claim to have ownership of this dragon, and indeed I cannot think how anyone might make such a claim. However he and I are acquainted and so far he has not given me any reason to justify the ending of his life."

"Young man, you may not have travelled enough in the world, or you may have been closed away in a farm where you've been kept ignorant. Of your background I know nothing, save that Queen Viola has requested that we escort you safely to her throne room in Ghiadon. However, you will have to learn that the red dragons are not to be treated as pets. They are our enemy and have been responsible for the death of many of my kind. I will not allow this creature the opportunity to roam our land freely and to strike at its leisure when we are less well prepared for it."

Theo looked more closely at the nymph. He was tall, even by their standards, standing half a head taller than the rest of his companions. His hair was long, reaching down to the curve of his back. His face was handsome with eyebrows arched above piercing green eyes. He reminded Theo of a wolf, the way he stood there with his long sinewy form and with those eyes that studied their surroundings like a hunter. He recognized this Malgor as one of the three figures he had seen kneeling before Queen Viola in his dreams.

"You may not know me or my friends, but your queen has placed some importance to our visit. And there is one among us who has been to your city before and wishes to return there again. Surely you will give us the benefit of the doubt, the same benefit your queen has given us?"

Malgor studied him for a while longer, mulling over his words. Then his grip on the spear softened and he lowered it, beckoning for his companions to let Theo move closer.

"Since you feel some responsibility for this dragon, then I suggest you come forward."

Theo stepped through the group of nymphs who continued to hold their spears threateningly, but lowered as they followed his every move with care. He noticed that their cloaks blended completely with the surrounding woods, which explained why he had found it impossible to see them from a distance. Even now their heads seemed to float, bodiless, as the rest of their form blended into the background. He tried to avert his eyes from them, feeling a heightened sense of unease as he gazed upon them.

Now that he stood so close to the dragon he felt his breath catch in his throat. It was not the first time he had stood in the presence of such a one. But this creature that was the colour of blood awoke in him feelings of mixed awe and fear. Seeing it there, in the flesh, was very different from his dreams. Now it stared at him with reptilian eyes filled with loathing. He was surprised and taken aback by the look.

After all, was he not the one that had stayed the nymph's hand–at least for the moment?

"We meet face to face, as you requested, however not under the circumstances that I had imagined we would," Theo said. He marvelled at the strength that exuded from the beast. Everything about it was large and imposing, from its beak, that was as long as a horse, to its arching neck that was lined with long spikes, down to its pointed tail. He looked with displeasure at the silver ropes that bit into the dragon's scaled skin, making grooves where they pressed into it.

"If you are truly one of Zarzbudin's disciples then you would not allow these few here to deter you from your task of capturing me for your master," the dragon answered back, exhaling from its lungs that Theo imagined were as large as a good sized room–that explained why its words sounded as though they were being uttered by a dozen voices speaking in unison.

Malgor cast Theo a suspicious glance at the mention of the Witch Lord's name. "What do you know about this boy and Zarzbudin, lizard?" he growled, lowering his spear threateningly to the dragon's throat.

"You have all been deceived by the boy, forest gnome. He is one of Zarzbudin's pets, and there are surely many more in your forest making their way here as we speak. You should never have allowed him to enter your woods with his friends."

Malgor's eyes narrowed as he gazed at Theo.

Theo felt two sharp points biting into his back as the Forest nymphs poked him with their spears from behind.

"Malgor, what the dragon says makes sense," one of the nymphs said. "We all noticed the Mountain nymph in their numbers. Perhaps they have tricked us, and we've been following five when there are many more in our woods, hiding from us till the right opportunity presents itself for them to come at us."

"Nay, Zalof. Do not give credit to the lizard's smooth tongue until we have thought things through with a clear mind. I will know the truth before we leave here this day. What have you to say in your defence, manling?"

Theodor did not flinch from the Forest nymph's gaze but stood erect. "I and my companions are not aligned with Zarzbudin or any of the enemies of the Leonese people. We came to your kingdom to seek the guidance and aid of your queen. My master has been after this dragon ever since it escaped from its domain in the Dragon's Foot Mountains. Unfortunately Archon was ambushed at sea before he could complete the task."

"Archon!" Malgor exclaimed, arching his brows. He looked genuinely worried. "The Wizard of Aldorn is dead?" Theo nodded solemnly. "You bring bad tidings, manling. Our queen will be distraught at the news. Archon has long been an ally and friend to Leonium and to Ghiadon."

"We too have been saddened at losing our friend." Theo felt the spear points withdraw from his back.

"What is your name?" Malgor asked him suddenly.

"My name is Theodor Marentherin." Theo said, both for the benefit of the nymph but also for the dragon.

"Far Strider," the nymph translated. "Where are you from, Theodor Maren' Therin?"

"I am from Cyrus Island, my Lord Malgor, and have been as far as Alcavia. I do not do my name justice, I must admit, since, till seven months ago, I had not ventured further than my home island's shores."

"You are young still, Theodor, and there is more to a name than you may know. Now tell me, what are we to do with this dragon that your lord and master had been charged to capture?"

Theo stared at the dragon which returned his gaze. "Maybe we should ask the dragon," he said.

The dragon turned its head slightly–it was too tightly bound to do much else–and looked around at the nymphs that surrounded it. Theo fancied he saw a grin forming on its lips as the teeth lining its jaws were revealed. "Release me," it commanded as if it was fully in control of the situation. "Release me and I will spare your lives."

Malgor leaned closer to its head, which made him look small in comparison. The dragon's one eye was as large as Malgor's torso. "You'll have to be more persuasive than that lizard. If it wasn't for Theodor Maren'Therin, you would be dead now."

The dragon turned its reptilian gaze back to Theo. It licked its lips and considered what it was to do next. "What is it you want from me, wizardling?" it growled.

Theo stood for a while, looking at the dragon. The way it rested, they were at eye level. "Firstly I deserve to know who it is I have saved," Theo said, looking obliquely at the dragon so he did not have to stare directly into its eyes.

"I wouldn't be too hasty on the 'saved part'," Malgor stressed. "That still depends on the dragon."

The dragon remained silent, apart from its breathing, which was like a saw cutting through a thick bark of wood. Then at last it spoke. "Varw'Raker." The dragon made a growling noise in its throat so Theo almost did not distinguish it had given its name.

"Good, Varwraker," Theo tried to pronounce the name correctly. It seemed to be in an ancient dialect, much like his family name, and was pronounced in two words: "Varw" and "Raker". "Now, perhaps we can come to a mutual agreement," he said encouragingly.

The dragon grunted in reply, letting off a thin trail of smoke from its nostrils.

"I happen to know a bit about dragons, Theodor," Malgor said. "Being a Dragonstrider, I know a bit about their ways. A dragon, once it swears its allegiance to its strider, is oath-bound to obey his commands. If Varw'Raker, here, swears on its honour as a dragon to be your steed, then I will give the command to have him released. If not, then he dies." By the look of the tall nymph, there was no doubt he meant every word.

Varwraker made one final attempt to break his bonds, straining at the ropes, but he was firmly held. "I have not escaped from one wizard tyrant, to be made a slave to another," he bellowed. The sound reminded Theo of the screeching of a hawk, only it was tenfold louder.

"I am no tyrant, Varwraker," Theo said, controlling his fear, and keeping the tremor out of his voice. Then he summoned up the courage to speak in a more commanding tone. "You heard Malgor. Now make your choice."

The dragon tried once again to break away from its bonds. Theo heard the trees creak as the ropes were pulled taut. For a horrid moment, he wandered what would happen if the ropes snapped.

But the ropes held fast.

Finally, the dragon blew its breath out of its nostrils and sighed resignedly. "Alright, I will do as you request. Release my bonds and I will swear my allegiance."

"Swear it first dragon, and do it soon. I am losing my patience with you," Malgor answered curtly.

The dragon stared long and hard at Theo. It was probably thinking how unfair it was for a beast its size to be forced to be servile to someone so small. "Very well. I, Varw'Raker of the red, do pledge to obey Theodor Maren'Therin of Cyrus Island till he releases me from my bond and to do all in my power to ensure his safety."

Theo felt he had to offer something to the dragon in return. It was not called for, but he felt it was the proper thing to do. "And I, Theodor Marentherin, do pledge to take care of Varwraker's needs and to treat him as a friend and not as a beast of burden with no will of its own."

And with that the bond was sealed.

Malgor gave the signal to his men and they began to untie the silver strands that held the dragon fast.

Before the last of the ropes were released the dragon fanned out its large canvas-like wings till they covered the entire glade. Theo half-expected the red beast to start feasting on him and the nymphs. Instead it gave out a loud cry which was so high-pitched it hurt Theo's ears, so he had to clutch his hands to his head.

"Varw'Raker, a most unfortunate name for a dragon, Theodor Maren'Therin," Malgor said, in a low voice so only Theo could hear.

Theo looked questioningly at the nymph flight commander.

"In the old tongue 'Varw' means 'War' and 'Raker' means 'deliverer' or 'bringer of'. You have placed more of a burden on your shoulders than you realize, my young friend."

Just then Nem and the rest of Theo's group burst on the scene. They stood back gaping at the red dragon. Finally Roxette seemed to gather up her resolve.

"Theo, are you alright?" She stepped forward with the feline movements which were so characteristic of her. She had washed her hair and it glinted with the tips looking as if they were on fire, so deep red were they. She had drawn both her swords and looked around at the Forest nymphs with distrust, but the dragon occupied most of her attention.

"I'm quite alright, Roxette. I and Varwraker, here," he said, pointing to the dragon, "have just come to an agreement."

He explained to his friends what had transpired, and then introduced them to Malgor and his men. They decided to leave the dragon behind at the glade. It was not as if it could follow Theo to the Forest nymphs' city. The Silver Dragons there would never allow Varwraker to come to within twelve miles of their territory. In fact, him just being so close was putting everyone at great risk. It was Serilia who had hit on the idea that Kerta, north of Cyrus, would be a good spot for Varwraker to make his home. The only dragons close by were Vracho and Celeste of Alunda Island, and they would keep to their own territory. Since Kerta had no dragons of her own it was the ideal home for the red. Varwraker informed Theo that he would be setting off at daybreak for the island.

Meanwhile Malgor led the group back to the river bank. There, they sat by Roxette's fire whilst the Forest nymphs built fires of their own. A few joined the group bearing game they had hunted in the woods. Theo and his companions ate till their bellies were almost bursting. The Forest nymphs had brought wine with them. Apparently, the Emerald Forest was richly supplied with wine by the orchards of Ameron which were amongst the finest in all Leonium, though not quite as good as the nuns' at Sulicia Island.

The next day they arrived by canoe in Ghiadon. They disembarked at the quay and were led by Malgor before trees with their trunks knit close together to form a wall. Two of the largest trees stood apart so they formed the entrance to what could only be the forest palace. They entered to be greeted by a sight that was totally unexpected. Theo felt as though he had inadvertently stepped back into the forest. The interior, instead of using columns for support, had interspersed the trunks of trees. As their eyes adjusted to the feeble light from the torches, Theo could distinguish carpets lining the floor; they were adorned with earthly colours which was why he had not noticed them before.

Malgor led them through the tree columns until they came upon an area in the palace where the trunks were sparser. There was a large gathering of nymphs waiting for them and they opened up to allow Malgor and his group forward.

Then they saw her.

She was more beautiful in the flesh than Theo remembered in his dreams. He felt a pang of guilt at the feelings of desire that threatened to overwhelm him as he gazed at the queen's rich brown hair and those mesmerizing eyes that were green like her forest in early spring. He looked around at his companions who were also gaping at the queen. *Where is Zoi?*

He looked back at the queen to find standing beside her a warrior figure with broad shoulders and a short cropped beard. *He must be Anathel.* Theo recognized him from the description Malgor had given of the naval commander. Standing on the other side of the queen was a shorter and slimmer nymph with long silver hair matching his beard that fell almost to his knees. *And this must be Xion, the bard.*

At their approach the queen rose from her throne and bent her knee bowing her head in reverence along with the rest of the nymphs in the hall.

"Great Mother, we welcome you back to our realm with gladdened hearts."

Theo looked about him at his companions and was surprised to find a new addition to his team. There, between Roxette and Serilia, stood a tall woman wearing a thin pink dress with a wreath of an olive branch on her head. She turned to look at Theo with hazel eyes. For a moment he had the eerie feeling they had met before.

"I too am glad to be here, my child, and owe a great debt to Theodor Maren'Therin and his friends for escorting me from my hide-away in Jandaea Island," the mysterious woman answered.

Theo could hardly believe that this young woman who looked in her mid-thirties and was in the prime of her beauty was the same old woman with the gnarled hands and humped back that had accompanied them on their journey from Jandaea Island. The transformation in Queen Viola's hall had caught him completely by surprise. He could not help but blush as he tried to avert his eyes from Ellodiere's skimpy dress. *What is it with these nymphs and their desire to provoke?* He realized all at once that, apart from Roxette and his aunt Emeralda, the rest of the female nymphs he had met, enjoyed exposing their bodily charms for all to admire. At least that had been the case with Queen Crystal of Alcavia, Queen Viola of the Forest nymphs, and now Ellodiere–not to mention the nymphs in their sea realm of Alunda.

In the evening Theo and his friends got reacquainted with Zoi–or more correctly, Ellodiere, as she was known by the Forest nymphs. When they had eaten and drunk their fill they retired to the queen's guest chambers so they could discuss freely matters troubling them.

Queen Viola got straight to the point. "Tomorrow, Theodor, you and those of your companions that will be going with you must leave for the north and onwards to the highlander's realm in the Brakkand's Throne Mountains. You cannot delay in the task you have set for yourself; if you are to free my niece you must do so as soon as possible. Already you are needed for other errands and will be occupying our time on a mission with little hope of success."

"Then it is time we decide who will be venturing forth with Theodor," Ellodiere agreed, with a silky smooth voice that was nothing like the voice of the hag she had been using for the past seven months.

"I'll be leading Theo into the mountains, Queen Viola," Roxette said with determination. "Archon charged me before he died with the safe-keeping of the youth."

Queen Viola nodded her pretty head then turned a worried look at Ellodiere. "Great Mother, his strength in the gift worries me."

"We've been through this before, my child. Let's not dwell on those things we cannot change. Theodor is young. He will grow stronger in time and with training."

"I will escort my brother also," Serilia added.

Ellodiere shook her head. "I have studied you all carefully for the past few months, my child. Your destiny lies elsewhere. You must gather up your courage Serilia and accept the role you will play in forthcoming events. Your strength in the gift is admirable for one your age and must be nurtured like a rare rose till it blossoms. No, my sweet. Your path lies south then east to the Wizard's Keep in Hendon, where you will be trained by capable tutors till you have fully developed your gift as a sorceress."

Serilia was about to protest but Ellodiere cut her off, raising a hand. "That leaves young Nemarchus." Ellodiere cast a hazel-eyed gaze at the youth who stared back with a confused expression. Theo could imagine what was going on in his mind. Nem was being torn by his loyalty to his friend and his brotherly love and protectiveness towards Serilia.

Theo answered in his friend's stead. "Nem will accompany my sister to the city of Hendon and, once he takes her safely there, will be free to do as he wishes. I can trust no other man with my sister's life." He realized suddenly, how much danger his friend had shared with him ever since the day they had fled from the cottage. It was unfair of him to ask more of his friend. Nem looked at him with saddened, tear-filled eyes but nodded in agreement.

"That settles it then." Ellodiere looked in turn at each of the companions, finally resting her eyes on Roxette. "Do not forget what we discussed back in Jandaea, daughter of the Mountains." Roxette lowered her eyes, surprising Theo: he had never seen her give way to anyone in the time he had known her.

"And what will you do now, Zo–Ellodiere?" Theo asked. He was curious to learn more about this woman who had entered their lives under guise and who the Forest nymphs treated like a goddess. Apparently she was one of the Ancients: a semi-divine race that walked the earth and had in the past played a major role in shaping Thalagia's future but who had then retreated to the sidelines allowing mankind to lead their own lives.

Ellodiere gave him a sombre look. "I will be leaving tonight. I have witnessed much in the short time I have spent with you and must hasten to meet with my brothers and sisters to decide on our next course of action. There is a quickening of events. The time draws near when the Dark Champion will ride forth once more to reclaim what was once his. You have had but a taste of what lies in store for the free peoples of Thalagia. Already the Dark Lord's manipulations have yielded results in the free cities of Leonium. Ameron and Ramila are at odds whilst Alcavia prepares to face alone an enemy that far outweighs her in size. The Dark Lord's desire has always been to conquer and enslave the free nations of the world.

"Theodor, do what you must for the one you love and return to us quickly. Archon's great loss must be replaced. We have but a few gifted to rely on. Do not waste the time allotted to you."

♦ CHAPTER 28 ♦

Highlander hospitality

That night Theo slept cradled in the confines of the forest palace. But he did not feel safe in his sleep. His dreams wrenched him away from the trees and threw him in a dark pit where his nightmares ravaged his spirit. He dreamt of *Sed Muthin*, the knight with the red eyes. *Sed Muthin* called to him as he fled followed by his taunting laughter.

"You cannot run from me, Athuddir. You cannot run from the dark. You must bow down to the Dark Lord. You have no other destiny. All must bow down to the Dark Lord, Athuddir, or be consumed by his wrath. Riches and beauty will be offered to you aplenty. We have many fine creatures to satisfy your loins' needs, or your heart's desire. Your every whim will be satisfied. You will wallow in riches. My lord will shower you with gold and precious stones so you will drown in a pool of wealth.

"All you need do is surrender to my lord, Athuddir. Who else can offer you so much, and so freely?"

"Never." Theo was shaking his head to clear it of the dark knight's voice. "NEVER!"

He awoke to find himself drenched in sweat. He changed into a clean shirt and stood staring down from his bedroom window. He was inside the palace in a wooden tree house suspended several feet above the ground. He considered whether he should go back to bed, then decided against it. Instead he put on his pants and ventured out of his room. Finding the trap door in the floor, he scrambled slowly down the ladder placed beneath and alighted on the ground.

Looking round he found a few of the Forest nymphs keeping watch. They greeted him with a nod as he made his way slowly forward. He followed the path they had taken to enter the palace. Soon he ventured outside and passed through the wooden huts that earlier during their visit had been alive with the voices of people. All was silent under the pale light of the moons. Their lights mingled so the forest trees glittered an uncanny bluish silver. Somewhere off in the distance he heard a wolf howling. A vision of Whitefang sprang to mind, the wolf standing on a rise throwing his silver head up to the moon to send out his hunting call.

He moved forward till he crossed the drawbridge and found he was following the path to the dockside. Before him, for as far as his eyes could see, lay sprawled, like a giant mirror, the Silver Lake. He moved closer to the edge of the lake and placed a hand gingerly on the water's surface. He half expected, as he withdrew his hand, to find the silver of the lake sticking to his fingers. He shook his head at what he had done on impulse. Throughout the trip upriver he had been afraid of what might lurk beneath the water's depths, and now he had sunk his hand in it up to his elbow.

He looked up suddenly as ripples began to appear on the water's surface. His eyes bulged with fear as the ripples became larger. He got up slowly and began to inch away from the bank's edge. *What have I gotten myself into, again?* Had he summoned a beast from the depths without realizing it? He placed one foot behind the other but kept his gaze fixed before him.

The head burst forth like a catapult from the lake. He fell back as the beast towered above him. It gave out a shrill call as of the baying of a hundred trumpets and flapped its great wings a couple of times before settling on the bank to stare at Theo with huge reptilian eyes.

"You have summoned me, mistress?"

Theo looked at the beast in wonder. He mistook, for an instant, the Silver Dragon for Adelayne's dragonsteed, Assima. Then he became aware of some differences between the two. This dragon was larger and older.

"Yes, Solla." Theo was startled by the voice, and turned around to find Queen Viola standing by the quayside with Roxette and Malgor. "I have summoned Teina as well, my sweet. Where is she?"

The water surface bubbled once more and a second dragon, almost as large as the first emerged. She shook her scaled body like a large hound, great drops falling to the ground. Theo was soaked by the drops as if he had been standing in the rain.

"What's going on?" Theo asked perplexed.

"I think you know, Theodor," Queen Viola answered simply. She looked down upon him as he lay sprawled on his back. He stood up swiftly and looked at Roxette, Malgor, and then back at the queen. "But Queen Viola, I have not had the chance to say goodbye to my friends, and my things are back in my room...Your Majesty," he stammered as an afterthought.

"It's better this way, Theodor. They might be tempted to change their minds in the morning. In any case, I meant what I said about you running out of time."

"And your things are with me," Roxette added, holding out a small bundle, and his sword. That was all that belonged to him now. This bundle and the sword his great grandfather had given him. He fingered the dolphin amulet that hung from his neck. That was still there also.

"So this is it then?" he asked with finality.

"Yes, my friend," the queen answered.

They soared together above the lake once, before the dragon pair tilted their wings and flew for the source of the Silver River. Somewhere to the south, Theo heard the call of another dragon, and the image of the red filled his vision. Varwraker was bidding him a safe journey. *You too, my friend*, he answered knowing in his heart that his message had been relayed somehow to the red beast. He clutched tighter about him the cloak Queen Viola had provided, and found it was surprisingly warm for a material so light.

It was daybreak by the time the two silver dragons had reached the high tips of the Brakkand's Throne Mountains just north of the source of the Silver River. They sped along casting dark shadows on the snow-covered peaks so it seemed as though two black lizards were worming their way through the whiteness. On their backs they carried two riders each, bent over and clutching cloaks which shimmered in the light, changing colour so the forms blended with the silver scales of the beasts till they became one. The north wind blew with increased fury as Autumn wrapped his rusty cloak about him and prepared to leave Thalagia to make way for his sister Winter, who hungered to reclaim the ground she had lost to her siblings Summer and Spring. However, at this altitude, the temperatures were never warm, even in the heart of summer, and the bluish black rock of the mountains was always cloaked by a white blanket of snow.

The silver dragons, at a faint signal from their riders, began to bank sharply, losing altitude swiftly. Just before they were about to collide with the mountains, they beat their titanic wings, sending a shower of snowflakes whirling about. Defying their large size, they alighted elegantly on the mountainside. The riders behind the Forest nymphs jumped off the dragons' backs and sank knee deep in the snow.

"Head down the other side, away from the river." Malgor was shouting so he could be heard from atop Teina's back. "You won't reach far. The highlanders will find you and take you to their lair." Roxette nodded her acquiescence.

Take care of yourself, Farstrider. Theo heard the queen's voice clearly in his mind. *And remember, the sands of time are running out for us.* He looked over at the queen, but her face was hidden in her fur-lined cloak. He cast his gaze over at Roxette and found that she too was listening attentively to voices only she could hear.

With a resounding painful shriek that brought Theo to his knees, and which must have been heard all the way to Ghiadon, the two dragons took to the sky and were soon lost to sight as they headed back to their watery home.

Roxette wasted no time and began to shuffle through the snow. She turned once to make sure Theo followed then set a pace that soon had him panting for breath. Theo looked about but could see nothing but blinding whiteness that gave him dizzy spells. The blizzard did not help matters either. It clutched at his cloak like a spoiled child that wanted it for itself and would not take no for an answer. As they waded through the snow going downhill, Theo rubbed at his arms to bring warmth to them. He was sweating profusely but the edges of his arms and feet were frozen so he could not feel his fingertips or toes. His nose was running and tears filled his eyes as though he were suffering from a cold.

He soon would be if Roxette kept this up much longer. "Why do we have to keep up this impossible pace?"

Roxette halted to place the water skin to her lips and drank a swig before handing him the skin. "Not too much!" she warned. "You'll give yourself the cramps." Then, in answer to his question she added, "We need to get out of this blizzard or we'll not make it to the dwarves' lair."

"Dwarves?" Theo asked, astonished.

"The Highlanders." Roxette's dark eyes were staring at him like the eyes of a mountain cat. They were more prominent in the snow and Theo noticed they did not water weakly like his own green ones. "Here, wear this for your eyes. I don't want to have to spend the next two days waiting for them to recover from light blindness." She handed him a thin kerchief from her pockets. He bound it around his eyes and tied the ends behind his head. It was a black cloth that allowed him to see vaguely but kept most of the glare of the snow from his eyes.

They set off without another moment's delay.

He was breathing hard by the time they reached a small creek that was cutting into the snow as it trickled down the mountainside in search of a stream. Roxette bent to fill their water skin and then they were off once more.

After what seemed like hours of wading in the barren white snow, Roxette halted. She sat behind a boulder that afforded them some protection from the biting wind. "Here, have some of this." She offered him some food from her pack and a small skin to drink from. She had to shout to be heard above the screeching of the wind. Theo could hardly feel the tips of his nose and ears. He bit into the food. It was smoked salty meat, probably pork. He ate greedily. He had not realized just how hungry he was. He lifted the skin and let the contents pour down his throat.

"Gently!" Roxette had been a trifle too late in her warning. He coughed and spluttered as he tried to recover from the burning, choking sensation of the liquid. The second time he sipped it. It had a biting taste but he found it warmed his chest and stomach and loosened his tired limbs. It also seemed to dull the headache he had developed.

"Mountain holly," Roxette explained. They had not been sitting for long, when Roxette hurled herself to her feet. She pulled at Theo's arms and yanked him along.

"Come on. We need to find the dwarves before nightfall or we'll not last the night out here."

Theo forced himself to shuffle behind the Mountain nymph that kept ahead of him, always at a merciless pace. The drink had helped bring back the feeling to his extremities; this was a mixed blessing, since now he felt the pain of almost having experienced the effects of frost bite.

Is that a shape separating from the white snow? He looked again, but saw nothing. He decided it was the blizzard casting shadows, or maybe his mind playing tricks on him. He moved his limbs faster. Roxette was getting too far ahead and he had no breath left in him to call out for her to slow down. As he laboured to push forward through the thick snow, he slipped and fell head first into the wet mush. He freed his nose so he could regain his breath and rolled on his back.

What if I just remain lying here? Wouldn't it be nice to just lie and rest for a while? Why should he push himself so hard? Suddenly he did not feel all that cold any more. True he felt numb, but the numbness chased away the pain. *Was the wind dying down?* He could no longer hear it screaming with the same intensity. It was getting darker too. His eyes drooped then shut. *Warmth at last.* He had found a spot away from the blizzard. Winter was wrapping him in her warm blanket of ice. He was immune to its chilling bite. Instead he felt comforted in her embrace. Soon he would be able to leave his fleshy shell behind and all the pain it brought him and travel with Winter to find some more companions to join them. Winter was hungry for new friends. She thirsted for blood like bees thirst for the nectar of blooming flowers.

Who was this who dared to invade his fun and frolicking with Winter? Oh why couldn't they just leave him alone to enjoy her?

"Theo...come on...hear me?...die...come on...out of the storm...wake up!" He felt his body being shaken like a rag doll. His throat was burning as he spat and coughed the hot liquid that had been poured down it. He ventured to open his eyes. His lids were heavy as if pebbles hung from them.

The shaking continued. He managed to open his eyes into slits.

At first his vision was blurred. Then it began to clear and he saw an oval face staring at him with concern. She had dark eyes below arched eyebrows and a small pinched nose above a red mouth which was like a spill of blood on her white face—her perfect beautiful face. Somewhere in the back of his mind he felt sure he knew this lovely creature with hair tinged red at the tips. He was about to call out her name when he saw a bearded face come creeping up behind her. It was a weather-roughened face with fierce ginger hair that sprouted from its nose, eyebrows, and cheeks leaving only the wrinkled skin around its eyes free of hair.

He saw the bearded man rise above the woman. He was twice as wide as any man and lifted burly arms. He held a kind of club in his calloused hands and was about to bring it down on the oval-faced creature that crouched oblivious to his presence. Her attention was firmly fixed on Theo. *Theo, yes that's my name.* He opened his mouth to warn the woman but no sound escaped his dry throat. The club began its descent. As it followed the curve downwards, Theo's eyes must have bulged, for the nymph's face changed expression. She looked at him baffled.

It struck her.

She tilted forward and stretched senseless on the ground. Theo was about to utter a protest when darkness enveloped him once more.

He felt the pain in his head first. Then, as he began to move his limbs, he felt the pain in his fingers and toes as well. The headache was the worst. It beat at his scalp till he feared it might split his skull in two. He opened his eyes allowing them to adjust to the spluttering light that spread from the only torch in the room. As he gazed around, he realized it was not a room at all, but a prison. The floor, like the walls, was cold black stone. Stout iron bars kept them locked inside their rock prison. He was not alone. He forced himself to his knees. He regretted it instantly. His head swam and he rocked on his knees as the dizzy spells threatened to overwhelm him. Somehow he managed to get to his feet. He shuffled over to the still form that lay on the other side of the room. She looked as if she had lain there in the same position for a long while.

He crouched down going to his knees once more. He pulled at the body on the floor and rolled it over. A small groan escaped its throat and it placed a slim hand to its head. Somehow Roxette looked naked to him without her swords. Not one of her daggers had been left on her person. Whoever had brought them here was taking no chances and had frisked them thoroughly. His nymph sword was missing as well. He looked at his companion and found that dried blood was stuck to her hair where the club had struck. *I suppose we should be thankful we're still alive,* he thought wryly.

Roxette opened bloodshot eyes and stared at him with dilated pupils. Then they seemed to focus. "Where are we?" She jerked up onto her elbows and plastered her hand to her head, wincing with the pain the movement had brought on.

"I don't know." Theo got up slowly, dragging his feet as he approached the bars to peer out of their cell. He placed his hands to the bars and pressed his head against them till they bit into his skin as he strained to look down the dimly lit corridor. There seemed to be other prison rooms to the left and off where the corridor ended was a wooden door held by firm iron hinges. It had a small hatch in the centre that was now closed.

"Let us out of here! Can anybody hear me? Let us out!" He was not sure if anybody would respond to his calls. He hoped there would be a guard at the door to hear his shouting.

He looked back at Roxette and found she was able to stand, though she still kept a hand on the spot that had been split at the side of her head. *What a fine mess we have managed to get ourselves into, once more.* They had travelled through the blizzard, not knowing where they were going or whom they should meet, and now here they were, locked away in a cell whilst Adelayne waited to be rescued. If any rescuing was to be done, it seemed it would not be at his hands.

He looked down at his fingers and discovered, to his astonishment, that they were covered by a yellowy salve. It was probably all that had saved them from being claimed by frost bite. He wrinkled his nose at the salve's smell. It reminded him of decaying pig fat. His shoes also had been removed and his socks were oiled at the tips. They had obviously placed more of the salve on his feet. They had not treated Roxette with the same kindness. Though she did not look like she had suffered from the frost, her head wound had been left to bleed into her hair. He turned around sharply as he heard the door lock scrape and grind with the turning of a key. The door swung open with a squeaking noise. He peered down the corridor as the group made its way towards them. They held torches to light their way. Theo noticed how the light fell upon their hairy faces giving them the appearance of cave men.

He recognized the red-bearded fellow as the one who had clubbed Roxette on the head and had probably slapped him senseless with one of his meaty hands.

"I see our unwelcome visitors are back on their feet." The rough voice that could have been mistaken as belonging to a pirate captain came from the fellow beside Red Beard. His black beard was neatly tied with gold clips so it split in two down his mid section to end at his wide leather belt that was clasped around his ample belly by a golden buckle. All five of the bearded men were no taller than a child of thirteen. "Who are you and what are you doing so far from your homes?"

Theo cleared his throat and grabbed at the iron bars. "I am Theodor Marentherin and this is my friend and guide, Roxette."

The dwarf that had spoken to them stood looking at Theo with dark beady eyes which reminded him of a mountain bear. "By your speech I understand that you are Galipan. Your features are Aldornish, though you could be from further south, Hendon perhaps."

"My lord, I am from Cyrus Island. My friend here–"

"Needs no introductions." Black beard interrupted. "We have been at war with her kind long enough to know where she is from." He glared at Roxette with an inborn hatred that had been instilled into his people over the passing of many centuries till it became part of their heritage. "You keep very bad company, Theodor Maren'Therin. I believe I have heard that name before, though I cannot place it right now."

"It belongs to my grandfather's house, my lord. He is Nestor, son of Prium, brother to King Rufous of Alunda." Theo did not usually divulge so much information about himself but he felt the dwarf would be able to wring it out of him in other ways, and he did not want to start off on the wrong foot. He had to reclaim lost ground with the dwarves. He realized now that because of Roxette, they had mistaken them for enemy forces who had wandered into their domain to spy upon them.

The dwarf's eyes widened at the mention of Nestor and Prium, and of the king of the Sea nymphs. "We know of King Rufous and, now you mention it, this Nestor has been through our land before."

"You have a good memory, my lord...?" Theo left the question hanging, hoping the dwarf would be courteous enough to divulge his name.

"I am Feduwin the Black." Roxette drew in a sharp breath at the mention of the name. "Yes, mountain rat! I see you are aware of me. I have had the pleasure of spilling much of your people's blood," he growled menacingly so the noise reverberated from the prison walls. "If I remember correctly, Theodor Farstrider, your grandfather had been a friend of the free kingdoms of Thalagia last time he passed through on his way south from the northlands. He had a fierce-looking red-bearded fellow with him and a maiden with blond hair."

"Yes, my lord," Theo's voice croaked, as he almost choked on the memory of his uncle Tiber and his aunt Fiona. "But that must have been close to two decades ago, my lord Feduwin!"

"That is correct, young Farstrider. You see us dwarves have long memories like our long lives. Nymphs are not the only ones who live for centuries. Now tell me, what makes a young Sea nymph prince keep company with a mountain rat from the Dragon's Feet?"

"My lord, *Roxette*," he emphasized her name, "has been one of my closest friends and my mentor ever since she came with the mage Archon to my grandfather's cottage near the Triad Woods of Cyrus. Archon was her friend and she led him faithfully before he charged her with providing the same service for me."

"You expect us to accept all this at face value? I admit you bear some resemblance to your grandfather: the proud set of your shoulders and back, though the colour of your eyes and your hair is inherent from the other side of your family, it seems. How do I know you are not here to spy on us?"

Theo reached for the amulet that hung from his neck. "This was given to me by my great grandfather Prium. He said it would protect me if I was ever caught in rough waters out at sea." He held the silver dolphin out for the dwarf to look at.

"White gold!" Feduwin looked at the dolphin in awe. "That is truly a precious and rare gift. But how do I know that you have not stolen it, or that you have not followed down a darker path?"

"Would ones such as ourselves be holding *this* without treading on the lighter path, as you put it?" Roxette walked forward fishing out what looked like a green leaf from her coat pocket. The dwarves stepped back from her as if she might still spring upon them from behind the iron bars. Then Red Beard reached out with his hand and snatched the green leaf from Roxette's outstretched palm.

"It looks real enough, King Feduwin." Red Beard held the leaf made from emerald stone up to the torch so it sent forth its green light to fall upon the dungeon walls.

"Truly it is an emerald leaf from Ghiadon, Baulkin." King Feduwin of the Brakkand's Throne Mountain dwarves turned his dark gaze upon the Mountain nymph. "How did you come by this, she-nymph?"

"Queen Viola gave it to me. She said it would convince you of our tale as nothing else would."

Before Roxette had a chance to finish what she was saying, the leaf began to glow with an inner light. Baulkin placed it hurriedly on the ground and backed away from it, spreading out his arms to guard his king. The emerald leaf turned a bright yellow. Then a white light as bright as a small sun shot forth from the leaf. Theo, Roxette and the dwarves shielded their eyes from the bright light. It lessened in intensity till an ethereal shape remained standing before them, glistening with sparks that shimmered on the shape as if it had been rolling in golden star dust.

"Feduwin Coalbeard of the house of the Axewielders, harken to my call. Theodor of the house of the Farstriders seeks your aid. Do not deny him. My niece lies in the hands of the Warlock. Help him and those that would accompany him on his mission to set her free of her bondage."

When the message was delivered, the figure vanished. All that remained of the emerald leaf was green dust. The dwarves shook their heads as if to clear them from troubled thoughts. Then Feduwin motioned to his men. One of the dwarves who held a collection of keys on his belt, pulled one out and turned it in the lock to Theo's and Roxette's prison. The gate swung open and they motioned for Theo and the nymph to follow them.

"We'll need to make this up to you." Feduwin pointed at Theo's and Roxette's sorry state. "How were we to know you were sent by the queen of the Emerald Forest? Come now. We will dine and feast. Let it not be said that the highlanders do not know how to treat their friends to a warm welcome."

They were led out of the dungeon and slowly upwards till they arrived in a vaulted hall that seemed to stretch for as far as the eye could see. Theo stared at the many carpets that lined the walls and floors of the great hall. People were coming and going in their tasks giving the group hardly a glance, though they bowed respectfully to their king. A few looked on with distrust at Roxette, but seeing Feduwin with her and apparently at ease, they carried on with their work without comment. They passed several workbenches where dwarves were grouped together. Some were working on preparing skins to be sown into garments. Others were carving wood into toy shapes, whilst another group was chipping away at precious stones to shape them into jewels that could be mounted on rings or necklaces.

True to his word, Feduwin led them to a long table where, at his order, it was filled with all manner of fruits, nuts and meat: there was wild boar, hares and pheasants. Ale also flowed aplenty that Baulkin informed them originated from Seldavia's rich fields.

The two companions ate with their hosts till their bellies were full. Then they were led away through tunnels carved from the mountain rock that branched away from the great hall. Finally they arrived at their rooms, one each, that were nothing more than small caves carved from the tunnels, like grapes from a stalk. That night Theo was too exhausted from his travels to dream.

Their pace could easily have matched a swift racehorse. The wagon took the curves without reducing speed, forcing its passengers to clutch tightly at its sides. Theo glimpsed the tunnels they passed catching sight of sparkling gems lining the walls. Torches situated every hundred paces to keep the wagon routes lit formed a blurring line above the wagon as its passengers hurtled onwards.

They were deep in the dwarves' mining routes. They had set off at daybreak–so Baulkin Redbeard had told them, for Theo had not seen the light of day since they had arrived at the dwarves' hall two evenings ago. They had taken two days to recover from their trip and their wounds, and to gain their strength before deciding to move on. Theo would have preferred to have remained a few days longer, for the dwarves' hospitality was great, but he knew every day he delayed was a day longer Adelayne would be forced to spend in the Witch Lord's prison. Roxette too, was eager to leave the Brakkand's Throne Mountains. Even though she had aligned herself with forces supporting the dwarves' cause, they still felt distrustful towards her; she felt uncomfortable in the company of people she had spent most of her life warring against.

The wagons were specially designed by the dwarves to traverse the mountains at impossible speeds, so they could get their gold and precious gems from the depths of their mines to their storage chambers near their great hall. They were descending now, the wagon covering close to fifty miles for every hour it travelled.

Theo had a thought. "Baulkin, once we reach our destination, how will you get the wagon back uphill?"

Baulkin grinned at him and pointed at his companion dwarf with the brown beard. "That's why I brought him along. You see that lever there, the one in front of the steering rod?"

Theo nodded. It was a horizontal wooden bar that pierced the bottom of the wagon and was positioned at the rear end, close to the "rudder".

"On our return journey, Glum and I will work that lever to push the wagon back up. It's much slower going than downhill, but it's the only way."

When Baulkin finally hit the brakes, Theo felt his stomach rumbling, so he estimated it was close to midday. They halted at a spot were the tracks of the wagons seemed less used. The tunnel was not lit further on. Baulkin explained that they were a day's walk away from the Brakkand's Throne and Dragon's Foot Mountain border.

"We dare not go further than Wagon's End," Baulkin explained. "From this point onwards you enter the 'No Man's Land'. Anyone who ventures further down this tunnel," he said, pointing at the dark hole, "does so at their own peril. We seldom come this far west, for it is a common event for the hordes of the Dragon's Foot Mountains to lay ambush to anyone who ventures too close to the border. Though, I must admit that we've been tempted in the past to mine this area. It is rich in precious gem deposits. I myself have dug up my best stones from the mines in this area." Baulkin spoke regretfully, peering about the tunnel walls as though he could see the gem stones buried beneath the rock. "But after we lost a good number of our men a couple of years back to the Mountain nymph raiders, King Feduwin ordered us to abandon these mines."

They ate a quick lunch of salted meat and drank some of the dwarves' wine. Then Theo and Roxette shouldered their packs and bade the dwarves a safe journey back to their hall.

"You could not have chosen a better companion to lead you through the nymphs' realm," Baulkin said, placing his bear-like arms on Theo's shoulders. "I suppose now is the time for you to prove your worth to your friend,' he added, turning to look at Roxette. She remained silent, her face expressionless.

"May our father Barrack of the mountains guide you and protect you," the dwarves called out as they clambered onto their wagon. Soon Baulkin and Glum were lost to sight as they worked on their lever, pushing the wagon uphill at a steady pace. When the wagon and its squeaking wheels had departed, Theo turned to gaze at Roxette. She met his gaze. Theo could tell that she was restless at having returned home. Shortly they would arrive at the places were she had grown up, and where she had spent the larger part of her life–a life she had abandoned for Archon's sake as repayment for having saved her from certain death. Theo wondered how she would feel should she come across her friends and family. *What if we come across her comrades, the ones that betrayed her and left her for dead?* he thought.

"Are you ready?" Roxette asked, though the question could have been for her benefit as much as his. He nodded. They set off for the dark tunnel.

They did not take a torch with them. Instead, Roxette fished out a small blue stone from her pocket and held it aloft. "Blueshine," she explained to Theo's questioning look. "We use it to light our way but at the same time not draw attention to ourselves."

The light emanating from the sapphire stone was just bright enough to illuminate the space directly ahead of them with its ghostly blue. Soon Theo found his eyes had adjusted to the feeble light and they were able to move along at a slightly quicker pace.

They were still following the dwarves' tunnel downwards, though there were several openings at the sides of the tunnel that led in other directions and sometimes opened up to chambers where the dwarves had mined the rocks in the past. After they had been walking for a long spell, Theo realized the wagon tracks had seized. The tunnel too was a lot more winding, like a desert snake moving on sand. The walls were beginning to encroach upon them as they moved further down the tunnel.

At some point Roxette halted.

The tunnel had become a slit barely wide enough to allow a man to pass.

"So, what do we do now?" Theo asked. "Do we turn back and seek another way west?" He was whispering, fearing he might alert some creature lurking in the dark of their presence.

"This is the right way forward." Roxette shook her head. "If memory serves me correctly, the tunnel widens further on."

"Yes, but will we be able to fit through?" Theo was already suffering the effects of claustrophobia. His breathing was ragged and he felt panicky, like a small animal caught in a trap it wanted to sprint away from. "Is there no other way around?"

"This is the least-used route by my people. We need to use caution. We are entering Mountain nymph territory now. In any case the other routes will take us a good two days longer to traverse."

"We don't have that time to waste," Theo agreed. "Alright, Roxette. Lead on."

"Remove your sword and your pack and give them to me," Roxette motioned. Theo did as he was told. She added his things to her own then advanced towards the slit. He heard her throw their belongings through.

"Great! If we're unable to squeeze through, then we'll be left defenceless as well as without food," he said, in a sudden fit of sarcasm. He was definitely feeling uneasy about being trapped between so much rock. He felt as though the entire mountain was pushing at him and might come crashing down on them without a moment's notice.

"Two more reasons why we'll make sure we get across," Roxette answered with conviction.

Roxette was the first to go. She inched forward, her back to the wall. Inch by inch she came closer to the slit. She reached its centre and Theo feared she would remain stuck there.

Then she was through.

"Come on Theo. If I can do it, so can you. It's not as bad as it seems."

Theo summoned up his courage and drew in a couple of breaths before he moved towards the opening from which shone Roxette's Blueshine stone. As he got closer, he felt his breathing become more laboured, as if an invisible hand was clutching at his throat. He felt his chest rub against the stone and found he could not draw in his breath fully for his chest was being compressed against the rock. Instead he had to draw smaller and more rapid breaths. He shifted his feet to crawl sideways till he felt himself get lodged between the stone walls.

He tried to pull himself forward but his belt buckle caught on the rock. No matter how he pulled he could not break free. He was panicking. He could not move forward nor go back the way he had come. A small cry escaped his throat and he banged his nose against the rock as he tried to straighten his head.

"Shhhhh!" Roxette admonished him. "Are you trying to bring the entire Mountain patrol down here? Theodor, give me your hand."

Theo kept his face sidelong. His nose was gushing blood from where he had scraped it on the rock. He extended his arm and Roxette took him by the hand. She yanked at him and he felt his pants tear against the rock. He was held fast and the rock was biting into his inner thigh. Then Roxette gave a mighty heave and he felt himself being wrenched loose. He fell to the ground clutching at the tear in his thigh. He pulled his hand away to find it was moist with his warm blood. Otherwise he had come out of his ordeal relatively unscathed. The way Roxette had grabbed at his arm, he was afraid he had dislocated his shoulder.

He took a moment to gulp musty air into his lungs then straightened to take a look around. He retrieved his sword and his pack and stood looking at the tunnel that now opened up into a cave that appeared to have been shaped without the aid of men–or dwarves. They moved along guided by their stone. Roxette stepped carefully around gaping holes in the tunnel floor and at some places they were forced to jump over crevices that dropped off into the chasms of the mountain. Gusts of cool wind were blowing upwards from these fissures in the tunnel floor so every time Theo jumped over the wide gaping holes he feared he would be blown off balance and fall into the darkness.

They began to lose all sense of time. Even Roxette, who was accustomed to living below ground, could not tell Theo with certainty what time of day it was. After hours of walking, they halted to take a drink from their water skins and to bite into the salty dwarf meat. Theo soon realized he had lost count of how many times Roxette had called for a halt. They had also taken short naps at intervals to refresh themselves. It was at those times that Theo felt most vulnerable. In his sleep he would be visited by his worst nightmares. Large beasts with gaping maws lined with rows of teeth and horned heads would appear to haunt him. He would wake up drenched in a sweat, only to fall back to sleep doubly tired. In the end, sleeping was tiring him more mentally than walking did physically.

It came to a point when Theo felt as though he had been in the underground tunnels for an eternity. He had almost forgotten what the sun's light looked like, or how the soft breeze blowing from the sea felt on his face.

He grabbed at Roxette's arm. "What's that?" he whispered.

She had heard it as well. It sounded like the moaning of a cave lion, only the sound emitted was from a larger throat. Roxette remained still, listening to the shuffling noises coming from somewhere further down the path they had ventured on. Whatever manner of creature was lurking in the dark ahead, it was not far from them. Roxette had closed her hand around the Blueshine stone as soon as she heard the moaning noises. They remained there, dead still, listening to the sound of their breathing, and to the beating of their heart in their ears.

The creature up ahead was sniffing at the air with huge intakes of breath. *Has it picked up our scent?* Theo wondered. He heard the faint ringing sounds of Roxette's twin sword blades being drawn from their scabbards. "Wait here," she whispered in his ear, and then she was gone before he could respond. He strained his ears to hear even the faintest sound of Roxette's feet, but could not distinguish any sound other than the sniffing and shuffling of the beast up ahead. He imagined a bear, as large as an elephant, would have sounded similar to this cave creature.

He jumped, as a hand clamped firmly around his mouth. "It's me," Roxette hissed in his ear. "It's about twelve paces in front of us. I think it may have picked up our scent, so we better get moving before it locates our precise position. That's what it's trying to do now with all that sniffing."

"What manner of beast is it?" Theo asked in a low voice as soon as she took her hand away from his mouth.

"It's an Orgul, and judging by its size it is most likely a female. They are larger and fiercer than the males."

"Great." Theo's sarcasm had returned renewed. Roxette tugged at his sleeve and he followed at her heels clutching like a blind man at her hand. They were giving the Orgul a wide berth, as they moved around it and further down the cave they had entered. They were edging their way forward when Theo caught his breath as the Orgul gave a discontented grunt and then sniffed at the air.

Theo was totally unprepared for what happened next.

Roxette grabbed him by the nape of the neck and was heaving him bodily forward as fast as his legs could carry him. He heard the sound of stones skittering across the cave floor as something large was lumbering along behind them. He fancied he felt a hot breath on the nape of his neck, and that gave him the extra spurt of energy he needed. His shoulder was jarred as it impacted on the side of the rock face and he realized Roxette had led them into one of the tunnels once more.

Behind he heard skidding noises and stones being scattered in all directions, followed by howling and pounding noises as the Orgul beat on the tunnel entrance with its huge arms. Roxette unclenched her fist and they sped onwards, the Blueshine stone lighting their way. When they were well away from the Orgul's frustrated calls, and just when Theo felt his lungs could not take any more punishment, Roxette halted. Theo bent over placing his hands on his knees, his mouth watery as he gulped in great volumes of air. He wiped away at the sweat on his brow with his shirt sleeve and looked up at Roxette's face that was blue-tinged in the light of the stone.

"Let's try and avoid anymore surprises like that one." He pointed in the direction they had come.

Roxette smiled wryly and nodded. "Come," she said, and they moved on. It was not long before the tunnel opened up into a second cave, only this one had a lower ceiling but was much wider than the previous one. Theo cocked one ear to listen more intently and fancied he heard the noise of running water. As they approached in the direction of the noise, Theo became aware of a change in the surrounding air. There was a freshness to it, like someone had opened a window in a stuffy room. Roxette held up her blue stone and he saw a rivulet of water gushing from a fissure in the rock splashing on the cave floor where it formed a small pool.

Roxette bent down and drank from the pool till she had her fill. Theo followed suit and then they filled their water skin. They decided to rest by the pool and pulled out a bundle tied with a clean cloth from their pack. They unfolded the napkin and sat to eat their cold meal. They daren't start a fire in the cave, so as not to draw unwanted attention to themselves, and in any case they had no fuel.

"This water seeps through from the springs of the Koran River," Roxette informed him, speaking in a low voice. "Depending on where exactly we are beneath the river, I would say that we have been travelling for two or three days."

Theo stared at her disbelievingly, but could not distinguish her features in the pale blue light of the stone. "Three days? We have been travelling for three days?"

Roxette nodded, as she took a bite from a nut and berry pie the dwarves had given them. She munched at it slowly and helped wash it down with some water from the pool.

"So how much further till we reach our destination?"

"Anywhere between twelve and fifteen days."

"What! We will be travelling in the dark for another fifteen days? Are there any breaks along the way where we can come out into the light and get a breath of fresh air?" he asked, morosely.

"There are tunnels that lead to the surface, but I wouldn't recommend we use them. They are frequented too often by my people. I'd rather not take the risk."

Theo pulled Roxette before him and peered into her eyes. "Roxette, I must feel the fresh air beating upon my face once more or I will die of suffocation. If there is such a tunnel nearby then take us there. I cannot last much longer buried beneath so many tons of rock. I was born to live above ground, not underneath it like a mole."

Roxette remained motionless for a while then nodded. "Alright, Theo. Finish up your meal and we'll find a tunnel leading above."

They were off once more. Soon Theo found he was labouring for breath as they climbed upwards. At some point a light far brighter than that of the Blueshine stone beckoned ahead. As they approached, whistling noises were being emitted by the wind beating against the tunnel entrance. He felt fresh air kissing his cheeks and sped towards it like a moth to flame.

They burst out into a world of whiteness. The mountainside was covered in snow, as was to be expected at these altitudes. But Theo was glad to be out into the open once more. He took in a few deep breaths to fill his lungs with the crispy air and let his eyes adjust to the bright noonday light. After he had had his fill he followed Roxette grudgingly back into the tunnel from whence they had come.

They came face to face with the Mountain nymph patrol as soon as they entered the tunnel. Roxette whirled around but froze. Behind them, from the snowy sides of the mountain, a dozen more nymphs had appeared.

They were surrounded. Roxette did not bother drawing her swords. It would have been a futile venture.

♦ CHAPTER 29 ♦

Alone

"Rise Commander Barack!"

The Mountain nymph stood at attention before his lord whilst the warlock blew on his long freshly lacquered nails.

"The time draws near when we will set our dragon's claw on Alcavian soil, commander." Zarzbudin spread the fingers of one hand so he could scrutinize the work of the pedicurist who lay half-naked by his throne. She was a delightful creature from the eastern isles of the Kalim Ocean whom the Witch Lord had found was talented in other areas as well. She had been given to him as a gift by the Kaidir of Neba who wished to pay homage to the new ruler of the Mountain nymphs.

"We are ready to do our master's bidding." Barack let his gaze caress the lines of the pedicurist's lithe form. *I wouldn't mind adding this one to my tent*, he smiled inwardly.

"Have you taken the required measures concerning the infiltrators?" Zarzbudin let a fingernail trickle down the woman's throat; she purred in response.

"I have increased our patrols south of Wagon's End, my lord, and I've posted more men at all the tunnel entrances from above. Nobody will be able to squeeze through, I assure you of that." The woman opened up her knees and stared at the commander invitingly as his eyes were drawn to her pale thighs. Barack wet his lips as his dark eyes focused on hers.

She smiled and looked pointedly at the bulge in his leather pants.

"Very good." Zarzbudin's voice was like a caress given to a favourite kitten. "What of the other matter, my faithful servant?"

"Our new guest has arrived, my lord, as per your orders. He is currently enjoying the same hospitality we have granted the princess."

"He deserves no less." Zarzbudin's laugh was like a crow's cawing. "See that no harm comes to him, Commander Barack. He may prove useful to us if matters go awry with Georgile of Ameron."

"As my lord wishes." Barack bowed his head, keeping his eyes fixed on the woman throughout.

"Let the princess enter!" Zarzbudin called to the guards beyond his throne room.

The doors were opened to admit the princess of Alcavia who was looking decidedly weaker than when she had first arrived at the mountain fortress. Some of the fire of her fighting spirit had been subdued, and it showed in her thinning form. Her garments also were becoming tattered as she fell into a state of self-neglect. She dragged the ball and chain that were tethered to her ankle with greater difficulty than before.

"Aah, Princess Adelayne. So nice of you to join us, my dear." Three pairs of eyes stared at the princess: the warlock with mock amusement, the pedicurist with a measure of jealousy as she caught the gleam of interest in Barack's eyes.

"I was just explaining to the commander how we would not be considered good hosts unless we righted a wrong which we have committed against you–out of necessity of course!" Adelayne's blue eyes were like icicles as she stared at her enemy. The warlock continued unperturbed. "You see, princess, we consider it only fitting that, since we are about to annex your kingdom, we owe it to you to provide you with a new one. To this purpose we have arranged for a friend of yours to be brought here."

The warlock nodded to his commander. Barack walked to the throne room doors and exited. Meanwhile the princess stood looking dejected, her shoulders slumped and her legs hardly able to support her weight. She wondered what new devilry the Witch Lord was brewing. In answer, the throne room doors were flung open to admit a presence that caught the princess completely by surprise. She gasped placing her hands to her mouth. She let out a weak cry and fell to her knees unable to cope with the emotions that threatened to undo her.

Barack grabbed his prisoner by the arm and led him to stand beside the princess. The prisoner was a young man, roughly Adelayne's age, and looked as though he had been through an ordeal. The princess reached out and wrapped her arms lovingly about the familiar youth. She sobbed uncontrollably whilst the young man cradled her in his arms and brushed her hair lightly with one frail hand.

"How touching," Zarzbudin commented, winking at his concubine who grinned back at him. "Let it not be said that Zarzbudin does not appreciate the value of true love. Princess Adelayne, I present to you your future husband, Prince Armend of Ameron."

When Adelayne eventually recovered, she wiped away at her moist cheeks and turned to look up into Armend's eyes which had deep dark rings around them. "Oh Armend, I'm so relieved to see a familiar face after so long, though it grieves me that you have fallen into the Witch Lord's hands."

Before Armend could respond, Zarzbudin called out, drawing their attention towards him. "Your Highness...or should I call you by your new title, Your Majesty?"

Armend took a while to register what the warlock was saying. His face grew even paler when he finally comprehended the meaning of the warlock's words.

"Yes, Prince Armend, I see you have not been kept abreast of recent events. I'm sorry to be the bearer of ill tidings but it seems your mother, the recent queen of Ameron, saw fit to dispose of her husband and bring an end to her troubled marriage."

"Noooo!" A look of disbelief and agony disfigured the prince's face. Armend sealed his ears with the palms of his hands in an attempt to block out the warlock's taunting voice.

"Oh come now, Your Majesty. There is always a silver lining to each dark cloud. By all rights, you are now the next king of Ameron. All that remains is for us to prepare you correctly to assume that role."

"You lie, Zarzbudin!" Armend spat. "My father is alive."

"I would not jest over a matter so serious. I assure you, as my name is Zarzbudin, that your father is well and truly dead."

Armend shook his head whilst keeping his hands plastered over his ears as if to block out the wailing voices of the dead–but he knew, deep down that the warlock was right. His world was falling apart all around him. His father had been everything to him. Sure, at first, as a child he had been close to his mother but as he grew to manhood his father had played a more central role in his upbringing till his entire being and reason for existence revolved around his father and pleasing him. He had done all in his power to meet the high demands his father had placed upon him and to what end? He was an addict barely able to control his weakened body and now he was without a kingdom as well. Perhaps the warlock offered him his only salvation. He looked resignedly at Zarzbudin.

"Now that the grieving is over with, it is time to face a few hard facts, Your Majesty." Zarzbudin ploughed on like a relentless battering ram. "Events have surpassed you, my prince, whilst your so-called friends have kept you locked away at the nun's infirmary. Your uncle Georgile has stepped into the void left by your father's death and is readying to seize the throne. Unless you move quickly, your heritage will slip through your fingers. That is where we come in."

A crocodilian smile crept over his lips as he hunched forward on his throne so he could peer more closely at the sick prince. "You need my aid, young princeling. Only my influence can ensure you wrestle the throne from your uncle." Armend clasped his hands together tightly in a futile attempt to keep them from trembling. His face was contorted in a grimace and his eyes were watery as his entire body began to convulse. "Bring the prince's medicine!" Zarzbudin shouted at one of his guards.

"And what will I have to sacrifice in return for your aid, Zarzbudin?" The prince managed to ask between short breaths. He cast Adelayne a reassuring look but her concerned expression did not alter.

"That we will discuss in due course. Meanwhile you are free to accompany the princess to her quarters. First thing you will need to do in achieving your goal is obtain a wife worthy of your kingdom. I believe the princess meets the criteria." Armend gave Adelayne what bordered on an apologetic look. "Good. Your medicine has arrived, Prince Armend." One of the guards held out a vial filled with a green liquid. Armend grabbed it with shaking hands and gulped down the contents.

"Now leave us!" the warlock commanded. The prince laid his arms protectively about Adelayne's fragile shoulders and led her slowly out of the hall. He was accompanied by Kakledur, Zarzbudin's personal servant, who was assigned the duty of looking after the princess.

As soon as the doors to the hall closed behind the couple, Barack turned to look at his master. "The princess is a wild minx, my lord. Armend is a weakling and will never be able to control her. Why not let me do away with the prince?"

"And what of the girl, Commander Barack?" A sly smile formed on Zarzbudin's lips as he gave Barack an amused look.

"The princess needs a strong man to stand beside her."

"And I suppose you are just the man for the job?" When Barack did not answer, the warlock added, "You're ambitious, Barack, and I admire that in you. But let us not be too hasty. The prince may serve our purposes yet–at least until we are sure that Georgile will do our bidding. Once we have established firm control over the lands occupied by Alcavia, and we have Ameron's full support in our endeavours to strike Ramila, then you may do as you wish with both the prince and his unwilling bride."

Meanwhile, in another part of the fortress–a cold, windowless part–the prince was escorting Adelayne to her tiny room. They entered together, shutting the door behind in Kakledur's face.

"That skeletal man gives me the creeps." Adelayne shivered with more than just the cold in her room. Armend removed a woollen shawl from the cloak stand in the corner and moved over to where the princess was sitting on the bed. He placed it around her shoulders and sat beside her.

Adelayne looked up at him with those blue-green eyes that haunted his dreams. "You know," she said, wrinkling her nose to show her annoyance, "he has been constantly by my side, shadowing my every move since I arrived here. I hate listening to his shuffling feet behind me and the way he stands crouched over all the time, looking at me side-on like a crow."

"I wouldn't let him worry you, Adelayne. He seems harmless enough." How his heart ached now that he sat so close beside her. The smell of lavender in her hair aroused his feelings of desire for her. *If only you could be mine,* he thought, but he knew it was a hopeless thought–and yet, perhaps now that they had need of each other's company, *perhaps.* He felt a faint hope rising within him. He had steeled his heart all those months that the princess had spent together with that villager from Cyrus. But Marentherin was far away and forgotten.

"That may be so but I still don't like him."

The prince was brought out of his musing and stared at her for a while. "Let's have a look at your ankle," the prince said, changing subject as he bent to examine Adelayne's leg. The iron clamp had rubbed the skin raw till the red of the flesh was showing. "That could get infected," Prince Armend said with concern. "Have you been given anything for the wound?"

"They apply a poultice three times a day. It smells foul but keeps the wound clean."

"I can't imagine why they would insist so much that you carry on wearing this blasted thing!" Armend turned red with anger.

"It's Zarzbudin's way of breaking my spirit; I think it's working too."

Armend pulled her towards him cradling her head in his arms. "My poor Adelayne. How we have all failed you." He rocked her to and fro like a child whilst she sobbed in his arms.

Then, Adelayne pulled away and looked at him in earnest. "Armend, you must stop taking that awful medicine they're giving you. Surely it's not going to do you any good."

"Not to worry, Adelayne." The prince smiled weakly. "I stopped taking any form of drugs whilst I was in the care of the nuns," he assured her.

She did not seem convinced. "But I saw you drinking that green liquid in the warlock's hall."

"I spat it out as soon as we exited, and when Kakledur was not looking."

"Good," the princess said with relief. At least that was one less problem they would have to deal with. They needed to be extra careful now.

"We must bide our time," the prince said, as if reading her thoughts. "Perhaps the opportunity will arise for us to escape from the warlock's fortress."

"Armend, I'm truly sorry for your father's death," Adelayne said, placing a slim hand in his. His heart leapt in his throat as she stared with a sullen expression deep into his eyes. Her face, which was like marble carved by an artist with loving hands till it was perfect in every aspect, filled his vision. He could not bear to be so close to her and not have her for his own. He felt a strong urge to kiss her soft trembling lips. "I know what it is to loose a loved one." Adelayne stroked a stray hair from his forehead.

Armend cleared his throat breaking the spell momentarily. "My father meant everything to me, Adelayne," he said fiercely. "I don't believe for a minute that my mother had anything to do with his murder. Zarzbudin is a lying, scheming cur. I'm sure he had a hand in all that has come to pass. In any event, I swear to make them all pay–all who were involved in the plot to end my father's reign."

Adelayne nodded grimly then a look of renewed hope lit her pale face. "Armend, I'm so glad you're here. I've been so desperately lonely these weeks."

"Can I hope that your feelings towards me will change with time?" Armend fixed her with his beseeching eyes.

Adelayne could not hold his gaze but looked down at her hands in her lap. "I...I don't know, yet, Armend. I still...I..."

"You are still in love with the Islander." Armend could not hide the note of bitterness in his voice. Adelayne simply nodded without raising her head to return his gaze. "That may be so, Adelayne, but I am by your side now, whereas he is miles away. Of what use is he to you now?"

Adelayne remained silent. She placed a finger tenderly to the emerald earrings she wore; she never took them off during the day. She remembered that night, the night Theo spirit travelled to her in this very room. She still harboured a slim hope that Theo would come after her to try and save her. As much as a part of her wished for this to be true, another part did not want him risking his life needlessly. She knew any attempts at rescuing her were futile.

Armend took her silence as a rejection of his offer. He got up from the bed and exited the room, leaving Adelayne with her thoughts. She felt completely wretched and alone.

***

Serilia could not believe her brother had left without saying goodbye. Of course Queen Viola had explained the circumstances under which Theo had been taken away. She felt so hopelessly alone. Suddenly she wanted to be on her way as soon as possible. It would be good for her to see her grandfather Nestor again. She needed to be near a member of her family. And her aunt Emeralda would be with her grandpa as well.

It had not taken them long to pack. Before noon, they were ushered onto one of the Forest nymph swan ships and were heading down the Silver River. Serilia had enquired as to Ellodiere's whereabouts but was informed that the Flora Ancient had left the previous night.

She stood at the ship's prow looking out over the swan figurine's head. They were moving swiftly through the Silver Lake, propelled forward by a prevailing north wind descending from the mountains. Nem came to stand beside her placing his hands on the ship's gunwale.

"Hard to believe he's gone, isn't it?" he asked simply.

"Yes. I suppose deep down inside I knew our paths would have to split someday. I just didn't expect it to be so suddenly. Oh Nem," she cried, flinging her arms about his neck. "How will I ever be able to cope with the grief," she sobbed.

Nem stroked her hair gently and placed a comforting arm around her shoulder. "It's alright, Serilia. I'll never leave you."

"Nem," she said, pulling her face free from his tunic. "Do you think Theo will be alright? I am worried about him, out there in those mountains all alone. I've always taken care of him, Nem. You saw how weak he is in his use of the gift."

"Serilia, you forget. Theo has Roxette with him. I'm sure she will keep him out of trouble. She's real tough, that Roxette is."

"Yes, I suppose you're right," Serilia drew in a deep breath. "It's just that I can't help worrying about him, that's all."

They stood for a while, huddled close together staring out at the deep sluggish moving waters of the river. Nem pulled his curly hair back from his face and tied it in a warrior knot. He fingered his scimitar feeling comforted by its touch and drew Serilai's cloak more tightly about her shoulders, tucking in a flapping piece that had freed itself from her grasp.

"Nem?"

"Hmm?" he answered, still deep in thought.

"Do you think Theo will be able to free Adelayne and get back to us safely?"

"I have to believe that he'll be successful, Serilia. It's a tough task but we've been through a few difficult situations and have come out of them alright in the end. Theo is a lot more resilient than we give him credit for. He may surprise us all in the end."

"Thank you Nem." Serilia beamed a smile at him and placed a slender arm in his.

They ate lunch then retired aft to rest. Nem was busy sharpening his scimitar's blade, though it did not seem to need it, whilst Serilia busied herself with repacking her things. She folded her dresses more neatly so they would not become crinkled then got up to check on the horses. She remembered her parents just then and felt the time was drawing nearer for her to see them again.

The first thing she would do once she was in Ameron would be to find her grandfather and aunt and set forth for Hendon without delay. There they would make a short stop before they would again set out for Aldorn where Archon had told them they would find her parents.

Next day the sun's light was weakened by an overcast sky. The wind battered the ship as it wound its way through the deep murky waters. By noon it completed its journey to Ameron's Silver Bridge and came to berth beside the other ships of the harbour. Soon the crew began to unload its goods. Nobody noticed the solitary pair that led their steeds slowly along the dock road and onwards to the city gates.

Nem accompanied Serilia to the *Horse Shoe Inn* where they had stayed with Nestor when they were last in the city. He was thankful that only the innkeeper seemed to recognize them. The fewer people that did, the better. The innkeeper, answering Nem's enquiry concerning Nestor, informed him that he and a woman who fitted Nem's description were staying at the inn but had gone out for the day.

Nem ordered lunch as they sat alone at one of the smaller tables. No sooner had they started eating, than the inn door opened letting the cold wind blow into the common room. He lifted his head to stare at the couple that entered with their cloak hoods pulled well over their heads. The more slender figure was wearing a green cloak Nem instantly recognized. The other figure's hawk-like nose protruded characteristically from his hood. The figure turned to look in Nem's direction and froze. Nem could sense those blue eyes fixed upon him. Then the figure moved forward and came to stand close beside him and Serilia.

"Leave your meal and come with us to our room. Quickly now and don't let on that you recognize us. Follow a few minutes after we have left."

When the figures had departed, Nem got up slowly and beckoned for the serving girl to come over so he could pay for their meal. They made their way swiftly up the inn stairs and found the door they were looking for left slightly ajar. They entered and closed the door behind them.

Nem turned to find Serilia had already flung herself in Nestor's and Emeralda's embrace.

"Nice to see you two again," Nem said, after he had taken his turn at embracing his companions.

"It's good to see you too," Nestor answered, and Emeralda smiled her agreement. "I suppose Theodor and Roxette are already on their way to the Dragon's Foot Mountains?"

Nem nodded.

"Nerus be with them both. I believe the boy will be able to take care of himself. We Farstriders are a tough lot," he said, turning to grin at his sister. Emeralda returned him a warm smile as she hugged Serilia closer.

"Nestor, why all the secrecy?" Nem asked, implying the way they had met downstairs.

"I believe we are being watched," Nestor explained. "I have had my suspicions over the past few days and today I think I recognized one of them."

"Oh, who is it then?"

"I believe Serilia is well acquainted with the brute, Nem; our vagabond knight has caught up with us."

"What! You mean Grimshaw?" Serilia asked, dismayed. She shivered at the thought of the black-hearted knight being close. Grimshaw would come at them with a vengeance now that they had given him the slip.

"I'm pretty sure it was him, though he tried to hide his large frame –unsuccessfully I might add."

"So what do we do now?" Serilia asked worriedly.

"We wait for dark and we make our way out of the city. Things have started to become heated up in Ameron since you've been away. These people are all war crazy. Georgille has got them all thinking that Ramilan assassins were responsible for King Philander's death, and they're all hungry for revenge. It's become dangerous in the extreme to remain here for much longer."

"What about your shoulder?" Nem remembered the vicious wound from the arrow.

"Zoi did a good job healing it. All the physicians here were left to do was prepare me some more salve to put on the wound till it closed. It should be as good as new in a couple of weeks, but I can ride without any problem."

"Eh...Nestor?"

"Yes, Nem, what is it? You look like you've just swallowed a bug."

"Well...it's just that...you know Zoi..."

"Yes, boy?"

"She's not what we all expected."

"Whatever do you mean?" Emeralda was also listening attentively.

"Her real name is Ellodiere."

Emeralda gaped at Nem in disbelief. "The Flora goddess," she murmured with awe.

"I should have guessed," Nestor chided himself. "Why else would the mage have made that detour to pick her up?

And I had my suspicions about him knowing her from before; it was apparent from the moment he brought her onto the *Sea Breeze*."

That night four figures clad in cloaks, with the hoods brought well forward to hide their faces, rode out of Ameron City's eastern gate. Shortly after, and keeping at a safe distance, a group of riders followed behind.

***

He raised his sword and brought it down as fast as he could. But however fast he had become over the months, he could not match her fluid effortless movements. She side-stepped his stroke easily and dealt him a soft blow with the flat of her blade on his back. He reached out for his gift. If he could not tear her to pieces with his blade then he would try to do it the other way. He came up against the barrier once more which cut him off from his gift, like a tent seals away its occupants from the outside elements. He felt at the corners of the "tent" and found it was being held down firmly at three points. He lifted hate filled eyes and met those of his captors. They were all three black-haired and brown eyed like the Mountain nymph that sparred with him.

He sensed that the old man, even though he was the feeblest looking of the three, was in fact the strongest in the use of the gift. The other two, one male and one female seemed to be about his age, though he had learned that nymphs did not suffer the effects of time as humans did. The old nymph gave him a toothless grin and shook an admonishing finger at him.

"Theodor, you disappoint me." He turned his gaze to the nymph that stood before him with the dark leather pants and tunic and the red fringed jet-black hair. She was in peak form her swift movements keeping her well ahead of his most ardent attempts to knock her flat. He realized that he hated her with an intensity that astonished him. *How could she have gotten so close to us without revealing her true nature? How could Archon have been so easily misled?* "Tell me, Nolath. Has he tried to use his gift again?"

The old nymph nodded to the warrior she-nymph that stood before Theo with both swords drawn. She turned a scornful eye at her sparring partner. "There is a time when you must rely on your gift, Theodor, and there is a time when you must make do with whatever weapon you have at hand. You must learn to use both talents to the best of your ability if you are to survive."

"Why should you care, Roxette?" Theo spat the words at her, like one cat in a fight does to another. "You've managed to deceive us all. What could you possibly want to achieve with me, still? You have the princess and there will be no rescue attempt. So what is it you want?"

Roxette looked down upon him scorfully. She lifted the right side of her lip in a sneer. "Why, Theodor, have you not guessed yet? I want *you*. I want what you can offer to me and my people."

"Never! I will never succumb to you and your Witch Lord. Never!"

"Well, your only other choice then, Theodor, is for you to remove me from your path. Come," she crouched down low, beckoning him forward with the tip of her right sword.

Theo sprang at her with renewed fervour. Maybe he could keep at it until he wore her down. All he wanted was the chance to run his blade across her slim throat and see the blood blossoming there. After all, he had not done too badly with the princes in Alcavia. Perhaps he would get lucky with Roxette.

After he had been sparring for what seemed like an eternity, his knees and arms aching, he lowered his sword and knelt on the ground to recover his breath. He had a few nicks on his arms and legs but Roxette stood before him without a single scratch. She wasn't even breathing hard.

"You've improved a lot," she said, kneeling close to him so he could hear. "Maybe tomorrow we will start you on your forms." As Roxette turned around to leave, he heaved himself up and lunged at her with an overcut move. She deflected his blow, bringing her sword up without even turning around and delivering him a back kick that sent him crashing to the stone floor clutching at his mid-section in pain. "That's enough training for today," she said, still not bothering to turn around and face him.

Theo estimated that a day had passed since he had been captured by the nymph patrol ...since Roxette had betrayed him. He looked around at his captors and saw there was no way of escape. There were a score of nymphs, not counting the three gifted that were keeping an eye on him, and they were all well armed with blades and pikes. The only reason they had not killed him was that they had recognized Roxette as one of their own, and she had convinced them that he was worth more to them alive than dead. He still remembered her words clearly: "*If he does not yield to our master Zarzbudin, then we can always use him in our mines as we have done with the rest of our slaves.*"

Theo was uncertain of the direction they were taking but when he inquired of one of the Mountain nymphs it confirmed that he was being led south. *At least I'm going the right way*, he thought, gaining little comfort from it. He was allowed to keep his sword only during sparring practice, so he grudgingly handed it over to the tall grim-faced nymph that reached out for it. He walked slowly to the side of the cave and sat on a small outcrop of rock looking at the nymphs going about their work. They had found the cave after they had spent many hours walking in the dark tunnels. Theo had lost all sense of time underground but his tired limbs and complaining stomach were all the signs he needed to know that it was close to midday. A half dozen of the nymphs were turning a small animal on a skewer, whilst the rest had been sent out to keep watch at the cave entrances or to fetch wood and water from the surface.

Theo was not allowed to venture far from the camp site. Who knew when he would see the light of day again? If they threw him in their mines, then he would probably never see the blue skies of Thalagia–ever–nor her bright golden sun. He tried to keep his mind focused on the task at hand and not let it wander aimlessly on what might happen. He would find a means to escape. *I just have to.* He wondered what his sister and Nem were up to. Hopefully they had met up with his grandfather and aunt Emeralda by now. At least they were safe and being well taken care of. It would not be long before Nestor would unite Serilia with their parents. How he longed to see his mother's face once more, and to gain comfort from his father's strength.

Elron had always been as tough as bull hide when dealing with problems, but at the same time gentle with his family and forgiving of Theo's and Serilia's weaknesses. He knew the siblings needed space and time to mature and nurtured them with advice and solid ideals so they would grow strong and able to tackle the hardships life had in store. Theo tried to think what his father would do in such a situation. Elron would make the most of Roxette's sparring lessons and would wait for the opportunity to present itself before striking. That's what Theo decided he would do. They were still a two-week journey from the Witch Lord's fortress. He would wait. Surely the three gifted nymphs would grow weary of shielding him from his gift? And then, when he broke through to it–then he would wreak his vengeance. Then he would strike out with all his might–and to Ushud with them all!

The gifted nymph maiden approached holding a tin plate upon which rested a piece of steaming meat and dry bread with some roots. She grinned at Theo and offered him the plate and a cup filled with crystal clear mountain spring water. "Eat. This will help keep up your strength for the trip ahead." Theo accepted the plate and cup from her and sat to eat without comment. He was very hungry and the food tasted good. "Mountain goat," she replied to his questioning look. "I am Madura of the Black Bear tribe."

Theo met her brown eyes. "I suppose you already know who I am?"

"Yes, I overheard Roxette earlier on when you were sparring together. You are lucky to have her for a teacher, you know."

"How so?" Theo sneered.

"Roxette is amongst our most notorious warriors. She is of the Mountain Lion tribe. They are well known for their fighting skills, but Roxette is unique. She was sent at the age of twelve to the Kamtai Island Temple and spent another twelve years there before she returned to us a fully trained Weapons Master. We were all distraught to learn of her death at the hands of our enemy. Now our hearts are gladdened to see her alive and the false rumours of her death laid to rest."

"That is what they told you, that Roxette was killed by your enemies?" Theo saw an opening that he might be able to use to his advantage.

"Yes," the nymph looked inquiringly at him. "Why, did you hear otherwise from Roxette?"

"No, he did not." Roxette chose that moment to come sit beside them. She had finished her meal and was nibbling at some berries. She held Theo's gaze, daring him to tell the truth. He knew he had nothing to gain from it. She would deny everything. For now he would play along with her.

"He has the ability to become strong at using the gift," Madura said to Roxette, ignoring Theo completely, as though she was speaking about a prize puppy she had picked up on her travels.

"Yes, the sorcerers of the Light sensed this in him as well, which is why I feel he can be useful to us–once he realizes there can be no victory against the Dark."

"That can be a hard lesson for one of the Light to learn." This time Madura turned to look at Theo, and two pairs of dark brown eyes stared at him from oval faces that seemed to be made from porcelain, so perfect were they in shape and their skin so smooth. *Appearances can be very deceiving, as I have learnt before*, Theo decided.

When they had all finished their meal, the nymphs broke camp and shouldered their packs before setting out. Several of the nymphs held torches to light the way. At least Theo could now see clearly where he was going. The blue shine stone had been taxing on his eyes. Large gaping holes crossed their path as they made their way down the tunnels. They were forced to step or jump over them depending on their size. When they entered caves on their way south Theo noticed stones glinting reflecting the torch light. There were green stones of emerald, blue of sapphires, red of rubies and many more. Baulkin had been right about the deposits of precious minerals that were to be found on the border of the Dragon's Foot Mountains.

They had not gone far when they came across another group of nymphs, only this one was twice their number. Theo could not help but gape at the creatures that loped alongside the nymphs. They were large but bent over so they stood only a head taller than Theo. Their arms drooped by their sides dragging wooden clubs studded with mean spikes, and their forearms were hairy like a bear's. Theo sensed that a single swipe by an arm that size would incapacitate a man. What caused him to stare, however, were the creatures' faces. They had no facial hair but were completely bald. In the centre of their face was positioned a single eye as large as a saucer and below their solitary eye they had large snouts the size of coconuts that were dripping incessantly. Warts covered their faces, necks and bare backs and arms. For clothing they wore a fury loin cloth and a woollen cloak thrown over their backs. On their feet they wore boots made from tough hide laced with rope up to their bulging calf muscles.

"You've never seen Cave Trolls before?" Madura realised, sensing his astonishment at seeing the beasts. Theo shook his head without uttering a word. "If you think Cave Trolls are a sight, just wait till you meet up with an Ogre, or even worse an Orgul."

"Oh, we've met an Orgul," Theo answered, coming out of his stupor, "or, rather, we managed to escape from one in the dark."

"So you haven't seen one face to face then?"

"No."

"Well you should count yourself fortunate. Even we Mountain nymphs cannot fully control an Orgul. They are massive beasts as tall as one of your three floored dwellings. And they know no master. Only when chained and flogged with steel whips will they bend their will to do our bidding, and even then they do so grudgingly. Many trainers have lost their lives to Orguls."

"So why do you keep them, then?" Theo asked, looking at his nymph captor. She had tied her hair in a knot behind her back so her face was kept clear. It was not an unpleasant face to look at, though Theo felt only nervousness around her.

Madura looked at him as though she did not fully comprehend his question. "We keep them for the same reason we keep slaves for our mines, or other beasts of burden. The Orguls are able to carry great loads on their backs. We use them to mobilize our war machines, and they give us a fighting edge over our enemies. If you ever come up against an Orgul you'll understand what I mean."

The nymphs from the second group moved on to carry out the tasks they had been assigned. They hardly gave Theo a second glance. For them Theo was just another slave.

Theo's group kept on marching through the tunnels till he felt his legs could not carry him much further. His stomach was rumbling again. *Is it time for supper so soon?* They found another cave and were about to lay down their packs and settle for their meal when they heard moaning noises followed by howling and clicking. The nymphs drew their weapons and formed an arc so they faced the direction from whence the sounds came.

Suddenly, the creatures toppled into the cave; the flames of the nymphs' torches lit their hideous features. Unlike the cave trolls, these were without a nymph escort. There were five in the pack and they blinked at the torch lights with three eyes to each gruesome head. They had gaping holes at the side of their heads for ears and their snout was flat on their faces. Their projecting jaws were square and heavy, and horns protruded on either side of their chins. They had three fat fingers to each hand and their feet ended in cleft hooves. From their rear extended long tails covered in tough hide. In their right hand they clutched long-handled double-edged axes surmounted by a tip that could be used as a spear. They took one look at the nymphs and peeled back their lips in a snarl revealing rows of sharp teeth with long incisors jutting out from their mouths like the tusks of wild boars.

The leader of the nymph group stepped forward and held his sword aloft before him. "I am Kasak, leader of the Black Bear Clan. What are you Ogres doing in Zarzbudin's tunnels without your nymph masters?"

One of the ogres stepped a little closer to Kasak. It towered above him but the nymph stood his ground without flinching from the ogre's gaze. "We are tired of being led by the nose by your lot, nymphling. Who decided to make you our masters? It's time we took matters into our own hands." Theo was surprised by the intelligence displayed by the creatures. These were not the words of dumb brutes. He realized the ogres might pose a problem for the nymphs.

"These are words of treason Ogre." Kasak lifted the tip of his sword till it rested below the ogre's chin and pressed it to the creature's throat menacingly. "I will give you one chance, and only that, to submit to my clan."

"And you think you and these few around you will be able to stop us?" the ogre asked menacingly. Theo did not fancy placing a wager on who would come out the victor in a potential fight between the two groups even though the nymphs had the weight of numbers on their side.

In the blink of an eye the ogre swang his arm up striking Kassak before he could react, sending him sprawling across the cave floor. The rest of the nymphs sprang into action striking with their pikes and swords at the ogres, trying to keep them at arm's length. The ogres felled five nymphs with their axes in the first few moments and moved on unscathed to meet the attacks of the rest of the nymphs. Soon another half dozen nymphs lay decapitated on the cave floor. Theo realized the ogres were close to overpowering their opponents. He felt a lifting of one of the restraints that had been placed upon him to keep him from his gift. He looked towards the ogres to find that one of the nymphs that had shielded him from his gift lay sprawled on the cave floor with his head split in two halves and blood and white brain matter oozing out of the mutilated skull.

Theo seized the opportunity and made for one of the cave tunnels. As he entered the tunnel he heard scuffling movements close behind him. He was about to send out a searching spell when he realized the two remaining restraints on his gift were still in place. He did not turn to look behind him but chose instead to run as fast as he could through the dark tunnel. He had nothing with which to light his way but stretched out his fingers and felt the tunnel walls to guide him in his mad rush. He turned at a fork in the tunnel and chose the path from which a soft breeze of chilly air seemed to blow faintly.

As he climbed the tunnel path, he realized there was light at the far end. He raced towards it hungrily and emerged from the tunnel entrance into the dawn-lit mountainside. *Free at last!* he thought.

He was face forward in the snow. Something had hit him in the back. He lifted himself from the snow and felt the icy tip of a sword blade beneath his chin. He raised his eyes slowly and gazed at the Mountain nymph that held the sword to his throat.

"There is no escape for you, Theodor. You may as well come to terms with it. The sooner you do, the quicker you will get over the pain," Roxette sneered. His hatred for her was like a burning coal in his gut. He would see her dead, even if it meant he had to give his own life to achieve his goal.

Kassak had been fortunate in that he had encountered the ogres deep in his own clan's territory. Shortly after his units had been deployed to rally aid, they returned with reinforcements; but it was not their added numbers that had finally overpowered the ogres but rather the ten trolls the clan kept as pet slaves. Now subdued, the ogres shuffled forward with their eyes averted, responding to their new masters' commands mechanically. Kasak swore as his patrol came across the ogres' previous owners. None of them had been spared. The patrol counted over a score of the nymphs littering the tunnel floor with most of their limbs torn from their broken, mutilated bodies. Kasak would not be so careless.

No matter how long Theo spent in the company of the ogres and trolls he could not overcome his feelings of revulsion for these creatures. They were the stuff nightmares were made of. Some of them approached him snuffling at his hair and lolling their tongues at him whilst drool dripped from their fangs as they stared at him contemplating. One of the creatures earned a well-aimed kick by a gifted nymph youth that had been placed beside Theo to replace their fallen comrade. After that, the creatures did not pay any notice to Theo, which suited him just fine.

Theo turned to Madura who was walking in silence beside him. "How many days have we been travelling?" he asked.

She turned her pretty face to stare at him, and smiled before answering. "You lowland plain dwellers have no sense of the passing of time. Unless your eyes see the sun rising and falling, you are unable to count the days."

"Yes, well excuse me for not being born a mole," Theo retorted, his feelings of restlessness being heightened by his extended stay in the tunnels. "Now are you going to tell me, or not?"

"Alright, Islander, don't work yourself up into a frenzy. By my estimate we have been travelling for six days, since we came across you and Roxette. We should arrive at our master's fortress in another week."

Six days. To Theo it seemed as if he had been in the tunnels for at least a month. As they moved along, Theo imagined he could hear a steady beating noise coming from the far end of the tunnel. The closer they got, the louder the noise became. He could now see a bright light illuminating the path ahead. The nymphs picked up the pace and soon the group emerged into a large cave. It was easily the size of the underwater cave of the Alunda Sea nymphs.

Theo beheld a sight that left him speechless in wonder. Massed in the cave, like a colony of ants, was a horde of

Mountain nymphs. A lot of them, mostly able-bodied males, were dressed in stout dark garments carrying an assortment of weapons with their faces painted in bright colours. The booming noise was coming from a creature larger even than the ogres and trolls. It was beating on a drum the size of a wagon and was surrounded by a score of warrior nymphs holding heavy chains that were wrapped around the beast's neck, arms, and ankles to keep it restrained. The beast's skin was yellow, like a species of lizard that could be found in the swamps, and large red warts dotted its naked body. It had two saucer-sized brown eyes and curved horns protruded on either side of its head. Sharp teeth and tusks lined its wide ugly mouth and a thick tail extended from its rear end. A simple loin cloth hid its genitals and around its arms and ankles it wore thick iron bands.

"Now you have seen an Orgul as well." Madura came up close to him to peer at the gathering of nymphs. Countless torches lit the vast cave and there was a cacophony of sound as the nymph tribes conversed with one another.

Roxette was restless. She tried to hide it but the set of her shoulders was unmistakable. As they moved sluggishly through the nymph host, she turned her head scanning all before her, clenching and unclenching her fists which she kept firmly plastered by her sides. Some of the nymphs they passed scowled at Theo as if to chase away the intruder with their glare. Others, upon seeing Roxette, rushed to their companions pulling at their sleeves and nodding in her direction. A small gathering was forming around them and Kassak's group had to push past.

"Roxette!" a young nymph warrior cried with glee, flinging her arms around Roxette's waist. Theo judged her age to be no more than twelve, though she was dressed in warrior garb and held a sword, a bow and several smaller blades around her belt and tunic.

"Hello Ilssa." Roxette returned the young nymph's hug caressing her hair affectionately.

"Roxette, it really is you!" Ilssa turned her face up to look at her friend lovingly.

"In the flesh."

Then another nymph made her way steadily through the crowd and halted before the other two who were still embraced.

Roxette, noticing the other's presence, tilted her head in acknowledgement and placed her hand to her heart and temple in a formal greeting. "My heart is gladdened to see you once again, Kandara, Chief of the Mountain Lion Tribe. May your blade forever remain sharp."

"May fortune smile upon you, your blade spill much of your enemies' blood before you leave Haulbrakk's embrace," Kandara answered the formal greeting. "We are glad to see you returned to us. We were led to believe that you had been killed in an ambush."

"Haulbrakk, in all his wisdom, has decided my time is not yet nigh. It seems he still has a use for me."

Kandara smiled with genuine pleasure at Roxette. As the three nymphs exchanged further words, Theo realized that Ilsa was also of the Mountain Lion tribe and that her fellow young female nymphs had been devastated at the news of Roxette's death. Apparently she was held in high esteem in the women's ranks and all the youngsters aspired to become warriors of equal skill. Theo gazed carefully at the chief she-nymph and realized she had the same red tipped hair as Roxette. It was the method used to identify each tribe. He looked around and realized that other tribes used different colours to dye their hair; there were oranges, purples, greens and blues. Some had their scalps shaved completely whilst others allowed a central band of hair to grow to the nape of their necks.

Kasak stepped forward interrupting the three nymphs.

"Come, Kandara. Roxette must accompany my tribe. She was caught above ground with this plain dweller," he said, motioning at Theo. "We will deliver her and the prisoner to our commander. He will decide on their fate."

Kandara peered at her counterpart with a contemplating look. "By all rights Roxette and her prisoner are your responsibility until they are brought before the commander. However, Roxette still belongs to my tribe; we will escort you to the commander."

"So be it," Kasak responded without argument; the Mountain nymphs were governed by a strict code of conduct which they did not easily defy. Roxette nodded her thanks to Ilsa and Kandara and allowed herself to be led away.

The group made its way steadily forward into the crowd, nearing the far end of the cave where a group of warrior nymphs were standing in attention with spears held aloft. Kasak motioned for the rest of his group to remain behind, but beckoned for Roxette, Theo and the three gifted nymphs to make their way forward.

"Halt! State your business." One of the warrior nymphs placed a spear point in front of Kasak to stop his advance.

"I am Kasak, Chief of the Black Bear Clan. I seek audience with the commander. I have in my custody a prisoner that might interest him."

One of the warrior nymphs disappeared into the circle of guards and came back a moment later. "The commander will see you now, Kasak of the Bear Clan."

The small party made its way through the warrior guards' ranks till they came upon a section of the cave which was raised higher so it afforded a clear view of the entire chamber. There, sitting on a wooden chest covered by an assortment of animal skins, was the golden-haired nymph that had abducted Adelayne.

Theo was about to go for his sword but felt Roxette's restraining hand clasping his wrist firmly. "Don't be a fool!" she hissed in his ear. "You'll be dead before you draw it."

Theo decided to heed her warning and settled instead to casting the nymph commander a hate-filled look.

Barack, Supreme Commander of the Dragon's Foot Mountain Forces, was busy speaking in hushed tones to two other nymph warriors.

"The Commander wears six red feathers in his head band," Roxette whispered in his ear. "His second in command wears five, and so on down the ranks." Both the nymphs standing close to the commander wore red feathers. One was a tall brutish fellow with a shaved scalp and four feathers. The other, with five feathers, was a woman with long black hair tinged with blue locks.

Roxette noticed Theo staring at the tall warrior woman with the red paint splashed across both cheeks. "That is Second in Command, Lizelle. She is of the Clan of the Mountain Hawk, and is a member of Barack's flight squad...and his lover."

"I thought you had that honourable position," Theo answered wryly.

"That was before Barack and Lizelle almost beat me to death," Roxette answered, her voice cold and devoid of emotion, reflected in the vacant expression of her eyes. Whatever she now felt over Barack's traitorous act, she hid it well.

Barack turned at their approach. A look of recognition and surprise dawned on his face as he laid eyes on Roxette. He grabbed at the swords protruding from his back, bringing them out of their scabbards with a ringing noise. The surrounding nymph guards, sensing their commander's unease, lowered their spear points at the new arrivals. Theo stood with a dozen spear heads held close to his throat and face. "Who let this dog near my sight?" Barack growled, coming towards Roxette.

In answer, Roxette fell to her knees and crouched on all fours lowering her head submissively. Barack let his sword tip hang above the nape of her neck.

"What brings you crawling back to the people you abandoned, Roxette?" he asked, his voice filled with contempt.

Roxette lifted her face. Theo was surprised to see tears streaming from her eyes. "I have come to seek forgiveness for my wrongful ways, commander. I was unable to deceive you, my lord. You saw me for the scheming, ambitious woman that I was. Your love for me did not blind you to the fact that I was unable to accept you were the one destined to lead our people. I coveted your position in our ranks and was hungry for power. Your justice was dealt swiftly and mercilessly. I have had time to come to terms with this and to accept my errors."

"Fine words, Roxette, but how am I supposed to trust you. We all believed you had died. Now you return to us like a ghost from the past. How do I know you will not revert back to your treacherous ways?"

"Kill her, my lord!" The she-nymph with the blue locks stepped close to Roxette and kicked her viciously in the ribs, sending her coughing and sprawling on the cave floor. Roxette raised herself slowly to a crouching position but averted her eyes from Lizelle.

"I will decide for myself what I will do with her, Lizelle." Barack threw his lover an admonishing look. She flicked her curls back in annoyance, but stepped away. Barack turned his gaze back to Roxette. "Well, what have you to say for yourself?"

"I have no way to convince you, my lord. Only my actions can speak in my defence."

"I will vouch for Roxette's honesty, my lord." Kandara stepped up boldly and held the commander's angry gaze without flinching.

"You should not be so hasty to provide your protection, Kandara of the Mountain Lion Tribe." There was a dangerous undertone to Barack's voice.

Barack turned to look at Kasak, then rested his gaze on Theo. "Who is the plain dweller you have brought with you, Roxette? Is he your pet lover, or have you brought him to work in our mines?"

"No, my lord, he is neither. This is Theodor Maren'Therin of Cyrus Island. He is a gifted, and I have brought him as a present to our master Zarzbudin. He is highly prized amongst his people, for he holds great promise in the gift. I deliver him to you, my lord, as a sign of my fealty to you and your leadership."

"Aah, yes," Barack said, a triumphant look crossing his face. "I remember you now, plain dweller. Last time we met, we left you alive to deliver our message to King Dreyfus. Now we are told there is more to you than meets the eye. My lord Zarzbudin has charged me with the task of locating you. We have been eagerly awaiting your arrival. What of the rest of the rescue party?" He turned to Roxette.

Roxette stared at Barack for a while, but managed to conceal her astonishment at how well informed he was about their movements. "The party split up west of Ameron, my lord. We encountered the Ameron City Patrol when this foolish boy and his friends rescued Queen Paula from the hangman's noose."

"Really," Barack exclaimed with interest. "It's just as well. Ameron and Ramila will be occupied with warring against each other, whilst we" he said, spreading his arms out wide to encompass the cave filled with his troops, "make our assault on Alcavia. As for you and your gift to Zarzbudin," Barack's eyes narrowed on Roxette, "I have decided to let you live so you can present him before our master. Should you disappoint in any way, then Kandara will pay for your treachery with the annihilation of her entire tribe." Kandara's face for the first time showed emotion–it was paler than the blind eels living under the nymph mountains. She looked down at Roxette in a meaningful manner.

When his threat had sunk in, Barack grinned roguishly at Roxette. "Seeing you like this, Roxette ...on your knees–I mean–reminds me there's another way you may prove your loyalty to me. Come to my tent tonight and we'll have the chance to catch up on old times ...and to test your devotion." The group of nymph warriors surrounding Theo and Roxette snickered. Lizelle however was not overly impressed and stormed away flicking her blue locks behind her in annoyance. "Oh...and Roxette," Barack said as he held out his hand to help her rise, "leave those blades behind when you come."

The beating noise from the orgul's drum continued steadily throughout the night, sounding the summons to the forces that where massing into the cave in preparation for the onslaught on Alcavia. Theo was exhausted from the quick pace Kasak's group had kept on the steady march south, but he barely managed to get some much needed sleep now the drum was beating . At some point during the night, his sleep was disturbed by Roxette making her way silently towards commander Barack's tent.

The next day Theo awoke to find the cave packed full with the Dragon's Foot Mountain forces. Everywhere he looked, to the furthest edges of the chamber, he saw dark-haired warriors dressed in their black garments and chain mail, bristling with weapons. There were many trolls and ogres in the fighting ranks and also several orguls. The Witch Lord's army was complete.

Barack pushed back his tent flap and exited, bare-footed, dressed only in a fur cloak that was tied at the waist by a leather belt. Behind him filed out a half dozen nymph maidens followed by Lizelle. Last to come out, clutching at her torn garments and with a cut above one eye and a split lip was Roxette. A gasp escaped Theo as he caught sight of her. Roxette averted her gaze and moved, hunched over, towards her pack where she proceeded to pull out garments with which to replace her torn ones.

Barack stretched out his arms and yawned. Then he turned to his bald third in command. "Gather up the army. We march in an hour." The officer saluted, then gave the signal for the horn to be sounded. The orgul drum beating began once more in earnest and soon the army was emptying out the cave from the many exits available. It took several hours before the last of the Warlock's army marched out of the cave, leaving behind Theo and his captors.

Kasak was charged with delivering Theo to the Witch Lord. He wasted no time in carrying out his task. They set out shortly after the cave had been abandoned. Over the next few days Roxette continued with Theo's training. Theo felt he was progressing much quicker than he had done in the past. His eagerness to learn was heightened by the thought that he might be able to strike a lucky blow against his enemy. He fought without restraint since his aim was to kill, whereas before he had simply been going through the motions till he could learn from repetition. Now he clung to Roxette's every word and hungered to learn more moves and techniques. He promised himself once more silently that he would take his revenge on Roxette before he drew his last breath, and added her lover to his list.

When they had made their stop to eat their meal and to take a few moments' rest, Theo felt tentatively at the barrier to his gift; he identified the "knots" that kept him barred from it. The old nymph, Nolath, kept the strongest knot of the three gifted. Madura was more or less at Theo's level, and the third nymph was barely able to use the gift. This gave Theo courage, for it meant the Mountain nymphs had no one abler to place as his guardian. Whenever Theo slept, Nolath would sleep also, so when Theo was awake the other two could rest. Nolath was confident that he could maintain the restraint on Theo's gift unaided. This was true, for Theo had tried to push back at Nolath when Madura and the other gifted nymph were asleep, but it was like trying to push against the tunnel walls. Nolath was as steady as the rocks which surrounded them.

For some reason Theo could not explain, when any of the gifted nymphs went away their knot remained intact. Perhaps this spell, once cast, maintained itself, unless the victim could find a way to break the knot. Theo bade his time. An opportunity would present itself. *It must*, he thought. The shielding of his gift added to the sense of depression that had descended upon him from being weighed upon by the mountain for so long.

His thoughts went to his sister and Nem. He wondered how far they had travelled from the Emerald Forest and if they were safely on their way to Aldorn and his parents. How he missed them all. *Will I ever see my family again? Will I ever be able to escape from the Dragonmaster's tunnels, or will I be forced to spend the rest of my life in the Warlock's dungeons, as a slave in one of his mines?*

Their clothing was being drenched by water falling from above. Madura informed Theo that they were passing beneath the springs of the Apalachus River. They were only a couple of days–three at most–from the Warlock's fortress. They moved with care over the slippery rock surface as they made their way south. Intermittently there were openings in the cave ceilings they passed under, and Theo would stare up into the light infiltrating down to the depths of the caves.

His longing to break away to the surface was at times maddening but he kept a fragile control over his impulse.

When they descended, steadily, to the lowest depths of the mountain, they came across large man-made openings. Theo stared in astonishment at the precious gems lining the tunnel walls. Further on, they came across a scene that wrenched at his heart. Holding picks, hammers and chisels, stooped over like hags, was a group of people who were busy breaking away the rock and sifting through the broken shards to separate gravel from precious gem. The group was a pitiful lot with no sign of flesh on their bony frames which were covered in sooty rags. Eyes stared forlornly from hollows beneath their wrinkled brows and their cheek bones protruded from their drawn faces. They passed through the nymphs' mines where slaves were used to do their dirty work. Theo recognized a few dwarves in the groups of slaves from their shorter stature and their hairy faces, though all the slaves had long unkempt beards.

"How long do you keep these poor people working in such conditions?" Theo asked quietly of Madura.

"Most do not survive more than five years." *Is that the sound of guilt in her voice?*

Mercifully, the group soon left the slave miners behind. Theo had added another reason to renew his vow to dispatch as many of the nymphs as he could before he himself was killed. He cast an accusatory glance at Roxette but she avoided meeting his eyes.

♦ CHAPTER 30 ♦

A question of trust

They were riding along the west bank of what Nestor had informed them was the east fork of the Dolomidur River. It had been four days since they had set out that night from Ameron to travel to Hendon. No sooner had they crossed the bridge over the west fork on their way to the County of Lenci, when they had encountered what was to become an additional member of their group. The man in question was a cleric who had fallen off his mule and had been trying to chase the animal down. The group had recovered from their fits of laughter to aid him in quartering the mule. Unfortunately for Nestor, who was ever mindful of strangers—even men of the cloth—the father had decided he much preferred to travel in their company than on his own. And so, Father Faith became the fifth member of Nestor's little party.

Father Faith was a jovial fellow with an ample belly and a long black beard. His full head of hair was covered by a straw hat to keep out the rays of the sun; even though winter was approaching, the sun's light was blindingly bright on a good day. They had been lucky to encounter the cleric along the way. He had informed them of a route through the Hills of Halum where the hills ended and the Brakkand's Throne Mountains began. Apparently, this mountain route would bring them safely on the other side and have gained them four days on their original planned route east through Hendon.

Serilia stared at the hills that lay before them. "Hills" was a misleading term to use to describe them. They were not as tall or imposing as the Dragon's Foot or Brakkand's Throne Mountains, but in other parts of Thalagia they would have been considered mountains. Father Faith had informed them joyfully that, at the rate they were going, they should reach the foot of the Halum hills by dusk. Serilia was glad they were approaching Leonium's border. She was anxious to get across to the other side and to meet up with her parents in Aldorn. It had been almost a year since she had last laid eyes on them and she missed them terribly. If it hadn't been for her grandfather Nestor and her aunt Emeralda, she was not sure how she would have coped.

Sensing Serilia's mood, Emeralda heeled her mare and came up beside her. She was wearing her riding clothes and thrown over it all was her favourite green cloak. She looked towards the hills with her hawk-like gaze then turned her attentions to her niece. "What are you thinking, dear?" She smiled at Serilia warmly and touched her affectionately on the cheek.

Serilia returned the smile admiring her aunt's blue eyes. They were so like her grandfather Nestor's. "Oh, I was just wondering how nice it would be to meet up with my mother and father, is all."

"My sweet, sweet child," Emeralda cooed. "You miss them terribly, don't you my dear?" Serilia nodded in return. "I'm sure they'll be glad to see you also, my sweet. We certainly have been through a lot over the past year, as have they, I'm sure."

"It's just so good to finally be heading for them. All this time, we've been travelling away. I just wish Theodor could have been with us."

"Theodor will join us, dear, in due course. I know it in my heart that he'll return to us."

"I worry about him, aunt Emeralda. He rides into the face of great peril...alone."

"Well, not completely alone, Serilia. He still has Roxette to take care of him, and Theodor is a resilient young man."

They rode on in silence for a while then Serilia turned back to her aunt. "What are your plans once we meet up with my parents, aunt Emeralda? I mean, you're always welcome to stay with me, though I'll be heading for the Wizard's Keep after I've been to visit my parents."

"Oh, Nestor and I will not burden you or your parents any more once we've escorted you safely to them. We've already decided to return to Cyrus as soon as we have completed our trip to Aldorn. We are not as young as we once were and need the comfort of what we've come to accept as our only home."

"Aunt Emeralda, you and grandfather have never been a burden to us, but rather a blessing. As for Cyrus, what will you do there? Our cottage was burnt down, from what grandfather told us."

"We will rebuild the cottage, my sweet, so you and your family will always feel you have a home to return to."

Suddenly, Serilia was overwhelmed by her feelings of love for her aunt. Tears filled her eyes and she reached over her saddle to place a kiss on her cheek. "Thank you. Thank you for always being there for me. You will always hold a special place in my heart."

Emeralda wiped the tears from Serilia's face with her hand. "And you and your brother will always be my most precious gems."

The remainder of that day they rode in silence steadily making their way upwards. All around them they could see scattered needle-leaved trees that formed the flora of this area. The path they followed was a dirt track forming a winding scar on the hillside where the shrubs did not grow. Father Faith had informed them that most travellers crossing from Leonium to Seldavia chose to cross further south, where Nestor had originally intended to take them, but explained that the more used path would have brought them through Hendon which would have added an extra three to four days to their journey to Aldorn.

That night they made camp at the side of the hills under the cover of a spruce tree which offered them some protection from the biting north wind. Nem and Nestor had found dry wood and soon lit a fire. Then they left the group at the camp site and ventured into the hills to hunt their meal. Game was plentiful in these parts and they soon returned with a pheasant and two hares.

When they had all eaten their fill, Nestor sat by the fire and puffed smoke rings into the air from his long-stemmed pipe. Father Faith sat close beside him and was telling stories of the people he had met during his travels to and from Seldavia. Apparently, the church kept him busy with conveying messages from the patriarchy at Ramila to its counterpart in Aldorn. It seemed the dealings between the religious regions were not restricted to an exchange of spiritual ideals but included an exchange of goods as well so the church built its commercial empire with the same zeal and professionalism it exhibited when carrying out its ecclesiastical role. Over the ages, the church had become the legal owner of much of the arable land of the Midland Kingdoms of Leonium, Seldavia and Renderon. To run this vast empire required the combined effort of all the clergy, which was why a lot of their time and energy was expended in administration and keeping an account of the church's wealth.

A lot of the church's land was rented out to farmers who cultivated it, and from their produce made their living and met their obligation towards their landlord. Some of the land was managed by the church directly, as was the case with the monasteries, where nuns and monks carried out the farming work themselves. The church's produce had managed to gain a prized position in the Midlands and abroad. Items such as wine, olive oil, honey and many more, had earned a reputation of being both relatively affordable and of high quality. With such a strong commercial base, it was no wonder the church was respected, and in some cases feared, by the ruling classes of the Midlands. The church was also prone to using its ecclesiastical role and its resources to influence the administering of these kingdoms.

"It's a wonder how you find time to carry out all these tasks the church sets for you," Nem was saying to Father Faith, as he listened attentively to the father relating the business ventures he had been involved in this year alone.

"The work of a holy man is never completed, my child. We cannot tend to the needs of our spiritual world and ignore our obligation to the material world we live in. But for every hardship we deal with successfully in this world, we gain a reward in the next. That is what gives us the strength and fuel with which we tackle our tasks. Perseverance and patience are both virtues, my son." Father Faith smiled warmly at Nem before raising his cup of steaming tea to his lips. The flames from the campfire played their game of light and shadow with his jovial face, emphasizing his round cheeks and lighting a sparkle in his eyes. It was difficult not to warm to this man, with his merry manner and his tales filled with adventures in various parts of the world.

Nem had a thought. "Tell me father, have your travels ever taken you beyond the Midlands?"

"Why yes, Nemarchus. I've been fortunate enough to see much of central Thalagia. When I was about your age, I travelled as far as Lisandria, across the Meldenyan Sea. I've even been as far as the Anvil Lands of Neba and Ishbad, though I did not spend much time there." The cleric's eyes took on a far-off look as he recalled the adventures of his youth.

"What made you venture as far as the lands of the Hadir Empire, Father Faith?" Nem asked with renewed interest. He clutched his cloak tighter about himself as the night chill began to settle on them like a blanket. He took a sip of the tea the father had offered and turned to gaze at the cleric.

"Well, my journey to Lisandria was to deliver documents from the patriarchy of Ramila to the primate of Lisandria. Then, I was requested to visit the Anvil Lands to secure a contract with merchants there, so our produce from Leonium could arrive safely to the kingdoms there."

"Some day, I would like to see these kingdoms of the south for myself." Nem stared out into the night, envisaging what it must be like to travel to such far-off places and to gaze upon the splendours of these lands. He had heard stories from his father about the wealth of the Hadir Empire, and how their buildings were adorned with golden domes and towering spires.

"Maybe some day you shall, young Nemarchus," the priest answered.

The companions agreed on how they were to share the guarding of the camp. Serilia was to take the first watch and would then be followed by Nem. Nestor would take the final watch and would wake the companions early the next day so they could make their one-day trip across the hills. Soon they had all settled down, huddled close to the fire, to sleep.

It seemed, no sooner had Nem laid his head to sleep than he was being shaken out of his dreams of travelling in a desert land where the buildings were made of gold and precious gems, and where he crossed oases with tall palm trees filled with fruit.

"What is it?" he asked, wiping the sleep from his eyes. He looked up to find Serilia bent over him, the faint scent of lily blossoms upon her.

"It's your turn to watch the camp, Foresight. It's pretty quiet up here, apart from the occasional scuttling of the bush animals. Oh, and I heard the wolves howling a while back, though they are far from us."

"Thanks for the information," Nem commented dryly.

"Enjoy your watch, Nem." Serilia stepped over to her spot near the campfire and laid a fresh log on it before curling up in her blankets to sleep.

Nem stood up and walked over to a small boulder near their camp where he sat and stared out into the night. It afforded a good view of the camp, and the moon and starlight lit up the side of the hill so he could see clearly enough for about a furlong. It was not long before he was nodding and his eyes drooping. When he had almost fallen from the boulder twice, he rose from it and decided to sit on the ground and place his back to it. No sooner had he done so, than he was sound asleep.

From the campsite, one of the companions rose slowly to his feet and came up slowly to Nem's boulder. The father remained looking at Nem for a while longer to make sure he was sound asleep. It seemed the sleeping potion he had placed in the youth's tea was doing its work perfectly. It would be several hours before the effects wore off, and by then the father would have finished what he had to do.

He wandered off into the night and followed the path up through the hills. He knew where he was going and needed no more than the moonlight to guide him. After walking for about an hour he found who he was looking for. There were five of them and they had taken all the necessary measures to remain hidden in the night. They had not bothered with a fire so as not to alert the cleric's companions to their presence.

The father stepped towards the sleeping forms gingerly and was about to lay a hand on the dark figure closest to him when he felt a sharp blade being pressed to his throat.

"Looks like I've caught myself a church field mouse," he heard a familiar voice saying from behind.

"Release me, Grimshaw. You've proven your point." The former Templar knight withdrew his blade from the father's throat and came around to stand before the cleric. The rest of his companions also sprang to their feet. Even in the moonlight, the father could see they were a rugged group of cutthroats. "So where did you pick up your crew?"

"Ameron has no shortage of talent, father. They're just what we need to get the job done, I assure you."

"Yes, well, let's see if you can do a better job of it this time than you did back in Ramila."

"I heard no complaints about the assassination in Ameron, father. Surely that is worth more to our master than a couple of youths with ambiguous talent at the gift."

The father gave him a sharp, admonishing look then looked around at the cutthroats. "Can they be trusted, Grimshaw?"

"Their lives belong to me. They would rather cut their own tongues out than squeal on us, ain't that so my lovelies?" he asked, turning to his crew of ruffians. Their teeth glinted white in the moonlight in answer. "Now, tell me father. When can we move on your companions? We've been riding ahead of you for the last three days waiting for your signal. Why did you wait till we reached the hills?"

"I wanted to be sure we would not be seen, Grimshaw. This is the least travelled route and it took me a while to convince the old buzzard that it was worth coming this way. Beware of that one. He's a tricky old blighter."

"Don't you worry about the old man, father. I owe that one big time for getting through my defences outside

Ramila. He won't be so lucky this time." Grimshaw's rough tone left no doubt as to his sinister intentions.

"Yeah, well you better make sure of it." The father eyed the knight and his men critically. "You will move on our unsuspecting friends tomorrow, at noon, when we will have stopped in the hills to have a bite to eat. The rocky terrain will afford you the cover you'll need to get up close. Shoot the old man and his hag sister. But don't hurt the boy or the girl. The young man has an impressionable mind and can be turned to our way of thinking. As for the girl, I'm sure our master will find a use for her emerging talent."

"Talking about the witch girl, what are we going to do about that talent of hers? Our blades are no good against witchcraft," Grimshaw growled.

"You leave the girl to me. I'll make sure she gives you no trouble. Now, get some rest and be sharp tomorrow. Our master will not be as forgiving, if you fail, as he was the last time."

"Oh yes, he was very forgiving last time." The huge knight ran his fingers across the ridges on his back and shoulders. It had taken him a week to heal from the bleeding welts that had been left on his back from his master's whip.

The father stared uneasily at the knight, a shiver running involuntarily down his spine. What had been done to the knight–and worse–could be repeated with any of the followers of the Dark. It did not pay to disappoint the Dark Lord, and his punishment was swiftly and mercilessly dealt by his vassals.

When Father Faith entered the camp, he found his companions sleeping soundly, including young Nemarchus, who would remain so for a few hours still. The potion would wear off before daybreak. The father smiled as he settled down to sleep close to the fire. In the morning he would arrange to have a little something put in Serilia's drink. With her out of the way, the other three would be no match for Grimshaw and his cutthroats.

Nem felt his shoulder being shaken and awoke instantly. He clutched at his head which throbbed painfully, and waited for his vision to clear. When it did so, he found Nestor staring at him with eyes matching the morning blue sky.

"How long have I been asleep?" he groaned, the pain in his head still strong.

"Oh, I don't know, Nem. I only woke about a couple of hours ago, just before daybreak. Come, no harm has been done. I've checked on the rest and they're alright, though we all need to be more careful in the future. Being on watch is a serious task, Nem. Our lives depend on the one who guards us while we sleep." The admonition in his voice was gentle, which made Nem feel even worse.

"I know, Nestor," Nem answered guiltily. "It won't happen again."

"Alright, lad, now help me get the rest awake. We have a trying day ahead of us."

When they had woken the rest of the group, Emeralda placed a pot on the fire and prepared tea for everyone whilst Nestor brought out some biscuits, crusty bread, and dried fruit from their saddle bags.

"Good day to you, father." Nestor approached the cleric who was bent over a cup of tea Emeralda had placed in his hand.

"Yes it is a fine morning, is it not?" The cleric turned, beaming one of his merry smiles at him. "Emeralda has been kind enough to prepare some aromatic tea for us. I'll take this cup to young Serilia. Please help yourself to some. I've tried it. It's quite tasty."

"I'm sure it is, father." Nestor returned his smile. "My sister makes a strong brew and is particularly fond of esselberry tea. Here, let me take that to Serilia whilst you get a bite to eat."

The father's smile became tainted, but then he seemed to recover and handed the cup to Nestor. "Yes, I believe I'll help myself to the fine breakfast Emeralda has prepared for us. For some reason I'm feeling ravenous this morning."

Nestor made his way to Emeralda and collected two more cups of tea before moving on to Serilia. He handed over her cup then returned to the campfire. There, Nem and the father were already chewing on some fruit and some of the meat that had remained from the previous night's meal.

"This is very good still." Nem lifted one of the biscuits Emeralda had baked before they had left Ameron.

"Yes, they will keep for a few more days," Emeralda informed him. "Dried cereals and such foodstuffs usually last a week or more."

"Here, father, have another," Nestor said, offering one of the steaming cups of tea to the cleric, before settling down to join the group at breakfast.

When the companions had finished with their meal, they struck camp and packed their belongings in their saddle bags. They were about to set off for the hills, when Nestor suggested the group remain a while whilst he and Nem went hunting, for he argued that in the hills game would not be so plentiful and they were running out of supplies. Father Faith was reluctant to agree to the delay but, unable to find a good enough reason to oppose Nestor's decision, submitted to his wishes in the end.

"Don't worry, father, we will travel into the hills in time to eat lunch there," Nestor assured him.

The father paced nervously about the camp as the minutes wore on into hours and as the sun began to rise into the cloudy skies. Whereas the previous night had been clear, the north wind had pushed long trailing white clouds across the hills during the morning and the grey fringes to the clouds promised rain. Emeralda busied herself with collecting berries and leaves which she could use for the preparation of their meals, and Serilia was sent out to forage for dry wood to use for the fire.

When Serilia returned to the campsite, the father made his way towards her.

"How are you feeling, child?" he asked, giving her a scrutinizing look.

"Quite well, Father Faith," she replied. "I must admit, this walking through the foot of the hills revitalizes one's spirits."

"Indeed, my child," the father agreed, though he looked puzzled as he pulled his hand wearily across his sweaty brow.

Serilia looked at him intently. "Father Faith, are you feeling alright? You look a bit pale."

"I'm alright, my child. I'm just feeling a bit fatigued, that is all. It seems that I've had a bit too much of the fresh mountain air. I'll join your aunt by the campfire to regain my strength. Maybe a little rest will help."

"Yes, father, I'll tell aunt Emeralda to prepare some more tea for you."

It was almost midday before Nestor and Nem returned with two hares hanging from their belts. They walked into the camp and laid their game on a napkin Emeralda had provided. When they had finished wrapping their quarry in the clean cloth they placed it on Nestor's saddle.

"What's the matter with him?" Nestor asked, pointing at the cleric who was sound asleep next to the campfire.

"Father Faith fell asleep about an hour ago," Emeralda informed him. "He was complaining that he felt drained of his strength."

"I bet he did," Nestor answered cruelly, bending close to the cleric. "Out cold like a sleeping infant," he murmured in a soft voice, as he placed a hand on the father's hair and curled his fingers around it.

"Nestor, what are you doing?" Emeralda asked, a slight tremor entering her voice.

In answer, Nestor yanked at the father's hair. It peeled off his scalp. Emeralda gasped as Nestor held the toupee aloft for all to see. Then he bent over once more and grabbed at the cleric's long beard and pulled. The long hairs came off leaving behind a neatly and closely cropped beard.

"I knew I had seen him before," Nestor said, pulling the cleric's shirt open and revealing the bands of cloth that had been wrapped around his mid-section to make him look plump. He turned to his companions who had gathered round to witness the father's identity being exposed. "Allow me to introduce you all to Father Prudent, a snake of a man, who is responsible for spreading false rumours about queen Paula of Ramila, and who I have no doubt is guilty of aiding the culprits responsible for the assassination of King Philander of Ameron."

The companions remained dumbstruck. Emeralda was the first to recover. "And you left us for an entire morning with him? Nestor, by your admission, this is a very dangerous man."

"This is why I had to act carefully, Emeralda, so as not to rouse his suspicions. Serilia, my dear, be so kind as to bring the father's travel sack close." Serilia went swiftly to the mule and returned shortly after with the cleric's sack. "Emeralda, have a rummage through his belongings and tell me if you recognize some sort of potion in there."

Indeed, after a quick search, Emeralda pulled out a violet vial and removed the cork to sniff at the contents. "Phew," she said, pinching her nose and making a face of disgust. "Forkleaf! It's a hypnotic made from the juices of the leaves of a certain type of spruce. How much did you give him?"

Nestor smiled mischievously. "I did not measure out the quantities, exactly." Then, in answer to Emeralda's confused stare, "I switched Serilia's cup with the father's this morning."

"You mean that was meant for me?" Serilia asked, in a shocked voice. Nestor nodded in reply.

"How did you know about all this, Nestor?" Emeralda gazed at him in wonder.

"Last night, when Serilia handed the watch over to Nem, I remained awake, for I had a premonition that something dubious was about to happen now that we were getting close to the hills. The father had been too insistent about choosing this route, so I've been on my guard ever since.

"Shortly after Nem drowsed to sleep, no doubt suffering the effects of the forkleaf poison you just discovered, Father Prudent got up from his sleeping spot and made his way to Nem. After making sure the boy was fast asleep, he vanished into the hills. I followed at his heels till, an hour later, he came across his companions. They're waiting for us in the hills right this moment.

"I overheard Father Prudent speaking with Grimshaw–"

"Grimshaw!" Serilia uttered in shock.

"Yes, it seems our villain knight found a way to circumvent us on our way here and is waiting to ambush us, with five others. Grimshaw was boasting, last night, of how he had successfully carried out the murder of King Philander."

"Why, that's absolutely horrid, Nestor." Emeralda's blue eyes were wide and nervous looking. "Let's not wait here any longer. We need to leave *now.*"

"I couldn't agree more, sister. Nem, be a good lad and fetch me that rope I have hanging from my saddle."

"What do you intend to do with him, Nestor?" Emeralda asked. "Why not just leave him here, and we can be on our way?"

"No, sister. I'm going to travel with you part of the way south, then the father and I are going to make a trip to Ameron, whilst you and the youngsters make your way around the hills to Hendon."

"Ameron!"

"Yes, we have to halt a war which is going to be fought on false pretences."

When Nestor had tied Father Prudent's ankles and wrists together, he and Nem hurled the cleric across his mule like a sack of potatoes and the group set out at a canter in the direction they had come.

"We need to travel as fast as possible for the first few days," Nestor shouted from atop Brigadier's back. The mule was trailing behind him from a rope Nestor had tied to the beast's bridle. "It won't be long before Grimshaw realizes something has gone awry with their plan and will come after us. We can't afford to let him catch up with us this time. Maybe the rain will cover some of our tracks." The approaching clouds were turning a darker grey and there was a moistness to the air.

The wet spell had lasted for three days whilst the group moved sluggishly south. On the fourth day, Nestor bade his farewells to the group. He felt uneasy about leaving his companions to make their way on their own, but it could not be helped. He had to get Father Prudent to Ameron in a hurry, whilst there was still time. In any event, the rain would have washed away their tracks, he hoped. Every day he had let the group move on ahead whilst he doubled back to make sure they were not being followed. So far, he had not caught sight of any pursuers.

Nestor tugged at the mule's reins and brought it closer to his steed. Brigadier laid back his ears and bared his teeth at the mule, not liking the proximity of the other animal. But he settled down after Nestor placed his hand on the gelding's nose and spoke to it softly. Nestor had a way with animals, something he had passed on to his grandchildren. He exchanged a flat look with the cleric. He dismounted and approached the father with care. The cleric had tried once or twice to break away from the group, but Nestor had overpowered him every time. For punishment, Father Prudent had been denied water for the rest of those days. He didn't think the cleric would try anything again, but it wouldn't hurt to be cautious.

"We will make camp by those trees," Nestor pointed at a group of pinewoods. "It's as good a spot as any. In any case, it will be dark soon."

The cleric put his leg over his mule and landed on the ground beside Nestor. He made his way wordlessly towards the trees.

That suits me just fine, Nestor thought. *I prefer a night without conversation. It will give me the chance to get some much needed sleep*. When he had been with the group, he had been forced to spend most of his nights watching over them. Now there was no reason to be so cautious. After they ate, Nestor gagged and tied the cleric up firmly. Then he lit his pipe and sat puffing smoke rings into the night. He stared up at the sky that had cleared of clouds. Both moons shone down upon him. He cast his gaze around the plain, wondering if they were too conspicuous. He was satisfied with the cover the trees afforded. As long as they kept in the shadows, they would not stick out like a mole hill in the fields.

On the sixth day of their travels, they arrived without incident at the city gates of Ameron. Nestor was surprised to find that all the inhabitants of the city were still in place. Not a single soldier had marched west. He made his way on foot through the busy streets of Leonium's capital city. The Amerons carried on with their daily chores as if the threat of war was not looming over them. Nestor tried to be inconspicuous and had dressed the cleric and himself in dark cloaks to conceal their faces. He also held a dagger to the priest's ribs, *"in case you get any fancy ideas"*, he had promised him.

They moved in the shadows, keeping away from the main flow of people. Nestor sighted a beggar close to one of Ameron's municipal buildings where the city taxmen resided.

"Good day to you." Nestor dropped a few copper coins in the beggar's hat.

The beggar looked at him and grinned showing his three remaining front teeth. "A good day to you too, kindly sir," he said.

"Tell me," Nestor said. "How is it that the city soldiers have not marched west yet? I thought Commander Georgile was preparing to ride forth to Ramila."

"Preparations have been made, sir, but just when the army was ready to move out, the order was given for the soldiers to remain at their posts and be at the ready."

A *strange turn of events*. "Thanks all the same for the information." Nestor nodded to the beggar and urged the cleric forward with a prod to his ribs.

Nestor was determined to get to the church grounds. They were at the west side of the city. They did not need to go very far before they reached the domed structure surrounded by a ten foot wall allowing entry through a wide iron gate that looked towards the city centre. After he had made a few enquiries, Nestor was shown to the primate's quarters. He stepped into the primate's office and found the cleric sitting alone at his desk.

"Primate Karat." Nestor kept his dagger to Father Prudent's ribs as he nodded to the Ameron primate.

"Nestor! I am pleased to see you." Primate Karat beamed a smile at him. "Last time we met, you and your group were making preparations to leave Ameron in a hurry." Then Karat's attention was drawn towards the priest by Nestor's side. "Father Prudent, you returned earlier than I anticipated. Did you complete your mission to Seldavia?"

Father Prudent was about to speak but Nestor pressed the tip of his blade into his ribs. "I've instructed Father Prudent not to speak unless I give him permission to do so." Nestor said, staring at Primate Karat with frosty blue eyes.

"What is the meaning of this?" the primate asked, worry creasing his brow as he looked uneasily at Nestor, the father, and back at Nestor again.

"You preach that confession cleanses the soul, Your Eminence," Nestor said, holding the primate's gaze. "In Father Prudent's case, it could not be any truer. Tell him!" Nestor hissed, placing his dagger to the cleric's throat. "The truth," he added, placing pressure on the tip so Prudent's eyes bulged.

"Have you gone mad?" Primate Karat shouted, as he stood and backed away from Nestor's blade. "I could have you in chains in an instant, sir."

"Your Eminence," Nestor said in a dangerous tone of voice. "The father and I have gotten to know each other quite well over the past few days. I'm afraid he has misled you. Listen carefully to what he has to say before you act in haste."

Primate Karat looked at Nestor and his dagger, then at the man that had served him faithfully for so many years. "Father Prudent. Please explain what this is all about."

The father looked at his superior with an expressionless face. When Nestor pressed the blade harder, blood began to trickle from his throat. That seemed to disturb the cleric somewhat. "I was on my way to complete the task you gave me, Your Eminence, when this mad man attacked me and ..."

Nestor punched the cleric in the ribs and grasped Prudent's hair, pulling back his head so his throat was bare to the blade. "Tell him the truth, you two-faced bustard, or I swear I will gut you like the swine you are right here and now."

The cleric swallowed a couple of times, blood still dripping from his cut. He looked at Primate Karat, who was waiting anxiously to hear what he had to say. Father Prudent began to laugh hysterically. When he regained his composure he smirked at his superior. "We fooled you Karat. We fooled you all. You sent the princess away and sentenced her mother to death for a crime she did not commit. The king was slain by my own men. Queen Paula had no involvement in the matter. No matter. It's too late for you to do anything now. The Dark Master's time is approaching. In the west the Warlock's forces will have overpowered Alacavia's futile resistance. And then the Dragon Lord will come for all those who do not bend knee to him. Don't worry yourself though. Ameron's aid in getting rid of Ramila will not go unnoticed. And I will put in a good word for you when my master has seized control of Leonium. After all, *you* are chiefly responsible for setting Ameron against Ramila. Without your aid none of this would have come to pass."

Primate Karat was left speechless. His face went pale like the bones of a corpse. He slouched in his chair and stared at the father in disbelief. "How is this possible? Why would you do such a thing, father?"

"Why else do you think, Karat? What have you managed to achieve all these years serving a non-existent god? Whereas the Dark Lord is real, Karat. And he rewards his followers well. For those who stand against him, the punishment will be severe." Father Prudent still wore a self-satisfied smirk on his face as he looked down upon the primate haughtily.

Primate Karat turned to Nestor, fuming with anger. "We must inform Georgile at once of this traitor's acts. We have greatly wronged the queen and must seek her forgiveness and her reinstatement to the throne. We still have a chance to right this error. We are fortunate that you discovered Prudent's involvement in the king's assassination. Thank Athud our army has not yet been commanded to march against Ramila. Come Nestor, if you please. We need to seek audience with Commander Georgile at once!"

They made their way hastily out of the church grounds and headed under an escort of a dozen Templar Knights towards the Ameron palace. It was not long before the group arrived before the palace gates and was admitted into the grounds. The Templar Knights escorted their primate until they arrived at the throne room doors and remained outside whilst he, Nestor and Father Prudent were granted entry.

They found Georgile sitting on the lion throne of Ameron surrounded by the royal councillors and the royal guard. As they approached, Georgile motioned for the councillors to leave till only his guard was left in the throne room and Grand Master Samarass.

Primate Karat nodded his head ever so slightly, refraining from bowing which he reserved for when he was in the presence of a king. "My lord Georgile. Is it not too soon for you to be sitting on your cousin's throne? We have not had a coronation ceremony yet."

Georgile showed his teeth to the primate as he wore a scornful smile without warmth. "Perhaps it's time we had one then so we can get the whole business over and done with."

"I'm afraid we may never get the chance, my lord," the primate answered with a solemn face.

"Whatever do you mean, Primate Karat?" Georgile's smile withered and was replaced by a glare. "Get on with it man! What is the purpose of your visit?"

Primate Karat cleared his throat and pointed at Father Prudent. "I believe you remember Father Prudent from the court proceedings where we ruled that Queen Paula was guilty of orchestrating our king's assassination?"

"Yes, I remember Father Prudent. What of it?"

"Well, I've just heard the father confess how he was responsible for organizing the king's assassination and that the queen is completely innocent of all charges."

Georgile's face went pale then flushed a deep red. He rose from the throne and walked slowly towards the primate. "Interesting piece of news, Karat, but it has come a trifle late, wouldn't you say?"

"How so, my lord?"

"What do you think will happen if we approach Queen Paula and admit that we judged her wrongly? How long will either of us last when she returns to power?"

"We were not aware of this treachery before, my lord. It was a mistake. We acted in the interest of our king. We were not to know that the queen was innocent."

"Oh? I am not as sure as you are, my dear primate, that the queen will be as forgiving as you believe. We both betrayed her trust, and no matter how we present our case, she will not be convinced of our having acted purely in our king's interest." Georgile looked at Father Prudent, Nestor and lastly at Samarass. He returned to sit on the throne.

"No, my dear primate. I am done with bowing my head to Paula of Ramila. The seat of Ameron belongs to me now, and nobody is going to take it away from me."

Primate Karat looked as though he had swallowed a toad. He looked back at Samarass, to make sure that he was not the only one who had heard what had just transpired, then his back stiffened as he turned to confront Georgile once more. "The church cannot condone this behaviour, Lord Georgile. You must relinquish your command of Ameron and return the kingdom to its rightful ruler. I demand that you act accordingly!"

"You are in no position to make demands, Karat," Georgile answered in a menacing voice.

The primate's face turned red beneath his greying beard. "You are not the rightful ruler of Ameron, Georgile! With the queen you have a chance at redemption. If you move against me and the church you will not be given the same chance."

Samarass interrupted, clearing his throat. "I'm sorry to inform you, Your Eminence, that you no longer have the authority to threaten Lord Georgile with retribution from the Holy Seat of Ameron."

Karat looked at the fox-like expression on the grand master's face to ascertain whether he was speaking in jest. He harrumphed. "Samarass, have you gone completely mad, sir?"

"No, Karat." Now Samarass's face was wolf-like as he snarled at the cleric. "By the power invested in me by the patriarchy of Leonium, I place you under arrest, Primate Karat!"

The primate looked as though he was about to explode. "On what charge?" he bawled.

"On the suspicion of having collaborated in the murder of our king. By your own admission, your accomplice, Father Prudent, was involved. Guards, seize them!" The guards snapped to attention and proceeded briskly till they held the two clerics and Nestor firmly by the arms. "Throw them in the dungeons!"

"That's outrageous! You will never get away with this, Georgile!" Primate Karat was trying to heave his large frame away from the guards as he and his companion were escorted away together with Prudent.

"I think I already have." Georgile shared a wicked smile with Samarass as the primate was led away.

"What a delightful stroke of luck," Samarass said with glee, as the throne room doors slammed shut behind the prisoners.

"Are you sure we have enough to hold the primate?" Georgile did not sound so convinced.

"Now that we have him in our clutches, we will be able to keep him there until he is forgotten. Once we spread rumours of his involvement in the king's murder, his own mother will renounce him."

"Shouldn't we order an investigation to find out the truth about Philander's death?" Georgile eyed the grand master carefully.

"There is a saying, my lord," Samarass answered in a cold voice.

"Oh?"

"Yes. The saying goes that it is sometimes better to leave matters alone when you have profited from someone else's misfortune. When you poke muddy waters you may inadvertently draw out the viper that bit your enemy."

Georgile swallowed, averting his gaze from the grand master's frosty stare.

♦ CHAPTER 31 ♦

Captivity

That night the princess had a fitful sleep. She woke the next day with a headache and feeling nauseous. She barely touched her breakfast of hard bread, smelly cheese and lukewarm tea.

Then Kakledur came for her. "Come on, plain dweller!" the man yapped at her. "Master's calling for you. You know how he hates to be kept waiting."

She was led swiftly through the series of passages carved out of the fortress rock which led up towards the throne room. They entered and Adelayne stopped beside Prince Armend who had also been summoned.

"You have arrived. Excellent!" Zarzbudin seemed to be in good cheer this morning. He was dressed in his customary maroon cloak with the upturned collar and the red dragons embroidered down the front. In his right hand he held his staff which was crowned by the figurine of the golden dragon. In his left he held a diptych with silver gilding and a golden clasp that could only be opened using a key. Beside him stood the tall nymph commander, his hair falling around his shoulders like a lion's mane. Barack was looking slightly apprehensive, as if he was preparing for something.

For a fleeting moment, Adelayne had the terrifying thought that they might be readying to go ahead with their war campaign, but then she remembered Barack saying that there were still a few matters to be settled.

"Now that you're all here we can begin our trip west to Dagorhind."

Adelayne's heart missed a beat. "Why are we going to Dagorhind?" she asked, fearing the worst.

"Aah, I wouldn't want to ruin the surprise, princess. Suffice to say that I want you to be witness to a tumultuous event that will affect us all."

Always Zarzbudin spoke in riddles. It was one of the things Adelayne found most annoying about him. They were led to the opening at the far end of the throne room where three red forms crouched in waiting. Barack straddled the largest dragon and pulled Adelayne up with one hand to sit behind him. Zarzbudin sat alone on another red dragon which Adelayne realized, by the shape of her smaller head, was a female. Lizelle, a nymph commander Adelayne had seen once before in Zarzbudin's hall, straddled the third together with Prince Armend.

They took off with a flap of red wings and headed west with the cold wind blowing in their faces. Dragons fly at incredible speeds so it was not long before the three reds had cleared the mountains and were descending the western slopes towards a deep green forest.

Adelayne cast her gaze beyond the forest to the blue of the Nerus Ocean. It was good to be away from the confines of the fortress, even if this luxury was afforded her on the back of one of Zarzbudin's beasts. She clutched her arms involuntarily tightly about Barack's muscular torso. Under any other condition she would not have allowed herself to be so close to her arch enemy. Her skin crawled at his touch. However, she was several thousand feet in the air with only the dragon between her legs and a plunge to her death, so she held on. The wind was catching her hair and blowing it behind her together with her cloak. She felt alive once more. She missed her dragon, Assima, but she did not dare to call to her; they were in the heart of the warlock's territory now.

As they began their gradual descent, Adelayne peered at the legendary city of Dagorhind.

They alighted in a courtyard surrounded by tall pyramids. Zarzbudin explained, for Armend's and Adelayne's benefit, that they were in the ceremonial part of the city where the leaders of Dagorhind were laid to rest. Apparently, at the top of each pyramid–there were four altogether aligned around the central courtyard like the points of a compass–were rectangular temples where one could find the coffins of past kings.

They left the dragons behind at the courtyard and made their way towards the eastern pyramid. Adelayne and the prince stared dumbfounded at the ancient structure before them. Large stone blocks as tall as two floors and twice that in length had been used to form the sides of the pyramid. The corners of the stone blocks had been eroded away by the passage of time but otherwise they were largely intact. Adelayne wondered what manner of engineering had been employed by the Ancients to transport and place them in position. The stairs they were using to climb the pyramid were carved into the stone and led steadily upwards to the pinnacle which was so high they could barely discern the temple at the apex. The braziers standing like sentries bordering the steps had been lit. They approached the top out of breath and became aware of a group of figures standing waiting for them.

Adelayne stared at the figures who wore red cloaks with hoods well drawn over their heads to conceal their features. One of them broke away from the rest and stepped closer to the warlock. He fell to one knee and bowed his head with arms outstretched above his hood. Adelayne noticed the figure was holding a small box with the lid left open revealing a golden key. Zarzbudin took the key and placed it in the lock of his large diptych. A distinct click was heard as the key turned and the clasp fell open. The warlock murmured a few words to the hooded figure. They were led towards the temple entrance.

They entered the temple leaving behind the wailing sound of the wind. It was stuffy and substantially warmer inside. Torches cast their light revealing the multitude of inscriptions and paintings on the walls. Adelayne did not recognize this ancient form of scripture which was largely hieroglyphic. She marvelled at the paintings that showed people at work: some were fishing in the river with their long wooden crafts, a few were foraging fruits and nuts, whilst others were tending their flocks. The Dagorhind's ancestors, it seemed, were no different from any other nations. However, as they moved further into the temple the pictures on the walls changed in context. These paintings were depicting scenes from wars which the Dagorhinds had waged against their enemies.

Some were very graphic in their outline, showing severed arms and limbs and sparing no thought to the feelings of revulsion they provoked on onlookers–in fact it was as though the creators of these images were deliberately trying to be gruesome. The group halted at the far end of the temple before an ancient sarcophagus. The room was well lit. The lid to the coffin had been partly moved to one side so a gaping black hole peeked through the opening. A chair carved from stone stood close to the coffin alone in the centre of the room that was bare of any other adornments; even the walls were plain yellow rock.

The figures in the red robes–there were a dozen of them–took positions around the chair and began to hum in low deep voices. They removed their hoods revealing their shaved scalps. Zarzbudin beckoned to Lizelle to pull Adelayne and the prince over to the far end, as far away from the chair as possible. Another fist of red-robed figures surrounded the prince and princess.

Zarzbudin used his staff to carve an image on the sandy floor. Adelayne peered from above the shoulder of one of the robed figures at the inscription the warlock was forming on the floor. It was a five pointed star enclosed in a circle with symbols drawn within each point of the star. Upon completing the inscription, the warlock sprinkled silver grains of sand in it and set fire to it with his wand. A bright flash exploded from the spot then burned away just as quickly. The inscription was now pulsating with an amber light as if alive.

"Go, Commander Barack." Zarzbudin pointed at the chair. "Your destiny awaits you."

The nymph commander looked with trepidation at the chair, as if it held his doom. But they had been over the ritual with the warlock many times before. He knew what sacrifices were required of him to reach the next level. Zarzbudin had promised him power beyond his expectations. It was time to seize what was on offer. The commander sat on the chair and allowed two of the robed figures to strap him down firmly. He was held by the wrists, ankles and neck; around his waist had been placed a wide belt. There was no escape for him now.

Zarzbudin stepped into the pulsating inscription he had drawn on the ground. He began to read from his book and held the staff up high till the golden dragon of his staff glowed with a red light. As the warlock continued his incantation the light spread down his arm and engulfed him. Then it swelled outwards enclosing him in a cocoon with its base contained within the circle he had drawn on the ground around the star symbol.

Something was happening.

Adelayne felt her skin crawling and a shift in the air. Even though the gift was dormant within her she could still sense the warlock's use of it. The light of the torches was spluttering as if a wind was blowing through the room, though the cloaks of the robed figures remained motionless. A bright shaft of light burst forth from the sarcophagus, where the lid had been partially opened. The light grew in intensity till Adelayne was forced to cower with her arms around her head to shield her eyes. There was a loud cracking noise and the lid flew open and was hurled across the room landing only a few feet away from where Adelayne and the prince stood. One of the robed figures lay motionless beneath the lid. He had been killed instantly.

A moaning sound drew Adelayne's gaze towards the depths of the coffin. A red ethereal shape with a beak, wings and a tail emerged from the sarcophagus and hung above the warlock screaming its discontent at having been awakened from its slumber. It grew in size till it seemed it would fill the entire room. The robed figures' voices now began to rise in tempo till they were almost screeching.

The red being uttered a cry that froze Adelayne's heart. Its fiery eyes were trained on the crouching form of Zarzbudin who averted his gaze from the being. The torches in the room spluttered and winked out. They would have been thrown into darkness but the ghostly light emanating from the creature of the sarcophagus bathed its surroundings in blood red. The warlock's shield burnt intensely.

"Who dares to meddle with the spirit of Rolgath?" the creature howled. The sound was as that of a hundred voices of the dead screaming whilst the flames of hell burnt their souls away.

"I am Zarzbudin." The warlock stood tall and defiant before the spirit. "I am a descendant of Dagorhind and a wielder of the red flame of Kaldarass. You will bow down to my will demon of Rolgath, by the laws set down before me by Zarrtoul the usurper." Then the warlock read a few more lines from the book he held in his left hand.

The demon shrieked in dismay as it pounded on Zarzbudin's cocoon shield without effect. Then, unable to harm the warlock, it looked around the room searching for other victims to satisfy its rage. Its gaze passed over Adelayne. She shuddered in horror. She could not have moved even if she was not being restrained by her captors. The demon flicked out a forked tongue at the robed figures that stood around the chair wherein sat the nymph commander. Its tongue licked the robed figures' bare heads. One by one the heads exploded in the tongue's wake filling the room with brain and skull fragments.

Then the demon became aware of Barack's presence and bent down to peer at the nymph commander with its fiery eyes. Barack howled with fear and wrestled with his bonds but was unable to break free. The commander turned a horror-filled countenance on the warlock. The whites of his eyes were showing and he searched the warlock's face pleadingly. "Save me master," he pleaded, his lower lip trembling. Sweat poured from his brow down to his neck. "I no longer care for what is on offer." He clenched and unclenched his fists, wriggling in his confinement thrashing his head from side to side. "I feel its hot breath on my soul," he gasped as tears streamed from his eyes. "It hungers for me. Don't repay my homage to you thus." The nymph commander was weeping like a babe as the demon crouched before him, an evil snarl disfiguring its gruesome features.

"Stand firm, Commander Barack!" the warlock snapped, holding out his staff at the nymph warlord to draw his attention. "In moments you will be repaid a thousand fold for the service you have rendered."

"What is this morsel you have provided for me, manling!" the demon snapped, its tongue flicking in and out of its fiery beak as it peered down at its prey.

Zarzbudin resumed his incantation then cast a beam of light at the demon. It shrieked its unearthly cry once more till it seemed the temple walls would surely collapse from the tremors of its howling voice. The room shook as if it were being rocked by an earthquake. The demon stamped its feet and flung itself time and again against the warlock's cocoon.

But it held.

Finally the demon unable to escape the beam of light emanating from the warlock's staff began to thrash its wings and tail against the walls. Pieces of rock were showered down at Adelayne and the robed figures around her who crouched in fear, having witnessed the fate that had befallen their comrades.

"Spirit of Rolgath!" Zarzudin called out in a reverberating voice that echoed off the walls of the room. "Answer the call of Zarrtoul your master. Accept the offering I have laid before you." He pointed at Barack who was wriggling on the chair in torment. "Your master has need of you. Come. The time of your reawakening is nigh."

The demon screamed repeatedly as it began to shrink in size. Then something happened that Adelayne would remember for the rest of her life. The demon turned on Barack and tore into his chest. Barack thrashed about wildly but there was no escape. The demon pushed its head into Barack's chest then folded its wings as it drew the rest of its body into the commander. Last to disappear was its pointed tail. Barack lay limp on the chair, hanging from his bonds.

The group remained in eerie silence staring at the mutilated form of the nymph. A sob escaped Lizelle's throat. "Master, what have you done to him?"

"Silence!" the warlock spat at her. He was still surrounded by his defensive shield.

Barack lay like a broken toy on the chair.

Adelayne let out a cry of shocked surprise as a tremor ran through the commander's body. Barack's head which was slumped forward on his chest came up slowly. He straightened in his chair and stared ahead at his master.

"Barack," the warlock called out. "Is the transformation complete, my faithful servant?"

Tears rolled down the commander's cheeks. "It burns master. Pleaase...help me...get it out of me...plea—" His voice was cut off as his body convulsed violently. First one then the other wrist were freed as he tore his arms away from his bonds with inhuman strength. Then he clutched at his throat and tore away the restraint. He unclasped the waist belt and stood squarely facing the warlock. Where a gaping hole in his chest had been was now an angry wound.

"You are not Zarrtoul the usurper!" He pointed an accusatory finger at the warlock.

"Barack?" the warlock enquired.

"Barack no longer has claim over this body, necromancer. I am Rolgath of the House of Dralco, Red Knight and Demon Lord of the Dargulheind." As he uttered the words, the rest of the red-robed figures knelt facing the demon knight. "Let all earthly men hear my name and bow in terror for none who stand before me may live. The mothers of this earth will bleat like ewes in the field as I tear their sons' limbs from their bodies.

"I am the wielder of the sword of flame with which I sear men's souls. I have returned to claim my lost heritage."

"Hear me Red Demon of Dargulheind!" Zarzbudin said in a mighty voice. A smile of triumph formed on his lips. "I am Zarzbudin, your life giver and your master."

The demon knight turned a cold-eyed stare at the warlock. "You are but a mere man. I have no master here on this earthly realm. Flee before me, manling, lest I take your head as my first trophy."

"I may not be Zarrtoul himself, mighty Rolgath, but I am a son of Dargulheind and the new ruler of this realm. You swore to serve your lord, Zarrtoul, and his descendants. I am such a one and I demand that you honour your pledge or I will send you back to the depths of Ushud's realm from whence you came."

They remained staring at one another. Adelayne and the rest of the group held their breath. It was apparent that the demon and the warlock were locked in a duel of wills.

Zarzbudin felt the burning presence of the demon scratching against his shield. It was trying to tear away at his defences and consume him. He kept muttering the chant from Zarrtoul's book. It was all that kept the demon at bay. To an outside observer the warlock and the demon knight appeared to be simply standing still, as if mesmerized, inactive like statues. But any gifted would have been aware of the battle waging between the dragon lord and the demon. They dealt blows at one another not visible to the naked eye. The demon was strong but it was held by the chains binding it to its previous master, Zarrtoul.

The demon fought with all the might it could master. It knew that it would not be able to overcome the necromancer–not whilst he used Zarrtoul's spells against him. There was another reason for his struggle, however. He needed to test the boundaries of the man's strength, needed to search out his weaknesses; all men had a weakness that could be exploited. Zarzbudin was no different. He was talented. Rolgath sensed that he was adept in the use of several agents of the gift. As a servant of the Dark, he had a firm command of that agent. Rolgath also sensed a strength in the Earth and Spirit agent. Zarzbudin's strongest point was his use of the Fire agent–he was indeed a skilled wielder of the flame of Kaldarass. Perhaps that was also where his weakness might lie; his arrogance and his confidence in his abilities as a sorcerer.

Rolgath ceased his struggle against the warlock. Zarzbudin moved, breaking the spell that had kept him and the demon locked in battle. Adelayne heard Lizelle and the rest of the group let out the breath they were holding.

"What is it you command, master?" Rolgath bent down on one knee.

Zarzbudin wiped the sweat from his brow and straightened placing most of his weight on his staff. He could not hide his fatigue. "Rise Red Knight. Your first task awaits you. Leonium is ours for the taking."

Rolgath rose and glared at the group huddled to one side of the room. The robed figures bowed their heads to their lord. Lizelle also cowered before the man whose only resemblance to her lover was the human shell he wore. Then Rolgath's eyes passed over Armend, who cringed before him, and came finally to rest on Adelayne. She shivered, trying to peer back defiantly at the man, but Barack no longer stared back at her. This demon brought terror to her heart and made her limbs weak like a newborn calf's.

Adelayne was wrenched away from that gaze by Zarzbudin who held her arm firmly whilst he led the procession away from the tomb. Zarzbudin gave her one of his reptilian smiles. "Enjoyed the show, Your Highness? There's more to come. Barack informed me before he was taken from us that a friend of yours is making his way to my fortress as we speak." Adelayne's heart jumped to her throat. *Could it be true?* "We will offer him the same hospitality we dealt you, princess."

Adelayne tried to pull away from the warlock's grasp but Rolgath was close behind with Lizelle and the rest of the red cloaks.

***

"Serilia, why are we heading in the opposite direction to the city?" Nem nudged his mare forward so he could speak more freely with his companion.

"Aunt Emeralda and I have been over this already." Serilia proceeded to make her way forward without giving him a second glance.

"Well, do you mind letting me in on your decision?" Nem asked sourly. It was a grey day with the promise of rain in the heavy clouds above; his mood was sultry like the weather.

"It's quite simple, really. We've decided that it's not yet time for us to go to my parents in Aldorn. It would only upset them gravely if we arrived without Theo. So we've agreed to travel by sea back to Ameron to seek out grandfather. Then we can all make our way back to Alcavia."

Nem stared at her dumbfounded. Here they were, only a five day's ride away from Aldorn and safety, and now Serilia was proposing they hurl themselves back into the snake's pit. Anyone who had any sense was fleeing Leonium in a hurry, what with the impending war in Alcavia, and the strife between Ramila and Ameron. What Serilia was proposing was lunacy. Nem expressed his feelings over the matter.

"You don't need to come along, Foresight. There's nobody forcing you to stay with us. You can stay here in Hendon, or buy passage to Cyrus. We won't hold it against you."

Nem gave her another flat look. He felt responsible for Serilia's and her aunt's safety. Nestor had placed him in charge of the women's welfare. He wasn't about to let the old man down, or Theo. What would Theo think if he discovered that Nem had left his sister and aunt to make the hazardous journey alone? *How will he take it if I leave him stranded in Alcavia just when he might need me most?* Nem blew out his breath in an annoyed puff. "You're wrong Serilia," he admonished her. "You need me to come along. I *must* come along," he said, in a way that sounded as though he were trying to convince himself that none of his arguments could outweigh his obligation.

Serilia bent across her saddle and planted a soft kiss on his cheek. "I never doubted you for a minute."

No sooner had they arrived at Hendon's port, than they had to rush in order to board before their ship set sail. They had rented a small cabin in a cutter roughly the size of the *Sea Breeze*, only their ship, the *Tenora*, was wider in berth and had a more generous hold, being a merchantman. The captain was in a hurry to drop off his cargo in Ameron and return to Hendon, and safety. News of Philander's murder and the state of alert in Leonium had spread fast to nearby Seldavia. Travellers were weary of the destinations west.

The *Tenora*, however, was not fated to arrive in Ameron. It was the second day of their voyage when they caught sight of the man of war. Serilia felt the presence of the ship's occupants almost as soon as it was sighted by the sailor on duty at the bow.

"Ship ahoy, cap'n!" They realized by the sharp edge to the sailor's voice that he was troubled by what he saw.

"Does she fly her colours, lad?" the captain yelled from the cockpit. He was a bear of a man with a weatherbeaten face hardened by a long life at sea. Covering his cheeks up to his eyes and down to his chin was a week's old stubble. Even though winter was approaching, he wore only a shirt opened at the front to reveal a hairy chest with the sleeves rolled up to his elbows; his arms were thick and hairy like the rest of him. What made a most profound impression on Serilia about the captain was the strong smell of whiskey on his breath. He had agreed to let them board his ship, though he had found it strange that there would be folk foolish enough to travel to where he was heading. He said as much but Serilia kept her silence concerning their reasons for going west.

"She flies no colours, cap'n, though by the looks of her she's not of these parts, and she's not friendly either," came the reply.

The captain motioned to his helmsman to take the wheel whilst he made his way forward so he could take a closer look at the approaching ship. Serilia was already at the gunwales well before the captain came to stand beside her.

There, ahead of them, about half a mile away was the brooding form of a battle cruiser with twin lateen sails and a predatory look to her hull which was built for speed. Her sails were full as they caught the north wind descending from the plains of Leonium; she was bearing down on the *Tenora* at an incredible speed.

"Turn about!" the captain yelled at the top of his voice. The sailors flew into action to obey the shrill command. They were not used to seeing their captain flustered. "Let out all the sails as soon as we have the wind behind us. Get a move on you curs, or this will be the last trip you ever make!"

Nem came rushing up on deck to see what all the commotion was about. He saw Serilia at the bow and moved swiftly beside her. Then, as he stared out at sea, his breath caught. "It's them, isn't it?"

Serilia simply nodded. She was unable to speak. She could feel the evil presence on the ship, now that it was looming up so close–except now there was no mage to come to her aid. She was all alone.

"We should never have left Hendon!" Nem snapped, with equal measure of annoyance and fear in his voice.

Emeralda came up to the youngsters and looked with trepidation at the approaching ship.

The captain of the *Tenora* was employing every tactic he knew to shake off his pursuer but the small cutter had no chance of outrunning the *Unrelenting Condor*.

The larger ship was almost upon them. With each gust of wind it loomed larger in their sights. The cutter was in full swing with its mainsail and two flying jibs straining at their tack. But it had to contend with the two larger lateens of the Kalkador battle cruiser that was now sailing beside them. Serilia looked up from the lower deck of the cutter and beheld the shadowed cowl of her enemy. Though she could not see his eyes beneath his hood she could feel them burning into her being. She stood transfixed. She felt her gift waiting for her call but dared not use it. Somehow she felt she would not be given the chance. In the fleeting moment she had gazed upon the dark sorcerer, she realized just how futile it was to resist.

She shuddered as she felt negative energy flowing across towards her from her opponent, like an approaching storm electrifying the surrounding air, chilling the living to their bones. He was an abomination, an entity that fed on the fear it instilled in others, so much so that Serilia almost did not notice the three cloaked forms that stood by his side. She turned to look at them and realized they created the same feelings of revulsion in her as did their master.

Several ropes were thrown over from the *Unrelenting Condor*. Sharp hooks attached to the ropes lodged and held fast on the gunwales. It was not long before the *Tenora* would be boarded. The captain barked out commands to his sailors and rushed forward to dislodge the ropes. Some he managed to throw back into the sea only to find that more were being thrown over.

The darklings descended on the cutter like a flock of crows upon a tasty morsel. The captain gathered his sailors around him as he drew his sabre in a last ditch attempt to save his ship. Swords flashed in the air as the two parties clashed. The *Tenora's* crew was hopelessly outnumbered.

"Hello, my pretty." Serilia looked up in a daze at the familiar face of the man that stood before her. "Didn't think you would see me again, did you, my sweet?"

"Here! Stay away from–" Nem's voice was cut off by a dagger held to his throat by a dark man with a red scarf tied around his head and an eye patch across one eye.

"I see you have become acquainted with my colleague, Maleb." Grimshaw grinned at the youth. "Watch out for his dagger, though. He's not shy when it comes to using it."

"What's the meaning of this?" the ship's captain bawled, just before he was kicked in the belly and forced to his knees before the rebel knight.

Grimshaw turned an enquiring gaze at his master aboard the *Unrelenting Condor*.

"Kill all on board and burn the ship," came the apathetic command. "Bring the girl to me, unharmed. She will not offer any resistance."

Serilia looked about her as the carnage unfolded. It was as if she was experiencing it all through the eyes of another, as though she had been removed from her body. Somewhere in the corner of her mind she heard a small voice screaming at her to act; but she was powerless to move against the force that had command of her will. She was paralysed to the extent that she could not move her limbs and had to be carried bodily by Grimshaw on board the warship.

She gazed at the *Tenora* as if in a dream–or a nightmare. Grimshaw's men proceeded to slaughter the crew of the small cutter ship as though they were cattle. The captain had tried to offer resistance but his sabre had been wrestled from his grasp. He was stabbed several times in the neck and belly before he toppled into the sea with a loud splash. Serilia looked around the *Tenora* one last time, anxious for any sign of Nem or her aunt, but the bodies strewn on the blood-soaked deck were unrecognisable.

"Lay her before me," ordered the High Sorcerer of the Brotherhood of the Dark. Serilia was unceremoniously flung on the dark deck of the battleship. She looked up to find she was staring into death's own face. Even in her state of paralysis, she could still feel a shudder going through her body.

"I know you!" the dark sorcerer's eyes widened as he peered at Serilia more closely. "Who would have thought I would see your familiar face on the other side of Thalagia." His words troubled Serilia deeply. *How was she acquainted with this man, this creature of the Dark?* she wondered.

"Let us feed off her, master," one of the three cloaked forms said, in a voice like the winter winds howling across a barren landscape.

"Patience, my pets," the dark sorcerer answered in a soothing voice as though he was speaking to his children. Then he turned to Serilia and grabbed her cheeks squeezing them in his hand causing her lips to pout. "These, my dear, are wraiths, wizards of the past who gave their souls to Ushud for the gift of eternal life. Behave yourself whilst you are in my custody, and you will be rewarded. If not, I will be forced to hand you over to them so they can feed on your life-force."

Then the hooded face looked up at the renegade knight. "Our work is complete here. You have done well and that will not go unnoticed. Now to the task at hand; we sail for Alcavia with all due haste. I will not leave Zarzbudin alone to collect the spoils of war."

***

He could hear the moaning of the man in the adjacent cell. The previous night they had arrived to interrogate them, to extract any further information they might divulge concerning Philander's murder. But they had been unable to offer anything more, though the interrogators used all the means at their disposal; Karat's occupation as a cleric meant little to them. Their orders had been explicit.

The man passed his tongue gingerly across his cracked lips. They had been cut in several places by their punches and were swollen. He felt the aching of his bones as well, though thankfully there were no cracked ribs.

The questions had all been the same.

"What do you know about King Philander's assassination?"

"What is your involvement with Father Prudent?"

"Who were his accomplices?"

"Who was the mastermind of their plot?"

The answers were short and did not satisfy them.

He limped over to the corner of his cell furthest from the smelly shit hole. He lifted the tin cup to his lips but it was empty. They only fed them once a day and gave them precious little water in the morning and late at night–after the interrogations.

He tried to speak but his tongue was swollen and he could not work up the spittle to utter the words. "Kar–rat," he croaked eventually. "C–an you he–ar me?" It sounded like a hoarse whisper.

From across the separating stone wall came a moan in reply. The primate was evidently delirious and was not responding. It was no use. They had been stuck in the dungeons of Ameron now for what he estimated to be a week. Nobody other than their interrogators came to visit them. Even the primate was forgotten, as though he had not spent his entire life in the service of the city and its faithful. It was a sorry state of affairs.

He shuffled over to the iron bars to try and peek through at the corridor. Blank stone walls stood on either side of him so he could not see his fellow inmates. There were several cells, he remembered faintly from when he was being dragged kicking and screaming into the dungeon. What struck him as strange was that Prudent had not been led to the cells with them.

There was a rattling of keys and he turned to the corridor entrance. He heard the murmuring of voices and a shadow was cast across the entrance bars of his cell. He moved back in fear. *Is it time for the interrogators so soon?* He gazed in expectation at the approaching shadows that were shrinking in length as the jailers came closer.

"Here's the old geeser." He heard the now familiar voice of the guard. "Can't imagine what you would want with the likes of him. Any case, that's your business."

"Your damn right, and you make sure you remember that when they ask questions." The second voice was also familiar to him, though it did not belong here. They stepped up to his bars and the second figure turned to gaze at him from within her cowl. He could not see her face except for her grinning gums which were toothless. She was dressed all in black and the hands she placed around the bars were gnarled and knobbly from old age.

"Looks like you'll be needing my help to get you out of this fix, old man. Ain't taken you long to get yourself in trouble again, has it?" she chaffed.

'Er, not meaning to sound rude...or unappreciative, but do you mind hurrying things along?' he meant to say in annoyance, but all he managed was a croak. The relief on his face, however, must have been evident for the old woman's grin widened.

"Now don't go getting yourself all flustered, dearest. Old Wecka will have you out sooner than you can say deliverance, ain't that right chief," she said, removing her cowl so she could glare at the guard.

"Alright, old woman," he answered quickly. "Keep your skirt on. A deal is a deal and you paid more than he's worth." He rummaged through his keys in a hurry and looked around in earnest at the solitary door that led into and out of the dungeon. He was straining to hear any noises coming from the other end. Finally he located the key he was looking for and placed it in the lock.

The prisoner let out the breath he was holding as he heard the click in the lock with the turning of the key. The door swung open and Wecka came to stand beside him. She touched his face gingerly and raised her hand. In it she held a waterskin. The prisoner drank greedily, spilling some of the precious liquid down his shirtfront. Then, when he had quenched his thirst, Wecka offered him her arm and led him briskly out of the cell. He grunted as he was forced to move his limbs faster than he would have liked. His entire body was aching from his cuts and bruises and every motion was causing him to wince with pain.

"Let him out as well," he said, stopping outside the primate's cell to peer inside. Karat was huddled in a corner, curled up in a ball. The prisoner called to him but the cleric continued to mumble unintelligibly, completely overcome by the punishment he had been through; what had been his previously majestic robes were now tattered rags hanging in shreds from his arms and back. His eyes were purple, swollen and sealed shut. His hair was dishevelled and dried blood and spittle hung from his grey knotted beard.

"Come along, Bones." Wecka tore him away from the primate's cell. She was surprisingly strong for one so old. "There's no helping that one. Even his own people have forsaken him. They will not fret over you for long. You are small fry to them. The primate, however, they will not release. He will be made to pay dearly for having chosen the wrong side. Such is the justice meted out by Georgile's men now he's in charge of Ameron."

Bones peered behind and stared dejectedly at the primate's cell as he was being dragged out of the dungeon. The taste of freedom would be bitter in his mouth every time he would contemplate the trials the cleric had still to go through. He prayed silently that Nerus would take pity on the cleric and offer him a swift end.

***

Theo sensed the nervousness of his companions as they approached the end of their journey. Madura had informed him that they would soon exit the tunnels and would make their way across the mountain to the warlock's fortress. It seemed the nymphs harboured an intense fear of their master and, though they were completely loyal to him, preferred to keep a safe distance from him. Zarzbudin was notorious for his magic craft which he used to great effect against his enemies but was also prone to use on his own subjects for his amusement, or for his experiments in his underground dungeons. The nymphs would not go anywhere near the fortress unless they were summoned. Theo imagined that the warlock kept the rumours alive of his ill-treatment of visitors so as to dissuade anyone from approaching his den.

They finally stepped out of the tunnel. Theo stood for a while, breathing in deeply the crisp mountain air relishing the late autumn's cool finger on his face. He looked about with pleasure at the white snow that covered their surroundings for as far as he could see. Anything was better than the grey walls of the tunnels. Then he laid eyes on it. At first he thought it was another mountain peak. Then he saw the marks where openings had been carved into the rock to form windows and the central entryway. A slender bridge arched like a dragon's spinal column over a deep chasm that led from the tunnels Theo and his party had just exited to what was unmistakably the warlock's fortress.

The company moved forward in silence, crossing the bridge carefully not daring to look down, or to come too close to the edge. Once on the other side, they stared at the two towering statues standing guard at the entrance to the fortress. They were shaped from the dark rock of the surrounding mountains in the form of dragons captured in a crouching position with mouths gaping and sharp teeth bared. Theo approached the dragon forms with apprehension. He fixed his gaze upon them. This was a sorcerer's fortress. He shuddered imagining the stone dragons coming to life to descend upon them. He looked at the rest of his companions and saw the same look of trepidation in their eyes.

"Is it safe to cross?" he asked Madura in a hushed voice, fearing any louder noise might stir the stone dragons. He gazed up at the eyes of one of the statues and immediately averted his gaze; he felt the same feelings of unease he had experienced in the presence of the Alcavian and Alunda dragons. Made of flesh or made of stone, those eyes held the same mesmerizing power–instilled the same terror.

"I do not know." Madura stood frozen where she had stepped down from the bridge. She too was staring at the stone statues, like a frightened child. "I've never been so close to the fortress before."

"Well I have." Nolath moved to the fore of the group and nodded to Kasak.

The nymph chief beckoned to the group and they moved forward towards the stone statues. As they approached, Theo noticed the intricate detail that had been used in carving the dragons from the stone. *Or had the dragons existed in the flesh before they had reverted to this form?* Theo mused. He wandered what became of dragons when they lived beyond their given one thousand years. *Is this the fate of the older dragons? If so, how had these been frozen into this crouching position of readiness?*

They passed by the statues and were still staring behind them at the large figures when they suddenly arrived before the entrance to the fortress. It was sealed by two doors so large they seemed to have been made to allow entry to giants. The gargoyle door knocker fashioned into the hideous grimacing face of an ogre was man high and unwelcoming.

Kasak knocked at the door thrice and waited for the fortress occupants to respond. There was a creaking, grating noise as of chains being drawn and locks being turned. Then, a crack appeared in the centre of the two large doors and they swung open sluggishly, their weight not allowing them to move faster. They opened barely enough to allow the visitors to enter one by one. Nobody appeared from within to acknowledge their presence. Kasak stared at Nolath who nodded back at his chief signifying it was alright to proceed.

The chief entered first followed by the aged nymph mage. After half a dozen of the nymph warriors had passed through, Theo was led forward with Roxette and Madura close behind. Theo entered through the slit in the large doors and stepped onto a cold stone floor that was completely bare of any adornments such as carpets or even a crude rug. His eyes took a while to adjust to the absence of light in the entrance hall. Torches hung from circular columns supporting arcaded vaults forming the interior. They afforded what little light they could to visitors of the fortress. The walls were as stark as the stone floor. Somewhere up above, white shafts of light filtered through the punctured walls of the mountain shell falling upon the group to remind them of the world they had left behind.

Theo felt the same claustrophobia he had experienced in the tunnels, the same crushing weight on his consciousness. Kasak barked out his commands and the nymph warriors formed two neat lines with their captives in their midst. They marched steadily forward to an arched opening at the far side of the bleak hall. When they reached the centre, Theo looked down at the stone floor and realized he was stepping on the snout of a dragon that had been carved there. He walked gingerly on the carving avoiding placing his feet anywhere near the teeth and eyes, fearing the dragon might surge from the floor and take shape. His companions also stepped swiftly to distance themselves from the carving.

Then they entered a long corridor lined with columns supporting arches on either side. Tall portraits hung from the corridor walls depicting battle scenes between red and silver dragons. On occasion the red dragons would also be shown combating blue dragons out at sea. There were fighting scenes showing a lord dressed in red armour with a dragon surmounting his helmet and shield, also forming the emblem on his breast plate. The red knight towered above his enemies bringing down a heavy sword on his opponents who grovelled with fear at his feet. Roxette stared long and hard at these portraits of the red knight and Theo imagined he could sense her searching for a weakness.

"He is truly magnificent!" The awe in the warrior nymph's voice was unmistakable. "Here and here," she said, pointing to two of the portraits. "Do you see now Theodor, how you must position your feet and your shoulders in order to deliver the death blow without losing your balance?" Roxette was speaking to him in the voice of a tutor to her apprentice once more. Theo nodded his reply.

"This is the first lesson a pupil learns when practicing the fighting arts and it is also the most important. With the passage of time and with repetitive and correct training the stance is perfected till you are able to do this." She pointed at the red knight's opponent who was felled across the chest by the red knight's masterful stroke.

"I wonder who he is, or who he might have been," Theo murmured with mixed feelings. If the Dragonmaster had such a knight at his disposal, then Alcavia was in greater peril than they originally thought. With such a warrior heading Zarzbudin's army, fear would be instilled in Alcavia's ranks. *Will King Dreyfus or his brave son Leon be able to face such a demon knight and come out of the encounter victorious?*

"The Red Knight lives no more, though it is rumoured the Witch Lord has found a way to resurrect him." Zolath came up close to peer at the portraits with Roxette and Theo. "Our new master has left nothing to fate. Alcavia will fall to our army and then the rest of Leonium. To resist the forces the Witch King has rallied unto himself is futile." He turned to rest his gaze on Theo, a small haughty smile crossing his chapped lips. "Our lord and master awaits your arrival in his mountain chamber. We would not be wise to keep him too long." Kasak pushed Theo forward with a shove at his shoulder.

They began to climb steps that led on to the higher levels of the fortress. They passed several great chambers and rooms sealed by doors, but nowhere in the fortress did they come across any of the occupants. It all added to the eerie feeling Theo had about the place. *Does the Witch Lord live alone in this mountain castle of his?* In answer to his question they finally came to a corridor where nymphs were dressed in black livery with red dragons imprinted on their left breast. The nymphs stood at attention lining either side of the corridor. At the end of the line was a double door now sealed. By the door stood several guards wearing chain mail and carrying spears in their hands and swords hanging from their belts. There were a dozen of the guards at least, whereas the rest of the nymphs were dressed in simple slacks and tunics. They most likely were the staff responsible for the care-taking of the fortress.

A skinny tall fellow with a drawn face stepped away from the group of servants and came closer to the visitors. He was dressed in plain white garments that fell loosely over his bony frame. His robe fell short of his feet revealing his knobbed ankles as he approached. "Our master has been awaiting your arrival."

The visitors stepped closer and Theo felt restraining hands being laid upon him by the nymphs in his group.

"I am Kasak, Chief of the Black Bear Clan." The Mountain nymph chief stepped forward to make the introductions. "This here is Roxette of the Clan of the Mountain Lion, a nymph daughter who was led astray but who has now returned to her people bearing a prized gift in recompense."

"The she-nymph's repentance will be confirmed by our lord. As for her prize, whether it turns out to be useful to us, or just another useless titbit to be thrown in our mines till it withers away, remains to be seen. Bring the boy closer so I may look upon him."

Theo was ushered forward by his captors till he was face to face with the skeletal nymph in the pale garments. The nymph stared back at him with dark eyes filled with inquisitive intelligence. For all the absence of living tissue on his bony frame his gaze was filled with vitality and eagerness.

"I have heard of this boy's promising talent in the gift. Who have you placed as his guardians and restrainers?"

"I, Nolath, have been charged with that task, along with my colleagues here." The elderly nymph mage stepped forward and pointed at Madura and the other gifted in their number.

"Aah, Nolath. I well remember you from our meeting three years ago when my master last required your services. But what is a magus of the Clan of the Grey Wolf doing with Chief Kasak's tribe?"

"Alas, my tribe is no more, master Kakledur. We were set upon by a pack of Orguls and I am all that is left of the tribe. Chief Kasak offered me food and the shelter his tribe could provide, and in return I have been given the task of training those nymphs in his clan that show promise in using the gift. These two are my remaining pupils. The third was killed a few days ago by Ogres."

"Chief Kasak," Kakledur said, turning to the group leader. "You and three of your warriors will be permitted to enter the master's hall, along with your captors and the three gifted in your number. The rest must remain outside."

Kasak nodded his concurrence and proceeded to choose the three warriors that would flank him when he entered the Warlock's presence. When Kakledur was satisfied that his commands had been carried out, he put his frail weight to the chamber doors and pushed them open.

They entered together without being announced.

Theo had a few moments to absorb his new surroundings. Behind him he heard the doors closing, like the doors to a prison cell being sealed shut. There, before the stone throne of his dreams, stood the Witch Lord, Master of the Dragon's Foot Mountain forces. He was dressed in his splendid robes with the ruff of his cloak raised about his head. His hair spilled over his garments down his back like the long mane of a dark stallion. He was more splendid in real life than Theo remembered him in his dreams. In his right hand he held his staff, the tall shaft made from a dark wood that was so polished by use it reflected the light from the fireplace. Surmounting the staff was the figurine of a golden dragon in flight with wings outstretched and mouth agape in a snarl, lips peeled back to reveal sharp teeth and a forked tongue protruding from its maw. A faint red glow enveloped the golden dragon signifying the Dragonmaster was in command of his gift.

"Aah, Nolath. At last our honoured guests have arrived, and not a moment too soon I might add. I have some surprises lined up for this visit. Come, bring our visitors closer so I may become better acquainted with them."

The group was led forward by Kakledur then genuflected before the Warlock. Theo tried to remain erect but was punched in the stomach by one of Kasak's warriors and pulled to a kneeling position by Roxette.

The incident was not lost on the warlock, however. "I see our gifted Islander has the spark of defiance burning in him. We will soon take care of that as we have done with our other guests." He clapped his hands twice. The doors to the hall opened from behind to admit an addition to the group.

Theo turned around and looked with puzzlement at the scantily dressed maiden that was being escorted into the throne room. Her face was thin matching the rest of her frame, as though she had been fasting for days. As she drew closer he noticed the absence of life in her eyes. She did not respond to his look but peered about the throne room with an empty gaze devoid of thought and emotion. Her heels were shackled by iron clamps, a chain and ball dragging behind her as she shuffled forward.

Tears rolled down Theo's cheeks as he gazed upon the woman he loved. He could barely bring himself to believe the spirit of the woman he had met that day when she had stood defiantly before Archon had been broken by the warlock. He was angered by the thought of the torture the princess must have undergone to reach such a state of submissiveness. Gone was the warrior princess he had known. Gone was the guardian of Alcavia's skies, the maiden who had taken upon her shoulders the legacy of her uncle.

Theo turned around to meet the warlock's amused stare. Unable to do anything more, he flung all his hatred in his gaze. "The surprises do not end here, Islander. From what I understand, you tried to wheedle your way between the princess and her true love. I have arranged to right this wrong." The Warlock clapped his hands once more and the door to his hall opened.

The man that stepped into the hall was the last person Theo expected to meet at the fortress. Prince Armend of Ameron stood before him with intense hatred in his eyes. But he was not attired in the brown garb of Ameron with the golden lion emblem. Instead he wore the black garments and red dragon livery of the Dragon Lord's personal guard. Prince Armend placed his arms protectively about

Adelayne's shoulders, escorting her forward till they stood close to the warlock. Adelayne looked about with glazed eyes, unaware of what was going on around her.

"Still here, farm boy?" Prince Armend sneered, looking at Theo. He grinned maliciously as Theo stared with longing at the princess. Armend placed a protective arm around the princess's waist. Adelayne's eyes remained vacant.

"What you once tried to snatch away has returned to my embrace where it rightfully belongs," Armend added, placing himself between Theo and the princess so she was hidden from Theo's view. "My new master Zarzbudin freed me from the clutches of the whores at Sulicia to whom your foul sorcerer had delivered me. I hear your mentor has met his rightful end and that his broken body washed upon the shore where its bloated form was fed upon by the worms. A rightful end for those who oppose my master."

Theo realized the prince still behaved as though he were under the influence of the drugs. He spoke as one who had been hypnotized. Why else would he turn against his own people and shun his royal household to don Zarzbudin's colours? "Are you aware, my prince, that as we speak, your uncle Georgile rules your father's kingdom and has sent an armed force to Ramila to arrest your mother so she can be brought before the hangman's noose?" Theo said dryly. "Are you aware that your new master Zarzbudin is responsible for the assassination of your father and for implicating your mother?"

A look of pain crossed the prince's face momentarily but was gone almost as soon as it appeared. "Lies! All lies to discredit my lord Zarzbudin. I have heard of my mother's treachery and her involvement in the plot to dethrone my father. Georgile moves to reclaim Ameron's honour. Ramila will pay for her involvement in my father's assassination and her support to my murderess mother and her kin whom I renounce. Those who stand against Georgile, stand against me and my deceased father." Theo shook his head morosely. There was no convincing the prince. His head was too mulled by the poison cursing through his veins.

"Now that we have cleared that up, let us move on to the next course of events for the evening," Zarzbudin offered smugly. The warlock approached the opening to his chamber lifting his staff. Outside a wind had risen and was blowing snowflakes into the hall from the gaping hole. Theo fancied he caught sight of a flash of red in the whirling snow. Then he saw the dragon alight before the warlock's outstretched arms. A tall warrior slithered from the dragon's back and planted his feet firmly before the warlock.

"Come commander. How goes the campaign?"

Barack stood proudly before the warlock, his long flowing hair tinged by gold locks falling across his broad heaving chest. "Master Zarzbudin. Our forces march east to lay siege to the city of Alcavia. Before the week is out we will have razed the city to the ground."

Theo took in a sharp breath. *Something is wrong here*, he thought. He cast a quick glance at Roxette and realized she too had sensed it. Barack had changed somehow. He was formidable. The very sight of him sent cold chills down Theo's spine. Even though he was shielded from his gift it still sent out a sharp warning to him that all was not well. He could feel Nolath's discomfort through their link. He looked at the elderly nymph and heard him muttering as his breathing became more rapid.

"My steed awaits me, my lord," Barack said, pointing back to the red dragon that waited at the chamber opening, "to take me to the heart of battle."

"Ah yes. Voltan, my pet. Are you ready to feast this day on the blood of your silver brothers?" The warlock asked, laying an outstretched hand on the dragon's large head that was twice as long as the Dragon master was tall.

"I have an appetite hard to satiate, my lord," the dragon rumbled, "but I dine not on my brothers this day but on my enemy. The silver ceased to be our kin the day they turned against us."

"Come, Rolgath," the Warlock beckoned. A gasp escaped Roxette's lips at the mention of the nymph's newly acquired identity.

"So it is true!" Nolath exclaimed in disbelief.

The warrior nymph followed in his master's wake. The warlock laid his hands on the stone walls of his hall. The red glow from his hands pulsated; the rock split as an outline of a door formed on the wall. The rock moved and the face that had been turned towards the hall swung inwards. Hanging from the opposite rock face was a red plate of armour. Theo was certain it was the same suit of armour that had been depicted in the portraits of the red knight in the corridor.

"Put this on Rolgath," the Warlock commanded. The nymph warrior took the suit down from its perch and began to place it piece by piece on his body. It fitted him clumsily, as if it had been tailored for another. Then the suit began to shift as though it were alive. It hugged the nymph's form till it looked as though it were one with his skin, like a lobster's shell. "How do you feel Rolgath?" the Warlock asked, grinning maliciously.

"I feel I have returned, Witch King," the red knight answered in a grating voice that sounded like rusty steel parts moving on joints that had not been greased. The red knight snatched the heavy two-handed blade from the rock face, hefting it easily in his muscled arms as though he held a stalk of wheat. Then he bowed to his master before turning and making his way to his red dragon.

What happened next caught Theo completely by surprise.

"Die red devil!" He heard the screech and saw Roxette hurling herself in the path of the red knight. She delivered successive blows with twin blades in quick repetition. Rolgath deflected Roxette's blows easily and dealt her a back-handed slap that sent her skidding back from where she had launched her attack. Roxette crushed into Kasak and his group of nymph warriors, bowling them over. Theo too almost lost his footing. In the commotion, Theo drew his sword and rushed forward to sink the blade deep into the gifted nymph that stood closest to him. The nymph gazed at him in shocked surprise as he slid from Theo's blade leaving a trail of red hot blood on the shiny surface of the blade.

Theo turned around and came face to face with Nolath. The mage nymph grinned confidently at him and advanced unperturbed by Theo's blade. Theo lifted his sword but felt a constricting pain in his chest. He fell forward on his knees, his sword clattering to the ground from his useless fingers.

"Do not resist, Theodor." Madura was by his side and wrenched him by the scruff of his neck till he faced her. There was a pleading look in her face. "Do not resist plain dweller or they will surely kill you."

"Better to die a free man than to live as a mindless beast in your Witch King's mines," Theo spat the words back at her and made to rise. He felt the restraining hand of Nolath's gift clutching him by the throat, forcing his life's breath from his lungs. Theo sank back on his haunches unable to counter the old mage's attack. He had no access to his gift.

Theo lifted his gaze to see Roxette exchanging blows with Kasak and his men. She had managed to dispatch one of the three warriors but the rest combined with Kasak were strong enough to keep her at bay. Meanwhile Rolgath had placed himself astride Voltan's back. Red knight and dragon steed launched into the air and with a battering of the beast's large webbed wings they disappeared into the snow-capped peaks.

"Nolath, bring the Islander to me on his knees," the warlock commanded. "Kakledur, open the doors and bring in my house guard to take care of the traitorous bitch you have brought to my throne room."

Kakledur moved his bony form towards the throne room doors and flung them open. Before he could bark out his master's commands, a sword pierced through his back and pointed rudely at the warlock from between Kakledur's ribs. Zarzbudin looked on in silence as his loyal servant fell in a heap from the attacking blade. His gaze was cold.

Theo saw a tall warrior with a shaved scalp, apart from his top knot, standing above the slain manservant. Rude scars criss-crossed the warrior's face. Theo could hardly believe his luck. "Colonel Ajax!" he shouted with relief.

Ajax turned to smile at him. Beside him stood a hooded figure dressed in a grey woollen cloak that hid his features down to his polished black boots.

"Glad to see you too, lad," Ajax said, stepping forward with the hooded figure.

"Guards!" Zarzbudin shouted.

"I wouldn't expect any to answer your call," Ajax called out mockingly. He made to move forward towards the warlock, but his hooded companion placed a restraining hand on him. Theo could see the corridor walls beyond the throne room doors were marked with black soot and the floor was littered with bodies. The furniture had been overturned and was still burning. Theo had seen Ajax in action when he sparred. However talented the colonel was, he and this grey figure could not have slain all those standing in the corridor without aid.

The hooded figure lifted a finger and pointed it at Theo. Theo cringed from the grey figure's finger, not knowing what to expect. Then he felt Madura's and Nolath's knots on his gift being severed as easily as a blade cuts through flesh. Nolath gasped in shock and turned to face the hooded figure. The grey figure reached up to his hood and pulled it away letting his silver and gold locks fall to his shoulders like a shower of golden sunlight.

"I thought you were dead!" Zarzbudin cried out in disbelief. He was not the only one, for Theo stared in shock also.

"Archon of Nexedor and Ullanda will not so easily fall to the servants of the Dark, Bastiele." The wizard fixed the warlock with his stone grey gaze.

Roxette, who had ceased her struggle with her opponents, stood transfixed by the sight of her lord. Then she attacked Kasak and his men with renewed fervour whilst tears of joy streamed from her eyes. The warlock rushed towards the opening to his chamber and hurled himself into the abyss. No sooner had he flung himself seemingly to his death, than Theo saw a red dragon rising up from the opening, bearing the Witch Lord on its back.

♦ CHAPTER 32 ♦

Falling stars

Theo came to his feet delivered from Nolath's grasp and reached out for his gift. It surged to him, like a dry pond filled by a torrent of rain. He felt more in touch with it than ever before. Every fibre of his being ached at having been kept so long seperated from it. He felt he could accomplish anything. He turned to Madura and saw her gazing at him with a mixed look of awe and fear.

"Do not come between me and your teacher, Madura, or I will be forced to kill you." Madura crouched before him, tears rolling down her cheeks.

Nolath was still looking in Archon's direction. Theo turned towards Archon and colonel Ajax. He saw a movement in the corridor. A woman dressed in a purple dress was moving through the bodies littering the floor and was being followed close behind by a fellow with a limp. Theo recognized them instantly, though he could not believe she was still alive.

"Archon, look out!" he called as the Black Widow came up behind the mage. But Archon sensed the sorceress's presence with his gift, and was waiting for her approach.

"My master sent me to take the boy," Loxandra pointed in Theo's direction. "Don't bother to stand in my way, wizard. I have survived the attacks of far greater men than you. Perhaps you are acquainted with First Sorcerer Sharman." She paused whilst a look of foreboding crossed

Archon's face. "Ah yes, but of course you are." A smile broke her lips showing her white teeth in a grimace of cruel joy. "The old ape would mention you often. Well, I have helped rid the world of Sharman's meddling influence. It was a task I relished. Now, unless you intend to meet the same fate, I suggest you make way and let me take the boy."

Theo remembered that day at the manor house in Ramila. He remembered how Loxandra had utterly vanquished the brown wizard, leaving behind a charred body where once had stood a great sorcerer. Then, Serilia had thrown such a blinding bolt of light at the sorceress that Theo was sure she had been destroyed. Yet here she was, without a single blemish on her blond head to show for the ordeal.

"It is unfortunate, what befell my colleague Sharman," Archon countered, deep regret mirrored in his face but also a look of grim determination. "He was a good man and had served the Council of Light well. You will not find me such an easy adversary, Black Widow." Archon stood before Loxandra. A magic shield surrounded him.

Loxandra moved to strike, hurling bolts of red flame towards the mage who retaliated with his own fire. The air around the sorcerers crackled with expended energy. Witch and mage were firmly locked in battle.

Meanwhile, Foreman Rogue had moved around his mistress and the mage and was readying to launch himself at colonel Ajax who was waiting for his foe to approach. Theo was about to give Nolath fair warning before engaging him in combat when he saw at the edge of his vision a movement. He turned to come face to face with Prince Armend.

"You haven't forgotten me, have you Islander?" Armend advanced to strike at Theo's head. Theo lifted his sword to meet the blow. Armend threw blow after blow at Theo with inhuman strength and ferocity that was fuelled by the drug coursing through his veins. However, Theo had become more proficient in the use of the sword since they had last met. Weeks of training under Roxette's tuition all came to the fore. Soon the prince had expended his energy and was panting and sweating from his efforts. Theo kicked Armend's shoulder, sending him crashing backwards on the stone floor. He lifted his nymph blade and prepared to ram his sword into the prince's chest to end his miserable life.

"No Theo! Have pity on him!" Adelayne placed a restraining hand on his arm. Her eyes stared deeply into Theo's, beseeching him to control his anger. "He is not himself, Theo. Stay your blade. Don't do this. Theo I love you. I only realized this very moment just how much. Do not taint our love with the blood of this innocent. Stay your sword, for Ellodiere's sake!" Then she turned to the prince. "You lied to me, Armend," she sobbed. "You said you had stopped taking the drug."

Theo calmed his anger with great effort and lowered his sword to his side. At his feet, Armend was shaking violently, his body racked by convulsions from the salith weed poison. Theo felt the warning of his sixth sense. It was all that saved him and Adelayne. He flung up his shield in time to deflect the bolt of red light. At first he thought one of Loxandra's fire bolts had strayed from their target and had inadvertently fallen upon him and the princess. Then he saw Nolath standing opposite with outstretched hands.

"It is futile to resist, plain dweller," the nymph said, his lips curled into a vicious sneer. "You are no match for me, boy wizard. Surrender to me and I will spare you and your girlfriend's life."

Theo placed Adelayne behind him protectively and stood before the nymph mage. Nolath hurled another bolt of flame at him. This time Theo was barely able to deflect the blow. The nymph mage was truly as powerful as Theo suspected all along. Theo retaliated with all the strength he could muster. He sent a long beam of blinding white light arching towards his opponent.

Nolath deflected the blow and extended his empty hand with the fingers spread wide in the shape of a claw towards Theo. At first Theo saw no flame enveloping the fingers and thought the nymph had lost his ability to draw forth flame. Then it hit him–an invisible force like a stone wall –sending him flying into Adelayne so they were both knocked to the ground.

When he managed to shake away the dizziness, he raised himself to his knees and stood swaying slightly from the after effects of the blow. He had a headache and his eyes could not focus properly. When they did, he saw Nolath advancing towards him.

"Now prepare to meet your doom." Nolath raised his arms and red flame enveloped his fingers. Theo reached out for his gift but was too exhausted to call it forth. Nolath kept up his advance. He clutched at Theo's throat and lifted him bodily into the air. Theo felt his throat being singed by the mage's burning fingers. Suddenly Nolath staggered forward. He released his hold on Theo and placed his hands around the sword tip that protruded from his chest. He fell to the floor and let out his last breath. Behind him stood Prince Armend.

"Tell my mother and sister that I am sorry for all the pain I have caused them, Islander," the prince said, before he collapsed on the floor.

Adelayne raced to the prince's side and fell beside him cradling his head in her lap. She placed her fingers on the prince's neck to feel for his pulse. Then she lifted tear-filled eyes to Theo and shook her head morosely. "He is dead, my love. Prince Armend is dead." Theo placed a comforting arm around Adelayne. He rocked her gently to console her. She was as light as a feather and the bones of her shoulder seemed so fragile he feared they would break if he clutched her too tightly.

"Hurry Theodor! You and the princess must get your friends out of here. The Warlock will have alerted his troops and they are sure to send men back to slay you."

Theo looked up from where they sat with the dead prince in their arms. Madura was beside him looking anxiously in the direction of his friends. Roxette had felled two more of Kasak's men and only she and the clan chief remained. She was bleeding from several wounds, bearing witness to the fighting skills of Kasak's warriors. On the other side of the hall, Ajax was fighting for his life against foreman Rogue. Rogue was the larger of the two and had managed to slit open Ajax's old side-wound. The colonel's shirt was bloodied and he clutched at his side with one arm whilst deflecting Rogue's sword thrusts with the other.

Archon and Loxandra were still locked in battle. There was a rip in the Black Widow's purple dress and her face was bruised where she had been hit by Archon's blows. Archon had a sleeve missing, and his grey cloak was charred in several places. Theo took a moment to make his decision then sprang to his feet. "Madura, stay with Adelayne!"

He moved in the direction of Roxette. He did not want to get anywhere near the Black Widow. Ajax seemed to need his help more than Roxette, but the colonel was too close to the warring sorcerers. As Theo approached, Kasak changed the direction of his sword thrust in mid-air and caught Roxette on the shoulder. She pulled back clutching at her shoulder. Kasak kicked her in the stomach and finished off with a kick to her head. She fell backwards losing her grip on both swords. They clattered on the stone floor. Kasak poised for his killing blow.

Theo flung himself desperately at the clan chief. He fell hard on the nymph chief baring them both down to the ground. Kasak brought up one of his knees to stop his fall but instead landed on it heavily, breaking his knee cap. He roared with pain and clutched at his leg. Roxette wasted no time seizing the opportunity. She rolled towards her swords, sprang to her feet and landed on the clan chief sinking both blades deep into his chest. Kasak coughed up blood. His head flopped to the side his lifeless eyes staring at Theo who lay on the floor beside him.

"Quickly, Theodor. Back on your feet!" Roxette urged, pulling the youth up.

"Glad to have you back on our side, Roxette," Theo said, as they approached the other end of the hall.

"I never left your side, Theo," Roxette answered. "It was just necessary to make you think so."

"What about that night you visited Barack's tent?" Theo did not know why he had picked that particular moment to bring this up. He almost regretted asking the question.

"That night, had I not acted the way I did, Barack would have suspected me of treachery, and I wouldn't be here to save your life, now would I?" Roxette's voice broke, heavy with emotion.

Theo remembered the state she had been in the next morning. She had suffered humiliation–and worse–to ensure they were given the chance to approach the warlock's den and rescue the princess. He felt ashamed at having pressed her into confessing.

"Come now. All that is finished with," the nymph beckoned. "Stay by your princess's side and protect her. This is far from over."

Theo approached Madura and Adelayne who was still sobbing over Armend's death. "Come, princess. We must seek a way out of here." Theo bent close to the woman he loved and fingered her ankles tenderly. They were bleeding and sore from being abraded by the iron clamps at her feet. Theo brought his sword down sharply and broke the chains.

He removed the iron ball then placed his hands on the iron clamps.

He tried to recall the weaves old Wecka had used that day to release his wrist restraints. He could not. However he was so angry at the warlock's treatment of the princess, so infuriated by the weakened state of Adelayne that his hands began to burn with a white hot light. Before he realized what he was doing, the clamps melted away at his touch. Adelayne felt at her ankles, a look of complete astonishment on her face, then beamed a smile at Theo that lit up his world.

"Nooooo!" They turned at the screaming sound. Roxette was running towards Ajax and his burly opponent. Somehow, foreman Rogue had managed to wrestle the colonel face down on the ground. He clutched Ajax's hair tightly with his left hand, yanking back the colonel's head so his throat was bared. In his right hand he held a sharp dagger. He grinned at the distress in Roxette's face as she raced towards them. A red line formed across the colonel's throat as Rogue drew across his blade. The colonel's life blood emptied on the stone floor.

Theo stood looking at the scene in a state of shock.

Rogue let Ajax's head flop to the ground into the pool of blood that was collecting on the floor. He got up calmly, the grin still plastered on his face. "Come, my sweet," he beckoned. "Come to me and I will send you to be reunited with your lover."

Roxette screamed a war cry as she hurled herself into the air and landed a kick squarely in the foreman's mid-section. Rogue was pushed back a few steps but he recovered quickly and back-handed Roxette across the face with a stocky fist, causing her to release her grip on one of her swords. As she found her footing and prepared to strike once more, he punched her with all his might in the face sending her crashing to the ground like a puppet that has had its strings cut.

"Stay with Adelayne!" Theo ordered Madura as he raced to the aid of his friend. He had to reach Roxette before Rogue had a chance to strike at her again. He saw Roxette rise to her feet slowly. She was swaying dangerously from Rogue's last blow. Theo could tell that she had trouble focusing. Had she entered the fight fresh, she might still have suffered the same fate. Rogue was a large man.

Rogue moved with a speed that defied his large frame and his limp. He pulled his arm back and lifted himself in the air before swinging his fist in an overhand stroke. As he landed he brought down his fist with all his might impacting on Roxette's jaw. Theo heard a loud cracking noise as his friend crumbled in a heap on the stone floor. He arrived too late by her side.

"Aah. Theodor, my young friend. You've come to join your companions I presume? Let's see what you have learned since the last time I laid eyes on you." Rogue held a heavy sword in his right hand. It was a two-handed blade used by knights to pierce armour. He hefted the sword with ease as the muscles rippled beneath his torn shirt. Theo could still distinguish the emblem of the black widow spider spread across the purple shirt that was darkly stained with dried blood and sweat. Some of that blood was Rogue's, but most was not.

Theo lifted his slender nymph sword and looked at the shiny surface of the metal which had been blemished by the blood of the young gifted nymph he had killed this day. Theo realized the young nymph was the second person he had killed in his life. Would he be lucky enough to add Rogue to that list? Colonel Ajax had been a fierce warrior with years of training and battle experience behind him. Roxette was legendary amongst her people. Yet the foreman had overpowered them both. Theo knew he was doomed to failure.

Theo had no time to finish his thoughts. Rogue came at him whirling the large blade in his right hand. Theo offered a silent prayer to Athud and prepared to meet the burly giant. He remembered old Prium's words that day as he had handed the nymph sword to Theo. "A *spark of light in the dark*" the aged sea nymph had said. Theo brought up his lithureal blade and met his opponent's downward thrust. Rogue's larger sword caused Theo to flinch with the weight of the stroke, but the nymph blade held. He slipped over to the foreman's weaker side, the side with the limp. Rogue turned to strike out at the youth. They circled each other with Theo keeping at arm's length desperately deflecting the mighty blows.

Theo realized with relief that his opponent was drained of most of his strength. Beads of sweat had formed on his brow and his shirt was thoroughly soaked. His breathing also was ragged. Theo forced the larger man to keep swinging his heavier sword. What may have proved a formidable weapon, had Rogue been fresh for the fight, was now an encumbrance. If Theo could wear him down then perhaps he could move in for a quick and lethal jab. Rogue sensed this and kept swinging his weapon to keep the youth at bay. Theo employed all the hit and retreat tactics Roxette had taught him. He saw an opening on his opponent's weaker flank and took it. He moved in swiftly and prepared to sink his blade in Rogue's side at the point in the back where the vital organs were, just below the ribs. Roxette had instructed him that a blow in this section would kill almost instantaneously.

Theo saw stars in his vision and shook his head to clear it. He wondered what he was doing lying on the ground face downwards. He turned around and saw Rogue standing on top of him. Only then did he realize what must have happened. Theo reached out for his blade but the foreman had kicked it away. He remembered the blow to his head. At first he had thought a huge lump of rock had fallen on him from the ceiling of the warlock's mountain hall. Then he recalled that the blow had come from Rogue's left fist. He felt at the lump on the back of his head. Rogue was a master of deception and packed a solid punch.

"I would have preferred to have given you the chance to meet our master, boy. However you have forced my hand. I must end your puny life here and now." Rogue lifted his heavy sword with both meaty hands.

The death stroke was soon to be delivered.

Rogue looked up in surprise and met Adelayne's cold stare. Adelayne, seizing Roxette's sword, had rammed it into the foreman's chest whilst his attention was trained on Theo. Roxette was lying on the ground in a heap where he had left her. However, he had forgotten about the princess. He looked down in disbelief at the sword that protruded from his chest and the blood pouring down his shirt as his heart continued to beat. Then he toppled over like a felled tree.

Theo pushed with all his might, but Adelayne and Madura had to add their weight to dislodge the large frame of the foreman from on top of him. Theo stood up slowly and retrieved his sword.

"Theo, the mage may need our help." Madura pointed at the two sorcerers who were still locked together in combat.

Theo sensed from the expenditure of energy that both Loxandra and Archon were using up huge amounts of the gift. They seemed equally matched. For every blow Archon delivered, Loxandra delivered the same in return with equal intensity. Perhaps Madura was right. The two of them might tip the balance in favour of the mage.

Theo reached for his gift and felt Madura do the same. They united their energy and sent forth a bolt of flame towards the sorceress. Loxandra broke away from her battle with the sorcerer and deflected the new attack. She turned around and prepared to flee down the corridor from whence she had appeared. "You have not seen the last of me, wizard. And your apprentice has much to answer for," she screamed as she made her getaway.

Archon stood hunched over with his hands on his knees and remained so for a while whilst he regained his breath. Theo came up to his tutor and waited for him to recover. The mage straightened and took Theo into a warm embrace. "I'm so glad to see you again, Theo. You have done well this day."

"I'm relieved to see you also, Archon."

Adelayne stepped up carrying Roxette on her slender shoulders. The nymph shifted her weight and embraced the wizard. "I knew you were alive, master. I would never have believed you were dead unless I had seen your corpse for myself. But nonetheless I am relieved to see you in the flesh."

"I am glad to be alive also, Roxette. But let us not linger any longer in this hall. The Warlock will have alerted his men to our presence. Soon the hall will be overrun with Zarzbudin's foul beasts. Come, Theodor, Adelayne. Call forth your steeds and let us make our way back to Alcavia in all haste. War is upon us."

Archon sealed and barricaded the doors to the throne room. Then he motioned for his friends to make their way to the opening at the other end of the chamber.

"Archon, wait!" Roxette cried out. "I will not leave our friends lying thus," she said, pointing at the colonel's and Prince Armend's bodies lying on the ground. Theo helped Roxette and Adelayne drag the bodies to the edge of the precipice. They offered a silent prayer to the gods to accept their fallen comrade's spirits. Then they threw the bodies into the void.

"Now call your dragon steeds," Archon commanded Theo and the princess.

"How do you know about the red dragon?" Theo asked in puzzlement.

"I passed through the Emerald Forest only a few days after you and your sister had left."

"Serilia left?" Theo asked in earnest at the mention of his sister.

"Yes. She was accompanied by Nemarchus and was on her way to Ameron."

"Is she well?"

"She was when she had left the forest, Theodor."

"And I suppose the queen told you about my meeting with the red dragon?"

"Well, actually it was Flight Commander Malgor who had informed me of your encounter with Varwraker."

Theo stood looking at Adelayne. The princess closed her eyes and remained so for a while. Then she opened them and smiled.

"What is it?" Theo asked.

"Assima is alive and well," Adelayne answered. "She is on her way here."

"Archon, how did she do that?" Theo turned to his tutor.

"Do you not know, Theodor. A dragonstrider's mind is bonded to his dragon. Try it and see for yourself."

Truly, no sooner had Theo shut his eyes and recalled the image of his dragon, when he heard a voice in his head. *"I'm already on my way over, Maren'therin. I have seen my sire's brother soaring through the skies and have guessed at your location. You are foolhardy in the extreme to have wandered into the Dragonmaster's den."*

"Well?" Archon asked of his apprentice.

"The red dragon is on his way here."

"Archon, tell me. What happened to you back at Sulicia? You plainly managed to deliver the prince safely to the

Sisters of Athud." Theo was sitting with Roxette and Princess Adelayne beside the mage, waiting for the red dragon to come.

"Yes Theodor. I delivered the prince into the care of Abbess Emilia and my sister Lucinda. I was surprised to find him here at the Warlock's hall."

"What happened to you after you left Sulicia Island? Why did you not contact us?" Roxette asked, looking at the mage intensely with her dark brown eyes.

"I could not, my faithful guide and guardian," the mage answered gently. "I barely managed to escape death at the hands of the dark sorcerer. He came upon us when we least expected it; he had the aid of three wraiths whereas I was alone and unprepared for his attack."

"Wraiths!" Roxette spat with disgust. "The walking dead have not troubled our lands for more than a millennium."

"That is so, Roxette, but we will be witness to many changes now that the Dark Lord's forces have been mobilized. Zarzbudin is but a small part in Ushud's design." The mage fixed her with a cold stare. "Our ship was split asunder and all on board perished," he said, continuing with his tale. "I was fortunate enough to grab onto a piece of ship wreckage or else I too would have met with a watery grave at the bottom of the Valdoric Sea."

"But you survived," Theo stated.

"Yes, I survived and, when I eventually washed up on shore, I came looking for you–and here I am."

"How did you know where to find us and how did you and the colonel meet up?"

"Well, as I have told you before, Theodor, I arrived at the Emerald Forest shortly after you left. The colonel arrived on the day I was preparing to leave. He had delivered Queen Paula to her brother in Ramila and sped back to the forest to resume his mission. Queen Viola did us the same courtesy she did for you and dropped us off at the entrance to the

Dwarves' caves. There we met up with Baulkin Redbeard who informed us how, a few days before, he had taken you to Wagon's End. We took the same wagon route and followed your trail."

"In any event, we are glad you survived Archon of Aldorn," Adelayne added. "Your aid will be sorely needed in the struggle ahead. My people are far outnumbered and from what I have been told so far, Ameron and Ramila will be preoccupied with squabbling amongst themselves."

"Oh it is more than just a squabble, princess. When I left Ramila's shores to make my way to Ghiadon, the city dwellers were anxious as if expecting a siege from Ameron at any time. I'm afraid that Leonium has been shrouded by the Dark's treachery. These two kingdoms have for millennia been allies. The Dark Circle's manipulations have led Leonium to the brink of destruction. But I will do whatever is in my power to help you in your hour of need."

Just then, a loud banging noise was heard on the hall doors. Theo heard the same grunting and moaning noises he had heard that day when he and Roxette were wandering through the nymph tunnels alone.

"Orgul," Roxette confirmed.

"I want you all to listen to me," Archon said, with a note of urgency in his voice. "I will tackle the beasts alone. Flee as soon as the dragons arrive. You may need to leave me behind."

"Archon, we have not come so far together to—"

"Hush!" the mage interrupted Theo. "Do as I command or we will all perish. I will not be able to face the orgul and guard your backs at the same time."

Theo nodded grudgingly, as did his companions.

There was a rattling noise as the orgul began to pound at the doors with its fists. It howled with fury, tearing away large strips of wood from the doors. Its hideous face was revealed from the opening it had ripped in the door.

It wouldn't be long now.

Archon placed himself a few yards away from the door and spread his arms out from his body. A silvery white flame surrounded him as he touched his gift. The orgul was employing a huge axe to chop away at the doors. With a mighty final stroke it shattered the doors and left the splintered wood hanging from its hinges. The horned beast burst through and came straight at the wizard.

A red blur passed in front of Theo and he felt the wind from the large figure's passage batter him. The red creature crushed into the orgul sending it flying back towards the broken doors only an instant before it would have struck Archon with its axe.

It was Varwraker!

The dragon recovered from its plunge and made to come back towards the opening but was being held fast. It clawed at the stone floor but could not move forward. The orgul had gotten a hold of the dragon's tail and was pulling it back. Varwraker roared in anger and blew flame at the orgul. The yellow beast however seemed impervious to the flames and proceeded to pull the dragon closer with its powerful clawed hands. Varwraker panicked. He thrashed and kicked his feet and whipped the orgul with his tail but the yellow beast did not flinch from the blows. Instead it wrapped its arms about the dragon's mid-section, lifting him up and squeezing tightly so the air was expelled from Varwraker's lungs.

Once the dragon had ceased his thrashing and was beginning to lose his senses the orgul grabbed his tail and began to swing Varwraker. The orgul released the dragon after a mighty swing, sending him crashing into the walls of the hall. Then it turned its attention back to the mage. Behind the orgul, a group of trolls and ogres were emerging from the hall beyond. Theo felt a feeling of utter despair. *How can Archon face so many?* The mage would not hold out for long. Archon shot forth white flame from his outflung arms, causing the ogres and trolls to recoil. The orgul however advanced steadily. Then, for a second time the beast was flung back at the doors of the hall. This time it was the arrival of Adelayne's steed, Assima, who had smitten the orgul with her silver tail.

Varwraker recovered from his battering and stepped closer to the mage. Assima turned her head at the red dragon and hissed a warning.

"It's alright, Assima!" Adelayne shouted. "He's a friend."

"Come let us leave before the yellow beast gets to its feet," Assima urged.

"I couldn't agree more," Archon said, as Roxette and Adelayne straddled Assima's back. The mage and Theo clambered onto Varwraker's back. Theo motioned for Madura to sit behind him.

"No Theodor, I'm afraid our roads part here. This is where I belong." Madura shook her head and inched back from Theo and his friends. "Run Theodor. Run whilst you can! Never return to the Witch Lord's kingdom again." Madura turned and fled towards the shattered doors of the throne room.

"Come, let's be off," Archon called out, and the two dragons launched themselves in the air.

However, as soon as Assima and Varwraker cleared the hall, instead of climbing upwards, they started falling rapidly towards the abyss. Theo stared behind in horror to find the orgul holding on firmly, a dragon's tail clutched in each mighty hand. It must have sprung at them before the dragons had taken flight.

Theo swallowed as they sped towards certain death. He looked around at his companions and saw fear in their wide eyes. The dragons were beating their wings frantically but they were nowhere near powerful enough to lift the orgul's massive body. Theo heard a rumbling, laughing sound being emitted from the orgul's throat and realised it was mocking them. However slow of mind the beast might have been it felt pleasure at having accomplished its task. It was going to plunge them all to their death.

Roxette stood up from her riding position and held one sword in her hand like a spear. She hurled it at the orgul. The sword flew towards its target and planted itself deep into the orgul's throat so only the hilt protruded. The horned beast gave out a gurgled cry. It released the dragons, spinning slowly as it fell into the abyss.

Mercifully, Varwraker and Assima halted their fall as they beat with their powerful wings to begin, at first, their slow ascent. Then they gained height faster and soon were soaring well above the mountain peaks. They tilted their wings when they had gained their desired altitude and made their way due east towards Alcavia's coastline.

They sped through the mountains like shooting stars from the heavens, one a streak of red, the other silver. Theo heard a bird call and turned to gaze upon the hawk with red plumage flying beside them. Archon called out Farwing's name and the Valdoric sea hawk responded with a cry of pleasure at having been reunited with his master. Winter's cold breath was descending as they fled before her. Only a couple of weeks remained till autumn would retreat to make way for its sister.

Their flight did not last more than an hour. Soon the two dragons were descending the skies above the city of Alcavia. Theo looked down to see a widespread black body milling around the city. The body, like black paint spilt on a canvas, was spreading out from the foot of the Dragon's Foot Mountains all the way to Alcavia's coast and the river Ankadar, and to the north almost as far as the Apalachus River. Smoke was rising from the city and Theo gazed with horror at the siege machines that were hurling large blocks of stone at the outer city walls.

"We need to proceed with caution," Archon screamed above the noise of the dragons' passage through the air. "Zarzbudin and his four reds will be somewhere close by and might come upon us in stealth and strike when we are ill-prepared."

"I feel the presence of the red dragons further south, wizard, among those peaks yonder." Assima indicated the spot where the lower peaks of the Dragon's Foot Mountains bordered with the sea; a scattering of islands spread into the Valdoric Sea from the coast.

"Keep alert until we reach the confines of the inner city walls."

As they approached the city, Theo could see the nymph army brandishing its weapons. In the front line, nymphs with shields were trying to scale the walls with ropes and ladders. The city defenders were shooting arrows into the nymph ranks and were trying to dislodge the ladders to throw them off the walls. The nymphs in the second line of attack were returning fire and the air was filled with arrows whistling to and fro. Away from the range of fire, orguls were loading huge boulders into the catapult machines and hurling them unto the city walls.

As they flew over the enemy, Theo could distinguish the nymphs' faces snarling with hatred and shouting their battle cries at the city dwellers. They passed the outer wall, where the Alcavian soldiers were massed together to repel the nymph attacks. Most of the soldiers were wielding their bows to fire at the offending army, whilst a few clusters were engaged on the walls in combat with nymphs who had managed to scale the walls. The Alcavian defences were still holding.

They came within the vicinity of the fortress and alighted in the palace grounds. There they encountered King Dreyfus and his queen. The royal couple rushed forward to embrace their daughter.

"Oh Adelayne, I knew you were coming," Queen Crystal exclaimed gleefully as she planted kisses on her daughter's cheeks and brow. "I've been feeling elated since morning, and when Assima took flight to answer your call my heart leaped with joy."

"Daughter," King Dreyfus said, beaming a smile at the princess and hugging her fiercely. Tears were streaming down the king's face. "I am so relieved to see you again, my child. Love of my life you are so thin and pale... but no matter. You are returned to us now and we will protect you." Then the expression on the king's face darkened. "I only wish you had returned under better circumstances."

The king turned to the rest of the companions. He pulled Roxette towards him and hugged her. "Thank you, Roxette. Thank you for all you have done for us. And you too, Theodor. You are a very brave young man; Alcavia owes you a great debt. Archon, I am glad to find you are alive, my age old friend. Last we heard your body had washed up on our shores."

"All vicious rumours spread by mine enemies, my lord Dreyfus. As you can see I am very much alive."

King and mage clasped arms as warriors do. "Your presence gives us strength at our greatest hour of need, son of Nexedor."

"My only wish is to serve you, my lord, and to fight at your side."

"Come. Our enemy is at our gates and requires our attention. Let us show them some Alcavian hospitality." The king ushered his friends towards the safety of the palace, where they were permitted to wash and eat a hurried meal.

♦ CHAPTER 33 ♦

The siege

King Dreyfus and his son were bent over a large table with a map spread out showing Alcavia and the surrounding countryside in great detail. Small statues on the map depicted the enemy and allied forces. The figurines representing the nymph army outnumbered the allied forces ten to one.

The king and his generals were using a tower in the palace as their command post. They could hear the sounds of war dimly filtering though to them from the city outer wall; the *boom, boom*, noises of the orgul drums were beating incessantly, filling the city inhabitants with dread. Every so often a loud crashing and pounding sound accompanied the drum beats as missiles wreaked their havoc on the city walls. Even so close to the palace, men could be heard barking out commands in earnest. The command room in the tower was high enough so the king was afforded a view of the city. In a corner, poking out the window like a rude finger, was a looking lens that had been presented to the king as a gift from the astrologers at Jade Island. It was now trained on Alcavia Port harbour.

There was a knock on the door. King Dreyfus nodded to one of his generals to open it. Archon the mage was the first to enter, followed by Roxette, Theo and lastly Adelayne. The princess returned her father's cool stare; she was defying his wishes to stay away from the fighting. She looked stronger in her black military garb than she had at the Warlock's hall. Her face was still drawn, but the spark of life had returned to her eyes.

Theo recognized many friends in the group standing around the king's table. He nodded to Templar Commander Baxter of the Sulician Order and to Prince Leon. "Primate Zerum!"

The primate stepped up and gave the youth a welcoming embrace. "You are a sight for sore eyes, my young friend." A warm smile lit his bearded face.

"As are you, Your Eminence, and the rest of your delegation," Theo clasped hands with Sir Duel. He was dressed in his customary Templar surcoat covering his chain mail beneath. His braided hair hung down his back adding to his formidable aura.

"Where are the rest of your comrades?" Theo enquired of the warrior knight.

"On the outer wall–where I should be." Duel gave King Dreyfus a meaningful stare.

"I had to send a special summons to wrench our Templar, here," Dreyfus smiled, tilting his head towards Duel, "from his duties on the wall. In fact I had to give him a royal command to get him to come here–grudgingly by the looks of it." Then he added in a softer, more sorrowful tone, "We feel Colonel Ajax's loss acutely."

Theo glanced over at Adelayne, who moved closer to Roxette and placed a comforting arm around her shoulders at the mention of her lover. The two women's attitude towards each other had turned full circle from that first day they had met. It was not surprising after all the sacrifices the nymph had made for the princess and the ones dearest to her–Theo included.

"Yes," agreed Duel. "Ajax will be sorely missed, especially at this hour when his military skills would have proved most useful."

"Which is why I have gathered you and my trusted friends and generals to this room, Sir," King Dreyfus explained. "I will be listening quite attentively over the coming days to your advice. As war-hardened veterans, you are most suited for the task."

Next to greet Theo was another knight similarly attired in Templar white. The large-framed knight was almost as tall as his comrade in arms, the troll-high Sir Brand of Ramila. He grinned at Theo as he took him in a bear hug that squeezed the air out of his lungs.

"I did not expect to find you here in Alcavia, Templar Commander Dionar," Theo smiled, pleasantly surprised. "Could this mean that King Ionid has had a change of heart and has decided to give aid to Alcavia?" The glum faces around the room, however, dashed Theo's hopes.

Commander Dionar scanned the room with a grim expression. "I'm glad to be here to offer aid to my brothers at arms, though I am ashamed to confess that I did not arrive in Alcavia as part of a relief force from Ramila. Our king's decisions are still being governed by his primate. All in this room are familiar with the sorry events that led to my being here.

"I was cast out of Ramila when a fist of Grand Master Samarass's Black Gloves—twenty men in all—accompanied by a hundred of Primate Orinor's men entered our Chapter House a week ago. It seems I laid all my hopes and confidence in a man without scruples—more treacherous than Orinor himself; Grand Master Samarass charged me with spreading false rumours about the Ramilan primate and causing discord in the Templar's ranks. He further charged me with acting in a manner not befitting a Templar Commander.

"His faithful hound, a Galipan dog going by the name of Redvik, Captain of the Templar Leonese Guard, was sent to deliver Samarass's message and to clamp me in irons. Our

Grand Master saw fit to relieve me of my duties. Redvik was appointed the task of placing me under arrest and to take me willingly or by force to Ameron, where I was to be tried–and probably thrown in prison–for treason.

"However, things did not turn out quite as Samarass had planned. The news that I had been placed under custody by the Black Gloves spread throughout the Chapter House like wild fire. Upon exiting the building and entering the front yard, Redvik and his band of a hundred came upon more than twice their number of my own knights.

"Redvik read Samarass's letter out to my comrades, but the words fell on deaf ears. As a sign of respect to the position of the Grand Master in the ranks of the Templars, they agreed to relieve me of my duties. But Redvik was told in no uncertain terms to leave the city empty-handed. Redvik, being a wise man, in the crafty way that a foxhound is wise, chose to leave with part of his dignity intact.

"The following day, I left with two hundred of my most trusted knights and friends who were willing to relinquish all bonds with their Order and their home city, to join me on my voyage to Alcavia. I would have arrived here sooner, had I been able to find a ship bound for my destination. But in the end we were forced to travel by horse over land."

"And we are glad to have you here," King Dreyfus said, breaking the uneasy silence that had followed the commander's astonishing tale.

"Do you have any news of my grandfather and Nem, Your Eminence?" Theo enquired of the primate, a note of worry creeping into his voice.

"I'm afraid I lost touch with your friends when they set out with you for the Emerald Forest, Theo. I have not had news of them since."

"I just hope they have had the sense to heed Queen Viola's warning and have headed for the safety of Aldorn," Theo sighed.

The king looked around the room at the grim but resolute faces. "I will not fill you with false hope, my friends. By our last count, we have been able to marshal together close to ten thousand able-bodied men, of which almost a quarter are young boys with no war experience or old men with too many years behind them. Commander Baxter has brought five hundred men from the Sulicia Chapter House, the sum of his force, two hundred of whom are knights, to add to Commander Dionar's equal number. The abbess and three hundred sisters have also evacuated their abbey and were accompanied by three thousand inhabitants of the island. Just five hundred of the islanders are able to take up arms.

"The news from Jade Island and the Astronomer's Guild is more encouraging. They have sent five hundred men at arms, though the rest of the islanders have barricaded themselves behind the walls of the astronomer's fortress. Let us hope they will survive Zarzbudin's attack, though personally I fear for their safety–in retrospect, they would not have fared any better in Alcavia. So that brings our military number to nearly twelve thousand. Slade, our Minister of Commerce," he said, turning to the short bald fellow, "informs me that from our sister cities of Ramila and Ameron we have been amply supplied with grain and additional clothing, thanks to the delegation's efforts, though I would have preferred men rather than supplies, which we have ample of to last the short siege.

"Our enemy has been estimated by our scouts at over a hundred thousand, and they are still crawling out of their mountain." The king fixed the group surrounding the table with his stare. He stood, proud and tall, giving courage to all in the room.

"Over the next week or so, our enemy will come at us with all the will and strength they can muster. My aim is to break them against our defences and to draw as much of their blood before they take the city, for I harbour no false hope that we will be able to drive them back. The more we hold out against the Mountain nymph forces, however, the more we take with us to the grave. Let it be written down in history that the Alcavians of our generation fought with the same zeal and courage as our forefathers before us. We will make the days to follow, the worst nightmare Zarzbudin could ever have imagined possible. We will teach the Witch Lord what it is to cross swords with an Alcavian. May your blades find their way to your foes' lifeblood. Death to our enemies!"

"Death to our enemies!" The group shouted in unison.

Theo felt an elation he had never felt before. He was caught up in the excitement of the moment. He knew it would wear off as he faced the grim reality of war, but for now he was filled with the blood lust.

King Dreyfus turned to the warrior nymph beside him. It was strange to have such a one as an ally when all her people had turned against the city. But Roxette had proved her allegiance many times over. The information she would divulge would prove most useful in tackling Zarzbudin's threat.

"Can you tell us a bit more about the enemy we face, Roxette?" The king offered her a glass filled with dark Sulician red.

She accepted it graciously and took a sip from the wine. "I take it the figurines indicate troops?" The king nodded. "Each figurine, judging by the two you have placed within the city walls signifies a force of five thousand." Again the king nodded. "Then, I'm afraid, Your Majesty, that the figurines outside the walls do not paint a true picture."

"Go on, madam," the king pressed. "If we err in our estimate of the foe's strength, then correct us. We will face them on the battlefield soon enough, so it is not our intention to hide their strength in numbers."

Roxette began her count of Zarzbudin's horde. "The mightiest clan, numbers more than your entire forces put together; that would be Barack's clan. You have all been briefed on who this war commander is?" There were nods of confirmation from the generals in the room.

"Adelayne," Archon interrupted, "mentioned that Barack has fallen foul of one of Zarzbudin's schemes. Can you confirm the new identity the commander has now assumed, princess?"

All eyes focused on the princess. "I saw Barack consumed before my very eyes by a demon of Dagorhind." Adelayne shivered despite the warmth being spread by the burning coals in the fireplace. "The demon identified itself as one Rolgath of the House of Dralco, Red Knight and Demon Lord of the Dargulheinds."

There was general silence in the room, though some of the older men became ashen-faced. One such battle-hardened veteran now stepped forward. "Forgive me for seeming to sound doubtful, Your Highness. But I was told about such a knight by my great grandfather, before Athud took him. This Rolgath you mention is but a legend. Some of our elders had heard the myth of the existence of such a knight who fed off human blood. It was a tale spread by our women to chastise our children when they misbehaved."

"Many events in history with the passage of time revert to legend and myth, Lord Alvenor," Archon said, drawing their gaze. The grey-haired veteran waited for the mage to continue. "It appears that Zarzbudin has found a way to bring the demon spirit of Rolgath back to life. I have read the palace library scrolls; they mention events that transpired in Dargulheind—such was the name by which the ancient city of Dagorhind was known more than a millennium ago. The scrolls are written in an ancient form of Galipan, that I am familiar with. They were recovered from the ruins of Phica, a

Galipan city built in 855 BA, when the Galipans were expanding their realm into Leonium."

Theo remembered with nostalgia that day he and his grandfather had been travelling with Ajax and their group just south of the Apalachus River, on their way east to Ramila. He recalled how they had come across the ancient Phican ruins and how his grandfather had told them the fateful story of the Galipan city with tears in his eyes. It seemed such a long time ago, though only two months had passed since that day. The mage's voice brought him out of his musing.

"The scrolls are dated 1704 by the Galipan calendar, roughly six hundred years before the Great War. At the time, a Dargulheind necromancer of notorious fame known as Zarrtoul was rumoured to have been carrying out experiments on his men. One such prominent figure was his military commander-in-chief, Rolgath. It was said by those closest to Rolgath that his association with the necromancer had a profound effect on him. There were whispers amongst his men that Rolgath was possessed and acting in a manner out of character.

"Rolgath led several successful campaigns against the Galipans from his base in Dargulheind. He was aided in his war efforts by the necromancer Zarrtoul, who was also brother to the king of Dargulheind. It is written that Rolgath drank the blood of his enemies in a golden chalice so their spirit and strength would flow through his veins. For reasons unknown, Rolgath murdered Zarrtoul. The king was furious and shunned the Red Knight, throwing him out of his kingdom. A group of Galipan warriors hunted Rolgath down, cornering him and managing to slay him after he had killed a dozen men.

"Rolgath's remains were retrieved by a group of Dargulheind monks known as the Red Cloaks. After the king's death, and well after the Dargulheinds had forgotten the Red Knight and his necromancer lord, the Red Cloaks placed Rolgath's bones in a coffin in one of the royal temples. They have been keeping vigil over their knight ever since. Their doctrine taught that the Red Knight would be raised once more in the future to feed off the blood of Dargulheind's enemies."

Archon drew in a sharp breath. "Which brings us to the present. It seems Zarzbudin has uncovered the necromancer's ancient tome and with it has been able to reincarnate Rolgath's demon spirit and place it into the body of Barack."

Sir Alvenor's ashen face matched that of the rest of the group huddling around the table. The light from the fireplace lit their faces as Duel placed more wood on the burning coals.

"Demon or not, he will be slain along with the rest of Zarzbudin's men when the time approaches," Prince Leon uttered defiantly.

"Heed me well." Archon pointedly fixed his stone gaze on the listeners. "No earthly weapon can defeat or harm the demon. The Galipans had a group of sorcerers with them when they went after the Red Knight. And they had in their possession a weapon said to be able to defeat a demon of Ushud.

"Should you come across the Red Knight, you are not to engage him in combat, unless you would squander your lives away. You *must* leave him to me." The prince looked away in anger.

King Dreyfus cleared his throat. "Rolgath is not our only concern. Roxette, please continue with your account on Zarzbudin's strength."

Roxette cleared her throat. "Your Majesty. Barack's tribe, the Clan of the Red Dragon, is twenty-five thousand strong. There are fourteen other tribes bringing the total to close to one hundred thousand. These numbers have been swollen by an added fifteen thousand trolls and ogres."

"Fifteen thousand, you say?" Commander Baxter exclaimed incredulously. "It takes two to three men to overpower just one of those beasts."

"That's not counting," Roxette continued, "Zarzbudin's countrymen the Dagorhinds who number at twenty thousand."

"I thought Zarzbudin was a nymph like *you*," Sir Duel said in disgust.

"A common misconception," Roxette answered dryly.

"One hundred and thirty-five thousand!" General Alvenar's tone matched their sultry mood.

"One hundred or two," King Dreyfus drew himself up from his slouching position, "Our task remains the same: to bleed our enemy dry. We will not give up our city easily."

Theo was assigned the task of furnishing the archers with fresh arrows. He wished to play a more glamorous role but Archon and the king insisted there would be time enough to engage the enemy. As he made his way to the parapets, he crouched down low to avoid being picked out by enemy fire. Arrows whistled above his head. A few of them hurtled from the sky carrying at their tips burning cloths dipped in oil. Down in the streets, young boys were running to and fro with buckets to quench the flames. They were losing the battle with the fire, as most of the city's outer reaches were up in flames. Princess Adelayne was placed with the group of boys and their fire-fighting task in an attempt to keep her away from the front line. She was as frustrated with her role, and more so, as Theo was.

Theo approached one of the archers and handed him a fresh quiver of arrows.

"Thanks, son." The archer was a man in his early sixties. He was one of those two thousand the king had mentioned, who made up the elderly or the very young in the fighting ranks.

"How is it going down there?" Theo pointed in the direction of the battlefield.

"Not too good, my lad." The elderly man shook his head. "For every one I kill, ten more take his place. I don't remember ever having to fight against such odds."

"Well, be strong, sir. We are all depending on you." Theo did not know what else to say. These men knew already they were fighting a losing battle. He took the decision and dared to peak through an opening in the wall. Below him, the nymphs massed around the city walls so they packed the grounds like a school of fish the sea. He fell sharply to the ground and covered his head with his arms as a torrent of arrows hurtled towards them. When the main body of arrows subsided, Theo looked up from where he crouched. The elderly man lay sprawled beside him with several arrow shafts jutting out from his neck and chest.

Theo prized the bow and the quiver of arrows from the dead man's stiff fingers and moved on glumly to the next group of archers. All day he moved from the parapets to the grounds below where boys were placing fallen arrows into quiver pouches to be reused. They tried to use as many of the enemy arrows as possible so as not to deplete their own resources. There were countless arrows to collect so this did not pose a problem. When night fell upon the combatants, Theo returned to a section in the city where a barricade had been set up to afford some shelter from the assailants' missiles. Here, the soldiers took their turn at getting a bite to eat and snatching a few hours sleep before returning to the battle front.

"You look gaunt," Freida, the palace cook, said to Theo in an admonishing but soft tone. She had volunteered along with the rest of the royal servants to offer what aid she could to the men battling at the walls. Theo recognized a few more of the palace staff. He sat at a crude bench and ate hurriedly a hot beef broth with pieces of bread dipped in it.

The missiles from the enemy siege engines continued to make thumping noises throughout the night as they fell upon the city walls. The Alcavian military had set up their own catapults to answer the enemy fire, and these contraptions were kept manned throughout the battle to deliver death to the enemy.

King Dreyfus moved among his men, shaking hands, patting them on the back and offering words of encouragement. He could see they were becoming exhausted from their exertions. Already the makeshift centres he had set up to house the wounded were filling up. The front lines were holding up against great odds. Several times, groups of nymphs had been successful in scaling the defences, but they had been beaten back every time. Dreyfus had taken the extra precaution of sealing the outer gates with a wall of stone. Now, the only way to enter or leave the city was by going over the outer wall. His problem, however, was covering its entire circumference which was six leagues long.

He knew this was an impossible task and that he would soon need to fall back from the outer limits. Inevitably, a section would be weakened enough for the nymphs to break through. Then it would become a race to get the Alcavians behind the second wall. Had he more men, he would have been able to hold the outer defences till every last one of the Witch King's nymphs lay dead in the surrounding fields.

"Templar Commander Baxter, it gives us courage to have a man of your stature fighting by our side." The king exchanged a firm handshake with the burly Sulician knight.

"I would not have missed this battle for the world, my liege. History is being made as we speak." The Templar Commander fingered his moustache grinning encouragingly at the king.

"Commander, you have been involved in many war campaigns against the Anvil corsairs. What are your views concerning the progress of the battle?"

"My king. Fighting at sea is quite different from a land battle. However I will assist in any way I can."

"Will the wall defenders hold out the night, you think?"

"To be honest, my lord, I am surprised you managed to keep the enemy at bay for so long. My personal feelings are that Zarzbudin is waiting till nightfall to mobilise the main body of his attack force. I have not, as yet, noticed a full-scale assault being launched at any point along the walls. He has spent the day testing your strength and locating weaknesses."

"I must admit, the same has occurred to me, commander, though we have already lost a thousand men without the nymphs breaking sweat. What do you suggest we do?"

"I believe your forces should fall back to the middle wall, my king. It will be easier to defend since your men would not be spread out so thinly."

"I agree with the commander." They turned to the bear of a man who now approached. The Ramilan Templar commander nodded to his counterpart and to King Dreyfus as he adjusted the long sword hanging from his broad belt.

"And leave the outer ring for Zarzbudin to devour without a fight, Commander Dionar?" Prince Leon walked briskly towards the older men. He had just returned from his position on the wall. There were several nicks and abrasions on his face and arms but no serious wounds. "We Alcavians are not used to fighting that way, my lords. My people would rather die than offer an inch of their homes without a fight."

"Not exactly without a fight, Your Highness," Baxter insisted. "A thousand nymphs at least, will have fallen to your army by the end of this day. That is an accomplishment for your forces. All I am saying is that you should retreat in an orderly fashion, whilst you still have the chance. This way you will control your losses and you will have the chance to deplete the Warlock's numbers further at the middle wall."

"It will not do any good for our men's morale to see part of their city being offered up to the enemy so easily, commander," the king answered.

"In war, my lord, sacrifices need to be made."

"Well I, for one, am against a retreat." Leonar threw an angry glare at his seniors.

King Dreyfus mulled over the commanders' words. Perhaps their luck had held out long enough. Maybe it was necessary to give some ground to the enemy in order to better oppose him later on. However his pride as an Alcavian and his fighting spirit told him otherwise.

"All men to the walls! To the walls!" Theo was awoken in the middle of the night by the screams coming from the battlefront. Somehow, exhaustion had overcome him and he had been able to snatch a couple of hours' troubled sleep. He splashed cold water across his face and strapped on his sword before exiting the house he and his comrades were using as temporary lodging. As he entered the streets, he was greeted by burning residences and soldiers rushing frantically to and fro; some were shuffling along carrying the heavily wounded to the infirmaries. Nuns in white robes with arms dipped in blood to their elbows moved amongst the men helping to lay the wounded on stretchers.

Theo realized that the commotion from the walls had built up to a frenzy. He had to find Adelayne. He had lost sight of her during the night when he was forced by lack of sleep to retire. The last he remembered, she had been collecting fallen arrows from the streets along with other women and young boys. An uneasy feeling crept through him. He felt certain, deep down inside, that the princess had not remained at that task for long. He ran towards the battlements.

As Theo sped along, a young maiden crossed his path halting his advance as she placed a restraining hand on his arm.

"Theo! It really *is* you!" He gazed down at the golden locks that hung around her pretty face. Her dress was torn in several places and smudged with blood and soot marks. Her cheeks were smeared where she had tried to wipe away the ash from the fires that blanketed the entire city, like a volcano smothers its surrounding landscape after it erupts.

"Irene," he said, recognizing the woman now standing before him. "Are you well?"

"As well as can be expected under the circumstances, Theo," she answered glumly. "I was woken by the soldiers calling for aid." Then a look of longing marked her pretty features. "Is Nem with you?" She pulled at his arm in earnest.

Theo shook his head sadly. "I'm afraid we parted ways when I left him behind in Ghiadon."

Irene's eyes widened with wonder. "You visited the Forest nymph kingdom?"

Theo nodded, smiling in response to the brightness in her eyes.

"Is Queen Viola as beautiful as the tales say?"

"More so." Theo blushed as he recalled his meeting with the queen in her hall.

Irene startled him by falling in his arms hugging him fiercely. "Oh Theo," she sobbed. "I miss him so much." Theo did not know how to respond as Irene buried her face in his shoulder and wept. He stroked her hair gently and waited for the crying to subside. He was in a hurry to locate Adelayne but his heart went out to Irene in her suffering. Finally she looked up at him through tear-filled eyes. "Does he mention me?"

"All the time," Theo lied.

"I know you're just saying that to make me feel better," Irene said, wiping at her nose with a torn sleeve. "Perhaps he thinks about me once in a while."

"Irene," Theo said gently. "I'd really like to stay and keep you company but I have a friend on the wall who urgently needs my assistance. Maybe we can meet later on when I return," he offered.

"My father's on the wall, Theo." Worry creased her face. "If you see him, tell him I'm alright."

"Irene, I've never met your father," Theo said, as he broke away from her embrace.

"Ask for a man named Eular," Irene said to him, as their fingers touched briefly before they parted. "Athud go with you, Theo."

"And with you, Irene," Theo called out as he raced towards the wall.

He climbed the steps two at a time. At the top he came face to face with Duel.

"Good, you've arrived." Duel wiped at his sweaty brow and flung his long braid behind him. He pulled Theo in to a crouching position as a volley of arrows sped past.

"How's it going with the defences?" Theo asked.

"Can you not tell?" Duel looked around at the carnage that littered the walls. "Half our numbers are involved with removing the dead and wounded. The bastards are hell-bent on breaching the defences tonight. We barely managed to hold them off thrice in two hours. Our men are in need of a breather. Dreyfus has decided to defend the outer wall but we are spread out too thinly."

"My lord," Theo interrupted the knight. Duel looked up as he detected the note of urgency in the youth's voice. "Have you seen the princess, sir?"

"Shouldn't you be looking for her behind the lines, man? You know well enough the king ordered her to steer clear of the wall."

"Yes, my lord, but something tells me that she has defied her father's wishes."

"It won't be the first time." A smile crossed the Templar's face. Then he said, in a more serious tone. "Well don't just stand there gawking, man! If you are so certain that the princess is on the walls, go and find her."

Theo moved in a crouching position along the parapet. As he proceeded forward he came across Miranda cradling Evenar's head in her lap. She turned to peer at Theo with dilated pupils. She did not recognize him at first, so dazed was she by the feelings of remorse that had overcome her. Theo noticed that Evenar's blond hair was mottled with a dark streak of blood.

"Is he...?"

Miranda shook her head. "No, Theo, but he's been struck a heavy blow on the head by the hilt of an ogre's axe. Had I not intervened his head would have been lopped off." Her voice was as cold as iron. "I fear for his life; the cut is deep."

"Miranda...have you...has the princess passed by here?" He dreaded to think that Adelayne may have been involved in the fight to repel the ogres' attack.

"I'm sorry, Theo." Miranda stared at him morosely. "I was too preoccupied with fending off our assailants. I sincerely hope she was nowhere near when they came over the wall."

Theo looked down at Evenar with trepidation. He sped along the parapet hastily, no longer bothering to crouch. An arrow narrowly missed striking him in the head. He decided he would be of no use to Adelayne dead so he proceeded with more caution.

"Aaargh!" He heard the scream as one of the Alcavian soldiers was run through by a nymph's blade. Behind the nymph towered a troll with its hideous mouth twisted in a snarl. It swung its club at the Alcavian soldiers, swiping them off the battlements and sending them plunging over the other side to their deaths.

Suddenly, Theo found he was all alone on the wall. The troll blinked at the fires from the burning city, the lights of which reflected off its single oversized eye. The troll wiped at its coconut-sized nose with one bare, hairy arm, then noticing Theo standing alone, it loped forward tilting its shoulders from side to side like an ape; it stepped on the bodies of its dead comrades and opponents without a second thought; its feet were larger than any bear's and were wrapped around in tough hide boots and cord. The troll lunged at Theo with a wooden club as large as Theo was tall.

Theo made to parry with his lithureal blade but it was knocked out of his hand by the larger club. Theo winced with pain as his arm was jarred by the impact. Meanwhile the nymph was approaching behind the troll brandishing twin blades. The troll drew itself up before Theo to its full height; it was almost as tall as a house. As the club descended Theo brought up his left arm to ward off the blow and save his skull from being crushed. *I can at least use the right arm if I get out of this one alive,* he found himself thinking, as he braced for the blow that would surely shatter his arm.

Just as the club was about to strike, an object half the troll's size collided into the beast sending the club off target. The troll recovered its stance and turned to face its new opponent. He was a Templar Knight with straight black hair, a characteristic long, twirling black moustache, and bulging biceps. Theo caught a whiff of cologne as the knight helped him to his feet. "I'll handle this one, young Theodor. You take care of the nymph." The nymph had a grin on its face, sure of its ability to overcome its opponents–in light of the protection it was being offered by its far larger companion.

"Thanks, Sir Bold." Theo nodded to the Templar before he retrieved his sword.

"You looked like you could use a helping hand." Bold grinned beneath his long moustache. "Now let's see what we can do about our two friends," he added grimly, turning to face their opponents. Theo noted that Bold's mace was long handled and had several cruel jutting edges to it.

They came at them simultaneously.

Theo was barely given enough warning to parry the nymph's blows. His training with Roxette came flooding back to him as he naturally adopted the fighting stance. He was more suited to fighting opponents of this size. The nymph's long black hair was tinged with white. Theo recalled from Roxette's description of the nymph tribes the day they had gathered in the cave that the nymphs with the white streaks in their hair belonged to the Ice Clan; they numbered ten thousand strong. *Well, it is time to lessen their numbers by one*, Theo thought, as he lunged forward.

The nymph was quick on its feet and battle-hardened. But Theo had been through a lot in the months that had gone by. He was not the same youth that had fled the cottage in Cyrus almost a year gone by. He screamed his battle cry as he launched himself at the nymph.

"Maren'Therin! Denam ked dosa!" he exclaimed, as he struck his foe repeatedly.

"Pagos! Pagos!" the nymph called out its own battle cry as it fended off Theo's blows. Then, the nymph made a fatal error in judgment, swinging too wide and leaving its side open to an underhand attack. Theo seized the opportunity and brought his blade up under the nymph's guard. It slid into the nymph's soft spot, under the armpit and pierced its heart. The nymph made to utter a cry but blood splattered from its mouth showering Theo's face. It slithered from Theo's blade and fell lifeless at his feet. It was the third life Theo had taken this year. An image of Loxandra's maid, Sophy, came flooding back to him. He remembered how he had sunk the pitch fork in her breast as she fell upon him with a kitchen knife in her hand. Then he recalled the gifted nymph he had killed at the warlock's den.

He was brought out of his ruminations by the sound of wood thumping on steel. He peered in Bold's direction to find that the knight had been backed against the wall by the troll's heavy blows. Bold had managed to crush the troll's left knee cap with his mace, causing the creature to limp and rub at its leg. However the mace was now proving ineffectual against the troll. Bold kept battering his opponent on the shoulder, arms and stomach, but the blows did not do extensive damage to the creature's tough hide. Theo caught Bold's eye and the knight indicated to him subtly to come at the troll from behind.

Theo inched forward till he was almost overcome by the creature's foul stench. He took a swipe at its leg, just behind the knee. The troll moved with surprising speed, catching Theo's blade before it struck with one calloused hand as tough as bark, sending it flying out of Theo's grasp for a second time. Then it reversed its lunge, slapping Theo across the face, sending him sprawling across the parapet floor. Theo bumped his head against the wall. Stars crossed his vision from the head injury. He gulped to recover the air that had been expelled from his lungs by the troll's heavy backhanded blow.

He recovered shaking his head to clear his vision and stumbled to his feet. This time he sought a more appropriate weapon to use against the beast. He found it lying next to an Alcavian soldier who had been killed in the first assault. Theo seized the halberd and inched forward. He would not make the same mistake of underestimating his opponent's speed and stealth again. The troll fended off the knight's blows with ease whilst keeping Theo in his sights from the corner of his saucer-sized eye. Bold was fatigued from having to lift his heavy mace repeatedly. Theo moved to place himself behind the troll. The creature shuffled sidelong so it somehow managed to keep them both in its sights.

"Go for the legs!" Bold bawled, as he delivered another blow to the troll's shoulder which bounced off leaving a small tear in the tough hide.

Theo lunged with the pointed end of the halberd. The troll howled more in anger than pain as the tip pierced its bulging calf muscle. It swiped at the halberd almost knocking it out of Theo's grasp like it had done with the sword. Then Theo hit on an idea that might just work. He waited till the troll's attention was diverted by Bold then sprang forward holding the halberd tight with both hands. He found his target, like an arrow falling true to the mark. The halberd sunk deep into the saucer-like eyeball and lodged firmly into the skull.

The troll flung out both arms narrowly missing Theo but impacting with Bold's chest with its left, sending him flying into the masonry wall. It shrieked an unearthly cry like the howl of a pack of wolves and grabbed at the halberd's handle snapping it off. The head remained planted in the troll's eye. The creature swayed like a drunken sailor then fell in a heap on the stone floor with a heavy thud.

Theo wasted no time but rushed to his companion's side. Bold was wiping away the blood from the corner of his mouth with one sleeve. "I think it may have broken my ribs," he coughed.

"Can you get up?" Theo asked, placing Bold's arm around his shoulder.

"I can try," Bold answered. The blood had drained from his cheeks. He winced as Theo brought him gently to his feet. "You...you did well," Bold said, between gasping breaths.

Just then, two more Alcavian soldiers arrived. They threw an uneasy look at the bodies of their comrades and approached the troll with trepidation. They poked at itl several times with their swords to satisfy themselves that it was dead before they turned their attention to the youth with the long wavy brown hair and the Templar with the blood on his moustache and lips.

"Take Sir Bold off the wall and to the infirmary." They were not used to taking orders from one so young but there was something different about this youth, something that made them obey without question.

Both soldiers were required to help the knight walk away slowly in the direction Theo had come; Bold was a heavy built man. When Theo was satisfied that the knight no longer required his attention, he turned, retrieved his sword and carried on his precarious journey along the parapet wall. He was weary of what new threats he might meet on the way. The smoke from the burning roofs of the residences was so thick now it reached up to the walls; Theo found it difficult to breathe. Tears ran from his eyes as he coughed to clear his lungs.

He ventured forward through the smoke that was as thick as clouds round a mountain. His terror was increased by the sounds of battle and the occasional scream and his inability to see further than arm's length. A soldier stumbled past him, clutching at his mid-section that was torn open at the belly so his guts were spilling out, then lurched ahead and toppled off the wall to his death. Another ran screaming, tearing his clothes off his back that had caught fire; Theo side-stepped just in time to avoid being scorched alive. He tripped over an object that was blocking his path and almost fell over. He gazed down at the hairy bundle and realized it was a woollen cloak. He pulled it away to reveal a man beneath it curled in a tight ball with white hair and eyes red from the smoke and his tears.

"We're all doomed...doomed I tell you...all of us are going to die...horrid deaths..."

"Get a hold of yourself, man!" Theo wrenched the old man to his feet. He pulled away sharply as the white-haired fellow brandished a dagger.

"You're one of them!" he screamed. "You're one of those demons with their hair dyed in blues and greens and reds to taunt us. So much hate in their eyes...so much hate."

"I'm not a Mountain nymph, sir." Theo knew that in the man's present delirious state he was a danger to himself and to others, unless Theo could make him snap out of it. He looked carefully at the man's clothing and the official crest on the front of his tunic. He had a long white moustache and his garments were made of the finest material. *Could it be possible?* "Duke Eular. Are you Duke Eular?" he asked. The chances of him coming across the duke in all the multitude that manned the walls was so slim, *and yet.*

The man seemed to recover from his daze; the whites of his eyes lessened and his pupils seemed to focus now on Theo. His breathing also was becoming more regular. "Are you Irene's father?" Theo repeated.

"That I am." The duke stood taller now. He was recovering some of his dignity and brushed at his sleeves with one hand as if to brush away the terrors that had haunted him before Theo arrived.

"Your daughter, sir. She told me to relay to you that she is well and that her thoughts go with you whilst you war against those that would do her harm." Theo's words had a profound effect on the man. Tears of joy ran down his cheeks to replace the ones he had shed in fear.

"You are acquainted with my Irene?" Duke Eular asked, gathering up his bloodied sword from where it lay abandoned on the stone floor next to his cloak.

"I am Nem's friend, who harbours feelings for your daughter, sir, and I'm sure would have wished to be here to fight alongside you."

A pained look crossed the duke's face at Theo's words. "I am sorry you had to see me in such a state my lad; but I have killed more men tonight than I can count on both hands...and still they come through the mist." His bony frame shuddered and Theo feared he would revert back to his previous pathetic state. But then the duke looked at him warmly. "I owe you more than my life, young..."

"Theodor, sir. Theodor Marentherin."

"Aah. Your reputation precedes you Theodor of Cyrus Island. Irene has told me much about you and your mission to save the princess. By the looks of it you have succeeded as well, though I cannot for the life of me imagine why you would let her fight on these walls after such a struggle to wrench her away from the warlock's clutches."

"You have seen her..." Theo clutched the older man tightly around the shoulders, "...here, on these walls, you say?"

Eular nodded grimly.

"You are quite sure?"

"I could not mistake our princess for any other woman, young Theodor. She has a certain way of dressing and carries herself with a military gait the best warrior would envy. I am quite certain it was her I saw passing by."

Theo didn't know whether to feel gladdened by the news or remorse that Adelayne was facing this hell without him, alone out there with who knew how many of her foes trying to tear her to oblivion. "How long ago was this, Your Grace?" Theo rattled the man's bones more vigorously than he intended.

"I couldn't say, Theodor. I was...how shall I put it...beside myself, for I don't know how long. Is it my imagination..." he bent over as his body was racked by coughs "...or is the smoke a lot thicker than before,' he wheezed.

"Yes it is," Theo's throat was also being tickled by the smoke.

"Come!" Eular almost wrenched his arm out as he pulled him through the smoke.

They sped forward at a dangerous run. The smoke was thick. Theo strained to listen to any tell-tale signs of a skirmish or an approaching foe. Eular was revived completely, for he slew another three nymphs who had blundered coughing and spewing through the smoke before them.

Then, for an instant, the smoke cleared. Theo stood transfixed as he gazed at a group of nymph warriors surrounding a crouching form. Their opponent held two long swords with slightly curved edges, like those favoured by the Kalim Ocean warriors of the east. She was outnumbered ten to one, but the swords she held identified her as a weapons master. Already a small pile of bodies had formed around her from the nymphs' previous failed attempts to get at her.

Theo did not give the nymphs a further chance to hurt the woman he loved. "Maren'Therin. Denam ked dosa!" he yelled his battle cry, flinging himself at the two nymphs closest to him. One fell instantly to his blade as a thin red line formed across its throat in the wake of Theo's lithureal blade. The other just managed to parry Theo's blow but was run through by Eular's long sword.

"Blood and glory! Death to our enemies!" Eular uttered his challenge as he engaged two more nymphs.

Theo moved on to tackle two more opponents. The nymphs had recovered from their initial surprise and were blocking Theo's blows retaliating with their own. Theo was facing a nymph with its face covered completely in white paint, contrasting with its black hair. The White Fang clan member blinked brown eyes at him through its pale mask, grinning maliciously as it wielded a throwing axe and dagger.

The other nymph, a member of the Stag Clan, had green tinged hair and held a sabre with a serrated edge. Such a weapon could inflict a terrible tearing wound.

They circled each other looking for an opening. White Fang was the first to spring to action. He jumped in the air throwing his axe at Theo as he descended. Theo swung his sword knocking the axe aside but was too slow to parry the dagger thrust. White Fang retrieved his dagger from Theo's arm and slashed once more. Theo flung himself backwards as the dagger blade missed his throat by inches. Meanwhile the she-nymph with the green tinged hair sprang at him from the side and cut open his leg. Theo stepped back to distance himself from his foe. He had never faced two opponents simultaneously. He tried to recall what his father and Roxette had taught him. "*Bring them in line,*" Roxette's words came to him. He remembered. "*You must force them to move the one behind the other. Keep circling so they get in each other's way and have to come at you one at a time, and concentrate on hurting the one in the front whilst the other tries to circle around their comrade.*"

White Fang came at Theo first. Theo circled forcing the she-nymph behind.

"Now you die, plain dweller!" The nymph used its dagger to poke at his opponent. Theo side-stepped neatly and brought his sword down slicing off the nymph's hand by the wrist, then swivelled on the spot bringing his blade in a horizontal motion. He felt the sharp blade bite into the nymph's throat then cut clean through. The nymph's head lopped off and went rolling towards his she-nymph companion. She shrieked with loathing and sprung at her opponent. Theo reversed his stance and plunged his blade deep into her soft abdomen, then stood up wrenching his sword away.

Eular had also dispatched one of his opponents and was parrying with the other. Theo looked in Adelayne's direction and saw that she was being hard-pressed by two nymphs. The other two she had dispatched.

Theo screamed once again to attract the attention of Adelayne's opponents. They came at him without pause. One of the nymphs had half of its hair painted red along with that half of its face.

Theo was beginning to tire. He barely managed to deflect the two nymphs' blows and was bleeding from several wounds. From the corner of his eye he saw Eular coming at one of his opponents. The nymph turned to meet its new assailant and managed to sink its blade in Eular's side before it was slain. Eular gasped and fell in a heap on the stone floor.

Theo was left to fend for himself. He glanced at Adelayne and found she was staggering from exhaustion. The red-masked nymph came at him relentlessly. She kept getting through his guard and managing to graze him. He was losing a lot of blood and his clothes were sticky and torn.

"Soon, plain dweller. Soon all your troubles will be over," the nymph taunted him.

A flash of blades passed across Theo's dull vision. He looked up to see a nymph staring at him with anger in her eyes. "I am forced to slay more of my people for you, Marentherin." Theo collapsed in Roxette's arms.

He recovered in time to see Roxette tending to Adelayne's wounds. Eular also had been wrapped around the waist by a broad bandage. Roxette held him up and they peered over the wall. The first rays of sunlight bathed the battlefield before the outer wall. Tears streamed from Theo's eyes as he beheld a sight that drained him of all hope. Zarzbudin's army spread out before them like the ocean spreading around an outcrop of rock.

A great outcry was raised by thousands of throats in the nymph ranks and carried across the walls to the cowering residents within. "Haulbrakk eni méges! Haulbrakk eni méges! Thrinatos de Feldarheim! Thrinatos de Feldarheim!"

"What do the words mean?" Theo asked in a hoarse whisper, turning to Roxette by his side.

"They are saying, 'Haulbrakk is great! Haulbrakk is great! Death to the plain dwellers! Death to the plain dwellers!'" Roxette translated, unable to conceal the tremor in her voice.

Adelayne slithered her arm around Theo's waist and stared out defiantly at the enemy who would wipe out her people. "Haulbrakk is the Mountain nymphs' god of War."

A trumpet sounded the retreat from within the second wall. The outer rim was to be abandoned by the Alcavians.

King Dreyfus stood at the parapet of the middle wall. At first he had been sure that his decision to abandon the outer rim, even with one day's delay, had been correct. But now he was not so sure. The middle wall, like the inner one, was not as tall, nor as wide as the outer. He scolded himself for his lack of providence at not having maintained it in a better condition. Large chunks were missing from the surface where time had eroded some of it away. *But how was I to know that I would one day be required to fall back from the outer defences which our predecessors had built to withstand the Mountain nymphs' most arduous efforts?* That was no excuse, of course. He was responsible for the safety of his people and should have had more foresight. He had been overly confident in Alcavia's ability to fend off an attack.

King Dreyfus had given the choice to two thousand of his bravest men to offer themselves as sacrifice to hold out for as long as they could so their comrades could withdraw in relative safety. The Templar commanders had been right. Before the last of the Alcavian troops had been ushered to safety, the nymph forces had launched a concentrated attack with siege towers that were pushed forward by a score of orguls. The trap doors to the towers fell open and trolls and ogres poured out accompanied by a multitude of nymphs. The fighting lasted for most of the morning.

By midday, the Warlock's forces had breached the defences. The outer bounds of the city were filled with the Dragon's Foot Mountain forces. Not a one of the brave two thousand Alcavians survived, though historical accounts written years later confirmed that the Alcavians had killed twice their number before being wiped out. The fires burnt unchecked, blanketing the defenders with a cloud of smoke which every so often broke up as the north winter wind descended from the mountains. Dreyfus prayed for snow. It would encumber the siege towers' progress and would make the walls slippery and harder to scale.

He shook his head in dismay. He had lost almost a fifth of his army in just two days. At this rate they would not last more than a couple of weeks. He needed to do something to halt the Warlock's advance, even for a week more; then by some merciful act of Athud, Zarzbudin would be forced to retreat by the winter conditions. A siege could not be maintained if the assailing troops were not fed properly, and winter would force the nymphs to seek out their mountain refuge. *Why is Ghiadon not sending any aid? Has Queen Viola abandoned us to our fate, as did Ameron and Ramila?* He could not blame the Forest nymph queen. She had to fend for her own people. With Ramila and Ameron fighting each other, Ghiadon would be left alone once Alcavia fell to the Dragon's Foot Mountain forces. *How have we allowed matters to reach this point?* Archon had informed him that the Dark Disciples were involved in the plot to deceive Ameron and to fuel the city's senseless hatred for Ramila.

He saw the grey clad figure coming towards him with a hawk resting on his left shoulder. Archon halted before the king and leaned heavily on his staff as if all the cares of the world were weighing on him. The hawk, sensing its master's discomfort, ruffled its rufous feathers. "My king," the mage said solemnly. "We must do all we can in the next few days to hold the enemy back. We cannot allow Alcavia to fall so easily. Our friends in the east are depending on us."

The king's face reddened with fury. "You feel I am not doing everything in my power, wizard? Can you not see that we are outnumbered? And why should we care about the rest of Leonium? I do not see any of their numbers coming to our aid. Do you?"

"Your anger is justified. But we are all servants of the Light. We must all play our part to keep the forces of the Dark at bay, for the greater good of our descendants. I am not saying you are not doing everything you can. I am just speaking out of frustration. Forgive me."

The king's face softened and he placed a comforting hand on the mage's shoulder. "There is nothing to forgive, my friend. After all, you are here amongst us fighting a war with no chance of victory. You are allowed to feel frustrated. I would ask you to take heart, however. We have still not dealt our final blow on the Warlock's forces. He will bleed badly before this is over. This I swear to you Archon of Aldorn."

Theo was walking through the streets in search of Adelayne. He had been informed by the page boys that she was helping to tend to the wounded massed in the church closest to the city gate. He reached the grounds to find a group of sisters there from Sulicia Island. He looked around to discover with dismay that there were many casualties to the war; it was only the third day.

"Theodor? Theodor Marentherin!"

Theodor looked up from the broken bodies of the men lying in the church grounds. It took him a while to recognize the woman standing before him. Her blue eyes were tired and her pale skin and fair hair were stained with blood where she had wiped at her face. "Lucinda. I am pleased to see you, sister." Theo bowed his head formally to the nun.

"No need for such formalities between friends, Theodor." Lucinda took him in a warm embrace. He hugged her back with greater fervour than he had originally intended. He missed his sister and all day he had not been given the chance to get close to Adelayne. To him Lucinda, being Archon's sister, was almost family. In the absence of Serilia, Lucinda would serve for the time being to comfort him.

"There, there, my dear Theo." Lucinda sensed his pain and stroked his hair returning his hug lovingly, kissing him gently on the brow.

Just then both Lucinda and Theo turned to find Adelayne gaping at them with wide eyes.

"Adelayne, this is..." Theo began to explain, but the princess turned around and fled from the church grounds.

"Go after her," Lucinda urged, as Theo turned back disbelievingly to look at her.

Theo shook his head. "I'm too tired now to deal with such a matter. I'll catch up with Adelayne later on and try to explain."

Adelayne fled towards the palace. She knew what she had to do now. She could not blame Theodor for finding another love. He was young and in need of affection. She could not offer him what he needed. She was a warrior maiden of Alcavia. Her duty to her people and her kingdom would not allow her to seek out a love of her own. She could not be both a guardian of Alcavia and a woman living a natural life. She had been wrong to allow her feelings for Theo to get the better of her. Better they split up this way. Better that Theo had a comforting embrace to help him get over her. In the end, things would work out. Her place was by her father's side, fighting against the enemies of Alcavia. It was time for

Adelayne, daughter of King Dreyfus and Queen Crystal, princess of the Silver Dragon kingdom to carry out the duty which her uncle had spent all those years preparing her for.

She entered her room and seized her two blades, placing them in their sheaths behind her back. Then she placed an assortment of daggers and small knives in various parts of her war suit. When she was sure she had not left anything behind, she made her way swiftly through the corridors of the palace and out towards the sound of the fighting. She encountered a warrior woman, much like herself, on the way to the middle wall.

"Mind if I come along, princess?"

Adelayne threw a cold blue-eyed stare at the warrior with the black hair, tipped with red as if it had been dipped in blood. "Do as you will, Roxette. Just make sure you stay out of my way. I don't want to mistake you for one of *them* in the heat of battle," she said petulantly, nodding in the direction of the nymph attackers.

They made their way to the palace yard where Adelayne used to train with Theo under Roxette's guidance. There they encountered the Lord of Alcavia surrounded by his fiercest warriors. King Dreyfus had donned his plate of armour. It consisted of a wide silver breastplate with the emblem of the silver dragon carved on the plate of steel. His shield was shaped like the pointed head of a spade and was coloured red on the one half and plain silver on the other. A silver dragon adorned the red half. In his right hand, he held a two-handed sword. Leon was by his side and wore similar armour. Adelayne was blinded by the sun reflecting on the brilliance of their silver armour.

"Princess. What are you doing here? I gave orders for you to stay with the fire fighters. Why do you not obey me, daughter?" Although his tone was rough and commanding, King Dreyfus stared at Adelayne with gentleness and warmth.

"I cannot, my king. My place is by your side, as much as it is your son's duty to be here." Adelayne stared pointedly at her brother.

"Is there nothing I can do to dissuade you from the decision you have taken?" The king looked at her beseechingly. But he knew the answer, even before the princess shook her head.

"Then be welcome, daughter. May your blade smite many of our enemy before the day is over." The rest of the warriors exchanged the same battle cry.

"May we join you, my lord?" Commander Baxter stepped up close to the king in battle gear with Athud's flame forged across his chest. He was accompanied by the towering form of his colleague, Commander Dionar. Standing beside the bear-like commander and fully a head taller than him was the knight Brond, the largest man Dreyfus had ever laid eyes on. Ancient Dromid was also in the group of Ramilans, wearing a suit of armour fashioned when he had been a young knight: the suit was intricately carved in silver and bronze with heavy plating and a snarling wolf embossed on the front breastplate. With his long flowing white hair, he looked majestic.

"We have but four hundred knights of the church with us," Baxter said, pointing at the ranks of the Templars gathered in the square. They were dressed in chain mail and brandished wicked-looking weapons of various types. "All of them will fight, however, my king with such ardour that they will equal any four hundred the enemy may throw at us."

"The knights of the church are always welcome, my friends." The king beamed an appreciative smile at the commanders.

"We too would like to join you, my king. That is if you will have us fight by your side." Archon stood before King Dreyfus, holding the reins to his dappled grey stallion. Mist had arrived with Roxette's shaggy mare a week before the mage and his friends had flown to Alcavia. The bond between mage and steed was strong; no river crossing or rocky path could stop Mist from finding his way back to his master.

Archon was dressed in his customary grey cloak and pants, but in his right hand he held a long sword and in his left a black shield with a silver sword imprinted on the front. "I have long had this Aldorn sword and shield in my saddle bag in case I would ever need them. They used to belong to my father, Nexedor. They will serve me well, I think, for the task that lies ahead. I have Mist to thank for this opportunity," he said, gently stroking the stallion's soft nose. Mist neighed and flicked his ears as he prodded the mage's shoulder affectionately.

The king laid a hand on the mage's shoulder. "Your presence gives us strength, Archon of the house of Thendelin. Roxette too is welcome. But why have you brought young Theodor with you? I thought we agreed to keep the lad back from the front line for as long as possible?"

"Alas, my king. Theodor is as stubborn as your daughter, with whom he is smitten and it is plain for all to see. He wishes to remain by the princess's side to offer what protection he can. My authority as a sorcerer of the council does not give me the power, or the right, to interfere with matters of the heart, my king. So here we are before you."

"And who might be the fair lady who stands by your side with a knight's sword in her hand, dressed in nun's clothing, if I am not mistaken?"

"You are not, my lord. This is my sister Lucinda, my lord king, and she too insisted that she help in this hour of greatest need," Archon said, introducing his sister. Then turning to the princess, he added, "Lucinda loves both Theodor and his sister Serilia. She sees them both as her cousins, you might say." Adelayne blushed profusely. She turned to Theo and smiled, then lowered her eyes.

"I suppose we should send someone to make sure the queen does not come to the wall also," the king jested.

"I would say that it is too late for that, my lord," a feminine voice answered from the group gathered in the courtyard. They all turned to find the queen dressed in chain mail and wearing a conical helmet on her head.

"Oh, this is too much!" the king retorted. "This is no place for the queen of Alcavia. It is our duty to protect you from harm, my lady, not throw you in its way."

"That may be so, my husband, but I was a warrior maiden of the Forest nymphs many years before I became your wife and queen. We face a common foe to both Ghiadon and Alcavia. I and the three hundred nymph archers with me," she pointed at a group of nymphs fully dressed in battle gear, "have a duty to our countrymen. We will not shy away from it now." Some of the nymphs Theo recognized from that night he and Adelayne had visited Ellodiere's chapel.

The king looked as though he had not said his last word, but then realized that his wife's mind was made up. "I want you to remain behind me at all times," he commanded his wife.

"Of course, my husband," the queen answered, smiling sweetly.

"Now all of you," the king turned to his men, "will accompany me to the middle wall. Our enemy is preparing to strike and we must be ready to meet him."

The king called out a battle cry sending up a chorus of answering voices.

The nymphs did not take long to gather their numbers. When all the buildings within the outer rim had been torched, they turned their attentions to the defenders on the walls. Soon arrows were blotting out the sunlight as they flew through the air at the Alcavians. There was retaliatory fire, but this time the attacking force had a chance to shield itself behind the rubble of the torched buildings. However the same buildings provided an obstacle to the siege engines.

In the night the fighting was continued with renewed fervour. Ogres and trolls were deployed to clear the rubble for the siege engines. The defenders shot a hail of arrows at the thick hides of the foul beasts. Many were brought to the ground exhaling their last breath as they lay in a pool of their own blood. But many more managed to flee unharmed, only to return hauling the siege towers with ropes bound around their waists and shoulders.

"Keep firing at them," Archon screamed from atop the parapets. "Don't let them get close with those towers." The Alcavians responded with a new shower of arrows. Many arrowheads had been wrapped with cloth dipped in pitch and were set alight. They were fired at the towers, but only a few of their targets burnt, for the occupants of the towers carried buckets full of sand and water and had also drenched the covering tower skins thoroughly before pushing the siege engines forward.

The towers reached the middle wall and their trap doors were released. The beasts from within howled with rage as they descended on their foe. Theo found himself staring at the gaping maw of a large troll. He took only an instant to recover from his initial shock; it was smaller than the one he had faced the previous day; this one was almost his height. Then he was crossing swords with the beast. The troll with one large swing of its arms had managed to swipe two Alcavians off the wall. Before it could swing back, Theo moved in swiftly and pushed the blade of his sword deep into the creature's back, just below the rib cage. The troll gave out a shrill screech before toppling off the wall like a falling boulder.

Theo had no time to recover fully, for a group of nymphs was coming at him from the siege tower. He caught

Adelayne in the corner of his vision. As he looked ahead at the approaching nymphs, three of them fell to their knees clutching at throwing knives that were stuck in their throats. They looked disbelievingly at the princess then fell to the stone floor. The rest of the nymphs were shouting curses as they raced towards the pair. Theo sliced a nymph in two before it could get at the princess then turned around to find that Adelayne had dispatched two more opponents. He turned back towards the siege tower where Roxette was in the middle of a group of nymphs, slicing with her swords and kicking her opponents in the groin and knees. A few of the church knights came to her aid and together they managed to fell the remaining foe. The knights set fire to the tower and pushed it from the wall with long poles, sending it toppling to the ground where it crushed underfoot more of the attacking force.

Theo turned to find the king fending off three ogres; their mouths were filled with rows of teeth and their three-eyed faces were even more hideous in the daylight. The king was not alone; Prince Leon, Archon and the queen were by his side. The beasts offered a good fight, and even managed to graze the prince's shoulder with their chopping weapons, but they were soon overpowered. Archon wrenched his sword away from the chest of a fallen ogre and proceeded to engage a group of nymphs. The king and his family followed close behind with Theo and his group. Soon they had the wall secured once more.

The fighting carried on throughout the night till the early morning hours. At dawn a great horn was sounded by one of the orguls in the Mountain nymph's ranks and the siege towers were drawn away from the defenders' firing range. The siege engines continued to batter the middle wall throughout the day and the enemy archers kept their assault going, diminishing the number of defenders on the wall, but also suffering great casualties themselves. The attackers had not retreated, but their main assault teams had been called back.

"It seems we have managed to hold out the night and this day," the king said, turning to the Templar commanders and Archon.

"Yes, my lord," Commander Baxter agreed, smearing his brow as he wiped at it with a gauntleted hand spluttered with blood, "though we have suffered great losses." He looked around the parapet, which the remaining soldiers had not had time to clear of fallen comrades.

"There are many of our foes lying amongst the fallen," the king said, wiping at his brow with a trembling, bloodied hand. He had taken off his helmet and his hair was plastered on his head with sweat. He unfastened his dented plate of armour and placed it against the wall beside him.

"Father." Prince Leon came closer to the king and saluted. The prince had already taken off his suit of armour and was wearing a fresh change of clothing. He and the rest of his group had been excused at the crack of dawn to take a much earned rest, whilst the king remained stubbornly behind with a small force of men to ensure that the walls were kept manned until the majority of his army had taken its breather. "Father, I have the report with me. We have made a count of our men."

"Report," the king said, grimly.

"We stand at just under eight thousand strong, my lord," the prince answered glumly. Then a wicked grin crossed his face. "We have made an estimate of our enemies' fallen. They number at close to seven thousand, my liege. Last night's attack was a resounding failure for the Witch King and his minions."

"That may be so," Archon murmured, staring out at the enemy lines that were massed before the walls of Alcavia and stretched out for as far as the eye could see, "but at this rate, we will not last till winter." Then, he added morosely, "and seven thousand are small loss for an army of Zarzbudin's size. We still face an army of over one hundred thousand." The mage shook his head in frustration. His grey cloak had been torn from his shoulders and his white shirt was ripped in several places. A wound above his right arm had reddened his sleeve and his pants were slit open where blades had bitten into his legs. It had been a tough night and they had paid for the defence of the wall dearly with their blood.

"How are your mother and sister, Leon?" the king asked, his voice thick with concern. He had kept his finest soldiers close to his queen throughout the night's skirmishes. His attempts to protect Adelayne from the full brunt of the enemy's attack had proven a tougher task, since the princess was used to being in the thick of battle.

"Queen Crystal and the princess are both fine, father," the prince answered. "They are resting."

"Good. I'm relieved that we managed to keep harm from coming to them last night. I must admit there were several moments when I felt we were losing control of the battle."

"We came out alright in the end, my lord," Commander Baxter offered encouragingly.

"We barely kept them at bay, commander, though I thank you for your words. Tell me sir, how many of your fine knights are still standing with us?"

"I'm afraid I lost a lot of my men, my lord. Many have been my companions and steadfast friends for years. Half our number survived, though they did not die easily." The commander's voice was filled with pride for his men.

"Indeed your Templar knights have proven exemplary in their fighting skills, commanders," the king turned to include Dionar in his praise. The knight bowed in acceptance, though his face was grim at the loss of his friends. "It is rare to come upon such finely trained men. I only wish there had been more of you."

"My lord?" the prince interrupted.

"Yes, son?"

"My lord, I am here to relieve you. We'll need to keep up our strength for the fight ahead."

Theo was being cared for by Lucinda, who had once again laid her weapons aside to tend to the wounded. Lucinda gave him a potion to ease the pain in his head. It was still pounding from the punches foreman Rogue had given him that day in the Witch Lord's hall. Roxette too was treated to the same. She was missing a molar tooth from the ordeal and Lucinda had wrapped her jaw and head in a bandage to help mend the bone which had been badly bruised from Rogue's fists. Last night's cuts and bruises added to their wounds, but they could not afford to stay away from the fighting. The Alcavian forces were dwindling and every man and woman who could wield a sword was needed—for a thousand women had also joined the fighting ranks, despite the king's strongest protests.

Lucinda had not managed to come out of the fight unscathed. She too had a gash across her cheek and her left arm was cut open at the muscle. One of the sisters had helped to tie it up in a sling so it now hung useless by her side. To Theo's disappointment Adelayne was also cut in several places, though to his relief none were serious injuries. Theo hoped he could dissuade the princess from going back to the front line again, but he knew he would not have much success. Instead he concentrated on being close to her and on offering her words of encouragement, and his love.

They all looked towards the coming of dusk with dread.

Zarzbudin's forces were falling into a repetitive pattern. By day they would harass the defenders keeping a steady stream of arrows flying at their opponents on the walls. Catapults would hurl their load of rocks to crush unsuspecting soldiers or to weaken the walls further. By night the siege towers would be rolled forward to deliver the main thrust of the attack. It was at these times that the enemy forces struck their fiercest blows and caused the heaviest fatalities to the Alcavians.

Nightfall inevitably settled over the city like a dark sinister storm and, as the last rays of sunlight were chased away, the sky released a heavy rainfall which added to the defenders' misery. Wearing chain mail or suits of armour and being drenched by heavy rainfall tended to dampen a soldier's spirits.

"Roxette, you are the sharpest eyed amongst us. Tell me what you see yonder. *There*, where that large group of nymphs has massed together." King Dreyfus indicated a distant spot just beyond where the nymph forces had torn down the outer wall to let through the main body of their army and their siege engines.

Roxette strained to see what was approaching them from the distance. "I'm not entirely certain, King Dreyfus but it looks like a giant ramp built from wood. It's being drawn by a score of Orguls."

"A score you say?" the king asked in disbelief. "They have a score of those beasts massed together? Commander Baxter, what do you make of all this?" The king turned to the Templar.

"It seems the Dragon's Foot Mountains are preparing to launch an attack with their most prized weapons." The commander answered, stroking his chin with one hand.

"Oh, and what might that be, commander?"

"Why, the Orguls themselves, my king. The beasts are too large to place in the siege towers and you have sealed the gates. The only other option left to the Orguls is to scale the walls. I believe the ramp is the method they will employ."

"Commander, I do believe you are right." The king stared at the approaching ramp that was looming larger every minute. Drums beat steadily to mark the ramp's slow progress as it was being pushed forward. "I believe it's time we put a stop to our enemies' advance," the king said with decisiveness. "Instead of sitting here waiting for the Orguls to come, we will take them by surprise."

"My lord?" Commander Baxter looked at the king questioningly.

"Prince Leon!" the king shouted. His son answered and came running to his side. "Order the cavalry to mount up. Oh, and get me my charger as well. We ride out to meet our foe." The prince saluted and went to deliver the king's orders.

"My lord? You propose to open the gates?" Commander Diorn asked with trepidation.

"I have been preparing for just such a need, my lord Diorn," the king answered solemnly. Then he barked out another command. "Bring the archers!"

At least a hundred men with bows answered his call. They briskly climbed the steps leading to the parapet and spread themselves along the wall above the gates.

"They will keep the entrance clear of our enemy," the king stated grimly.

"We'll need to ride out fast," Diorn warned. The king nodded.

When the cavalry had been massed together at the gates, the king turned to face his men. He had a force of a couple of hundred select knights. Amongst them were his son Leon, commanders Baxter and Dionar, knights Templar Duel, Miranda, ancient Dromid and towering Brond. Lastly Adelayne with Theo. The king raised his sword and saluted the men and women on horseback. "May your spears find their targets with their first strike and may your sword blades decapitate your foes with their first swing. Death to our enemy!" The cavalry took up the battle cry.

Roxette and Archon had been ordered to remain behind to guard the queen.

"Be careful, Theodor," Archon called out as the youth passed him by.

Theo heeled his sorrel stallion forward. It had belonged to Ajax and was given to Roxette at the news of his death. Roxette, unwilling to give up her shaggy brown mare, gave the stallion to Theo who had been left without a steed after Queen Paula's rescue and the narrow escape from the Ameron Guard. The sorrel war horse snorted as it fell in beside Adelayne's large white.

The orguls were completely caught unawares by their charge. Several of the beasts fell to the cavalry's spears as they pierced the unsuspecting beasts in the belly. However the rest of the orguls massed together when they realized the fate that had befallen their kin and howled with anger, frothing at the mouth as they unleashed their malice for the riders.

King Dreyfus bore down several nymphs with his first pass and circled round to meet the remaining orguls. They charged and slammed once more into the horned beasts that stood as tall as three horses. The orguls were better prepared for the second rush and most managed to swipe the spears away with their arms that were as thick as the horses' torsos. The orguls swung their clubs and began to bear into the riders. King Dreyfus, sensing the danger to his men, sprung forward with his black charger and cut the hamstrings of two orguls, bringing the beasts crashing to the ground screaming in agony. He then delivered the killing thrust by slicing through the orguls' jugular with his broadsword held in both hands so he could deliver the power required for the death stroke. His men, seeing how their king had dispatched two orguls simultaneously, followed their lord's example and proceeded to attack the beasts with thrusts and jabs from their axes and swords. Soon men, horses and orguls were a milling mass.

Theo was by Adelayne's side, trying desperately to stay alive. Gnashing teeth, horns and claws were coming at him from all directions. At some point he felt his steed being snatched from under him. He fell to the ground and looked up in time to see his stallion being flung to one side by an orgul, like a hare is flung by a man. The sorrel stallion landed heavily on its back, its spinal column snapping. The orgul blew out through its dilated nostrils its contempt for man and steed, then it advanced towards Theo brandishing a cleaving knife like the ones used by butchers to chop meat, though this chopping tool was six feet long. The orgul raised its weapon and brought it slamming down. Theo managed to roll away only seconds before the cleaver hit the spot where he had lain. The orgul ripped the weapon out of the ground and came at Theo once more. Ordinarily Theo would have brought up his sword to block his attacker, but he knew that in this case his arm would be severed from the force of the orgul's thrust.

So he sidestepped. The chopping blade grazed his left arm–he had been a tad late. The orgul came at him again and Theo flung himself between its legs and emerged on the other side. He ran and heard the sound of the orgul's large feet pounding the ground as it followed after him. He remembered that night in the cave with Roxette. They had not been able to outrun the female orgul. If it hadn't been for the tunnel they had crept into, the orgul would have had them. He continued to run towards the safety of the city walls, not daring to look behind him. Then he felt something grab his shirt and haul him into the air. For a frightful moment he believed himself close to death.

To his relief he found himself sitting astride a white stallion racing at breakneck speed towards the gates of the middle wall. He felt slender arms around his mid-section whilst the stallion surged forward. He smelled Adelayne's unmistakable lavender perfume. Looking behind him he could see a diminished group of riders heading back to the walls with them. The riders were being closely followed by a half dozen orguls that had not been slain. The orguls fell back as the riders neared the city wall. The Alcavian archers fired arrows incessantly at the horned beasts to keep them at bay. At last they made their way through the gates to safety. Theo looked around and found that King Dreyfus and Prince Leon were amongst the survivors. He estimated there were fifty riders left.

"Where's Commander Baxter?" he asked.

"I'm afraid the commander did not make it back," Dionar answered, as he removed his dented helmet. "I saw the commander falling to an Orgul's cleaver after he had killed three of the foul beasts."

Theo dismounted from Adelayne's tall stallion and patted the horse's neck in thanks. The charger had protected his princess. He extended his arm and helped Adelayne dismount. Then he caught sight of Duel cradling a slim figure in his arms. It was Dame Miranda. Blood gushed from a wicked wound to her head. A group of sisters stepped up to the knight and took Miranda away to the infirmary. Duel stood there morosely, his sullen gaze fixed on the sisters. Brond followed behind, carrying Dromid on his broad shoulders. Dromid's plumed helmet had been lost in the skirmish so his long white hair hung down his comrade's back as he lay there limply; his bronze breast plate had been dented and parts of his armour had been torn off.

The remainder of the night the siege towers rolled forward once more. Archon was hard-pressed to keep the enemy at bay. The king and those that had accompanied him during the attack on the orguls were unable to aid the mage in his task. So the weight of the defences rested on Roxette's and Archon's shoulders. Lucinda and Queen Crystal were there to help as well. Several times during the night the queen had dealt a surprise blow with her sword, saving the mage's life. When it seemed they could hold out no longer, the first rays of sunlight broke through once more and King Dreyfus returned to his post to chase away the last of the night's attackers.

The city's defences had held for a fourth night.

King Dreyfus sat alone in his command tower looking out at the city that had supported generations of Alcavians. It was not the most magnificent city in Leonium, for it was built like a fort with three tall walls and much attention given over to defence, though to Dreyfus it was home. The bleak rainy weather matched his mood. Winter would not come while there was rain. There was a plus side to the wet conditions. The fires that had been blazing around the city for the past seven days were now being brought under control. *Seven days of torment*, he mused, *with each attack fiercer than the one before.* Zarzbudin sensed that he needed to bring an end to the siege before winter arrived. He was throwing all his efforts into his campaign, wasting away the lives of his troops in daring foolhardy attacks that resulted in heavy losses on his side. But he could afford to be wasteful.

A bird flew through the window and landed on the king's desk. It ruffled its white feathers to shake off the rain. It was a messenger dove employed by the king and his generals to relay news. Dreyfus bent towards the dove and untied the little scroll round its leg with apprehension.

> "My lord Dreyfus,
>
> First let me begin by informing you, my liege, that we your humble servants will do everything in our power to support our city and to defend our seas from the foe with our lives.

> I am sorry to inform you, my lord, that though we have been relatively unhurried by Zarzbudin's land forces and have successfully kept the port clear of his minions, that effort can no longer be sustained.
>
> We are under attack, my lord.
>
> Our scouts have returned to us bearing the ill news that twenty Dagorhind galleasses are sailing towards us from the south. They crossed the Giant's Fiord two nights ago and will have reached us before you receive this letter."

Dreyfus sprung off his chair, startling the dove that fell flat with its breast touching the desktop. He seized the looking glass and trained it towards the port. He fumbled with trembling hands at the adjusting knobs. The enemy fleet was brought sharply into focus. They had already descended on the Alcavian ships and were preparing their onslaught.

Dreyfus looked away grimly. He turned to the crumpled letter in his hand and read the last few lines.

> "I do not need to remind you, my liege, that their twenty battle cruisers will face your royal flagship, the 'Western Star', and our three carracks. To this we add our relic cog which is a century old and five cutters with half the length and a quarter of the archers and marines of the larger battleships.
>
> That brings our archers and marines at a total of close to four hundred, less than half that of our enemy's.
>
> May Athud have mercy on us all.
>
> Your faithful servant,
>
> Admiral Heonar."

Dreyfus flung open one of his office drawers and pulled out a small parchment of paper and a ball of red wax. He dipped his feathered pen in the ink bottle and scribbled some hurried words on the parchment. Then he placed the ball of wax in a small tin saucer and held the saucer with miniature tongs above the lit candle on his desk. He tipped the molten contents of the saucer on the little parchment and pressed the signet ring of his left finger firmly on the page before rolling it up and attaching it to the dove's leg. Then he clutched the bird in both hands and brought it close to the window. He released it into the drizzly morning rain.

"Athud's speed, my friend." The dove sped south towards the sea.

"Fire!" The lieutenant in charge of the quarterdeck gave the command as their carrack pulled up close to the foe's galleass. He was young, only twenty summers old, but had learnt a lot about naval warfare at the academy. The carrack, he knew, was outnumbered in archers two to one by the flanking enemy ships, and the galleasses had ballistae and catapults on board.

The galleasses discharged their catapult bolts as they pulled up alongside the Alcavian carrack. These missiles were similar in appearance to the grappling hooks used to tear down defensive walls but had thicker wooden shafts mounted by sharp iron heads that could pierce a ship's hull. With this type of warfare it was a race where each crew tried to fire as many volleys into their opponent's side as possible; the objective was to damage the enemy hull sufficiently so the ship capsized.

The carrack retaliated with its own volley of archery fire but with little effect. A loud crashing sound was heard. The marines clutching bows fell back in terror as a missile pierced the hull and pinned the lieutenant to the opposite wall. He hung there with his body limp and broken as blood drenched his clothing.

Below, in the hold, men were screaming as more catapult bolts struck the ship. "There's a breach in the hull!" It was the call they had been dreading. The sailors abandoned their posts and rushed up the companionway in a panic. The ship lurched and some of the sailors were thrown off the rails, sent careering back into the depths of the ship where the sea water had already rushed in. Up on deck the hatchways had been thrown open and the sailors on top were pulling their comrades out of the lower decks that had flooded. As the ship careened, the surviving sailors dived to save themselves whilst the enemy fired arrows mercilessly upon them.

Admiral Heonar watched with dread as another of the carracks sunk before his eyes. There was only one left now, the *White Pilgrim* manned by the Templars of Sulicia, and three cutters, and–surprisingly–the cog was still afloat, though her hull was letting out huge clouds of smoke; her crew was desperately trying to put out the flames–the galleasses were armed with pitch! The admiral had lost the other carrack along with two of his cutters in the first half hour of the battle to the Dagorhind's superior force.

Already longboats had been lowered from the *Western Star* and were proceeding with all due speed to retrieve the survivors from the recently afflicted carrack. Heonar knew that most of the other ship's crew would have perished in the water from enemy fire.

"Sir, two galleasses have pulled up on port and starboard!"

Heonar's thoughts were torn away from the strugglers in the sea by the need to protect his own ship.

"What are we to do, sir?"

Heonar looked down from the cockpit to his third lieutenant, Gregori, whose chestnut hair and dark brown eyes were so characteristic of Alcavia's youths. *How many of our sons have died this day?* he wondered. Gregori, a naval officer with a ready smile on his lips, was now glum. He waited for the admiral to respond.

"We do what we have been trained for, Gregori," Heonar answered. "We fight!"

Heonar nodded to his first lieutenant, a man who had spent many of his years as a youth at sea with his father as a fisherman, before he had signed up to the navy. Colben was in his mid-thirties and had served as a lieutenant on several ships both in the Alcavian fleet and abroad before he was assigned as first of the *Western Star*, a post that had elevated him to new heights and was due to result in him being promoted soon as captain of his own ship.

That was before we were called upon to fight in this futile war. Heonar had never felt so defeated before. But he had been a sailor long enough to realize when a situation was hopeless. "Lieutenant Colben!"

"Sir!" The lieutenant snapped to attention.

"Look sharp, man! I want all our ballistae manned and ready to be fired at my command, and only at my command!" he barked.

The lieutenant sent a pair of officers rushing along the quarterdeck to spread the word. Admiral Heonar waited for the galleasses to fall in line with the *Western Star*. He knew that the galleasses had three ballistae each whereas the *Western Star*, being the king's flagship, was the only Alcavian to be armed with no less than eight ballistae and two catapults; the Dagorhinds would not be expecting such firepower. The element of surprise was on the admiral's side. Timing was everything. *At least I'll take some of the bustards down with me,* he thought grimly.

"Fire!" The command came just as the galleasses pulled alongside the carrack.

A whooshing sound was heard as missiles from both sides were fired. The galleasses also got off a few rounds before the next command was given.

"Let out all sails. Full speed ahead!"

"Sir, what about the rest of the longboats?" Colben asked.

"We have no more time lieutenant," Heonar answered gravely. "Those that have not returned yet must be left to fend for themselves." They both knew what that meant; the longboats and their occupants were doomed. "My first priority is to my ship and the two hundred lives aboard."

The *Western Star* surged ahead whilst the crippled galleasses remained behind. Already one of the ships was tilting dangerously as the sea flooded its punctured hull. The other was swaying out of control as its useless rudder hung from its stern. It careered into its partner ship and they both split asunder as the sea claimed their crew.

Heonar looked up to the heavens to offer thanks that his prayers had been answered. A white dove was descending and alighted on his outstretched arm. He untied the tiny scroll on the dove's foot and read the message within.

> "Get your men out of there, NOW!
>
> Flee east, well past the Twin Islands into Ramilan waters and remain there till I summon you.
>
> Dreyfus."

Heonar read the message once more and studied the seal carefully to be sure. When he was satisfied it was genuine he turned to Colben who was looking back at him expectantly.

"Sound the retreat, first officer. Our work here is done."

Back in the tower the king observed through his looking glass as the remainder of his ravaged fleet set full sail bound due east. He noted with satisfaction that the *Western Star* surged ahead relatively unscathed leaving behind the slower galleasses. The carrack and the three cutters were not faring so well. They were equally matched in speed with their foe. The old cog, however, could not escape.

Dreyfus watched with bated breath as six enemy ships gave chase whilst the remaining twelve bore down on the port. He saw the rowers of the leading galleass heaving at their oars. It collided with the cog's starboard side and embedded its metal-plated bow deep into the older ship's hull. The cog shuddered as the galleass oarsmen reversed their direction and pulled their ship free of their prey. Within minutes the cog pitched and sank into the sea.

Dreyfus next turned his looking glass towards the cutters. One had fallen behind and was being approached by a galleass. As the larger ship pulled up beside the small cutter it released its missiles. The cutter's sails caught fire. Its mast was severed and fell overboard dragging the rigging and several sailors with it. Another missile attack was launched and the cutter blew up in flames and was consumed. Dreyfus placed his hand to his heart and forehead murmuring a silent prayer for the deceased. He turned away from the window as a knock was heard on his door.

"Enter."

Prince Leon's face was even grimmer than his father's and covered in soot and grime. He had come straight from the battlefield.

"Report, my son." The king stood, bearing up to his fatigue.

"My liege, during the last week we have lost half our men. There have been civilian casualties from the fires as well and from the missiles thrown by our foe's siege engines. Morale is low, my lord." The prince was downcast.

"Less than half our army survives on the seventh day." The king murmured in distress. *We are being beaten by both land and sea.* "What of the enemy's fatalities?"

"Their dead number at twice that of our own, my lord—hardly a dent on Zarzbudin's armour."

"We will be hard-pressed to hold the middle wall with so few." Dreyfus poured whiskey in two glasses and offered one to his son. "Your mother and sister?"

"Are well, my lord, though they too are low in spirit, as would be expected. We have had word from our lookouts that a force of Dagorhinds has landed on our shores."

"The twenty thousand Roxette warned us about." The king emptied his glass and got up from his chair. "Come, son. Help me get my armour on. Our men will need our encouragement now more than ever."

The rain had turned from a drizzle to a torrent. The king looked round at the remaining soldiers. Some were involved in removing the bodies of their fallen comrades. They were all tired men, grim and with all hope vanquished from their faces. *It will soon be over now,* the king mused. *And what have we accomplished? More than a hundred thousand of the enemy waits outside the city walls to destroy us. And then? And then Zarzbudin will move on to the rest of Leonium. City after city will fall to this superior force. Leonium cannot stand if the kingdoms fight alone. A united front has always saved us. Now, matters have taken a turn for the worse. So this will be how the western flank will fall.*

King Dreyfus stepped off the parapet wall and walked towards the church grounds. There he saw a large number of his men lying battered and wounded whilst nuns moved from soldier to soldier to administer what aid they could. Most would not make it through the day. Dreyfus found Primate Zerum amongst the group of sisters. Zerum had removed the suit of armour he had donned when he had joined the fighting and was now aiding the sisters in caring for the wounded. Dreyfus recognized the abbess of the Sulicia Island sisters standing alongside the primate. He bowed his head formally and the abbess made a gesture with her right hand, murmuring a blessing for his benefit.

"Thank you, Mother Superior." The king acknowledged her gift.

"Emilia, please," the abbess insisted. "You are most welcome, Your Majesty."

"Just Dreyfus will do," the king returned in kind. Abbess Emilia looked exhausted, like the rest of her nuns and her hair was streaming out from beneath her veil. Even so, she still managed to smile. Dreyfus was smitten by the bravery of these women that had fought with all the means they possessed; some, like Sister Lucinda, had even taken up the sword, following their primate's example; it made what Dreyfus had to say next even more difficult. "I want you to round up the wounded, Primate Zerum. We need to get them behind the inner wall. We will not be able to hold this one for much longer."

The primate was about to protest, but then nodded his head silently. The king was proposing they abandon the church to the enemy. Abbess Emilia hid her face in her veil so the king would not witness her tears. The primate placed his arms gently about her shoulders, then nodding at the king led her away.

Theo had found a house within the middle wall where he and the princess could rest and eat in relative safety. They sat together at the kitchen table and were having a hurried breakfast. Outside the sounds of war were muffled and seemed further away.

"Theo?" Adelayne moved closer and placed her slender arms around his neck.

Theo stared deeply into her blue-green eyes. Her oval face filled his vision and his heart leaped with the feelings of love he felt for her. They had grown even closer over the last few days. He was worried about her being at the war front and risking her life along with the rest of the fighting men. But he knew there was no changing the princess. She was born a warrior. He had come to accept that side of her. He respected her wishes too much to force her to stay behind. In turn he tried to protect her as best he could. As it turned out, she had saved his life several times during the fighting. "What is it, my love?"

"Tell me about your parents, Theodor. Tell me about Russilda the sorceress and Elron the former general of the Hendon forces."

Theo's eyes misted over as he recalled the warm moments he had passed with his family at his grandfather Nestor's cottage. *How I miss them all.* He had not seen his parents for close to a year. He wondered how they were faring at far-off Aldorn. He hoped they were well. At least they were far away from the war. He remembered his mother fondly, how her rich brown hair cascaded down her shoulders. Elron had said she was beautiful, and it was plain for everyone to see. He felt a wrench in his heart as he recalled his father's gentle ways, how the man had patiently guided his every step, teaching him how to fend for himself and giving him his first lessons in how to wield a sword and use a bow and arrow. Elron had lost an eye and was crippled down the one side from a confrontation he had once had with followers of the Dark. This had left a scar on Elron's soul, and perhaps it was for this reason that he had chosen to abandon his position in the Hendon army. Elron had chosen to remain at his father's cottage together with his family.

It was much later on, when Archon came for Theo with a posse of pithiks and a dark sorcerer at his heels, that Theo learnt the truth about his parents; they were hiding at Cyrus Island away from the forces of the Dark. Much had changed in their lives after Archon's visit. Theo's family had been split up with his parents seeking sanctuary at the capital city of Seldavia: Aldorn. Theo had been enlisted by Archon to serve as his apprentice and to learn how to use his gift. His sister Serilia, aunt Emeralda, and grandfather Nestor had chosen to go with him. Nemarchus, his best friend had also left behind his boyhood years to travel with him and share in his adventures. Now Theo hoped fervently that his sister and friend were safely across the Hills of Halum and on their way to Aldorn.

"Theodor?"

"Hmm?" Theo was brought out of his musing by Adelayne's gentle voice.

"Will you tell me about your parents?"

Theo smiled at her and began to tell her everything he knew. The princess returned his smile as he described his family, and they laughed together as Theo recalled cherished moments when he had been caught doing one mischievous act or another. Adelayne stroked his hair fondly and kissed him gently on the lips. Theo clutched her close and hugged her fiercely. He felt Adelayne trembling in his embrace and heard her sobbing. "What's the matter, my love?" He pulled her gently away so he could look upon her tear-stained face.

"Oh, Theodor, I'm so sorry for landing you up in this mess. If you hadn't come after me, if you had gone with your family across the hills east, you would have been safely away by now. Now...now you..."

"Hush." Theo placed her head on his shoulder and stroked her long wavy hair. He noted she still wore the emerald earrings he had given her. "I would do it all over again, my princess. That night, when I first laid eyes on you, when I was spirit travelling, I fell instantly in love with you, Adelayne. From that moment onwards our lives have become entwined. What happens to the one happens to the other."

Just then a shadow filled the doorway. Theo looked up to find the mage staring at him. Farwing was perched on his shoulder and uttered a cry in greeting as it laid eyes on Theo. Archon looked years older than the day Theo had first met him in the Triad woods. His cheeks were indrawn and hollows had formed around his tired eyes. His hair also was tangled and dishevelled and his beard was unkempt.

"I've been looking for you two," he said, entering the house. Farwing took flight; he was not comfortable being cooped up inside.

"Oh?" Theo answered trying to read the mage's thoughts. Archon's face was as grim as a grey cloud bearing the promise of rain.

"We are nearing the end of the war and I just wanted to express my thanks to you Theodor, for all the aid you have given for our cause ...and to you of course, princess." He smiled weakly at Adelayne who returned him a brave smile. Then the mage sat opposite Theodor. He looked once more like an eagle as he fixed the youth with his stone grey eyes beneath arched brows that crossed over his beak-like nose.

"This is not how I intended it to end for us, my apprentice. But we will all die in the end, and to die fighting for one's freedom and for the freedom of one's friends is as good an end as I can think of. But you can still flee Theodor–you and the princess. Varwraker awaits you within the palace grounds. All you need do is mount your dragon and take flight. Zarzbudin will not go after a solitary dragon and its riders. His interests lie with the city."

Theo considered briefly the chance at life the mage was offering him. He took one look at Adelayne and his thoughts went to her brother and parents who would be left behind. He shook his head. "I cannot, Archon. I cannot abandon my friends. I cannot abandon you to face the Dragonmaster alone."

The mage placed a hand on Theo's shoulder. "I'm proud of you, lad. We will not fall easily to the Witch Lord. He will learn what it is to face Archon Thendelin and Theodor Maren'Therin."

Theo placed his hand above the mage's and nodded in agreement. He had every intention of making the Witch King pay.

That night the siege towers rolled forth before the sun set in the west behind the peaks of the Dragon's Foot Mountains. Zarzbudin was in a hurry, it seemed, to annihilate the last remaining defenders of the city. The fighting became fierce as more and more siege towers came against the middle wall. Trolls, ogres and nymphs and a few of the remaining orguls came in their thousands. Now there were tall, dark-haired Dagorhinds in the ranks attired in grey apart from their cloaks which were blood-red like the dragon emblem on their shields and the left breast of their surcoats. This was to be the largest assault Zarzbudin's forces had launched so far.

At some point during the night, the frustrated calls of the Alcavian defenders were heard. "The wall is breeched! The wall is breeched!"

King Dreyfus barked out a command for the defenders to retreat behind the inner wall. A horn was sounded and the city soldiers moved back with the attacking forces cutting and slicing at the retreating Alcavians. When daybreak came, the last of Alcavia's soldiers were behind the inner wall. It was the city's last defence.

♦ CHAPTER 34 ♦

The final blow

She crested the hill astride her white mare and gazed at a sight she had dreaded to witness but which she was fated during her lifetime to behold. There before them lay the proud city of Alcavia, only from within its ruined walls the city was charred and aflame, like a bed of dark coals that were fed till they glowed red at the edges.

"We are too late," she uttered, tears streaming down her pallid cheeks.

"All is not lost, my queen," her first in command answered. "Look there, yonder to the palace towers. The red flag of Alcavia is still flying defiantly. Dreyfus has not yet succumbed to the mountain beast."

"My lord Anathel," a red-bearded dwarf drew the commander's attention. "How are we to pass through *that*, my lord?" He pointed at the dark mass that milled around the city walls for as far as the eye could see. Zarzbudin's forces stretched from the sea to the east right up to the foot of the Dragon's Foot Mountains and all the way up to the Apalachus River. It was a heart-wrenching sight.

"What is wrong, dwarf?" Anathel sneered at the red bearded dwarf who was straddled over a shaggy pony with a fat belly like a wine barrel. "Have you lost your nerve, highlander?"

"Baulkin has more courage in his little finger than most men have in their entire body, my lord Anathel." Another dwarf answered, only this one's beard was coal black and split in two held by golden clips at the ends. The dwarves made a formidable pair; they were dressed from head to foot in chain mail and on their heads they wore conical helmets with ogre horns jutting out from the sides. On their saddles were hitched heavy two-bladed axes. "But his question is a valid one," the black-bearded dwarf added.

Anathel bowed respectfully to the dwarf. "King Feduwin, the answer is simple. We ride through them, sir. Are you up to the task?"

"Ready when you are," Baulkin answered in his lieges stead.

"Wait," the lady atop the snow-white mare requested.

"Queen Viola?" Anathel gave her a questioning look.

"My lords, perhaps the direct approach is the best. However, I would prefer to use the edge I have on our enemy, that of surprise, to save Dreyfus and his family, if I am not too late, before you go charging down the hill."

"Then let us draw our army back until you are ready, my queen," Anathel agreed. He pointed down the hill. "We are close enough to be seen by Zarzbudin's men."

The four riders disappeared once more behind the hill.

***

King Dreyfus rushed out of his command room taking his broadsword with him. He fled down the steps as fast as he dared; they were winding and steep and with the chain mail he wore–he seldom took it off since the siege began–he was in the precarious position of losing his footing; the fall might very well kill him or at best result in broken bones at this height; the tower was tall and the stair landings few and far between. Another unearthly shriek shook the fortress walls as though they were made of paper rather than stone. His sword fell from his hand and went clattering down the stairs ahead of him as he plastered his hands over his ears squeezing tightly in a desperate attempt to shield them from the alien cries that belonged to another era.

Run! Run! came again the warning through the mind link he maintained with his dragon steed. It was all that had saved him, for in the next instant he felt a breath of hot air surging towards him from the control room at the top of the tower. He growled with fear and rage as his back was singed. Then he began to cough and gasp for breath as the poisonous fumes from the dragon's breath enveloped him.

He tripped and fell.

He shook his head, clearing his mind from the dizziness induced by the fall. Thankfully he had been close to the bottom when he lost his footing. He felt at his arms and legs. *Only bruises; no broken bones*, he thought wryly. He retrieved his broadsword and rushed out into the open expecting the worst.

He emerged into the front courtyard where a week ago he and a group of two hundred brave knights had assembled in preparation to meet the orguls' onslaught. Now, the courtyard was empty as Dreyfus cast his gaze around searching for any soul that might have remained on duty to protect the fortress. But it was too much to expect mere men to stand firm before the colossal forms that were now locked in a titanic struggle above.

Dreyfus looked up at the flutter of giant bat-like wings and tearing teeth and claws that could rip a horse to shreds in an instant. He recognized his three remaining silver dragons and Theo's red steed. The other four reds he had never met in battle, though he knew only too well to whom they belonged. One red in particular was far larger than his companions and was striving to knock Dreyfus's steed out of the sky. The alpha she-dragon had lost her mate to this foe; she screamed her loathing and brought up her talons like a hawk to scratch at the red's face. He retaliated by blowing flame at her belly. She howled in dismay and Dreyfus caught the nauseating smell of charred flesh. He couldn't bear to look. He already knew what the outcome would be. The other three aiding his steed were young and inexperienced at fighting.

"Aah, King Dreyfus. Nice of you to join us." Dreyfus turned in the direction of the baleful voice and came face to face with a knight dressed in armour unlike any he had ever seen before; it hugged the knight's form to the extent that it seemed to be a part of his flesh and did not impair his movement in any way.

So this is the Red Knight of Dagorhind! he realised with dismay. At the edge of his vision, Dreyfus caught sight of a group of the knight's men. They had emerged from behind the tower and were running towards the pair. The king realized they must have ridden over the walls on the red dragons' backs. There were seven of them.

"Your time on this earth is long overdue, Your Majesty," the Red Knight said, tauntingly. "I have been sent to ease your passage from this world to the next." He held a two-handed sword in both hands and was not encumbered by a shield–evidently he felt he didn't need one.

Dreyfus recalled Archon's words of caution. *Warning be damned!* he thought petulantly. "The only one who will be going back to the underworld from whence he came is *you*, sir knight," Dreyfus growled as he sprang at his opponent.

"Hurry Theo!" Adelayne came rushing into the *Dancing Maiden*. She and Theo had been using the abandoned tavern ever since the defenders had withdrawn behind the inner wall. It wrenched at her heart as her happy memories of the place were replaced by the desolate scene before her. The fireplace had long gone out. The wooden benches and tables were overturned–those that had not been demolished.

Theo yawned and rubbed at his eyes to clear them of sleep. It was the crack of dawn and he had only managed to get a couple of hours' fitful sleep. They had spent most of the night before on the wall defending it from the continuous onslaught of Zarzbudin's forces.

The eleventh morning since the siege began. Theo counted the days in his mind. Eleven gruelling days fighting from dawn till dusk and right through the night. Every bone in his body was aching, every muscle strained; he was ridden with fatigue. His head throbbed incessantly and his spirit was troubled night and day by the sight and smell of death spreading all around him. *How long can we go on like this? How long can we go on struggling without knowing when it will end?* But struggle they must, for they were given no other choice. They could not give in to the foe without a fight. They were too proud, too hungry for life. Whilst they fought, hope still remained.

"What is it, Adelayne? Has the wall fallen?" he asked, fearing the worst.

The princess shook her head. "Can you not hear their call?" Her face was twisted in agony.

Theo shook his head to clear it of the pain from his headache. There was something...a faint voice in the distance...a voice that meant something to him...a friend asking for help. "Varwraker!" he exhaled his breath sharply. "He's in danger!"

"Assima also," the princess confirmed.

Theo pulled on his pants and tunic in a hurry and wrestled with his sword belt whilst he stamped on his boots. Adelayne pulled him along by the arm, not allowing him time to tie up his laces as they exited the house. It was just as well, for an instant later a huge chunk of what had been part of the middle wall came hurtling towards them. They flung themselves to the ground as the missile landed on the roof behind them reducing the tavern to a pile of rubble.

Splinters of wood from the rafters caught in the youths' hair as they were covered in dust from the wreckage.

They got up and brushed themselves down, looking at each other in stunned disbelief. Theo took the time to tie his laces whilst Adelayne recovered from her shock. Then they raced to the palace with the pleading voices ringing in their ears. They skidded to a halt as they emerged from the vaulted arch of the palace entrance and beheld a sight that stilled their breath.

There, lying on the charred ground of the front courtyard, were two silver dragons. Smoke was rising from their bodies so they resembled antelope caught in a field overrun by fire. Adelayne drew her hands to her mouth in horror. She looked up to the sky and let out a breath of relief as she sighted Assima, still struggling to stay alive. Varwraker was beside her. The red dragon lying on the ground next to the dead silver pair was one of Zarzbudin's.

They turned together and caught sight of King Dreyfus and Prince Leon fending off the Red Knight's attack.

Adelayne grabbed Theo by the arm bringing him around. "Theo, listen to me carefully," she said in a voice that brooked no argument. "I want you to run to the battlements and fetch Archon immediately. Do you understand me?"

Theo nodded grimly. "Adelayne what about you? What..."

"Theo, there's no time," she said, shoving him back towards the vault. "Go now, with all due haste, if you love me." Tears were filling her eyes as she drew the swords from her back.

Theo took a good look at her, memorizing every detail on her face, every feature of her form. Then he turned and fled.

Adelayne moved with caution as she approached her father and brother. The Red Knight was not alone; there were seven more warriors with him fighting with the palace guards who were armed with halberds and trying to fend off the warriors from their king and prince. Adelayne counted a dozen guards. Of the foe, she recognized Lizelle with her blue locks and Barack's formidable third in command with the shaved scalp. The other three were nymphs she had never laid eyes on before. The last members of Rolgath's group were two Dagorhind knights. The one held a tall shield in one hand and a morningstar with cruel spikes in the other. The other knight held a mace and a round shield smaller than his companion's.

Adelayne picked the knight who was furthest from the palace guard and closest to her. She came at her opponent from the left flank. She was trying to avoid his right hand which held the ball and chain. The knight was swinging the spiked ball when he caught sight of her. He grinned at the princess maliciously. She flew at him with both swords. He retaliated bringing up his shield so her blades bounced off harmlessly. Then he swung the morningstar at her. Adelayne flung herself backwards to avoid the weapon and almost lost her footing. As the knight advanced towards her, she brought her sword from under him and sliced his arm causing him to release the shield. She brought her other sword down expecting to bury it in his chest. Somehow the warrior avoided her thrust and, before Adelayne could recover, the ball buried itself in her shoulder. She yelped in pain and fell to the ground.

Adelayne almost fainted from the pain in her shoulder. She could not feel her arm and had lost her sword. She brought herself to her knees and rose, staggering forward as her head swam, her vision becoming blurry. She managed to remain on her feet and raised her other sword. The Dagorhind stood looking at her with an amused smile.

Adelayne advanced more slowly. The knight lashed out with the ball and chain again. Adelayne managed to grab a hold of the chain and yanked at it. The knight lost his footing and came crashing into Adelayne. His eyes dilated in surprise. Then he slipped from her grasp and fell to the floor clutching at the sword in his belly. Adelayne placed her boot on his chest and ripped her sword from his gut. The feeling had come back to her injured shoulder and she retrieved her fallen sword. She did a practice stroke in the air. The arm was stiff but she could still use it. She turned to face her next opponent.

"Leave this one to me, Your Highness." Sir Duel had arrived with three more knights. One was a woman who looked at Duel with special interest. She was a tall woman with sun-darkened skin, long black hair and a perfect oval face, though most of it was covered by the bandage she wore around her head. It was Miranda, who thankfully had recovered from her head wound. *Funny how a woman's mind works at times like this*, Adelayne thought, smiling despite the gravity of their situation.

"By all means." Adelayne moved on to the nymphs and left the knight and Rolgath's two commanders–Lizelle and the bald nymph who was as big as a house–to the Templars. The princess noted with chagrin that the dozen Alcavian guards with the halberds had been slain by the group of assassins; they had evidently been well picked by Rolgath. She decided to be extra vigilant.

The princess and the nymphs circled around one another. One nymph, with a patch across his eye, held a sabre. The other had a snarl permanently fixed on his face and was missing an ear. He held two throwing knives he was whirling in his hands; a dagger hung from his belt. The third, a she-nymph with purple hair, was hefting two long swords with the tips slightly curved. *Weapons master*, Adelayne realized woefully, her blood chilling in her veins.

She forced the nymphs to align themselves so the she-nymph was behind.

One Ear made the first move. He threw his knives, simultaneously leaping in the air and snatching his dagger from his belt. Adelayne knocked both knives out of the way and brought her sword up as the nymph landed. The sword plunged deep into One Ear's chest. Adelayne yanked her sword free and brought it up just in time to fend off the second nymph's sabre attack. They exchanged blows and Eye Patch retreated making way for the she-nymph.

They circled each other once more. The she-nymph attacked with such speed that Adelayne could barely follow her moves. The nymph's blades flashed before Adelayne's eyes and she felt a cut across both thighs, her left arm, cheek and her right hand. Adelayne's right sword was struck from her grasp. She could not believe the ease with which she had been disarmed.

She backed away from the nymph pair searching frantically for a way to stall them. The she-nymph smiled triumphantly and made way for her companion to finish the princess off. Eye Patch raised his sabre and came rushing at Adelayne. The princess fell backwards dragging the nymph with her. Eye Patch landed hard on his back. Adelayne grabbed the nymph's head and twisted. The nymph's neck broke with an audible crack. Then, as she lay on the ground she made a flipping motion, like acrobats do, and was on her feet once more. The she-nymph was still smiling–this time with amusement.

"I would have you know my name, Feldarheim, before I send you to your maker," the she-nymph said haughtily.

They crossed swords and she brought her face close to Adelayne's. "Celta of the Blue Lake Clan," she hissed, pulling away. As she did so, she cut Adelayne across the other hand as well. The princess barely managed to hold on to her remaining sword. She was becoming outraged, partly from fear and partly from frustration. *"Rage is the road to death,"* her uncle Eschalion's words echoed in her mind.

"Know this, Celta of the Blue Lake Clan. I am Adelayne, Princess of Alcavia, the last person you will see before you die."

Celta's eyes widened in surprise, then she smiled with genuine satisfaction. "You honour me, princess. I could not have hoped for a greater prize: the head of Eschalion's favourite niece. Prepare to meet your uncle soon." Before she had finished delivering her threat, she sprang in the air. She came down on the princess whirling both swords.

Adelayne ducked, narrowly missing the she-nymph's death strokes. Then she rolled on the ground and came to her feet several paces away from her opponent. She had managed to retrieve her other sword. She advanced more slowly, recalling everything her uncle and Roxette had taught her. With Roxette, she had advanced to the next level of her training, but she was still several steps away from being a weapons master–unlike her opponent.

Theo was searching frantically for the mage. One would have thought it would be easy to locate a sorcerer of Archon's standing. However the city was under attack and the defenders were too preoccupied with staying alive to note the movements of any one particular man, even if it was the infamous Archon of Aldorn. Theo was desperate. Which part of the wall should he search? The king was running out of time. Why had he left Adelayne alone back there? Archon had warned that no man could stand up to the demon knight.

I have to find Archon. He was panicking. *No, I must stay calm.* Archon would be where the battle was thickest, where the defenders were in direst need.

"The wall has been breached! Our defences are down!" Theo's first instinct was to run back to the palace and escape.

Then he realized where he would find Archon. He ran in the direction of the calls of distress.

"Get reinforcements over to quadrant twelve!" he heard an officer yelling. "All reserves to quadrant twelve! Hurry or we are all doomed!"

Theo was being pushed and shoved along by the mob of soldiers who were rallying all stray men to the wall. He tried desperately to keep from falling. They arrived at the portion of the wall that had been torn down, affording a view of Zarzbudin's force massed beyond the opening and flooding through like water erupting from a ruptured dam.

Theo's gaze fell upon the towering form of Sir Brond who wrestled with an ogre using his bare hands. The beast had opened its maw and was trying to shut its jaws around the knight's head. Brond placed the fingers of both hands in two of the ogre's three eyes and gouged them out. The beast howled with pain and outrage, knocking the knight aside with its arms. It could still see with its central eye and advanced towards its opponent. Brond leaped up at the beast and punched it repeatedly on the head. The ogre fell back stunned. It shook itself to recover but Brond clasped its head under his arm and gave a mighty yank. A loud crack was heard as the ogre's spinal cord snapped. Brond threw its lifeless body on the heap of dead bodies that was accumulating all around the defenders and moved on to engage a troll.

There! Theo saw Archon clasping a staff to steady himself on the rubble of the demolished wall. He faced several nymphs who Theo realized from the tingling on his skin were gifted. Archon stretched out his hand and three of the nymphs were flung backwards cracking their heads against the wall. The other seven advanced resolutely. Madura was amongst them.

Theo sped to Archon's side.

"Theo what are *you* doing here!" Archon reproached him gruffly, as he threw up a shield to protect them from the nymphs' retaliatory blasts.

"The king needs your help, Archon. He faces the Red Knight alone!"

"The Red Knight, you say!" Archon exclaimed incredulously. "How is that possible? The wall only fell moments ago."

"He and a band of his assassins flew over the wall on the red dragons' backs."

"Hurry!" Archon grabbed him by the arm and they sped away from the wall, closely followed by the nymph gifted. Archon sent a bolt of flame flying at the closest two nymphs. They exploded into live torches as the mage's flame engulfed them.

Archon jumped onto Mist's back pulling Theo behind him. He heeled the grey stallion forward and soon they left behind the mayhem at the broken wall. Theo cast his gaze wearily behind and saw a lone rider with red tinged hair on a shaggy mare following in their wake. He felt comforted by her presence.

They arrived in time to see Varwraker and Assima fighting for their lives against three red opponents. But they could not give aid to their dragons for the king was lying on the ground wounded. His son was before him fending off the Red Knight who was eager to finish off his prey. Queen Crystal was beside the king cradling his head in her arms.

"I think his back is broken, Archon," the queen looked up at the mage tearfully as he approached.

"Stay with him." Archon turned on the Red Knight. He was about to engage him when a bolt of red flame arched towards him, forcing him to divert all his efforts to the new threat.

"Son of Nexedor!" A booming voice called out from the vaulted entryway of the palace. They all turned to behold the warlock with a triumphant smile on his lips. He was dressed in his customary maroon cloak with the upturned collar and the red dragons embroidered down the front. In his right hand he held his staff that was capped by the figurine of the golden dragon, now glowing red as the warlock enveloped himself in a protective cocoon. "I have come to finish off what we started at my fortress."

The sorcerers engaged in a battle of the minds. Theo was aware of the large amounts of energy being expended, though to the rest of the observers it appeared as though the mage and warlock had frozen.

Theo moved away from the mage and hastened to locate Adelayne. She was fighting a nymph who held two long blades with points upturned. By the incredible speed with which the nymph moved, Theo could not mistake her identity as a weaponsmaster. Theo looked around at the rest of his companions who were battling for their lives: Roxette and Lizelle were squaring off on one side, Duel and the large nymph commander on the other.

Duel was not faring too well. He had lost his sword to his opponent and was being squeezed in a bear hug by the nymph commander with the shaved scalp. Duel raised both hands and brought them down in a chopping action. The nymph released him and Duel rolled away to recover his breath.

Theo turned back to Adelayne and was about to move towards her when he caught the fluttering of something purple at the edge of his sight. *Could it be? But how had she descended so fast from the Warlock's fortress?* He was reminded by Archon's notes of caution that the Dark employed many means to accomplish its tasks.

Theo put up his shield mere seconds before the Black Widow flung her bolts of fire at him. They deflected off his shield but she retaliated with another spell. Theo felt his shield being wrenched away as if by a groping hand; he could see from the weaves Loxandra wrought that she had used the element of Air to do this. *Ingenious,* the academic side of him observed.

He seized upon the idea and did something he would not have thought of before. Loxandra yelped in surprise as she was raised in the air by an invisible force. She was being pushed rapidly towards the wall when she raised her hands and halted her mad rush. Theo felt the backlash of her counter-spell and almost capitulated to the force. He shook his head to clear his vision and looked in the direction of the sorceress. She looked back at him with an amused smile, though there was fear in her eyes as well.

"You have learnt much since we parted, my pet." Her voice was like honey spread to mask the loathing beneath.

"I am nobody's pet, Loxandra, least of all yours." Theo gathered up all his strength and sent white hot flame bursting forth from his arms. Loxandra countered with a shield which exploded as the bolts impacted upon it. She blew on her scorched hands and threw Theo a look so venomous, he expected her to choke on her own poison.

But he was not given the chance to strike again.

A black shadow passed over him as a mighty condor larger than a horse and with a wing span to match alighted before him. A figure slithered down from the condor's back. It wore dark garments that concealed its features utterly except for its beaklike nose protruding from its cowl. It freed its hands from the sleeves of its coat and began to weave its spells. Theo was knocked off his feet by a force that struck him with such intensity that he felt as though a stone wall had fallen upon him.

"Time to redeem yourself, Loxandra," the shrouded figure reproached his servant whilst wasting no more time on Theo. He trained all his attention on Archon as he approached him like a menacing dark cloud. "I have come to claim what is mine Bastiele," he said, turning to the warlock. "Our powers combined will destroy Nexedor's son."

Just then a mighty screech was heard as another of the red dragons fell between the dark sorcerer and the mage. Its throat had been slit and it lay with its belly upturned and its legs curled towards its stomach. Archon inhaled sharply, gathering his breath as he broke off his mind duel with the warlock. Zarzbudin and the dark sorcerer stared up at the dragons that were fighting above them. Varwraker and Assima were alive as were two of the red dragons. But the reds gave out a call of dismay as two more silver dragons descended upon them.

A nymph flew off the leading dragon's back and floated to the ground beside Archon. Another figure clad in black robes and bent over like a hag sprung off the second dragon's back and landed before the Red Knight. No sooner had she done so, than she began to chant in a loud voice that reverberated off the palace walls. Rolgath's sword fell from his fingers as he began to convulse. He fell to his knees and tore off his helmet, clutching at his ears as he screeched in agony.

"Demon of Dargulheind, I call you forth!" the hag spread out her arms above the knight's crouching form. Her cowl fell away from her face.

"Zoi," Theo breathed, feeling elated at the sight of her.

"I command you! Release this body which you have defiled. Go back to your master! Your time to roam this earth is not yet nigh."

Rolgath let out another howl that turned to a fit of laughter. At first the laughter sounded human. Then it grew in magnitude and became distorted as though it were being uttered by a larger throat. "I WILL RECALL MY PET, ELLODIERE," the voice uttered using Rolgath's lips, "THOUGH YOU SHOULD NOT SLEEP LIGHTLY. MY

SERVANT AWAKENS. SOON YOUR WORLD WILL BE MINE."

The dark sorcerer fell to the ground, crouching in a show of subservience. "Master," he murmured, just loud enough for Theo to hear.

Then Rolgath snapped his head from side to side and screamed. A red light burst through as a hole appeared in his armour at the chest. The light grew stronger as his chest exploded, showering Zoi's face and garments with blood. It reached for the heavens and grew in size taking on the form of a demon twice the size of the dragons that fought above.

"Claim your abomination!" Zoi screeched, bringing her arms down. A tremor shook the earth and a chasm formed beneath Zoi's feet. Zoi stood firm. Flames leaped up and engulfed the demon that fell into the chasm screaming its loathing towards the figure that had expelled it from Barack's body.

The hole sealed up and the screams were cut off. The dark sorcerer gave out a shrill whistle and mounted his steed's back. "Another time and place, Nexedor's son," he said, as the condor fled south. Zarzbudin, sensing the imminent danger, called to his pair of remaining red dragons. They descended allowing the warlock to mount. Loxandra sprang and grabbed a hold behind the warlock just before the dragons took off. Lizelle and the commander with the shaved scalp were mounted on the other red as both flew to the west, abandoning the palace. Theo looked with apprehension towards Adelayne; her nymph opponent had vanished.

The nymph queen turned to her sister. "Come," she beckoned. "Gather up your sire and let us be off. I have come to retrieve you and those few I can carry on Solla's and Teina's backs." She pointed at her two silver dragons.

"What about the rest of my people?" Queen Crystal asked of the nymph queen. "Am I to flee whilst my people remain to perish?"

"No, sister. Commander Anathel descends on your city as we speak from the north accompanied by ten thousand nymphs and dwarves."

"Too few," Prince Leonar said, with grief.

"They will be enough to help you evacuate the city, nephew."

"Evacuate?" The prince asked, incredulously.

"Yes," Viola answered bluntly. "Surely you don't believe Zarzbudin has abandoned the siege. What we have accomplished is a minor setback. He will regroup and hit us hard. We must evacuate the city whilst we have the advantage of surprise on our side."

"Wait!" Adelayne stepped up to the nymph queen. She held a small scroll in her right hand and a dove in her left. "It's addressed to father, but under the circumstances..." She gave the scroll to the nymph queen and turned to look glumly at her father. Zoi was bent over him and studying his back closely.

Viola finished reading the message, then handing it to Archon looked up at the rest of them, her face brightening. "It seems we are not entirely alone. We will split our forces. Those too old or too young to fight will flee north with my army. The rest will divert Zarzbudin's army south. Take heart. All is not lost."

♦ CHAPTER 35 ♦

A southerly breath of flame

Griffin had given over the command of the *Flying Duchess* to Kober Splitjaw. Apart from being the leader of Ameron's underground network, Kober was also a seasoned sailor. Nem looked around with satisfaction at the group of shifty characters that now manned the rigging. He and Emeralda were lucky to be alive. After they had thrown themselves overboard to save their necks from the crew of the *Unrelenting Condor*, they had spent the remainder of the day watching the fateful cutter, *Tenora*, being reduced by flames to a pile of charred timber. However, the flames had drawn the attention of another vessel, this one being a top-of-the-line clipper. Nem had stared in amazement as the *Flying Duchess* pulled up beside them searching for survivors.

Griffin retrieved his friends from the sea by some incredible stroke of luck. He was on his return journey from Cyrus when the Anvil corsairs set upon him just as soon as he cleared the north port of the island. The corsairs gave chase blocking his route west so he was forced to flee to Sandora, thus delaying his promised return to Ameron. It was during this journey that he had come across the pair swimming feebly in the cold waters surrounded by the burnt wreckage of the ill-fated cutter.

Nem was in a rush to go after Serilia, but Griffin advised him that it would be wiser to return to Alcavia with reinforcements. So they continued their journey to Ameron.

They met up with Griffin's cousin, Solitaire, who needed no convincing in joining his ships with the *Flying Duchess* to provide the aid promised to primate Zerum. Close to Ramila's shores they encountered Admiral Heonar who was delighted to accept them and informed them that he had sighted the predatory form of the *Unrelenting Condor* only a few days before heading west.

Now the admiral led a renewed fleet: Griffin's and Solitaire's new evolution carracks: the *Flying Duchess* and the *Ocean Queen*; King Dreyfus's full-rigger, the *Western Star*, along with two of Solitaire's full-riggers; four older carracks: the Templar's *White Pilgrim*, the other three Solitaire's; five cutters: two Alcavian and three Ramilan mercenaries. That meant nine large ships and five smaller ones against an opposing fleet of eighteen—nineteen if one counted the dark sorcerer's ship. The allied ships might be hard-pressed to defeat Zarzbudin's galleasses, but that was not their objective. The city was falling and they had to evacuate as many of the citizens as they could.

"Fire!" Kober commanded as the *Flying Duchess* pulled beside the *Unrelenting Condor*. Griffin's ship, like the rest that had sailed west, had been furnished with the latest missile launchers with the money they had raised in Ramila and Ameron by citizens and merchants who espoused Alcavia's cause.

The dark ship returned fire but it was outgunned by the larger carrack which carried eight ballistae armed with flaming bolts dipped in pitch compared to the Kalkador dhow's two. Grappling hooks were thrown over and lodged into the enemy ship's gunwales. Nem was amongst the group led by Kober the Black that boarded. Nem feared they would meet up with the sorcerer as they made their way on the burning deck. He was not prepared for the horrors that confronted him. There were three of them. Nem felt as though a cold hand had seized his throat and was squeezing the life out of him. He fell to the floor, clutching at his throat as the wraiths approached.

One of the wraiths screeched as its garments caught fire from a flaming torch thrown upon it. The wraith took a dive over the keel and a splash was heard as it hit the water. The other two wraiths backed away as an elderly woman advanced from Kober's group holding out her hands, waving them about in the air as she murmured a spell.

"Come, Nemarchus." Nestor helped the youth to his feet. Nem and Emeralda had been overjoyed to be united with Nestor, though the plight of Primate Karat had left them stunned. "We still have an entire ship to search," Nestor added, looking around uneasily at the fires consuming the ship. "No good you lying on your backside whilst we do the dirty work, now is there?" the old man grinned.

Nem looked over the ship's keel. The water hissed where the wraith had fallen in. Nothing remained of the creature but its cloak. "They dissolve in water," Wecka explained. She sent bolts of flame at the other two who turned to flee. They lit up like fire demons and dived overboard to suffer the same fate as their companion. "There's nothing I detest more than Sparks than these undead bustards." Wecka spat.

As they made their way to the cabins below, a large-framed fellow burst out and bowled Nem over. He kicked Nestor in the stomach sending him careering into Kober's men. "You old bugger," Grimshaw growled. "You refuse to die."

A ruffian with missing front teeth lunged at the renegade knight. Grimshaw slammed the hilt of his sword in Snitch's throat, crushing his jugular. Jewels yelled with outrage at the death of his friend and came rushing at his foe. Grimshaw side-stepped and plunged his sword deep into

Jewel's bowels. Wecka screamed and fell beside Jewels cradling his head in her arms.

"My son." Nem turned to look at Kober as he murmured the words of despair. The bear-like man glared at Grimshaw who just smiled back tauntingly. "Now you die!" Kober growled in a low voice filled with malice. He moved with incredible speed, driven by the rage of his son's death. They clashed, oblivious to all around them. Grimshaw's men moved to engage the rest of Kober's crew. The fight could go both ways for they were equally matched in numbers.

"Hurry!" Nestor hissed in Nem's ear. "We must find Serilia before the ship sinks."

Nem looked around at the burning ship. Only moments remained. They entered the lower decks. Nem searched frantically all the cabins but could not locate Serilia. He went through them once more. He coughed and wheezed, almost overcome by the smoke that now spread thickly below.

Was that a thudding noise he had heard in one of the cabins? "Nestor, this way!" They entered the cabin and looked around. There was nothing there but bed bunks and a chest used as a table. Maybe he had imagined the noise. They were about to leave when he heard it again. *There, beneath the chest!* They pulled it aside to reveal a trap door. Nestor prized the lock with his knife. The knife's blade snapped in two. "Hurry," he screamed at the youth. "Go find an axe!"

Nem coughed and spluttered as he plunged out of the cabin into the thick smoke.

"It's alright, Serilia," Nestor said, beating on the trap door. "We'll get you out soon enough." The moments passed and still there was no sign of Nem. Nestor got up and exited the cabin. He entered another where he had seen a pitcher filled with water. He wet a rag thoroughly and tied it around his mouth and nose to keep out the poisonous fumes, then made his way forward along the corridor. He tripped over something and almost fell. He regained his balance and stared at Nem's form. He turned the youth over fearing the worst. Nem was pale in the face but Nestor felt a strong pulse at his neck. He would be alright if he got clean air in his lungs.

Nestor grabbed the youth and carried him on his shoulders towards the end of the corridor. *He weighs a ton*, Nestor thought, as he climbed the stairs. He almost reached the top when a man with a knife in his throat came crashing into them sending them careering down the stairs. Nestor recovered, wincing at his strained wrist. He grabbed Nem by the scruff of the neck with his good hand and hauled him up the stairs with the youth's feet trailing behind and thumping on the stairs with each pull. Finally they arrived at the top. Nestor gave another heave and placed the youth near the gunwales. He retrieved a bucket from the deck and splashed some water on Nem's face.

Nem stirred and began to cough. Nestor laid him on his side and left him to recover. He continued to search frantically for the tool he needed. He saw a masked fellow lying on the deck with two sabres and a knife impaled in his chest. *What had Wecka called him? Brass. Yes, that was the ham's name.* But Nestor was more interested in the weapon the torturer held in his right hand. He prized Brass's fingers open and snatched up the axe. Then he fled down the stairs blindly; he could not see through the smoke. He felt his way from cabin to cabin till he sensed he was close. He considered pulling the rag from his face and calling out Serilia's name, but decided against it. The smoke would overpower him in an instant. He was breathing with difficulty even with the wet rag. He fumbled blindly till his hands felt something round and cold. He prayed to Nexus that it was the lock to the trap door.

The axe descended and sliced the lock. Nestor heaved and the trap door fell open. He was surprised to find that the chamber below was relatively free of smoke but almost flooded with water. Serilia jumped up at him and wrapped her arms around his neck. "Grandfather," she sobbed.

Nestor tugged the rag free and gulped in the air from the chamber. It smelled of excrement but it was clear of poisonous fumes. "Quickly now." He motioned to Serilia to follow. She tore off a piece of her tunic and dipped it in the dirty waters before wrapping it around her face. They fled through the smoke and felt their way along the corridor till they stumbled on the steps. They climbed them on all fours and emerged above to cleaner air.

The ship was ablaze. Serilia recognized Grimshaw's form amongst the dead. His stomach had been opened and his entrails lay in his lap. Next to him was the lifeless body of Kober face down, a sword embedded in his back with only the hilt showing.

They found Nem where Nestor had left him by the gunwales. The trio grabbed a hold of the ropes that had been used to board the *Unrelenting Condor* and made their way across precariously, using all the acrobatic skills they could muster. Finally they were across and back in the safety of Griffin's ship. In the absence of Kober, Griffin was back in command.

"Cast off the grappling hooks!" Griffin barked out the order. "We're finished here." The *Flying Duchess* surged ahead leaving behind the *Unrelenting Condor* which hissed as its flaming hull sank into the surrounding waters.

Admiral Heonar was signalling to his fleet to regroup around the port. Already Zarzbudin's galleasses had rammed several of the smaller cutter ships and had exchanged fire with the bigger ships as well. But the admiral had been successful in his first wave of attack in breaking through the enemy fleet's lines. Now it was a race to get the citizens of Alcavia to safety before the galleasses launched their counter-attack. The ships took it in turns to approach the docks and to load their passengers. The rest were positioned across the port and kept firing their missiles at the enemy ships to keep them at bay.

Nem looked in awe at the masses of Zarzbudin's forces gathered around the thin stream of survivors who were struggling to get to the port from the city. Above the refugees he could see two dragons, one silver and one red, battling with two opponents. He fancied he recognized the striders on the dragons.

Theo looked down with trepidation at the four thousand brave Alcavians who had been deployed as a decoy to draw Zarzbudin's main force away from their families which were heading north accompanied by Queen Viola's force of ten thousand dwarves and nymphs. He and Archon, who was riding behind him on Varwraker's back, were powerless to act as the Alcavians were set upon by a force many times their number, a force eager to tear them apart, like hounds grappling with a fatigued deer. Archon sent another bolt of flame arching towards the red dragon that was harassing them; Barack's steed, Voltan, was a dragon larger and more skilled in combat than their own, so the mage tried to tip the balance as much in favour of Varwraker as he could.

Adelayne and Roxette on Assima were faring worse. The smaller silver dragon was trying desperately to keep away from her opponent's talons and dragon fire. Her size, however, aided her in that she was swifter than her antagonist. Theo's heart constricted in his chest every time the red took a plunge towards Assima. Archon had to shout at him several times, to draw his attention back to saving their own necks, for Theo's contribution was essential to maintaining the link with Varwraker and to giving the correct signals that would keep them alive.

Archon breathed a sigh of relief as the first of the Alcavians reached the docks. There was a ship waiting for them. Theo recognized it as King Dreyfus's full-rigger, the *Western Star.* Admiral Heonar was still afloat! Barack's red dragon also watched the port with discontentment. He diverted his attention to the ships massing at the docks and changed tactics; he dove towards them.

"Hurry, Theo!" Archon yelled from behind. "Don't let that dragon reach the ships before we do."

Varwraker had already sensed the imminent danger and followed close behind his larger foe. They plummeted from the sky, like giant birds of prey readying to strike at their quarry.

Theo held his breath as the docks loomed closer. Now he could see the startled faces of the sailors on their ships as they turned upwards to gaze at this approaching menace from the heavens. Varwraker had caught up and was above Voltan.

Are you sure? Theo heard Varwraker's voice in his head. *It's worth a try*, he answered.

Varwraker responded by folding his wings. They lurched and Theo felt his stomach surge up to his throat as they fell. Varwraker landed on the red's back with a thud, then just as quickly he spread out his wings and flapped them vigorously to gain height. Voltan cried out in anger and frustration as he was plunged into the sea, half a mile short of the port. The waves caused by his dive were high enough to disturb the ships nearest to his point of impact.

Then something totally unexpected occurred. Voltan, after his plunge, continued to swim rigorously towards the port like a sea serpent. Theo realized the red dragon would reach his target before Varwraker could turn about. He watched in horror as Voltan's snake-like form made its way determinedly towards Heonar's fleet.

Voltan dived beneath Zarzbudin's galleasses causing them to bob up and down like corks in a barrel in his wake as he passed beneath. He came up on the other side and crashed into one of the allied cutter ships. The small craft broke in two as the rest of the fleet looked on in horror. Voltan emerged from the depths and reared before Griffin's *Flying Duchess*.

Nem had been firmly rooted on the spot, looking at the red dragon's advance. He witnessed the attack on the small cutter and the sailors diving into the sea, moments before, in an attempt to save their lives. Then he watched in horror as the dragon approached Griffin's ship. The dragon surfaced, rearing its ugly head before the terrified eyes of the hundred souls on board. It opened its maw revealing sharp teeth and a forked tongue. It was preparing to launch its destructive breath of flame. All on board froze as they awaited the inevitable.

Flashes of light scorched Nem's vision and he fell to the ground. He grabbed at his face expecting to find the flesh had been seared away. Instead he felt at his stubble. *I'm alive*, he thought, feeling relief and elation flooding through him. *But how is this possible?* He grabbed at the ship's gunwales and pulled himself to his feet. He opened his eyes but was momentarily blinded by the bright light that had scorched his vision. Then as it cleared he saw the dragon thrashing before the ship. Its snout was blackened by fire and its right eye had been reduced to a weeping, molten mass. It howled with outrage and pain as the sea water seeped into the wound.

Nem turned to see Serilia bent over a tiny form dressed in black rags. He approached the pair and laid a hand on Serilia's shoulder. Serilia looked up at him with tears in her eyes. "It's Wecka," she explained. "She used her magic fire. In her attempt to save us she expelled too much energy. She's dead, Nem." Overcome by her grief she grabbed him and wept in his arms. Nem bent down and placed his arms around her as her shoulders were racked by sobbing.

A screech was heard and Nem feared the red dragon was about to strike again. He placed Serilia behind him to shield her with his body and peered over the gunwales. The screams had indeed come from the dragon but the ship was no longer in danger. Griffin had given the order for the catapults to be launched. A sharp stake protruded from the dragon's throat as it uttered its last cries before the sea claimed it.

Queen Viola looked on at the dilapidated state of her army. Though the diversion had been a success, a large number of Zarzbudin's forces had still been left around the city when Anathel's force had descended from the north. The Forest nymph army had managed to retrieve the remaining thirty-odd thousand survivors—all but four thousand of them had been women, the elderly and the very young. These four thousand Alcavian soldiers had combined with Anathel's force to push back the enemy. Half that number had survived; losses had been staggering.

"We need to get the convoys moving along faster," Anathel said gravely, pulling up beside his queen. "Zazrbudin's warriors are still giving chase. They are like hounds on our trail. They feel we are weak and will nip at our heels till they corner us. Then they will set upon us."

"What would you have me do, Anathel?" the queen answered vehemently. Her patience was wearing thin. "We cannot make them go any faster. They are exhausted and have lost the will to go on struggling. Look at them," she added, sorrowfully. "Most of them have lost sons and husbands in the siege. Women also have not been spared. Mostly the elderly and the very young now survive."

"And these will not live long either if we don't get them across the river by nightfall. The four thousand we sent south will have reached their destination—if ever they did—by now. Our enemy will come at us and quash us if we don't get across the border by dawn."

"Hush now," Viola cautioned, as her sister pulled up beside her. Viola's heart went out to her. Crystal had lost the home she had known for more than two decades, and had almost lost her husband as well. The fate of Prince Leon and Princess Adelayne was unknown. The prince had insisted on being part of the force deployed as a decoy, and the princess had flown south with Theodor to keep them safe from potential air attacks by Zarzbudin's dragons.

"How is he?" Viola reached across from her saddle and placed her hand lightly across her sister's.

"Ellodiere says he will recover, though he will never be able to wear armour again or wield a sword; three of his spinal disks were dislodged and pressing the nerve. Ellodiere and I managed to align them once more but the nerve will need time to heal, and he must avoid placing strain on his back in the future, else he risks becoming paralyzed from the waist down."

"I'm glad he's recovering." Viola smiled encouragingly at her sister. Crystal's face was more careworn than she remembered. She had been through a lot this year; Adelayne's abduction would have cost her, and the war was the crowning of her troubles. *I must get them to safety*, Viola thought desperately.

Nem stood beside Serilia as the battered fleet made its way silently past the shores of Sulicia Island. The fleet had managed to recover a thousand Alcavians. The rest never made it to port. Heonar paid dearly for these thousand lives. He lost both his cutters and the three from Ramila in the conflict. Also, the Templar's carrack, the *White Pilgrim*, was the sole survivor of the four older carracks that had set out for the port. The last-of-the-line, Griffin's *Flying Duchess*, and Solitaire's *Ocean Queen*, had fared better than the full-riggers:

King Dreyfus's flagship, the *Western Star*, was in desperate need of repair whilst Solitaire's two full-riggers had been sunk. Zarzbudin's fleet of eighteen galleasses had been halved–a fact that did not go unnoticed by the surviving allied crews and that helped to sweeten the bitter taste in their mouths from the deaths of their fallen comrades.

"I am glad to find you are well, Nem."

Nem stared at the solemn man beside him. He was a tall figure, dark-haired with penetrating eyes. Primate Zerum was a survivor. He had donned armour above his cleric's robes and had led the Alcavians, giving them the inspiration and the extra spurt of courage they needed in their struggle to reach the port. Sir Duel and Prince Leon had been with him, both of whom were having their wounds treated on Admiral Heonar's ship.

"I too am glad to be alive, Your Eminence, and to find you are likewise so. I feel lucky to have survived all that we have been through."

"Luck?" Zerum cast his gaze over the calm sea. "Luck had very little to do with it, my friend. It was thanks to our efforts and our perseverance that we survived, Nem. You know," he said turning to face the youth, "our race has proven resilient both now and in the past when facing an oppressive force. We may have lost this battle, Nem, but mark my words, we will never relinquish the hope of one day returning to our homes. As long as even a single Alcavian lives and breathes we will spread the word of how our brave nation of twenty thousand fought against a superior force many times larger and how we managed for two weeks to hold out alone against our foe. We will wake our neighbours in Ramila and Ameron from their slumber. Every survivor of the siege will be an ambassador abroad, stirring the plain folk, forcing them to face the threat that looms over their heads. Those leaders who now oppose us will be expelled by the common folk who helped build Leonium.

"I have not lost my faith in the people, Nem, though their leaders have fallen short of my expectations. And our struggle will be carried further east, to Seldavia. The war, my friend is far from over. Zarzbudin has woken the lion within our hearts. We will make him feel our wrath. This I swear to you."

Theo cast his gaze to the north shore, then at the small group of ships below. They would arrive at Ramila's port soon. He turned about at the familiar cry and acknowledged the presence of their small feathered companion. Farwing had returned. Then he looked over at the silver dragon that flew alongside. Adelayne and Roxette were crouched forward against the cold north wind. Flakes of white fluff were falling all around. It was snowing.

Then, unexpectedly, he felt a warm breeze, like a finger stroking his back, passing over him from the south. He straightened and looked behind. Archon was slouching beside him asleep. He felt a ghostly hand clutching him around the throat and loosened the shirt buttons to his collar as he continued to stare south. Off in the distance he imagined he saw a group of black ships bobbing in the waters like flies caught in a soup. Behind the ships was a line of flame on the horizon. He blinked and the vision disappeared.

Perhaps his mind was playing tricks with him.

Then why is my sixth sense alerted?

Look out for "The Golden Menace" the next thrilling episode of 'The Hearstone Talisman' series.